Piece by Piece

A story of medicine, women, and wildfire

Donna Ashworth

Small Mountain Books

Quilt squares designed and created
by Shirley Payne

Small Mountain Books
Box 1113
Carefree, Arizona 85377

ISBN: 0-978-5874-0-5

Library of Congress Cataloging in Publication Data
Piece by Piece/Donna Ashworth
    p. cm. Includes index
  1. Flagstaff (Ariz)--History--Fiction
  2. Coconino National Forest (Ariz)--History 2000–2001--Fiction
  3. Doctors and Medicine in Flagstaff (Ariz)--1881–1931
  4. USFS Fire Lookouts--Coconino NF (Ariz)
  I. Title

for Beth, Amy and Scott
for all the years

Acknowledgements

Fiction is no excuse for error; history should be as accurate as the writer can make it. I am grateful to people who contributed time and information to help make this story true.

Donna and Sylvester Allred
Allen Ames
Emma Jean Bader
Louise Black
Joyce Browning
Fran and Ed Elliott
Kathy Farretta
Therese Fronske
Rita Gannon
Henry Giclas
Babs and Alan Gordon
Maya Granger
Cynthia Leigh
Della Lusk
Caroline Schermann Mackey
Richard and Sherry Mangum
Joyce Maschinsky
Jean Mason
Joe Mehan
Mary Lou Morrow
Sue Ordway
Ricardo Pardo
Shirley Payne
Anne Pomerene
Fern Rabe
Cindy Rabe
Gilbert Sechrist
Rayma Sharber
Art Thornsley
Steven Verkamp
Bee Valvo
Art Welch
Susan Wilcox
Loree Williams

Thank you once again to Sheryl Tongue who designed the book and prepared it for publication.

Flagstaff's General Practitioner M.D.s
1881–1930

Dennis J. Brannen
Percy Gillette Cornish
George Felix Manning
Edwin Seymour Miller
Wilbur S. Robinson
Wilbur P. Sipe
W.M. Slernitzauer
John E. Adams
Raymond O. Raymond
Albert H. Schermann
C. W. Sult

George Felix Manning Jr.
Thomas Peyton Manning
Martin George Fronske
H.K. Wilson
Peter Paul Zinn
Eric St. Clair Flett
Richard M. Francis
William C. Hendricks
Charles Nicholas Plousard
Charles W. Sechrist

The Doctors' Wives

Sarah Manning
Kathleen Brannen
Clara Cornish
Felicia Brannen
Mira Robinson
Ethel "Effie" Sipe
Margaret Adams
Nellie Sult
Josephine "Josie" Manning

Lois Manning
Hilda Fronske
Mary Wilson
Annis Zinn
Pearl Regina Schermann
Elizabeth Francis
Elizabeth Plousard
Ruby Flett
Ethel Sechrist

$\mathcal{F}$lakes of crust and pumpkin were scattered across Gwen's dessert plate. "Mother, you can't do that. You should come to Denver and live with me."

Gwen's house was a maze of modern technology that totally confused me. During last year's visit, when I was trying to mute her television, she began to laugh, "Mother, that thing you have in your hand is the cell phone." How could I live with all the buttons there were to push in my daughter's house?

Life has changed her into a director of other's affairs, including mine. I leaned forward, hands folded under my chin, elbows on the table. "That's good of you, Sweetheart. But I'm not infirm yet. I'll let you know when I'm ready to be tended."

"Mom, is there something you're not telling us?" Oh, Baxter—my sweet child had become so large, so male. "We understood Dad's estate left you well-provided for." His perky little Texas wife perked up. Estate?

"It's not about money, Baxter. I just need to prove I'm alive. New, challenging, fun—remember fun?"

Aging with nothing to look forward to, no possibilities, no future: some things you don't discuss with your children.

Abby was frank, as usual. "Frankly, Mom, it sounds a little, well…"

"Flighty? Whimsical? What you'd expect from an Arizona girl?"

"'Wacky' was the word that came to mind first. You've always had a strong wacky strain…"

I sighed. "Hey, gang, what's with the negative vibrations?"

Abby raised both hands. "Wait, wait. On second thought, Mom, 'gutsy' might be better. Rad. Awesome." Her partner, Jane, watched. "I say, way to go, Mom. Go for it." For all her modern language, Abby had old-fashioned hair. Late afternoon sunlight slanting through the west window turned it to a golden halo. "Unless…is this some kind of joke or something?"

It wasn't that Baxter was pompous, just weighty. He'd probably never in his life had too much to drink. "Did Dad's death damage your social position?"

"Of course it did. When you're no longer the wife of a man who saves lives, your social position changes. There's no getting away from politics."

"Is this because of the accident?" Gwen didn't ever give up. "Post-trauma or something? You want to escape? Beanie, quit kicking your brother under the table."

Escape from memories of that headless torso in the road? Oh surely not.

My son folded his napkin carefully. "You don't feel guilty about Dad, do you?"

Abby glared at him. "What's with you, Baxter? Playing hardball?"

"I have a responsibility to Mom."

"Oh, barf."

Let's hear it for family values.

He turned his eyes back to me. "You want to work as a lookout? On top of a mountain?"

"I'm thinking about it."

"But how... I mean..."

"Loreen at the medical library knows somebody who knows somebody who knows who I should see and where I should go. It might be a possibility, if there's an opening on a tower nobody else wants."

Gwen's agitation radiated. "But why, Mom? This is such an abrupt decision. Cazz, stop it."

"One of my childhood dreams was to live in a mountain cabin. I was a romantic little creature, once."

For the past twenty-five years I'd tended a house that sprawled on three desert acres in north Scottsdale, impressing—as it was intended to do—the people I'd invited to dinner parties. Until Don began to wear thin in significant places...

Gwen nudged her plate farther across my yellow table cloth. "You don't need to camp out, you know, you have this big lovely house."

"I plan to sell it and find a place that's more personal, more my size. What I have in mind is an apartment that I can furnish to suit no one but myself. Or maybe just one big room, so I can be in my whole shelter at one time."

"Mother, you can't mean it."

"Oh yes I can. Be thinking about what you want, something you grew up with, paintings, anything. I'd like to keep my desk, the rocking chair, the Mahaffey landscapes, but anything else, you're welcome to."

"What if you should fall, alone up there on a mountain?"

"I won't fall."

"Mother!"

"I promise."

"You can't be serious about this. Boys, I mean it."

"Gwen, being serious makes me feel old."

I stand four feet away from mirrors now and my hands look like an ad for life insurance, but I don't want to feel old. Anyone who doesn't understand that hasn't lived long enough yet.

"What's the point of being older if you're not freer?"

"Mother, I can't believe you said that." Gwen's husband stayed out of it. So did Beanie and Cazz, watching grown-ups across flowers on a holiday table, fidgeting through an hour's wait so they could go back into the pool. Don had insisted on having it heated—even in Phoenix water in swimming pools is cold in November—but Gwen was a stickler about safety rules.

What does a woman say to grown children who don't understand? "Life is phases, a series of phases. New century, new millennium, I'm ready for a new phase." I needed a new one, but I didn't want to sound pathetic.

If I have forty more years, and I might—or only four, who knows?—I want to live them in some kind of, I don't know, affirmation? I prefer that to resignation.

An idealist after all these years. I'm such an American.

There were no blacks in my schools until I was in college, none in my neighborhood. The whole issue was an abstraction. That's how old I am.

It's less than two hundred miles north of Phoenix, but I hadn't been to Flagstaff until Don and I drove through one October day in a thirty-six-foot motor coach. He would have preferred forty-five feet, "top of the line," he said.

That meant a monster so long that in some states it couldn't be driven legally off the highway system. And could cost up to $700,000, thousands more to register. And weigh several tons.

"Don, we couldn't do anything with a behemoth like that but park it and keep it in one place."

"I want the best."

"Biggest isn't necessarily the best. If you're thinking to get far off major highways, you don't want the biggest."

His mouth had looked handsome to me once upon a time; I'd loved the sweet curve when he smiled. "I don't want to drive down the road in a buggy. No, don't pour me any more coffee, it's bitter."

I was the one doing research and shopping, learning words like invertor, deep cycle marine battery, slide-out. "Longer would weigh more, and once you get above twenty-six thousand pounds, you have to get a commercial license even to drive it home."

"What's that supposed to mean?"

"It means you'd be considered a trucker."

"That's ridiculous. You believe anything you hear."

"Here's the brochure, look at this one."

"I like that, it's fine. Get that one."

"Wait a minute. It costs almost a million dollars. It's over forty-five feet long, and it doesn't bend in the middle. You wouldn't want to take it on a rough, crooked dirt road. This one is for parking. You want to move around, don't you?"

"OK, show me one that bends in the middle."

"I was trying to make a joke. None of them bend, but you can get something shorter that would be better for scenic roads. Please, Don, the numbers are important, it's all numbers. The bigger you are, the more experience you need and the more gas you use. Top of the line might go less than eight miles to the gallon."

"*Eight*! That's outrageous. Put that pencil down, damn it."

"If we were to buy a diesel pusher…"

"I don't want diesel."

"With the longest model our turning radius would be a big problem—you'd need two lanes just to go around a corner."

"I could handle it."

"You couldn't find places to park. Couldn't stop as quickly with the extra mass. Couldn't go far off pavement." I covered the table with facts, and we compromised at thirty-six feet.

It had been years since I'd had driving lessons, and there I was again—first on a course with built-in problems, then on dirt roads, finally on city streets—with an instructor sitting beside me issuing advice.

"You can't forget for a minute how long this rig is."

"Put on the brakes hard and we'll measure the distance it takes you to come to a full stop."

"Give yourself plenty of room turning this corner."

"You're cutting off that little car! Please. Remember. Remember the tail when you're turning."

But Don hadn't been behind the wheel until we'd set out that October morning. He claimed that maybe I needed practice sessions but he didn't, he'd been driving since he was sixteen. So had I.

It was all of 11:30 before we started moving. Fortunately our driveway was circular, so he didn't have to learn backing up right off the mark. We barely missed a palo verde tree and bumped off the curb, lurched down the block while Don figured out that he had automatic shift. Driving west on Phoenix streets, looking into the eyes of semi drivers, I was alert, those little cars below us zooming in every direction.

"Don, we don't have to be right in the middle, half in one lane and half in another. Our width is designed to fit the street."

"Relax, Marlene. And, damn it, quit gasping. They can't help but see us, they won't hit us."

"I hope not. Yellow light ahead."

The back end of our moving house tried to make right turns shorter than the front had. Once Don changed lanes too soon and forced a car onto a sidewalk and into someone's front yard. He didn't notice.

"You know, Don, I had quite a time learning to use the side mirrors so I wouldn't get too close to the edge of the road."

"Marlene, I don't need your subtle hints."

It was a relief to get onto I-17, where everything on our side was going in our direction. Most of it wanted to go faster than we did, especially the 18-wheelers, until we got past Black Canyon City and started up hill.

I remember when that interstate was finished, something to do with Eisenhower. Forty years ago?

A vigorous wind nudged us off course now and then—we were very high profile. The central highlands, Black Canyon to Camp Verde, were spare and spacious, elegant, no extra detail. I rather enjoyed moving past the scenery, looking at everything through the huge windows.

My roadside geology book said that whole faulted band across the state used to be—like more than a thousand million years ago—a great mountain range. Let's hear it for Time.

We started winding down into the Verde Valley without stopping to check the brakes. Don used them on every curve, on every corner, even on the straighter stretches until I reminded him: "You know, you can gear down with this vehicle."

"Don't tell me how to drive."

"Just doing my job, passenger responsibility."

"This is like driving a car."

A sign on the highway above Camp Verde read HIGH WIND ADVISORY, USE CAUTION. If we'd been pulling a boat, we'd have been in even more trouble. But Don wouldn't hear of stopping in the lee of something.

Ten miles to the west, the cliffs of Oak Creek Canyon reared up, exposing part of earth's history. The Redwall sandstone well above the river at the Grand Canyon is at the bottom of the Oak Creek Canyon pile. I'd like to have seen the cliffs closer, but in a big motor coach and all, it didn't seem the right time.

The approach to Flagstaff was straightforward enough once we'd crawled up the long slope to the Rim at 25 mph and pines closed in. Leaves of oak and aspen were gold in the forest, flaming in sunlight. As we approached the town, elevation 7000 feet, traffic began to congeal, and construction crimped the lanes down. I asked Don if his mirrors were in good positions, if his little rear-vision camera was on.

"Everything's under control."

Yeah, sure. I'd driven it home: I knew how intimidating the size of it was. I was on my knees on the sofa behind him watching for bicycles, motorcycles, small foreign cars, teen-age drivers. Fortunately everyone had sense enough to hold back for us.

We eased past the university, survived a traffic light and confronted a railroad under-pass, a curve, decisions about highway signs. I rushed back to my seat in a panic to consult the map, and a train blew its whistle right beside me. Nearly scared me out of my shoes.

"Stay in this lane!"

"Right."

"Traffic light!" I was shaking.

"I see it." He was leaning forward, intent on just ahead.

"There's a curve coming up, but don't take any exits."

"Okay, okay. Shut up." Like a slap in the face. I turned my head away from him and retreated inside, slammed the door, piled up furniture against it. An old hand at protecting myself.

Driving into town again on an April day three weeks ago, seeking the ranger station, my new blue 4Runner loaded full, I saw rocks and pines, stone buildings, a gritty wind tearing at pedestrians' clothes, dead volcanos everywhere. My home for the summer.

Out back of the ranger station, where I signed forms and promised not to overthrow the government by force, people in the fire shop—men and women four/five decades younger than I am—handed me radio, keys, binoculars and anemometer and told me how to find Woody Mountain. I guessed there was a problem somewhere; they didn't have anyone to spare who could show me the way. Just sent me out to learn. Maybe I didn't look as close to panic as I felt.

Leaving town, leaving cars and buildings and people. Going alone into a forest. I hadn't been on a dirt road since the accident, and I expected speeding cars to skid toward me around every curve. I was not a novice, I was alien, tense and twitchy, trembling from the inside out. Since the breakdown, or whatever it was, I do that sometimes— heckuva a way to handle tension. At a side road I pulled over and sat for five minutes.

It was easier when I located the narrow road winding among pines to the mountain. Got through the gate at the foot and locked it behind me, locked danger away. Illusion is better than no safety at all.

The road turned steep, circling up. Slopes rose sharply on my left and fell away sharply on the right: I was on the skin of the mountain, no more than that. Through gaps in the trees, forest hundreds of feet below appeared now and then. Bushy-tailed squirrels dashed across the road. A wild turkey ran ahead.

On a rocky two-track just barely wide enough, the road dodged through a tunnel of oaks and burst out into a little clearing right at the top—forty feet wide at the most— skirted the feet of a tower, stopped beside a one-room cabin that looked pitifully small and lonely standing there in the wind.

I was slow to turn off the engine and open the door. This was it? This was what I'd applied to live in? Well. I could see why I'd been hired: probably no one else wanted the job. The cabin was eleven feet by fifteen feet on the inside. Bed and table, stove, sink, refrigerator: room enough for one. One.

Wind was loud in the pines that first night, and I was grateful for the walls around me, the CDs I'd brought. Add wind and night to solitude, stir in an unknown place: that's quite a recipe. After my books and clothes and cooking pans were unpacked and my blankets were on the bed, and Ella was singing, I felt reassured a little. Sort of at home. Just twenty pounds of wet laundry on my chest…

The tower that rose forty-five feet over the cabin was only seven feet square at the top. All those hearty work-boots types in the shop no doubt couldn't stand such restricted movement. The walls were windows though, the view forty, sixty, eighty-plus miles. The huge old volcano to the northeast, sloping up into the sky, looked close enough to touch.

My first day on the job was rated Red Flag: wind was nearly fifty miles an hour on the mountain because of a cold front approaching from the Pacific. It talked around the corners of the tower, blew down trees in Flagstaff, tore the roof off the Hutch Mountain lookout. Climbing with my heavy Forest Service radio, I was careful about bracing against gusts. Ravens flashed by, strong and glossy black in the sunlight. Am I a heroine or what?

The forest radio was broadcasting voices that talked in numbers and letters. "What's your 40, Bill?"

"S.O."

"Could you grab some TnAs and bring 'em out?"

"Affirmative."

"Thanks. Crew Two."

One mysterious exchange after another. "Flagstaff, 2-32. we'll do a small test, 6-22-14. No approval for full treatment."

"Copy that."

I was in a first-day panic. Didn't know the language. Didn't know what was expected of me. Insecure? Whoo, boy, fragile as a kleenex. I listened to anything that might be other lookouts for a clue.

"Flagstaff, Moqui in service. Southwest fifty to sixty, gusts to seventy. No precip."

Did that have something to do with wind? Hadn't they given me a device to measure it with? I scrambled in my pack to find the little instrument and stared at it—I ought to be able to figure out how it worked. I hadn't felt so clueless since my first day in geometry class more than half a century past.

"Flagstaff, Baker Butte in service. Wind is west southwest sixty to seventy with higher gusts."

OK, they were reporting wind speed and direction, but did 'southwest' mean from or to? I stumbled down to the top landing, swiveled my head until I could feel wind the same on both ears, and held up my anemometer with a trembling hand. There was no one within miles I could turn to for help.

"Flagstaff, Elden in service. Gale up here gusting southwest to a hundred."

Why were they all so different? I was measuring only fifty to fifty-five—was I doing it right?

Finally, in despair I picked up my microphone and looked at it, pushed a button down and said, "Flagstaff"—my voice croaked

—"Woody Mountain in service. From the southwest fifty to fifty-five."

"Copy, Woody Mountain."

Five whole minutes behind me, and I'd done something right. Then a voice right out of Texas: "Woody Mountain, Apache Maid lookout. Welcome. Good to have ya with us."

"Thank you, Apache Maid." I was so grateful to him I almost cried.

Another voice. "2-32, 2-3. Let's hold off for today."

"Copy. I was just gonna suggest that."

Every minute there was something new. "Engine 5-2, Flagstaff."

Flagstaff, Engine 5-2."

"We'd like you to stage at Happy Jack."

"On our way."

"Hey, Clyde, leave that gate open for us. We're right behind you."

"You got the cat at Blue Ridge?"

"Flagstaff, Engine 2-2. We'll be at Brookbank if anything breaks."

In the middle of my seven-foot space a heavy wooden platform two feet square supported a contraption that would obviously be important if I could figure out what it was. A circular map of the forest with a tiny spike poking up through the center at Woody Mountain. A metal ring with compass numbers, 0 to 360. Was it supposed to be some way of deciding where a fire was? That would make sense. But I've learned that if it makes sense, it's probably the wrong thing to do.

The fire season of the year 2000 started before I'd had a chance to become acquainted with the landscape. Little smokes were reported here and there, most of them I couldn't see even with the binoculars. "I think I'm a little long on my mileage." What did Turkey Butte mean by that?

There was no water in Rogers Lake two miles away, just grass and a moist spot in the middle. This is a lake? On roads, dust was a brown powder that blew up in plumes and followed vehicles for miles. Air was full of it; effective visibility was limited. In my tower I was cold, even with all the windows closed.

Restrictions on open camp fires were announced, but next day there was a fire at the top of Schnebly Hill. I could see half an acre burning near Chimney Spring, so a voice reported when an engine arrived. NAU graduation celebrations (on the radio voices said "tearing up the place," "refusing to douse open fires") kept ground units moving around. Citizens were cutting green trees for a camp fire outside Pine Flat in Oak Creek Canyon and other citizens were reporting them on cell phones.

I had only the vaguest idea of what to do; the job is a case of self-training. Pay attention and stay alert. Figure out what all those numbers mean. Listen to voices on the forest radio. Use the map every day to identify places, decide how far away they are. The hardest section for me was all those Government names to the northwest—Government Prairie, Hill, Mountain. Why Government?

Weeks ahead there'd been speculation that we were in for trouble, given low snowfall, high winds, and warm temperatures. My first day off I went into town and bought books about fire fighting, about anything relevant—I didn't know a thing. The second day I drove out to Turkey Butte to ask for a lesson and got lost twice before I found the right road.

She lives in her own trailer near the foot of the tower. Her name is Sandy. Brilliant blue eyes, blonde hair pinned up, a good nose, nice smile, a woman who wears bright colors and matching bows in her hair. (Good for her, I say: today's teen-agers tend to dress drab and dreary.) Her tower is ten feet square, bigger than mine. She's done it up domestic—carpeted floor, curtain swags at the top of the windows. Comfortable chairs. Desk and book shelves.

"Have a seat. That table is oak, it's very heavy. Last spring when I carried it up here, I got it stuck on a landing, I mean I was *stuck*, between the table legs. I couldn't go up or down, afraid I'd get a call on the radio and I'd just have to stand there helpless. I like to never got that table loose."

Some women can tell you enough right away to make you feel familiar. "I came out here hunting with my dad for twenty years when it was really remote. After that for twenty-five years I camped out here every summer with my friend, and we didn't worry about a thing. But I tell you what, there's too damn many weirdos any more."

Only sixteen miles from my tower, and I was in a completely different landscape. "You're OK with being up here alone?"

"Oh, sure. I can lock the door from the inside." She laughed.

"I like the feel of your tower."

"I think of it as an old-fashioned porch or a tree house. I carry all this up here and back down at the end of the season. You don't dare leave anything—it'll get stolen."

"Sandy, I…if I were to see smoke, I wouldn't know what to do."

"Well, the first thing you can count on, I won't steal a fire out from under you. I think that's just plain bad manners. We have to stick together out here. I'll call you on the radio and say something like 'Woody Mountain, what's that northwest of you?' or 'If you need my cross on that smoke at Budweiser Tank it's—what ever it is.' That'll help you figure the distance."

"That's so neighborly."

"Well, *sure*."

I pointed to her map-in-a-circle. "What's that thing?"

"We call it a fire-finder. You use it to tell just where your smoke is. C'mere, I'll show you." She explained the thing and put me through half an hour of tests. "If you have any questions at all, call me on channel five. Does your radio have that many?"

"I don't know."

"Here, see this dial?"

The last thing she said before I drove away was, "Eddie will come up to your tower every two weeks to pick up your time. Save any questions that aren't emergencies and he can answer them. He's been hunting and wood-cutting out here in this country all his life."

"He's…?"

"My husband. The patrolman out here."

That means he tends about 150 sections in this part of the Coconino. By my math: each section a mile square means his district is 150 square miles of pine. (Is that right?) Three ranches, three lookout towers, the Arboretum and the City Wells. South boundary is the rim country above Red Rock-Secret Mountain Wilderness; on the west he patrols to the bottom of Sycamore Canyon.

The next day he came tromping up the stairs; Sandy had told him to stop by. "Howdy, howdy." Ed Piper. Sixty or so, a retired sixth grade teacher. I've learned since then that in this district he's a Hero of the West. He knows every foot of it, every road, every gully, every hill. When four different units are hunting a smoke, Ed is the one who finds it and knows what to do about it. When he runs across teen-agers misbehaving, he barks out their names. "I know your daddies. You know I do."

Authentic: his mother's family traveled to New Mexico in 1910 in a covered wagon, his father's arrived in Flagstaff early. So he's been here all his life, hunting, cutting wood, working fire.

Ed's is the only face I see up here from one week to the next. Every other Saturday he climbs my stairs to get the paper on which I list the hours I've worked. For a few minutes he answers my questions, tells me what's going on down below.

"Woods are crawling with people, you should drive down Fry Canyon."

"We don't have a helicopter, but we can get one right away from Green Base over by Williams."

"Red Flag means hot, dry and windy: fire danger weather."

Hurray, I say, for people who make you laugh. "I could see his runaway horse over there by the corral, but I didn't give him a ride. It was only half a mile, wouldn't hurt him to walk it." Or "I said, 'You give me a hard time about cleaning up this camp, I'll write you a citation'."

Sandy is another retired teacher, Ed says, another Westerner: she was born in Prescott. They leave the administrative channel to talk. "Turkey Butte, Patrol 2-4, go to twelve."

"Patrol 2-4, Turkey Butte on twelve."

"Can you see smoke on the Rattle fire?"

"No, I sure can't, but this wind could be keeping it low in the canyon."

"OK, I'm gonna be out of my truck for a while to hike into it."

"Copy. Let me know when you get back."

I envy that kind of work-together marriage. Most of the couples I've known have lived two separate lives—my marriage was nearly a vacuum finally. I'd hear love songs and cry and volunteer for another committee.

The Pipers talk. "Keep an eye out over toward Little Round Mountain. This country got hardly a drop of rain last night."

"Rats, that's where all the lightning was yesterday."

"That's what I thought. OK, I'll talk to you later."

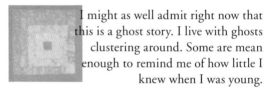 I might as well admit right now that this is a ghost story. I live with ghosts clustering around. Some are mean enough to remind me of how little I knew when I was young.

Doctors can't have any human weakness, not when I was living with one, they couldn't. Don projected competent and certain at the world; listen to my voice—I Know What I'm Doing.

He didn't expect confirmation of his value as a doctor, as a person, from lesser mortals like patients. Like nurses, although they know what's going on. Like the children and me. It had to come from those who mattered—other doctors. No wonder wives became involved in auxiliaries. We were second to medicine, maybe fifth or tenth. It can be quite a put-down never to come first, in case anyone's curious.

When he had a crisis, Don would come home late with tension all over his face, ready to argue it away. "By the time his mother brought him in, his face had been swollen for a week. It looked like an allergic reaction to me, so I prescribed an antihistamine. But they were back two days later—his face wasn't any better, and his hands and feet were swollen. I told her to give the medicine time to work. But when his belly and scrotum swelled up, she took him to the ER, and a resident diagnosed nephrotic syndrome. I should have made that diagnosis, god damn it, I should have. I blew it completely."

He became agitated about any mistake, pacing back and forth in the kitchen with a glass of Irish whiskey. I'd try to listen sympathetically, with intelligent comments, but it didn't do any good. You'd think his problems were all my fault.

"That's a stupid idea—what the hell do you know? Her glucose level is fifty, blood pressure way too high. Left arm is motionless, and she's barely breathing. I thought at first she'd had a stroke, but her CT scan was negative. She'll die if I don't figure out what's wrong with her."

"Have you…"

"You think I'm a moron? It's not a stroke. Not epilepsy, not diabetes."

I'd lean against the sink, frozen, watching him pace. "Would it help if I…"

"No, I don't want you in there interfering. I have authority in the office, I don't need my wife running things, undermining me. I just need some understanding."

"Is there anyone you can talk to? One of your doctor friends…?"

"What's wrong with you, you think it wouldn't get around that I was losing it? Do I have to explain malpractice to you again?" He'd slam out of the kitchen, and I'd hope the children hadn't heard.

Usually he'd come home late, eat dinner in front of the TV, give orders he expected to be obeyed when he wasn't there. I tried, I really did. But he was a difficult man to love. Years of that, and I felt worthless. I should have seen the signs…

If I had a problem, Don reacted by pulling away. A doctor has to distance himself from emotion if he is to do his work, didn't I know that? I was being unreasonable. He had important responsibility. There was a patient at the hospital he had to look in on, he'd be back late, I shouldn't wait up.

It's painful, the embarrassing things we do for the hope of feeling love. Or the memory of it.

May of the year 2000

To my children grown and my grandchildren growing,

Here I am, and I'm taller than any of you, even Baxter. You won't dare to talk back to me now, the top of my head is 8,045 feet above sea level. For a while anyway, I've got you all beat.

The other day a hiker climbed to the top of my mountain. I unlocked the trap door in the floor and invited her into my seven-foot-square, glass-walled tower room. She looked around—on Flagstaff, a toy town from here, and beyond it the Painted Desert sixty-five miles away, at the Mazatzals eighty miles to the south and the cliffs of Oak Creek Canyon and the mountains west of Prescott, at the long line of old volcanos across the north—she looked around and said, "Wow, this is really neat, I'd go crazy in a place like this." She meant the size of the view and then the size of the room.

I gathered she didn't understand me. "What are you trying to do, be a hermit?"

Retreat from a world of speed and noise and pressure? From people who complain and throw temper tantrums? In the morning I stand in the open doorway of my cabin brushing my teeth and looking around at sunrise shadows, looking down on ranch buildings two miles away. There's no need to hurry through tasks. I am responsible to no one but myself and the dispatcher—no meetings, no shopping, no driving to work—I'm free to stand brushing my teeth, listening to birds, and looking at the sunrise. Nights in my little cabin, alone on its mountain top, are a joy. The moon shines white on treetops and makes long inky shadows on the ground. If I look directly at it, I'm nearly blinded by the moon. Hermit doesn't sound so strange to me.

Well, OK—it's not a job that would suit everybody, but she was curious. "How long do you stay up here?"

Eight hours a day, five days a week until the end of the federal fiscal year in September.

"Don't you get lonesome?"

On the Coconino radio I hear the voices of other people, but I don't have to deal with gossip or office politics. All day the university radio plays music I like and news I don't like, often as not. In books I'm in touch with the most interesting minds in the country. Lonesome? It doesn't occur to me.

She wanted to know, "Don't you get scared?"

I'm not afraid of heights, obviously. Coyotes sing in the evenings. A dozen vultures ride the updrafts above me. Wind shakes the tower. I'm more likely to be hurt driving a car on city streets. But I am afraid I'll panic when I see smoke. The first time, I turned in circles saying, "What'll I do? What'll I do?" And I'm afraid of going to sleep after lunch and missing a fire.

My hiker didn't think to ask, "Why did you take this job?"

I could have told her I wanted privacy, quiet, trees, a long view, company rather than contact. Freedom. Time.

She could see books, pen and paper, knitting, an exercise bicycle, and she asked, "What do you do up here?"

I scan the land for fire, for one thing, but I can't rotate slowly all day. I have to provide something to do, and I have so many possibilities that I'm never bored.

Finally, leaving, she asked two more questions: "How much do you get paid?" And "How did you get this job?" I'm still laughing about how quickly she'd changed her mind about me.

Love,
Your Bear in the Air

Together Emily and I knew almost every song composed before 1970. Emily specialized in show tunes. We'd be up to our volunteer elbows in hours of paperwork and she'd start to sing, "I'm just a girl who can't say no." We always watched when she told a joke—her face alone made it hilarious, and she'd do a funny little waggle with her tongue.

Another Mrs. Doctor. She was soothing. It was her voice, I think—gentle, smooth, the voice of, let's face it, a lady. She made English a beautiful language.

Emily battled with her weight for years. "My motto is: Old you gotta get; fat you don't." When a horse from a neighbor's corral escaped into her garden, she went out with bare hands and pushed at it until she turned it and put it back. "It looked embarrassed for me, so I reasoned with it. 'Now, you know you don't belong here. You go right back home.'" In that wonderful voice.

Summer days she'd come to my house or I'd go to hers and we'd spend hours drifting around in the pool up to our armpits in inflatable rings, the current babies in front of us in the shade of our big sun hats, churning water with their fat little legs while the other children played Marco Polo or shouted "Mom! Watch!" inventing new ways to jump into the water. Sunny winter weather we took them to parks and sat on a blanket talking while they climbed on monkey bars and shouted "Mom! Watch!" inventing new ways to go down slides.

In the hours we spent keeping an eye out, we small-talked and turned ideas upside down and compared notes about being doctors' wives. "He's never home. That's wonderful, Baxter!"

Emily had this wicked little smile. "Don't you just feel like a single wife sometimes?"

"Oh you bet. When we drive two cars to a dinner party because he might get a call…"

"…and there's that empty chair at the table…"

"…and I have to be interesting and entertaining for two, I'm single."

"Darn it, why do we bother inviting them? We should do luncheons instead…"

"…and let the men concentrate on saving lives. Gwen, no running beside the pool."

Emily was the best friend of all my life. "Does Don fuss about coming home three days early from every vacation? That's great, honey! I'm impressed."

"My heart sinks. Sometimes he says he's running out of money, and sometimes he says he needs to get back."

"Does he always have you tagging in late when you're invited out?"

"I learned a long time ago to tell him we're due at seven when it's eight."

"So you'll be on time, I do that too. Oh, we're sly."

But Emily was fair. "Here we are drifting around in your pool on your three-acre lot. I drove here in my BMW."

"I have more clothes than I can wear in a year."

"Now me, I fly to L.A. to shop."

"I never even look at prices in the grocery store."

"Marlene, let's take the kids to La Jolla next week and let them play on the beach."

I loved to hear her laugh. "And we're complaining. I'm glad we don't have really bad problems."

Our husbands didn't hit us, our children weren't in wheel-chairs. We had no money worries. There was a black hole at the center—at least, there was for me—but we weren't homeless. Emily said, "Our husbands are old enough to know not to go for the jugular. Travis learned a long time ago that it feels good to be nice." I smiled and nodded and didn't dare respond.

Her doctor husband was the same cheerful man he'd been when she'd married him. "I know med school and internship are so stressful for some men that they never recover. But Travis loved it, loved the excitement, the problems he solved. I didn't see much of him—I still don't—but he just sailed right through it. I suspect it's like everything else, individual chemistry."

By the time Don finished his intern year he was crippled inside, and he was not the same after that. One of those who never recovered.

But Emily and I had each other, sitting in the shade on a blanket at the park. "Gwen, not that way please, honey, you need to watch your feet. I've been listening to the whole Nixon thing. He may be guilty as charged, but he's been effective in foreign policy."

"I don't feel good about the impeachment talk. It's not in our long-term best interest to make the country cynical about government."

"I'm glad we have Goldwater. Can you imagine that man lying? I don't believe he can hide a single thought."

"Remember when he said that most of the country's problems could be solved if we sawed off the east coast and towed it out to sea? I loved it."

We could talk about anything, no arguing. There were no touchy areas between us. We wanted a definition of marriage. "It's not political anymore. Or economic, like adding one fortune to another."

"It isn't enforced servitude, the divorce rate proves that." "The way things are changing, it doesn't have to be about children. Or sex."

"What's it for then? Self-realization?"

"Nah."

"We need to re-think this institution."

And we chanted a litany we'd learned from a woman at an auxiliary meeting: Who needs it? Life is hard enough as it is. Why look for trouble? You can't be too careful. And we laughed at ourselves.

Do little girls play with paper dolls these days? Jacks? Jump ropes? Do they draw Hop Scotch squares on sidewalks with chalk? Those games were handed down to us through generations as if they had always been.

One year Emily and I volunteered to put together an outline of the medical history of Phoenix—when services began, how they grew, that sort of thing. It was a revelation. I hadn't known anything but what I could see, which isn't much when you're talking about time.

After the Civil War, the population in Phoenix was, as they said, "few and far between," not enough to justify much in the way of a medical presence. Falls from horses were common, so were gunshot wounds. The usual. There were such afflictions as malaria, smallpox, scarlet fever, diphtheria, typhoid, cholera. The twenty or so doctors in the whole territory mixed their own medicines and sent their lab samples to Los Angeles or St. Louis. Surgery was performed on kitchen tables if it was absolutely necessary and couldn't wait.

Untrained women in private homes or boarding houses tended the sick and injured, as they always had, time out of mind. The only hospitals in the territory were Army, often just a couple of tents. In 1868 Camp Verde had three beds in a log house fifteen by eighteen feet. Fort Whipple could accommodate all of twenty-four men. To add to the bleak picture: Lister's antiseptic surgery for combatting "hospital gangrene" was opposed and ridiculed, and few American doctors sterilized anything.

Far as I'm concerned, the Golden Age is in the future, not the past.

Most full-time nurses were nuns. St. Mary's Hospital opened in Tucson, then there was a sanitarium in Yuma and the Cochise County Hospital opened in Tombstone. In 1877, four years before Flagstaff was founded, the territory's first surgical hospital was built in Prescott. The Arizona Territorial Legislature authorized a mental hospital in 1884, but it took a couple of years to get that going.

When the Maricopa County Medical Association and the Arizona Medical Association organized in 1892, the population of Phoenix was about 2,000. That's all. Tuberculosis victims who had come to seek a cure lived in tents in the desert or in rooming houses. Recognizing human need when they saw it, the Sisters of Mercy founded a sanitarium in 1895 in a six-bedroom house near downtown (as it was then), set up beds for twelve patients, and called it St. Joseph's.

That was the beginning. One hundred years later there are somewhere around fifty full hospitals in the Salt River Valley, counting medical centers, the state hospital, behavioral and surgery and heart facilities, hospitals in six cities adjacent to Phoenix, and including St. Luke's (1907) and Arizona Deaconess (1911) which became Good Samaritan ten years later.

I don't live in Phoenix any more; now I'm in Flagstaff. Has anybody done a history of medicine in Flagstaff? I've been wondering. Smaller than Phoenix, younger. How did this town compare to that one?

On my two days off each week, I've wandered around in libraries, seeking an answer or even a clue. The county court house too, it's always a good source of what happened. I've met quite a few people.

Finally a librarian suggested the Pioneer's Museum, which was the county hospital once upon a time. Susan and Joe were helpful as if they'd known me for years and showed me a history Art is compiling. Sleuthing, I went into the old carriage house at the Riordan house and talked with Kathy. Finally we assumed what we guessed might have happened. That's what's called History.

In 1881 a crew arrived in what was to be Flagstaff to build a sawmill for the Ayer Lumber Company. The seven cases of smallpox that broke out among them a month later were isolated in a "sick tent," where two of the men died. Was there a doctor or a nurse to tend them in that little camp in the middle of practically no where? Seems unlikely. At any rate, it was the beginning of our medical history.

The Riordan brothers bought the mill from Ayer in '87; it burned the same year and was promptly rebuilt with "modern improvements." The company, the only employer of any size in a town that was not much more than a water stop on the railroad line, was just big enough to justify rudimentary medical care.

The past swarms with ghosts. A note Kathy turned up hinted that in 1888 Mrs. W.H. Carroll—thirty-one years old, born in Germany, a practical nurse—opened a hospital for the saw mill. She was evidently a distant cousin of the Riordans. A local historian named Dick Mangum said that W.H. Carroll worked for the Riordan company and "ran" a boarding house. Guess: the sawmill's hospital was a room or two in the boarding house, and Mrs. Carroll was the nurse who kept the men clean and fed and reasonably comfortable.

She cooked their food—a guess here, informed by the Montgomery Ward catalog—on a black iron stove with a fire box to hold burning splits of wood. A reservoir for heating water was on the right side, a warming shelf above at the back. Her pans could have been nickel-plated, wrought steel, aluminum or tin, but she probably used heavy iron ones that were cheapest and lasted longer.

She washed their sheets on a scrub board in a round tub, sewed hospital shirts on a steel and iron machine with a foot treadle that she tilted back and forth to make a rod move up and down and turn a wheel that operated the needle.

Like any respectable woman, she wore layers of under-clothing: vests and drawers, a corset and corset cover, chemise, at least one ankle-length underskirt. When she went to church, she strapped on horsehair pads under her skirt to augment her hips if they needed it—the curves of big hips were considered feminine in those years. At home she wore house dresses of no particular fashion, no bustle, train, tucks, folds, drapes or bows. Merely a serviceable garment with a high neck, long sleeves, hem brushing her buttoned boots, a big apron tied around her waist. Come to think of it, my grandmother probably did too.

I'd already gathered my books. As soon as the bell rang, I hurried out the door, dodged through crowds in the hall, skimmed down the stairs, rushed past the library, jerked my locker open. And there he was beside me with a malicious smile, jeering. "You make good time."

That skinny swaggering boy followed me everywhere, enjoying himself. I barely saw or heard anything around me I was so swollen with the nightmare of it. I was fifteen.

That summer, drunk, speeding, he skidded into an irrigation ditch and hit a culvert. His car exploded. I was fiercely glad he was dead, and I'm still not ashamed of it.

My eyes are brown, and I loved it that Don's were such a brilliant blue, his hair a rich golden beige. He was too studious to be a Big Wheel. A girl I knew called him a Drip, but I thought Brain was a better word. He was a Brain. He was going to college on the G.I. Bill and working part-time and maintaining high grades. (We didn't say G.P.A. then.) That didn't leave much time for fun and games.

We walked to the A.S.C. library in warm evenings, when sunsets were red on Tempe Butte. We were "going steady," as we called it then. "This hand I'm holding,"—he raised it to his lips and kissed it, and I was thrilled, of course—"this hand is mostly molecular space. Gamma rays given off by stars can pass through it without hitting anything."

I had a blue plaid skirt that swung around my legs as I walked. We wore skirts on campus then.

"Just my hand?"

"Your head too. What isn't space in the human body is about ninety-five per cent water. That's true of everything that lives. Water is a solvent for chemicals, and life is chemical reactions."

"That's not terribly spiritual, is it?"

"Marlene, spiritual is not my field. Human physiology has no room for it. Think about this: a whole suite of flora and fauna live in your gut, bacteria and like that. You couldn't get by without them, they're always busy digesting your food for you, breaking down three-carbon compounds, for instance."

"Don! That's gross!" (I don't think we said 'gross' then. What did I say?)

"No, it isn't. We're part of everything, and everything's related to us. You'd be surprised how little separates life forms. For example, the big reason you can talk and your dog can't is because his larynx is lower than yours."

I was majoring in history—he gave me a new perspective. Synapses, the complexity of life processes: he explained, using gestures and similes. When he'd act something out and I'd laugh, he was pleased.

It was a challenge to make him laugh. College does that to some people, makes them serious. There was sweetness in him. Tenderness. One day when we were driving in that old brown Ford of his, we saw a car coming toward us on the other side of the street, slow, the right wheels bumping against the curb. The driver looked as if she might be having a seizure of some kind. I'd no more than realized that when Don had pulled over and jumped out, running after the other car.

By the time I'd taken the keys and followed him, he had caught up, opened the door and turned off the engine. It was smooth the way he lifted the woman out and carried her to grass beyond the sidewalk and laid her down. I was so proud of him I tingled: he held her loosely in his arms so the convulsions wouldn't hurt her and, when she was conscious, reassured her in a low soft voice as if he were already a doctor.

He proposed during my junior year with both my hands in his. "I've given it a lot of thought, it's not a frivolous decision. We complement each other. You'd be interesting to live with. I like your company. We're nice to each other, that's a good sign. A doctor's wife should be special, and I think you are."

I reminded him: "I want to go into public affairs, maybe politics or government or journalism. There's so much to do in the world. (I was young, therefore an idealist.) I'd sort of like to go to graduate school."

"You could apply at U. of A. I'll do a year there first—practically nobody from A.S.C. is accepted at medical schools."

"Mmmmm."

"Med training is demanding, it wouldn't be easy for either of us, and the G.I. Bill doesn't provide much money to live on, but someday I'll have a good income. And the thing is, Marlene, when I'm with you I'm the happiest I've ever been. I'm not sure what everybody else means by love, but I think being happy together should be part of it."

My college sweetheart. How was I to know how life changes people one step at a time?

They weren't easy years. I earned a PhT, Putting Hubby Through, worked as a teaching assistant and let my degree go so I could find references for him, type papers for him, cook meals for him, wash clothes for him. Live in a basement apartment where pipes snaked across the ceiling. Listen to him. Be company and comfort for him. It was a purpose we had together.

At first it was safe to love him: it didn't make him mean. Safe to sleep close against him. Safe to take coffee to him in the morning. I could bring a colored pebble and put it in his hand and trust him not to say, "I already have a rock."

But for Don medical school was a regimented, grueling ordeal. His textbooks were biochemistry, anatomy, pharmacology—not really good topics for pillow talk. One boy in his classes suffered a psychotic break. Another was a suicide.

When street lights were coming on, we went out for tacos and beer. Later, on a student-size mattress, we held each other close.

"Marlene, you're the most important thing in my life." He touched my face, stroked hair back from my forehead. "I couldn't go through this if I didn't have you."

"Oh, Don. I'm glad to help any way I can."

"It won't always be like this. Things will be better soon."

"I know. We'll look back and laugh."

Youth. You can accomplish wonders that you'd never try for again.

The residency years were worse, punishing to his health, hard on his mood—it's a wonder anyone survives the strain. Some don't. He was on duty eighty to a hundred hours a week, new to the job, living on coffee, sleeping at the hospital, coming home worn out, worn down, exhausted by responsibility, earning less than minimum wage. (No, I don't think there was such a thing then as a minimum wage…or was there? That was after Roosevelt…so maybe.) He faced one crisis, one horror after another. The skin under his eyes turned dark. Sometimes his speech was slow, slurred.

I tutored for a while, but after that I was a lunch waitress, smiling at strangers for tips. I was afraid it would make me into someone I didn't like.

But Don was so nice. "Have I told you today how grateful I am to have you?"

"Not yet. But you can go on touching my face like that."

"Well, I am grateful. You're the most wonderful thing in my life. It won't always be like this, Marlene. Things will be better when I finish my residency."

"I know. We'll look back and be proud."

The change was so gradual that I didn't recognize it for a long time. There was no conversation over the dinky kitchen table or holding each other close at night. Two people living one life, but separate. Finding books that would fill emotional holes didn't fit my idea of marriage.

His training lasted eight years. After that came board certification: oral and written exams. He didn't specialize because, he said, he didn't want any more punishment.

We came back to Phoenix because a good situation was open—at $10,000 a year. There was a practice to build, social duties, an increasingly expensive series of houses. It was expected that I have children to establish Don in Phoenix as a family man. I didn't have a graduate degree to match his, and it bothered me. Sometimes I was angry.

> By the time a breast tumor is palpable, it has undergone about thirty doublings and contains about 100,000,000 cells. Oh dear god.

1882 I've learned a lot. When Flagstaff was new, medical training was uneven; many schools were criticized by the federal government as "substandard." In that time, when only six percent of all Americans had graduated from high school, ninety percent of all U.S. physicians had no college education.

Dennis James Brannen, born in June of 1857 to Irish parents who had emigrated to Ottawa (reason, famine), entered the United States when he was three years old. He graduated from the E. M. Institute in Cincinnati in 1881, practiced medicine in Ohio until February of 1882, then traveled to Arizona when Flagstaff barely had a name and made a career here that lasted a quarter of a century. I can't say I'm impressed by the fashions in face hair of those days, and the doctor was "a fine figure of a man," which meant he was on the well-fed side. No matter: he became a Leading Citizen of the town.

At age twenty-five, D.J. Brannen was Flagstaff's first doctor, as well as one of its settlers—the town's population then was less than 600. His first office was in a tent. That wasn't remarkable, almost everything in Flagstaff was in a tent for a few years. An old photograph of Brannen's "office" shows only four medicine bottles.

I wonder what they were—heroin and morphine were sold over drug store counters all over the country. Maybe one of his medicines was a frontier tradition: whiskey.

Probably Dr. Brannen had a thermometer and a stethoscope—they'd both been around a few years—and a steel forceps for extracting arrowheads and such. But microscopes were not yet widely used, rare even in bigger cities. Rubber and surgical gloves would not be standard medical equipment for another two decades.

On the plus side, anesthetics (ether, nitrous oxide, chloroform, cocaine) had been part of a surgeon's arsenal since the Civil War. Blood-letting was going out of fashion.

But these infectious diseases didn't disappear until well into the Twentieth Century: influenza, measles, hepatitis, chicken pox, mumps, scarlet fever, whooping cough, syphilis, tuberculosis, diphtheria, typhoid, typhus, small pox. The transcontinental railroad that ran right through town brought infection as well as passengers and dry goods.

Cholera and dysentery, caused by unsanitary conditions, had come west in the great 1849-51 migration. Flagstaff had no drinking water except for what was brought from springs and emptied into barrels outside back doors and no sewage systems apart from outhouses behind each home and business. Horses, cattle, pigs, goats and dogs wandered in the streets. I wonder how the town smelled in the summer.

Population minus 600—not a large patient pool. D.J. Brannen signed on as physician for the Atlantic and Pacific railroad as division surgeon along the line from Albuquerque to Needles. Settlement in the whole of northern Arizona was so sparse at the time that priests served on the same route, stepping down from a train to visit Flagstaff only occasionally.

The doctor established a consulting room in a real building in 1884, moved to a new office and dispensary in 1886, then in '88 to a structure on Front Street—it fronted the railroad tracks—where he set up the town's first drug store. It was common on the frontier for a doctor to be proprietor of his own pharmacy, where bulk shipments of roots, herbs and leaves were ground with pestle and mortar. I never can remember which was which.

Within a year D.J. had located his office around the corner on the west side of San Francisco Street. Neither of the buildings nor any place else in town had electricity—the Riordan brothers didn't organize the Flagstaff Electric Light Company until 1895. Ah, the Romance of the Old West.

There was the usual variety for a frontier doctor. Brannen treated sick babies and children, also adults with fevers, skin cancers, broken bones, pneumonia, and gun shot wounds; he performed amputations and was called to accidents caused by fights, horses, trains, logging and the sawmill. Definitely a General Practitioner, he was on the payroll of Arizona Lumber and Timber Company which had its offices south of the railroad tracks in Mill Town. In '88 he tended the fire chief, Sandy Donahue, who had been burned fighting one of the town's frequent blazes.

1885 Doctor number two in order of arrival was Percy Gilette Cornish. Raised in Alabama, he was in Flagstaff by 1885, almost the beginning. Twenty-eight years old that year, as was Dennis Brannen, he was fresh from Jefferson Medical College of Pennsylvania. Reading about him in the local newspaper, I gather that he was rather livelier than his colleague.

The local newspaper referred to him as P.G. to distinguish him from his brother A.T., who had arrived earlier. Dr. P.G. Cornish treated the same variety of illness and accidents that Dr. Brannen did and worked with him on amputations and the like. In ads he said he too would answer calls on the A & P line. One: when the boiler of an eastbound freight train exploded near Ash Fork, killing engineer, fireman and brakeman, Cornish was one of the doctors called to embalm their bodies. Doctors on the frontier were hardly specialists.

1888 Then a third doctor came to town, a man twenty-five years older than Brannen and Cornish. George Felix Manning had been born in 1837 in Alabama, down on the Gulf of Mexico, to southern parents. A Confederate veteran, he had been a private in Company E, 3rd Alabama Infantry, and a Sergeant in Company D, 2nd Battalion Alabama Light Artillery, according to State of Alabama Department of Archives and History. By the end of the war he was a Captain. Or maybe a First Lieutenant: sources differ.

Manning attended the Universities of Virginia and Alabama Medical Colleges—two medical colleges affiliated with universities?—studied two years in Europe. Two years in Europe? In a time when much of American medical education was mediocre at best? On paper, at any rate, George Felix was well-prepared to do the job.

Then he moved to Texas, where he was appointed to the first state medical board and accumulated a touch of Old West color. His brothers, who were operating a saloon in El Paso—about as far west in Texas as you can get—were feuding with a deputy U.S. Marshall, and George Felix got involved.

On a September day in 1882, Manning and the marshal, in good old Western tradition, engaged in a gun fight in which the doctor was wounded in his right arm. His brother shot and killed the marshall, but George's arm was nearly useless for the rest of his life. Six years later, thin as a fence-post, he moved to Flagstaff, bringing wife and family with him.

For the first ten years, Manning doctored in town only if he was needed and apparently concentrated on running a drug store. That was something of a tradition too, an informal way of seeing patients, diagnosing and prescribing medicines. It's a wonder anybody survived the treatment. Frontier druggists dispensed a list of medicines that would have alarmed 21st century patients:

Laudanum: tincture of opium
Ipecac: dried roots of a South American plant

> Jalap: roots of a Mexican plant
>
> Tartar Emetica: antimony and potassium Dover's Powder: opium, ipecac, sugar of milk
>
> Calomel: mercurous chloride

Blue Mass: metallic mercury and licorice

Paregoric: opium and camphor

Nux Vomica: strychnine

Belladonna: deadly nightshade

Quinine: bark of a Peruvian tree

Morphine: alkaloid of opium

Arnica: flower heads of a native plant

Digitalis: leaves of Foxglove

Ergot: rye fungus

Blaud's Pills: carbonate of iron

Asafetida: gum resin

Seidlitz Powder: bitartrate of sodium and potassium, bicarbonate of sodium and tartaric acid

Dr. Manning was not licensed to practice medicine in Arizona. Neither were Brannen and Cornish. Thirty years earlier most states had repealed—in the name of freedom (!)—their laws requiring doctors to pass a test and earn a license. By 1879 opinions were changing, but still only seven states had effective licensing. It was not until 1903 that the 22nd Legislative Assembly of the Territory of Arizona approved "An Act to Regulate the Practice of Medicine." Only after that date were doctors required to file applications, register their qualifications and pass examinations.

Some American doctors had adopted Lister's sterilization; maybe Brannen, Cornish and Manning had as well. In Flagstaff there was always a lot of germ-killing whiskey around. When your only water is in a barrel outside the door and you have to start a wood fire to boil it and you're 7000 feet above sea level…

Midwives cared for women giving birth when doctors were busy or too far away, delivered most of the babies in Arizona's territorial years. Experienced and practical, they were indispensable; even the doctors said so. But who were they? The doctors' names are on record. The names of most of the midwives have vanished.

As a doctor's wife myself, I sought Manning's wife in far flung records. (I like that image: far-flung.) Her name was Sarah Ellen Alexander. Born in Tennessee in 1859—just before the War Between the States—she moved, probably with her parents, to Texas. In 1879, according to Bell County Marriage License Records, when she was twenty years old, five feet four inches tall, she married George Felix. Tennessee, Texas—I wonder how her voice sounded.

Dr. Manning was twenty-two years older than she was. Her figure was "pleasingly plump," his was unfashionably thin. When they came to Flagstaff, he was fifty, she was twenty-eight. They brought three children with them: Henrietta whom they called Yetta, George Felix jr., and Althea, all born in Texas. There had been one other baby who had died.

Sarah Manning was the first doctor's wife in this dusty little town, not yet a decade old. There were more vacant lots than buildings when she arrived, and most of the buildings were saloons. She raised her children in hard-work conditions—otherwise I could find barely a clue to the person she was. Except for 1888, when she was mentioned as attending a Knights of Pythias Ball and a July 4th Ball, Sarah's name didn't appear anywhere in the Flagstaff newspaper in the 19th century. Why not?

Her husband was not as prominent as Brannen and Cornish, and she was ever busier at home: two other children were born after they arrived, Thomas Peyton and Julia. Or maybe George Felix sr. was the kind of old-fashioned man who preferred that his wife stay at home and out of the newspaper.

> People in a family are too close to help—emotional illness affects them all like a plague in the house. How could we tell who had the illness? All of us had the symptoms finally.

"Hello?"

"Gwen, in your voice I can see your face."

"Mother, hello. Is something wrong?""

"I'm in town on a day off, standing here in front of the laundromat, and I thought I'd call."

"Laundromat? You don't even have a washing machine?"

"The only water where I'm living comes from a pump outside. It doesn't hold a prime, but I don't complain, it's a fair trade-off for the view. How's the family?"

"Fine. Your letter came yesterday. I feel as if I'm becoming acquainted with you for the first time in my life. Is everything really as wonderful as you described it?"

"It is. Air is clear, brilliant. Swallows flash past and change direction so quickly they disappear. Trees move in the wind. One evening I walked on the mountain and saw a doe with twin fawns. Everything is goodness."

"I hope so, I worry about you."

"I'm letting my hair grow out."

There's a pause. "I like it that ash blonde."

"This summer I'm washing it in the sink. Not convenient for coloring. Besides, it's become so white that the difference barely shows. I hope."

"Are you careful on the tower stairs?"

"Coming down I put my feet sideways on each step so they'll be completely supported, and I keep one hand on the railing at all times. Going up I'm slow and careful."

"Are you comfortable?"

A noisy truck drives by. I wait until it passes.

"My cabin is about the size of the closet I used to have for my clothes, and the tower's only seven feet square. Very personal space, especially at night or when wind is blowing. Small shelter, barely separate from the forest—glorified camping. It's luxuriously intimate. I didn't feel anything so personal in all those rooms I had in Scottsdale."

"Speaking of the house, have you sold it yet? I should come down and handle it for you."

"I've had an offer. We'll see how that goes. It's clean and empty—after you all took what you wanted, I put what I'd like to keep into storage and sold the rest."

"Don't you miss it?"

"I remember, but I don't regret. Don't wish it back."

"I'm turning my fourth bedroom into a separate suite with its own bath so you can come to Colorado in the fall and live with me. You don't have to be alone."

"Thank you, Sweetheart, that's good of you, you're a good person. But I might stay in Flagstaff for a while. I like it. Leafy trees, libraries and book stores, good restaurants. Bells in the Catholic church steeple chime every hour. Strangers smile at me in the grocery store. It feels human."

"Mother, I've been thinking. You've always been slim, but lately you're looking— well, vulnerable. Are you safe?"

Slim, she says. This summer I'm noticing the bones under my skin, but she should have seen the waist I had before children.

"I suppose I'm as safe here as I would be anywhere. The tower's only twenty feet from the cabin door—I think we can cross off being hit by a drunk driver on my way to work."

"That reminds me, do you know what the boys asked me the other day? It was so funny, 'Did Nana buy a motorcycle?' Oh my god! Beanie's snake just poked its head out from beneath the microwave—it's been missing for days—I gotta go!"

What had she and her husband been saying to give their boys the image of me on a motorcycle? I liked it: Grandma in a black leather jacket and a neon helmet taking curves at a forty-five degree tilt. I'll show you vulnerable.

I doubt there's a formula that could predict what it takes to bring a mind to collapse, but I'll bet you could figure what kind of impact at what speed would cause a body to fly to pieces like that one did.

A magazine item I read lately says that weather exists on planets, stars, brown dwarfs, maybe everywhere in the universe. Really? Comes under the heading of Things I Never Knew Until Just Now.

Maybe it's peculiar for a woman my age to be interested in astronomy. Or in doctors' wives in Flagstaff—I didn't know the town, the people, anything, and it was over a hundred years ago. I'm learning only the skeleton of a story, but imagination begins to fill it out, and in no time at all I have real people in my head, living in a real town.

Maybe the difference between weird and "normal" is a matter of degree.

The first doctor in Flagstaff, Dennis J. Brannen knew everybody for miles around— which wouldn't have been hard, there were so few. He represented them in 1885 in the Territorial Assembly that met at Prescott; in 1887 he was the postmaster. His financial interests included ranches and cattle, mines, real estate. All over the West doctors, regarded as men of substance, lined their bank accounts from business, ranching, politics.

According to the federal census of 1900, eighteen adults living in Flagstaff had been born in Ireland; there were twenty-five whose parents had been born there and twenty others whose Irish immigrant parents had been born in Canada. It was the largest single group in town. Flagstaff was an enclave of Irish, which might have been unusual for a northern Arizona settlement. That has to have been a factor in what it became, doesn't it?.

Anyway, like other Irishmen in town, D.J. was an active member of the Church of the Nativity from the time it was organized. In 1887 his cousin P. J. subdivided a tract of land "on the southside"—south of the railroad tracks but east of Mill Town—in the expectation that Flagstaff would grow in that direction. (It didn't, not right away.) P. J. donated a site on Ellery for the church, and Nativity was finished in time for a Christmas mass in 1888.

1889 Active in his little town, Doctor Brannen remained unmarried until March of 1889, when the local paper printed that he was on vacation in Canada—in Ottawa, I think.

It is reported that when Dr. D.J. Brannen returns home, he will be accompanied by a bride. He is having a neat little cottage built for him on the Brannen addition.

That woman was in for a big change—I wonder if she knew. Ottawa had been the capital of Canada for the past thirty-two years, a busy sawmill center and market town with dominion judges, legislators, administrators and executives to leaven the mix. The National Academy of Arts, the Academy of Music and the Royal Society were well established. Flagstaff was seven years old, still part of Yavapai County.

The population of Ottawa was more than 20,000, the population of Flagstaff a twentieth of that. Ottawa had been built among rolling hills in the St. Lawrence Lowlands where three rivers watered fertile farmland. Flagstaff lay at the base of a 12,000-foot volcano where the only river was the seasonal Rio de Flag and rainfall was sparse; potatoes and hay were the most reliable crops.

Ottawa had been laid out with broad parallel streets; Flagstaff huddled at the base of Mt. Elden. Soaring Gothic buildings crowned Ottawa's Parliament Hill; houses in Flagstaff straggled away from a town center of mostly one-level stores. Ottawa's Department of Public Works had provided the city with water ten years earlier; there would be no water piped into Flagstaff for another decade. Ottawa provided hydroelectric power within a fifty mile radius of the city; Flagstaff was still using candles and kerosene. Ottawa had sewers and "sanitary facilities;" Flagstaff was dotted with outhouses.

The bride was 24-year-old Kathleen O'Donnell. I wonder what she felt when she stepped down from the train in northern Arizona and saw the town. Maybe excitement: "Oh good, an adventure!" Maybe dismay: "I've made a ghastly mistake." That looming mountain. Unpaved streets, the few sidewalks wooden.

The Brannen Addition was a dusty (and muddy), treeless neighborhood. "Tidy" cottages were single-story, four-room, red brick houses. Perhaps at first Kathleen set up housekeeping in the back of the doctor's office: it was a while before the paper informed readers that the Brannens had occupied their new home.

She was a woman of what were then called "genteel accomplishments." In November of 1889 the newspaper described a Catholic fair featuring fancy work:

> *It is but just to make special mention of Mrs. Dr. Brannen's oil painting, which represented Welsh scenery. It was pronounced by all present the most beautiful piece of work on exhibition, and Mrs. Brannen can justly feel proud of her work.*

The local newspaper didn't tell everything, no more than the Arizona Republic does. Again, I needed to make an educated guess: as the doctor's wife, she wore in public clothing which signalled her status. Her bodices were fitted and heavily boned to squeeze her into a tiny waist. Collars stood high under her chin. Sleeves were slightly gathered at the shoulders. National magazines that arrived on the trains decreed no more bustles, just flared skirts with back pleats and padding on her hips to make her look feminine. For evening there was decoration on her bodices and drapery on her skirts, as much as could be accommodated.

In the style of the day, Kathleen's front hair was probably padded and featured a frizzed fringe over the forehead; the back was swept into a high-set knot. Bird feathers and wings decorated her hats.

As a respectable married woman, she was nearly as invisible in the newspaper as Sarah Manning. While she lived in Flagstaff, she was mentioned in the paper only eight more times, so says an index. But issues for all of 1890 and half of 1891 are missing from all libraries in the state which could be expected to have them—Flagstaff, Phoenix, Tucson. I don't know what part she took in that frontier society, which was surprisingly active.

Like: in February of 1884, only two years after the little water-stop logging town was settled, a Literary Society had begun to meet Thursday evenings at the schoolhouse, a twelve by fourteen foot log cabin—the size of the one I live in—with a brush covering for a roof. I'm impressed: bear were on the outskirts, the Peaks were alive with lions, water was carried home from the few outlying springs, and a handful of the pioneers started a Literary Society. After 1886 there was no further mention of it in the paper.

In 1887, two years before Kathleen arrived (no public library in Flagstaff yet), a book salesman came through town offering sets of books by respected writers and sold several Shakespeare volumes. The newspaper reported in November that another literary society had been organized at the Methodist Episcopal church but did not print a list of members nor of books to be discussed. With her Ottawa background, Kathleen might have been a member. Or maybe not. She was Catholic, after all, and the ladies seem to have been inclined to segregate their socializing.

The 1887 group may have been the Shakespeare Reading Circle. It persisted, possibly into 1892, but expired after the women became too busy with babies to read and discuss. The Shakespeare Club was organized again by 1904 and, I'm told, continues today, claiming to be the oldest active women's group in Arizona. Good for it.

The Chautauqua Literary and Scientific Society was organized nationally in the late 19th and early 20th centuries to provide general adult education with lectures, classes, and directed home reading. There was a chapter in Flagstaff by 1888. Again, the paper did not print membership lists. Nor for the Authenian Literary Society set up in March of 1890. Ambitious, weren't they? For culture, I mean.

Mrs. Dr. D.J. Brannen may have been a reader, but there's no way of knowing. In that case, I choose to believe that she held barbarism at bay during the doctor's frequent absences with the companionship she found in books. Why not?

Early in 1891, she gave birth to a girl, probably at home: ninety-five percent of births in the United States took place at home. I remember that whole uncomfortable experience—three times was enough—and I imagine what it must have been for her to be pregnant, needing to get rid of urine two dozen times a day in a town that had only chamber pots and outhouses. My sympathy, Kathleen.

She wasn't well. The Arizona Champion told its readers:

> On Tuesday the 13th of February, Dr. D.J. Brannen left with his sick wife for San Bernardino, California, hoping the change of climate and scene would improve the health of his wife, who was suffering with consumption, but on Wednesday the last the sad news reached here that her death had called her home. She leaves a kind husband and an innocent babe to mourn her loss.
>
> Mrs. Brannen was a native of Canada and came to Flagstaff nearly two years ago as a bride. The body was taken to Ottawa, Canada for interment.

She was only twenty-six when she died. I suspect her baby, a girl, was sent to D.J.'s parents to be reared on their farm in Illinois.

No one knew at the time what cured tuberculosis; Kathleen's fingers-in-fifty-pies doctor husband was as helpless to save her as he would have been with anyone else's wife. He resorted to what most people in Flagstaff did: used the transcontinental railroad to take her to a larger city, hoping. The "professional courtesy" that we enjoyed wouldn't have helped at all.

I have only a foggy idea who she was, but I set this name here as a memorial.

Kathleen

What else can I do?

2

Dear progeny, near and far, and my two grandsons,

It was a thrill to open my post office box this week to find letters. OK, it's an old-fashioned way to have a conversation, especially for those of you who are in your beholden years, when leisure is a quaint idea. For me, isolated here on this mountain with no e-mail, writing letters to you is not just a way to keep in touch—it's an opportunity to say things I might not in a voice-to-voice.

But don't feel obligated to match me page for page or letter for letter. I've been where you are. I remember that sometimes a week can go by with nothing new to say and no time to say it anyway.

Beanie, your drawings become more colorful and imaginative with every month. I love the ones you sent of me on my tower, especially the wings that you put on me. It's true, it's true. I've bought some colored pencils so I can draw something to send to you.

Cazz, the poem, my goodness. I'm proud of you. I had no idea such thoughts were in your mind, and I like the way you say them. Here's an Arizona poem I've written for you—Arizona because what isn't there is important. With that as a clue, do you see what I mean?

> *Bad weather—*
> *the Anasazi walked away*
> *from their beautiful houses,*
> *leaving only footprints*
> *on the dry earth.*

Gwen, I can see the evidence of your influence, the time and effort you invest in the job. It isn't easy, is it? I'm proud of you too.

Baxter, congratulations on your promotion. I hope the company won't be expecting more work from you now, but it probably will. Companies are like that. Will you have time to tend your little trees? That's been important to you.

Abby, your analysis of the economic role of domestic servants for your dissertation is not just intelligently written, it's quite provocative. Yes, please do send pages from your work. I understand: the research is a chronicle of your life right now. Does it leave you time to work on lectures for your teaching assistant class or are you winging it?

Is everyone happy and in reasonable health? I hope so. My life is grand and glorious these days, and I wish the same for everyone. What a world that would be.

I've been exploring Flagstaff on my two days off every week, discovering, choosing a section and driving slowly through it. I have no guide book, so there's the excitement of finding things for myself.

First I identified all eight blocks of downtown: a park with tall shade trees, a library with big windows, an old stone courthouse, a corner bookstore, an artists' co-op. I've been to Lowell Observatory, walked around the university campus, spent a whole afternoon at the Museum of Northern Arizona, got lost at the Country Club. (An odd sort of name, now that I think about it. Country. Club.)

There's a clarity in newness. Edges are sharp, light is brilliant, colors mean more. Truth lurks behind everything. Every person is significant, every detail is art. Now I can say there's more to Flagstaff than I thought at first. And it's quite cosmopolitan: both kinds of Indian. Black-Hispanic-Anglo-Oriental-Pakistani. University students, professors, scientists. Green Forest Service engines are in the streets; so are foreign travelers of every accent.

I come back to my lookout cabin on a mountain top. A room of one's own…

A professor at U of A thinks that after a long stretch of wet years, the southwest is returning to the dry climate which is normal to it. Because of a Pacific Decadel Oscillation (ten year swing, in common speech) and snowpack projections of less than seventy percent of average, a mean fire season is forecast for the Southwest this year. You've read that efforts to burn off ground fuels on the North Rim and in New Mexico produced wildfires? Out of control near Los Alamos through 47,000 acres and 250 homes charred? News magazines are reporting a problem: "The West's Hottest Question/How to Burn What's Bound to Burn."

My job has been downright exciting. Day after day for the past two weeks there were Red Flag warnings: wind was strong, and humidity was in single digits. A fire north of Apache Maid lookout burned two acres in heavy fuels. Abandoned camp fires grew to half an acre near I-40, a fifth of an acre on Mt. Elden. A few days later, rapidly growing smoke was spotted on Mars Hill, upwind of Lowell Observatory, and a flock of firefighters in green vehicles raced toward it. The forest radio was full of excited voices shouting unit numbers and road directions, and Law Enforcement was dispatched to keep sightseers away.

Only ten minutes after that, smoke was reported at Harding Point on the red-rock rim, one acre of ladder fuel (fire climbs it) burning on the edge. Two hours later an acre was burning, smoke was huge and black, trees were torches, the helicopter from Green Base was looking for a dip site for its long-cable bucket, and the radio was a tangle of voices. Television camera crews were requesting permission to film both fires. Does that come under the heading of "the American public's right to know"?

With hardly a quiet day between, a fire started south near Clint's Well and burned 120 acres and—did I hear this right?—a Forest Service fire engine. Nearly trapped a man inside it.

"Possible" clouds were forecast, coming from California. In town on a day off, at noon, I saw white billows rising beyond a flank of the Peaks. They didn't look quite right, but I accepted the prediction of an advancing storm, perhaps because I wanted one. Leaving town on old Route 66 at four o'clock that afternoon, I saw the cloud again, huge, black and brown, alive, changing shape by the moment. I said: "That's smoke!"

I was concerned about me, of course, how close fire might be to my things in the cabin. Driving, I estimated. OK, beyond the Peaks, not on them. Too far north to be a danger to me and mine. For miles it would be out of sight, and then I'd have a brief glimpse before trees closed in again. Afternoon light slanted through pines; sky was peaceful blue. "It must be out near Kendrick Peak." (A volcano, extinct a million years or so—they all are, including Woody Mountain.) The first thing I was going to do when I got back to the cabin was switch on the Coconino forest radio for information.

It was only when I turned onto the tower road that I got a clear look. Roiling billows of smoke were surging up from the west side of Kendrick. (…photographs of Pearl Harbor sixty years ago…) In the cabin the Coconino radio was silent. "It's on the Kaibab," I guessed. "Not on us." I climbed the tower stairs in a strong southwest wind, and the whole picture twenty miles away spread out. The source of the smoke was behind a ridge. Was it caused by human error?

Human Error—is there any other kind?

From KNAU and the forest radio I pieced together: 500 acres burning in wilderness, moving northeast at thirty MPH (away from me), an increase of 100 acres an hour, and the Kendrick lookout had raced to his car at the bottom before a helicopter could get there to lift him off the top. The start had been near Pumpkin Center, so they'd named the fire Pumpkin.

In the middle of the night I woke to a smell of smoke and stood shivering in the cabin doorway in my nightshirt, testing wind against my face. It had veered to the north, blowing Pumpkin smoke toward me across the miles. All the next day Kendrick was invisible behind a pall of it.

Early in the morning the fire boss radioed, "Out of control. All lines are lost." It was going to be what they call a "project" fire. Big organization. Swarms of people.

Pumpkin would have been challenge enough for any district fire organization without the competition for resources that developed. At 2:30 three afternoons later Sandy spotted smoke near the old Winter Cabin down in Sycamore Canyon; helattack plus "a lotta folks" hurried toward it. At 3:15 Scott on the East Pocket tower reported smoke on a ridge between Vultee Arch and Slide Rock in Oak Creek Canyon. Within fifteen minutes I could see that one too, huge and brown. Slide Rock was evacuated, campers were advised to leave, Highway 89 through the canyon was closed at both ends.

A big skycrane helicopter was overhead, and a portatank dip site had been set up in the parking lot at Slide Rock. I relish the jargon of fire fighting, it's like learning a code.

The Sycamore Canyon fire didn't become a problem, but by evening twenty-five acres in Oak Creek Canyon had burned. By morning the total was sixty.

And the Pumpkin Fire was still active. Columns of black smoke moved farther across the back side of Kendrick every hour, covering six miles west to east, approaching Highway 180, drifting out behind the Peaks. On Memorial Day the *report was that a line was around half the fire to the south above Slide Rock, but 5000 acres north of Kendrick mountain had been scorched, and only fifteen percent of a perimeter had been cut. So many aircraft were working it that two frequencies were issued for their radios. Hundreds of firefighters were on the scene, for all the good it was doing. "Raining sparks," they said. All electronic equipment had been taken out of the tower on the top, and sheets of insulated aluminum sheathing had been delivered (by helicopter?) to wrap an old log cabin in hope of saving it. Crews were digging a line.*

My radio would not pick up the frequency the firefighters were using, so I watched a silent show, hypnotic smoke clouds surging hundreds of feet into a blue sky. Then, oh no! fire was obviously climbing the mountain over there: black smoke boiled up from slopes out of my sight. Wind here was blowing in fierce gusts, southwest 30 to 40. Temperature in town was 85 degrees. No hope for the Kendrick tower? I could see it through my binoculars standing alone against the sky.

KNAU announcers did not break into their Memorial Day Sousa marches to shout, "Do you know what's going on?" I thought it would have been fitting—they were broadcasting news of a chemical fire in Louisiana instead.

By three o'clock the tower on Kendrick stood not against the sky but against smoke rising behind it, some orange (orange?) among the black and brown. Next morning the radio reported total acres burned at 7,000.

Tuesday, another Red Flag, and Kendrick had been burning for six days. The tower still stood on the peak, but smoke began to inch over the ridge and down the south slope in three places.

I watched, concentrating on holding fire to the north side but not really convinced I was having much effect. Just, you do whatcha can, and the practice wouldn't hurt.

Gwen, Baxter, Abby, you grew up on super heroes—I suspect only Batmom would impress you—but you've known me a long time. You know I'm up to this adventure.

Love,
Mom

I wanted them to admire me for more than my clothes and my house, my charity work and cooking, not to mention what I tried to give to their lives. Their mother could live interested and unafraid, that's what I hoped they'd think.

"Hey, she's really something."

"You betcher booties."

Fantasy is better than no praise at all.

It wouldn't occur to them that juggling duties, poised, always available, had been courageous. I never, ever, wanted them to know that, right under their noses, I could love without being loved in return. And do it maimed, but then we all are, aren't we?

I considered an encore letter that described the night I was up in the tower at ten o'clock watching fountains of flame on the summit ridge of Kendrick, billowing smoke lit from beneath in golden-red. But I decided not to push it.

A total of 15,000 acres burned. The tower on Kendrick was saved after all, and the lookout went back. Smoke rose for more than another week while I tried to figure out what was happening over there—back-fires or burning off ground fuels or creating a fire line completely around the mountain? After days of watching it, I can say that smoke is beautiful. It rises out of the slopes and soars upward, not a straight line anywhere, fragile as blossoms.

Ten days went by without smoke on the forest. Then two-thirds of the Coconino was closed to public entry because of fire danger. Individual freedom gave way to communal safety, as it has a way of doing. The result is that my part of the forest is mine, not to be shared.

Don was good at remembering the details a G.P. needed to know. At his fingertips, on the tip of his tongue—the Latin words for everything. He could stitch a suture with his right hand and follow, tieing off the knots, with his left. When Baxter cut his foot, Don took him into the emergency room and told the duty staff, "Just like to tend to my boy here." But diagnosis frightened him. He had no problem treating patients, but for some reason deciding what was wrong with them gave him the shakes. It was part of what brought him down finally.

1890 Dennis and Percy and George doctored in a lively little town out here on the frontier. Did it form them or did they form it? And Sarah (Mrs. Doctor) Manning, how did she feel about it? I wonder—education was not free and universal in the South for years, could she read and write? If Sarah had a scanty education, maybe that would explain her apparent reticence in a little town full of book discussion groups.

Sarah, are you out there somewhere?

Eva Marshall was Flagstaff's first school teacher, 1883-1885, when the town's Sunday services were held in the school house. Mr. Van Horn, teacher for 1886, did his best to control boys who were as tall as he was and carried their six-shooters to class. I've been told a story—maybe apocryphal, good stories usually are—that once he gave the students an algebra problem and told them not to come back until they had figured it out. They all cheerfully stayed away from school for three days.

In September of 1887, Miss Weatherford and Miss Coffin, so the paper reported, went to Prescott, the county seat, to take a Board of School Examiners test. They passed and were hired by the Flagstaff school board as assistant teachers in charge of the younger children for three months each. In July of 1888 Clara Coffin was hired as teacher of the primary grades.

Coffin. Wasn't that a Nantucket name? One of the Coffins whose men were merchants in town, she was a former resident of Leavenworth, Kansas, a granddaughter of a prominent Kansas Republican.

Dr. Percy Gillette Cornish, Flagstaff's second doctor, knew the schoolteacher. She was a lively girl, a very visible presence in town, a social feature at balls and dances and card parties. On stage in amateur theatricals, available for spirited recitations at Chautauqua meetings—she seems to have had a wonderful time.

When John Hawks held a reception in his hotel in honor of his visiting married daughter, Clara was a guest, as were the P. J. Brannens, Dr. D. J. Brannen, the D. M. Riordans, the G.A. Brays, and Dr. Cornish. When the Protestant ladies held a fair with a raffle, music, dancing, and food, in the Hall of the Arizona Wood Company, Clara and Nellie Downes of Winslow competed for a gold watch with their recitations. Probably she was pretty. Center-stage girls usually are.

Dr. Cornish was reported several times in the newspaper as being in attendance at events which Clara attended but was not mentioned as her escort. It wouldn't have been considered seemly, would it? On January 1 of 1889 she attended a Leap Year Ball; Cornish was also there and at an Inaugural Ball at Wood Hall, where Clara danced in black lace over black satin—so the newspaper reported.

She was what they called a "corker." My parents would have said "a live wire." Definitely "popular."

I suspect Dr. Cornish was delighted with Clara Coffin. Who could blame him? She was so alive. They married in December of 1890. As a respectable newly-married woman, Clara was of course no longer a teacher: a married woman's career was her home. She appeared less often in society news for a few months. But Mrs. Dr. Cornish couldn't be repressed for long. In June of 1891, both she and Percy were in attendance at the Odd Fellows Ball; in July she went off to Prescott for a two-week visit with her sister, Mrs. E.S. Clark. There was a short trip to Albuquerque, probably on the train—given the condition of the roads, it was the only comfortable way to travel—another trip "east and south," a two-month-long visit to San Diego.

She and Kathleen Brannen were aware of each other, had to be, in the eight-year-old town, but after reading about Clara's exploits, I doubt there was a close friendship between them. Or with either and Sarah Manning. Three wives. Three very different people.

On windy days when I was, I don't know, twelve or thereabouts, I climbed a pecan tree thirty feet tall beside the house, almost to the top, and swayed back and forth pretending I could fly. My parents would say, "Marlene isn't afraid of anything," but I'm not sure that pleased them.

Moving out of my big house, going through drawers, I found a collection of old photographs, me at sixteen, and sat looking at them, thinking: such a bland, unmarked face. I wouldn't go back to adolescence for anything—it was a painful time—but I thought I wouldn't mind looking young again. Next morning I had a PIMPLE! A part of being young I'd forgotten. I laughed at myself. Emily would have too, she made life funny. Emily, I miss the laughter.

We didn't work for money. It was one of those unspoken understandings that make up a culture. We were doctors' wives, we just didn't work. We made big clever parties for the children on every birthday and holiday—oh, the Halloween costumes!—took them to movies and museums, to the zoo and the circus and the rodeo parade. We seized every opportunity Phoenix offered to civilize our little barbarians.

"Marlene, Maria Tallchief will be dancing with that touring ballet company next month. Shall we take the kids for a matinee?"

"I'd like to see Tallchief. I'm not sure how Baxter would feel about it, lately all he wants to do is read adventure comics."

I settled onto a stool at the breakfast bar and reached for a nail file. Emily and I talked so often on the phone that I used the time for basic maintenance on hands that always looked a little ragged.

"I'm contending with an escalating case of male hormones here too, but I thought it might be worth a try."

"I'm game. We can leave at the intermission if we see signs of rebellion."

I prepped my three for a week ahead with glowing comments about movement as art, the beauty of the forms, the athleticism of the dancers. Emily picked us up in her big station wagon, and we drove in to Phoenix Union High School with sounds of covert squabbles from the back.

The auditorium at P. U. was the only place in town big enough for a performance to be staged. We climbed those broad steps to the entrance doors and settled our group into front-row balcony seats with the boys on either end, separated from the girls by their mothers. I was enchanted by the whole delicious spectacle, and the kids were quiet, but at the intermission Abby said, "Mommy, aren't you glad to get out of there?" and I knew they weren't ready for ballet yet.

I was dedicated to the mother job. It was everything, my legacy to the future. Eventually, in the nature of things, the material with which I worked grew up and left me. It was only after the children were in school all day that Emily and I began to do volunteer work, charity work, reports and money-raising and the like.

I never did tell anyone about Lyle, not even Emily. It wasn't that I was afraid she'd tell Travis, she just didn't like Lyle. "I don't trust bachelors who are that smooth with women." But she usually was reserved with dermatologists, suspecting them all of looking at her skin, deciding what could be done with it.

Emily is gone but, always my special friend, she didn't abandon me. Lyle left me feeling like Joan of Arc after the Dauphin dropped her.

There is no language for such love as I felt. Or for such wild anguish. Words would have bled them into ordinary. The beginning was so gradual that there was nothing to say, the middle transcendent as a vision—I understood everything—the end left me too stricken for talk. It defined humanity for me, and it was private. I hope it was private. I hope nobody guessed.

That was thirty-five years ago. Afterward I told myself I had needed someone who would love me and make me feel valuable, which was true. In the years since I've admitted that sex was a factor lying under all my idealism. Of course it was.

Until I was about forty, I had secret power. When anyone taunted me or gave me orders or criticized me or hurt my feelings, colored rockets and pinwheels would burst out of my head and scream around me spelling out insults. Now we'd call that stress management.

Don wanted an adventure into isolated country. Life in action with all the comforts of home: phone, refrigerator and freezer, air conditioner, shower. Couldn't be done.

"There are dozens of kinds of coaches we can get. Let me tell you—I've learned a lot. Sit down, I'll get my notebook." I was quite proud of the information I'd collected.

He pointed at a brochure. "What's that? Top of the line?"

"It's ten feet shorter than the top, still big but better. It has a steel chassis and aluminum walls, but I'm not sure about the torque, and I don't know whether it has a diesel engine. I'll have to go back."

"I told you I didn't want diesel. What's torque?"

"The ability to turn the wheels against a load. It's important. A diesel engine has a lot of torque at low RPMs, fewer moving parts, no spark plugs or ignition system. It lasts longer."

He turned pages. "What's glide-out?"

"Here, look at these floor plans. *That's* a glide-out."

"What does this mean?"

"Gross axle weight. This one has dual wheels and electronic fuel injection."

"Why are you bothering me with all this?"

"There are all kinds of options, that's why. Air conditioning units, washing machines, cable TV, phone jacks. Do you want twin beds or a big double?"

"Two big doubles."

"I don't think we can get that, these coaches are only nine feet wide."

What he finally decided he wanted was what was called "a luxury coach" with blue squiggles along the sides, micro-wave and oven, upholstered furniture. Length was thirty-six feet. And it was a diesel pusher. He said that was what he'd preferred all along.

Actually, it was a house that could begin to move before the dishes were washed in the morning, and that was how Don wanted it. I learned that if I turned on television before he was out of his pajamas, I could hold him still long enough to get breakfast out of the way. By 9:00 a.m. he was behind the wheel, agitated. "Let's get on the road, come on, that can wait."

He had to keep moving. "No, I don't want to look for a place to stop, just bring me a sandwich so I can make some time." It was pitiful to see, I guess, but it drove me crazy.

We'd planned—that is, I thought we'd planned—to park the first night at Cameron. That would be a six-hour day at the speed we were going, longer if we stopped by Wupatki, which I wanted to do. But he was anxious to go on, north on 89 to Zion Canyon, all night if necessary. I could go to bed in back, and he'd keep driving.

I sighed. "Don, pull over a minute. Look at the map. Here's Flagstaff. It's still a long way to Cameron."

"That's a short day."

"The wind is very strong, and we're top-heavy. You'll be tired if you don't give yourself time to get used to driving such a big vehicle. We've never been on the Colorado Plateau before—people come from all over the world to see it."

"What's so special about it?"

"The scenery, the geology. Since before dinosaur time it's been intact, all one piece, 130,000 square miles that have moved en masse for millions of years. It's like no place else. Miles of driving roads, you told me that's what you wanted."

"I said I wanted to go through all those national parks, and I liked the idea of a place where there aren't many people, that's why I thought we should come up here."

"Would there be anything wrong with a little side trip to Wupatki? We're supposed to be on vacation, not in a race."

"Okay, okay, have it your way, but then we go on to Zion."

We'd been through all the reasons several times. "We'll do that if you want to. But I reserved a place in the RV park at Cameron, right across the highway from the trading post, hook-up, pull-through parking. Gas station at the post so we can fill up, which we need to do at every possibility if we don't want to run out. After that, it's miles and miles until we can get gas again. We'll be stuck in the middle of no where, and this thing is too big to push."

We took the Wupatki loop. All the colors of the Painted Desert opened ahead of us. Pines disappeared, then junipers, until most vegetation was only knee-high. Don complained that the land was bare and ugly, but I soared in the huge sweep of it, stretched my legs out on the console in front of me and let my spirit roam.

Don walked through the National Park visitor center but refused to go down to…beautiful…remnant of a building …empty for centuries…silent on its ridge above a dry wash…red stone walls leaning. "You can see it just as well from up here."

See it? I could feel it, and standing back was as good a place as any. Ghosts…life gone centuries past…rock-still and unmoving, except for the tourists. I wanted to wait there in the wind until the stars were bright. Not to understand, just to be there.

Don turned away and went back to the security of aluminum walls, and after a few minutes I followed him, climbed in and shut the door. The sound of it, closing out Wupatki, was sad.

Then on toward the Little Colorado, struggling with the wind that was pushing us sideways.I'd brought along books and maps, anything I thought might make the country we'd be driving through more interesting. Far as I could tell, the colors went way down, maybe six hundred to a thousand feet. Whether there's color deep in the dark is a separate question.

I tried to tell Don about it. "The rocks around here were laid down by a succession of ancient oceans that were more shallow in some places than others. And there's been movement, pressure, so some of the layers bent. We're driving on rock that's pre-dinosaur. On the right we've got cliffs that are about a hundred million years younger than the sandstone on the left."

"It doesn't make sense to me."

No, I suppose not. That's how it goes.

"Why'd you bring all that stuff?"

"These books and things?"

"Doesn't look much like a vacation."

"Since we came up out of the Verde Valley, we've been on the Colorado Plateau. We won't leave it until next week when we drive down off the Rim again. I wanted to learn something about it, we'll be going right across the middle."

"Plateau? A plateau's small."

"Not this one. It's huge, vast, massive. Almost half of Arizona, two-thirds of Utah, east to the Rockies in Colorado and New Mexico."

The motor coach was groaning up a long swell in the land. "Since when have you cared about geography?"

"I'm trying to understand what's under my feet. Anything wrong with that?"

"Sounds like a mid-life crisis to me."

"Don, that's mean."

"Don't you want the truth?"

When sun was lower and we turned at the Cameron RV sign, he complained. "Look at this, it's shabby."

"Well, spare. Compatible with the country. And they've tried. Planted trees."

"These sites aren't long enough."

"I told her how big we are. Turn left here, see, she said she'd try to leave another space open so we can turn into it and drive through up to the fence. No problem."

"How will I get out in the morning?"

"Probably in reverse. You've got that rear view monitor so you can see what's behind you."

"Dust is blowing everywhere."

Being cheerful against the odds can wear a person down. "Aren't we lucky we have walls around us? Do you want to eat dinner in here, or walk across to the trading post? The freezer's full of casseroles. Honey-glazed chicken and rice is thawed."

He didn't want to go outside into the wind. I think he felt safer isolated inside, removed from other people. Protected from other people?

Twenty years had passed since we had slept in the same bed, even the same room, together. We had twin beds in the back, but around midnight Don got up and went to the front to sleep on the couch.

It was about then that a question appeared in my mind from no where. He was so volatile, so agitated, erratic, unreasonable. Did he, as a doctor, ever hurt anybody? Wrong diagnosis? Wrong prescription? My god, the way he was acting, it would have been easy.

That headless torso was not the first corpse I'd seen, but it was the first one I'd discovered in the middle of a road. Ordinary life doesn't prepare you for that kind of thing.

1891 In the nine years since Dr. Brannen's tent, the raw little frontier town in northern Arizona Territory had managed to get by with no proper hospital. (Fine as far as it went, but a boarding house is not a proper hospital.) People who could afford to or who had enough advance warning went by train to Los Angeles for specialized care. The three General Practitioners in Flagstaff did what they could for the rest, making house calls to deliver babies and treat sickness, patching up injuries, both minor and ghastly, in their offices.

Mumps, measles and scarlet fever were reported in town. If ads for patent medicines are to be believed there was practically an epidemic of scrofula, salt rheum, dyspepsia, catarrh, and la grippe as well as such exotic ailments as "weak nerves, enfeebled skin, torpid liver, impure blood, debilitated system, biliousness, chronic grumbling, and nervous prostration." I love it, especially the chronic grumbling.

Probably I should mention here that there was a change in newspaper editors in 1891 when Clarkson M. Funston, a thirty-eight year old man born in New York, bought the Champion and changed its name to the *Coconino Sun*. To my frequent amusement, Funston reported Flagstaff news for the next sixteen years. Such as: Dr. Brannen treated a man with a skunk bite on the nose. An ad read: House and four lots to trade for cows. "Brute" was a description for men who committed "heinous crimes" and "dastardly devilish deeds."

In 1892 a Territorial Medical Society was organized in Phoenix for alumni of "regular and respectable schools of medicine." Apparently some schools were not.

Flagstaff that year: the frame Front Street building owned by Dr. Manning was destroyed by a fire on "wooden row." The next week he moved a building from the south side—that is, he had it moved—and set on the lot.

From 1888 until 1902 Dr. Manning bought and sold lots in Block 5, which I think was north of the center of town. Did he and the family live on them? I don't know.

1893 In October of 1893 Clara Cornish was back in the news. The Ladies Aid Society of the Methodist and Presbyterian churches offered a "comical musical production" for Flagstaff's entertainment. The newspaper didn't say exactly what the details were, but listed the ladies involved, one of whom was Mrs. Dr. Cornish. Ice cream and cake were served afterward. Ladies' activity was limited to that kind of thing in the Land of the Free. That was the world she lived in.

In the mid-west, Chicago's Columbia Exposition was attracting attention with innovations. By act of Congress the fair had a Board of Lady Managers (separate from the men) which was responsible for a Women's Building—designed by a woman, representing women. The Bureau of Music and the Women's Musical Congress took as their mission the demonstration that art music was the pinnacle of the evolutionary ladder. Interesting idea.

Weeks ahead Bertha (Mrs. Potter) Palmer commissioned composer/pianist Amy Beach to prepare an ode for the dedication of the Women's Building on the opening day. The male Board of Managers decided that as a woman Beach was very good but of ordinary merit compared to men (I'm not exaggerating—that's what they said) and rejected her music. The Lady Managers delayed the dedication of their building and used Beach's work anyway. Women had lived with such put-downs from self-confident males for a long time, and they were beginning to rebel.

Bicycles were a national craze, "all the cry" in Flagstaff. The paper advised readers, "Don't dodge a bicycle. It will confuse the rider." The new town council created an ordinance forbidding cyclists to ride their "wheels" on the few sidewalks and providing for a fine if they did.

Until the 1890s voluminous skirts and public opinion had kept the ladies earth-bound. Women did not "have the right" to ride. It was "not done," not good for their health, their morals, their families, their complexions, their hair and their reputations. They were "not ordained by nature" as cyclists, but if they insisted on being so bold, two-person tri-and bi-cycles provided space for a chaperon; side-saddle mono-peds maintained propriety. Side-saddle cycles! With one pedal. Shall I laugh or weep?

There were hundreds of kinds of bicycles in those years. Hobby-horse, celeripede, pedomotive, celeremane, lever and carrier and sociable tricycles, Ordinary (high wheel)—all with a fascinating choice of experimental saddles. Finally the "Safety" with its chain drive, direct steering, diamond frame and pneumatic tyres supplanted the others. Finally, anybody could ride. Even—gasp—the ladies!

Clara Cornish was one of the four married women who were chaperon to one another as they rode their new Safety bicycles around town. Well, bless her heart, of course she was. Flagstaff's newspaper, like others in the country, discussed them and their accidents in mocking tones.

They rode ladies' cycles—no rod from seat to handle bars to interfere with their "cycling skirts", which were of a length to below their boot tops, unlined but faced with fine leather in two layers. The outer part—listen to this—cut to provide a little fullness in the back and hips, of course, was not divided. Inside was a partition from the front to back seams on either side which enclosed their legs loosely. Thus: decorum but practical convenience, worn over heavily-boned corsets that created "wasp waists" with twenty-five pounds of pressure per square inch. Yikes!

Shirtwaists were all the rage, starched white linen collars almost to the ears, buttoned down the front, finished off with ascots or ties. From shoulders to elbows, sleeves grew wider every year until (leg-o'-mutton) they reached their most absurd in 1895.

Seems to me it might be difficult to be a lively, popular girl in such a get-up, but what do I know?

Dr. Cornish was a member of the new all-male Coconino Cycling Club, which organized picnics and expeditions. When the men rode to the Grand Canyon, Clara and five other ladies followed after them for quite a distance on their bicycles.

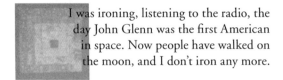

I was ironing, listening to the radio, the day John Glenn was the first American in space. Now people have walked on the moon, and I don't iron any more.

Thinking I might write another letter to the family about my adventures, I took notes one day.

9 a.m.: This morning the sky is blank and blue. Air is clear with visibility to the horizon in most directions. Along the east lies a thick band of white smoke from the monstrous Rodeo-Chediski Fire on the Apache-Sitgreaves Forest, the largest fire in Arizona history. Where the heat is most intense, huge billows of black and grey rise high into the air, creating their own caps of shining cumulus. I track the progress of the burning by where the billows are behind the mountains that stand unmoving here on the Coconino, between me and the smoke.

Hourly news broadcasts repeat: 190,000 acres so far, no, 200,000, no, 300,000—Show Low evacuated and expected to be swept by fire today, several small towns already destroyed, 25,000 people in shelters—a fast-moving front fifty miles wide (That can't be right, can it?)—Apache and Navajo counties experiencing adverse health conditions due to low smoke, which reaches all the way to Durango in southern Colorado—Hot Shots and air tankers withdrawn because conditions are dangerous. I'll bet they are. It's hot here and very dry, and strong erratic winds blow every day.

All of the lookouts on the Coconino are on overtime until further notice, just in case, and we all have evacuation plans. But so far wind through my tower is cool. I have tree shadows and bird song, books to read, music on KNAU. It's incongruous—peace and beauty here with hell (literally) within sight. We're taking it day to day and looking around anxiously.

10 a.m.: Fire has not reached Show Low yet. Now the estimate is 30,000 people evacuated. (I didn't know there were that many people over there.) Pinetop and Lakeside have been on one hour notice for a couple of days.

Most of the public is cooperating beautifully with the forest closure, and the few who defy the emergency restrictions are chased down by horse patrols, engine patrols, and air patrols with help from reports by the aforementioned cooperating public. So far none of the human-caused fires on the Coconino have grown to more than two acres. So far we have no forecast of rain either. Just hot and dry, pressure high. The big fear is that we might have dry lightning storms with all our people off fighting fires in other places.

The district ranger has collected all lookout home and cell phone numbers in case of a sudden catastrophic wildfire. I expect no problem getting away if I have to.

11 a.m.: One of our engines and another Hot Shot crew are going to the Lakeside fire camp. Three-hour driving time, they say. Smoke over there is boiling up into view far east of Mormon Mountain. Fire must be "making a run," as we say in the Forest Service.

Tension. Apprehension. But no excitement for us yet. A quiet radio.

12 p.m.: Wind is blowing from the southwest 10 to 15 MPH, lifting plumes of dust into the air from roads and construction sites. Traces of cirrus clouds are drifting from the south—I've noticed to my surprise that clouds seldom move as the wind down here is moving. I'm hoping in this case that there's no shift to southeast, which would put me downwind from the Rodeo Fire.

By the way, it started, probably arson, near an old rodeo ground on the reservation. Fort Apache?

Animals of all sizes left behind when their people evacuated have been brought out by Humane Society workers and are being cared for in several locations. What kind of people would abandon dogs and horses in the path of 200-foot-long flames? Frightened people.

1 p.m.: The smoke over there behind Mormon Mountain is black at the moment. Fire has not yet reached Show Low, but 126 houses in the area have been burned.

The public is running our ground crews ragged by reporting the plumes of dust I mentioned an hour ago. I'm very smooth saying, "Flagstaff, Woody Mountain. There is no smoke visible from here at that location. However, there is dust."

For several weeks I've spent nine to eleven hours a day up here in my little glass perch. Sometimes I'm told to spend a sixth day. My math is weak, but even I can figure out how much time-and-a-half I'm getting paid.

2 p.m.: Roads in the eastern central part of the state have been closed as a safety move. And officials are trying hard to maintain order—the radio says mail is being re-routed to Eagar and McNary, lists have been compiled of evacuees and their present locations, phone centers are taking calls from families and friends, Red Cross and United Way are collecting and distributing necessary personal items, even games and toys to children in shelters.

In this country, which we criticize whenever we feel like it, we expect such responses to emergencies without thinking about it much.

3 p.m.: The fire is approximately 100 to 120 straight-line miles away—beyond Mormon Mountain, which is 8000 feet high, 18 miles from me—but a black smoke monster soars above it, twice as high as the mountain is and just as broad. Is Show Low burning?

4 p.m.: What I know is what I hear on KNAU; now it's saying McNary has been evacuated. Five hundred square miles blackened, 330,000 acres. Sixty-one crews are on the lines. Cost of fire fighting is one million dollars a day. Three hundred and thirty-five houses have been burned so far. Show Low has escaped so far because of a back fire; probably Pinetop/Lakeside will be saved. Is that enormous black smoke hundreds of pine trees burning?

The Pres will visit the site tomorrow. (The Gov has already been.) Will this result in a debate on forest management policy?

5 p.m.: Some of the lookouts are signing off for the evening, but the five of us on the north end, around Flagstaff, will be here mostly alert for another hour.

Articles in the Journal of the American Medical Association say that personality style may render an individual vulnerable to specific psychological stressors and thus to emotional illnesses like depression. Personality style? What's that?

Today's nurses are medical professionals, and we absolutely couldn't do without them. When Clara Cornish was pedaling her bicycle around Flagstaff, the practice of training women to be nurses was barely more than twenty years old in America, that's all.

In the census of 1900 there was only one listed for Flagstaff: Johanna Yost—born in Austria, forty-eight years old, a widow with no children—who had immigrated to the United States fifteen years earlier.

Over fifteen percent of the nation's wage workers were women—young, single factory and clerical employees, a few professionals, and servants, of course—but

Flagstaff's lumber companies did not hire females even as secretaries. The six, the only six occupations of women listed in the census in 1900 were wife, schoolteacher, dressmaker, housekeeper, prostitute. And nurse, one. There had to have been domestics, hairdressers, laundresses and maids. Were they not listed, or did I miss something?

At the outbreak of the War Between the States, there had been no group of trained nurses in the country—it apparently had not occurred to either army. Maybe war clarifies the mind: Women's Hospital of Philadelphia started a training school for nurses in 1861; Boston's New England Hospital for Women and Children included a nursing school in 1863; in 1869 an A.M.A. committee on the Training of Nurses proposed that large hospitals should have schools for the training of nurses. In 1871 Godey's Lady's Book suggested an educational program that would graduate "professional nurses." More "training schools" were established instead. Nurses were not much more than housemaids anyway, and shouldn't be, in the opinion of some people. Is that outrageous or what?

Emily and I, reading about it, were indignant. "And look at this, Marlene. 'Midwives received no training or encouragement in any school or program. Doctors opposed recognition of their work in the belief that every delivery should be assisted by a physician.'"

"Male, no doubt."

"You know, I love my father, my husband, and my sons, but there are times…"

"Women have been the target of gender profiling for about 8000 years."

"Yeah, well, darn it, (Emily never said anything stronger than 'darn it.') who thought up that indignity?"

"Who let them get away with it?"

"You think we've been too nice?"

A training school saved its hospital money by putting nursing students on ward work. They were expected to labor twelve hours a day and were paid a modest stipend for a program that sometimes lasted only six weeks. It was better than nothing, but not much, not compared to the 21st century.

Nurse's training at the time was not professional education. Students learned sanitation—keep the patient, wound, bed, ward and yourself clean—and nutrition, bandaging. Practical care. Organization, standardization, and discipline were the basic principles.

Did anybody then think to say, "I'll bet she's a good nurse?"

Don was my first ghost, but it was a long time before I realized that the young man I had loved was gone. No certificate, no funeral, no consoling phrases marked his passing, and I didn't think to mourn him. He should have had tributes, spoken and written in the papers. He deserved that much, he was a good person when he was young

.

end of June, 2000

Dear kids,

What shall I tell you this time? I could talk about the map of the human genome sequence. The news was published yesterday, and it's already being called the beginning of biology, the beginning of understanding the genetic story of humans…a book of 3.3 billion letters…entirely mysterious. "We stand on the brink of a continent of new knowledge." "…ranks alongside the revolutions wrought by Euclid, Copernicus, Newton, Darwin and Einstein." Well! If that isn't dramatic!

I ponder the possibilities in law, ethics, philosophy. Religion? The media focus seems to be on changes in medicine. I suspect that we can't even begin to imagine what the future will be as a result of this big event. Strange and unknown land, the future, with strange and unknown people in it.

Baxter, you have such strong opinions it will probably offend you to hear this: I approve of what Bruce Babbitt is doing as Secretary of the Interior, and I think next November I'll vote for Eleanor Roosevelt for president. I wonder whether I'm growing more liberal as I get older. And whether Jimmy Carter is the closest thing to a political saint we have in this country. I can remember when George McGovern and Eugene McCarthy and Ronald Reagan had saint reputation in some circles. Woodrow Wilson did too, a saint once and for a while.

After a month of high fire danger and campfire restrictions and forest closures, the summer storm season has arrived even though people are hesitant to say so. It's early—July 4th is the traditional date—and therefore not to be announced too boldly, although after a few hours of rain in the Verde Valley someone said on the Coconino radio, "There goes the fire season."

I've become very interested in clouds. What beautiful things—they fill most of what I can see from my tower. Maybe you know—they've been organized into five categories with subdivisions, one of which is "unusual." I'm trying to learn to recognize them with the help of a book I bought in town. It's complicated: there's usually more than one category moving around up there, visibly growing or dissipating. At the moment three huge cumulus (I don't think they're cumulo-nimbus) are swelling hundreds of feet straight up over my head, blinding white and all shades of grey, with streaks of cirrus high above them, and rain is falling in four places, and bright sun is shining through my tower windows. The cumulus are drifting slowly to the east. I think the cirrus are going west.

People have asked—social chit chat—what I'd like to come back as after I die, and I've thought it a strange question. But I finally have an answer: a cloud. Always moving, changing, disappearing, appearing again. Looking down or ahead, watching. Nothing could stop or confine me. Nothing would have to die so that I could eat. It would be better than flying. I would be incredibly beautiful, especially at sunset, and the world would be more beautiful because of me. Yes, definitely. A cloud in Arizona where I would be welcome as a shelter from the sun and a carrier for rain.

That's rather Hopi, I think, but never mind.

I've been in ballrooms that were glowing with color, every color imaginable, every tint of every hue that could be dyed into a designer gown. Jewels glittering in the light of chandeliers, men's tuxedos setting it all off—it was dazzling. Medical Society Christmas Balls and later Barrows and Symphony balls were peacock displays.

The Coconino Forest after summer storms begin is softer, more subtle than those dresses, but I find its colors simply lovely. The Painted Desert sixty-some miles east glows pink in the washed air. There are indigo shadows in the folds of the Peaks. Down the ridge what I can see of the Oak Creek Canyon cliffs is a sort of peach. The forest rolls away from me in shades of green and yellow and pale gold that turn to blue and then blue-grey. Sky is Arizona azure at its most intense. I hear Louis Armstrong singing, "And I say to myself, 'What a wonderful world.'"

Air is so clear it vanishes, my books say that's a sign of an active atmosphere. I've seen green and pink in the clouds and a pale green low in the afternoon sky. At sunset, mountains to the west are rich purple. And sky colors—satin! Several kinds of butterflies wave their wings as they rest on the few flowers that came up early. In my view are three cinder pits dug into volcanic ridges; those openings in earth are magenta. Hummingbirds and mountain bluebirds are accents of moving color.

I'm in love with the view from my tower, the way it spreads, the way the moods change. You know how it is when you love a person, how you can't stop watching the expressions on that face? That's how I feel. The sun moves, and shadows change, light changes; therefore landscape changes. Clouds pass, bending over the hills and sliding down their sides. I'm in love with it. Hope that doesn't embarrass you.

In the mornings when I stand in the open doorway and look around, there's no need to hurry through tasks. I am responsible to no one but myself—no meetings, no dinner guests, no shopping, no papers on my desk—so I'm free to do nothing as casually as I like. Luxury beyond remembering: I can stand and look at the world.

As of this morning the road closure has been lifted, and people can surge into the forest again, though I've measured less than a third of an inch of rain, total, so far this season. Campfire and smoking restrictions are still in effect. It seems to me that this area is dry enough to be dangerous, especially since July 4th is coming up.

Maybe personnel are worn down after two weeks of running after potential arsonists, I don't know, or maybe past experience is that it's easier to police holiday campers than exclude them. Or maybe there's a forecast of heavy rain I haven't heard about. Stand by, as we say in the Forest Service. I will report to you.

Love,
Mom
a.k.a Eye in the Sky

1892 Doctors in Flagstaff saw patients in their offices, in private homes, hotels, rooming houses, but there was no place where single men without resources could be cared for if they were sick or injured—until the newly-organized Coconino County decided to establish a hospital "for the indigent" in 1892 and solicited bids.

Local hotelier John F. Hawks said he'd charge $1.20 a day per patient lodged upstairs in the rear of his building and was awarded the contract. Thus the first officially designated hospital in Flagstaff (distinct from two rooms in a boarding house) was two rooms in a hotel across the street from the railroad station. Capacity: eight men.

Hawks was not a doctor, no more than Mary Carroll. He had several interesting sides, but doctor wasn't one of them. Born in Maine in 1836—that much I found in federal census records. His mother was born in Maine, his father in Ireland. The catastrophic potato famine started about 1845, so Mr. Hawks senior immigrated well before the huge wave of poor, starving Irish arrived. I'm not sure what that means.

In 1880 when John F. was about forty-three, he moved to a collection of tents on the route of the Atlantic and Pacific line: the origins of Flagstaff. His wife, an Irish woman named Sarah Kelly, had died in Kansas, and he brought with him eight children. Other settlers called him "Dad."

He set up a saloon in a log cabin and then a rooming house with meals for boarders, then a restaurant on Railroad Avenue. And raised eight children without a wife? Hard to believe.

This was a down-to-basics country at first; I would think pioneers had to be enterprising and hard-working. And tough. When most of the town burned to the ground, Hawks started again—a hotel with a large cellar, twelve sleeping rooms upstairs, a bakery complete with oven [sic], and a restaurant. The local newspaper reported the opening: "Such an establishment is bound to succeed." His daughters served guests that first day. In no time at all he was proposed as a school trustee and began buying and selling property, town lots and such.

Two years later the hotel burned. He built another one of brick on the same site and rented downstairs space to wedding and dancing parties that paused for midnight dinners. He'd been doing nicely until he was 54, in about 1890—Flagstaff population up to 965. His daughters were getting married and his sons were getting shot. The financial panic of 1893 was just around the corner.

John Hawks was a frontier entrepreneur, alert to what the terrain offered. He had hotel rooms that were sometimes empty and a facility for cooking food, but as far as I could tell there was one thing he didn't have. The county board specified that the wife of the Superintendent of the new hospital for "the indigent" be hired as matron to run the place at sixty dollars a month, and there was no Mrs. Hawks, not that I'd found, not in the newspapers. When John was mentioned as being in attendance at social events, one of his daughters accompanied him, not a wife.

But wait a minute, the federal census of 1900, Coconino County, Flagstaff precinct, listed a wife for John Hawks and said they'd been married ten years: Anna B. Kelly— born in 1844 in Ireland—father and mother both born in Ireland. She'd had no children of her own. Later county probate records confirmed the name.

There was no record of a marriage license in either Coconino or Yavapai counties but "Anna Hawks" began feeding prisoners in the county jail at twenty cents per meal and tending indigent patients in rooms at the rear of the hotel.

I finally learned something about her, but it took some effort. According to her obituary in the local newspaper a few years later, she was the sister of J.F.'s first wife. But here's the surprise: she had been in Flagstaff from the very beginning "when there were but few houses," even before the first through train passed on the new railroad tracks. Well, of course. That's how John Hawks managed without a wife, ran a saloon and a rooming house, raised eight children. They knew Anna as "aunt and mother," but in the old records she was even more invisible than Sarah Manning. There's a story there, I think.

After the small county hospital was designated in a hotel in the center of town, it came to be used for anyone who needed something like an amputation with care afterward. A logger, for example, with a broken knee was taken to the Hawks Hotel for treatment by Dr. Brannen, the county physician, whose office was just around the corner.

Until I was a grown-up, we had to rotate the dial on a telephone to choose the number of the person we wanted to call. There was no such thing as buttons to push.

I sacrificed my education to Don's. It's too late for me to take up ballet or basketball or roller blading—anything that requires stamina from my tired body—but it's not too late for learning anything I want to know. I have time now to be a teacher with me as my only student, and what I want to know is merely everything.

In the NAU library I went hunting for a paper I'd read about: paleoecology by Thomas Swetnam at the U of A dendrochronology lab. I didn't know there were such fields. Or such words. If I understand his paper, Swetnam said:

> Most areas of the western United States lack written records of weather before the late 19th century. But there are natural archives in sedimentation, packrat middens, and tree rings that indicate plant migrations in response to climate during the most recent geological epoch. ("Plant migrations"—scientific writing has such delightful images.)
>
> After the last glacial period, pinon pine, which had been widespread in the northern Chihuahuan Desert, began expanding north to higher sites until it was established in the lower third of Arizona, land which is desert now, and then it displaced conifers like spruce and fir in some northern parts of the state.
>
> That happened because of weather change, increasingly dry climate. (The Petrified Forest lying on rock in northeast Arizona comes to mind.) More recently the state's climate has been the result of the El Nino/Southern Oscillation swing from wet to dry years and back. Extreme phases of the Oscillation affect wildfire activity. La Nina following El Nino is a time of increased fuels which dry out and create burning conditions.

Well! We have a good example of that right now. Or maybe I should say a bad example, if you can use words like good and bad when you aren't talking about humans. Anyway, I've discovered curiosity, and I finally have leisure to learn, and I'm enjoying the situation.

I sense that I'm younger than I was. The world is not exactly leaving me behind—more that I'm going off in another direction which feels natural and quite nice. Rebelling against years of public appearances in expensive suits, I've bought bright full skirts, underwear covered with flowers. For breakfast I eat exotic fruit and fresh

Parmesan cheese that comes in a small block. My Day-Timer is in storage with my panty hose and my cosmetics.

I do not plan to have my nose pierced and decorated with a stud, nor will I get a tattoo of any kind. There's a limit.

I wonder whether growing older is realizing truths you hadn't dreamed were there. Growing, yes that's a good word for it, growing older. Not what I can't do any more, rather what I couldn't do until now, couldn't see until I got here.

The star nearest to us is 26 trillion miles away. Those of us who are on this planet inhabit—I have to say this slowly—the outer edges of a supercluster of galaxies. Ours probably contains two hundred billion suns, and it is only one galaxy in at least 10 billion in the universe. Ten billion. Galaxies. In a multi-verse, as William James said.

Astronomers at a meeting in England on Monday brought the total of confirmed planets around other suns to fifty, and not one of the systems resembles ours. They all look serene from here, yet each sun is violent, with temperatures more than ten times that of our sun. Some are nearly as large as our whole solar system.

Is that impressive? All the stars visible when I look out (not up) at night are neighbors, but there are three dozen galaxies in the local group. That ought to expand human perspective, if anything can. At least for those of us who are edging elderly. Which is one thing I mean by what I couldn't see until I got here.

I might just make lists of why growing older is so exciting. First, the world is more beautiful than we are aware when we are so busy building lives. I wouldn't go back for anything: I'm finally old enough to know something. "When I was seventy, it was a very good year."

In high school, we wore pointy-toe shoes with heels that were spikes, the ends no bigger than dimes. We felt quite glamorous in them—we never wore them with slacks or shorts or swimsuits. The balls of our feet hurt, and we had to re-align our weight to keep our bottoms from sticking out. It was possible to walk and dance on smooth surfaces, but we couldn't run. Good grief, it's a wonder we didn't all break our ankles wearing those things.

1894 One week when I sat down in the library to read microfilm of old newspapers, I found that another doctor had come to Flagstaff, for a total of four. Edwin Seymour Miller, thirty-six years old. Born in 1858 to parents who'd been born in Vermont and New York, he graduated from the University of Buffalo Department of Medicine in 1879. Ah, a university-affiliated medical school.

Miller's office was upstairs on Aspen Avenue one door east of the post office, which was in the Coalter building across Leroux from the Weatherford Hotel. Like Brannen and Cornish, he came to town unmarried. I wonder where he lived—and how.

The Arizona Medical Association had been founded two years earlier with only nine members. Twenty-three states had licensing laws for doctors when Edwin Miller arrived in Flagstaff; Arizona Territory still did not. Doctors in the East were learning about X-rays; there was no X-ray machine in Arizona and wouldn't be until 1898.

In Flagstaff a new school was being built; committees were set up to plan a "waterworks" with pipes into town from springs on the mountain. Battle Ax Plug Tobacco was advertised in the paper. Twenty cyclists pedaled out to Leroux Springs for a picnic. Roads into the surrounding country were still dirt; they would be rough for automobiles for at least another decade, which was OK because there wasn't an automobile here anyway.

Three of the doctors (not Manning) were listed in a box on the front page. Three lawyers. Three churches: Catholic, Presbyterian and Methodist Episcopal. And seven secret societies for men. No such groups for women far as I could tell, secret or otherwise.

Big progress: the Riordan brothers organized the Flagstaff Electric Light Company and built a generating plant south of the railroad tracks. In early November of 1895 the company installed a dynamo, got up steam, and turned on the lights. There was no current during daylight—power was not available until dusk.

What's the point of my trying to learn anything so late in life? What's the point of being exposed to learning so early that you're too young to understand its value? Anybody know what the point is?

We bought the house in north Scottsdale when Abby was in the 4th grade. Frankly, I was intimidated by it and a little embarrassed, it seemed so much more than we needed, even with two teenagers in the family.

"It's a touch ostentatious, isn't it, Don?"

"I don't agree. I have to look successful if I'm going to be taken seriously."

"That's what I said: a show, a display."

"We can have all kinds of recreation for the kids—a whole separate rumpus building out back by the pool where they can have their friends and you can keep an eye on them. And there's plenty of room where we can entertain."

Entertain, yes. Dinner parties for a dozen. Cocktail parties for fifty. Not to mention committee meetings and readers' circles. Work expands to fill time; entertaining expands to fill available rooms.

"It would cost a fortune to furnish. I'd need somebody full-time to keep it clean."

"Oh, come on, Marlene, it's not that big."

"Three living rooms?"

"That's not true. Each has a different function."

"Oh, Don. I'd feel lost in that house, there's no space that's intimate. Can we afford it?"

"Yes. I need a house that looks successful."

"You're hardly ever home. I'll be the one who…"

We bought it, and I set myself to furnish and decorate. Touring gallery after gallery in Scottsdale, I bought a few big expensive paintings, western landscapes with no cowboys or Indians in them, to fill the big expensive walls. Then a decorator came to furnish around them, which wasn't too bad: I liked the paintings for the way they made me feel. Don liked them for their price tags.

The entertaining I treated as part of my job and located a good caterer. Bought dresses in impractical fabrics, what we called "cocktail" dresses, to stand around in looking successful. Hired small chamber groups of musicians, violins and guitars, sometimes a harp.

I liked to think I was doing it gracefully, but that house was never my home, those guests were seldom my friends, not real friends. No one knew how I felt except Emily.

"You think your dinner guests should be people you want to talk with?"

"Don gives me guest lists. Names I don't even know."

"You're an idealist, Marlene. In a cynical world."

"I didn't mind when we invited two or three other couples. It didn't seem dishonest. Or luncheons for half a dozen of the wives, I liked doing that. But these men I'm inviting now, they are their positions. It's a drag. As Baxter says, a major bummer."

Or maybe this is a horror story. People who disappear and leave no trace except in legal papers. Minds that can't stop transformation. Skin that crackles into something alien. Children who become bent and bitter before your eyes. A killer that patiently destroys from the inside. Victims who can't escape. That's horror. Oh yes. Even without viruses.

1895 Dr. Brannen went on as always, traveling hither and yon, busy treating illnesses and bones broken in bicycle accidents, building a grand new two-story structure for his offices on San Francisco Street, half a block north of the railroad tracks. In 1895 he was chairman of the 4th of July festivities, delegate to the National Irrigation Congress in Albuquerque. In December, the paper told Flagstaff:

> D.J. Brannen expects to leave next week for a month's visit to the home of his parents in Champaign, Illinois. He will also visit relatives in Canada before he returns.

I read microfilmed newspapers carefully, anticipating that he'd come back with another Ottawa bride, but he returned alone seven weeks later and resumed his duties as attending physician at the county hospital. Brannen was spoken of as "the right man for delegate to Congress, a true Democrat."

His parents visited him, and he escorted them on a ten-day visit to Pomona, California, where he owned a "prune orchard." The paper reported frequent trips to check on those prunes.

Meanwhile, Dr. Cornish, the only one of the four doctors in town who rode a bicycle, joined the League of American Wheelmen and became first lieutenant of the Coconino Cycling Club, which rode all around the Peaks now and then. On July 4th in 1896 they paraded and invited "all persons who have a wheel" to join them, "especially the ladies."

1896 The big news was the election, Bryan and McKinley competing for the presidency. Ungentlemanly political cartoons, usually ridiculing Bryan, and urgent arguments about free silver versus "sound money" dominated the pages of the paper, which was partisan Republican; it referred to "the so-called democrat party."

The 1896 campaign went on issue after issue in a tone no more civil nor thoughtful than that of the 2000 campaign. (Is that inevitable in a democracy?) The furor built to a November climax culminating in the triumph of Republicans and Sound Money, a.k.a. McKinley. In Flagstaff, Dr. Brannen and Miss Sampson from Phoenix led the grand march at Flagstaff's Inaugural Ball. I have no idea who she was.

Through the early 1890s, Dr. D. J. Brannen was mentioned often in the columns of Flagstaff's newspaper. One wonders whether the man ever stopped moving. Vice-president of the library association (What library? Was there a library? Or were they just planning one?), president of the company that ran stage coaches to the Grand Canyon, major in the National Guard, member of the Ancient Order of United Workmen and of the International Order of Foresters and of the Democratic Party, he was anything but a nose-to-the-grindstone doctor. In 1894 alone he 1) returned from Chicago, where he had been chairman of the Arizona World's Fair Commission, 2) went off to San Francisco as an Arizona delegate to the Trans-Mississippi Congress, 3) traveled to Prescott three times and Los Angeles twice and Montezuma Well once. Through the '80s and '90s, Brannen bought and sold real estate and lots in town as if they were peanuts. In '94, he acquired a ranch north of town and leased it to W.H. "Spud" Anderson.

Late in November of '96, when he was thirty-nine, the town learned of "one of the society events of the coming month," the wedding of Dr. D. J. Brannen and Miss Felicia Marley of Pomona, California." Pomona! All those trips to check on the orchard. Well! Born February 1870 in Michigan to a mother who had been born in France, Miss Marley was a sister of Mrs. J. X. McDonald of Challender.

She was twenty-six when she married "one of the popular physicians of Flagstaff, well and favorably known throughout the territory," and she jumped right into the role of Mrs. Doctor, setting a standard of social activity we tried to live up to through most of the 20th century. Thanks a lot, Felicia.

Before half the town had had time to learn her name, she became the Secretary of the Catholic Ladies' Benevolent Association and joined the group that played whist—D. J. was president and Clara Cornish vice-president. (Whist was a four-handed card game that had been popular in Europe for three hundred years. In simple terms it was bridge without bidding. I didn't know that.)

In February the group held a private dance at Babbitt's Opera House and met at the Dr. Brannen house, Felicia as hostess. "A very enjoyable time was had."

The paper gave fulsome coverage to her first dinner party:

> *Mr. and Mrs. Dr. D.J. Brannen entertained at dinner a party of young men—*
> *"the homeless four"—at their cozy home Sunday afternoon. Covers were laid*
> *for six, and at the table besides the host and hostess were Professor C.W. Wassen,*
> *F.W. Smith, Thomas Jasper, and the writer. The elaborate dinner was the*
> *product of Mrs. Brannen's skill and was most delicious, appetizing, and inviting,*
> *the homely four doing excessive justice to it. After dinner Mrs. Brannen favored*
> *the young men with a taste of her rare and gifted musical accomplishments. She*

*made a very pretty figure as she sat at the piano playing her own accompaniment
to those old songs that have never lost their sweetness, and from the frequency of
the encores it was apparent that such musical treats are few and far between in
the lives of the four "homeless." Dr. and Mrs. Brannen were most hospitable,
and the guests departed, deeply feeling that there was no place like home, and
that the doctor's home was the most pleasant of all.*

Every mention of Felicia was decorous and respectable and quite Victorian. It
was no surprise to me that in May when three students (the first class) graduated from
Emerson School, she was on the commencement program, singing "When Day Is Done."

Did she enjoy her position as a leader of community society? I'll bet she did. If not,
she thought she should do it, which is not the same thing at all. I speak from experience.

Notes on Medical History:

1872: The American Public Health Association was organized.

1889: The Mayo family opened a small hospital—the beginning of the Mayo
Clinic.

1889: Johns Hopkins Hospital opened.

1890: The National Association of Medical Colleges was organized.

1890s: A yearly average of 500,000 pounds of crude opium was imported for
medical use as well as 20,000 pounds of morphine. Alcohol was also a basic ingredient
of medicines.

1892: Viral research began. In the late 19th century bacteria responsible for tuberculosis, cholera, typhoid, diphtheria, bubonic plague, and pneumonia were discovered.
That did not mean those diseases had been eradicated.

1893: Johns Hopkins School of Medicine opened with a four year program and the
unprecedented requirement that all entering students have a bachelor's degree. The first
medical school in America of the university type, its emphasis was on laboratory and
clinical research. The Johns Hopkins program, a radical departure from the old regime,
eventually influenced all medical institutions in the country.

1893: New York City's Health Department began using its bacteriological lab for
diagnostic purposes.

1895: Doctors first used rubber gloves.

1895: Research into nutrition was initiated.

1897: The first American use of x-rays in surgery was at Johns Hopkins Hospital.

3

The years 1890 to 1910 brought greater changes in medicine than at any other time in history. I wonder whether that was too fast for some people.

mid-July, 2000

Dear family,

First: Beanie, I loved your drawing of all of us dancing and running around in a meadow. You've obviously been paying attention to how people move. How modern of you to color the trees pink and our faces blue. The question of what is a "real" color is something we could talk about sometime. (His art is quite good for a six-year-old, don't you think, Gwen? So are the poems Cazz is writing, for a nine-year-old.)

Cazz, the Colorado poem is quite impressive, very visual, and so is your ear for loose rhythm—you push me beyond my limits. Nevertheless, I send my latest effort.

You too?
Even the hardest rock
is changed by water
running, wind blowing,
Time, the tread of feet.
My bones are wearing thinner.
My roof will soon be old.

Did Baxter send you his poem about Texas? I laughed and laughed. Who would have expected a man who moves money all day could be so funny?

Second: the weather, always a good topic of conversation because it's endlessly fascinating. Why it's fascinating is a topic for another day.

Mornings here are bright blue and breezy. Sun pouring through the east windows is hot on my skin. Down the slope, noise hisses in pine needles, rustles through oak leaves. Tree tops below my windows are still. Surf sound rushes up through branches. Papers lift, fly out, and here's the wind.

A few little clouds show up out of nowhere, and first thing I know, the sky is full of them. They get bigger and darker, some of them rain, some shoot out lightning. It's very dramatic.

Up in the air as I am, I live with birds: ravens, swallows, jays. Now and then there are turkey vultures, sometimes a dozen of them at a time. And so many small flying bits and pieces moving through the branches of the pines that I went into a bookstore in Flagstaff and bought a guide to Western birds.

There are hummingbirds around the cabin, three dozen at least, both broadtail and rufous; I think lookouts in previous years must have put out feeders for them. I've bought some feeders too.

Several times a day hummingbirds visit the tower, whirring in with flashes of red and green that blaze out when light is just right. They examine book covers, my shirt, a flowered cap that keeps sun out of my eyes. If I imitate a statue, they rest on my shoulder.

Last Tuesday I was sitting at an open window, reading, when a bird no more than two inches long buzzed in. I moved my eyes but not my head, and it perched on my book and looked at me. It's fascinating to see one so close—the feet are almost thready.

Wings blurred they moved so fast and it approached my face until I could feel moving air, closer and closer until I couldn't focus. Tentatively, gently, it put its bill into my left nostril. About the size of a darning needle. Clean and smooth against the membrane. Whoop! When I laughed, it zipped out the window.

I'll bet I'm the only woman you know who has had her nose mistaken for a flower.

Weather has been erratic, and so has fire activity. There was a little rain at the end of June; campfire restrictions were lifted; afternoon storms faded away, and we were back to a couple of weeks of hot, dry and windy. The best thing you can say about drought is that there are few mosquitos. Flies, wasps and spiders of all kinds, but few mosquitos. There are no roaches up here. No. Change that to—I've seen no roaches.

Drought still and again? In the city library I tried to find out why. Yes, drought is prolonged absence of rain; what I was after was the reason behind the reason. I don't understand it yet, probably because there are several factors. Droughts develop over continental deserts—as Cazz would say, "Like, duh-uh"—and are associated with high pressure. High pressure equals heavy sinking air, but I don't know why it's heavy. I'm not finished with this yet.

A few small fires here and there occupied some of the ground units, but there wasn't much excitement until July 3rd, when a days-old lightning strike smoldering eight miles west in a drainage came to life just before noon. Four of us could see only top drift smoke, and in the strong wind we couldn't be sure where the base was.

Smoke was growing and blowing while Ed tried to find the fire on the ground. Three engines, two trucks, a dozer, the Hopi 8 crew, water tenders 2 and 5, and a helicopter—at least three dozen people—headed in from several directions. Given hot and dry and so windy my tower was shaking, it wasn't an over-reaction.

Ground units couldn't reach each other by radio, so they relayed messages through me. I filled a legal- size page with notes. Which road shall we take? Shall we come in through Garland Prairie? We're in this big bus, would 530 be better than 526? Is anybody on the scene yet? Has anybody flagged the road? Does that Type 3 helicopter have a bucket? Everything fast and urgent—I loved it.

Even with, or maybe despite, advice from four towers, it was an hour before Ed found the fire. Three acres on the ground, he said, in grass and medium fuels with a few heavies. Then he went back to tie orange ribbons on trees at junctions in the roads so everybody else could get there. Three hours later those three dozen people with all their tools and machines reported containment at about ten acres.

I know I shouldn't like wild fires. Nobody wants to see the forest burn. But finding a fire is what I'm up here for. Sometimes I stand looking around and fretting, "Come on, let's have some lightning." I finally have a smidgen of confidence about reporting smoke, I'm happy to say.

On the 4th there was a Red Flag wind coming through on a dry southwest flow of air, but no fires developed, and we entered two more weeks of quiet. A few clouds in the afternoon, sound of breeze blowing through the pines, windows open to eighty miles of scenery, all very nice, but no lightning. So quiet I checked my forest radio several times a day to be sure it was tuned to the right frequency. This morning a band of dark clouds seems to be moving slowly in this direction. Dare we hope for some action?

Love,
Good ol' Mom

At work Don hid behind his professional facade and managed to convince nurses and patients that he was a genial, courteous man. I heard comments about how easily he smiled, how sympathetic he was, how thoughtful, how willing to explain and reassure, like the young man I'd fallen in love with in college.

Another side came out at home with the people he said he loved. He was tired and angry, dark-faced and sullen. Controlling, complaining, critical. We didn't see courtesy or sympathy.

He was too hard on the children, I thought, and they stayed away from him.

"Mom, could I eat dinner in my room tonight? I have a big report due tomorrow."

"Me too, Mom, I'll eat at my desk."

Poor kids, they thought they were fooling me. I set up trays for them, but Don shouted that we would sit together for meals as a family in his house. Not ours, his. As if the rest of us were there on his sufferance. We didn't have a home of our own?

I told Emily about the Jekyll-Hyde man I was living with. "He used to be so sweet, but now I don't even recognize the doctor people describe to me."

"You know, Marlene, something's wrong there."

"Yeah, tell me about it."

"No, really. There must be something going on inside."

"Something going on with the rest of us too by now."

"Medical training is hard for a lot of people. Some men have complete changes in personality."

"It's hard on wives too, Emily, as you no doubt noticed years ago."

"True. I've known wives with real problems because of it."

Don never threatened any of us physically—you don't have to hit to hurt—but there was a breach in our security. I could see the children building walls around themselves, and I did all I could to compensate, to reassure, but I wasn't feeling too good myself.

For a long time my husband and I went to social events as always, and when we did, he was open and friendly, far as anyone could tell. On the way home he'd let me know what I'd done wrong because I was so gauche, and he'd grumble that he didn't like those people and claim he hadn't wanted to go but I'd insisted.

I got through those parties because of Lyle. He'd sit down beside me and begin a conversation. Had I seen a certain movie? Read a certain book? What did I think? Oh, he was smooth. And patient. The I'm-your-friend approach went on for two years before he asked whether I'd seen the paintings at a particular gallery in Scottsdale.

"No? I'd like to have your opinion. Why don't I meet you there at noon next Wednesday, just a quick look for you to react, and grab a sandwich afterward to talk about it."

I met him mind to mind, or so I thought. I was a fool, and he was a vampire feeding his ego on a woman. After that sandwich, when I was standing in the breeze beside my car and he was saying it was a pleasure to talk with me, he raised his hand and brushed a strand of hair away from my cheek.

He was an ordinary size and he had an ordinary face, an ordinary voice, but slowly he built a magic spell. Men who know how women like to be treated have considered it too coldly. They can't be trusted, more's the pity.

Misty rain soft on my face. A dark sky. Grass under my back. My hands curving to the muscles of his back. Slow, sensuous, skin on skin. Out of time and place, past and future.

Yes, this is a horror story and a ghost story. With Sarah Manning, it's a mystery. It's a love story too, a love story without a happy ending. I could have done without the anguish of the ending, but if I had reached this age without having loved like that, it would be a sin and a tragedy and a waste of life, wouldn't it? Or would it? Am I just older now, therefore wiser?

Well. I love sunrise through trees, moving clouds, little colored birds, large colored bowls for pasta. I love being on this mountain. Books and music and paintings for the joy I have in sharing the world with them—that's love, isn't it? I don't expect to be loved in return.

Don I loved for his intelligence and youthful goodness, for the pleasure I felt in the things we did together. And because he seemed to love me. When we were first married and he was in medical school, I collected recipes from everywhere and didn't repeat one for two months, proud to keep him well-fed and healthy and happy, to cook things that would make him laugh. That love left me open to pain. Love does that.

The children—love exquisite as no other, especially when they were young and dependent on me. I won't say 'when they were innocent.' Anyone who really watches children knows they're appealing but no more innocent than sharks. But they were part of me, and I loved them with consuming fervor until they were grown, and then it became a steadier feeling. I've known them all their lives, but I don't know how they feel about me, not really.

They're all unique, aren't they, all the kinds of love? Emily. Emily was agape not eros. Affection, admiration, concern: comfort contact. She kept my soul alive until it could learn compassion; because of her, I came to love the world and skirted around the edges of God. Wait. That's altogether too purple. Let me change it. She was my friend, and she brought out the best in me. I loved her. Looking back down the length of it, I have to say she was the most important person in my life.

Lyle was a six-month body-frenzy obsession, not a mind response, not a spiritual condition. More being in love than loving. Recovery from him was an illness. I'm embarrassed that I was so easily duped but grateful to have had the revelation, if that makes any sense. And I'd rather not, thank you very much, have the experience again. But I'm not ashamed. I believed where there is no love, no kindness, no companion, no comrade, there is no marriage and thus no marriage to betray.

That's what I believed. Now I don't know what a marriage should be. There are a lot of things I'm not so sure of anymore—that's how old I am.

There are other kinds of loving probably. I should leave myself open to them too, but I doubt I have the energy. How complete a person do I have to be?

My mother went to a one-room school near Chandler. One day she went out to the pump for a drink of water and saw a strange metal thing rattling toward her down the dirt road. Ran back into the school room shouting, "A car is coming!" The teacher and all the children rushed out to see it pass—their first automobile. What I'm talking about is Time and Change and Generations.

1897 On my days off, faithful as a robot, I spend a few hours in the city library reading microfilm copies of the *Sun*. Still seeking news of medicine and doctors and their wives and some kind of pattern or trend. Sometimes I can't find much, but I move on.

Late in the 19th century a fifth doctor came to Flagstaff, a young man apparently modern in outlook. I haven't been able so far to discover where he was schooled to be a doctor. Historical research isn't as easy as it looks, in case anyone is curious.

Brannen—E.M. Institute in Cincinnati
Cornish—Jefferson Medical College of Pennsylvania
Manning—Universities of Virginia and Alabama Medical Colleges
Miller—University of Buffalo Department of Medicine
Robinson—??

Like E. S. Miller, Dr. Wilbur S. Robinson, born in 1866 in Indiana, was single, so there were still just three wives to consider: Sarah, Clara, and Felicia. At first both Robinson's office and his residence were in the Presbyterian parsonage. A couple of rented rooms?

In February he was called to a case of frozen feet. Mr. Cartnell, trying to return from Jerome cross-country with a pony and a packhorse, had been found near collapse three quarters of a mile from the pumphouse in what's now Kachina Village, walking and leading the horses with his feet frozen. Three weeks later Wilbur Robinson amputated Cartnell's left foot above the ankle; later he amputated the toes of the right foot.

The *Sun* reported that Robinson tended a man who had been trying to "steal a ride" under a railroad freight car. His foot had been caught in a lever working the airbrake. Welcome to Flagstaff, doctor.

A county seat is a good place for historical research. Big, dusty, old ledgers, records of taxes on personal property, were preserved in the Coconino County court house from 1894, spare, dry, and full of clues. In the 19th century, Dennis Brannen owned more than the other four doctors in horses, cattle, farm and ranch implements, stock of goods, money at interest. He and Cornish and Robinson had books, watches, and jewelry, but only Cornish and Robinson claimed surgical instruments.

Felicia's piano was there on the page. Clara had a piano at home too. Sarah didn't. George Manning owned little which the county wanted to tax except for several lots in Flagstaff. Manning didn't own a bicycle. Neither did Dennis and Felicia, and after reading about them in the newspaper, I wasn't surprised.

No sooner was Robinson established in Flagstaff than Cornish left taking Clara with him, all that life and sparkle moving on. Moving—a major theme in American culture. I must remember to talk with Abby about it.

In March Dr. Cornish was called to Albuquerque to attend a meeting of the Board of Examiners of the Atlantic and Pacific Railroad, which met to appoint a successor to the late chief surgeon at the railroad's line hospital there. Flagstaff's editor wrote: "It is most gratifying to us and to his many friends here to learn that Dr. Cornish was the unanimous choice of the board for the position...a fitting mark of distinction."

He moved to Albuquerque shortly afterward, missing the fourth annual cycling run to the Grand Canyon, but Clara stayed on in Flagstaff for a few months, active as always. The newspaper mentioned solemnly that she was one of three members of a Presbyterian committee that sent a message of sympathy on the death of the synodical missionary for Arizona and New Mexico.

The next month Dr. Cornish traveled along the line to visit A & P facilities and stopped briefly in Flagstaff to pick up Clara. Editor Funston later printed a paragraph which *The Needle's Eye* in Kingman had published:

> *Accompanying Chief Surgeon Cornish on his westward trip last Wednesday evening was his charming wife, who visited the shops and offices with her husband and appeared delighted with all she saw. The chief's good wife is quite as popular with the employees as is the chief himself, and in the name of our good people the Eye cordially invites her to come and visit our little desert hamlet as frequently as is convenient and pleasant to her.*

The Cornishes went back and forth on the trains. In May Clara took "her little son"—she'd had a baby? how'd I miss that?—to Albuquerque for a week. The doctor stopped off in June while he was on an inspection of "sub-hospitals" along the line. In July he was back visiting. Even after they rented their house and relocated the family to Albuquerque, the Cornishes visited, i.e. in October, again in December to spend Christmas with Coffin and Cornish relatives. Her sister's husband was district attorney; P.G.'s brother was chairman of the County Board.

So long, Clara. It's been good to know you.

It was easy to travel on the Santa Fe, easy and quite comfortable compared to other ways of moving about the West. At Albuquerque one could board Number One at 7:30 in the evening, relax in the elegant splendor of a Pullman Palace Sleeping Car, wake to breakfast in a "beautifully appointed" dining car, and step down into Flagstaff, clean and rested, at 10:30 in the morning.

One winter evening I left a late class and walked through the campus between big old trees that lined the sidewalk. On the corner The Devil's Den, I think it was called—I don't know if it's even there any more—was bright lights and colors, images of warm cheerful welcome. The night air was frosty. But inside was noisy, smokey. Crowded with bodies. Faces I didn't know. I stood next to the door a minute and went back out into the dark. Some things look happiest from the outside.

Despite the prevailing myth, life as a doctor's wife was not a ramble through sweet peas, but I doubt it was different from the lot of wives of other high-earning professional men. Politicians' wives probably have a harder time, facing publicity and criticism. Policemen's wives deal with all that plus danger.

For me the years of Don's education and training and what they did to us—that was a crucible. I could only imagine what it was to be an intern, dealing with crisis every hour, seeing people die under my hands, being Superhero a hundred hours a week on insufficient sleep. It was years before the effect on young doctors was investigated. Talk about a horror story...

Medical reports: Residents face considerable financial burdens and educational debt in addition to stresses that seem designed to break a human psyche. Residency requires that they be responsible for patient welfare for several years in conditions that include fatigue, sleep deprivation, loss of control over schedule, long on-duty assignments, information overload, frequent rotation, high technology equipment, and complex procedural tasks.

That's true, every item. When Don was home, we didn't quarrel—he was asleep most of the time—and we barely talked. He was usually so deep in brooding about something at the hospital that he didn't notice when I tried to distract him, didn't even look at me. Week after week I didn't see him smile.

Medical reports: Fatigue has a detrimental impact on small muscle coordination and complex decision making, but sleep deprivation, coupled with continuous work, is the greatest source of stress in residency. The effects are inevitable and disturbing: increased electro-cardiogram reading errors, decreased mathematical abilities, slow reaction time, compromised ability to respond to new information, affected cognitive function, altered behavior and biochemical functions—especially in the early morning hours of 2 to 6 a.m.

Emotional states can't be separated from internal physiological changes. Didn't they know, those administrators, what they were doing to young people with their residency programs?

Medical reports: Without sleep, experimental animals die. The toll on medical students has been well-documented: they are likely to develop drug and alcohol abuse, psychiatric disorders, anxiety, depression, under-confidence or over-confidence. Forty percent of residents are so depressed or anxious that performance is seriously impaired.

Oh, that's great, that's just the kind of doctor we want to see walk into our hospital rooms. Really the kind we like to see walk through the door at home.

One in three interns suffers frequent or severe episodes of depression and emotional distress and higher than the average percent of dysfunctional marriages. Twenty-five percent of those interns have suicidal thoughts; suicides are second in number only to accidents as a cause of death among medical students. The dropout rate hovers around ten per cent. It has been estimated that up to half the students who eventually graduate need psychotherapy.

Not too long ago parents watched their children develop sore throats and headaches before a red rash emerged on their faces and bodies, even in their mouths, followed by peeling skin and frequent complications. Heart damage, for one. That was scarlet fever.

1899 A Flagstaff station to make daily records of weather was established in a cottage on the corner of Aspen and Park—"a step forward," Funston called it—and Mrs. E.L. Renoe (widow) was hired to tend the instruments. A one-story wooden school-house, thirty feet by forty feet, was built by the Catholic congregation. Over four days the lumber mill south of the tracks was reduced to ashes by a raging fire; hundreds of local men converged to save what they could of the cut timber in the yard.

I don't know exactly what it meant, but since the churches seemed to engage the energy of the women, I noted it: the Women's Christian Temperance Union held their monthly meetings alternately in the Presbyterian and the Methodist Episcopal churches and a "New Woman's" congress was held in Babbitt Hall—upstairs above the store—under the auspices of the M. E. ladies.

About medicine in Flagstaff I could find only a snippet of detail here, a snippet there. Or tangents. Not a coherent tale.

After long negotiations, water from a spring on the Peaks was finally piped into Flagstaff, much to the delight of housewives. Clean water—that can't be separated from medicine, can it? William Friedlein advertised that he was available to install plumbing in private houses.

The editor considered it worthy of mention that a woman doctor had passed through—Elizabeth Snyder, who had been trained in diseases of the eye at Woman's

Medical College and Hospital in Philadelphia. Dr. Snyder went to the Moqui villages to work with Dr. Fewkes, *the* Dr. Fewkes, the anthropologist.

There was no end to the injuries Flagstaff's doctors were summoned to deal with through those years. A man got his right elbow caught in a moving circular saw at the Enterprise mill; the blade cut through the bone. Oh, ouch! Dr. Robinson removed the joint. Dr. Brannen treated a woman who had been kicked in the back by a horse, also George Hochderffer whose head was injured when a limb fell from a tree and hit him. Robinson and Miller amputated a leg that been run over by a freight train and a hand that had been mutilated in a saw at the AL&T mill. Miller tended a man who had been "badly crushed" between the bumpers on a train and the skidway. D.J. Brannen was called for a broken leg, a crushed hand. One sickness or another felled townfolks. Babies died right along. There was a smallpox scare. Smallpox, that dreaded disease.

End of July, 2000

Dear Baxter, Gwen, Abby, and those associated,

By now you've surely realized that I write one letter for all of you and have it copied in town. I hope you don't mind the labor-saving strategy.

First topic in this letter: night. The black sweep of night, horizon to horizon, has been astonishingly clear. I stand in the door of my cabin looking at thousands of stars, hundreds of thousands, millions, the naked-eye kind. I've never seen so many so clearly. I think of Ray Charles: "Oh beautiful, for spacious skies." Next time I'm in town, I'll buy a star book.

Second: weather bulletin. Hotter, drier, and windier. Temperature all over the West is at record highs—in the 90s for Flagstaff. Still trying to find a Unified Field explanation for the drought afflicting us, I've learned that it might be part of either a long term cycle or a world-wide trend toward extreme weather events consistent with global warming. Or both. My first thought was, "Oh, great. Hotter, longer, drier summers in Arizona," but according to articles I've been reading, it could mean more heavy rainstorms because of evaporation of melting ice at the poles and disruption of El Nino patterns. I'm still confused. Maybe meteorologists are too.

Up here in my tower I'm not suffering. Wind blows constantly and keeps me cool, and as the sun moves, I shift to the shady side. Before the sun goes down, air becomes quite pleasant. At night in my little cabin, I sleep under a blanket and remember what people in Phoenix used to boast about when they went to the coast for summer vacation. "We slept under covers!"

Public radio has been announcing that this fire season is setting records for activity, with blazes in every Western state except Oregon, double the average of the last decade. As of today, half a million acres are burning—8000 acres on the Apache Reservation (rattlesnakes are an extra problem there); 15,000 near Sequoia National Park in California; 23,000 at Mesa Verde in Colorado; 60,000 acres in Idaho. Prisoners from jails are on fire lines, 500 soldiers, 500 marines.

There was news on the 15th of a major solar disturbance that would produce magnetic storms on earth. I don't know whether that's had anything to do with our fire situation, but the human mind likes explanations, so I noted it.

From the 10th through the 20th there was a high pressure dome stationary over the Southwest, and I didn't see smoke in any direction. Well, there was what looked like smoke, but it was white dust thrown up by a well-drilling rig starting up in the morning—so the engine crew told me when they reached it. "False Alarm" is an embarrassing report to go out on the radio for all to hear.

On the 21st we had cumulus that reared high overhead. (My cloud book describes storm cumulus: sharply defined edges, many rising bubbles of warm air, downward air movement around the perimeter, flat base produced by onset of condensation.) More than twenty fires were started all over the place by lightning from those clouds, the same on the 22nd, seventeen or so on the 23rd, but there was almost no rain to douse them.

I spotted and reported smoke west of Rogers Lake. The engine responding to it saw another fire in one of my blind spots, thought it was the one I had reported, and stopped to put it out, leaving my smoke to itself while I sat up here wondering why it was growing steadily instead of sinking away. Ed finally found it. Another day I thought there was smoke on Observatory Mesa, it certainly looked like it, but the source turned out to be out of sight four miles farther on.

Ground personnel were spread thin, moving from one place to another, in service until after dark, back at work by sunrise. We were so short of trained firefighters that "line 'em and leave 'em and go on to the next" was a necessary tactic.

On the 25th Ed went for a routine check on a small blaze north of Bellemont and found it had crept out of the line that had been cut to contain it. He called for a dozer, a plane, people, anything. Within an hour his little blaze had grown to ten, thirty, a hundred acres, torching, flame length four feet, strong winds blowing sparks out ahead. The smoke was a dark, billowing presence.

Somewhere around 300 people with their tools and machines came from all over the landscape. At the same time smoke turned large and black on a fire north of Cosnino. Both grew to 600 acres before they could be stopped.

I managed to pick up more fire jargon for you. "The drag is in the upper bone yard." That was my favorite, isn't it marvelous? "We've got a bird dog for you," a man plus truck who leads an off-forest crew like Hopi or Navajo into a fire in unfamiliar country. "The Anderson Type Two Team for Northern Arizona has been activated." (? I don't know what that is.) "Assembly point is at Camp Two Flat." A helicopter pilot reported that he couldn't respond until he had stopped at the airport to pick up either rapellers or propellors, I couldn't make out exactly what he said.

Since then the days have been silent, no drama. Down on the Tonto there's a large fire near Globe, and requests are coming over the radio: for "bodies," for a water tender if we can spare one. The past eight days air over the Coconino has been so heavy with smoke that effective visibility from my tower has been only ten to fifteen miles, making distant mountains almost invisible.

Radio reports are that dry lightning (a reporter on NPR called them "rogue storms", I love it) could so strain our already "stretched thin" resources that the long-predicted Arizona inferno could be a reality. I guess we'll just have to wait and see.

Love,
Your prodigal mother

P.S. I hope you're sharing your poems with each other. Abby's rhymed academic comments on California are hilarious. I think Cazz is having a good influence on all of us.

P.S. again. I'm sharing the mountain with chipmunks and golden mantle ground squirrels and big Aberts squirrels that travel through the pines along the branches, so I've been putting vegetable trimmings outside where I can watch through the windows. Basic recycling. It's a kick to see those little creatures dash in to grab carrot tops and broccoli stems and canteloupe seeds, their tails twitching. I imagine a squirrel finding an avacado seed and shouting, "I'm rich! I'm rich!" and then trying to figure out how to carry it away through the trees.

A couple of things I've learned from living so long:

1. Don't talk so much. Listen. Pay Attention.
2. Sometimes trauma is invisible. Treat people with compassion, kindness, interest.

You never know.

I sit in a dim room the size of a small closet, turning the handle on a bulky machine, scrolling slowly through microfilms of newspapers more than a century old. There's no door on the room, so no claustrophobia, but it's tedious work, and it makes my shoulders ache. I scan for doctors' names—-Brannen, Manning, Miller, Robinson— but other things catch my attention. The Babbitt name, for instance, is in nearly every issue for one thing or another.

Early in the 1890s, Congress passed legislation that gave the President power to establish forest reserves to protect natural resources like timber, and McKinley set aside three million acres in north central Arizona as the San Francisco Forest Reserve. Well! You'd have thought he'd sent in a thief in the night. "Fiendish," Flagstaff's mayor fumed. Other words used were "evil…outrage…wicked…injustice…diabolical," which goes to show that environmental issues excited people then too.

1898 The supervisor of the new government group was Fred Breen, a twenty-nine-year-old newspaper man from Illinois.

In September of 1898 he stepped off an A & P train to face stockmen threatening to "hang these U. S. tree agents to the trees they had come to save." Apparently he charmed them into changing their minds, but it must have been a tense first day on the job.

Thanks, Fred. I just might owe my tower to your social skills.

That was the year when Dr. Ancil Martin, Phoenix, brought the first x-ray tube to Arizona. And the Spanish-American War—war being the filthy business that it is—resulted in ten to one more deaths from typhoid fever, malaria, dysentery and food poisoning than from combat. The Nurses' Associated Alumnae of the United States and Canada offered assistance, but—for reasons I don't want to speculate about too long—the Army accepted help instead from the Daughters of the American Revolution, which placed 8000 volunteers, only 1600 of them graduate nurses, under contract.

There was no Army nurse corps until after the war ended, also in 1898. Really. It didn't last a year.

John and Anna Hawks still held the contract to maintain a county hospital for the indigent in the Hawks Hotel. In 1895 it was renovated, and electricity was installed in the rooms, which seldom held more than four men at a time. Dr. Brannen had turned over the task of attending physician to P.G. Cornish in 1896. In 1897 Dr. Robinson had the job. Doctors who treated men in the modernized hospital submitted their bills to the county board. (Or to the local logging company? Did it send injured employees in on some kind of agreement? There was nothing in the paper about a boarding house hospital near the sawmill. More mystery.) The names of a few of the nurses survived. Mrs. A.C. Morse was paid $1.25 a day in 1898 for services, which didn't mean she'd had nursing training. Later Mrs. David Miller and Mrs. G.E. Lake were employed. But nurses were sometimes male too.

So there were meals and clean beds and attention for impoverished men with such afflictions as frozen feet and broken bones, often caused by fights or accidents along the railroad tracks. But there were no hospital facilities for anyone else, especially not for women, who were nursed at home.

On VJ Day, my father drove up and down Central Avenue with all of us in the car. Everyone in Phoenix was there, seemed like, driving up and down, honking and cheering and celebrating the end of World War II.

Now and then Emily and I rebelled. There's only so much perfect you can stand, only so much poise and efficiency, so much public performance, so much Nice. Now and then we'd cut loose, saying that Westerners can behave with restraint for only so long without damage to their nervous systems.

Usually I did the rebellion and Emily did the imagination. "Marlene, let's keep all the kids out of school tomorrow and ride horses in the desert."

"Where will we get the horses?"

"I know of a place—they'll send a couple of girls with us to keep us out of trouble."

"It'll take more than two to keep the boys in line. I can just see it."

"OK, we'll assign the chaperons to them."

We were the ones who caused the trouble. On a long stretch of dirt road, we looked at each other, kicked the horses and whooped, went galloping off for half a block, laughing like maniacs. When we turned around, the boys were kicking furiously, but their horses didn't even lift their heads.

Emily had as many facets as a diamond. She was our official fun director. "What do you think, Marlene? I've had this fantasy about water-skiing, let's arrange lessons for the kids and sign ourselves into the classes too."

That one was no end of therapy, outdoors in sun and wind, moving every muscle, thrashing around in the water pretending that falling down was funny. Saying we were doing it for the children. It lasted three years. We were pretty good finally, jumping from ramps without falling. I never did learn to balance on one foot, but Emily did.

One late afternoon we picketed her house, walked solemnly back and forth in front with signs CHILDREN UNFAIR TO MOTHERS. The kids watched from the windows until they couldn't stand the embarrassment and came out and said all right they'd clean their stupid rooms.

Another time we had a water fight with hoses in my back yard, and Gwen called us Mrs. Pecan and Mrs. Almond. When it rained we went outside and ran around and celebrated and told the kids goofy was better than cranky any day.

The most hideous of the Halloween masks we reserved for ourselves. "I'm pulling rank on you, Abby, this red one's too scary for a little girl."

"If I had it on, I wouldn't be able to see it."

"Enough of your logic. The cook has some privileges."

Children are strange creatures. We broke no laws and damaged no property, but maybe they'd have preferred June Cleaver with an apron over her bouffant skirt. Maybe they've never recovered from seeing their mothers stomping in rain water running down the neighborhood street, competing to see who could make the biggest splash. Maybe staid mothers would have made it easier for them to establish their own identities, poor dears.

We weren't always goofy, just when we needed to be, and I for one did not admit that hysteria was sometimes dangerously close. Once I laughed so hard I cried and couldn't stop, and Emily put her arms around me. I pulled myself together when the children when began to look frightened.

For a few years we kept them, that is, we hoped we kept them, safe from the monsters that swim just below the surface in every life, waiting to burst into view in all the disguises of human power. Wars in Asia, in Africa, in the Middle East, in American cities. Neighborhood tyrants and torturers. Plane hijackers. Gunmen who open fire in school playgrounds. Family terrorists. Drunken drivers. Jealous lovers.

That's in addition to loss. Death. Unexpected disasters. Run-of-the-mill heartbreak. The sickness, the cruelty that injure every brain.

We tried to make a shelter for our children but could not keep ourselves safe from monsters.

When I learned to drive a car, I had to put my arm out the window to signal which way I intended to turn. That's how old I am.

1899 Flagstaff's doctors traveled frequently, as usual. The Manning family spent several months in Texas and came back saying that they preferred Arizona. He went to Los Angeles for a few weeks; there was no mention of Sarah and the children going with him.

Her son Tommy fell from the rafters of a barn where he was trying to catch pigeons. "The little fellow" broke his right arm in two places, displaced the wrist joint in his left arm, and had to have four stitches taken in his nose. Sarah probably did the nursing. Basic nursing was expected of a married woman, had been, would be.

D.J. Brannen was still the prize traveler, up and down the railroad line to see patients, to Prescott as a delegate to the Democratic territorial convention. When he went to Champaign, Illinois, I thought he might have visited his parents and his daughter, but nothing was said about it in the newspaper.

In addition to everything else, Brannen was a member of the Normal School Board of Examiners, chairman of a St. Patrick's Day celebration, a brother in the Ancient (1868) and Honorable Order of United Workmen, and president of still another literary society. According to the editor, he "addressed audiences in his usual affable style."

Foreshadowing: a citizen's committee (another one?) was formed in August to consider the possibility of a Flagstaff hospital. D.J. and Felicia were members.

Felicia Brannen, well, that woman was aware of her position. When the Ladies Beneficent Association of Church of the Nativity decided to hold a three-day fund-raising fair, Felicia was appointed manager and Caroline Riordan, wife of the president of the lumber company, assistant manager. The ladies booked the Opera House and worked for two months on decorations, booths, concerts, a grand ball, nightly suppers, and hand-crafted "articles too numerous to mention" offered for sale. It was a financial success: $1100 gross.

Caroline was one of sixteen guests when

> ...a most pleasant pre-Lenten reception was held at the residence of Dr. D.J. Brannen...Guests were received by Mrs. Brannen. Progressive whist and many new and exciting parlor games consumed the early part of the evening, while vocal and instrumental music followed the refreshments.

Felicia and Caroline sang soprano in a musical program in August and in Millard's Mass in G at Christmas, which Caroline directed. Both met with the Whist Club once a week.

It's not good to be cynical, and I hope Caroline and Felicia were congenial, but it fits what I learned from years of social implications: money and position establish friendships. Brannen and Riordan were prominent and successful men—one would expect that their wives would be associated. No criticism intended. That's just how it goes.

In that last year of the century, an ad for a patent medicine appeared in the columns warning parents and husbands that young women who rode bicycles too often were likely to damage their health by the exercise. The recommended cure was Pink Pills for Pale People. I did not make that up.

Emma Catherine was the oldest of the three Verkamp sisters from Cincinnati who had married three of the Babbitt brothers. David, the oldest, doubted she would be happy in a dusty little town on the frontier, but she waved the doubt aside and married him in 1886. For thirteen years, she worked to civilize Flagstaff. Only fourteen percent of the homes in the whole country had bathtubs then; she installed the town's first in her home. (Notice: Flagstaff's first bathtub was in a Babbitt house.) She also brought in teaching nuns for a Catholic school and along the way bore six children.

For each birth she went to Los Angeles in the final weeks for facilities available there—the women all did if they could afford it. Expecting the seventh baby, Emma Catherine became seriously ill. There was no question of surgery: the first Caesarian section in Arizona was not performed until 1920, in Phoenix, by Dr. E. Payne Palmer.

Emma Catherine, in critical condition, was carried onto a train for an over-night trip (that poor woman) by her husband David, her sister Mary, who was C.J.'s wife, and her doctor D.J. Brannen. In Los Angeles a dead baby was removed surgically. Emma died of peritonitis.

Felicia too was seriously ill that year with a diagnosis of peritonitis—the paper didn't say why—but she recovered. After a convalescence, she went to Los Angeles to spend a month or so with her mother. Rose Lockett died of "cerebral spinal meningitis" after six weeks of nursing by Grandma Lockett.

The good old days, so simple, so peaceful. Yeah, right.

Menstruation would have been hard enough to accept. Sixth grade boys turned it into ridicule. They'd sit in a row and wait for a girl to walk by and then shout, "Hey, you dropped something!" and laugh the way boys do when they've said something nasty, and I guessed what they meant—bloody pads. They made me so ashamed of my body I couldn't talk about it to anyone. There were no tampons then.

In the third consecutive year of drought, the West is suffering the worst fire season for five decades, so commentators say. Three and a half million acres have been blackened, twice the annual average; almost a million are burning today in seventy active fires. In the Sequoia National Forest alone 1700 acres were charred in the past two weeks.

Heat and drought and wind and lightning. According to this morning's news, 74,000 lightning strikes on the West have been picked up by radar in the past forty-eight hours. What was that? By radar?

In all of July, usually a wet month with a mean of 2.45 inches of rain, only 0.29 fell on Flagstaff, a little over an inch on Woody Mountain. Cumulus clouds drifted around on this north part of the forest, but they didn't develop lightning to start grass or single trees to burning. Hard as I looked, I didn't see enough smoke in one day to keep me alert.

Weather is emotionally important to humans. Physically too, of course, there's no question about that: too much sun or too little, ditto rain and wind and snow. The effect on our emotions is more subtle but no less real. We respond to difference, variation. Our brains evolved to create routine—and they crave novelty. That's how contradictory we are. We want order and slide into a blue funk because of sameness and too-muchness. At least, I do.

High pressure moved this week, and allowed a difference. There were thirty-six lightning fires here last Thursday, thirty-one on Friday. On Saturday, a mere twenty-one with too little accompanying rain to put them out. Seven new fires were reported before I went into service at eight o'clock. The radio was thick with voices sending, discussing, asking, responding to new fires and old ones not yet controlled.

"We need more bodies."

"Send the water tender."

"On the scene of number 28 from yesterday."

By ten o'clock cumulus was massing above the Peaks, to the northeast and southeast. Kendrick lookout reported smoke; O'Leary lookout said it was number 29 from yesterday. Numbers 2 and 6 for the morning did not yet have anybody on them— no one was free to send.

Sky was freckled with smallish clouds in all directions, brilliant white in sunshine. The underneath was a grey soft as a bird's breast that I could feel in my fingertips. A southwest breeze was picking up.

"Copy, Brush 23."

"Who do you want to send to the Common fire?"

"No contact, Russ."

Kendrick reported number 8 at 10:37. Rain falling above Schultz Pass was not even reaching the ground, but there was storm activity north and south of me. The Air Attack plane was up.

"Patrol 2-7, respond to number 8, Township 24, Range 6, center of Section 24."

"Stage at Happy Jack."

Smoke number 9 was reported by Patrol 2-35 at Bear Jaw Canyon, and there was thunder far to the east.

At 11:06 Air Attack reported a storm with lightning north of the Peaks. He moved out of the area. I closed the east window. Clouds were merging. Woo hoo! Rain was falling behind Mormon Mountain, north of Baker Butte, above Hochderffer Hill!

"ETA on the hose?"

"Air Attack, check on your time and fuel."

Baker Butte reported ground strikes along the Rim. Hutch Mountain reported number 11, smoke south of Happy Jack. Storm clouds stretched across 180 degrees, from the Peaks to the Rim, there was rain at the airport, and things looked promising, much to my approval. I locked down the south window.

"Snag on fire three miles south of the ranger station."

"Unable to read you on the repeater."

"Reese fire has doubled in size."

"Give me a topography reference."

Elden lookout reported smoke north of I-40 at 12:07. I crossed it at 67 degrees 30 minutes: a cameo appearance. Brief rain was a mist north and west, loud on the metal roof. I closed the north window.

"7-31 wants to go for full control."

"Penguin I. C., you were covered."

"NPS Engine 500 at milepost 204."

"Can you cut loose Engine 5-3?"

At 14:00 the fire count was up to 16, at 14:20 to 19. Washes were reported running full near Black Canyon City, but the ground around me did not look muddy. By 15:50 our fire count was 21, but I had seen only one smoke. A pygmy nuthatch landed on a window frame and looked in at me—I was wrapped in a blanket, watching. A black storm hung above the Verde Valley.

My precipitation for the day was .07 of an inch. The airport, four miles away, measured .76. Rain had helped people on the big fire near Globe put a line around thirty percent of it.

Did I hear the radio correctly this morning? One third of the world's population is facing starvation due to drought?

Of the girls I knew in high school, one died when her heart stopped beating, three have died of cancer. All their parents have died. The houses sold, a whole world gone.

Life and other things went on in Flagstaff as the 19th century passed toward an end. Talk of building a railroad from Flagstaff to the Grand Canyon ("…it will become one of the greatest resorts in America…") appeared often in the newspaper, one issue after another, as did discussion about a forest conservation policy. Percival Lowell's observatory held open nights for citizens and informed them often of new theories, new research.

1899 Sometimes things happened suddenly in the paper, leaving me protesting "Wait, wait a minute." When Dr. Robinson, thirty-one, was reported leaving for a two-week pleasure trip to Pasadena early in September, I didn't pay much attention and almost missed the notice later in the month that Reverend C.P. Wilson, pastor of the Methodist Episcopal church had left for Pasadena to attend the marriage of his daughter Mira to Wilbur Robinson.

Born in 1870 in Indiana, Mira had been living in California with her mother, that much I know. It's possible that she wore a white dress with a high neckline and long sleeves for her wedding, perhaps a flowing veil with a coronet of orange blossoms. In the 19th century that fashion for brides developed into an unstated but understood requirement, a custom that no one questioned, which is the way customs are.

In early April the Robinsons returned from their honeymoon, and we were back up to three wives. When Mira stepped down from the train in Flagstaff, population up to 1,260, she saw Dr. Brannen's Pioneer Drug Store on Front Street and gaps in the row where buildings had burned and had not been replaced. Wooden sidewalks had been constructed here and there; streets were still dirt. There were no trees along Front Street. There was no public library and still no bond for a waterworks, but soon Flagstaff would have a "Dramatic Circle" and a symphony orchestra which played "beautiful and catchy" music.

Dr. Miller, still single, went to Phoenix to stay a few months and came back within weeks to serve as the fire chief and to move his office and place of residence to a house on Beaver Street, then to the Whipple house opposite Emerson School. Dr. Robinson, newly married, moved his office and residence from the Presbyterian to the Methodist parsonage, then leased rooms over the post office, then set up an office one door north of the Bank Hotel.

When I read that Robinson was proud to own the only dust-proof surgical instrument case in the territory, I paused. In the whole territory? He did have a bicycle which Mira may have ridden. According to tax records, she had a piano.

He and Mira joined a group that climbed to the top of the Peaks and later camped for two weeks south on Beaver Creek, maybe clues to the person she was. Strong and vigorous and comfortable outdoors in the clothes that women wore? She spent a good part of the summer in California visiting her mother, making the twenty-four hour trip on #3—which came through Flagstaff on Monday, Wednesday and Friday—or #4 on Tuesday, Thursday and Sunday. Felicia Brannen went in the other direction, to visit relatives for three months in "her former home in Michigan."

> Apparently nothing can be done about death. Or aging, worse luck. The long end of living, though, that's open to humor and courage and understanding and infinite adventure. Illusion is better than no opportunity at all.

Air was sharp and clear when Don and I left Cameron the next morning in our luxury motor coach. That is, air was clear and the landscape was sharp. Miles away the eastern horizon was penciled in straight lines: a long horizontal stretch, then a short vertical drop, then another long horizontal stretch. Did that have something to do with the Grand Staircase? I thought it was miles ahead.

We drove across the Little Colorado, which was not really a river that time of year, and onto ten layers of ancient history, five of them what was left of sea bottoms a few hundred million years old, the other five petrified deltas and deserts. Hidden beneath our tires. So I gathered from my books.

Vegetation, what there was of it, was about as high as our ankles. And—the oddest thing—what looked like conical mounds of melting mud no more than fifteen or twenty feet tall. Different sizes. Striped in layers. Mudstone and clay and volcanic ash, I thought. I persuaded Don to pull over for a minute so I could get out and touch one that was close beside the highway.

"It's gritty," I reported, climbing back in. "And crusty. Do you suppose it really is melting mud, and there just isn't much rain here?"

"Too much sky," Don said.

"What?"

"There's too much sky around here."

He was right about that, sky was most of what we could see.

Miles farther on, miles and miles along the red sandstone Echo Cliffs, with those same conical shapes on the plain in front of them, I noticed suddenly that they were emerging from the base of the cliffs, from under them, by the inch, partly visible, veiled sometimes in the red sandstone. Because I found them myself, without a book, I was excited.

"Look, Don, look! When the formation above erodes back, you can see that they're underneath."

He glanced at them. "Yeah. Neat."

"Well, it is. It's a language you can learn to read. Ultimate earth history, significant as any king or general or war or anything humans have done."

"I don't care about history."

We drove north up 89, comfortable in our big padded seats, watching Echo and Vermillion Cliffs converge until we came to Navajo Bridge over Marble Canyon. I wanted to stop and walk out over the gorge and look down on the Colorado River, but Don kept driving and didn't answer. I thought, "Oh, great, it's The-Driver-Has-the-Power game."

Across House Rock Valley (easy to see why there were no settlers in that place), up and over the Kaibab Plateau, he did not respond to anything I said, so I stretched my legs toward the front window and sang "King of the Road" and didn't bother to ask him to stop at the view point when the Grand Staircase spread in five vivid bands through ninety degrees of horizon. I could see it from the front window anyway, pink-white-grey-vermillion-chocolate layers, 155 million years of earth history, younger than the cliffs in the Grand Canyon.

I had made notes during the months of shopping for a motor home and planning the trip Don wanted through southern Utah.

1. The Colorado Plateau was relatively stable during most of geologic history, when it was close to or at sea level. Most of the rock layers were formed during sedimentation 570 up to about 230 million years ago.

2. About 65 million years ago the area was low in relation to the adjacent province. Then a great wave of compression rolled eastward through the crustal rocks of western North America, buckling and smashing them.

3. The Colorado Plateau began to rise—more than a mile— in at least two phases, with three phases of volcanic activity. During recent time the plateau has retained its stable integrity.

Driving across it, I realized that you can't understand the Colorado Plateau unless you think bigger than what you can see. The isolated places we'd driven past all the way from the Mogollon Rim are part of a mammoth whole, clues here and there to what it is, and I would need all the pieces to understand the puzzle.

Things I Learn from Reading: The stressors that some people face are related to their temperaments and personalities, which may give them a higher natural setting for anxiety than others have. Then 'you're too sensitive' is ignorant? It means 'you should be like me.'

I didn't think much about it. Abby was thirty, working on a Ph. D. (history) in California. No interest in marrying, far as I could tell. So? A woman who chooses an academic profession is no longer an immoral freak. I surrendered my career to help my husband in his; I wouldn't think of expecting my daughter to do the same. A mother lives by reflected glory as much as anyone does: I was very proud of her, am proud of her.

When she said she was sharing expenses in an apartment, I thought it was a sensible move. On my last trip to California, I'd met Jane and liked her. How nice that Abby had an intelligent, funny, pleasant room—well, house mate. I didn't even guess, which shows how unconscious I was.

When Abby finally told me how things were, I'm ashamed to admit I didn't take it in at first. She used the word "lesbian," and I cringed under the weight of cliches and stereotypes.

"Don't put a label on yourself, please don't, you might try to fit it. I mean, I'd probably love Jane too…"

"Get with it, Mom, I've known since high school that I liked girls better than boys." The things kids don't tell their mothers.

"I'm the same person I've always been."

I wasn't outraged or upset, just off balance. As if I'd learned after thirty years that I was adopted, that kind of off balance.

"Yes, well, give me a minute to make this one little change in the way I think."

I didn't tell Don, afraid he'd make a scene, but Gwen and Baxter were matter-of-fact.

"I don't see that it's any big deal, Mom."

"Right. So what if it makes her life a little different from ours? It is anyway."

Are my children really as conventional as I thought they were? Or do they just want me to be conventional?

"Hi, Abby. I'm glad I caught you at home."

"Mom, your timing's perfect—we've just finished dinner. Jane can clear the table while I talk with you." I heard Jane laugh. "Where are you?"

"I'm using a pay phone in front of a campground store. On my way back to the mountain with books and laundry and groceries."

"Is your forest burning like everything else? I hear the news. Four and a half million acres in the West on fire, fifty houses destroyed, nine people killed. I'm worried about you—it's off the wall to be on top of a mountain at a time like this."

"I think Arizona is one of the least affected of all the Western states this summer. Last night a strong windstorm in Black Canyon City blew mobile homes off their foundations. And the fire near Globe is still burning, up to 2300 acres so far. Southeast of Casa Grande 700 acres are on fire. One just started on the North Rim at the Canyon."

"See? What's wrong with this picture?"

"The closest to me is sixteen miles south on Wilson Mountain, in the wilderness above Oak Creek Canyon. It grew to seventy acres. Ninety people hiked in to fight it, with a helicopter to shuttle supplies to them."

"And you say don't worry. I'd be inconsolable if anything happened to you."

"Well don't grieve yet. That country is below my horizon, most of the time I couldn't even see the smoke. I heard about it though. Slide Rock parking lot was closed so it could be used as a staging area. A 250-man cache was sent there—extra tools and hoses: fire-fighting equipment."

"You having lightning around you?"

"Every day. It's a revelation to look out at it instead of up."

"Too much noise in the kitchen, I'm moving to the couch. Are you in any danger?"

"My cabin was struck the other day, fifteen feet away from me. Now, that's something to see. Pure power that lasted two seconds. Blinding and fierce, I can understand blaming it on somebody in the clouds."

"I hope it wasn't crazy to take that job. I love you. Please take care of yourself."

"Thank you, luv. Likewise."

"I mean it."

"So do I. But it happened too fast for me to be frightened, much less take protective measures. There are lightning rods on the cabin, and it's grounded. I admit I was concerned, but—no fire."

"Must have been quite a rush."

"The tower's been struck twice."

"With you in it?"

"Both times. Not nearly as much excitement. On the roof, you know, so I couldn't see it. A halo of blinding light and a deafening crack that made me jump, but I had the windows locked down, and the tower's grounded. No damage."

"Janey, she's taken two direct hits from lightning!"

A voice from the kitchen: "Lived through it?"

"Probably."

"There hasn't been a whole lot going on around me, mostly I listen to other people having adventures. Especially down on the Rim. And below it. Washes running, flash flood warnings. In the first week of August I had only two-hundredths of an inch of rain. A whole inch the second week, but when you live on top of a mountain, you don't worry about floods."

"No, I guess not. I'll mark that one off."

"I haven't understood this weather: it seems to me that it's influenced by high and low pressure moving around without any pattern. East, west, back and forth. Today in the city library I looked up atmospheric pressure, the weight of air, movement, things that are supposed to determine systems. Lows draw air in and produce storms. A lot of things I didn't know until just now, but I still can't figure out what's going on outside my windows. Maybe the university library has something."

"So 'student' is your new career. Jane, now she's studying barometric pressure."

"Good for her."

"I absolutely love these clouds. On the 7th I had my book out, counting the different kinds I could see, five, I think, but clouds are constantly changing. Ten minutes and they're something else. I wouldn't bother to figure them out, except that they make the invisible visible."

"Who has seen the wind?"

"Exactly. I turned back toward the Peaks and saw a five-mile-wide white cupcake in the sky that hadn't been there before. Huge and white, vertical sides perfectly straight, twice taller than the mountain, the top gracefully rounded."

"I've never seen such a thing."

"Neither had I. I was turning pages like mad, looking for a definition. I think it was a cumulonimbus with an ice crystal collar, but it loosened right away and spread and fingered out into the blue, turned black and advanced toward me, thundering. I had half an inch of gentle rain that evening. I'll never forget that cloud."

"What caused it?"

"Something invisible is all I can say. With the rain—over a month late—flowers are coming up and blooming everywhere like some kind of magic. And it's full moon again, that's magic too. It absolutely transforms the night, gives every tree a meaning that's hidden in sunlight."

Emily was crazy about Duke Ellington. We'd put on "Take the A Train" and dance all over her living room. Or "It Don't Mean a Thing If It Ain't Got That Swing," and shout "Doo wa, doo wa, doo wa, doo wa." All the children danced with us. Gwen was hilarious. Baxter and Emily's boys invented slam dancing. Sometimes we played slow tunes like "Mood Indigo" or "I Got It Bad" or "Sophisticated Lady" and moved independent of each other. Abby would turn circles and fall down.

We were heavy. Shopping, I had bought an RV rating book. Of course I did: what did I know? Going through it with pen and paper looking for wide body—which I hoped would keep Don happy—and thirty-six feet long, I found only nine models that had earned maximum stars for weight-to-wheelbase ratio and payload capacity: the gross vehicle weight rating (max load-carrying capacity of tires, wheels and suspension) minus average gross weight (unloaded vehicle weight plus gas, propane, water, batteries and optionals).

That did not include people, food, personal items, etc. I had to do some of the math myself, and it challenged me to my max. Most of the weight was in the bottom half of the vehicle: a welded steel-framed chassis which included the floor and the "basement" storage, equipment, pounds and pounds of fluids and equipment.

I covered my desk with books and cross-referenced papers. Long-term live-in? Highway safety rating? If any category was marked "dangerous," "fatiguing," "deficient," or "cautionary," I crossed that model off my list. Neither Don nor I rated high as mechanics, so we needed a motor home for dummies. Then I figured in durability and handling safety, selected three models, and asked Don whether he'd like to inspect them.

No, he wouldn't, just get the best. So I chose a blue one. I'm kidding. The wheelbase-to-length ratio was fifty-eight per cent and gross vehicle rating was 19,500 pounds, seventeen percent of which was 3343 pounds of payload. I trusted the book to have it right.

The day before we left Scottsdale that October, I finished loading everything and drove to a scale to weigh each axle to be sure I wasn't above capacity. I was rather proud of myself.

Weeks later, after we had gone west to east across southern Utah from one national park to another and were heading home across Navajo country, we filled our gas and water tanks at Tuba City, so when Don insisted on turning north again to Lee's Ferry, we were close to our top weight. I would think the speed at which he was driving would have to be factored in, also the speed that little sedan was going, maybe as much as seventy. Physics—the point of impact and all that. Maybe our Chevrolet engine made a difference, I don't know.

Late August

Letter to my inside group—

I've been on my perch for three and a half months. My reason for being here is to look for smoke, and I do that conscientiously, with greed even, I'm so eager to find a fire. I love the landscape, mountains and gullies, shapes and colors, the way it changes as the sun moves west, especially Pumphouse Wash down at Mexican Pocket. The landscape matters for reasons I hesitate to put into words—you'll think I'm icky.

But I spend my days in the sky. It forms three-fourth of what I can see. A lookout lives with weather. The sky moves and changes; the land doesn't unless something is happening in the sky, something like shadows of clouds passing over or reduced visibility because of haze or smoke. Wind blows from varying directions, a different speed every minute. Temperatures rise or plummet. Clouds in ever-changing textures move and combine, separate, re-form, turn dark, flare with lightning.

Like Monday: sunrise was turning clouds peach at six when I went out to look. I climbed the tower stairs at eight to find that the Painted Desert was the only area within a hundred miles that was in sunshine. At ten o'clock, rain was coming toward me from the southeast with a front that stretched twenty-five miles, everything behind it blotted out. The rain faded, the clouds began to evaporate.

When I turned to scan my territory, there was rain on Woody Ridge, in Black Pass, over the Arboretum. Those clouds backed away and others came toward me from Turkey Butte, from the southwest, black across twenty-four miles, and first thing I knew they had all closed in on me from every direction but down, the forest under them black in their shadow.

Wind turned icy. Clouds sank to tree-top shreds flying past my tower windows, then turned into thick cotton batts that crowded against the glass. I was safe and dry inside, but rain pounded on my roof.

By 2:00 I was in sunshine, entranced with the light, the extraordinary clarity of the air. Two hours later clouds moved in again, hiding the world, and I went down the stairs at 5:00 in rain, wind and cold, one shelter to another, to the comfort of my little cabin. Rain continued and cold wind blew and clouds moved around the walls. I stepped outside after dark and felt them swirl against my face.

That night there was a flash flood warning all over the Coconino. The next morning I poured .86 of an inch of water out of my rain gauge. Sandy reported .54, Shirley sixty miles away on Baker Butte had nothing, and my next-door neighbor, Ray on Elden, measured 2.4. Each of us in isolated cells. Some spots on the forest were still dangerously dry.

In Montana, ash from fires was falling on cities, and smoke was drifting east into other states—you must have read about it. Six million acres across the West had burned. Even with reinforcements from other countries, there were not enough people available to fight all the lightning starts. Drought. Weather, always weather.

We have fires here too, every day more starts. Our Hot Shot crews are in Idaho and California, so are many of our other trained people, which makes the lookouts even more important. Most of the starts we're having are along the Mogollon Rim, where air rises suddenly, and they're spotted and staffed/manned/personned while they're still small.

Every morning the sky looks as if we're going to have rain; some days we do. Cumulus comes low and heavy, moving fast. Ray on Mt. Elden says his tower has been hit by four lightning bolts so far. Pounding rain turns my clearing to a lake, *and more black waves of rain are coming, and I wrap in my old blue Mexican blanket against the cold wind. Sandy says she's turning off her radio because of lightning, then Scott on East Pocket does the same. My world is ominous black and shining white and very noisy. Flooding in Sedona, flooding around Prescott. Clouds move around, form, break apart.*

Clouds are not linear thinkers.

And the news is that our rain this season is still below normal. All summer the storms have followed no patterns. For years June has been part of a spring drought, but I measured two inches of precip in my rain gauge down on the ground. July is supposed to begin the summer rainy season—this mountain received not much more than an inch. August has been a little wetter, but I'm not much over four inches so far for the whole "monsoon." Ed says Shirley down on Baker Butte measured twenty-five inches last year; she too has only slightly more than four inches for this year.

Lightning strikes have been erratic, and so have fires. When I totaled mine, I was pleased to realize I'd reported nineteen until Ed told me Sandy had spotted forty so far and Shirley eighty-one. In 1999 there were few ground strikes near Turkey Butte and Sandy's total for fires was only twelve, in 1998—six. There's no pattern. Hey, how we s'posed to understand anything without patterns?

Heat wave in the mid-west, drought in Texas and Oklahoma. The forecast here was for a drying trend and perhaps the end of storms, then for a northeasterly flow aloft that would bring increased moisture. And an unstable low pressure system moving on shore in California that would push storms east toward New Mexico but maybe allow moisture to come up from the Gulf and return rain to us again.

Obviously there are big issues in all this, significant movements, serious lack of control, and from presidential candidates Gore and Bush, no leadership. I haven't heard them say a word about it. Have you?

Love,

Mom

Baxter, I'm adding this post-script to your letter. Your comments on the election were most interesting to me. I've known for years that you feel yourself more in sympathy with conservative positions than with liberal ones, but I didn't understand the reasons. Thank you for taking time to explain your thoughts to me. Do I have it right: you support not a return to past ideas nor a perpetual freeze on American culture but slow evolution of opinion rather than legislation that is too far ahead of the majority? You think that's the best way to preserve social order?

I follow your argument, and I'm proud that, given the tone of political discourse of the past years, you're not calling names. But then, you've grown into a reasonable man, I'm happy to say.

How would you answer those who say that, in matters of civil rights or environmental protection, the country hasn't time to wait for an evolution of ideas? Might we face angry revolution and social disorder if we do not address such issues sooner rather than later?

I anticipate a long conversation with you on this subject. I do love a thoughtful discussion.

Love again, M

I remember cars with running boards and Phoenix without Sun City. I remember when the border between Scottsdale and Phoenix was miles and miles of orange groves, when McDowell Road ended at the edge of the Salt River Reservation and irrigation ditches were deep enough to drown a child.

The Biltmore Hotel and the Heard Museum were new then. A dinky public library had books to lend in the basement of the Maricopa County court house, but I have no memory of a city library until one was built at Central and McDowell. There were art associations in Phoenix, but I didn't know about them.

We were not a cultural oasis, not like Santa Fe or Taos, and I read enough in books to feel poor about that, poor as in impoverished, lower class. For years I wished I had been born in Boston or San Francisco, someplace big and sophisticated, someplace with rain, snow, not in the middle of a desert. What a cliche, the youthful fantasy that life would be better in a different town.

Through my middle years I put myself to sleep at night with escape fantasies— running through crowds in streets and stores or panting through dark back alleys, dodging, escaping, hiding. A counselor would have asked what those bedtime stories meant, but I couldn't have admitted it was the prison I was in that I wanted to get away from. There wasn't a place I thought of running to, I just wanted out. Away from Don and marriage and Arizona. Probably a cliche too, but I didn't know that at the time. Women really do need to talk to each other.

Now? Now I can't think of another place in this country I'd prefer. I know the language here, the culture. I'm proud to be Western instead of Eastern, free of layers of crust, and I'm finally old enough to recognize the elegance of the Colorado Plateau and the Sonoran desert. What with libraries and television and the www, I have access to ideas, music, and art, maturity enough to discard the dross. And I can see a long way in this state. I don't mean a long way back, although that's true too.

There was a gorgeous girl—I've forgotten her name. Tall and slender. Black hair. Beautiful clothes. I was so jealous of her I couldn't stop looking. She cut classes to lie in her back yard in the sun, and only the girls whose parents had money could be her friends. Years later I saw her in a drug store, waiting in line for the pharmacist. The heels of her shoes were worn down on the outsides, and she was obviously drunk. She died of alcohol and a drug overdose, fifteen years out of high school.

1900–1903 A century's difference lies between then and now, and the past is no more like the present than the future will be, but those years in Flagstaff were taking on reality in my mind. The trouble was that I felt as if I were walking four dogs on four different leads: as the story went on, there was getting to be so much to it that I had a struggle to keep the lines clear. The town, the land around, medicine, doctors and their wives couldn't be separated. Of course. Nothing is separate, in case no one has noticed.

Coconino County was gearing up (Would they have said "gearing up" before there were cars?) for the census of 1900. In the *Sun*, Editor Funston advised his readers that they would be asked questions that would make them want to hit the surveyor with a club—"but don't do it." I read the final figures with some surprise.

Census of Arizona Territory—1900

Males—122,931   Females—71,795

Almost twice as many men as women? Not what you'd call a balance. Of that 194,726 people, 92,943 were labeled white, a minority among the Indians, Orientals, Blacks, Hispanics, etc. Over the past two decades, Flagstaff population had doubled to 1,271. Big city high schools now enroll more than that. There were sixty doctors in Maricopa County, four resident G.P.s in Flagstaff: Brannen, Manning, Miller and Robinson.

Under the heading of Statistics of Human Interest I include: In 1900 one in four children in the United States died before s/he could grow up.

Life expectancy for American women was 49 years.

American hospitals offered only a handful of paid staff positions.

Influenza, pneumonia and tuberculosis were the primary diseases of death.

During the first years of the new century Flagstaff turned twenty years old, twenty hard and hopeful years out in the middle of a lot of very wide space. People like Dr. Brannen who had been there from the beginning remembered the tents which had huddled around Old Town Spring.

A sewage system had been finished, and it was about time. For fifty years medical reformers in the East had been calling public attention to what they labeled "social disease:" typhoid and cholera. Dr. Brannen was vice-president of the sewer company and one of its directors. Worth speculation: what would the town have been without him?

The Twentieth Century opened, and the Santa Fe Railroad, which absorbed the Atlantic and Pacific in 1902, filed a notice of appropriation with the county that it was planning to build a dam at the head of Oak Creek Canyon 800 feet below Sterling Spring. WHAT?? Steam-powered locomotives needed a ready supply of water, which Flagstaff couldn't guarantee even with the new city system, so Santa Fe officials proposed building an Oak Creek reservoir and a pumping plant in the canyon with a pipe line that would carry 1000 inches of water north to its tracks. Daily, weekly, monthly? I wonder what stopped them.

An automobile road had been laid out to the Grand Canyon. It wasn't much of a road, but there weren't any automobiles (Planning ahead, were they?), not until 1902 when one was shipped in on a Santa Fe freight car from Los Angeles. At that point there was talk of building a real road.

Building News: Clara and Dr. Cornish, visiting from New Mexico, confided that they were erecting "a handsome new house" in the Highlands above Albuquerque. Dr. Robinson and Mira bought a house on north Beaver Street. Dr. Brannen had a new roof put on his drugstore.

I read carefully and faithfully through microfilm of the 1900 election year, but politics of a century ago don't seem particularly urgent compared with today's. There's a lesson there somewhere. McKinley and T. Roosevelt were chosen to head the Republican ticket; Democrats still liked William Jennings Bryan. He came to Flagstaff, and Sandy Donahue, incorrigibly cheerful, decorated his Front Street hotel in welcome. That was before Sandy agreed to "a friendly wrestling match" and broke two bones in his right leg just above the ankle.

I will never be pregnant again, I'm happy to say. I hated being pregnant, hated every detail: pain in my breasts and back, stretch marks, nausea—I couldn't stand the smell of cooking eggs. I hated not being able to sleep on my stomach or tie my shoes. I didn't develop swollen ankles or spots on my face, but when I heard a man say, "A woman is never more beautiful than when she's pregnant," I cringed. There was no Pill then.

I may not know myself—the who I was born with, the me apart from things and places—any better than I ever did, but I'm becoming familiar with the shape of my own skeleton. There's less muscle under the skin; I can feel the irregular shape of my shoulder bones, my elbows. My hands are thinning away to tendons and bones and veins. Be nice if vanishing muscle would take some skin with it, I have more than I need.

When I first noticed what was happening, a few years ago, I resisted, willing myself to look as I did when I was thirty-five. I'd bend my wrist and clench my fingers into a fist to stretch skin on the backs of my hands and make it smooth and began wearing long-sleeved blouses whenever I could. High-neck shirts too. When I saw women of eighty and ninety, I raged at the fate that arrives just as we're experienced and maybe worth something. I needed thirty years, maybe forty, to recover from adolescence, and I'm not sure I've made it yet. And now this. Send in the clowns.

Illusion is better than no progress at all, I guess. I indulge in whimsy: maybe my body is just refining. I should concentrate on refining my mind as well, pruning away what's not necessary or even useful, the clutter of old habits, old scars. If possible.

Sometimes, just when I'm getting somewhere with such cheery ideas, there's an ambush. In the grocery store parking lot I pulled into an empty space next to a bright red car. Bright red. Blood all over the windshield. Gobs of flesh. After shattering impact and explosion, silence except for fluids dripping and a suffering animal noise that was coming from me. Dust and something else in the air, falling. Smells I didn't know. Bad smells. Oh god oh god. Sitting there in the parking lot, I covered my eyes and shook until I heard the red car leave. Probably everyone is a walking wound and doing pretty well with what they have left, like Itzak Perlman, except that his damage is there for everyone to see. For some of us it's hidden inside.

The season has gone past Labor Day, too soon, too soon. No matter how hard I try, I can't will the summer to be longer, no more than I could will myself to be thirty-five again, so that I can have more time and pay more attention. I'm not paying enough attention now.

On Labor Day's four-day weekend, our Friday was overcast, cold and windy with soft light, soft rain here and there. The radio was quiet all day except for a helevac at Happy Jack: head injury from an ATV accident, no helmet.

A front blew in that night bringing colder wind, a colder climb up the tower stairs Saturday morning. Air was so clear that far mountains I hadn't seen all summer were visible. Mare's tails, cirrus, and small cumulus advanced as the day went on, and the radio was quiet except for: a Game and Fish call about an accident with cars off the road; a report from District 7 of an unconscious male down; City Unit 5 responding to a warning about a juvenile setting fire to things near Fanning Drive; and an accident with a trailer left on the side of the road at Mormon Lake. Holidays. Everybody out for fun.

Sunday morning we had campfire smoke everywhere. Ed reported a tree down across Road 231; he requested a chain saw and law enforcement for control of holiday traffic. In the afternoon, ground units responded to barbecues and campfires and tourists running wild. There was another accident at Happy Jack, a deputy confronting "juveniles," one of them injured. Enough clouds were in the sky for beautiful.

Monday was clear and sharp-edged, and people were getting help from strangers. At Long Valley a missing person was reported —Search and Rescue and a deputy responded to that. An injury accident at Stoneman Lake had a Guardian ambulance on the highway and a helicopter in the air. A motorcycle accident with injuries at Upper Lake Mary, deputy and ambulance responding, closed the road for a while.

A band of heavy cumulus across the east was followed by a day of grey overcast and ·gentle afternoon rain. Then a low moved in with strong winds, dramatic clouds, distant storms, cold nights. The forest radio was silent most of the day.

Now we're back to autumn brilliance. Just before sunset, low in the southwest, light lies warm and golden on walls and trees. Soon people will be going home and lights in town will come on and birds will settle to roost and bats will begin to flicker across the sky. It's a brief time, between the day and the night, a changing time, as autumn is brief and changing. I wonder whether anyone has figured out why the end of day and the end of summer are both so poignant.

When I'm walking on a sidewalk in downtown Flagstaff, I look at myself in store windows to see whether my back has slumped at all. Eleanor Roosevelt's was noticeably curved toward the end and, much as there is to admire about Eleanor, I want mine to be straight.

Women had always had a role in medicine as nurses, midwives, herbalists, et cetera, but before 1870 no major American medical college freely admitted them as students. There were a few schools, sectarian and homeopathic, that admitted only women.

The federal census of 1870 listed 525 women physicians, fewer than one percent of all American doctors. In 1868 a daring American woman entered the *Ecole de Medicine* in Paris, another the University of Zurich.

In 1880 all leading American medical colleges in the East were still closed to women, though a few in the West—California, for instance—accepted female students. The census of 1880 listed 2431 women physicians in the whole country, a growth of fewer than 2000 in ten years.

On to 1883: the new Johns Hopkins University School of Medicine opened to both men and women, with the result that enrollment of women in co-educational training jumped forty to seventy percent between 1890 and 1900, when 1,467 American women were enrolled in co-ed American medical courses. Seven thousand women doctors were practicing in the U.S. by then.

But no women doctors were resident in Flagstaff. I am not being sexist and ignoring doctors' husbands. There weren't any.

1900 Hypodermic syringes were in use early in the century. By 1900 there were diagnostic laboratories in every state. Arizona was still a territory; there might have been a lab in Phoenix, but I found no mention of one in Flagstaff. Sulpha, penicillin, and antibiotics would not be available anywhere for decades. Smallpox would not be eradicated until the 1970s.

Dr. Miller still didn't have a wife. Dr. Manning was gone for two months on a trip with his brother down the Colorado from Needles, but Sarah's doings were not considered newsworthy. Both doctors and wives went back and forth on the trains— Mira to Pomona "for an extended visit," D.J. Brannen to California for "hot baths" he hoped would cure his rheumatism. Dr. Robinson went into "the wilds of the Little Colorado" on a vacation.

For years, as a leading citizen, Dr. Brannen had been mentioned in nearly every issue of the local paper. In 1900 Dr. Robinson attracted attention with his innovations. There had been that dust-proof case for surgical instruments three years earlier. In the first year of the 1900s, he announced with pride that his new house would be connected to his office by telephone day and night. Doors to the office would be open all hours; he had arranged with the night operator to put through to his house any calls directed to or from his office. I hope Mira was a good sport about bells ringing, as we were expected to be—part of our part of the job.

On a Sunday, so the Flagstaff paper reported,

> *Mrs. L.S. Drum had her right arm broken by being thrown from her horse. She was going from her home at Stoneman Lake to the S.S. Aker ranch, a distance of four miles and when within a mile of the Aker ranch her horse became frightened and threw her among the rocks, breaking her arm in two places, the bone protruding through the flesh, and the shock made her unconscious. Not withstanding her injuries, she walked to the Aker ranch. The man in charge went to the Dunn ranch for aid, the Akers being in Flagstaff. Mrs. Drum was taken home and a man was sent to Camp Verde for a doctor. The doctor could not come and Dr. Miller was sent for, who reached the suffering woman Wednesday night. Mrs. W.W. Durham, her daughter, left Flagstaff on Thursday for the Drum ranch, and will bring her mother to her home here.*

J.F. Hawks, who served as Superintendent of the county hospital for eight years, fared no better. Thrown from his wagon in about 1893 while he was trying to stop a runaway horse, he "suffered from an injury" from which he had never fully recovered. In 1900 he "submitted to the amputation of his right foot above the ankle, Drs. Robinson, Brannen and Manning performing the operation" and "never left his room after that time." According to the newspaper, he died in January of 1901, sixty-four years old, "of paralysis," leaving his wife, four daughters and one son.

I checked probate records in the county courthouse. John's estate—$5000 in hotel and saloon, $1000 in personal property—went to Anna. The county awarded to her the contract for "medicine, medical attendance, food, lodging and clothing" at the hospital, as well as meals for prisoners in the jail, but she died a year after John did, aged sixty-eight, after an illness of eight weeks, also of "paralysis." Then everything went to his daughters, as he had specified. The hotel continued to serve as the county hospital for the indigent under someone else's supervision.

A grave site next to John's was part of the estate, but his wife was not buried in it. Rest in peace, Annie, wherever they put you.

1901 I turned through week after week of old Flagstaff newspapers for 1901 and couldn't find the names of doctors or their wives. A meeting of the Shakespeare Club "comprised nearly all of Flagstaff's social circle"—Felicia wasn't mentioned.

Where were the doctors? There was war in the Philippines, had the doctors been requisitioned?

Then there they all were in a flurry. Dr. Robinson attended a birth and a fractured ankle and a case of small pox, which he decided was chicken pox instead. He occupied "his new suite of office rooms over the post office"—upstairs in the Coalter building across the street from the Weatherford Hotel—"the most elegant appointed physicians offices in the territory."

Medicine in Flagstaff didn't seem much changed during the first four or five years of the 20th century. There was still no general hospital. Dr. Miller was Flagstaff delegate to the BPOE convention in Phoenix; he was a Mason as well. Dr. Brannen was remodeling his pharmacy. Dr. Cornish was in town as consulting physician for a tubercular man from New York.

Grisly cases, as usual. Leg amputations were common after men fell from trains and under the wheels. Robinson removed an injured eye (the patient lived) and a pine knot from a skull (the patient died). All four doctors removed a forty pound ovarian tumor (Forty? was that a typo? Four would have been large) from Alice Anna, wife of rancher Mose Casner. The *Sun* reported that the surgery was successful but did not say whether the patient lived or died. It would not have been an idle question: Mrs. A.T. Cornish, P.G.'s sister-in-law, died at thirty-two having "not recovered from an operation."

Surgical masks had come into use just before the turn of the century. Maybe the four Flagstaff doctors used them for the operation on Alice Anna.

> *A child living with Claude Emerson and wife undertook to drive a horse away from a sack of oats Thursday and was kicked in the face, fracturing the lower jaw and knocking all the upper teeth out. Dr. Robinson administered the anaesthetic, while Dr. Brannen performed a very neat operation, removing the broken particles of bone, stitching an ugly cut from the ear to the opposite point of the jawbone, and placing the injured member in splints. The little patient is doing well and will recover.*

Dr. Brannen attended Sarah Ashurst's eight-year-old daughter, who had fallen out of a milk wagon and suffered a dislocated shoulder and a broken arm. Mrs. Ashurst's older son Henry was an attorney in Williams.

More good cheer: In a fracas at 4 a.m. in the Parlor Exchange a man who had quarreled with a prostitute threw a revolver at her and then attacked a man who protested such behavior—who pulled out his knife and stabbed the troublemaker nine times. Robinson, Miller and Brannen tried to tend to four knife wounds in his abdomen, but he died two hours later.

Patients sometimes died of "nerve waste" and "paralysis of the heart." Does that mean their hearts stopped beating?

Social: doctors Robinson and Manning were charter members of a new golfing organization. I saw nothing in the paper about a course to play on, nor anything about Sarah Manning as a member of any group, even a church Ladies Aid. I hoped she liked to stay at home with the children.

Hi kids,

    Cazz and Beanie, I mean you and also your parents and your aunt and uncle—my once and present kids. I remember them when they were younger than you are. I remember you when you were younger than you are. Hey, I remember ME when I was younger than you are. I know things about all of us that nobody else knows, but I promise not to pull rank. That's a military term. You can ask your parents to explain it

    Beanie, I enclose a sketch of the mountains I can see out of my north windows. It isn't easy to do a landscape from up here—the problem is deciding where to stop.

    Cazz, here's a short poem for you. Short poem, long title.

A Geology Poem that Summarizes
the History
of the Planet Gaia
Dirt

    Green in aspen leaves is fading toward yellow; I can pick them out in this sea of pines. I'm told that most lookouts will be "terminated"—not as severe as it sounds, I hope—as of the end of the federal fiscal year, which is the last day of September. After that date the Coconino would be drawing on next year's budget, and no one wants to be so bold. Ergo, there are only three weeks remaining in the millennium fire season of 2000.

    Sunlight pours in through the south windows of the tower now, more than an hour less of it than there was at summer solstice. As the song says, the days grow short when you reach September. The sun's light, passing through more of our atmosphere than it did in June, is soft and gentle.

    For three nights the Harvest Moon was full, shining white on tree tops and making long black shadows on the ground. Air was still and mild, so I stood outside seeing the glory. Why have I never noticed? It's been there all my life.

    Politics—-moving right along: Bush and Gore tied in the polls, Hillary now the Democratic candidate for New York's Senate seat. The tone of the campaigning wearies me, surrounded as I am by peace and beauty. Unable to believe that Jefferson or Lincoln shouted such innuendos and alert to opportunities for determining the quality of my days, I switch off the radio.

    Absolute freedom, it seems to me, is impossible so long as we live in bodies. I make small gestures when I can.

    I've chosen my home for this winter. I had decided on the neighborhood, quartered it block by block mapping rentals, seeking something that would make me as happy as this mountaintop aerie has, eliminating one and then another as not quite right. Too large or too small. Too shabby or too sterile or not enough trees. This week I decided, signed a lease, paid a deposit, ordered my furniture to be shipped from Phoenix on October 1st.

    Perhaps you'll come to visit at Thanksgiving? I'll be in a new duplex group on an old street, two blocks from the city library, a quarter of mile from downtown. Big old trees that meet above the pavement will turn into a golden tunnel through autumn. The apartment is the right size for me: two smallish bedrooms and a bath upstairs, two rooms and a bath downstairs, but there's a B & B across the street where I can arrange rooms for an overflow.

Or would one of you like to be host this year?

I'm suffering pangs of regret, knowing I'll be leaving my mountain soon, my cabin, my tower, my spacious skies and spreading landscape. But beyond the winter is another summer; I'll be back next spring; and I love my house in town.

Since the Labor Day weekend, the forest has been calm and the radio quiet hours on end. I'm not bored: content is a sensation in my chest, peace a taste on my tongue, happiness soothing on my arms. Surely I must have learned something splendid from this, but I can't say what.

For a week days and nights were cold, clear and windy to thirty miles an hour. Ed reported on the radio that a pickup truck had "kissed a tree real hard" on road 231 and a wrecker would be needed to move it. There were a couple of small bow-hunter fires. Most of my attention, though, was on smoke high on the slope above Schultz Pass, visible from town and Fort Valley and Doney Park, attracting phone calls by the dozen, so a voice from the dispatcher's office said. It started in a lightning-and-rain storm during the last week of August and smoldered undetected for days.

On the 5th, smoke appeared. One of the men—named 2-35 though not by his mother, I'm sure—hiked to it and said it was in a rocky area, probably wouldn't go anywhere.

Next morning fire had "fingered out" to ten acres. I could see from here that it had spread a third of a mile along a ridge and down a slope. 2-34 and 2-35 burned a line around it late that afternoon and went home.

On the morning of the third day, somebody said on the radio, "If we don't do something, we'll have a mess up here," and there was apparently an argument about what action was best. At the end of the day, the report was "contained at forty acres." Next morning "It's picked up some acreage, but it's still inside the lines." Smoke was visible over there for another week.

I hear there was a "dust devil" yesterday, tall and tornado force, that bent pipe at Fort Tuthill three miles east of me and put people in the Flagstaff hospital. In town on a day off, I didn't see it. No damage on the mountain.

Love,
Mom

P.S. Gwen, I laughed both loud and free over your letter about driving the boys through traffic every day to lessons and practice so they could have "exercise." You have an unsuspected talent for humor.

Early in the Twentieth Century people in small towns made their own enter-tainment, if they were to have any at all. There were afternoon "socials" and teas, literary circles, amateur theatricals, and evening dinners with cards or dancing parties.

Mrs. Dr. Brannen entertained in honor of Miss Spellmire…Progressive euchre was the main feature of the evening. It was one of the most enjoyable events of the season.

With music, cards and "german" the hours slipped away on wings. A dainty luncheon was served...

According to the encyclopedia, euchre was a partnership card game for four, very popular. I have no idea what "german" was.

Felicia might have bought a new dress for that occasion. "Leg-o-mutton" sleeves were out and the bustle was long gone. Lace on everything was in. The style for a few years became pale, frothy, lavishly-trimmed gowns with modest trains in the back. "Pouter pigeon" bodices bulged and drooped from shoulders to waists and extended up to the ears, held in place by stays of whale bone.

I wonder how tall she was. In my mind she was stiffly erect because of her corset, dignified in carriage, gracious in manner. I knew women like her when I was a doctor's wife, women who played the role beautifully—perfect complements to their husbands' positions. I admired them for their poise and felt awkward by comparison. They set a standard some of us could never quite live up to.

The size of the Brannen household fluctuated. Felicia's niece Cecilia had been living with them in Flagstaff for the past two years. Brannen's mother began wintering on the desert with his brother who lived in Tucson and spending summers in Flagstaff, traveling back and forth on trains. There was no mention in the *Sun* of the doctor's father nor of Kathleen's daughter. Had they died? The girl would have been ten years old by then.

Mira Robinson's husband had recently bought "a handsome new phaeton" (carriage) for making calls on patients in style. One day, coming home from professional rounds, he stopped to water his horse outside the barn. A piece of paper blowing in the wind set the animal on a bolt for safety, and Mira grabbed at the harness. She was thrown under a carriage wheel, which ran over her and bruised her badly. The horse ran on into the barn, smashing the phaeton to splinters.

Kathleen and Sarah were shadows. Clara and Felicia had become real to me through clues in newspapers and tax records. In that one vigorous gesture, rushing forward in a flurry of skirts to grasp at a frightened horse, I saw Mira plain as any photograph.

I wonder whether those frontier women felt lonely sometimes, whether they ever had "vapors" or blues. Some of us did. Some of us went to pills or alcohol or psychiatrists to get through.

Formal education means a lot when you don't have it. I never did get even a B.A. All around me people had advanced degrees, and I didn't, and it ate at me. Don said, "There's a strange restlessness about you, Marlene." I don't forgive him that crack.

I've heard people say that when you love someone, it's forever. I don't think so. Or maybe I should say: in my experience it isn't. The feeling I had for Don when I was young wore out slowly through the years, but it was a long time before I realized what was gone. When the children were babies, there were whole days when I didn't see another adult except Emily. She kept me alive.

Looking back, I'm embarrassed by how volatile I was in those years. The running-around-laughing days with Emily and the kids were fun, but I grew to be afraid of them because usually I'd crash into hopelessness afterward, like falling off a cliff. What's the difference, nothing has meaning, suicide would be better, that kind of hopelessness. Every time I said anything about anything, Don puffed air from between his lips. And there was his jeering little laugh that convinced me I was worthless.

Fifteen years, and it wasn't safe to love him anymore.

At parties I was alone in a crowd, hesitant to say anything for fear it would be stupid. Half my soul amputated, half my life aborted. A standard human condition, I suppose. There are an infinite number of ways to destroy a human. All are effective; all are immoral.

Emily saw. "Marlene, you're losing weight, aren't you? You'll be looking gaunt first thing you know."

"It's just...I'm just not hungry. Nothing tastes good."

Through the window we could hear Abby and her friends in the pool. "Marco." "Polo."

"Hey, like the book says, you have to keep eating if you want to keep going."

"Oh Emily, I know. I'm tired all the time, I don't have any energy. There isn't anything I can think of I want to do. What's the point?"

"Well, for goodness sake, my friend, we have to do something about that. Marlene! What are you crying about? Heavens, your hands are cold as ice. Marlene, what's wrong?" She was on the floor in front of my knees, trying to see my face. "Did I say something?"

I was shaking. "My friend."

"Friend? Of course you're my friend. You know that. I love you."

"Not...not..."

"Not what?"

"Not..."

"Whatever you're not, who says so? I don't say so."

"Marco." Children's call and response, blind tag.

"Polo."

How can you find words to tell how gloom can build layer by layer until you believe you're not worth even liking, everything you've ever done is wrong, death is the only way out? How can you say that? It's too embarrassing.

"Here's a kleenex."

"Marco."

"Polo."

I blew my nose. "I feel like a fool."

"Well, you're not. You're hungry, you're bored, and you're too darned unselfish. Here's another kleenex."

Now I can say that tears are better than illness, better probably than murderous rage. Them I could not escape—female emotions are unprovoked hysteria?"

Emily knew. "The Heard Museum needs volunteers, let's join. It'll be one or two days a week, whatever we think we can do."

"Sure."

"A little more enthusiasm, please."

"I'd love to."

"Good for you." We did not say 'You go, girl' then. Or check it out. We're outa here. Get over it. Put it behind you. Fuggedabout it.

We served on all the committees, and I became fascinated with the culture of Southwest Indians. Until then, I'd thought they were all alike. I'd lived in Arizona my whole life, and I thought they were all alike.

Don accused me of neglecting my responsibilities to him and the children. After a while, I concentrated on medical auxiliaries—organized volunteers for the Heart Association, chaired the Maricopa County division. Ran the Ball a few times. Worked on soliciting physicians to donate to the United Way. I was president of the Arizona Kidney Foundation Board, ran the authors' luncheon, et cetera, et cetera.

I did Girl Scouts, Little League, PTA. Joined the Symphony Guild. The zoo auxiliary, A to Z horse show. Appeared at all the social functions. Charity work, scholarship committees—I demonstrated efficiency and fierce organizing skills all over Phoenix. When the county medical auxiliary set up a daily watch on the legislature, which was considering malpractice insurance, I was there to observe one day every week.

More stubborn every year, I fought Don for the right to do it. He said I should be "fulfilled" as a wife and mother. I hate that word.

And then, I was in love, and it felt delicious. I was so alive after years and years. All day and all night my body tingled, the world was beautiful, life had meaning. I hugged my children. I hugged Emily. It was transcendent.

Emily said, "You know, Marlene, you're more cheerful than I've seen you for a long time."

"I've been walking. Vitamin B. Little things."

"Well, they've made a big change, I'll have to try them myself." But the way she looked at me, I could tell she thought it was more than that. "Is Don feeling better these days?"

"No, he's still a grumpy bully. I've just decided I have to make my life separate from him, be happy by myself."

It was something Lyle didn't know; he wasn't in love. He'd pat my hand and glance around the little coffee shop that was conveniently unappealing to anyone we knew. "Your face is so open, Marlene, it shows every emotion. We're going to have to avoid public places."

A few months later, when it was finished, I was heavy with grief. Embarrassed that I'd been so dumb, so inexperienced, so ignorant of men's rules for the game that I hadn't seen what he was. Except for that, nothing. No disgust, no hatred, no anger. Something you learn as you go through life, that's all.

What I am ashamed of is that I went on living with Don. Shrinking under his ridicule, his criticism. Went from being radiant in a fraudulent situation to half dead in a legal one, as if I couldn't expect anything better—that was shameful.

"Hello."

A boy sniggered and said, "You really sound like a jerk." When the phone rang I didn't answer it. I couldn't tell my mother, anyone. I was ashamed that such humiliation could happen to me, as if I were so worthless I deserved it. I was only fifteen, naive and I didn't know it. We need to broaden our definition of girl abuse.

On September 9th, the end of a two-week pay period, Ed came to pick up my time paperwork.He climbed in pummeled by the wind. "Ok, here's the word I got this morning. One more pay period, to the 23rd. They're cutting us off a week early this year."

I supposed it made sense. The forest was very dry, but most of the people had cleared out after Labor Day, and there was no more lightning expected. No people plus no lightning equals no fire. I had hoped to be here long enough to watch the oak trees turn color. Oh well.

"Before we leave, Sandy wants to invite you to dinner on Turkey Butte. What night would be good for you?"

I hadn't felt lonely in my tower, no missing the face-to-face, but I was pleased. So Tuesday after I had said "Flagstaff, Woody Mountain out of service" to my microphone, I drove sixteen miles through shadowed canyons and across open meadows with late afternoon sunlight lying like a blessing and got lost only once in a maze of old rocky roads.

Ed was waiting for me outside under the pines. Without his brown Forest Service shirt and cap, he looked different, almost another person.

"Hi there, hi there. You didn't have any trouble?"

"The last hundred yards is quite a challenge. Do you actually pull your trailer over those rocks?"

"Oh yeah, no problem. Sandy ties everything down and we take it slow. Come on in."

A table was set bright-colored in the slide-out. Sandy was wearing blues and greens that matched. She stepped out of the little kitchen, came and, to my surprise, hugged me. "Well hi, fellow lookout. Long time no see."

I hugged back. "Almost four months. I know your voice well, but I'd forgotten your face."

"Sit down. Let me give you some wine. We have a white zinfandel." She held a glass under the spout on the side of a box. "Do you drink wine?"

"Every evening and earlier on holidays. Thank you." I moved to the table, and she put something into the oven.

"You know, I forgot to ask whether you're allergic to anything, so I avoided the obvious no-no's—pork and shellfish. wheat, milk, eggs. But I should have asked whether you're vegetarian. Can you eat halibut with pistachio crust?"

"I'm not allergic, and I love halibut. Sandy, your trailer is as homey as your tower. Both say nice things about you." I think she is ten or fifteen years younger than I am, but I forgive her. I haven't made friends by number since high school.

"Marlene, I have to tell you, I laughed myself sick the other day when you told the dispatcher to wait a minute, you had some jeep jocks on your mountain, and you couldn't hear him. Those people drive me crazy, they think they own the whole world."

"Actually, it was three all-terrain cyclists that came roaring up and turned around at full throttle."

"Quads? Four wheels? We each have one. I love to ride mine, but it is noisy, I wouldn't go around someone else's house with it. Not like some of them. They think if they're not driving a car, rules don't apply to them."

Ed slid into the bench seat on the other side of the table. "Some of those turkeys think in the forest no rules apply."

Sandy began to set bowls on the table, more food than I could eat in a week. "Here's something to nibble on until dinner's ready."

We talked while we nibbled. "Do you like having Ed work so close every day?"

"Oh, you bet. It makes the job more interesting. I like doing everything with him, he's the nicest guy I've ever known. He wakes up in the morning and starts to sing. When something gets broken, he doesn't get mad and storm around, he just says, 'Well, I guess we'll have to fix it'.

"And he comes home with the best stories. This high school kid went past him at ninety miles an hour around a curve and flew off the road and landed on some rocks, stuck. Eddie got out and walked over. The kid was rubbin' his head and lookin' up at him. Eddie said, 'Do you know who I am?' He meant Forest Service, but the kid recognized him. 'Yeah, you're married to my sixth grade teacher.'

"Eddie wouldn't give him a ride back to town. 'You can walk it, and you better get started, it's seven miles'. Three months after it happened, we were out to dinner and there was the kid bussing tables. I thought, no way was he going to be friendly, but he came over to us and said, 'That wasn't very smart, was it? Drivin' like that. I'm workin' two jobs to pay for the repairs to my car.'"

Private feelings are not out of bounds for Sandy. "To tell you the truth, I don't want to leave here. For me it's spiritual."

"Yes. That's the word."

"I wish we could stay all year."

"I've been feeling that way too."

Over the best fish I'd eaten for years, Ed told Forest Service stories and I laughed until I was worn out. "We were up on Wilson Mountain on a fire and we used a det cord to blast a fire line. With the sound and the echoes, we set off all the car alarms down in Oak Creek Canyon, and the dispatcher called and said, 'You gonna do that again?'"

He'd been Forest Service for years; there was no end to his stories. "My goodness gracious, he was so mad that he'd stepped into that bog, he stomped in it until he had mud all over himself."

He liked his own stories so much that he laughed too. "We put a pop can over the end and shot tennis balls down the hill. Bateman was trying to hit 'em with a bat."

I drove back through Treeworld drenched with moonlight, full of unseen creatures out in the dark watching me pass. I'd had a wonderful evening, though at my age there's an ease to being alone, a calm. Being here as I am with books and radios and long views of non-human country feels congenial. I like the openness to life I feel when I'm alone.

But is it true that humans need the company of their own kind? All the large animals I can think of live in groups, at least the females do, except for bears. Maybe I ought to invite Ed and Sandy to dinner when I'm settled into my house in town.

When summer sun was searing hot in Phoenix, I stayed indoors in the room that had an evaporative cooler in one window, reading books or playing with paper dolls. In the long evenings I played kick-the-can with the other children in the neighborhood.

By 1898 American schools of nursing had graduated 10,000 trained practical nurses. The American Nurses' Association was working for state registration of graduate trained nurses who could pass examinations, and it finally prevailed: the first nurse registration act in the country was passed in North Carolina in 1903. By then the U.S. Army Nurse Corps had been given permanent status by an act of Congress.

Anybody who has read about nursing in Phoenix knows about Barry Goldwater's mother, Josephine Williams, born in 1875 in Illinois and reared in Nebraska. She left home after high school to the disapproval of people in her little town and went to Chicago to learn nursing at the Illinois Training School, which had a good program for the time, the first to extend course work to two years. In 1903, when the first survey on tuberculosis was conducted in New York City, a doctor in Illinois told Jo that she was tubercular and advised her to go West for a cure.

1903 It was said at the time that half the population of Arizona had come west to die of respiratory problems—tuberculosis, asthma, emphysema, lung cancer, with tuberculosis the most insidious. Mortality in big Eastern cities was as high as forty percent; one-third of all deaths among patients between the ages of twenty-five and forty were attributed to the tubercle bacillus. If progress of the disease was rapid, the diagnosis was "galloping consumption." Galloping—I love it.

Young, small even for that time, Josephine Williams boarded a trans-continental train and traveled to Phoenix alone. Like other "lungers," she moved into a tent village in the desert outside of town.

"Spunky" was the slang with which people described her, a woman of "spunk," of courage, an individualist who refused to conform to the restrictions which applied to females. Why, she even smoked and sometimes wore trousers! I wonder: how did she manage to submit to the discipline imposed on student nurses?

By the way, she had been trained in a respectable school, but she was not a Registered Nurse. The Illinois State Legislature did not pass a Nurse Practice Act, which provided for a licensure examination, until 1907. It wasn't until 1921 that Arizona formed a Board of Nursing to license, register, and certify.

1903 was a significant year for doctors in Arizona Territory. A Board of Health was created in March by the Territorial Assembly, which also established county and city boards of health, and finally Arizona Territory required that doctors be licensed.

License to Practice Medicine
Act March 19, 1903

Board of Medical Examiners of Arizona

To Whom It May Concern:

Know ye, that _____, a graduate of _____, having a diploma thereof, dated_____has complied with all the provisions of an act of the Legislative Assembly of the Territory of Arizona entitled "An Act to Regulate the Practice of Medicine", approved March 19, 1903, to qualify him to practice within the Territory of Arizona, and is therefore entitled to practice medicine therein; and this is and shall be his license therefor, until revoked according to law.

The hard years are behind me now, the beholden years when responsibility was everyday and everywhere, and the welfare of other people was up to me. I don't miss those years at all, and I wouldn't go back for anything.

"Abby, it's your wandering mother. How are you?"

"Hi there, wandering mother. Fair to middlin', as I believe one used to say."

"That they did."

"Where've you been wandering lately?"

"The unpaved streets of Flagstaff early in the past century."

"Sounds like a hoot."

"I'm finding it interesting."

"I just finished my writing stint for today, and I was shutting down the computer. Hold on a minute while I get out of it. OK, hit me with some proof that Flagstaff a hundred years ago was interesting."

"Well, this ad appeared in the paper—'Take your girl to Timerhoff's drug store for an ice cream soda.' Crushed pineapple and strawberry were among the choices."

"Hey, the fast life."

"Timerhoff also had a long distance phone, available to customers, and advertised hot celery and tomato soups, Coca Cola on tap, and golf clubs."

"Golf clubs?"

"So the ad said. This was a town with character."

"I'm trying to visualize that drug store."

"Mrs. Sterns ran a 'reading room and lunch counter' on the east side of San Francisco half a block from the depot, open 7 a.m. to 10:30 p.m. I'm guessing she stocked newspapers that had come off the trains."

"So they knew what was going on in other places."

"Knew and were influenced by—about like any small town of the time."

"Like how?"

"OK, let me work up to this. Since the Civil War, American society had evolved in directions unforeseen by the combatants."

"Ain't it always the way."

"Industry and finance and governments were different. Cities had changed. And—horrors!—the ladies, no longer so willing to accept their traditional place, began pushing into public affairs for which any man could see they were not suited."

"*There's* a good argument for avoiding war."

"More women were educated than ever before; more of them had professional occupations. They also had household machinery that freed them from the worst of their drudgery. So they organized and agitated for suffrage."

"Out of the kitchen, by golly."

"In the 1890s four western states—Wyoming, Utah, Colorado, and Idaho—had provided women the right to vote in state elections, and they kept right on working for it in other states."

"I didn't realize the West was so far ahead."

"There was genuine alarm in some quarters."

"Well, I should think so."

"The Flagstaff newspaper didn't hide the bias of its editor in politics—decidedly Republican—and reported New Women with amusement most of the time. Occasional meetings of the Women's Christian Temperance Union were noted but not promoted. The New Women in this little town, with the exception of bicyclists, probably behaved for the most part as traditionally as the Old ones had, whatever they thought."

Abby probably knew about all that—she was a history major. "In 1899 Jane Addams established Hull House in Chicago to do what she could for people who were living in tenements. Any effect on your small town?"

"There were immigrants in Flagstaff too and poverty and subsistence struggle. But the entire population was only 1,271."

"That would have made a difference."

"Caroline Riordan accepted responsibility for the welfare of her husband's employees at the lumber company and expected her granddaughters to join her in visits to them. Churches helped parishioners. The town council took steps in some cases. But there were no tenements and no ghettos—more localized collections of shacks than anything."

"Thus *noblesse oblige*."

"Not much in the way of aristocracy around here, but I suppose the impulse was the same."

"Admirable, I've always thought, no matter where it came from. Good for Caroline Riordan and the girls."

"Decorum in women's clothing had changed only superficially. Skirts still reached the floor, neck lines were high, underwear was layers of cloth. Corsets still established a woman's shape and dictated her behavior."

"Behavior?"

"Of course. Wasp waist. Hour glass figure. Curves, that's what made her feminine, and she could achieve them with a corset of heavy-weight cotton, rigid boning, reinforced casings, and metal eyelet holes for lacing—you know, feminine. They didn't have sports heroines in those days."

"Croquet, maybe."

"For a while fashion was downright grotesque—the backward S-bend: a large, low, protruding mono-bosom, a tiny waist, and a round, exaggerated posterior."

"Didn't they notice the obvious emphasis?"

"I guess not, fashion being what it is, but I did."

"I can't imagine any woman in the West wearing such a thing."

"But maybe they did—the look appeared in ads in the local paper. It didn't last long. But here's a style that did hold a while: great masses of hair piled on top of the head, wide and full, supported by a frame or pad or hairpiece called a pastiche (French) or rat (American), the whole creation held together by pins and combs and topped with enormous hats heavy with decorations and trimmings."

"Egad!"

"I'm having fun imagining such a style in Flagstaff's wind."

You know what I think? Sometimes one person has the illness and the other person has the symptoms. It's complicated. Don said I was the one who had the problem, and he convinced me. He was a doctor, wasn't he?

Standing in the kitchen with a Courvoisier while I cleared up dinner dishes, Don said he was considering retirement. What did I think about that?

"I'm old enough." His voice was stiff. "The way I've got things set up, I don't see a financial problem. And to tell you the truth, I've had it with sick people. I hate to go into the office."

I stopped, poised over the dishwasher. He'd never given me even a hint that he felt that way.

"I can hardly get out of bed in the morning."

I groped for the right reaction. "Oh…well…what a surprise. Sounds like it's time for a change of direction."

"I'm not talking about frivolous little diversions, I'm talking about *retirement*. I'm talking about not seeing any more sick people."

I dried my hands on a blue towel and avoided looking at his eyes. "Do you have anything in mind?"

"I thought I'd buy a Winnebago and travel."

"Travel? Both of us?"

"Of course. I'd expect you to go with me."

"You would?" Obviously I was too stunned for sparkling dialogue. "I think Winnebago is a company name. Not all big motor homes are Winnebagos."

"You know what I mean. Find out about it."

That was the beginning. Alone, I spent weeks reading magazines and brochures, visiting show lots. Salesmen were patient and courteous, and at those prices they jolly well should have been. They cleared up for me the difference between vans, sedans, buses, and coaches and told me about so many different products and brand names that I lost track.

Diesel pushers. Raised rail chassis. Leveling systems. Insulation, aluminum frames, steel frames, suspension. A basement? I could have air conditioning, plush carpets, satellite tv, hardwood cabinets. Everything in the kitchen that I had at home just smaller and closer together. And they called it a galley.

Don wanted to go on a shake-down cruise across southern Utah: to Zion, Bryce, Grand Staircase, Escalante, Waterpocket Fold, Capitol Reef, Natural Bridges, Arches, Canyonlands, Glen Canyon. Which I knew about as well as I knew Inner Mongolia, so I read about that too, read words and numbers until I saw a drawing of North America in the millions of warm years—I mean *millions*—when ocean drowned the middle of our part of the continent. Then I could see sunlight, starlight, glinting on the surface for time beyond comprehending. Water rising and receding in climate changes. A slow falling of silt and tiny shells to the bottom. Dunes on the shores blown by winds, covered by sea again. Marshes. Sediment a mile thick. A mile. Now that's Time.

Movement is the key, continents drifting, sea level and climates changing. When the Pacific Plate began to grind against the North Atlantic Plate (it's still grinding, if I understand the process) the impact slowly—slowly like for seventy-five million years—pushed up mountains that squeezed a huge section of ancient sea floor, et cetera. Crumpling, bending and cracking but not turning into mountain ranges, it rose as a unit 5000 feet into the air, out of reach of waves, tipping toward the north. Later, volcanos burst out around the edges. All that sediment, solidified into stone, began to erode. And that's the Colorado Plateau.

It would be a state to itself if geography had had anything to do with it. But people elsewhere drew straight lines on a map and cut the plateau into four pieces. Three-fourths of Utah, the northern third of Arizona, northwestern New Mexico, Colorado west of the mountains. Ignorant disregard of reality—which is harder to deal with than politics, I suppose.

I wonder how many people who live in Phoenix today are old enough to remember open irrigation ditches that were dug through alleys to carry water from canals to residential lawns and trees and gardens in summer. The smell of rotting vegetation in the water was not pleasant.

I was counting the days left, memorizing the shapes of land and clouds, shadows and colors, the way trees move in the wind. Fixing images. Knowing I was going to miss my connections to what? to an invisible network? (I've read that trees have underground root networks with chemical connections.) Up in the air for months, I'd been solitary—and expanded. Would I feel restricted among people in town, able to see only down the block?

A man hiked up the mountain with his child and said to the boy that I was lucky to be so close to God. And did I feel that way? I couldn't think of a single word big enough for what I've felt close to. Definitions reduce things to my size.

Does wind itself make a storm? For three days "blew" was not strong enough to describe the cold wind that kept my tower shuddering and me huddled inside trying to keep warm with all the windows closed. The basin at the pump developed a layer of ice overnight. The morning climb up the stairs in coat and mittens was an adventure. On a calm day I had moved slowly and stopped to rest on every landing; those three windy days I was nudged off balance every time I lifted a foot.

How come I never get a medal?

Days were looking looking looking for smoke with overtime in late afternoon. Bow hunting season had opened, I'd seen several camps when I drove into town that week and half a dozen camouflaged men up here. Surely I could count on somebody throwing out a cigarette or leaving a live campfire.

Our only significant burn was in the wilderness on the north side of the Peaks east of Bear Jaw Canyon. (How long ago was the bear jaw found, I wondered.) The fire was never visible from here, so I listened on the forest radio. Two acres and moving. Request for resources. Three engines, two water-tenders, a city crew, assorted overhead, and some people from the Kaibab, all responding. Staging area for hike-in on road 418. Law enforcement dispatched to contact hunters in the area. Lockett Meadow evacuated. Barricades set up. Air Attack overhead. Two Indian crews sent for.

They managed to hold it to six acres despite winds that were gusting thirty to forty. And named it Jaw, of course.

Nights in the little cabin, alone on its mountain top, were a joy. In warm weather, bed is necessary. In a cold wind storm, it's a luxury. Trees roar and thrash. Wind whistles though cracks. The floor is icy. And I'm cozy with a book under quilts. I'm working on a theory that if phone calls and business decisions, lawsuits and legislation were conducted from bed on a stormy night, this would be a happier country.

I moved through two weeks of golden goodness. Slowly aspen became incandescent patches across the land, oak quietly antique, each yellow in its own way. Both retreating within, closing down for winter.

There were highs aloft and upper level lows and weak Pacific systems passing through, the usual movement of atmosphere, with one day of intermittent soft rain, another of fair-weather cumulus: nothing dramatic, nothing that would change anything. Days were warm and quiet, nights cold and clear with spectacular star shows. There were no fires of significance—I was paid to look at drowsy landscape, very acceptable duty.

Through the summery summary (I couldn't resist that) I drifted in limbo. One morning on KNAU I heard a report: some physicists claim that we live not in three but twelve dimensions, something to do with String Theory. I decided I wouldn't be up to investigating that one, but it gave my imagination something to play with through the silent hours of space that surrounded the tower.

> When Emily's terrier was old and feeble, my friend sat on the floor and stroked the little body and sang, hoping that love and tenderness would comfort the dog in its dying. Oh Emily.

1902 In January of 1902 there were calls for statehood, but a bill that would make Arizona a state was indefinitely delayed in Congress, partly because there were so few people here compared to states in the East.

The *Sun* also printed this:

> *Wednesday night about 11 o'clock Sheriff J.A Johnson received a telegram from Winslow to look for a man who had jumped from passenger train No. 8 at Agassiz, three miles west of this place. Half an hour later a freight train left [Johnson] at the siding and he commenced the search for the missing passenger, whose trail was easily followed in the snow. The man climbed the hill north of the track, and so devious were his windings that the sheriff did not find him for two hours afterwards, suffering from cold and exposure. The sheriff was satisfied that his companion was crazy and the sooner he got to the hospital with him the better it would be for both.*

During the walk to Flagstaff the stranger allowed himself to be guided by the sheriff and seemed to be rational enough. The patient on being put in the county hospital was searched, and from the papers found on his person his name proved to be James Minola, an Italian, on his way from Congress, Arizona, to New York.

Dr. Robinson attended Minola, but as he did not show any violent symptoms, it was not thought necessary to restrain him, and he was left in charge of the nurse.

Thursday forenoon Minola cut his throat with his pocket knife, which was not found when the sheriff searched him. The windpipe was cut through and a gash six inches long made across the neck. The wound is not necessarily fatal.

Dr. E.S. Miller was called, and while attending to the injured man, and while his back was turned, Minola made a vicious attack on him with a pair of shears, stabbing him in the back of the neck, cutting one of the arteries. The wound bled profusely, and might have proved serious but for prompt attention.

Minola made several stabs at the doctor, but they did not cut through his clothing. The nurse [male]), who was in the adjoining room, heard the noise, rushed in and pulled Minola away from the doctor. The crazy man turned on the nurse with his weapon, but failed to strike him.

It took the aid of three men to overpower Minola, and he was put to bed and tied to prevent any further injury to himself or others, and a watcher was placed over him.

Dr. Miller's injuries were not of a serious character, but he was weakened from loss of blood and is confined to his room.

Minola was examined before Probate Judge Layton yesterday afternoon and adjudged insane. He was taken to the territorial insane asylum by Sheriff Johnson today.

Town news was full of nuggets like that. Here's more. Specialists—opticians, oculists, dentists, osteopaths—came in briefly and solicited patients in the *Sun*. Mrs. A. Grant advertised her services as a nurse in private homes. Babies and children died almost every week. Dr. Manning, whose listing in *Who's Who in Arizona* referred to him as a specialist in treatment of children's diseases, bought the Thurber house on Aspen Street. Dr. Brannen was appointed by Governor Murphy as a delegate to the American Congress of Tuberculosis that would meet in New York. Progressive Dr. Robinson bought "new surgical instruments and appliances." And look at this: there was a "pest house" south of the tracks for quarantine of people afflicted with small pox. Pest house—charming name.

The day I realized that blood would no longer seep from my body every month, I realized I was free. And I wondered how it is for men, with no such event that liberates them to see their lives differently.

"Baxter, hello."

"Mom. Is something wrong?"

"No, no. Nothing's wrong. I assume you ask because you'd drop everything to help."

"Of course."

"That's one of the nice things about you, your acceptance of responsibility."

"Well, thank you, Mom. Don't ever hesitate. No, Honey, it isn't your little Texas Mama, it's my little Arizona Mama."

"Tell her I send greetings."

"She sends greetings. Ok. Greetings back at you."

"I have no current problems. Just wanted to hear your voice. I'm not one of those people who resist technological advance—for me instantaneous long-distance communication is a blessing. It preserves families through space and time."

"True, true. Do you have a phone on the mountain?"

"No, the mountain is quite primitive. I'm in town today, sitting in a private nook in a red-carpeted hotel hallway, using my phone card. When we say goodbye, I'll go into the restaurant for an early dinner."

"You're a study in contrasts."

"Thank you, Baxter, I take that as a compliment. I've just come from the city library, where I learned how to use The Readers' Guide to Periodical Literature on computer. I'm feeling quite proud of myself."

"Mom, I'm just beginning to know you. After all these years."

"Thank you again. We're both old enough to be people to each other."

"Hmmm. I hadn't thought of it that way. Why the Readers' Guide?"

"I mentioned that I'm seeking an explanation for this year's fire season, the Western droughts and heat waves?"

"Yes, you did."

"I think I'm closing in on it. Would you like to hear?"

"Of course. Better than reading the paper, which is what I was doing. I'll put my feet up."

"I gather the explanation isn't simple. Let me get my notes out…here's a phrase I love: normal chaotic variability of atmospheric circulation patterns. I love it."

"Chaotic patterns. Sounds like an oxymoron."

"Doesn't it? Big swirling global air currents that may be oscillating faster these days."

"Global warming?"

"That might be affecting it. Maybe sunspots. Maybe volcanic eruptions and resulting sulfates in the air. I'm getting into big issues like Ice Ages and such things, paleoecology, before I want to, but at least I can say that weather is wind, moisture, temperature and sun. Right?"

"That sums it up, I think."

I moved the phone to my other ear. "I suspect that recent weather in Arizona is tied to surface water temperature in a huge expanse of the southwest Pacific. And 'an erratically swinging pendulum of air and water.' I hope I'm getting this right, it seems bizarre to me."

"Does this have anything to do with El Niño?"

"As I understand it, yes. Trade winds pushing warm water west toward that giant oceanic pool and lowering sea level a few inches along the coast of South America—imagine!—thus cold water welling up from deep ocean. That's point number one, normal conditions."

"Equatorial."

"Yes, but number two—every three to seven years the arrangement collapses into warm water east, and next thing you know, you have a *giant underwater wave* speeding toward South America, the jet stream changing its path, and air pressure doing strange things. Thus lots of El Niño rain in some places. I may have this wrong, but I'm not making it up. My opinion is that the whole mechanism was invented in France."

Baxter laughed. "That's as good a guess as any."

"And then number three: La Niña reverses the process. Cool water develops in that big Pacific pool and an intense jet stream bends and that's likely to produce widespread drought—what we've had in the West lately. Are you clear about all this?"

"Not entirely."

"Neither am I. The cause of fire weather this year may be something else—I don't trust an outline where weather is concerned, given planetary interactions and all that. I'm not finished yet; I'll keep you up to date."

"Please do. You're never too old to learn from your mother."

"Good heavens, Baxter, you've become a philosopher."

"I've just now read in the paper that the projected cost of this year's fire season in the West is one billion dollars. And that this four-year drought has cost Texas four billion."

"I wonder how that compares with the annual sports budget for television networks."

"Mom, there's no end to the matters you don't know yet but probably will."

"Wonderful what you can learn if you live long enough to put it all together. The next forty years ought to be a revelation."

"Have you moved off the mountain now?"

"No, I haven't. I was being maudlin about the end of the season, packing clothes into boxes, when the assistant fire boss announced that, there having been lack of significant summer moisture, he'd received orders to keep lookouts up and patrolmen out indefinitely—until it rains or snows, maybe another six weeks. That took some adjustment. Six more weeks!"

"That would take you into mid-November."

"I might see leaves on the mountain turn color after all. On my days off I can take my time moving into the house in town."

That evening I was back at the gate while there was still light enough to see to unlock it: I'm uneasy standing there at night with my key, lit by car headlights like a target in the dark forest. Driving up, rounding a curve, I could see colored lights of Flagstaff sparkling ten miles away, a thousand feet below.

One inside turn on the east side always looked like potential danger to me. Raw in my mind: the man at Grand Gulch had said to Don, "Sure hope you aren't plannin' to take that big rig down the Dugway," so Don had done it. Who knows what he was thinking of by then?

— — — — — — — — — — — — — — — — — — — —

The road snaked across the face of a cliff a thousand feet at least, straight down, no guard rails, hairpin curves. I just knew we were going off.

"Don, let me out. I can go in front and tell you when the back wheels are too close to the edge. Please, Don, stop and let me out."

Statistics: People who suffer severe depression have dramatically shorter life spans: 40% die before sixty-five. This includes their families too, even infants. Infant death rate in families dealing with depression is five times higher than average. You mean it's contagious?

1903 In Flagstaff on New Year's day, Felicia Brannen and Ida Wittington received callers at the Brannen house. Miss Wittington had been born in Baltimore and had come to Flagstaff to teach music privately. For a year she had been unofficially engaged to Andrew E. Douglass, a Boston astronomer born to a family of intellectual achievement. Formerly at Lowell Observatory, he was a new probate judge in Flagstaff.

Later Ida was assistant principal and music teacher at Emerson School. In 1905 she married Andrew Douglass, studied at the Sorbonne (1910) and at Radcliffe (1912). She was not Catholic—at least, I assume not, the marriage to Douglass was in an Episcopal cathedral in Los Angeles—but she was Felicia's friend anyway. That's another clue to who Mrs. Dr. Brannen was.

Doctor W. P. Sipe, thirty-five, born in Pennsylvania, arrived that spring with no local fanfare in the *Sun*. The AMA's Directory of Deceased Physicians (very small print) reports that he had graduated in 1898 from Hospital College of Medicine, Louisville, Central University of Kentucky. He had previously been licensed to practice in Colorado, New England, South Dakota, and New Mexico. That's interesting, but I don't know what it means.

While I'm on the subject—the AMA's Directory does not list Wilbur Robinson. I don't know what that means either.

In Flagstaff Wilbur Sipe rented office space in the Pollock building above the newspaper office on East Aspen. In July his license to practice medicine in Arizona was filed for record with the county. So was a license for Dr. Miller—still not married—mentioned in the weekly newspaper often as a lodge official or delegate to one lodge convention or another.

W.M. Slernitzauer, described as "an old school physician and a young man of prepossessing (archaic for favorable) appearance," arrived from Denver in April with a specialty in obstetrics and diseases of women and children. No place of education mentioned in the newspaper. He rented office space at Mrs. Viet's—I suppose everyone knew where that was.

In May another doctor, twenty-seven years old, born in Illinois, was introduced by a formal announcement.

Dr. John E. Adams, a graduate of the College of Physicians of Cleveland, Ohio, and who served one year as house surgeon in the Cleveland General Hospital and six months in St. John's Hospital, and spent ten months taking special courses in the New York Post-Graduate Medical School in New York City, has associated himself with Dr. W.S. Robinson, for the purpose of the practice of his profession in Flagstaff. The doctor's office is over the post office, where he can be found during his office hours.

John Adams had worked on the staff of two hospitals and studied at a post-graduate school in New York. He'd had a better training than any doctor who had come to Flagstaff thus far—at least on paper.

As far back as anyone could remember, American undergraduate medical schools had been taught by traditional didactic, no-questions-asked lectures and had offered no clinical experience with real patients. Internship and hospital affiliation were available to very few.

Since about 1882 independent postgraduate schools in large cities (New York and Philadelphia were the first) had offered short courses catering to "the self-improving generalist who felt his clinical training to have been inadequate." Given the medical schools of the time, that had to have been a high percentage of the nation's doctors.

Termed "polyclinics," the schools offered courses lasting four or six weeks, sometimes as much as three months—clinics of one or several days a week—in surgery, neurology, dermatology, gynecology, pediatrics, ophthalmology, orthopedic surgery, but not much pharmacology for some reason.

By 1895 or so the New York schools were serving several hundred doctors annually. Therefore Brannen, Manning, Miller, Robinson, Sipe and Slernitzauer, yes and Adams too, had available to them as much advanced training as they wanted no matter how inadequate their initial schooling had been.

The addition in 1903 of Dr. Adams with his modern education brought Flagstaff up to, what, seven doctors? Yes, seven and three wives. No mention of wives for the three newcomers. Adams, Sipe and Slernitzauer advertised that they could be reached by messages left at Timerhoff's drug store, telephone #86.

Editor Funston was not above a little humor in his reporting of the minor medical situations the new doctors might face.

> *Bob Jennings was run over by the hose cart...while the team was practicing at Milton for the 4th of July hose race [between fire companies]. The incident would not speak well for Bob's agility with strangers, but we who know him understand that he is fast enough to keep out of his own way, but that he must have been hypnotized by one (or all) of the pretty girls who lined the sidewalks watching the proceedings.*

And then with no warning I could find, Wilbur Robinson, who in July was county physician and superintendent of the county hospital for the indigent—including blacks and Indians—was gone from tax records and voting rolls. The newspaper reported tersely that he had gone to San Francisco, "probably to engage in the practice of medicine." He had been in Flagstaff for seven years.

We were back to two wives again, Felicia Brannen and Sarah Manning. (Maybe she was shy.) I had barely begun to know Mira Robinson, to suspect that I might like her, and she had disappeared.

I've been taking an anti-depressant since I had that bizarre mental breakup after Don died. Most of the time I feel quite cheerful—get up in the morning and say, "Hello, face" to my image in the mirror—but now and then the reality of living slams into my chest, and I want to quit right now before the rest of the bad happens.

More notes on medical history:

1901: The Rockefeller Institute for Medical Research was established in New York City.

1901: Aseptic techniques to exclude bacteria from surgery were introduced in Germany.

1902: New York was the first city to send nurses into public schools.

5

My children are all adults, yet I find myself now and then swaying and bobbing, rocking long-gone babies. Mothers learn habits they don't recognize at the time.

Tag end of October, 2000

A la famiglia—

It's been a while since I've written, sorry, but I have reasons. I'm up to the 20th century now in my survey of medical people, etc., in Flagstaff, and I've realized that Expositions—"world fairs"—had been an influence, so I was reading about them in books I carried up into the tower. Also, I was busy with a move into winter quarters. And now...

Here I am! I occupied my half of this townhouse duplex in less than a day with the help of a moving van and six men in and out with furniture and boxes.

"Put that chair here, please."

"That goes upstairs."

"No, leave it. I'll unpack the kitchen utensils myself."

"I'll decide about the paintings later."

"The desk—upstairs in the north bedroom on the west wall."

I wrote a check and thanked them. Never in my long life having had a place that was completely mine, I'm quite excited about making myself a home my size, haven against cold and dark, refuge against winter.

Is it because I'm older and alone that bed is such a pleasure? My house-furnishing priority was a new double bed—I gave away my old king size—with silky blue sheets and four down pillows and a puffy comforter with a hint of blue flowers all over it. A bedside table big enough for books, a radio, reading lamp, and a small wooden bowl filled with cloves. I love the smell of cloves, in case you didn't know. The old rocking chair is in a corner by the south window.

My employment on the mountain was still indefinitely extended, so my little apartment was a place to come home to at night. As early as seemed decent, I retreated to bed each evening, humming with the comfort of it, and lay reading for hours. Memo to my grandsons: Fun is something that changes as you go through life. As you get older, it's not so noisy.

The one-room cabin on Woody Mountain was open to the world, a joy all summer. I loved listening to wind coming up the slope like a wave, loved lying in bed watching moonlight make moving tree shadows on the walls. But the forecast was for two strong Pacific systems to arrive from California with cold down into the twenties at night and snow at high elevations, so on October 11th and 12th I moved out of the cabin and locked it until next spring—Ed came and turned off the gas, unscrewed the pump. I began spending nights in town with street lights and train noise and traffic and campaign signs, driving morning and evening to be in the tower during the days.

In April I saw the cabin for the first time, hoping I wasn't making a mistake; when the time came, I didn't want to leave it. Those two Pacific systems gave me a brief idea how cold and dark and ominous winter could be on top of a mountain, how vulnerable I could feel, even in the daytime.

Five mornings a week, I started my 4Runner at 7:15 and drove past sunlight on the colored windows of the Federated Church, then through light and shadow on a dirt road. Going to work. Sometimes there was frost in the shadows of the trees. Sometimes there were running squirrels. North of Woody Mountain beyond the Arboretum, the yellow of oak leaves was a mosaic in the steady green of pines. Not a bad going-to-work drive, not at all, considering.

Several hundred thousand acres had burned in northern Arizona during the fire season, but there at the end, days in the tower were slow and quiet, timeless. Sun circled farther south every day, shadowing folds that erosion had carved in the hills. The beauty of the summer seemed concentrated at its ending—-I'd have missed it if I'd left earlier.

Five afternoons a week I went down the tower stairs and drove back through green-gold scenery. Rifle hunting season started: one Saturday after work I passed seven trucks full of camouflaged hunters in the two miles between my gate and Rogers Lake, ten more before I'd reached the Arboretum three miles farther on. I waved; they waved back. There were runners and bicyclists on the road—we exchanged waves. Communication. Traffic after I reached pavement was human contact, people going home, as I was. Daily routines. I felt quite warm toward everyone, but then I was separate in my car, and I didn't know them.

October is supposed to be a dry, sunny time in northern Arizona, but on the morning of Columbus Day a distant bank of cumulus stretched across the southern horizon, small clumps of cumulus hovered just above the Peaks. No wind—the tower was silent except for an occasional plane taking off at the airport four miles away. A day-long drizzle came out of that, not enough to affect forest moisture.

Then in the fourth week of October, something new! Every day crews invisible to me ignited prescribed burns to the northeast—150 acres a day of ground fuel and slash pile burning intended to reduce danger of wildfires. There was no wind to speak of, so smoke rose in thick columns straight up to somewhere around 11,000 feet. Then to my amazement, it ran into an invisible ceiling, flattened out, and drifted twenty-five miles at exactly that level. With shifting wind up there, it changed direction sometimes, but it never went higher.

Air is invisible unless there's something in it, moving. I think I've said that before.

Twice a day all summer the dispatcher had said, "all stations stand by for the fire weather forecast," and had read a detailed statement of what each district could expect for the next few hours, the next few days. So I was duly warned toward the end of the month when cumulus approached from two directions, gathered around the Peaks, darkened, lowered. Rain began about 2:30.

What I wasn't ready for was the cold. Sun through the windows is the only source of heat in the tower, and there was no sun. I huddled in my blanket trying to stay warm enough to last out the day as hail pounded on the roof, until I began to feel like a fool. Visibility was half a mile. I couldn't see a fire beyond that if one started, and nothing was going to burn anyway. "What am I doing up here?" Then, "Enough of this." Shivering, buffeted by wind, I struggled down the stairs and spent another half hour in my car with the engine running and the heater on. I couldn't seek refuge in the cabin: it was dark and empty.

Intelligence can over-ride duty. Advantage number three hundred of getting older: I'm able to say, "This is absurd." I put the car in gear and drove down a boggy road through a sodden forest, gold leaves shining through the gloom. I was sorry for all the creatures and glad I didn't have to stay with them.

For three days dark clouds moved above Flagstaff in waves, parting now and then to reveal snow on the Peaks, closing for more rain. The Hassayampa River ran full. Floods in the south central part of the state disrupted traffic in Phoenix and carried away people in Wenden and Salome—the governor declared a disaster area. I made no attempt to go back to the tower.

For three days I was warm and dry and safe in refuge, surrounded by unseen neighbors and the services of a community. Such a luxury. I had been sampling restaurants within walking distance and found some I approved, but I wasn't in the mood for strolling in damp and cold. Inside, I listened to rain and wind outside, untouched by them.

I wore comfort clothes, bonding with my house, baking bread, curling up on the couch in my grandmother's old patchwork quilt, reading comfort books. I didn't feel house-bound; I loved every minute. Freedom is relative.

When I called the Fire office to inquire whether the burning season had ended, the FMO laughed and said, "You bet."

As soon as the rain stopped, I drove back to the mountain to retrieve the things I'd left in the tower. Locked it. Drove away again, saying goodbye for a few months. Put the mountain to sleep in my mind.

Love,
Mother and Grandmother

(Those are roles, of course, not names.
My name is Marlene)

Exit, stage right, singing a song that Baxter taught me when he was in college: "You never even called me by my name."

P.S. to Cazz alone: During those rainy days, while I was happy in my
apartment, just for fun I put some of my old geology notes into a form that looks like
a poem, but I don't think it is. What do you think? Is this a poem or not?

100 million years ago
  during a long arid epoch in the continent's drift,
wind-blown sand dunes 3000 feet high (more than half a mile!)
  lay across 150,000 square miles,

dune desert covered what would be most of the Plateau.
  In the time of dinosaurs, mudflats buried the dunes,
  and other things happened,

and they turned to stone and rose a mile into the air.
  Everything moves, all the time.

When layers of the Plateau began to wear away,
  those dunes-turned-to-stone emerged

salmon-pink or grayish-white, massive cliffs and rounded domes—
  150,000 square miles of Navajo Sandstone.
Once it lay high above what would be the Grand Canyon.
  Now it's a step on the Grand Staircase.

Art is quite personal when you choose it to live with, and I just can't quite respond to Modernism. My offspring don't share my taste in painting, much to my relief. They'd left me the Southwestern landscapes: two Mahaffeys and a small Ed Mell. Knaub, deep blue storm clouds over New Mexico. Greg Hull, whom I discovered only five years ago. Gunnar Widforss. A Lynn Rowan Meyers that was not blue—they teased me about that, but I liked it, and that matters, doesn't it? I spent half of one day hanging them.

The Nobel Prize for medicine was announced in October, three men who'd worked on chemistry in human brains, the functioning of dopamine in billions of nerve cells. I was proud to be part of a species capable of such a search. But I thought of Don, whose tragedy might have been avoided had he been born a hundred years later. And all those suffering people who had plodded through our long traveling toward the twenty-first century.

A purple spot smaller than a dime appeared on the top of my left wrist. Red dots had been showing up there occasionally, pin-prick holes in capillaries, I'd decided, letting blood escape just beneath my skin. It didn't hurt or raise a bump, just reminded me that time runs out for all bodies, and I'd better pay attention to life while I have it. I didn't see a doctor, didn't tell my children.

People don't love you because you're sick. People love you because you make them feel well. Knowing I might lose Emily was pain I could hardly bear, but I already loved her.

"Oh, Emily. What would I do without you?"

"You want a list? Plant trees. Love a dog. Go to Tuscany and look at it for me. Make people laugh. Learn something."

At night on the mountain, full moon
illuminates white clouds drifting above,
and thought soars into the radiance.
There's also *more* and *part of* when the
bed is warm and the book is true and a
violin is playing on the radio.

The bottom of the Grand Canyon is walled by some of the oldest rock exposed on earth. It was formed maybe two, three billion years ago, and it's gone through a lot since then. Two thousand feet of rock strata are visible on top of it, all Paleozoic, before there was any life to speak of but algae. Another mile, a mile, of sediment was laid down above that for a hundred million years and then worn away. Formations to the north, not so eroded, are younger.

Come to think of it, this is a travel story too. Journey in more ways than one.

Zion National Park is only one hundred bee-line miles north of the Grand Canyon, but the rock layers in its cliffs are at least thirty million years younger—*younger*—than the top formation at the North Rim, which is Kaibab limestone. It lies under the river in Zion. The half mile of solidified Kayenta sandstone/siltstone/mudstone and, mostly, wind-blown Navajo sandstone that the Virgin River has cut through are aeons-gone from the Grand Canyon down one ancient river or another.

We used our new Golden Age card to enter the park high on the east wall, near the top, where the sandstone walls were white stone so close that we could see every line and swirl of the cross-bedding in the old dunes, layer after layer after layer. It was stunning, stupendous—fossil sand dunes half a mile deep, cliffs in that clear air. If words are ever adequate, they are not in Zion.

Signs along the road from Mount Carmel had warned that vehicles longer than fifty feet or taller than thirteen could not be accommodated in the tunnel. We were within those limits, but Don fussed anyway.

"You didn't tell me there would be a tunnel. What if they won't let us through? What if there's no place big enough to turn around?"

"I did tell you. The tunnel was finished before there were motor vehicles anywhere near our size. But the ceiling is an arch, and we'll get through if we stay in the middle. Guards at either end will stop other traffic so we can."

"What's the tunnel for? Do we have to go under a river? I don't want to get stuck under a river." His voice had a tense and ugly sound.

"The river's at the bottom. This route is along a side canyon so narrow there was no room for a road, so the tunnel was carved out twenty feet inside the cliff. It's a mile long. They thought they could do anything then."

"A mile? Damn it, Marlene."

"Please, Don. Please, it'll be an adventure. Big windows were cut to the outside here and there so we can see what we're going past. It won't be bad."

He drove slowly and carefully. When we inched out into sunshine again, the sandstone cliffs around us were pinkish from minerals that had seeped down into them for millions of years, and we were still high above the canyon floor.

Don never had been much of a man for scenery. "Look at that, hairpin switchbacks all the way. We'll never make it."

"I'll bet we can. They wouldn't have let us through if they'd thought we couldn't." Trying to jolly him along was wearing me down.

At the bottom there was a little river, a creek in October. Also big trees, their yellow leaves shining in mid-day sunlight, and a soft breeze. Rockrockrock soared straight up above our heads; in one place climbers were on it. Everywhere I looked were arrangements for moving hordes of people around painlessly, but summer tourist-clamor was finished for the year, and there was a feeling of peace and ease.

I had reserved a campground site at the lower end of the canyon long enough for our motorcoach, quiet, shaded by big trees, quite level. We found it with no trouble, but Don wasn't ready to stop driving.

"That wasn't so bad. Let's go up the canyon."

"Why don't we get set up here first and catch a shuttle bus."

"You mean with other people? A noisy crowd wasn't what I had in mind. I'm not going to ride any shuttle bus."

"Do you want to walk?"

"Walk?

"Or we could rent bicycles."

"Are you crazy?"

"Don, congestion is up to five thousand vehicles a day, and there's no choice but to restrict them to the lower end of the canyon, which is broader. Above the junction where we came in, we can't drive except in the winter."

"That's ridiculous."

"That's the way it is."

I thought the buses were not so bad. Their walls were windows three feet high; through skylights in the roof I looked up at the steep cliffs. And there was no fare. It was better than a car—especially for someone who would have been driving.

But it seemed to make Don anxious. Everything seemed to make Don anxious. After one ninety-minute trip, he went back to the coach to adjust the solar disk and watch daytime television. I rode the buses all day—a new one came along every seven to ten minutes, so I got off wherever I chose.

The only thing about the whole place that bothered me was the names that had been given to those ancient rocks. The Great White Throne. The Court of the Patriarchs: three monoliths called Abraham, Isaac, and Jacob. The Pulpit. It reduced them, I thought, to the size of the human brain. Which can be enormous, I guess, but all too often isn't.

The next morning Don was driving away before sunlight had crept down the west wall. I watched him after that, wondering, for all the good it did me.

Waiting for the school bus in the mornings, we jumped shadows. That was the year I was ten. We'd line up on the sidewalk beside the street and jump into the air as cars passed, trying to stay up long enough to clear their moving shadows. Some of the kids managed to do it, but I never could.

Just before my father died, he asked, "Who am I?" My mother told him his name, where he lived, what he'd worked at for so many years, and it upset him. "No. Who am I?" She told him where he'd grown up. The names of his children and grandchildren. The places he'd liked to go fishing. "I don't mean that. Who am I?"

That haunts me. What was external was not who he was. His real identity was inside, and he couldn't find it.

For the past thirty years I've felt the same emptiness at times, as if I've been set adrift in a place where I don't belong with people who are alien. I don't like the feeling at all.

Now here I am in a town, a house and a job, all new and strange. I don't know the names of the people around me, and I have no friends. Don and Emily are gone. The children I used to hold close are gone. There's no one in Arizona I can put my arms around, touch with my hand to find a sense of self in the connection.

OK, I am what I think and do and care about. Also a set of responses, learned or inborn, floating in a culture? So I go hunting in history for people to know, back almost a hundred years, the way things used to be.

1904 The *Sun* reported that the nation's Congress had defeated a bill that would have created a huge state joining Arizona and New Mexico. Debate about the idea continued anyway. Theodore Roosevelt was a candidate for a second presidential term. In newspapers "Yellow Peril" was used in reports about the Russo-Japanese War. A National Association for the Study and Prevention of Tuberculosis was founded—that was of interest to Arizona, we had plenty of tuberculosis in the state.

In Flagstaff Sarah Ashurst's lawyer son, Henry, had married Elizabeth Renoe, the woman who had come to Flagstaff to take charge of the recently established weather station. Described as "a noted speaker and orator," he was mentioned as a possibility for county office, but editor Funston was not one of Henry's supporters.

> *H.F. Ashurst was in town yesterday looking after his political fences, which look like they had been struck by a cyclone and long since past repairing. In other words, Henry is a candidate for nomination for district attorney on the democratic [sic] ticket, with the chances of the nomination going to his opponent.*

Ashurst received the nomination of his party anyway, and the newspaper battle was on. The Republican nominee for D. A. was incumbent Judge E. M. Doe, described as "a legal light."

Funston was an unabashed partisan, describing Democrats in lower case and trumpeting

COCONINO COUNTY REPUBLICANS
Meet in Convention and Nominate an Excellent Ticket
Harmony Prevails in the Party

But I knew how Ashurst's story went on and Funston didn't, so I wasn't surprised by the outcome. After the election, Henry was the district attorney by a margin of (total county vote) 577 to 524.

Twenty-nine "world fairs" had been produced since 1851, twelve of them in America. In 1904 the Louisiana Purchase Exposition opened in St. Louis after fifteen years of talk and planning.

The Columbian Exposition in Buffalo, New York, in 1901 had celebrated the electricity generated by Niagara Falls and displayed a machine based on the discovery only six years earlier by a German scientist of an invisible power he called X-rays because he didn't know what they were. The machine could photograph broken bones and dental cavities and foreign objects in human bodies.

Buffalo had been fine, but St. Louis had a song written in 1904 by Sterling and Mills, a waltz that all of America was soon singing: "Meet me in St. Louis, Louis. Meet me at the fair." The *Coconino Sun* published railroad fare rates and bank offers to sell money orders, and just days later Felicia Brannen, her sister, and D.J.'s mother went off to see the show.

At 1,272 acres, it was so big that doctors warned weak patients not to visit for fear they would collapse trying to see it all; a professor of neurology at Barnes Medical College urged doctors to do all they could to prevent patients diagnosed as neurasthenic from visiting the exposition because its dimensions would surely lead to their collapse. (They loved that word "collapse.") Ambulances were kept busy transporting "overweary" visitors to first-aid stations and hospitals.

Education was emphasized, as were technology and expectations for a better way of life in the new 20th century. Women's committees were part of the planning; there was a Women's Building. The Arizona building was "a modest and cozy place (one story, seven rooms) where Arizonans [could] rest and meet their friends."

But that popular waltz didn't mention the fair's underlying theme: imperialism buttressed by the anthropology of the time, which ranked humans based on the theory that

> *cranial capacity is correlated with culture grade so closely that the relative status of the peoples of the earth may be stated in terms of brain size. [And that]...a range in manual capacity is found in ascending the scale of human development from savagery to enlightenment...[and that] the forearm is better developed among whites than in any other race, yellow red or black.*

As proof of the theories, Geronimo, Chief Joseph, and Quanah Parker were exhibited to the gaze of the curious. Native people from all over the world, especially from the Philippines (recently defeated by guess who), were formed into living ethnological exhibits. Laboratories tested

> *sensitiveness to temperature, delicacy of touch and taste, acuteness of vision and hearing, power of coordination as expressed in rapidity and accuracy of forming judgment.*

The racial superiority of whites was considered manifest. Surprise.

Thus the White Man's Burden and the Strong Man's Duty to "uplift inferior races" which were "weak, dense and stupid". As if that weren't disgusting enough, there was this tragedy:

A FATHER'S DEVOTION

> *Although a pronounced savage, bloodthirsty, cruel and heartless, a villain of the deepest dye, Geronimo has a soft place in his heart. An attraction at the St. Louis fair, he became a weeping old man when he was introduced to his daughter whom he had not seen since she was a baby.*

Opinions and policies formed in St. Louis would last for years.

The Flagstaff newspaper announced that Dr. John Adams had purchased an automobile at the fair, "of the steam type." Steam—like a railroad locomotive. Six years earlier the Stanley twins had demonstrated a steam-propelled carriage that produced no odor but required half an hour to start: first the driver had to light a fire in the furnace to heat water in the boiler.

The doctor's machine, built in the Grout factory in Massachusetts, was a "light touring car" of eight horsepower that weighed 1300 pounds and traveled at the breath-taking speed of one mile in 2.2 minutes. The first locally-owned automobile in Flagstaff, it carried gas to heat enough water for one hundred miles, but only enough water for fifty. In December Adams, "an enthusiastic automobilist," drove it to the Grand Canyon but had to leave it there due to a snowstorm.

It was quite a year. Dr. Sipe's brother was injured when a velocipede car (railroad bicycle) he was riding was hit by the eastbound Limited. Thrown into the air, he landed on "the pilot of the locomotive." His left foot had to be amputated. Young Mr. Sipe's foot, that is.

Dr. Brannen was appointed surgeon to the National Guard of Arizona with rank of Major. An osteopath named Dr. Graves, who had decided to locate here, opened an office at the residence of Mrs. Kennedy. Dr. Miller, 46 by then, was called to Oak Creek by the illness of C. S. ("Bear") Howard. Funston said that "the old gentleman," past eighty-seven, had good eyesight and still hunted and trapped for his living but had been in poor health since he'd had pneumonia.

Other patients. The youngest child of John Hennessy was kicked in the head by a horse. And Sarah "Grandma" Pattee, 86 years old, fell and broke her hip. The mother of nine children, widow of a man who had served in the War of 1812, she died a month later.

A Sad Failure

I.A. Turnell about 9 o'clock yesterday morning took his gun and left the house, saying that he was going to commit suicide. Nothing was thought of his threat to take his life, but as the hours passed and he did not return, search was made without finding him. About six o'clock a man came to the store of Mrs. Turnell and told her that a man had shot himself and wanted to see her, and that he was lying on the hillside east of the courthouse. She immediately called for Dr. Sipe, who, with a number of men, went to the place indicated. Turnell was found lying on the ground under the shade of a pine tree, conscious and badly scared. Upon examination by the doctor it was found that Turnell had cut the small veins of both wrists, but had failed to cut deep enough to produce death, the cuts being about an inch long. He was taken to the county hospital, and this morning was able to go to his home. His experience will probably make him a wiser and better man.

So said Editor Funston.

It's allegorical: the way you see things depends on where you're standing. I've learned that from growing older. Life doesn't look the same from here.

"Good morning, Gwen. I'm sitting in sunshine at my kitchen table looking out the window at autumn leaves on the big trees across the street."

"Mother. I've been so relieved since you moved into town. Are there neighbors who can help you if you fall or something?"

"I'm awash in people, but I don't know any of them yet."

"You should introduce yourself to the closest ones and ask them to keep an eye out for you."

"Ummm. Thanks for the advice." I wasn't about to do that, but there was no point in saying so.

"You should make friends, you know."

"Oh, no doubt I will."

"It's not healthy to be alone."

"I'm considering inviting Ed and Sandy to dinner. They're quite friendly." Why must I defend myself against my daughter? Everyone knows it's supposed to be the other way around.

"Are you eating a balanced diet? That's important, you know."

Yes, I did know. "Thank you for reminding me, I'll be sure to pay attention."

"Do you exercise? I could send you a stationary bicycle."

"I drive to the grocery store, but I walk everyplace else I want to go. Sometimes I walk around this part of town for the pleasure of exploring. And I climb to go upstairs."

"Is your mental outlook good? What are you doing to exercise your mind?"

"Dad Hawks, Fred Harvey and Queen Victoria have just died. McKinley died some time ago. Shot."

"Mother!"

"Big headlines on the front page called it A Dastardly Crime. I had it on the screen of my microfilm machine in the library when a class of grade school children stopped at my closet to see what I was doing. I showed them the headline, President Shot, and one bright boy asked, 'Why?'"

"It's not healthy for you to live in the past like that."

"I'm following the 2000 election. It's so close I don't envy whoever wins. I do hope this will be the end of Buchanan, but I fear he's a weed that comes up no matter what you do."

"Mother, that's not nice. Some people like him."

"I know. But one good thing about this country is the freedom to express opinions. What are you doing that's interesting?"

"Driving Beanie and Cass to their schools and their lessons. Traffic is terrible in Denver."

"I imagine so. It is everywhere." If driving is the most interesting thing in her life, no wonder she bullies me.

"Mother, I've been wondering about you. I thought people become more conservative as they get older, but you sound almost like a liberal. I'm surprised at you."

"I don't know what I am anymore. I'm seeing the world differently these days—and it's possible that political definitions have slid around. It's my feeling that 'conservative' doesn't mean what it once did. I can remember when Barry Goldwater was considered a dangerous extremist. Now I hear people talking about going back to things. You can't go back, don't they know that?"

"Oh my god! What's that awful noise? Beanie! Cazz! I'm sorry, Mother, I have to go."

The Udall girl could make everyone laugh by the way she said some ordinary word. I used to wish I could be as funny as she was. I wonder where she is now. Is she still funny, or did life wear her down? Neurological erosion is one of the theories I'm working on.

Twenty years ago when I heard that Lyle had died, my reaction was to wonder what kind of person I might have been if I hadn't gone through that storm, hadn't learned that I could love like that. What meaning it lends to life for a while. How impossible it is, later, to define it.

I didn't decide. Lyle was too experienced to create a situation that required a decision. I wonder whether he had any idea of the power he was playing with.

He'd call me to read something—"I thought of you when I saw this—Mark Twain—'I have met the dragon, and I can run faster than he can'."

Or "Did you see 'Peanuts' this morning? Lucy is the strongest female character in modern literature, hands down."

I found little things to send by mail.

"I've just opened a card with the Laocoön sculpture and a message that reads 'You think you've got problems.' Signed Anna Freud. I think I know who that is."

And "What's this I find on my desk? A perfectly credible letter from Lewis Carroll describing Eisenhower's smile. I ask you!"

I loved how funny I was with him, that was it, how intelligent I felt.

I believed a man and a woman could be friends. There was nothing romantic in my mind at first, nothing secretive. Just phone calls to share stories, now and then lunch after a gallery visit. Weeks would go by with no more than a note or a phone call.

It seems naive to me now: I didn't even think of sex. It was such a pleasure to have a man interested in my opinions, in debating them with me.

"What's wrong with narrative paintings? People respond to them."

"That's true." I spoke slowly, finding exactly the right words. "And the figurative skill required is astonishing. Composition can be, often is, subtle and intelligent. But they aren't about art. A viewer's focus is on the story, not on painterly qualities like color and line. I suppose you could argue that an artist's technique should be like an actor's— best when you don't notice it…"

"No, no. I see your point: story telling is the province of literature. I would just question why it must be kept separate. Even paintings with nothing human in them are stories to the human mind."

I smiled. "When I was a little girl there was a painting on the living room wall. Trees and a fence along a road that curved out of sight. I used to imagine myself walking along that road." For the first time in years I felt that I was a thinking creature. Lyle didn't touch me except with his fingers on my arm to emphasize a point. Oh, he was smooth. Later, when he began to touch my face, he did it briefly, in a teasing way, to underscore praise.

"That's a perceptive mind inside there"...touching my temple..."Meeting it calls up the best in me."

What woman wouldn't respond to that? A woman's mind is her primary erogenous zone, in case no one has noticed. At least, mine is. By the time he began to show me that my body, all of it, was made for love, he had already captured my mind.

Love may not be blind, but it certainly does change the way you see. I had known Lyle for years, and his face had seemed merely ordinary until I loved him. Love made it fascinating, alive. I watched his expressions when he talked, collected them like money. And his voice, slightly abrasive before, made my whole body thrill when I loved him.

The muscles below his shoulder blades—*latissimus dorsi*, he said—I felt them under my palms, loving the ways his body was different from mine.

Even in the beginning, I didn't love Don the way I loved Lyle, an obsession that rules your mind for a while. With Don it was more quiet. A sweetness in my chest. I liked to talk with him, cook for him, find surprises for him. Like the time I made a picnic and we drove out to Saguaro Lake on a breezy Saturday to watch sail boat races. It was so long ago. I was barely twenty-two.

In those days he was a spur-of-the-moment guy. "Hey, Marlene! Sweetie. This book is making my eyes glaze over. Let's go get ice cream cones."

We walked through old neighborhoods, licking ice cream, looking at houses and wondering what their stories had been. "Lots of children," I'd say. "Happy families. It's so big and solid, and that wide front porch."

"You think so? I'm getting a feeling of danger. Bet it's haunted. Something malicious, wanting revenge."

"Oh, Don, no. If there's a ghost in there, it's wishing it could be a child again."

Or he'd say, "Let's go to a movie. What's playing?" And we'd see something full of singing and dancing, the way movies were in those years.

He seemed to be happy then or at least at ease with himself. For the first few years sex was a gentle wonder, really "making love." He would wrap me up in his arms, moving slowly, nuzzling and murmuring, for half an hour until we finally, well—it was quite exciting, and I thought he was wonderful. Next morning I would bring him coffee in bed singing "Good morning, good morning." Make tiny bouquets and put them in the bathroom for the pleasure of it.

I didn't feel all-over compulsion, never the can't-keep-my-hands-off, can't-keep-my-eyes-off. I was just glad to be with him. In the grocery store, at a movie. It was nice, companionable. On cold nights we slept close against each other and kept each other warm.

When we were young—long ago, when we were young—we made up the bed together. Sometimes we'd cook together, side by side in the kitchen. Meat loaf and spaghetti and beans-with-cheese that didn't cost too much. I need to remember those years, need those memories.

There was barely enough money, and we were more in debt for his education every year. We couldn't afford to drive far or stay in a hotel. Clothes had to last a while. I don't remember minding too much, except for shoes. I wished I had enough money for new shoes. But there was hope, and life wasn't really bad.

It was a sweet time, those first few years. Things changed so slowly that I didn't notice. He studied longer hours. He was often gone at night. No time for quiet walks or slow love-making or cooking together, and I went to the grocery store alone. When Don was home, he was drinking, just a little at first, to relax with. It was near the end of his residency that I noticed his personality had begun to change.

I'm too wary now to feel romantic love again, too unhappy about the game. But not having the opportunity, how do I know?

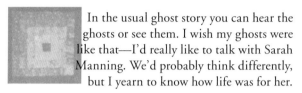 In the usual ghost story you can hear the ghosts or see them. I wish my ghosts were like that—I'd really like to talk with Sarah Manning. We'd probably think differently, but I yearn to know how life was for her.

In the city library a shabby black man sits quietly for hours every day at the same little table by a window that looks out to tall trees and the red stone walls of the old Federated Church. The hood of his jacket is pulled over his head to hide his face. He makes no fuss, speaks to no one, meets no one's eyes. There's a clumsy bundle tied with rope at his feet. A book is open before him, but he seldom turns the pages.

A woman at the reference desk told me that his name is Marvin. Every noon he leaves his bed roll and suitcase at his table, trusting to strangers, and walks to the soup kitchen for lunch. I don't know where he goes to sleep.

Through October, our night temperatures seldom rose above freezing and were sometimes below zero. Waves of storms passed through, some described ahead of time as "major," but we never had more than eighteen inches of snow on the ground. Sometimes I was house-bound by wind and icy streets; usually I could go out if I wanted to.

A 2000-acre wildfire in Florida. Thousands dead from earthquakes in Guatemala and India. The coldest winter on record in the eastern and central parts of the country. Warming warnings from a United Nations panel: rise of ten degrees over the next century caused by carbon monoxide pollution, thus more sunlight reaching the earth. Massive power shortages in California; other states close to the same problem.

But in Flagstaff I had everything I needed, everything I wanted and a whole library at my disposal. Reading. Always reading. I like reading, it opens the world to me.

In 1905 three groups formed the Council for Medical Education to begin reforms in the nation's medical schools. The Council requested the Carnegie Foundation to conduct a preparatory study. I filed a note with myself to watch for its report.

1905 At the beginning of the year there were—have I lost track of anybody?—six doctors living in Flagstaff: Brannen, Manning, Miller, Sipe, Adams, and Slernitzauer. Seven if you're not biased toward orthodoxy, and you count Dr. Graves, the osteopath.

Slernitzauer didn't stay long enough to be on any list of taxes for personal property. Graves was taxed in 1906 and applied to the territorial board of medical examiners—Dr.

Manning was a member—for a license to practice, and then Graves sold his house and moved to Portland with his family "to practice his profession." That left five. And only two wives: Felicia Brannen and heart-of-her-home Sarah Manning, age forty-seven. Through the year the situation changed.

Dr. John Adams, who owned Flagstaff's first automobile, began to offer "electrical treatments" (I haven't the foggiest what that meant) and "x-ray examinations." The progressive young man owned the town's first x-ray machine. In May at Flagstaff he married a woman named Margaret Cox Strain, "of legal age" and a resident of Los Angeles County. In June they returned from a few days trip to the Grand Canyon. In April she went to Los Angeles for a week or so. Otherwise I haven't the foggiest about her either.

Dr. W. P. Sipe went east and the *Sun* repeated a rumor: "When he returns, he will be accompanied by a charming bride." Sure enough, when Dr. Sipe arrived by way of Colorado, he had with him Mrs. Sipe, formerly Miss Ethel "Effie" Sawyer, twenty-seven years old, born in Iowa, previously a missionary at Tuba City.

Suddenly we were up to four wives. The Sipe-Sawyer wedding had been performed in Missouri, possibly in the bride's home, possibly in a Presbyterian service. That's assumption: within a month Dr. Sipe was part of a temperance program at a Presbyterian meeting speaking on "Alcohol and the Body," and he was occasionally mentioned in the Flagstaff Presbyterian church news.

So. Five doctors and four wives—Dr. Miller was still single. At forty-seven, he was perhaps out of the running, although one never knows about bachelors.

As always I learned little about the wives. It was frustrating. I made some guesses though, based on changes in the world around them, about what they wore, when their neighborhoods had sewer service and water piped into homes. No radio yet, no movies, no television. Occasionally traveling actors or musicians came into town, but what entertainment those people had was still home-made: socials and theatricals and parties of all kinds.

Bridge had arrived in America from England at least by 1894. Wildly popular, it was played at home card parties in Flagstaff early in the 20th century as Auction, in which each of the four players could bid for the right to nominate trumps. I imagine respectable Felicia Brannen entertaining friends in the afternoon with "delightful refreshments" and competitive bidding.

Sarah Manning had her home and five children to care for, clothes to scrub clean and iron, meals to cook on a wood stove, a fire to keep going all day in winter, a grocery list to have ready for when the boy came around. It's more difficult to envision her at the table, cards in her hand, calculating her bid, but bridge was said to have "invaded every grade of society and laid low the proud and the humble," so she might have played the game.

By the way, George Felix Manning was apparently not one of the men of the era who cultivated an expanded waistline by eating heavy, multi-coursed meals. He was always thin with a mustache that looked like a bird on the wing.

The *Sun* printed news like brief stories about patients the doctors were treating. In July, a young man named John Rawlings attempted to swing aboard Santa Fe passenger train Number 1 near Winona, and sustained serious injuries.

He was found and brought here on No. 7, and taken to the county hospital, where it was found necessary to amputate his right leg about half way between the knee and the ankle. His left ankle was also broken, but can be saved. His right hand was also mashed and one finger was amputated. Drs. Adams, Miller and Sipe performed the operations. The victim's mother and brother came in from California and accompanied him to Los Angeles.

It was the habit all over America in those years for newspapers to employ a light tone in reports of new fathers and other targets considered fair game. That was long before Political Correctness.

An Old Mexico Mexican filled up on booze last Saturday night and proceeded to show his compatriots that he was "un hombre mucho grande." After taking in the business section of the city, he returned to Mexican town and opened up an altercation with another Mexican; after the battle was over, he was moved to the county hospital, where on Sunday, Dr. Adams, assisted by Dr. Miller, took eight stitches in his left breast, over the heart, tied up three leaders and sewed up the left arm, taking fourteen stitches in that member, it being almost severed.

Medical news elsewhere in northern Arizona was sometimes reported. In June down on Oak Creek, Sedona Schnebly, horrified, saw her little daughter Pearl dragged to death by a frightened horse. Unable to stay where it had happened, the stricken family left Mr. Schnebly's brother in charge of the ranch and moved to Missouri for a while.

Henry Wickenberg, eighty-six, discoverer of the Vulture Mine, killed himself by his own gunshot, and Funston wrote: "During the last year he had been given to fits of melancholy probably due to old age and the lack of family ties." There was only the simplest understanding then of the causes of depression.

Mental/emotional illness, invisible except for its symptoms, was still considered a failure of character. Or worse. When the sheriff of Maricopa County shot and killed himself, the cause was reported as "temporary insanity."

Mose Casner, a well known rancher on Beaver Creek got up early in the morning and roused his wife and five children with a rifle and ordered them off the premises. He broke up all the furniture in the house and cut up the clothing. His family took refuge at the home of Nelson Hillingshead two miles away. Casner was arrested…Neighbors are so upset they think Casner should go to prison.

When his wife had needed surgery to remove a tumor, medical care had been available. When Mose was obviously ill, he was arrested.

Anna Hawks was gone, and the Coconino county hospital for the indigent was supervised for a year and a half by Dr. Robinson. After he left, W. H. Carroll, whose wife had maintained that boarding house in Mill Town, had the position for another year and a half. Then T. E. Pulliam "obtained possession" after a dispute, and Carroll leased the old Tinker house with plans to turn it into a private hospital, but I don't think he did. In August of 1905 the county Board of Supervisors called for bids to construct a new hospital for the indigent from plans prepared by Godfrey Sykes, one of the versatile brothers who ran the fix-and-mend bicycle shop.

Other news: New Mexico was admitted to the Union, supposedly eliminating the issue of joint statehood with Arizona. Utah wanted to annex the part of Arizona north of the Colorado River; Coconino and Mohave counties were opposed.

There were 5,335 children in schools in Maricopa County, only 741 in the whole 18,000-square-miles of Coconino County. Heavy storms washed out the Santa Fe railroad tracks, causing frequent delays. And Elizabeth Forster, "an accomplished lady printer" in Prescott accepted a position with the *Sun. Alors! Cuidado!* Also where would it end?

"You're so simple." Don, superior, stating a fact. My headaches, growing in intensity, came more often. Sometimes they gave me violent vomiting fits.

Until the day in October when I drove away from the mountain in a cold rain, 2000 was the driest year on record in Arizona. The 1990s went on the books as the warmest decade in the Northern Hemisphere over the past 600 years (!), the warmest decade of the 20th century on a global scale, but rainfall in the state was erratic: normal amounts in 1991 and '92, 1995 and '98; triple normal in 1993; below normal in the others. No pattern that I could see, just some blips that did not quite correspond to El Niño or La Niña. Chaotic variability, yessir.

Then the October and November storms of 2000 began. There was just time after those three days of rain for me to rush out to a grocery store, to the library for a new stack of books, to Babbitt's for boots and a heavy parka. A huge storm came in from the Pacific with two weeks of rain and snow.

Day after day wind blew and temperatures were below freezing. A man on contract came to shovel snow from the steps and sidewalks in our townhouse unit, but some of our neighbors didn't try to keep up with it. Afternoons I suited up in cold weather security—sweat suit, turtleneck shirt, polartec jacket, warm socks—and navigated through obstacles to the library with my notebook to read about a global climate system that includes oscillatory dynamics driven by long temporal lags in the transfer of energy between the oceans and atmosphere. About the North American Oscillation, the Quasi Biennial Oscillation. Yikes. Sun spots and carbon 14? I still wasn't sure I understood what I was reading.

There are churches in the neighborhood and apartment units and big old houses with many doors and windows and little one-car garages in the back. In the evenings I followed sidewalks under trees bowed so low under the heavy weight on their branches that they touched over the streets. Snow falling past street lights. The squeak of it under my feet. Light reflected from snow and clouds, a soft illumination that enchanted everything.

Sobering news: despite nearly record precipitation over the past few weeks, Arizona was still in the grip of a drought. The storms had not been able to make up for dry conditions in previous years; parched land had soaked up so much of the recent rain, that runoff into reservoirs was seventy-two percent below normal. That's seventy-two.

BELOW. If we have little moisture this winter and next, Salt River Project is prepared to begin water rationing.

America has survived a few bad presidents—weak, naive, greedy, et cetera—and a few good ones—cynical, clever, charismatic—and a lot of mediocre ones, so I wasn't a partisan in the 2000 election. I preferred one of the candidates, but my preferences have not always been elected; I wasn't apoplectic, as some people were, and I was fascinated by the process as it played out. Only a few votes separated Bush and Gore in Florida, in the national popular tally. The country was divided pretty much down the middle. Like the rest of the world, I waited to see what would happen since we had a president but no real winner, no real loser. Politics is a grand show if you can keep your sense of humor.

Gwen and Baxter and Abby each decided that a B & B in Flagstaff was not to their taste and it was about time everybody came to visit them for Thanksgiving. Telephone tension developed. Compromise may be required for politics, but I haven't noticed that families are so inclined.

"Mom, I don't understand my sisters, I never have. Now that you've sold the Scottsdale house, mine is the biggest. I have three extra rooms that would accommodate guests comfortably and privately. I think you should all come to Texas."

"I know, Baxter, it does seem logical. Neither of the girls can offer private rooms for us all, but Abby and Jane say they can't afford the plane fare or the time to drive that far. Gwen says she's lived in Colorado long enough to develop a poor opinion about Texans."

"That's outright prejudice, and she knows it. You can't judge Texas by what summer vacationers do."

"True, but she seems quite incensed."

"Mom, a lot of people live in Texas, they aren't all alike. I really had expected better of her."

Mothers spend a good deal of time trying to mediate. Long ago I realized that my offspring are neither like me nor like each other.

"Mother, Abby says that the only reason I'm declining her invitation is that I don't approve of Jane. That's not true; I have no problem with Jane. My boys think she doesn't like them, and they want to know what they would do all day in that apartment. I've promised that we'll go to the beach, but they say that's not enough."

"Gwen, I'm disturbed—my grandchildren splitting my children apart."

"Frankly, I don't think that's so awful. We aren't really comfortable with each other. I have a much better time with my in-laws."

I'd like to think she didn't know what a zinger that was, aimed right at me. "I didn't know you felt that way, Gwen. Maybe it's time to abandon our annual Thanksgiving-together tradition. Let you each build one of your own now that you're grown up."

"Well, I didn't mean I don't want to see you. You're welcome to come up here and have the holiday with us."

"No," thinking while I spoke, "I shouldn't play favorites. I think I'll stay in Flagstaff and build my own Thanksgiving ritual. I rather like the idea."

"Mother, don't sulk."

"I'm not. Really. Just intrigued by the possibility of a new phase. You've set me free."

"Mother, don't be mean."

There was no new snow before Thanksgiving, but days were so cold the old snow melted slowly and at night it froze drier and harder. It crunched under my feet when I walked to the library under tall bare trees, taking small steps, putting my feet straight down, feeling that I was living in a book. Living in a book.

By the third week in November I was indeed thankful. So I walked through icy streets finding delicacies—pate, ciabatta bread, Stilton, apple tart—my own private celebration. I arranged a single place setting of china and silver and crystal, opened a Monrachet, and watched football on tv. It's hard to impress me, though. I watched Joe Montana and Jerry Rice make touchdowns for the 49ers when Bill Walsh was coach and they still called it Candlestick Park.

The weeks between Thanksgiving and Christmas, fulcrum year 2000, were cold, sometimes windy, often grey. Golden leaves no longer skittered across streets. Crusty old snow lingered, stubborn in shady places.

A cyclone in northwest Australia destroyed aborigine houses. On our Pacific coast a hydroelectricity alert! threats of rolling blackouts! (English is so picturesque.) The culprits in California were unusually cold weather plus previous deregulation that had resulted in tripled costs to consumers.

I don't feel so naive when I contemplate the faith some people have that a market economy will create saints.

There's always weather news. Always. Storms closed down "Chicago, Chicago, that toddlin' town" with snow and eighty MPH winds south all the way to trucks blown off highways in Texas. Tornados in Alabama. More blizzards in the upper mid-west. A threatened eruption of Popocatepetal south of Mexico City. Winds in Africa have produced—get this—"several hundred million tons of dust a year" for the past twenty-five, blowing to the Caribbean with accompanying fungal spores that might be the cause of dying coral reefs. Has it always been like this, or am I just now noticing?

Flagstaff weather was staid except for flurries in the middle of the month. Conversations I overheard were about Presidential vote counts in Florida.

Here's another thing I've learned: God might reward you for being nice; people usually don't.

Don always worked long hours—fatigue was part of the role. He didn't show much enthusiasm but, for goodness sake, his job involved listening to people complain. Who wouldn't be bored after that? Getting older—weren't we all—so of course his appetite was off. He didn't enjoy anything. He had headaches.

I was having headaches too, fatigue, anxiety. And ashamed of it. Self-pity? Maybe hypothyroidism? A mineral deficiency? I made up lists of possible diagnoses, the more serious the better. But mostly I blamed myself for not being good enough. Don had become critical of everything. He'd say;, "What's the matter with you?" There's no answer to that, and it isn't a question anyway.

If I turned toward him, he turned away. "Busy day tomorrow." If I tried to touch him, he moved my hands. I thought it was my fault—I wasn't trying hard enough to be attractive and affectionate—but he refused to talk about it. I felt guilty. I felt like a failure. When he moved into a separate bedroom—"My hours are erratic, on call late, I don't want to disturb you"—I was sure he was having an affair with someone else, a nurse probably. There was always an ache in my chest.

He woke after two or three hours of sleep and sat in his study with the lights off, drinking Scotch. Thinking about a patient, couldn't I see that, and would I go back to bed and leave him alone? NO, he didn't need anything.

He'd go days barely speaking, looking glum. For me, dis-location: how did I get into this situation with this stranger? This isn't me, I don't belong here. I didn't talk with Don or any of his colleagues, not even Travis, afraid I'd be dismissed as exaggerated, emotional and dramatic, a hysterical woman. There were whole days when, truly, I didn't want to live anymore.

Well. I told Emily how I was feeling but not all of why. "Oh Marlene, what a shame. Would you see a counselor?"

"I mentioned it, and Don accused me of trying to destroy his reputation."

"Shame on him, that's not helpful. Maybe it's a medical problem, not something you can talk yourself out of. You've tried B complex and things?"

"In secret."

"You need information." She was a believer in information.

"Dietary intervention is recognized therapy in some circles. Mind affects body, body affects mind. Maybe it's a food allergy. That would be trendy."

What a friend—she sent me to the medical library and scientific tomes and a wooden chair at a big wooden table. I positioned my notebook, read every sentence twice, and tried to reduce it from medicalese to English.

> *Neurochemistry indicates a biological basis (for depression)…Interrelationships between sugar, hormones, light, exercise, B-vitamins and certain amino acids are involved in a complex chemical feedback loop…The brain requires certain chemicals to function normally.*

Okay, so far, so good. I'd had Psych 101. But the authors spread around me were talking about food and its effect on the human brain, and I didn't believe they had to be so stuffy. An insufficiency of neurotransmitters may be a cause of depression. Serotonin is a neurotransmitter. Tryptophan crosses the blood barrier to be converted to serotonin.

I muttered, "Wait a minute here. Wait a minute," and the librarian looked up. It took me only half a day to figure it out

    a. Availability of neurotransmitters depends on a precursor or the substance from which they are synthesized.

    b. Precursors are substances that must be obtained in whole or in part from *diet*. [my emphasis]

    c. Serotonin is synthesized from tryptophan, which cannot be produced by the cells of the body.

    d. An individual must consume a diet that contains a sufficient amount of tryptophan.

Great. WHAT IS TRYPTOPHAN?

Oh, it says right here. It's an amino acid, one of the building blocks of protein. Plasma tryptophan levels are decreased in depressed subjects.

Let me get this straight. Tryptophan loading [loading?] increases the synthesis of central serotonin. So I should eat more meat, right? Wrong.

> The behavioral effects of whole foods do not operate in isolation...With little protein in the diet, a greater proportion of the available tryptophan crosses the blood-brain barrier to be converted to the neuro-transmitter serotonin...The synthesis of serotonin involves the action of several enzymes, vitamins and minerals.

Don insisted, I mean insisted, on meat of some kind as about half of every meal. But I could leave it out of my breakfasts and lunches.

Another book: When people are feeling low, they consume more sugar, chocolate, and caffeine. No kidding? I didn't need a book to tell me that. You have coffee and a doughnut, you feel better for a while, then you feel worse, so you reach for a candy bar, but they may do more harm than good in the long run. So stay away from table sugar and coffee. I could do that.

Eliminate alcohol, nicotine, salt, saturated fat. It sounded depressing. Increase fiber, fatty acid, raw fruits, vegetables, whole grains, and complex carbohydrates. Maintain sufficient levels of B-1, B-6, B-12, C, A, niacin, folic acid, calcium, magnesium, copper, thiamin, and iron.

I tried all that and felt like a hypochondriac.

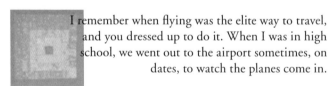 I remember when flying was the elite way to travel, and you dressed up to do it. When I was in high school, we went out to the airport sometimes, on dates, to watch the planes come in.

For almost 200 years the colonies-turned-states had had acts on their books regulating such important foods as bread. Since 1879 bills about American-made products that people put into their mouths had been introduced in legislatures, in Congress. Introduced and defeated. Articles in popular magazines exposed alarming conditions, but no action was taken.

Physicians at the time generally supported sanitary measures, public health laws, regulation of food and drugs, inspection of water supplies, vaccination programs—but that support seems to have had little effect on legislation. No regulation meant that through the last half of the 19th century meat, milk, and butter (commonly adulterated with lard) were sold under dishonest and unsanitary conditions. Chemical preservatives such as boric acid were in common use. Patent medicines included baby products containing cocaine. Whiskey was often made of raw alcohol and food coloring. Packers sold sausage—processed by workers who had active tuberculosis—that contained rancid meat and "foreign matter" like mouse droppings. No wonder the life span was shorter then.

In 1905, after two bills to regulate food and drugs had been dropped in the Senate, the Supreme Court ruled unanimously in favor of federal attempts to break up the "Beef Trust." The ruling had no effect on the powerful meat monopoly.

It was a situation made to order for political reformer Theodore Roosevelt and the thousands of women activists in the country, who turned public opinion against business arguments, especially after Upton Sinclair's novel *The Jungle* about the meat packing industry hit the nation's stomach. Political sentiment suddenly focused on the responsibility of the federal government for public welfare, public health, and public medicine.

1906 The result, in June of 1906, was the Pure Food and Drugs Act, the first federal action which made it a crime to adulterate or mislabel foods, drinks, and drugs intended for interstate commerce. If that was a loss of American liberty, well, it's all right with me.

Then in April the front page was full of purple prose: San Francisco, "the pride of California," lay "stricken to the death" due to "the fury of elemental forces." The Great Earthquake—what an opportunity for a writer. A relief fund set up to collect money sent off $1600 dollars from Flagstaff to San Francisco, which had been generous with help after a fire in 1884. Arizona as a whole contributed $97,400, including clothing and supplies.

Turning through pages of the *Sun*, seeking doctors and their wives, I noticed state news as I passed by. Preparatory work was under way at the confluence of the Salt and Verde rivers for Arizona's first dam, which would be named for President Roosevelt. Elk in the eastern part of the state having been eradicated by hunters, one hundred new ones—elk not hunters—were being brought down from Yellowstone National Park to be turned loose in Arizona forests. A "madman" had put the Southern Pacific railroad "on the bum" by setting fires in round houses and destroying signals and telegraph wires. The Colorado River, in flood, was six miles wide at Needles.

There was miscellaneous local political news. Democrat Henry F. Ashurst, strongly opposed again by Editor Funston, was re-elected county attorney by 609 out of the 1034 votes cast.

Mail from California came into Flagstaff on eastbound Number 4 at about 1:50 p.m. Former teacher Eva Marshall applied for appointment as postmaster, salary $1800 a year; Roosevelt approved and sent her name on to the Senate, where she was duly appointed. J. G. Verkamp was postmaster at the Grand Canyon at a salary of only $1100 per year, because there were fewer people over there to serve and less work for him to do.Leo Verkamp was Flagstaff's mayor in 1906.

> *Footnote:*
> *Were the Verkamp men related to the three Verkamp women from Cincinnati—Emma, Mary and Matilda—who married three Babbitt men and moved to Arizona? Curious, weary of sitting and reading microfilm of old newspapers, I wandered around the library, searching for the answer. It turned into quite a task: first the federal census of 1900 and again 1910; folders in the vertical file, obituaries; books written by Dean Smith and Platt Cline. I drove to the Special Collections library at NAU and to the Pioneers Museum. What I found was a family that had a lot to do with what Flagstaff became.*
> *Gerhard "Papa" Verkamp, a prosperous merchant in Cincinnati, raised five sons and four daughters who grew up with the Babbitt brothers. (Cincinnati. The E.M. Institute in Cincinnati was where Dr. Brannen had medical training. I wondered whether there was a connection.)*

*When three of his daughters married Babbitt men, Papa Verkamp was
liberal with money and advice that helped them all get started in business in the
West. The women were influential in Flagstaff social matters, raising the tone
and all that, civilizing the town. Producing children who became part of the big
Babbitt family.*

*Later three of their brothers were here—Leo and John and Oscar. Leo
arrived in 1904. Two years later when he was only 26 he was elected mayor,
which probably said something about him but I don't know what. A Republican and a sheep rancher, he didn't marry, did not send children into the next
generation. In 1919 he died, age 39.*

*Oscar married but had no children either, managed several retail outlets
including Verkamp Inc. at the Grand Canyon.*

*Brother John George sr. married Catherine Wolfe and lived in Flagstaff for
thirty years. He had financial interests in lumber and sheep, and in 1906 opened
a curio shop at the Grand Canyon that was still in operation almost a hundred
years later. The Verkamps in Flagstaff in 2000, including a federal judge, are
descended from John G.*

OK, back to the newspaper. There was just enough news about disease and injury
to reassure me that doctors were still in town. A few cases of scarlet fever showed up, and
Flagstaff doctors continued to respond to the Hawks Hotel hospital to treat men with
injuries suffered as usual in fights, shootings, accidents involving horses and unsuc-
cessful efforts to board moving freight trains. Would-be suicides included a man who
cut his throat from ear to ear and afterward nearly severed his right hand. A cripple who
had been in the hospital "for some time past" was taken to the territorial insane asylum
suffering from "the delusion that he was about to be attacked by some unseen person."

Dr. Adams' younger brother visited for a while. In what was known at the time as
"fine writing" the newspaper covered a social event at which the doctor's wife—what was
her name? I shuffled through my notes—Margaret

*acted as hostess to a jolly party of young people. The early part of the evening was
most pleasantly spent at bowling in the alley in the basement of the Banner drug
store, after which the party repaired to the cozy home of the hostess, where an
excellent luncheon and light refreshments were awaiting their disposal.*

There were fifteen jolly boys and girls in the group. The bowling alley was
downstairs at the south east corner of San Francisco and Aspen.

Margaret Adams—who was she? If she was fashionable, she wore taffeta petti-
coats, gored smooth at waist and hips, with flounces ruffled at the hem to maintain the
"princess line" of her dress, which was fastened with two dozen buttons down the back.
The doctor was taxed for a bicycle that year. If Margaret rode it, she wore an ankle-
length "safety" skirt, but did she ride? Was she a member of the newly reorganized
Shakespeare Club? A church ladies' group? I read carefully through the paper for news of
the various churches, but activities of their women were not reported.

The Special Collections archive at NAU held no photograph of Margaret and no
photograph of Effie Sipe either. I wondered if that meant they weren't here long enough
to leave descendants who would donate pictures.

Records of the doctors themselves were, as always, sketchy. Dr. Adams moved his office from the Banner Drug Company corner half a block west to the Pollock building. He and Margaret traveled to the Schnebly ranch at the mouth of Oak Creek Canyon—there'd been ads in the newspaper suggesting that it was accepting guests who wanted a scenic vacation—and then they boarded a train to Los Angeles "for the benefit of the doctor's health." Adams was thirty years old.

P.J. Cornish, "practicing physician in Albuquerque," was in town visiting friends and relatives; later in the summer Clara stopped off with their son on the way back from California. When the daughter of Saxton Seth Acker was ill, Mrs. Acker—Charlotte— took her to Albuquerque for a consultation with Dr. Cornish, who operated to remove an eleven pound cystic tumor.

Dr. Sipe and Effie (married one year), his mother and sister, went to the Grand Canyon "in their own conveyance". That fall Effie, who had been a missionary at Tuba, spent a month on the Navajo reservation. Doing what, I wondered.

Something was going on with Dr. Brannen. In 1904 he had moved from his office on San Francisco Street to corner rooms upstairs in the Coalter building. The telephone number for his house was 4, really, four (4); the office number was 50. In 1905 Brannen sold the Pioneer Drug Store. By 1906 he was talking with a thirty-year-old doctor in Willams, R.O. Raymond, a graduate of Washington University who had applied for Arizona certification in 1904. Was D.J. Brannen, nearly fifty years old, planning to take a partner into his practice? to retire?

The *Sun* reported trips to Tucson, speeches at various events, and then said that D.J. and Felicia would be in Los Angeles for several months where the doctor would "take a much-needed rest." Praising his twenty-three years of service to Flagstaff, it wished him success in any place he decided to live, any occupation he decided to follow. That sounded like a departure. D.J. and Felicia, who had been so respectable in this small Western town—what were they discussing?

Announcing the death of an old-timer, Funston wrote, "The old guard is slowly giving way before the young guard." But the news wasn't all sad. In June of 1906

> Ed Priest was sprinkling the street near Dr. Miller's residence last week when the hose was suddenly forced around by the swiftly running water with the result that one of the Doctor's windows was soon in fragments.

George Felix Manning, jr., the doctor's son, was twenty-two years old in 1906—old enough to go hunting with other men. His mother, Sarah, was forty-eight. Her children were growing up, and I know what that means: big parts of her life, her work, would be sliding out of her hands. I don't for a minute think she was a cipher because she left little paper trail, but I would like to know how she filled the growing space in her days.

Persons with social anxiety disorder fear that they will somehow humiliate themselves in a social or performance situation and assume that no one else suffers from similar symptoms. Research indicates that the limbic system may play a major role.

How's this for a theory? Trauma of any kind leaves an after-image on your nerves that fades very slowly. It's with you a long time in bizarre sensations. All right, I'm describing my own experience, but I can't be the only one.

Say your house is broken into or a tornado levels it, and for months you feel vulnerable to odd things—a convertible at a gas station, a voice behind you in a hardware store, a phrase like "another bombing" on the evening news—and your alarm bells go off: "Danger!" Your heart thumps in your chest.

You are raped. Or you lose something that was dear to you, or someone, and a worry sits on the back of your neck and chokes your throat while you are walking to your mailbox.

There's a crash, and everything reminds you of the crunch of metal on metal and the crack of breaking glass, and you remember that fluids dripping don't sound alike. Your muscles shiver. The tips of your fingers go numb. You cry in public places.

6

Clouds lean before the wind, piling up ahead—
there's no need to watch them move to know the
direction air up there is taking. Sometimes the
tops are ragged, blown up in waves and plumes.

My children decided a decade ago to do Thanksgiving with me in Arizona and
Christmas with their in-laws. Valentine parties had gone first, then Halloween and July
4th, all the zany decorations and games that Emily and I had produced. No more Easter
egg hunts of historic magnificence, no more birthday parties.

For years Emily and I had all kinds of fun with Christmas. Starting on December
first, we spent afternoons making messes together weaving wreaths and baking cookies
and singing, anything but "Frosty the Snowman." Emily didn't like that one. Or
"Rudolph the Red-Nose" either.

Christmas was the high point of the year for me. The day after Thanksgiving Emily
and her kids, I and mine, began decorating—pulled out old wreaths and hung them,
made red and green construction paper chains, popcorn strings, mistletoe bouquets
and red velvet bow-kays. All day we played scratchy old recordings full of bells and read
aloud the picture books we'd had since the kids were babies.

We bought our trees together, Emily and I and the children. Don and Travis
were too busy to be included. She and I put on the lights and let the children hang the
ornaments, with kitchen step-chairs for reaching the upper branches.

"Abby, there's a bare spot right here. It needs something."

"It does not, Gwen, you're not the boss of me. Do your side and leave me alone."

"Look. There's a bare spot right here, Abby."

"I can handle it myself, Gwen."

When it was just the two of us and we were young, working our way through
his schooling, Don welcomed Christmas as a few hours of respite. His gift to me was
always small and inexpensive and thoughtful, once a string of tiny blue glass beads. I
still have it.

By intern time, he was too harried to remember, didn't have the time off, wasn't
interested anyway. "I haven't done a thing about it, Marlene. You take care of it, I'll just
sign my name on the cards."

When he was forty or so, he began to complain. "Load of crap. The house looks like
a bar."

That didn't mean axing our annual Christmas party for his colleagues. "Are you f...are you crazy? We damn well have to." I did catered dinner parties with shining tables for six scattered around the house. Beautiful. Highly praised. Lot of work.

Oh well. If you look at things just right, there's a whisker's difference between gain and loss, it all depends on how you turn it. I wouldn't say I'm now re-inventing myself, because I doubt that I invented myself in the first place, but with all the usual duties behind me, I can do what I choose. Hurray for the advantages of being old enough to do it my way.

This year for my three and their children and their spouses, I ordered gifts from catalogs and had them sent. There were certainly sufficient catalogs in the daily mail. How did those companies find me?

It was time to invite—the custom of the season, and I had done so many Christmas parties. It would be a relief to have only two guests instead of two dozen, and who else did I know in Flagstaff?

Sandy said it sounded like fun, she and Eddie would love to, and what could she bring?

"Let me do it all, Sandy. It would be a pleasure."

"Well, I wanta tell ya, Christmas wouldn't seem like Christmas without a few happy get-togethers."

Pale green plates on a dark green cloth with red napkins and a small centerpiece bowl of red carnations, pots of poinsettias to separate the table from the cooking area—would that do? A green salad with bits of tomato and red pepper, some kind of hearty bread, beef stroganoff over rice, pinot noir, a little bowl of fruit sprinkled with rum.

The Pipers were as full of stories as before. He talked about his mother, how she used to saw down their tree herself. "Christmas was no big commercial deal in Flagstaff then, no elaborate decorations. You did things for yourself."

For Sandy (green ribbon in her hair) it had been different. "In the 50s and 60s we lived out on the army base. You know, NAD, only it was Navajo Ordnance Depot then, still functioning, the streets were all named after generals. My mom was secretary to the CO, and my dad was in charge of building the stretch of highway from Flagstaff to Williams that hooked up with I-17. The housing was in tip-top condition."

The past summer I had looked out on Camp Navajo from my mountain—out there south of Bellemont. "I no idea that families lived on the depot after the war."

"Oh, you bet. It was a great place for a kid to grow up. We had movies and our own bowling alley, a commissary, an infirmary, a non-denominational church. Let me tell you, Christmas was a big deal. The Army delivered a tree for each family, all on the same day, so everybody was decorating at the same time, it was real festive. We had a big party in an empty warehouse. Santa, a gunny sack full of candy and things for each family, the Hopis and Navajos too. From the Army. I don't remember Christmas without snow in those years."

I grew up on the desert. I can't remember a Christmas *with* snow.

"It was fun. We went caroling to all the houses at night, in the snow. We had sledding parties on the run they built. I just loved it. When I moved into town, I didn't feel as much a part of a community as I did out there."

"Was there a school for you too?"

"Nope. Everything but a school. We were bussed the thirteen miles into town. Cold! I can remember waiting for the bus when it was minus 23 degrees. Our nose hairs froze." She laughed.

"Weren't there enough children for a school?"

"Oh, there were lots of other kids. I had two sisters and two brothers myself. Some were there for only two-year stretches, but some of us were there for a long time. In high school, the parents would car pool us in to night games."

We sat long at the table telling stories and laughing. The next morning I wrote down my latest theory: Christmas parties are best with people who are easy company.

The day grew closer; UPS and FedEx deposited on my Flagstaff doorstep packages from Texas and Colorado and California. (As a long-time mother and giver of gifts, I still feel odd receiving.) Checking that there was colored holiday paper inside, I split the boxes open and made an arrangement on my grandmother's drum table.

On Christmas morning, drinking coffee with real cream and nibbling at a fruit cake from Vermont, I unwrapped my presents. Abby had sent blue satin pajamas, blue slippers, and a blue cashmere robe with lace trim. The Real Me. Also a book titled Yoga for People Over Fifty. My practical Gwen had chosen a state-of-the-art coffee maker—I didn't know such appliances were available in blue—and a small microwave to match. From Baxter there was a cell phone, my first, and a note that told me he had taken care of all paper work, that he had given his sisters the number, that bills would be sent to him indefinitely. On the card he had written, "So you'll never be out of reach and neither will we."

Christmas Day in Flagstaff was cold and windy, with a few flakes of snow. Phoenix temperature went all the way down to 40 degrees. Over half a million homes in the country were without electricity, but I had light and heat, and I was alone, and I was OK with that.

"Don? Don, please. Open your eyes. Please, Don. Don? Will you drink this please?"

1907 Back east (I love that term, back east) nurses were finally being taken seriously: the first professor of nursing was Mary Adelaide Nutting who took charge of the hospital economics course at Johns Hopkins Teachers College. However, trained nurses were still rare in Flagstaff.

I'm guessing here based on what I've found—it seems to me that in the decade before World War I, there were personal changes for the doctors in Flagstaff but no dramatic change in the kind of medicine they practiced. They weren't hopelessly isolated—Dr. and Mrs. Sipe went east and stayed three months so that the doctor could take a post-grad course at Philadelphia Polyclinic—but Flagstaff didn't have the resources for the latest equipment. The railroad could take serious cases to Los Angeles.

The Pure Food and Drug Act went into effect in January. The *Sun* endorsed the new law, saying that merchants had been complying for some time. It continued to print ads for patent medicines though: most Americans, when they were sick, first tried to cure themselves.

Cases requiring uncomplicated or emergency surgery were tended by the local doctors.

Dr. Adams, assisted by Dr. Miller, performed a very successful operation on Mrs. C.S. Harrison at her home last Sunday afternoon. At this writing she is progressing nicely.

Surgery in her home, that's the point. Respectable people, especially women and children, were treated in private houses in Flagstaff.

Accidents requiring special treatment were a different matter.

On Sunday while gathering cattle near Canyon Diablo William Roden lassoed a calf and his right hand got entangled in the rope and the calf nearly pulled his hand off before he could disentangle the hand. After the accident Mr. Roden rode five miles to the railroad station where a special train was given and he was brought to his home here. Dr. Adams attended to his injury and Dr. P.G. Cornish of Albuquerque was sent for and arrived Monday when the wrist and the broken bones were set. Mr. Roden while suffering from the injury is improving and is congratulating himself that his hand was not pulled off.

For fifteen years Coconino County had maintained in the Hawks Hotel a facility that had served as a hospital for some people, indigent men mostly. There may have been some kind of cooperative support from the Arizona Lumber and Timber Company [AL&T] so that injured loggers and sawyers, who often had no families in Flagstaff, could be treated. Did I say that before?

The big medical news of February, 1907, was that a grand new structure was to be built by the county on two hundred acres north of town and administered as a combined poor farm and hospital for the indigent. "Poor farm." How quaint.

The Board of Supervisors have taken steps toward the purchase of the north quarter of the Livermore ranch for the purpose of building a county hospital. It is a move in the right direction. The location is a desirable one, being near the city limits. A portion of the land is tillable and will give employment to the inmates in some capacity during a portion of the year. The distance from town will probably reduce the number of inmates, as a goodly number in the past who have gone on protracted drunks have found the hospital [in the Hawks hotel] a good place to stay during their recovery from the effects of their spree. The hospital is now a convenience to many who wish to spend a short time in town. While it is not expected that the [new county] hospital will ever become self-sustaining, it is expected that the expenses will be somewhat reduced and no needy one be deprived of the benefits of the hospital on account of its location.

In July the county Board of Supervisors awarded the contract for what is now the Pioneers Museum.

The main building will be two story, 25 × 60 feet, with an addition of 30 × 40 feet, with cellar under the addition. The material to be used will

*be the tufa stone, which can be obtained nearby…The building is to be
completed by the first of January.*

Surely it must have occurred to somebody—it did to me— that moving the county
hospital so far out of a community that boasted only two automobiles, moving it away
from its old position across the street from the railroad tracks, half a mile by spur track
from the sawmill, would mean that there would be no facility in which men injured by
trains and horses and accidents at work could be treated quickly, not to mention strangers
passing through who seemed to be of questionable sanity. Was anybody making plans?

Other medical news: The first Chinese baby was born in Flagstaff; the family name
was Foo. Lee Doyle sprained his knee at the skating rink; so did several other people—
their knees, not Lee's.

Dear Cazz:

*Since I moved into town, I've been communicating with the family by phone,
but I wanted to respond to your answer about my poem question.*

*I don't think it's a poem either. It's visual—that is, there are images you can see.
Ideas and truths are good for poetry, but turning words into pictures that make a
thrill in the mind, that's crucial. A poem should mean more than it says. At least, I
think so.*

But I like your argument—it looks like a poem, but it doesn't feel *like a poem.
Hurray for you!*

Love,
Nana

I wonder how it is to live in those little farming towns in southern Utah—not so
isolated as it used to feel, I'll bet, what with phones and television and satellite dishes
and the www. There might be more freedom of mind now than most people in the past
ever knew.

From a motorcoach those towns look peaceful and comforting, the houses a good
size for family shelter. The world is colored: red cliffs and brilliant blue sky and trees
that change with the seasons. Food grows all around for tending. Rhythms are obvious,
matters that crowded city people don't ever get to know.

I've never lived in a little farming town. There was no reason for me to be nostalgic,
but a surge filled my chest, longing for what I imagined, not what I remembered. That
may be more common than we like to admit.

Sitting in the passenger seat, books and things spread out on the console in front of
me, I was shocked out of my romantic musings when I realized what I was not seeing:
the farms were in air that wasn't there once; the cliffs around those farms were all that's
left of ancient stone so deep it's hard to imagine.

I tried to tell Don. "This is fantastic!"

"Yeah?"

"Less than a hundred miles separate Bryce from the bottom of the Grand Canyon;
it's only forty miles northeast of Zion."

"So?"

"The rock at the bottom of the Grand Canyon, at the foot of the Grand Staircase? It's 1.5 billion years old. There were no dinosaurs when it was formed. Zion is above the whole Grand Canyon; its stones are remnants of sedimentary layers millions of years gone in Arizona."

"You already told me that."

"But that's not the end of it. The top of Zion is below Bryce. Dinosaurs were around during the deposition of the stone of Zion, but no mammals until the creation of the rock exposed in Bryce, and those were small. The making of Bryce covers a short period of time, only a hundred million years of silty, limey lake deposits millions of years after Zion's rocks were deposited. Then, in less than ten million years, almost a mile of sediment was stripped from the land. One vertical mile."

"What's the big deal?"

"I've lived all my life in the Southwest and never guessed at the size of what's gone."

"You're nuts."

"No, look, Don. I can live a perfectly good and responsible life without understanding Einstein."

"Damn right."

"But knowing about the geology of this planet, the forces that shaped it, that's history, and it changes my perception of humanity and ethics and behavior, of everything I need to live a good and responsible life."

He laughed at me, he actually jeered. "Cut the melodrama, Marlene. What makes you such a simpleton?"

Let's hear it for life as we know it. I closed the door on him, shut him out, lived inside where he couldn't see. How's that for retaliation?

Bryce Canyon is not a canyon, which is something I figured out for myself. There is a canyon named for a family named Bryce way down the slope, but the part of the park accessible to cars—just a small part—is a pine-covered peninsula with its side eroded into scallops of amphitheaters in soft sedimentary rock at the top of the Grand Staircase. High on the Pink Cliffs, I looked out across the Gray, White, Vermillion and Chocolate Cliffs, all jumbled by synclines, monoclines, anticlines.

Bryce is smaller and younger than Zion—intimate, delicate, exquisite because of iron and manganese layers thirteen hundred feet thick that color the rock red yellow orange brown violet when it's exposed to oxygen. At least, that's how I understood the books. I wouldn't want to be quoted.

Three days on the road, and we had fallen into a routine. Don drove and ate and watched television. I cooked meals, washed dishes, checked tires and oil and fluids, pumped gas, paid fees and charges, read the map and told him which way to turn. In Bryce at Sunset Point I did my tour guide imitation.

"The park has eighty-three miles of hiking trails, and an eighteen-mile paved scenic drive with thirteen viewpoints, but a thirty-six-foot-long vehicle can't go any farther beyond this point because farther on there's no room for it to turn around. So we have to park here."

"Where?"

"Between those two lines."

"I can't park parallel in there."

"Sure you can. I'll get out and guide you. Pretend you're in a car."

Actually, he did a fine job, and I told him so. "Bravo! Let's go out to the edge and take a look."

"I'm tired and my back hurts. I can't breathe. I'm going to lie down for a while."

So he watched soap operas, resenting the noise our generator made, and I spent the day hiking the Rim Trail, alone with air and silence and a few hundred million years worth of rock a few thousand feet deep. Illusion is better than no freedom at all. I stopped to look when I wanted to at what was gone and what was left and moved when I decided to, amazed by the sculpting a little water had done. I can't say I figured out what was going on in the view, but I thoroughly enjoyed myself. There's a lot to be said for being alone.

At sunset I drove out of the park—he said, "I don't want to"—and settled our coach at Ruby's RV Park at the entrance, where I'd made a reservation for a long site with full hook-ups. Don went on lying on the couch. I opened the wine, pulled pork chops off the non-skid pad in the refrigerator, started potatoes in the microwave, set the table. And Don went on lying on the couch. As I mentioned, there's a lot to be said...

He didn't feel like getting up the next morning. "You drive. I think I'll just lie here and sleep."

"You're the doctor, what's your diagnosis?"

"It's the altitude, how high are we?"

"Almost 8000."

"Well, hell, no wonder. How do they expect people to function at this elevation?"

In La Jolla, we always stayed at the hotel with balconies that overlooked Scripps Park and Boomer Beach. The kids and I loved the cove and the tide pools and the seals that lay on the sand.

Don never wanted to go anyplace else for vacation, but when we were there he never stepped out on the balcony, seldom left the suite—just sat and watched television all day, all evening.

1907 News of doctors: Sipe and his wife Effie, purchased the Greenlaw house at the corner of Birch and Humphreys where his sister died soon after of tuberculosis. There is no residence at that corner now; the house must have disappeared years ago.

In August the *Sun* mentioned that Dr. Adams had gone to Los Angeles for a well-deserved two week rest. Apparently he went alone. In October there was this: Mrs. J. E. Adams (Margaret)

> ... returned Thursday from a five months' stay with relatives in Chicago, Ill. During her stay in that city, a fine son was born to the doctor and Mrs. Adams and is now eight weeks old. The doctor is overjoyed at the coming of a John E. jr. They are occupying the W.C. Bayless residence.

I could spin a tale here, I suppose, about a difficult pregnancy that required big-city care, and that might even be accurate for all I know, but the truth is—I have no idea why Margaret went to Chicago when she was six months along and stayed for two months after her baby's birth.

Dr. Manning was gone from home for six weeks "on a trip to the southern part of the territory where he has been looking after his mining interests." Do I recall that he had mining interests in other directions as well? He went to Phoenix occasionally because he was on the territorial Board of Medical Examiners.

No mention was made of Sarah traveling anywhere. Others wives did—Clara and her son Gillette came over from Albuquerque now and then to visit her Coffin relatives—but Sarah's name was never in the newspaper for anything.

Lacking information, I invented her. She would always have been older than the others and a comfortable person, comfortable to be with. Nothing showy, just calm and practical and kind, like the woman in a novel who lives next door and knows how to make pie crusts that are not tough. In other words, a cliche. So I gave her a sense of humor and a ready laugh.

In 1907 her two older daughters married—I found that much in the index to marriage licenses in the court house. Althea, age nineteen, married J. P. Wilson, age twenty-three, a bank clerk. Henrietta, age twenty-five, married Edward M. Brown, also twenty-five, a retail jeweler. Both remained in Flagstaff, at least for a few years, close to her parents, close to each other. According to the *Sun's* society (society!) column, both young women played bridge.

Nothing local was printed about Dr. Brannen, who for twenty-three years had been a significant part of the little town. He seemed to have left for good. The previous year he had sold his drug store and gone off to Los Angeles with Felicia. From California they had moved to New York, where he said he expected to remain for some time. The next news of him was:

> *A letter from Dr. D.J. Brannen states that since leaving Flagstaff he has not been in good health. The doctor and his wife have been spending the summer at St. Ignace, Mich. and will soon take up their residence in Buffalo, N.Y.*

Dr. Raymond, who had, I think, taken over Brannen's practice, had spent the past month on professional business in the east, and returned to Flagstaff, where Dr. Sipe had been looking after the office for him. The *Sun* printed, "Dr. Raymond will now receive patients as before."

Among the General Practitioners who had come and gone, Raymond could claim at least one difference: the tuberculosis that had brought him to northern Arizona four years earlier at the age of twenty-eight. He had registered as a doctor with the territorial board, but at first he had lived in a sheep camp for the fresh air and healthy outdoors. Feeling better, he had begun to "doctor" in Williams and then, after some kind of negotiation with Dr. Brannen, moved to Flagstaff to take Brannen's place on the AL&T payroll to tend injured loggers and mill workers.

Keeping track of the doctors' schools:

Sipe: Hospital College of Medicine, Central University of Kentucky
Adams: College of Physicians of Cleveland, Ohio
Raymond: Washington University Medical School, St. Louis

Dr. Raymond was another bachelor, so there was no new wife to report. With the Brannens gone, there were still five doctors in Flagstaff, and we're back to three doctors' wives:

Sarah Manning, fifty-five, born in Tennessee, mother of five children, married to a man of seventy-five; Margaret Adams, former resident of Los Angeles, mother of a new baby, married to a man of thirty-one who owned the first automobile in Flagstaff;

Effie Sipe, nearly thirty, born in Iowa, former missionary, president of Flagstaff's Presbyterian Aid and Missionary Society, married to a man of forty.

I suspect Effie might have been involved in the local chapter of the Women's Christian Temperance Union: she was invited to a dinner party at the home of its president, Mrs. Magistrate J.C. Milligan, whose personal name was Flora.

There were no pianos listed in tax records for those three women. The only items for which the doctors were taxed that had any hint of their wives were, in each case, household and kitchen furnishings. That's not a whole lot of information about who they were.

Three wives and four gone. Kathleen had died. Clara and Mira and Felicia had moved away from Flagstaff with their husbands. Sarah Manning, of whom no notice was taken in the newspaper, was the connecting thread. Over twenty years she had seen the others come and go. What was her story? I didn't even know her church affiliation.

One more detail: C. M. Funston, editor of the *Coconino Sun*, died in early December of 1907 at the age of fifty-four and stepped into the ancient parade. The newspaper staff continued to print weekly issues—shortened to four pages—but there was no name listed as editor at the top left corner of the second page.

For our honeymoon we went to Oak Creek Canyon and stayed one night in the Mayhew Lodge. I loved seeing that romantic old building standing at the entrance to West Fork looking as if thrilling stories were possible within. It's gone now. Burned by vandals, so the story goes.

"Mom! How're you doing? Just got back from walking the dog and thought I'd call."

"Abby, how nice to hear from you."

"I couldn't call this summer, you had no phone."

"True, true. That makes hearing your voice just plain thrilling."

"Thrilling? Hoo! How's the weather in Flagstaff?"

"Skies are blue sometimes, and there are stretches of no wind. But every day, every long dark night, is cold. Temperatures don't rise above freezing. Cold makes house into a haven, in case you hadn't noticed."

"Are you housebound?"

"Only when I want to be. I walk to the library to ferret out doctors' wives and come home to hot bubble baths with good books and Oscar Peterson."

"My decadent Mom. You're golden."

"And I'm trying to find out—photographs and paintings of galaxies show the centers as places of brilliant light. Dense concentration of stars? Active nuclei? Gas? The opposite of black holes? I haven't found the answer yet."

"If I happen to run across it, I'll check it out. That's a joke. I don't encounter galactic nuclei on a daily basis."

"Oh, there was something I read the other day I thought you might like to know. Wait a minute—now where?—ok, here it is, I photocopied it to read to you. Listen to this. By 1900 the General Federation of Women's Clubs (one million members) was investigating social conditions and conducting social reforms, forming corporations, reconstructing the judicial system, endorsing factory inspection and child labor legislation.

"In Arizona women's cultural and community clubs in the central and southern parts of the state joined together and applied for federation with the national organization in 1901 and 1902. Including people like Sharlott Hall and Mrs. Dwight B. Heard and Mrs. G. C. Ruffner, it established Departments of Work: art, civics, conservation, education, food sanitation…"

"Wow! That's impressive."

"…household economics, industrial and social conditions, legislative behavior, literacy and library extension, public health, juvenile court, philanthropy, press."

"I'm astonished."

"By the second decade of the 20th century, women had formed a veritable army of "social housekeepers," including 80,000 in the WCTU, 50,000 in the YWCA, 400,000 women union members, and two million in the suffrage campaign."

"By 1910? How'd we get the idea women back then were suppressed?"

"Beats me."

"How about Flagstaff? Were there social housekeepers there?"

"That's a puzzle I'm trying to solve. If there were, they didn't get into the newspapers. Now and then I see a hint about The New Woman or the WCTU, but no real evidence."

"In the newspaper? You don't suppose the editor…?"

"A definite possibility."

"I tell you, women must be downright threatening."

"Obvious, isn't it? But it might not be fair to blame Editor Funston for censoring, Flagstaff wasn't very big. Apparently the local literary circle, the Shakespeare Club, had been resurrected and organized with a constitution and by-laws by 1904. In 1909 it joined the Federation of Women's Clubs but withdrew in 1911. I don't know why."

"Maybe the ladies had trouble getting to Phoenix?"

"Maybe, but women's clubs in Winslow and Williams participated. I don't know yet where to look for this answer."

"Mom, you're an example for us all."

"Thank you. What a responsibility. And how are you, sweetheart? Staying healthy? You and Jane planning something big for New Year's Eve?"

"You betcha we're healthy. We thought we'd stay home this year and do yoga at midnight or something. What about you?"

"I've had enough noisy New Year's Eve parties—wincing at loud laughter, parrying vulgar passes, watching drunks stagger around dance floors. It was more chore than cheer long before I was free to avoid it. I don't go there any more."

"Me either. I'm into making traditions of my own instead of settling for things other people thought up."

"I agree with you. Alone on New Year's Eve is the way I like it."

"Yeah!"

"I don't think I have much hearing loss. It just tires my mind to listen to loud sound, even music I like. I'm beginning to appreciate silence."

"Way. To. Go. Mom."

"I guess Thoughtful is part of my private tradition, thoughtful with shrimp and chardonnay and ten-grain rolls. Examination of the year past—what did I make happen and what happened that I couldn't have expected? Goals for the year coming, the usual intentions. Good use of the time remaining. As always—we'll see."

In Arizona we don't have chiggers. But once when I was in high school I stumbled and sat down on a cholla cactus. Absolutely impossible to take off my jeans, so I spent the rest of the picnic lying on my stomach while people pulled cholla spines out of my behind.

Last year when the numbers rolled over from 1999 to 2000 there was palpable excitement. End and beginning. Would planes crash because computers would fail? TV tracked the changeover from Asia around the world with notables and fireworks every-place, and Alaska was at the end. There was hope for a new era, an improved kind of human to match our technology.

December 31, 2000, I watched the pros on television, Frank Sinatra with Count Basie and Ella Fitzgerald and Gene Kelly. One for my baby. The lady is a tramp. Let's take it nice and easy. I did it my way. Those songs were scored into my brain a long time ago, and I sang along with every one. Fun is a matter of attitude.

The people on the screen were part of my youth, and I wondered which of them was still alive. None?

In high school, once, my date and I drove to a night club because Ella Fitzgerald was singing there. We asked the man inside the door if we could stand against the wall and listen, and he called the manager, who said, "Let these kids in during the set if they stay in back and don't sit at a table." A man of understanding. We stood in back where we could see Ella and the musicians, and I'll never forget it.

I still have an old recording of Ella and Louie Armstrong backed by Oscar Peterson, Herb Ellis, Ray Brown, and Buddy Rich. Stompin' at the Savoy. Yes.

I was in bed nesting among pillows when the year turned over.

Birth was easy for Gwen and Baxter, but Abby was turned back to front, and her forehead was presenting. Afterwards I began to tremble violently on the gurney. The next evening I rang for the nurse and told her I couldn't stop crying, hadn't slept since the baby was born. My post-partum depression lasted for years.

The library in this medium-sized town is practically a community center, used by a full range of people all day. For public use there are thirty computers loaded with a variety of programs, five machines for reading microfilm and microfiche, two copy machines, forty study carrels, forty-three newspapers including the Navajo Times, and too many magazines to count. Videos and CDs can be checked out.

When I arrive in the mornings the bells at Church of the Nativity are chiming ten o'clock. Usually there's a crowd of a dozen or so people waiting for the doors to be unlocked, and we fan out, knowing just where we want to go.

There's a room for "junior" readers with papier-mache dinosaurs perched on top of the stacks and booster stools around the computer carousel. Adults at either end of lines of chirping children shepherd them in and out.

Volunteers from three different literacy groups, mostly upper-middle-aged women, use the library to tutor people of varying ages who are learning to speak English. They sit at small tables here and there talking, reading aloud one word at a time. No one seems to be disturbed.

Patrons are all sizes, genders, and national backgrounds. I'm aware of them because reading microfilm is tedious and it makes my back hurt, so I walk around every half hour or so to loosen up. An elderly man in a tweed hat and a sand-and-salt mustache sits in the same place every morning, reading a newspaper and working crossword puzzles. I'm told he's upset if anyone else has already done them. Another regular is a tiny fellow with dark hair who talks to himself loudly in a language I don't recognize and looks at the pictures in books. The curvature of his spine is quite noticeable.

I like all this diversity until two or three o'clock in the afternoon, when the public schools have released their students, and a rising tide of them floods in and overwhelms the computer stations. It's impressive how competent even the junior high kids are at the keyboard, how determined they seem in their search for information—surely they aren't playing computer games in the library, are they?—but they arrive in groups, and they can't seem to stop talking to each other. The collective hum is distracting; I have not yet found a spot where I can escape it. Even when I burrow into my closet or take material back behind the locked cases of the reserve shelves, they walk past. Talking, talking. Not shouting, just talking. Nevertheless...

My adaptation is to be there from ten when the doors open until two when school's out.

And this is a detective story, though not the suspense kind. I already know in general the how and when of their dying. It's their living...

"Hi. Woody Mountain?"

For a second I was confused—it had been two months. "Yes. That's who I am."

"It's Shirley from Baker Butte. I got your number from the district office. I hope you don't mind." It was the voice I'd heard all summer on the forest radio. A young voice, twenty or so I'd thought, she sounded so light and cheerful, but Ed and Sandy had said, no, she had to be older, she'd been a lookout for sixteen years and she had a daughter in college.

"No, of course I don't mind. Of course not."

"I just figure we work together, and we ought to know each other. It can get kinda lonesome if you don't know the faces that go with the voices. Visitors, you know, strangers? They don't count." She chuckled, not the nervous punctuation you hear from some women. She laughed at the world. "Your name is Marlene?"

"It is."

"I live way out here at Blue Ridge about fifty-five miles from Flagstaff, but I come into town now and then, and I thought it might be fun if we could have lunch somewhere. If you'd like to?"

"I'd love to. Really. I don't mind being alone, but I'm so touched by your…your friendliness."

"That's me." She laughed again.

"I'm free any day."

"How 'bout tomorrow? The Brewery? Whoever is first waits inside the door?"

After Don died, a heavy black line was drawn through my name on social lists in Phoenix—so it seemed to me. There were no more invitations to luncheons, to dinner parties. No more requests that I serve on committees. I'd been first name with a hundred women for years, but no one knew me when I was no longer the wife of a doctor.

That was lonely, there's no word for that kind of empty. Don and Emily were gone, the children were gone, and my position, my occupation, had evaporated. All I had left was a big house filled by a vacuum. I walked in the vacuum in those rooms feeling old and ugly. All my life had had no meaning.

But within three months here, two women who didn't care about my position or income or wardrobe had offered both hands to me. Another advantage of growing older? Or is it just an advantage of a smaller city?

Shirley is small, five feet or so. Blondish. Maybe fifty. Round but not plump. She came through the door laughing. "Marlene? Look what I did. I didn't realize I still had my slippers on until I got out of the car. They're so comfortable, I forget I'm wearing them."

They were brown leather clogs, and they looked all right to me. I held out a foot. "I'm wearing fleece clogs. Lands' End calls them slippers, but I wear them everywhere. Let's walk in proud of being old enough to be comfortable being comfortable."

"Whee!" She tucked her arm through mine and raised her chin and laughed.

We drank wine with our pizza and ordered dessert and laughed while we talked. You have to laugh when you're with Shirley. "I'm addicted to that job. If they fired me, I'd probably die or something. I have elk and bear and lightning strikes and wind at ninety miles an hour and wind chill at forty below. I mean, whoo! And I have sunsets and sunrises, birds, the sound of the wind. Fall is the saddest time of the whole year for me because it means I have to wait all winter before I can start again. You know?"

"I know. Do you have many visitors?"

"Hundreds! Some of them come back every summer and bring me presents!" She laughed. "Ooops! Almost dropped it, pizza is sloppy to eat. Anyway, that doesn't mean I don't have time to myself. I quilt. Old fashioned, huh? In the winter I piece it together, and then I hand quilt it in the tower. I have a round frame on a stand, it's really cool. Except I just had to wrap duct tape around it to strengthen it. This quilt that I'm doing now is really big, and it's heavy. What do you do?"

I wasn't sure how to say it, so I went slowly. "I'm trying to find out what life was like for doctors' wives in the early years in Flagstaff. I spend a lot of time in libraries and the court house."

"Well, that sounds neat. Why are you doing it?"

"My husband was a doctor, which is not as glamorous as some people think. I was curious about whether the wives here a hundred years ago…whether they had the same problems I did."

"That's great! Did they?"

"Maybe—it's easier to find the doctors. Some of the wives are nearly invisible in old records."

"Oh yeah, I'll bet they are."

We sat in that restaurant for two and a half hours talking and talking, and I loved it. Next time she comes into town, she said, she'll call me. Or maybe I'd like to come out to Blue Ridge for lunch?

Yes. I'd like.

> Don and I slept close together in the early years, in a great comfort of touch. I liked to lie close to his back, my skin against his from my face to my toes. Breathing against his shoulder, my arm around his chest, I was secure.

When New Year's Day is past and the colored lights are gone for another year, when trees are bare and sun is low in the south, and a strong wind is blowing at coats and parkas, and dirty old patches of snow linger in gutters, Flagstaff can look almost dreary. The big volcano stands above everything, white and hard. Cars drive through the streets, skis strapped to the tops, snowmobiles loaded into trailers behind, but the frolic is somewhere else, not in town. From the comfort of windows I watch pedestrians hunch against the cold, determined, going somewhere.

In the second week of January a series of storms was forecast, possible snow. To my disgust the first clouds tossed us a bare inch that melted by noon. The second was two days later than expected. Might drop three feet, the radio said, severe weather all over the state.

How exciting, I'd never seen such a storm. In anticipation I made a long grocery list, went out and bought enough food for weeks, stocked cupboards and freezer. Candles and matches were laid close to hand on the kitchen counter. A stack of library books was on the drum table.

Snow began to fall silently before dawn on a Friday morning. Several inches had piled up, an inch an hour was coming down when I woke. Schools were closed; highways in all directions were blocked—snow plows couldn't keep up with the accumulation.

I went out to walk through the falling flakes and discovered how they muffle sounds. My neighborhood was quiet, beautiful, intimate.

We had fifteen inches on the street by dark, eighteen inches when snow stopped falling that night. Big deal. By morning plows had pushed it aside. I went out and made footprints in soft powder, smiled at other people walking. They smiled at me. Next morning the temperature was minus two degrees, and I didn't even open my door. The radio reported that the winter so far was the coldest ever recorded in the East.

Also that wildfires in Florida and an 11,000-acre Santa Anna fire outside San Diego had been controlled—that Arizona's governor had called for a "war on wildfires"—that at A.S.U. there had been discussion of a ten-year plan to suppress and manage fires, restore Southwestern forests, foster cooperation and coordination between agencies, thin the small trees around towns and houses, and require flame-resistant roofs. An ambitious program, if you ask me.

Far as I could tell, not much was said about regulating development of sub-divisions in forests. And nothing about on-going drought, which they couldn't do much about anyway. But Congress did double fire prevention and recovery budgets for the next summer, with ten million dollars provided to the Coconino for more firefighters, for thinning and burning to reduce fuels on more than 19,000 acres.

Another snow storm eased in silently, then two more. Tall ridges of crusty snow sat heavy between sidewalks and streets; morning fog shrouded the world. On clear, freezing days when sun on icicles four feet long made rainbows through the window, I sat at the computer at my desk in the second bedroom upstairs, typing my notes on the lives of doctors' wives a hundred years ago. If streets were dry, I pulled on boots and went to the city library to read microfilms of old newspapers in the dinky closet room. Now and then I went walkabout among the stacks to find books that might answer my questions.

> A psychiatrist in Boston is urging fish oils, like a quarter pound of salmon every day, in treatment for depression with the argument that the human brain is sixty percent fat (WHAT?!) and needs omega-3s to function properly. I don't think I'm up to that much salmon.

1908 In Flagstaff the year opened with an announcement that within two months the *Coconino Sun* would be offered in Probate Court for public sale as part of Clarkson Funston's estate. Two months later the paper printed the news that Fred Breen, who had been Supervisor of the San Francisco Mountains Forest Reserve for ten years, had resigned citing unending problems—accusations of "prejudice, ignorance, partiality, graft, ulterior motives, laziness, salary grabbing and other such innocent pastimes"—and pay that had shrunk over the years. He promptly announced that he had bought the *Sun* and all its assets (plant and office, equipment, subscription list, et cetera) and that his purpose was "to make the *Sun* shine all over Northern Arizona."

Breen, nearly forty years old, had been a newspaper man in Illinois, and he took charge from his first issue. Headlines were bigger. The number of pages increased dramatically—from four to six. There was the same kind of news there had been under Funston: weather, church and lodge, politics, county and territory, the Normal School, snippets of Local and Personal. But there was a definite difference.

News about Forest Service and forest fires increased, especially after four Forest Reserves were merged to form the Coconino National Forest. That got lengthy coverage, which figures, since the Coconino surrounds Flagstaff. There were new features directed to ranchers—stock, range, and such things. Breen hired reporters or at least one reporter to find the local news:

The Pioneers Society plans a picnic out at the city reservoir.

Roaring Flood/Rio de Flag Overflows/West Side Flooded.

The California Limited, fastest train on the road, wrecked east of Winslow, dropped into a wash at fifty miles an hour because a seventy foot long bridge had burned, engineer and fireman killed.

The tone was more informal, lighter, with occasional slang: "a bum show," "the swellest program." A man who had hurt his leg was described as "rolling around town with one flat tire." "The two children were not lost, but home was." I liked it; it was more fun to scroll through the microfilm after Fred Breen moved in.

Advertisers increased. 1908 was an election year again. The *Sun* covered campaigning by William Howard Taft and William Jennings Bryan in a newspaper that sold for five cents a copy.

I read the local news carefully. The Electric Theater had equipment for showing moving pictures, but it was destroyed in a fire. Apparently the City Hall flew a "weather flag." The sewer system was extended to houses on Knob Hill, where the big hospital now dominates upper Beaver Street.

There was always news about doctors. Forty-one-year-old Charles F. Portz from Pennsylvania, the first resident dentist in town, had begun treating patients in the "second house north of the Arizona Central Bank." He didn't own property—at least, he was not taxed for property. He and his wife of four years, Clara, thirty-five years old, lost—well, their little girl died in the autumn.

Dr. Miller had surgery on his throat in Los Angeles; Adams visited in California, Sipe in Kansas City, the Manning boys, Tom and Felix, were home for the summer from Alabama, where they were both students at medical school. Toward the end of the year, Wilbur Sipe and John Adams formed a partnership and consolidated their offices in the Pollock block, but Adams immediately went to Michigan to take graduate courses and submit to an operation for "stomach trouble." The *Sun* reported that he was near death for a while.

In the East, medical research continued: into cancer, into measles transmission, into the role of iodine in thyroid function. In Connecticut the world's first Society for Mental Hygiene was organized. "Mental Hygiene." What a concept.

The U.S. Army's Surgeon General warned the public that in the past five years there had been nationwide 786 cases of tetanus from which 721 people had died. Wounds from blank cartridges fired on July 4th had caused 608 of those cases of tetanus. The Surgeon General's conclusion was that blank cartridges could kill people, fired on July 4th or not.

How old does an American have to be now to remember smallpox? I mean really remember what it was. Head ache and back ache, both excruciating. Fever and vomiting. Pustules in the mouth, nose and nasal passages; pus-filled bumps thick on hands and arms, feet, face, neck and back, sometimes merging into an oozing mass. A terrible smell.

Damage to eyes. Scabs encrusting the whole body. If the victim survived, there was pitted scarring. To make it more fearsome, it was highly contagious.

Smallpox had killed or disfigured millions of people around the world for at least three thousand years. Late in the 18th century Edward Jenner in England had announced that it could be prevented by vaccination, and half a dozen European countries had made the procedure mandatory. But there were technical problems, contamination of serum and so forth.

Americans, who had a tradition of resenting being told what to do, protested that compulsory smallpox vaccination was a violation of their civil liberties. They especially resented the procedure when it was required for their children before they could go to school. American parents are touchy about their children.

But there was hardly a year in northern Arizona without reports of smallpox somewhere. In 1908 Williams was under quarantine by order of Dr. Adams, the county health officer, who said that an epidemic was threatening. No one could leave town without a pass.

So members of Flagstaff's Board of Trustees took what they considered prudent action—they ordered that all children would be vaccinated in February or excluded from the public school. And the children were vaccinated, despite anger from expected quarters.

Come to think of it, my mother said her mother "didn't believe in it. None of us kids were vaccinated for smallpox." She doesn't have a scar on her left shoulder. I do though, or I did last time I looked.

In early April of 1908, the county hospital for the indigent was moved into its big new building out on the road to Fort Valley. At the end of summer the Board of Supervisors reported its first annual inspection: Dr. Adams had all the surgical equipment he needed there, and hot and cold water were provided in each room. Such convenience. There were beds for all of twenty patients although little more than half of them were occupied. (For contrast: in 1908 St. Joseph's Hospital in Phoenix, which ran on support from local citizens, had beds for sixty patients.)

There had been gradual developments in the story of another Flagstaff hospital, developments which left little paper trail. To follow it required going back to the beginning of the town a quarter of a century earlier, looking for small clues. I organized what I found in my research notes.

1. Almost everything south of the railroad tracks was known as Mill Town, and everything there—sawmills, houses for employees, offices, machinery, corrals for horses, all that was necessary for a thriving operation—was on land held by the logging company, Arizona Lumber and Timber..

2. The Riordan brothers who bought it from Ayer were, like many of the settlers, interested in literature; they had organized a Society for the Study of John Milton's poems. The Riordans changed the name Mill Town to Milton as a gesture toward life's finer pursuits.

3. In 1882 Mary Carroll opened a "hospital" south of the tracks. Fire insurance maps for the early years show in color each building there. A boarding house two and a half blocks from the sawmill, on a dirt road

with sidewalks built of boards laid on stringers, was the only structure south of the tracks big enough to take in injured loggers and mill workers.

4. Since back in the 1880s AL&T had employed Dr. Brannen to treat its sick and injured employees, charging them seventy-five cents per paycheck to pay for it—an early group insurance plan. 5) Dr. Raymond had taken Brannen's place on the lumber company's payroll, but neither man had worked in the convenience of a proper hospital.

5. When a county facility for "the indigent" was established, injured loggers and sawyers could be loaded onto any car available in the yard and delivered to the door of the Hawks hotel on the company's spur track if necessary. Example: in 1901 a paragraph in the *Sun* told of a man who had attempted to cut his own throat in the AL&T commissary building. He was taken to the Hawks Hotel for treatment.

6. About that time there was glancing reference in the *Sun* to a place on AL&T land called the "hospital in Milton" but no description or location and no mention of Mary's name or anybody else's. Maybe it was still a room in a boarding house, and doctors brought their own instruments. The fire insurance map for 1904 did not identify any building in Milton as a hospital.

More mystery, no Sherlock Holmes.

7. I went back to Kathy, ranger at the Riordan Mansion State Park. Her guess was that Milton Hospital might have been started by the lumber company when the county hospital was moved out of the center of town, but she called later to say she'd located quite by chance three pages headed "Milton Hospital Monthly Report" and dated 1907. Would I like to see them? It was lists of patients dated July, August, and September with a notation on the back of July—"Ed—note and file" and initialed TAR—Timothy Allen Riordan.

This is what's known in research as "a Eureka moment."

In 1907 six men were in the Milton hospital on July 1, ten on August 31st, twelve September 30th. They were there for injuries to faces, ears, toes, backs, knees, and legs. One man lost his hand, another his finger. Three times Ole Nygard had trouble with serious nose bleeds. An AL&T foreman, Mr. Harris, was in the hospital for a month after amputation of his foot. There had been two cases of pneumonia, four of gastritis, three of typhoid. Total days spent in the hospital for June: 60; for August: 10; for September: 119.

The *Sun* reported that a logger from the Greenlaw division of Arizona Lumber and Timber had been brought into Flagstaff with typhoid and taken to the Milton hospital, where he had died. A few weeks later landscape artist Louis Akin was brought in from a painting trip suffering from pneumonia. He too was placed in the Milton hospital.

On the fire insurance map of 1910 a house across the road from the mill, previously the residence of Fred Sisson, was labeled "Company's Hospital." Fred Sisson, treasurer of AL&T, had died in January of 1908 in Los Angeles; within a few weeks his widow had moved out of Milton into Flagstaff. There is no record in the Index to Deeds in the county recorder's office that the property was sold to the company. Of course not—it hadn't been transferred to Sisson in the first place; all property in Milton was owned by the company.

Why didn't any of the old documents say what happened? And why, if AL&T was taxed for such property as a cow and some horses, nine buggies and eighteen wagons, typewriters and mechanical tools, was there no mention in county tax rolls of hospital equipment?

In the County Recorder's Office I went through the Index to Incorporations, thinking maybe… I can now say that the Flagstaff Library Association was incorporated in 1891 as were the Presbyterian and Episcopal churches. (I didn't know churches could incorporate.) The Flagstaff Electric Light Company went on the list in 1895, Seventh Day Adventists in 1904. The sewer company incorporated in 1913, the Catholic church in 1914, the Baptist church in 1915. I examined every page: there is no evidence of incorporation for the Milton Hospital.

I looked everywhere I could think of, several county archives, Special Collections library at NAU, the Pioneers Museum (the old county hospital). I even wrote to Pat Sullivan at the Medical Society Library in Phoenix, but I couldn't find a trace of an answer.

On the advice of several librarians, I drove up to Lowell Observatory to talk with Henry Giclas, who was born in Flagstaff in 1910. He said, yes, the Sisson house—the operating room was in the study, which had the only fireplace in the building; a ward for male patients was set up in the living room/dining room; women patients were carried to the upstairs bedrooms. In 1916 his father Eli ran pipes to the house from the boiler at the saw mill to provide steam heat for it. Dr. Raymond organized the hospital, and the doctors ran it. The logging company charged no rent for the use of the building.

So the Sisson house was used by the company as a place to put sick and injured people, and they called it a hospital. Two private rooms, eight beds and an operating room. Probably it was bigger than the building they had been using, wherever it was.

Probably the hospital was never formally organized. There was a sick man, the Sisson house was available, they began using it with no change of policy. It didn't really have a name or a sign out in front. It was just the hospital in Milton, the Milton hospital, and it apparently accepted patients from the community as well as the mills and logging camps. Appendicitis and nosebleeds were treated. Injuries from knife fights went to the county hospital.

That made Flagstaff part of a national revolution: a rapid growth of hospitals. In 1873 there were only 178 in America; at the turn of the century there were around 4000. Care in them, especially in big cities, provided antiseptic surgery, clinical pathology, artificial respiration, blood transfusions. Terms like contagion, ventilation, x-ray, anesthesia, electro-cardiography, and pharmacology were becoming common. Tools of the trade would have amazed Civil War doctors: stethoscopes of course and microscopes, oral thermometers. Also autoclaves, sterilized dressings, rubber gloves, opthomaloscopes, otoscopes, test tubes, Petri dishes, hollow needles for hypodermic injections. And a cuff for measuring diastolic and systologic blood pressure was not far off. That was in the big cities.

Industry in more populated areas had sponsored hospitals for years before the practice began here. Elsewhere, respectable people with families were using hospitals for antiseptic surgery, but not in northern Arizona. I could find no evidence that AL&T provided its Milton hospital with any of the new-fangled devices, with a supervising doctor or with a nursing staff, which didn't mean there weren't, just that any paper record had disappeared.

Dr. Dennis J. Brannen, who had been Flagstaff's first doctor and the first doctor on AL&T's payroll, traveled down to Washington D.C. from Buffalo in March of 1908 to attend a clinic at George Washington University Hospital, whether as a patient or a doctor the newspaper didn't say. While he was there, he went to the Capitol building to talk with friends among Arizona Territory's delegates. In the middle of the conversation he suffered what was called an attack of apoplexy; we refer to it now as a stroke. He died in Washington, only forty-nine years old.

His will, drawn up in 1901, was taken through probate by attorney and budding politician Henry F. Ashurst. It bequeathed to his brother Paul in Tucson his ownership in the Brannen Farm in Illinois; Felicia received all other property, which included several pieces of real estate in Flagstaff and shares in several Arizona mines as well as Electric Light and Power of Williams. The estimate of the value of her inheritance was "several hundred thousand dollars." In 1908 that was what some people nowadays call beaucoup bucks.

Before the legal paperwork was complete, Felicia, age thirty-eight, "sojourned" in Italy for a while and then stopped off in Flagstaff on her way to "make her future home in Los Angeles." Of all the doctors' wives in Flagstaff in the early years, she was the prototype for the future—respectable, accomplished, socially active. I'll bet her clothes were impeccable, whatever the fashions were.

So goodbye to Felicia. Too bad she was going out of the story—I thought I recognized her, so to speak.

The most common of the breast cancers are those which develop in ducts. They can spread by clumps of cells breaking off and traveling through blood or lymphatic vessels to bone, liver, brain, lungs, just about anywhere.

Maybe it's true that male bodies need sex—human males, that is. I wouldn't know from personal experience. The whole pursuit and conquest and domination may be an invention of the human male mind and therefore a different issue entirely, a matter of culture not biology. One question I don't have an answer for at all is whether most men need love, like beyond the age of about ten.

Do women need sex? My generation didn't talk much about such things, so despite decades of experience as a woman, I hesitate to make a general statement. Just—liking and wanting and needing are not necessarily the same, and I'm not sure that physical response is a requirement for female sanity. But I'll say this with some assurance: for most women, sex is a part of love, and that's a need. Things your mother didn't tell you.

So for a man who wants (not needs) to seduce a large variety of women, understanding the difference is a key to success. Some of us women may consciously seek uncomplicated sex. Most of us, I'll bet, want (need?) love to go with it.

I'm talking about Lyle, of course. Seduction was by definition a goal-oriented activity for him. I needed a specific kind of love, needed it with a body hunger. Morality had nothing to do with it. Compliments, appreciation—well, I opened like a flower, grew wide like a tree. I loved and mistook it for his love.

"Marlene, I have a craving for your company. Your conversation. Your shining face. Tell me you have time for me today. I'll buy your lunch if you'll tell me your opinion of Bob Dylan, LBJ, Timothy Leary, and Haight-Ashbury."

That kind of thing was irresistible. He greeted me with one-arm hugs and laughed at my jokes. Seeing me to my car afterward, he kissed my hand and thanked me for making his day. A more sophisticated lady would have seen right through him.

"Marlene, I only have a minute. Would a teen-ager think I'm cool if I walk into the examining room singing "I love you, yeah, yeah, yeah?""

"Marlene, your judgment is impeccable. Should I invest in IBM or bell-bottom pants?"

"Marlene, did your parents name you for Marlene Dietrich and bring you up to be so exciting? Or is it natural? I'm just curious."

One day when we were having lunch in a cafe on the west side, we overheard a conversation at the next table:

"I was married for forty-seven years, and he got a lady. You know, things were not good between us. Then he died. And that was perfect."

"He was a Scorpio?"

We looked at each other wide-eyed and sucked in our cheeks trying not to laugh.

Seduction was Lyle's art form. He must have been refining it for years, he was so good at it. Later I could figure out when he moved from phase two to phase three, but it was so smooth I didn't see it at the time.

I'm glad I had the experience. I hope no one guessed. From the outside it would have looked like one more tawdry affair. Maybe it was, but it didn't feel like that to me.

Someone at UC Berkeley has announced that playing contract bridge requires the use of the brain's dorso-lateral cortex, which also produces white blood cells. Thus, playing bridge may boost the human immune system. Oh, brave new world.

"Residence."

"Baxter?"

"Oh, hello, Mom. Sorry, phone marketers have been pestering me in the evenings—I enter defensive mode the minute the phone rings. How are you?"

"Fine and dandy, as my father used to say. I'm calling to report that your instructions about how to connect my computer with the web were excellent. I'm now surfing away cheerfully. Well, not exactly cheerfully, and I'm not sure "surfing" is the word for it, but I've finally found information I wanted."

"Congratulations. Still looking for explanations about weather?"

"Explanations, yes. While it was so cold and I was staying home, I went upstairs and figured out how to get into a server, which caused some cheering around here. Only took me an hour."

"Hey, I'm proud of you."

"I found the National Oceanic and Atmospheric Administration, something called Downstrike, the Environmental News Network, the Department of Agriculture, and I survived the experience."

"So you're now enlightened?"

"Oh lord no. It's my private conviction that information is not as accessible to some of us as it used to be. I mean, I still miss the card catalogue. The Readers' Guide got me through college classes galore, but the city library no longer subscribes. Juvenile gearheads may have improved the world for their generation, but they've nearly crippled mine."

"Are you serious?"

"You just wait, your time for confusion will come. They aren't finished with us yet."

"Mom, I never know when you're kidding. But thanks, I guess. I'll consider myself forewarned."

"I never know when meteorologists are kidding me. I think La Niña and El Niño are other terms for the Pacific Decadel Oscillation, but I'm not sure. I've just learned that there's an Arctic Oscillation, much to my fascination. I may understand upper lows and lower highs. And I'm delighted by this report from U of A: a destructive monster is lurking in the Pacific Ocean that could negatively affect Arizona weather for the next thirty years, but scientists know very little about it. Want to know what it is?"

"Of course. I'm holding my breath."

"A gradual shift in ocean water temperature between China and California."

"Is that a big Pacific Oscillation?"

"I think so. A NASA satellite that measures water temperatures, don't ask me how, has provided data that foretells decades of low rainfall in the Southwest."

"That doesn't sound good."

"My first reaction was to a satellite that can measure water temperature in the Pacific. To quote the Wicked Witch of the West: "What a world, what a world.""

"Isn't it though."

"I've also read that our summer rains depend on whether sea surface temperature is seventy-nine degrees or higher in the Gulf of California, maybe because of a warm coastal current. Low temperature, low rainfall."

"I begin to feel sympathy for the weather service. No wonder it won't forecast more than five days ahead."

"No wonder. Anyway, having read and misunderstood pages and pages, I'm prepared to say that for the last six months weather in Flagstaff, Arizona, has been the result of vacillation between La Niña, El Niño, and La Nada—I laughed at that—producing wind patterns, pressure troughs and ridges, the usual collection. Vacillation meaning that it can't make up its mind."

"You know, when you started all this, I thought I knew quite a bit about weather."

"Me too. That's how it is when you can't see The Big Picture."

Definitions for cause of death are too precise to be accurate. If a man is so unhappy in his life that he becomes ill, gives up, and dies, is it murder, suicide or natural causes? If a woman dies from a cancer that grows from her own body (body killing itself), is it suicide?

"Have you introduced yourself to your neighbors yet?"

"Gwen…"

"You haven't, have you?"

"I'm touched by your concern…"

"What am I going to do with you?"

"My love, you aren't old enough yet to know how peaceful it feels to be alone. How secure. I just love it."

"Mother, I told you."

"Other people weary me these days. For years I was so often in a crowd and it was so often stress."

"Humans are by nature gregarious."

"I see people every day. The library swarms with people. There's Mariano, a small child with huge eyes who plays quietly while his father is tutored in English. I always speak to him— 'Hola, Mariano'."

"That's not the same, you need to talk with your peers."

"I do, I talk with people at the reference desk, they're very helpful. I smile at strangers on the street. But I'm happy to rest in my own company. Rest is the operative word there."

"Mother, that's not healthy."

"It feels healthy to me. Wouldn't you appreciate peace and rest now and then?"

"Oh gosh, yes. A day off occasionally would make such a difference."

"There you are. You might not understand me until you're my age, which you will be, I promise you."

"I won't want to be cut off from humanity."

"I'm not cut off, I'm very involved."

"Oh, I'm sure."

"I'm involved with women who lived before I was born. Doctors' wives. I just wish I knew them better."

"Oh, Mother."

"Just this week I learned something tantalizing about the woman who married Dr. Adams, the man who had bought the first automobile in town. There wasn't a thing in the paper about her personally, just that she went to Illinois for the birth of a baby and stayed five months, things like that."

"Five *months*? Was she ill?"

"I don't know. But she and the doctor didn't seem to travel together much. He went off to California for his health or to the Mayo Clinic in Minnesota for surgery. When he got home, she went to Los Angeles for a few weeks."

"She didn't like home when he was there."

"That's what I was thinking. They'd been married for three years when she took the baby to Los Angeles, where she had lived before, and 'willfully and without cause' refused to come back."

"Willfully and without cause?"

"That was the legal language. I noticed a single line in the newspaper that read 'Divorce Action: Adams vs. Adams', so I went to the Office of the Clerk of the Superior Court and asked for the court record of civil actions. There's something rather daring about doing a thing like that."

"Well, I'd think so."

"In August of 1909 Dr. Adams filed for dissolution of the marriage, charging Margaret's absence as the cause. She was served with notice but did not respond, did not contest, did not appear. Three weeks later Case #884, John E. Adams vs. Margaret C. Adams, was resolved in favor of the plaintiff."

"She didn't like John? Or Flagstaff? Or marriage itself? She obviously didn't like something."

"She could have been bored with Flagstaff—there was still more open space than buildings, even right downtown. Maybe she was tired of the trials of being a doctor's wife. Any one of us would have understood that reason."

"Never home. Always thinking about something else? What did the doctors do?"

"All kinds of things; they were all GPs, not specialists. A man whose skull who had been crushed by a shovel swung by another man died at the county hospital. Another man was riding across the railroad tracks on horseback and the horse's shoe caught between the rails; the horse fell, the rider's right forearm was broken badly. The newspaper didn't say what happened to the horse. A logger cut his leg open with an ax. Dr. Raymond treated two girls with scarlet fever, and Dr. Adams, who was the county health officer, had the house fumigated. An entire family in Williams was quarantined in the Pest House with smallpox. There was no end of drama."

"But not much in the way of dinner conversation for Mrs. Adams."

"You know, Gwen, I applaud her spirit, it makes her seem quite modern. Maybe she was an unpleasant person, always dissatisfied about something, but at least she didn't see herself as a prisoner of marriage as too many women have."

"Prisoner? Mother! What a thing to say! I don't feel like a prisoner."

"I'll bet you don't, my Gwen, not a woman like you. Anyway, in 1909 there were five doctors in Flagstaff, three of them single, and only two wives, Effie Sipe and Sarah Manning. Both apparently steady and respectable, proper wives of Victorian virtue. I wonder whether they signed the copy of the petition to Congress that the National American Suffrage Association was circulating in Flagstaff. The editor of the newspaper said there were "a large number" of signatures."

"Suffrage? You mean women couldn't vote yet?"

"Not in national elections."

"Well, I think that stinks."

"The saloon element was afraid if women could vote they'd outlaw saloons. And they did, of course, later, with help from tee-totaling men. In Flagstaff there was an active chapter of the WCTU."

"What's WCTU?"

"Women's Christian Temperance Union. The ladies opened the Flagstaff Reading Room that made magazines and newspapers available free to citizens. There was no library."

"I don't see that there's necessarily a connection between reading and drinking and voting. That's pure hysteria."

"And you don't see hysteria having any part in politics?"

"Ugh. You're right. They do every time."

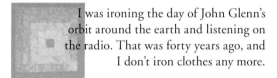

I was ironing the day of John Glenn's orbit around the earth and listening on the radio. That was forty years ago, and I don't iron clothes any more.

We called it "the blues" and said people were "weird" if they had "an inferiority complex." I never heard of depression being a medical condition, but when I went hunting for explanations, I found that a lot had been published. According to books and journal articles, there were two theories about causes of depression, and the two were not mutually exclusive.

One cause was supposed to be psychological: post-trauma of many kinds; loss, especially early; chronic reaction to stress; learned response to environment through reinforcement and conditioning. Well, I thought, that ought to include nine-tenths of the population. Who goes through life without stress and loss and trauma?

The second was biological, harder to see and understand:

1. Reaction to hypo- or hyperthyroidism, hepatitis, influenza, cancers, autoimmune disease;

2. Genetic factors (familial transmission) on the X/mother's chromosome;

3. Disturbances in the prefrontal cortex, fore brain, central nervous system—an insufficiency of certain chemicals at neuronal synapses; Abnormality in the activity of neurotransmitters;

4. Secretion of neural hormones—endocrine, adrenal, pineal, pituitary, cortical circadian.

Those were both theories, suspected because of the way patients responded to medication. The way they reacted to the psychological blows might be different because of biological factors. Was depression like fingerprints, different in each person? Stand by: there's something new out every year.

Another of Marlene's theories: beware of those who so use your virtues against you that they become your handicaps.

From my notes:

1. A woman's left breast is generally a little larger than the right. I didn't know that—didn't feel like it to me. Breasts are mostly made up of fat. Thanks a lot.

2. If metatastic disease is already present, it is pointless to subject a woman to removal of breast, division of underlying muscle and removal of axillary lymph glands.

I've never fought in a war or been anywhere near an explosion. I'd never seen human bodies blown apart until that accident with the motor coach. A few months later a man told me such a thing was impossible, and I could only stare at him. Didn't he realize what he was saying to me?

In all the advice and warnings and criticism and other such negative emphasis called "bringing up children" no one had thought to give us lessons in happiness. I'm sure I never saw either of my parents having fun. I didn't want that for my children, and neither did Emily.

"Marlene, it's been at least a week since I've heard myself laugh. I haven't even felt like it, that's a shocking state of affairs."

"Gadzooks. We're wasting our lives. If it's been a week for you, it's been that long for me. I laugh only with you."

"Gadzooks?"

"I've been reading an old English novel."

We built sets, invented dialogue, staged plays starring our children and their friends. Produced books every summer full of original drawings and poems. Arranged neighborhood 4th of July parades. Took everybody out for ice cream. Played Follow the Leader. Taught them to do the Hokey-Pokey and the Schottische. There were eight of us, just enough to dance one square. "Allemande left with your left hand. Left, Abby, left."

You never learn anything as well as what you teach yourself. I haven't seen Emily's children lately, but I don't think Gwen and Baxter know much more about having fun than my parents did. Sometimes they forget their dignity and carry on something wonderful, but I'm sorry to say usually they're too busy being grown-ups. There may be hope for Abby.

Emily and I were the ones—by what we tried to teach them, we changed ourselves. It was hard work, it took time and imagination; sometimes we ran ourselves ragged. But we taught ourselves, if not to be happy, then to behave as if we were, and that's almost as good.

We never did much exercising as such. I had three children, she had three; we both managed large houses and yards, both volunteered hours of work on charities and causes.

Some nights we went to bed too tired to sleep—had to lie there and rest for a while first. When the country turned into a perpetual jogging marathon, we laughed ourselves silly.

"Those people don't have enough to do, that's the problem."

We talked almost every day, on the phone or in the car going to committee meetings. I saw scads of other people in all kinds of situations, but Emily was my only real company. Contact is not company. I don't know whether that's widely known.

It wasn't that we agreed about everything; we didn't. We didn't need to. We had a way of talking that was curiosity rather than persuasion.

"Tell me what you mean by grace."

"Hmmm, a new perspective; I hadn't thought about the welfare program as promoting social order."

"What do you think might happen if President Johnson were to do exactly the opposite?"

So we learned about each other, and we were never angry or hurt or offended, and we laughed at everything we could.

We played 'what if?' "What if you were elected president? Who would you appoint to your cabinet?"

"Well, I think I'd start with Stew Udall as Secretary of the Interior."

"He already is."

"I know. That's what I mean."

"What if he wouldn't do it?"

"Then how about Ralph Nader?"

"He has to be Secretary of Commerce."

"You're right. Would you take the job?"

"I'd rather be Surgeon General. Or maybe press secretary."

"I kind of had Bella Abzug in mind for press secretary."

"Perfect choice, perfect. Though she might be good as Chairman of the Joint Chiefs."

Funny how alive a silly game like that could make me feel. Alive and awake in my mind. Because of Emily.

The children were half grown by the time I lost her. Don was deep into withdrawal. I had no company, and I couldn't bear mere contact. So. I carried books out of the library in stacks and forgot them as soon as I'd read them. Walked hours every day, through neighborhoods, along canals, up mountains, it didn't matter as long as I could keep moving. Wrote long letters to Emily and folded them into a drawer in my desk. But I wasn't completely daft, I always waited until noon to start drinking and I always stopped when the children were due home. I drank a lot of Irish whiskey before I realized it didn't really do any good. Dark years. Everybody has dark years. And then darker ones.

 My theory is different from Freud's. I say that sex is not the prime mover of human behavior. Power is. Unless they're the same thing.

Nights were either cloudy or too cold for going outside, and I couldn't see the sky through my roof and the big trees around me. I was content in my little home in town, but I seldom saw the moon, couldn't have told you what phase it was in without searching through the newspaper.

Nights were also long and dark. Icicles hung on street lamps. In the evenings everybody was indoors or in warm restaurants full of color and food and cheerful people. I saw them through windows if I decided to sally forth for a walk, and there was no one on the street but me. They looked communal and companionable in their eating and talking.

The sun was far to the south, and days were short and cold. Snow in shady places didn't melt. Bare tree branches moved in the wind.

I loved winter in Flagstaff, loved the drama of a storm coming whether it got here or not, loved being soft and warm in bed when the book was true and a violin was playing on the radio. I even liked walking with tiny straight-down steps so I wouldn't slide and fall. Slept late and wore heavy sweatshirts. Wrapped in my grandmother's quilt, I napped on the couch, a book open on my chest.

I didn't miss being outdoors—I'd been outdoors all the past summer. TV and phones kept my world huge. In a land awash in dour and sour, in cynics and complainers, in emotional hypochondriacs, in reformers and avengers and people who just plain like fighting everybody, I felt it was my obligation to humanity to be happy.

On the corner of my desk I was keeping, where I'd notice it every day, a line by Dorothy Sayers: "Time and trouble will tame an advanced young woman, but an advanced old woman is uncontrollable by any earthly force." Right on, Dorothy.

The first week in February was clear and bright. Water poured off roofs as snow melted, and icicles shrank rapidly. Wind became a breeze, but mud was on every unpaved surface, sticky, squishy, inch-deep mud.

I slogged through the wet to libraries, the County Recorder's office, the office of the Clerk of the Superior Court, the Pioneers Museum—still trying to figure out what life was like here early in the 20th century. Were there nickelodeons in Flagstaff? Did people sing waltzes? "In the Good Old Summertime." "Take Me Out to the Ball Game."

1910 In 1910 the *Sun*, which had over 800 subscribers by then, reported the usual accidents: Mrs. T.W. Davis, who had been cleaning a ceiling in her home, fell from the ladder and broke her shoulder bone. The usual causes of death: a young woman, married only thirteen months, died, probably at home, having failed to recover from childbirth a month earlier. Which local doctors attended them though, that was missing from the paragraphs.

OK—a recap to keep me from making mistakes. In the first thirty years, eight doctors stayed in Flagstaff long enough for their names to be entered in county records: Brannen, Cornish, Manning, Miller, Robinson, Sipe, Adams, and Raymond. There was constant coming and going, but those eight were in residence at least for a while. In don't know what happened to Slernitzauer, he disappeared from the newspaper and from the court house.

1910—Flagstaff population up twenty-eight per cent to 1,633—was a year of downright upheaval on the M.D. scene. Dr. Albert H. Schermann arrived expecting to remain indefinitely, so he said. The federal census of that year listed him as single, age thirty-one, born in Pittsburg, Pennsylvania in 1879.

The Coconino County Register of Physicians listed him as a graduate of Western Pennsylvania Medical College; the American Medical Directory listed first Western University of Pennsylvania and later the University of Pittsburg. The librarian at Maricopa County Medical Society Library said he had graduated in 1903 from the University of Pennsylvania School of Medicine, for more than 100 years a university-affiliated medical school, one of the first in the country. This is what you call historical research.

Schermann's family (I wrote to them) remembered that he did post-graduate work in eye, ear, nose and throat at New York General Hospital, that he left Pennsylvania because he was tubercular, that he went first to New Mexico. According to his daughter, Mary Caroline, he left New Mexico because he became tired of removing bullets from patients.

Flagstaff's newest doctor registered immediately with the Territorial Medical Board, but he did not buy property in town, was not listed in tax records for 1910, 1911 or 1912. Maybe that was because he was employed at the Milton hospital—as the census listed him—and living there, in a room in what had been Fred Sisson's house. It was the first clue I'd seen to a resident doctor. Was he hired and paid by the other doctors? Could have been if it was a loose cooperative, as Henry Giclas had implied. Brannen and Raymond had been on the company payroll, but as far as I could tell, they doctored all over the country as well. Schermann too was in general practice.

There was a nurse at Milton hospital, Catherine Power, single, thirty-seven, born in Ireland. And nurses north of the tracks—Mary Fairchild and Eva Yost, born in Austria—but I don't know where they were employed, maybe they took private patients. There's a limit to what you can learn from census records.

In May Dr. J.L. Halstead came in on the Limited and told the *Sun's* reporter that he would make Flagstaff his permanent home. He said he was taking the place of Dr. W.P. Sipe as a partner of Dr. J.E. Adams.

Wilbur and Effie were leaving? Yes, for New Mexico, where he had been hired to take charge of a church hospital near Gallup. Within the year he would be a patient in a Los Angeles hospital—surgery for cancer.

Halstead apparently didn't work out, that was the only time I saw his name. He didn't buy property or register to vote or receive a certificate from the Medical Board, didn't pay taxes, didn't appear again in the *Sun*.

Was all that moving around normal on the frontier in 1910? I've always thought of doctors as people who stay put and build a practice. Don certainly did.

Then John Adams, divorced, age thirty-four, left for Oakland, California, to enter into a partnership with a doctor there, and C. W. Sult, physician and surgeon, came to town and announced that he was the successor to Adams and Sipe with an office in the Pollock Block. He too was immediately certified to practice by the territorial board.

Sult was married to a woman named Nellie V. The Sults leased "the Julius Herman residence on the hill." Her sister Anna Taggart was the new assistant at the post office. Did she come to Flagstaff with the Sults or was she here first? History swarms with questions.

So within a few months the list of M.D.s went from eight to six, and three of them were new: Miller (listed in the census as rooming in the house of John Woody), Manning, Raymond, Schermann, Sult. And George Felix Manning jr.—in the spring of 1910 he returned from Alabama with an M.D. degree, intending to practice with his father. Felix jr. may have moved into the family home for a while: he wasn't taxed by the county for any property, real or otherwise, no furniture or kitchen equipment, nothing.

Keeping Track

    Brannen: E.M. Institute in Cincinnati
    Cornish: Jefferson Medical College of Pennsylvania
    Manning: Universities of Virginia and Alabama Medical Colleges
    Miller: University of Buffalo Department of Medicine
    Robinson—??
    Sipe: Hospital College of Medicine, Central University of Kentucky
    Adams: College of Physicians of Cleveland, Ohio
    Raymond: Washington University Medical School, St. Louis
    Schermann: University of Pennsylvania School of Medicine
    Sult: Georgetown University, Washington D.C.
    Manning, jr.: University of Alabama Medical Department

In November Sult, Raymond, Miller, and both Mannings were paid by the county Board of Supervisors for services at the county hospital out on Fort Valley Road. Not Schermann, who was at Milton hospital—an employee of AL&T died there in October.

Sarah Manning, what a position! At fifty-two, she was not only the first doctor's wife in town, the senior doctor's wife, and the only doctor's wife from the 1880s still in Flagstaff—she was also the only doctor's mother. But she was still a mystery. I checked: not a member of the Ladies of the Maccabees of the World. She wouldn't have been GAR auxiliary, not with a husband who was a Confederate veteran. Neither was she on the guest list of any of the parties reported in the newspaper. George Felix sr., seventy-three, was not listed as a member of one of the ten men's lodges in town. Kept to themselves, did they?

I have the impression that news of private citizens was reported only if they stopped by the office of the *Sun* and told Fred Breen or his reporter what they were doing. Maybe the Mannings thought it undignified for Sarah to do so. But it was all right for her daughter Julia, seventeen, the only Manning child left at home. Dr. Manning was finally taxed for a piano in 1910. For whom? Julia? She went off to Pasadena to school.

After 1909 many women in this land of the free adopted the hobble skirt, a very narrow construction which restricted a woman to small mincing steps and no running at all. Colossal cartwheel hats were all the rage. I've tried, but I cannot imagine Sarah Ellen Manning dressed like that. Or myself, either.

Felicia might have. She visited Flagstaff that year. Another reminder of the past: Clara Cornish's son, Gilette, who was nicknamed "Doc," made the freshman football team at Yale. Heavens, time was moving fast—he was a baby only a few pages ago.

Also in 1910, Florence Nightingale died. Over 1000 nurse training schools in this country were based on the program she established in England, and one of them was in St. Joseph's hospital in Phoenix, which opened Arizona's first nursing school that same year.

When I was in the 8th grade, I shaved my legs and used hydrogen peroxide to bleach the hair on my arms and make me look more "feminine," which meant less like a boy, I suppose. Now my arms are bare as a doll's and I let my legs go weeks before I notice anything worth mowing down. Then why do I examine my chin every morning with a magnifying mirror? When I was young, we plucked our *eyebrows*.

I drove southeast from Bryce on Highway 12. Until that October Sunday morning, I hadn't driven the motorcoach on the road, and I discovered I liked the feeling. There were more little farming towns—people walking to church in family groups or friendship pairs under big golden trees—but mostly it was open road, really open, hardly any traffic. Fall colors, bright blue sky. We were in the valley of a smallish river, so there were no cliffs-plus-air views to make me feel puny, just peaceful, human-size country mile after mile as we moved steadily across the northern edge of the Grand Staircase. Don slept on the couch with a pillow over his head.

I had finally figured out that Bryce is geologically part of the Staircase, and I'd expected to see it from the side in profile from Highway 12. I'd been looking forward to the Cockscomb, a hundred-mile-long north-south ridge squeezed up by tectonic pressure and eroded down into two parallel rows of sharp uptilted rocks that reminded some people of a rooster comb. In aerial photos it looked to me more like the back armor of a very long stegosaurus. I watched, hoping there'd be an overlook where I could pause carefully so as not to wake Don and see for myself how the Comb came up from the south and marked the east side of the Staircase region.

No such luck. All I could do, cocooned in the little valley, was slide across the top of invisible scenery that was accessible by only one crooked dirt road, "primitive...four wheel drive or high clearance vehicles," which wasn't us. Too bad.

The Staircase had just become a national monument. The presidential proclamation said "distances that defy human perspective," and I could confirm that. It certainly defied my perspective. A frontier, the proclamation said, "a geologic treasure," "the last place in the continental United States to be mapped"..."challenging"..."remote."

You know, I wonder whether there is a jeep tour that I could join or some hardy small-town entrepreneur whom I could hire to drive me down the Cottonwood Canyon road the whole length of the Cockscomb and back between the gray and white cliffs on the Skutumpah road to Cannonville. Probably take a long full day, might be a rough ride, but I think I could handle it. Gwen would be horrified; maybe Abby and Jane would come along.

And there's something else I'd like to see for myself. The Grand Staircase-Escalante National Monument is so big (double the size of New England) because it's three distinct geologic regions, each different from the others. On the west are the benches of the Staircase. In the middle—sharply defined by the Cockscomb—the Kaiparowits Plateau. On the east—beyond the Straight Cliffs and the Fifty Mile Bench—the Escalante River Canyons. Maybe I could jeep-tour them all. Where did I put those maps?

My father's old-fashioned handwriting was beautiful and refined until he was eighty years old and his hand began to tremble. I could read his letters, but they were no longer beautiful.

"Hi, Momsie."

I put down my pencil."Good morning to you, Abby. Momsie? Touch of whimsy there."

"What's wrong with whimsy?"

"Not a thing. I like it. Momsie is all right with me."

"In southern California it's a Saturday morning, almost spring, and I'm planning to spend the weekend working in the yard. Is it almost spring in Flagstaff?"

"Oh dear no, weather stays cold and windy. I'm beginning to think that in Arizona the mountains have fall and the desert has spring. Remember the poppies out on Camelback Road?"

"The smell of orange blossoms in March…"

"Spring didn't last long, but wasn't it intoxicating?"

"Of course we have orange blossoms here."

"Good. Then you're not homesick. Neither am I. New and different is keeping me alert."

"Are you doing anything now that's new and different?"

"Last evening I took myself out to dinner."

"Good for you. How was it?"

"Wonderful. I was the first person in the restaurant, quite an elegant place, so I chose a seat under the music speaker—Mozart and the like. Ordered half a bottle of Pouilly-Fuisse to go with Coquille St. Jacques. I had with me a new library book, a biography of Andrew Wyeth."

"That's my mom. Did you feel uncomfortable being alone?"

"Not at all, just the opposite. A couple, upper middle-aged, was seated near me. He was one of those odious men who never stop talking, pompous, slapped his opinions down on the table, painted the walls with them. She rarely spoke, but I noticed her duck her head now and then, trying to see what I was reading. So I ever-so-casually set my book up so that she could see the cover."

"Good for you. Poor woman."

"I'll bet I was much happier with my evening than she was with hers."

"So what will you be doing today, more library?"

"Hordes of people are in the library on Saturdays, I think I'll stay home and organize my notes at the computer in my upstairs office. My desk is in morning sun—icicles make occasional rainbows on the wall."

"You don't like hordes?"

"Not much, not anymore. My nervous system has been over-stretched by years of social obligations."

"Great image, a nervous system like an old rubber band." We both laughed. "How's your search and research going? Been saving bits of old trivia for me?"

"I have, yes, I keep a list headed Trivia for Abby. Wait a minute. Walking into my office. Sitting down at my desk. Shuffling paper. OK, the newspaper informed Flagstaff that Friday was Ladies Night at the bowling alley."

"Ladies Night—blast from the past."

"Isn't it? I wonder what they wore."

"Still a stiff corset?"

"You're probably right. Imagine bowling in a corset?"

"You know, I can't."

"Here's another one: street sprinklers."

"No kidding!"

"Yep. The streets were all dust and dirt. The Normal School had a girls basketball team. A 'lady forester' was here from L.A. on an inspection of ranger stations and such."

"Lady forester. That must have been a revolution."

"The editor apparently thought it was unusual enough to be worth mentioning. And, let's see, other local news. The Santa Fe was 'double tracking' across Arizona. The grading outfit included fifty-two mules."

"You mean there had been only one track all that time?"

"Surely there had been one for east bound and one for west. Maybe they were doubling that."

"Only one track would be invitation to head-on collision."

"Seems obvious, doesn't it? More than fifty men left the double track work because their time was increased from ten to twelve hours a day. Even with extra pay for the extra two hours, they refused."

"Good for them. Can't say I blame them."

"Is this being more than you wanted to hear?"

"No, actually it's interesting. Right up my sidewalk."

"Well, then. There was early environmental news. Roosevelt Dam was nearly finished. It had already begun backing up what they were boasting would be the biggest reservoir in the world. A bill was introduced in Congress to create Grand Canyon National Park."

"'Bout time. 'S a wonder it hadn't been turned into money by then."

"It wasn't because people hadn't tried. There'd been prospecting and mining. Men claiming they owned the hiking trails and charging tolls. Even a plan to build a railroad track through the canyon along the river. For a while they thought it could be done."

"What a species we are."

"The real unknown, as far as they were concerned, was that Halley's comet was approaching for the first time since 1833, and they were worried about what would happen if earth should pass through the tail."

"They didn't think about an impact?"

"Not that I can see. Just the effect of the tail."

"You know, Mom, you are a real treat to talk with. When I was in high school, I didn't know that."

"Maybe I wasn't back then. I like to think I'm growing into the real me."

"You're certainly setting an example for the real me."

"Thanks. My job description changes as I get older."

— — — — — — — — — — — — —

"One thing I called about—I'm doing a medical profile for myself. Was there ever cancer in our family? Either side?"

"Not in mine back, well, ummm, five generations. Not in your father's for at least three."

"Heart disease? Diabetes?"

"Not to my knowledge. Except for contagion or war, they lived into their 80s and 90s."

"War?"

"We had two men in the Civil War. Nobody in our background fought in the Indian wars. Or the Spanish-American."

"How about Dad's illness?"

I'd feared that would come up sooner or later, and I answered carefully. "It's possible it had a genetic component."

"Can be inherited?"

"Could be, I suppose, but that would depend on a number of factors and could be treated easily now with drugs."

"What early symptoms should I look for?"

"Oh, darlin', you don't think…?"

"No, I just wondered."

"Chronic fatigue/low energy level/reduced activity."

"Sounds like me at the end of a day in the library."

"Also irritability. Insomnia. Loss of productivity."

"That could mean practically anything: boredom, irritating job, bad love affair."

"You're right. Difficulty concentrating, poor appetite."

"*Everybody* feels those now and then."

"That's what makes it so hard to recognize."

"What else?"

"There's a long list. Are you ready? Inability to handle criticism. Guilt. Worry. Dependence on alcohol. Feeling unloved. Sadness that morphs into hopelessness. Even submissiveness."

"Dad? I never guessed."

"There's more: social withdrawal, loss of self esteem."

"My god, Mom!"

"Huge, isn't it? Like a mushroom cloud. Bigger than one well-intentioned spouse can hope to handle."

"But you're describing half the population."

"I know. You begin to wonder if it's an epidemic."

During World War II trains going through Phoenix were full of soldiers, and people were often standing in the aisles. I wonder if it was the same in Flagstaff. I'll ask Ed and Sandy.

I've always been such a wretched athlete that in grade school the position I played in baseball was bench. In high school I avoided gym class by signing into mixed chorus. My athletic credit in college was for square dancing.

So? There's a role for everybody. I watch.

When Don and I were at ASU, before we were married, we went to every home basketball game, and I loved it. Football too, but we couldn't get close enough to see the players, just the patterns—half the time I couldn't even see the ball. Basketball was more personal: muscles worked—the boys wore shorter shorts then—sweat shone, running feet were loud on the floorboards. Swift, powerful but graceful as a dance.

Don explained the rules to me until I understood what was going on. We'd shout and cheer and thump on each other, hug and laugh when our heroes made spectacular plays. There was an inclusive feeling—half of a couple, part of a crowd, belonging in a tradition. The learning in college was exciting, but basketball games were my happiest times.

When we moved to the U of A, we didn't know the players, and Don was ever busier, and there was no more basketball for us. Television began to broadcast professional games, but it wasn't the same, no more inclusion.

Later though, I don't know, maybe cameras were better. I could look right into the faces and see the eyes—football and baseball too—and I began to watch for the pleasure of seeing what human bodies could do. I guess I could say I became a fan. A cut-off, middle-aged female fan who hated to miss a game, and I was part of something that meant more than it appeared to be.

I don't think I'll tell Gwen, no need to add to her shock—sometimes on these cold nights here in my little Flagstaff townhouse, I watch NBA games. And I try to imagine being as big as Shaquille O'Neal, looking down at people, ducking to go through doors, searching for a chair I could safely sit down on. If my feet were as big as his, how would that feel? What would I be like? I laugh at the thought: a lifetime of wearing size twenty-two shoes.

Born and reared in Phoenix, I've lived in Arizona most of my life. Without knowing it, I was formed by the Southwest. How can I tell what that means if I haven't seen it from the outside?

The biggest storm of the season moved through Flagstaff with two days of snow, ten to eighteen inches depending on what part of town you lived in. None of it melted, but wind blew a lot of it around, and the temperature stayed below freezing.

After most of the clouds had passed to the east, it was very cold, of course, and KNAU reported that two unidentified homeless men had been found frozen, one in a dumpster and the other in his sleeping bag in a grove of trees at the end of a southside street. Usually such news is impersonal, but this time I thought, "Oh no! Not *our* homeless man, the one in the library!" He had become a mythic figure in my mind, monkish there in his big hood in front of the window.

As soon as ice had turned to slush, I went to the library looking for him. I rounded the circulation desk into the big reading room and didn't see him. When I was a little closer—ah, there were his bedroll and his battered suitcase under the study carrel. And he was coming out of the restroom hall. For a moment I could see his dark eyes, deep in the hood, looking at me. What's his story? Everyone is a story.

The older I grow, the more appreciative I am of House. Wind was a tearing gale which came right through the walls of my apartment. Through January, snow and ice did not disappear even during sunny days—driving to the library would have been as chancy as walking, and I didn't want to subject these thinning bones to unnecessary bumps. Just the right conditions for reading mysteries, if you ask me, good ones with real dialogue, easy style, fast pace, not too gruesome. During those cold days, tucked up on the couch under the quilt and a throw on top of that, I could go through one mystery a day. Do I know how to have fun or what?

The phone was next to me so I wouldn't have to untangle if it rang.

"Hello."

"Mother, it's Gwen."

"Well, hello, darlin'. What a pleasure." I slipped my left hand under the quilt to warm it.

"Are you all right? The weather map shows very cold for Flagstaff."

"I couldn't be more comfortable."

"Do you have everything you need?"

"Trust you to wonder about that. I lack nothing. I barely go outside. Only when the wind pauses for a few minutes, just to work on my snowman."

"How weird—I thought you said snowman."

"Actually, it's a snow woman. I'm building her out in my little side yard, it doesn't get much sun."

"Mother. What if you catch a chill?

"I wrap up. And I don't stay out long. We built a snowman once, years ago, remember? Emily and I drove all you children up onto the Rim above Payson so you could see snow."

"Now that you mention it, I do remember something. It was very cold."

"And snow got down your boots and made your feet wet."

"And you put me into the station wagon to warm them up. I watched the rest of you through the window."

"You had your face up against the glass with your mouth wide open, screaming."

"I don't remember that. Just that you were all having fun without me."

"We were, it's true, Emily and I were running around being goofy trying to set you children a good example."

"*Good?*"

"About cutting loose and having fun. That was when I learned how heavy snow is. We were rolling balls of it to make them bigger, and by the time mine was two feet or so diameter, I couldn't move it anymore. What a revelation. We finished our constructions by carrying snow in our hands and patting it into place. That's what I'm doing with this one, only I'm using a trowel and a big pan."

"But you don't have to, there are no children to build them with now."

"That's the important thing—I'm doing it for myself. You know, Gwen, it's as if I'm recovering something, getting myself back. Do you ever feel that?"

"I have no idea what you're talking about."

"Maybe you're not old enough yet. It's the most delicious feeling. Not un-aging or anything, more that there was a long interlude when I was meeting responsibilities—a necessary phase—and now it's finished, and I can go on with something interrupted."

"What's that supposed to mean? We took yourself from you?"

"No. No, no. I'm ever so grateful for those child-raising years. I learned important things about life and a special kind of love, about being human, about myself. Now I'm learning other important things. I'm telling you so you'll know you have it to look forward to."

"Thanks, I guess. Honestly, Mother, sometimes I don't understand you at all."

I laughed. She'd paid me a compliment and didn't even know it. "How are Beanie and Cazz?"

"They both have disgustingly sloppy colds—it's been snowy and windy here too. I'm running back and forth all day trying to give them medicine and keep them in bed."

"You know what my mother used to do when I had a cold? She'd put a mustard plaster on me."

"I've never heard of that."

"I'm not surprised, I haven't thought of it for years. It was some kind of poultice made with mustard, I suppose, and spread on a cloth. Folk medicine, no doubt. She'd put it on my chest and leave it there for a while to 'draw out the sickness,' so she said. It burned, as I remember. It seems to me I was about nine years old."

"Sounds awful. I don't think I'd try it on the boys."

"Speaking from experience, I wouldn't advise it—I hated it. I wonder whether she stopped doing it because I protested so loudly."

"Things certainly have changed. Which reminds me: how are you doing on your medical history research?"

"I'm still working on it, or I was when these icy days set in. Speaking of things changing, early in the century there was a man named Bernarr McFadden, widely known as an "advocate of physical culture." He was arrested for distributing obscene materials through the mail: a magazine issue explaining to men how venereal disease was contracted."

"That's *insane.*"

"The purity police had a lot of power in those days. It was also obscene to distribute information about birth control to women. Ho for the good old days, right?"

"I wouldn't go back for anything."

"Nor would I. Not even for curiosity. The question is: would I go forward if I could?"

The next time I was in the library, I asked Sue at the information desk where I could find a recipe for mustard plasters. She went right into alternative medicine on her computer and found it immediately: a folk remedy for colds, bronchitis, congestion, flu, etc. I wouldn't be surprised to learn that Flagstaff mothers used it a century ago.

Oil the skin on the patient's chest to prevent burns
Lay a thin clean cloth on the oiled area
Mix 1 Tbs dry powdered mustard
   4 Tbs flour
   Tepid water to make a paste the consistency of cream cheese
Spread the mixture on the cloth and cover it
Leave on 2 to 20 minutes or until the skin becomes red, but be careful: the
     treatment can cause blisters
Follow with camphorated oil

I remember it as an unpleasant experience, but I never was required to put my feet into a tub of mustard and hot water to "draw out" a cold. Or wear a bag of asafetida or boiled onions on a string around my neck. I'll bet children in Flagstaff did.

> I remember the first doctor in Phoenix who bought a car with air conditioning. The other doctors clustered around it in the Good Sam parking lot looking into the trunk where the machinery was.

1911 After the doctor turnover in 1910, 1911 was quite stable in Flagstaff. Dr. Sult bought a house "on the hill," wherever that was, and moved into it in time for his wife to give birth to a boy—at home, of course. Dr. Raymond was preparing to build a handsome new office building of tufa stone on Leroux, half a block north of Front Street.

The *Sun* carried homely bits of doctor news. Dr. Raymond and Dr. Schermann went out duck hunting together. Editor Breen reported that, accompanied by his friend Dr. Hanser of St. Louis, Raymond "went to Rogers Lake in an auto on a short pleasure trip. At one spot on the road owing to previous precipitation it took two doctors, two forest rangers, two horses and two ropes to make the machine come along." Breen enjoyed teasing drivers of autos.

Dr. G.F. Manning (probably junior, senior was seventy-four years old) fractured a small bone in his ankle while stepping off No. 10 as it pulled out of the Flagstaff station. He had put a patient on the train and was attending her when it started to move. His foot "turned with him" as he hopped down. Dr. Manning jr. was president of the Normal School alumni association.

There was a new M.D. in town, new and long-timer: Thomas Peyton Manning, who had tried to capture pigeons in the barn twelve years earlier and had fallen and broken his arm. He returned from Alabama a full-fledged physician, bringing with him his son Frank and his wife Frances Josephine (Josie), born in Tennessee, who had married him in Mobile in 1907. *Who's Who in Arizona* referred to him as the youngest person (at the age of twenty-two) to serve as a practicing physician in the state.

Minutes of the Board of Supervisors meetings reported within the year that there were three doctors named Manning practicing at the county hospital. I hope Sarah was proud of her boys. If her children had been the work to which she had devoted her years, she had earned the right to pride.

It wasn't M.D. news, maybe, but worth mentioning: a veterinary surgeon named H. M. Berry said he planned to locate permanently in Flagstaff, which was still dependent on horses. He set up an office in Babbitts' Livery Barn. Later he leased the Greenlaw barn. A fire that started in his new house near the kitchen stove burned through the floor, dropping the stove into the basement. The estimated damage was a hundred dollars, which at that time could have been one-fifth the cost of the whole house.

Other snippets. Six-year-old Alice Schnebly was brought in to the hospital from the family ranch on Oak Creek with pneumonia. She died. Measles appeared again among the children and killed a baby; therefore schools were closed through January, and Sunday School was canceled at the Methodist church. Back east viral infection as the cause of measles was discovered.

Milton hospital served both loggers and the community. A man employed at Flagstaff Lumber Manufacturing sawmill was taken there after his foot was crushed in the conveyor belt.

Births and deaths were almost even in Arizona Territory in those years. Coconino county, population 8,130, reported 122 births and 101 deaths.

The future looked bright. The population of Flagstaff in 1911 was 1,633. Number of automobiles: twenty. The first auto to go from Flagstaff to Oak Creek Canyon, a 25 horsepower Overland, went as far as the Thomas Ranch at West Fork and took three and a half hours to come back.

The town boasted thirteen lodges for men before the year was out, also four churches: the Adventists were new. E. B. Raudebaugh, the cement man, was building sidewalks downtown.

Probably few of the doctors practicing in Flagstaff, 1882 to 1912, had served as interns. Until the 20th century there were few interns in America working in hospitals as part of their medical education. The number grew as the century moved along—an estimated 50 percent in 1904, 75 percent in 1914 when the AMA recommended that a year or two of clinical experience would be useful.

There were thirteen independent post-grad schools in 1910, but by then internship had become a standard requirement at large hospitals, which had taken on an educational role. Large student enrollments in polyclinics faded as they joined with established medical schools and hospitals and as education of doctors lengthened and improved. By 1914 five universities operated their own post-graduate schools.

As late as 1932 only seventeen state licensing boards required an internship, and only fourteen medical schools required it for an M.D. degree. In 1940 a mere 732 hospitals offered programs. Standards were not uniform and neither was the value. Internship was characterized by: routine chores in some hospitals; lack of systematic training or supervision; little attention to chronic illness or patients as individuals; too much time spent as surgical assistants.

Now people defend long hours and little sleep as "the way it's always been." Not true. Sixty or seventy years is not "always."

My second year in college, good grades made me a member of an academic fraternity. When we had our initiation meeting in a restaurant banquet room, the only black boy had to come in through the kitchen rather than, heaven forbid, through the dining room. Now I see black patrons everywhere. It's been a rapid social change.

When I married—the whole legal and social and ceremonial affair—I was only twenty, no more than a child, not nearly old enough to understand the decades-long results of sentimental actions. Not choices, there wasn't enough thought to call it a choice. He asked me to marry him, and I said yes to a fairy tale. I wanted the thrill of loving without any real idea of what love was, any more than I knew what he meant. Love. Marriage.

I didn't tell anybody: I loved the feel of his erect penis, so firm and the tip velvety soft, a combination of strong and tender. There were moments when physical closeness seemed to be spiritual intimacy. When he wasn't too tired or too distant…

But mostly I played a role, did what I thought I was expected to do. Laundry, cooking, all that dusting and sweeping. Ironing. Ye gods, ironing! He built a career, which was what he was expected to do. But two people who were enhanced by their joining, their separateness eased by it, their lives given meaning? I doubt we even thought about it. Not knowing what could have been, we created lives so ordinary it was painful.

Would life have been better if I had lived it alone? Maybe. I can say that now. I am working on a theory that no one, male or female, should be allowed to do anything important like serving in political office or getting married until the age of fifty.

I was forty when Lyle began his campaign and no more mature about love than I'd been at twenty. He'd say things like, "Easterners have a long social tradition with answers for everything, but Western society is so new that we have to figure out everything as we go; therefore Westerners have to be smarter."

I agreed that Western culture, at least in Arizona, is centuries newer, but I wondered whether the real difference is that the initial migration from east of the Rockies was made up of people from such different places that there was no dominant group to impose a "right" way, and there's freedom in that, which explains the making it up. And I asked whether he had looked at a map to see how much of the state is reserved for Indians.

Lack of wide experience, that was part of why I was such a pushover, and then, I suspect that men live in such a different culture concerning carnal matters that some of us are hard put not to be naive. I hope I said that fairly. He was operating by a definite set of rules. I hadn't a clue. Was I more ethical than he was because I loved and he didn't? I don't know.

But I thought at the time that love is so necessary to a woman that she will do it any way she can, legal or not. Children, friends, home, church, beauty, even self—a woman will love. That's not an excuse. Not an explanation. Just seemed a fact to me. Maybe I was wrong. At any rate, I loved like a whirlwind, like a radiance in the heavens. It was the most intense emotion of my life.

My doctor husband was obsessed with his work and deep in his long illness. He didn't seem to notice except to scowl: "What makes you so happy?" By then I hadn't loved him for years.

He wasn't evil, not at all. He wasn't trying to make me unhappy, at least I don't think so, I hope not. He was sweet when he was young. If he'd lost a leg or had his face badly scarred in an accident and gone on being sweet, I could have gone on loving him.

I won't say Lyle was evil either, that would imply that he was malicious, that he hurt people with conscious intent. The longer I live, the less I'm sure about a lot of things.

I'd be out on my bicycle all day riding on canal banks and dirt roads, through orange groves, along irrigation ditches. That was grade school years. I can't remember how long it's been since I rode a bicycle.

Everywhere I go, people I barely know tell me how glad they are that days are now warm and brightly colored. I agree that the town has been looking bleak and shabby; I savor the crocuses that are blooming and daffodils that are budding. But I like winter. I like winter clothes, and I don't trust this early spring. I bet we'll have more snow before the month is out.

Shirley called late in the month. "Hi. I haven't seen you since just after fire season ended. How are you?" What a woman—she managed to make everything she said sound like a delicious joke. "I'm coming in to town Tuesday. Shall we meet for lunch or something?"

"I'd love to see you and be reminded of last summer and next summer—I'd love to. Say where and when," singing, "and I'll be there, yes I will."

She answered, singing, "You've got a furr-end." And we both laughed.

Well, why not? I could do worse for a friend than a woman who laughs her way through life.

"I'll have my errands finished by noon, I hope. Shall we invite Sandy too?"

"Good idea. Do you want me to call her?"

So on a bright breezy day the three of us sat at a window table in a building that was constructed in 1912 looking out on what used to be called Front Street, eating sandwiches and doing some serious female bonding.

Shirley was eating corned beef. "Have you guys heard yet when you're supposed to open your towers? My district gave me April 22nd to open Baker Butte."

Sandy had ordered a cheeseburger although she said she knew she shouldn't. "I haven't heard. Bet anything here on the north end nobody has thought about it yet. If they have, they're waiting to see."

"After the grass dries up and begins to burn is way too late."

"Oh, you know it."

I was working my way through roast beef. "Will they call when they've made up their minds?"

Sandy laughed. "Probably not. Sometimes they don't decide until I call them."

Neither of them have the pinched look in their faces that thin women often develop—both are roundish and cheerful-looking. Sunlight through the window shone on their hair and made halos of light. Madonnas of the West.

They both laugh easily, as if they're comfortable with who they are. Both are somewhere in the long middle of life, so they must have known painful times, but they act as if the personal bad isn't what they want to show. I'm working on a theory that women can learn a lot from each other.

Both have been lookouts for years, lookouts miles apart. "I didn't hear any Hopis on the radio last summer, Shirley. I thought there was almost a village of them at Long Valley."

"Not any more. They've all retired, I guess, and moved back home."

I looked from one to the other. "How could you tell it was a Hopi on the radio?"

"They spoke Hopi to each other." Both women laughed. "Nobody could understand a word."

"Remember when one of them switched to English and asked Hutch Mountain if she copied?"

"I thought they made the Coconino special."

All three of us have children grown. "Do you have any kids, Marlene?"

"Two girls and one boy."

"How old are they?"

I hesitated. They'd guess how old I was, and it might spoil the camaraderie. But they could see for themselves that I wasn't thirty anymore. And about the time I turned twenty-five, other people's ages stopped meaning much to me—maybe it was that way for them too. "Wait a minute, I have to subtract. It changes every year. Baxter is, let's see, ummm, forty. Gwen is forty-two now, and Abby is twenty-eight."

Shirley didn't pause long enough to do the arithmetic. "My youngest is still in high school, and she's driving me crazy."

Sandy: "I've got all mine out and gone, when they don't decide they need to move back home for a while."

We laughed and went on to what Flagstaff was like when Sandy was a teen-ager. "Saturday nights there were dances in the armory at City Park, we car-pooled in from the army depot. I mean to tell you, it was fun. Hundreds of cars in the parking lot. There's nothing like that for high school kids now."

Shirley laughed, as usual. "Do they even know how to dance any more?"

"How long have you been around here, Shirley?"

"About, let's see, twenty-four years, at the Grand Canyon—I worked over there—and Blue Ridge. I've never lived in Flagstaff, but I've been coming in all that time."

Napkin to touch oil off my lips: "What changes have you seen?"

"Oh, it's so much bigger now. A lot of places that used to be way out there are right in town now."

Sandy: "I miss Flagstaff when it was like that. Do you?"

"I liked it when there was no Wal-Mart, I miss the Yellow Front and Penny's General Store, but I wouldn't mind if they'd put in a Trader Joe's."

Two hours later, on the sidewalk beside her truck, Shirley said, "I brought a show and tell," and unfolded a four-foot section of a quilt—"This is the one I'm working on this winter"—and we held it open in the sunlight. "This one is for my friend's daughter when she goes to college next Fall."

"Oh Shirley, it's beautiful, look at the colors!"

"It's so beautifully done."

"It's art."

"How long have you been quilting?"

"I started when we lived at the Grand Canyon, but I didn't spend too much time at it until we moved to Blue Ridge. I must have made hundreds by now." She laughed. "Now I piece by machine in the winter and hand-quilt in the tower in the summer when there's nothing going on."

"Hundreds?"

"Well, maybe not quite that many."

"Do you sell them, use them, give them away, what? Hang them on the wall?"

"Yes. I mean, I haven't sold any, but each of my friends got one for a present. Every time a baby is born too.'

"That's some present."

"They're on all the beds in my house. I don't cover them with a spread or anything."

"You shouldn't. Shouldn't hide something so wonderful."

"If one wears out, I just make another."

"Well, sure."

"If I make one that's memories, you know, reminds me of somebody or something, I keep it and hang it on the wall."

"Oh, you'd have to keep those."

I can't say I really know those two women, we've never discussed Big Issues or anything, and maybe it's just as well we don't. We share jobs though, and I like being with them, they keep me smiling. That counts for a lot, I think.

The bird was soft and limp. I padded a box with cotton, dug a grave under a tree in the back yard and sang a song over it. Then I lay on my bed and cried for an hour. I was about eight years old. I still haven't accepted death.

"Mom, it's me."

"Abby, luv, how nice."

"I was out walking the dog which is like washing dishes, a job that's never finished, and I realized it's been a while. How ya doin'?"

"Just fine. Content."

"How's your weather?"

"Temperatures are up into the 40s, even 50s. Days are an hour longer than they were at winter solstice, but it's still winter and I'm still loving it. Any progress on your dissertation?"

"I told you that my committee approved the topic? I'm finishing the research, and dreading the writing."

"Why? You write so well."

"Research is fun. There are those moments, you know the Whoop! Look what I found! moments."

"I do know. It's exciting."

"Writing has to satisfy a committee."

"A committee exists to find faults?"

"Exactly. Not much fun to write when you're anticipating criticism on every sentence."

"You have my sympathy. I almost hate to mention that I don't have a committee. I won't have to submit anything to anybody."

"I'm jealous—fun all the way. "

"I think so."

"Well then, how's your research going?"

"Moving right along. I saved some social detail for you. Hold on, it's right here. Ragtime was a dance craze, with Scott Joplin the big name. I've got a definition of rag: music played in 'ragged time.'"

"That meant—-?"

"Broken rhythms, shifted accents, syncopation."

"OK, that makes sense."

"But that was just part of it. Rag was also a collection and integration, a medley of folk tunes."

"I didn't know that."

"It had a steady rhythmic pulse, so you just couldn't help dancing a two-step, a cake-walk, later maybe a turkey trot."

"Improvisation like in jazz?"

"Apparently not. There were sheet music and player piano rolls and in the years before World War I records and phonographs in homes. It was basically piano music for black clubs…"

"…which ended up in middle-class white homes."

"Right. The whole craze lasted only about two decades, 1895 to its peak in 1915."

"You know, every time I talk with you, I learn something. You're phat."

"Fat?"

"No, no. P-H-A-T. It's a compliment."

"Oh. I see. Thank you."

"Anything else? I bet you've got something else."

"Well, let's see. A telephone line reached the Schnebly ranch in what would be Sedona—Flagstaff central would place a call to the ranch for a charge of ten cents."

"Imagine."

"The national craze for bridge swept up local women who could manage the time to play. Invitations were issued for afternoon and night card parties at which prizes were awarded and 'dainty refreshments' were served in rooms 'attractively decorated.'"

"These were women who were still wearing corsets?"

"Absolutely. Bridge was a game of brain, but that didn't mean it was unladylike."

"Oh, heaven forbid."

"Here's something I thought you might be interested in: Andrew Carnegie was offering funds for establishing libraries all over the country, but I found no notice that Flagstaff requested his attention, perhaps because there was no Women's Club here to take an active part. At least, I don't think so. They'd organized a Women's Club and joined the state federation in 1909, withdrawn in 1911.

"Why?"

"I don't know. Their proper sphere was still debatable. It seemed to me that an editorial in the newspaper might have been part of a discussion about all that. Listen:

> The women of this town have labored earnestly and long in an endeavor to
> maintain truth and sobriety in the home, teaching their sons and daughters
> that these are cardinal virtues, and are to be prized far greater than rubies.

*They have recognized the fact that homelife is the foundation of all life and
that municipal, state and national existence is pure only as home life is pure.
The women of this city have been the silent force, the under current, that has
been working so effectively through the years, the result of which has meant the
ushering in of social conditions that are extremely wholesome.*

How's that for Conventional Wisdom?"

"Power-behind-the-throne was such an important role that the ladies shouldn't get
pushy about politics?"

"Sounds like it."

"I tell ya—propaganda works sometimes."

"Doesn't it though?"

"So except for bridge they were stuck at home?"

"I notice some groups, but I'm not sure they were exclusively for women, except for
Eastern Star, of course. There was one named Coronado and another called 500. 'Don't
Worry'—I haven't a clue what that meant, if anything. And the Swastika Sewing Club."

"Swastika?"

"I'll bet they changed it in twenty years or so."

"Whoo. Damn straight."

Do ear membranes wear thin or
something, like skin does? Loud
music bothers me now; I reach out in
irritation to turn the radio down. How
do teen-agers stand it, the ones you can
hear coming a block away?

1912 Local news: Several autos drove in the 4th of July parade; Studebakers were
introduced; the Good Roads Association agitated for better places to drive
them. School children in Coconino county totaled 966. A small group of people who
followed Christian Science had formed in Flagstaff.

The *Sun* printed only a little news about doctors and even less about their wives.
Felix Manning went to Oak Creek to attend a child ill with pneumonia. Dr. Raymond,
always to-ing and fro-ing, was on a month's vacation in St. Louis, Boston, Baltimore.
Dr. Miller, county health officer, was still an active Mason and an Elk.

In 1912 Flagstaff acquired a third Manning wife when George Felix jr. married
Lois Anderson, age twenty-eight, born in Tennessee. The wedding was probably not in
Flagstaff: there was no marriage license in the Office of the Clerk of the Superior Court.

Big national news about medicine: the Public Health Movement, a significant
approach to preventive medicine. An American Public Health Association had
been founded in New York in 1872 to address community problems like sanitation.
Progressive Era activists had been demanding for years that government take more
responsibility. Makes sense to me: the country had a lot of infectious disease, which is
not a situation that responds to individual action.

In 1912 the United States Public Health Service was formed to provide for investigation and research, interstate control of sanitation and communicable diseases, distribution of federal aid to state health departments. Eight years later a professor of public health at Yale (the movement had professors by then) defined public health as

the science and art of preventing disease...through organized community efforts for the sanitation of the environment, the control of personal hygiene, the organization of medical and nursing service for early diagnosis...

The Public Health Service became active in the control of smallpox and yellow fever as well as regulation of food and drugs, to name a couple of issues, and its scope was extended to the diagnosis of sick people.

Smallpox and poliomyelitis were fearsome threats then. Influenza, pneumonia, and tuberculosis were the primary causes of death; diseases of the heart came next. Patent medicines were still fulsomely advertised, despite the 1906 Pure Food and Drug Act. I could see that in the *Sun*, there were medicine ads on every page.

But deaths were slowly decreasing. The rate for children under one year was down to 131.4 per 1000; ages one to four years was 14 per 1000. Maternal mortality rate per 1000 live births had dropped to 6.1. Death rates in general were falling as communities took responsibility for clean water, sanitation, nutrition, and quarantine for communicable disease.

During the decade—a dividing line decade, actually—enormous improvements were made in the ways physicians were trained and hospitals were organized. At the behest of the AMA and the Carnegie Foundation for the Advancement of Teaching, an educator named Abraham Flexner chaired a commission which published an indictment in no uncertain terms of America's medical education, and attention was finally focused. The result was Carnegie Foundation money to foster higher quality medical schools. Weaker schools were forced out of business by higher standards. Let's hear it for higher.

Phenobarbital was introduced as a preventive against epileptic seizures; salvarsan came into use as a treatment for syphilis. There were advances in bacteriology, electrocardiography, and surgery. Investigation of the human brain. I'm not sure any of that did much to change medical service around here for a while—people who needed sophisticated treatment would have gone to Los Angeles, as they'd been doing for thirty years.

When I was in college, I was intrigued by the existentialist idea that life means what you cause it to mean by what you do. Now I look back down the years and ask What Did I Do? Raised three children who turned out to be good people. I hope that lives were lengthened by the work I did for the Kidney Foundation and improved by the hours I spent on scholarship committees, but I'm not sure that would satisfy Sartre. I planted trees. I tried to make the people around me happy. Does learning count as doing?

"Hi Mom. Thought I'd call *you* for a change."

"Baxter, how nice. Let me dry my hands. How's everything going?" I wonder whether he tries to make his voice that deep.

"Fine, fine. We're both well. Business is a little slow, but nothing serious. We've been thinking of moving to a house on a bigger lot—quieter, more elbow room, a garden maybe. That's on hold until we see which way the wind is blowing. Economic wind, that is."

"Is it just my imagination that it's always going in one direction or another? "

"You need to keep your finger in the air, all right, so you won't get hit with a surprise. What's new with you?"

"It's more winter than spring here so far, cold still, but I'm enjoying it. Staying comfortable. Feeling chipper."

"Glad to hear it. The past few weeks, seems to me, you've been short on action and heavy on what you're thinking. Is that because the weather's been keeping you indoors?"

"I suppose so. And then, I like to think internal is important."

"Well then, what's news with you?"

"Baxter, that bordered on a joke."

He laughs, pleased with himself.

"No boring stability in history. Right now there are Bull Moosers. Taft, Woodrow Wilson. The big political news of 1912 around here was that Arizona had at last been granted statehood after years of negotiation. You're such a political animal, you might be interested in that. Unless you remember what you were exposed to in school. I almost said 'what you were taught,' but if you don't remember, you weren't taught, were you?"

"Puts the responsibility on me—that's fair, I guess."

"The first primary elections were held in October, with much comment in the *Sun*. Democrat nominations: Henry Ashurst for Senate, Carl Hayden of Tempe for the one House seat, G. W. P. Hunt for governor. I grew up knowing those names, but that's not how old I am. Ashurst and Hayden were in Congress for decades, and Hunt's Tomb is still a feature of Papago Park.

"Do I remember that the statehood story was a triumph of sound thinking and all that?"

I laughed. "Depends on your point of view. Arizona was overwhelmingly Democratic for years; very few Republicans were elected to anything."

"Not a triumph then."

"A primary vote for a Republican was a vote thrown away up until the 1950s or so when immigrants streamed in from the East. I don't know why so many of them were Republicans."

"People of good sense came West."

"Oh, was that it? Well, they did change local politics."

"The state's Republican now."

"It certainly is, like a magnetic reversal. By the way, both major parties had their own factions when Arizona became a state. Republicans were either 'standpatters' or 'insurgents,' Democrats 'mossbacks' or 'progressives.' You can figure by the names which were opposed to reform."

"Standpatters and mossbacks."

"Give that boy a nickel. But the Progressive Movement was as strong here as it was anywhere. Progressive with a capital P. It urged reform, moderate political change, social and economic improvement. By government action, no less. So there were some new ideas in the state's constitution."

"Was the newspaper liberal?"

"Not in Flagstaff, Baxter, the paper here was Republican, for all the good it did. And 'liberal' wasn't necessarily an insult then. In fact…hmmm…I wonder…"

"What?"

"I was just wondering when Liberal with a capital L became a political point of view instead of an adjective…I'll look that up. Anyway, 'radical' was what some people thought of the new constitution. Free public schools—we're so accustomed to the idea that it doesn't seem revolutionary any more."

"Now charter schools are the revolution."

"Perhaps a revolution gone all the way around. Anyway, moving right along. Back in 1911 a clause that would have given women the vote was so controversial it was dropped by the convention. So was state-wide prohibition of alcohol. But—this was dangerously advanced—the new constitution said that 'eight hours and no more' were to be considered a lawful day's work. At the time a twelve-hour day was customary and labor was fighting for ten."

"You know, I hadn't realized that Arizona was so liberal in the beginning."

"Progressive. It was called the most progressive of the progressive states. But it was still sparsely settled. Population was adequate for statehood but… where is that note? I'm looking through the clutter on my desk. Here: there were 255,000 humans within the borders, 800,000 sheep, and one million cattle. The sheep and cattle had no vote."

"Talk about rule of the minority…" He laughed.

"The big challenge to tradition was that the constitution gave ordinary citizens power to make laws instead of having 'leading' citizens do it. A fight erupted over that 'extremely modern' idea. The document provided for Initiative—the people may pass a law without any action by the state legislature—and Referendum—the people may vote on an act of the legislature and veto it."

Baxter was good at following a discussion. "I'll agree with the word 'modern': majorly modern, as my nephews would say. But whether power-sharing was a good idea is worth a debate. Right from the beginning in this country there was reluctance to establish full democracy."

"I remember: opinion in the federal constitutional convention was that most people were too downright ignorant to make good decisions—the elite should do it for them."

"I don't know how you feel about it, Mom, but I'm beginning to think that letting everybody vote about everything is not necessarily a sound idea. I wouldn't say that to the CEO in my company, of course, he has strong ideas about what's not really American."

"I'm glad you feel you can talk with me, Baxter. Tell you what, I'll collect my opinions on the subject and write you a long letter."

"You're on, Mom. I'll do the same"

"Goodness, that sounds impressive. I'll probably argue that power in the hands of any class is inherently dangerous and ask whether there is a better way, one we haven't tried yet."

I've long suspected him of trying to convert me to his way of thinking. It can turn conversations into sermon monologues. Tedious sometimes. But one must stay engaged with one's children.

"There was one more issue that I should mention—judges. In Arizona they're supposed to be elected without reference to political party. That was a response to a national movement of the time to curb the power of courts. But the Arizona constitution specified that all elected officials could be removed from office by a vote of the people, and that applied to judges too."

"Can of worms there."

"Definitely potential for mischief. President Taft strongly opposed recall of judges, claiming that it would hamper independence of the judiciary, and he vetoed the constitution. So the provision was removed. Statehood was approved. Arizona promptly put recall of judges back in the constitution. So there for you, Mr. Taft."

"Independence from the Eastern Establishment, I suppose. It's always been strong in the West, hasn't it?"

"I suspect so. You have to admire their spunk. Let me mention in passing that one of the first actions to recall, in 1913, was against Arizona's governor G. W. P. Hunt. Something about his having neglected to execute four convicted murderers."

"The recall action was a surprise to him?"

"Well, I would think it was a surprise to everyone, coming so soon."

"Right on the heels."

"The legislators also made woman suffrage a statute right away, and 195 women in this little town immediately registered to vote."

"Was that a high percentage?"

"You bet. And a high level of interest, I would think. Of course I checked to see whether my doctors' wives were among them."

"And?"

"Yes. Raymond, Miller and Schermann weren't married. But Doctor Sult's wife Nellie registered and so did four Manning women: the matriarch Sarah, her daughter Julia, and both of her daughters-in-law Josie and Lois. Every doctor's wife in town."

"That's interesting. I'd have expected doctors' wives to be more conservative."

"A League of Women Voters was promptly formed in Phoenix."

"Uh oh. Still going strong, isn't it?"

"Oh yes. Prohibition of 'spirits' was law by 1914. One of the first bills the legislature passed put a five dollar tax on automobiles and set a speed limit not to exceed 15 MPH."

"Now that's radical." He laughed again. Thrice in one conversation!

"Another new provision was a child labor law restricting jobs for which people of fourteen, sixteen, eighteen and twenty could not be employed, the more dangerous ones allowed as the kids got older."

"I suppose that was majorly modern too."

"Exactly. I've been reading about all this hoping to learn how statehood affected doctors and medicine in general."

"And?"

"Another statute passed by the first legislature was for a Board of Health. You'll no doubt be interested to know that the act forbade doctors to prescribe opium and intoxicating liquor."

"As medicine?"

"Affirmative, as we say in the Forest Service. They were required to furnish birth and death records to the state and to report cases of and deaths from contagious diseases. I wonder whether that information is on computers yet."

"Everything's on computers now. Amazing how fast that revolution's been."

"Doctors, midwives and undertakers were required to register their names, addresses and occupations with the county recorder. The big effect of statehood was probably a Board of Medical Examiners to regulate the profession. Doctors had to be certified to practice but only after they had submitted testimonials of good moral character—hard to prove, I would think—plus a diploma from a legally chartered medical school, and they could have their certificates revoked for, among other things, intemperance in the use of alcohol and narcotic drugs or—gasp—moral turpitude. Do you know what turpitude means?"

"Not precisely."

"Neither did I, I looked it up. 'Depravity or inherent baseness.' I love it."

8

My aunt played baseball until she was almost sixty, when she hit a home run and didn't feel like running past second. When she was eighty, she was proud that she could still put on her slacks standing up. By the time she was ninety-two, she couldn't do that any more.

Every year more than ten times the number of women die of heart disease. Ten times. But it's breast cancer we're most afraid of. Aren't statistics reassuring? Cancer in the breast is relatively rare in women under twenty-five; most women who are affected are older than fifty. Most women who die of it are between the ages of forty and fifty-five.

Oh, I learned a lot. Breast cancer can be classified into more than a dozen main types and four different stages. Small tumors that have not spread to lymph nodes or other more distant sites are stage one tumors; stage two and three tumors are more advanced, larger and involving more lymph nodes. Stage four tumors have progressed to the point of establishing detectable secondary cancers elsewhere.

I switched off the vacuum cleaner and answered the phone. "Hello."

"Marlene…" Emily's voice caught on the second syllable.

"What's the matter?"

"All I said was your name."

"I could tell. So what's wrong."

"There's a little hard place in my left breast. Not rock hard, just sort of more dense. It doesn't hurt or anything, but I made an appointment."

"Oh no. Oh Emily. I don't believe it."

"I'm feeling kind of dark and scared. I was wondering if you'd come with me…"

"Of course I will."

"…to hold my hand and take notes and pay attention if I'm in shock or something." She laughed, but it was nervous.

"Travis is so involved at the office, you know. So busy. And I'd like to have someone there to take notes. I might not be entirely clear-headed."

"He doesn't know? Emily, you didn't tell him yet?"

"I will. I just didn't want to bother him unnecessarily."

As I've mentioned, a doctor's family is not always his front-line priority.

"Of course I'll go with you. When?"

"This afternoon before the kids get home from band practice."

"I'll drive, OK?"

When I picked her up it was raining, which usually excited me because it didn't happen often in Phoenix, but I was so concerned I barely noticed. Neither of us owned an umbrella, we so seldom needed one, and we went into the examination room together with damp hair.

There weren't many women doctors in Phoenix then, even for women's problems. The oncologist was a man, brisk, polite enough, but not really soothing.

"There's definitely a little lump there. We'll have to find out what it is, mammogram then sonogram, or we could skip those and go straight to a biopsy, which is what I would recommend."

Emily looked as stricken as I felt. Sitting on the rolling stool, pen and notebook in hand, I spoke for both of us. "Cancer?"

"We don't know yet, but it could be. The most common cancer in women is in the breast," he looked at the chart, "and she's the right age. Even if it is, breast cancer is not necessarily a death sentence, most women recover."

I scribbled on my note pad. "What does the biopsy procedure involve?"

"Oh, not much. Maybe we'll just remove a small piece of the lump with a needle— or maybe an excision—and have it examined by a pathologist. I'll have the office make an appointment for you. In a couple of weeks."

"Two weeks? No sooner?"

"It's not a medical emergency. That lump could have been growing five or ten years, it's not going to balloon overnight." He patted Emily's shoulder and started for the door. That made me angry.

"Wait a minute, wait just a minute. We need some information. What happens after the biopsy?"

"The pathology report will tell us the size of the tumor, if that's what it is, what kind of cells are in it, how aggressive they are. Maybe there'll be further tests to detect metastasis—blood test, MRI, bone scan, CAT. Ladies, I have other patients waiting, if you want to know more, have your husbands tell you how to find the journals you need."

"Will she need mastectomy, radiation, chemotherapy?"

"We won't know until we get the pathology report. Stop at the desk to make a biopsy appointment. 'Bye."

Furious, I helped Emily to her feet, shaking, both of us shaking. "What a jerk! Does he think because our husbands are doctors, he doesn't need to explain things?"

We told our husbands, who did just what the oncologist had suggested: they recommended books and journal articles. Maybe Travis was comforting and reassuring, but Don wasn't much concerned about what Emily might be going through. "She'll get the best of care, Travis will arrange it."

When the country was fighting World War II, there were ration books for shoes and sugar. People who had cars put them up on blocks and didn't drive them because gasoline and tires were rationed too. Doctors had extra allowances: they made house calls then.

Dear generations:

A giant sun spot, they said. Huge flares. Radiation rushing toward us. Disturbance of radio waves expected. Well, huzzah, I was excited. Bound to affect earth's weather. Since that initial notice, I've heard nothing about it. Have you?

Weather here has gone on in a regular succession since Christmas. A few days of grey storm, snow seldom more than a foot on the ground. Four days or so of bright clear weather with night temperatures below freezing, then another storm. For two weeks toward the end of March, skies were clear and bulbs were blooming bright and confident. That was followed by wind blowing an icy gale and snow bending daffodils to the ground, two days of clear but cold, another small snow storm. Two more clear days, another brief storm. Snow never completely melted; crusty old mounds of it were always lumpy ugly on the north sides of buildings.

Is that what's called a "storm train?" I assume the process arose somewhere in the Pacific, but I don't know.

After beginning with icy winds and snow flurries, April turned unseasonably warm. College students were bicycling around town in shorts, showing off their legs. Freezing winds and day-long snow returned; college students were still bicycling around town in shorts, showing off their legs.

The forecast for today was clear skies and much warmer. Skies are clear all right, but wind is so strong and cold that I'm wearing a big fleece shirt—indoors.

The idea of weather nibbles at my edges. I gather the principles that govern the atmosphere are understood or at least known, thanks to decades of investigation. Maybe I should say the principles are at least named. But what I'm wondering is, could weather be even more complex than we think it is, and we don't realize that because we've named it? You are quick to see that this principle could apply to everything.

In the past, chaotic weather has triggered huge changes associated with variations in the Gulf stream or the jet stream. Earth's whole climate sometimes changes drastically, so they say, in just a few years. We could go back to Ice Age temperatures in a couplethree decades. Does that agree with what you think you know?

I was afraid I wouldn't say this well, and I was right. OK, try it another way. The conscious human mind barely functions without order, patterns, categories, therefore we say things like "natural law." What if reality isn't order, patterns and categories, and we see what we do not because of what is but because of what we are? Is reality more chaotic than our brains can comprehend?

I know you're smiling now and shaking your heads because I've always depended on order, at least domestic order, for my own composure. That proves my point, doesn't it?

Oh, never mind. I've begun to distrust orderly explanations, that's all. For months now I've been trying to figure out the reasons for Flagstaff weather, and the more I think I learn, the more I doubt what I think I know.

I don't understand a lot of things, no matter how I try. I've read that the majority of matter in the universe is "hidden energy," invisible to us, and I bog down. I don't understand quantum mechanics either, at all, no matter how hard I concentrate. Like—I concede right away that individual human life, and probably group too, constantly "emerges from a haze of possibility." But the whole universe? Consists of "huge clouds of uncertainty?" Infinite variety is inherent in quantum mechanics? I read that recently.

Back to matters of more polite conversation. I expected my starting date on the tower would be well into May as a result of the repeated storms, (wet forest, etc.) but this morning I called the ranger station and was told I should plan to go into service on April 22nd, two weeks from now. That's the beginning of a pay period, so it probably makes sense to the fire office, but I'm already thinking about shivering in that exposed tower while the customary spring winds buffet me. Good for my pulse rate, no doubt.

My daily routine through the winter, safe here in town, has barely varied. I brew coffee in the morning, tidy up a bit, then walk a few blocks to read old records, seeking doctors' wives. Most of the personal news I could relate to you, as Baxter has said, has been what's happened in my head. You know, new understanding because of what I think or read .

Example: I recently read that bacteria can live and grow and reproduce on cumulus clouds. What does that mean about rain? DNA can protect itself from ultraviolet rays in sunlight by converting radiation into heat. What is it doing in sunlight in the first place? Beanie and Cazz, you're smart. Do you know?

Example: A couple hundred billion stars (suns in case you've forgotten) orbit the center of galaxies like ours. No wonder it's so bright in there.

Cheers,
Mom

When I was a little girl, my father would say, "Shall we go for a ride?" That meant in the car. We would drive up north Central Avenue under the big trees that met above the road and, in the middle of a desert, it was like moving through a fantasy. Years ago those trees were cut down so that Central Avenue could be widened to four lanes for the sake of traffic. I missed them for a long time.

1913 In 1913 Flagstaff was a small town with a resident osteopath, a couple of dentists and veterinarians. Optometrists visited for a few days and saw patients in hotel rooms. Enrollment in Flagstaff schools was up to 596 children. The ladies of the Women's Christian Temperance Union, who had been maintaining a public reading room, were finding it too much for them. Would their fellow citizens like to cooperate and turn it into a free public library?

The newspaper reported little about the doctors, just a clip here and there. Dr. Raymond returned from a two-month visit to medical institutions in the East. A barber was operated on for appendicitis by Drs. Manning—probably Tom and his father: Felix was working as physician at the Fort Grant school. Tom, Coconino County health officer, took a man with "a malignant (?) case of typhoid" to Los Angeles on the train. When a case of spinal meningitis was sent to the county hospital from Williams, there were people who were raising anxious questions. Was it legal to transport a contagious case from one town to another?

Early in the year Sult, Schermann, Raymond and Miller and all three Mannings registered their certificates with the Coconino County recorder as the new state constitution required. Sixty-nine years later the record is still there to look at in the vault in the county recorder's office.

The *Sun* reminded readers that they needed to inform a reporter if they wanted their activities to be included in Local Matters columns. Sarah Manning was mentioned as spending a couple of months with her daughter Julia visiting relatives in Waco, Texas, and I wondered, was it Julia who walked into the newspaper office to leave a note?

The *Sun* printed "It's Local News Local People Want," and that's what it printed. In Mexico a revolution/civil war led by such men as Venustiano Carranza, "Pancho" Villa and Emiliano Zapata would soon involve American troops; nothing about it appeared in the Flagstaff newspaper. There was no mention that the American Cancer Society was founded that year, that X-ray mammography was developed, that the American College of Surgeons was organized. Instead Editor Breen argued in bold headlines that a proposed national ocean-to-ocean highway should come through Flagstaff. He also felt that campers and picnickers needed better forest manners—too much trash thrown around. It's still true, Fred.

There was no warning in the *Sun*, none at all, of what was developing in 1913 in Europe: explosive industrial growth, labor and socialist agitation, imperialism, nationalism, revolution—more New than the Old Political Order understood.

Since the late 19th century men of the old order in every country had faced change with a system of alliances and mutual defense treaties and with an arms race: long-range artillery, machine guns, flame throwers, mine launchers, war planes, submarines, poisonous gasses, tanks. I may have the mind of a mere female, but that approach doesn't seem to me a reasonable way to deal with social ferment. And by the way, I do not remember 1913, that's not how old I am. I looked it up.

Newspapers and magazines which came into Flagstaff from east and west on the trains probably carried reports and analyses of growing trouble abroad, but there had been so many wars in Europe. How could anyone know what was coming? Or how it would affect a small hospital established three years earlier by a group of Americans living in Paris? Or what the effect was likely to be on medicine, on both young Manning doctors? On Dr. Alexander Tuthill, employed as an industrial surgeon in Morenci, who was a colonel in the Arizona National Guard?

Note: The first model of renal dialysis was developed in 1913 at Johns Hopkins.

Depression is a chronic (perhaps lifetime), recurrent illness that can result in serious mental and *physical* health problems if it goes undiagnosed and untreated.

Don didn't want to go east to medical school. It was a different culture, he said. He felt more at ease in the West among people who didn't feel they had to fight the world, like New Yorkers do. For four years we lived in Denver, with the Rockies right there in sight every day. He studied at the Colorado Medical School, worked hard to learn mountains of information. Grind, he called it. Lectures week after week. Boredom. Intimidation. Humiliation.

"I didn't know med school would make me feel so worthless. Sometimes I think I've made a mistake."

There was no Match program back when he did his hospital internship—students could finish their training any place they wanted, any hospital that had a teaching staff. He chose Good Samaritan in Phoenix. It paid two hundred dollars a month, more than other programs paid, more than we'd been living on in Denver. And he'd had enough of being among strangers in an unfamiliar city; he wanted to come back home.

Moving into that little duplex apartment on 7th Street, he seemed happy and excited, and I was glad. The strain of medical school had been hard for him. The night before his first day, though, he lay tense in the bed beside me.

"What's the matter, Sweetheart? Can't sleep?"

"God, Marlene, I'm worried. Scared I don't know enough."

"After four years of getting every question right? You have all the facts down cold."

"But I don't know anything important, things doctors are supposed to know." There was a catch in his voice.

"What things?"

"Everything, that's what. I'll go out there in the wards and be expected to know what to do in an emergency, what's wrong with little kids with high fevers, how to start an IV, how to do a spinal tap on a baby. If I have a cardiac arrest or a kidney failure, I won't remember the first step. I could hurt somebody, kill somebody."

There in the dark he turned to me and began to cry against my shoulder, racking sobs, tears that wet my nightshirt. I stroked his hair and hummed what I hoped were soothing little sounds, but I was stunned. My confident husband who could do anything he set out to do. My Don who knew the answers to everything. Sobbing like a little boy for half an hour. I'd never seen that in him.

When he came home at the end of his first day, he looked shaken. "I couldn't find a bathroom the first time I needed one. They sent me down to the emergency room to pick up a patient, and I got lost and wandered around in the basement. The head nurse yelled at me."

He learned where the bathrooms and the emergency room were and laughed about his first-day confusion. In no time at all he could do an admission form or a death certificate or an autopsy request. Technical work was easy after a while. But the pressure never let up. On call every third night, he was always tired, always sleepy, and sometimes when he had to make a decision, he said, his brain went blank and he couldn't think at all.

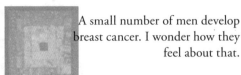 A small number of men develop breast cancer. I wonder how they feel about that.

1914 Accidents continued to be covered, as a gesture to human interest, I suppose. Dr. Raymond treated a man whose arm was broken in Ashfork when he was struck by a railroad switch engine. A blacksmith at Saginaw Camp No. 10 was stabbed in the abdomen with a chisel and died at Milton hospital. A month later a man whose chest was crushed by one of the big AL&T log wagons also died there.

News of doctors became ever more sparse in the newspaper.

Dr. Manning sr. still traveled widely to look after his mining properties; Dr. Miller traveled to take care of lodge affairs. Tom Manning, county health officer, was campaigning against bugs. He and Josie "gave a delightful rag party in the Commercial Hotel dining room New Year's night to a small party of friends." Well, now. Dr. Raymond had brought a woman in from St. Louis to help in his office as bookkeeper and nurse. Miss Hazel Neer—5'4" tall, 123 pounds or so, thirty years old—might have been quite attractive, but she was not the doctor's wife. She registered to vote in Flagstaff in May of 1914, listing her residence as Milton Hospital. Oh?

I suppose it's true anyplace, it certainly was in Flagstaff—a few of the doctors became The Big Names: Brannen because he was first and very active, Manning because of his sons, Raymond for several excellent reasons. In 1914 Dr. Martin George Fronske entered the story and became another Big Name.

He was born in St. Louis in 1883 to German-speaking parents and grandparents and attended German Lutheran grade schools until he was twelve, when he left to work. That was part of the American pattern, as I understand it, children had to be useful to the family economically.

When he returned to school at fourteen, it was hard for him because it was all in English, which his family didn't speak, but in 1903 at the age of twenty he graduated from St. Louis Central High.

I have that information from his daughter-in-law, Therese. Charming woman; she's lived many years with a remarkably pretty face, and it doesn't appear to have spoiled her at all.

From 1903 to 1907 Martin attended Washington University Medical School in St. Louis on scholarships, graduating as a member of an honorary fraternity. Licensed to practice medicine, he did so for three years (here's an archaic detail) in the front room of his family's home.

An older doctor named H.J. Harnish did what he could for Martin, including introducing the young man to his daughter, Hilda Ann. In 1911, age twenty-four, she married Martin Fronske, who was twenty-eight, and they went on a wedding trip to Los Angeles, San Francisco, Salt Lake, Denver and back to St. Louis. Probably on trains.

They hadn't been home from traveling long when he contracted scarlet fever from a patient, so the story goes. It's hard to tell from an old diagnosis what might have been going on—look at John and Anna Hawks' causes of death listed as "paralysis of the heart." When Martin began bleeding from his lungs, Dr. Harnish decided he was tubercular. Given statistics of that time, TB would have been a safe enough guess.

In the spring of 1912, Martin and Hilda went west to Albuquerque, where they lived for a while hoping for a cure in the high desert air. He seemed to improve, they went home to St. Louis, and his symptoms returned. Daily hemorrhages—bad sign.

Martin and Dr. R. O. Raymond, seven years older, had both attended Washington University Medical School. Raymond had moved to Williams, also with a diagnosis of tuberculosis, and then to Flagstaff to take on the practice of Dr. Brannen. In January of 1914, after Dr. Raymond wrote to St. Louis requesting Washington University to recommend a doctor, Martin Fronske came to Arizona for a few days to look the situation over and talk about the possibility of association with Albert Schermann.

In March, thirty-one years old, he traveled west with Hilda to Flagstaff in the new state of Arizona. Later he said, "When I came, pretty nearly every front on Front Street was a saloon, open day and night." For a while, they stayed at the Commercial Hotel while Martin placed his credentials on file and moved into Dr. Raymond's office. The *Sun* mentioned it briefly.

> *Dr. M.G. Fronske and wife of St.Louis are recent arrivals in Flagstaff. Dr. Fronske will assist Dr. R.O. Raymond during the absence of Dr. Sherman [sic] and may decide to make Flagstaff his permanent home.*

Schermann, who had made the arrangements for Fronske's visit, was going to Philadelphia for three months to study at the Polyclinic. Martin was tubercular, hemorrhaging daily, and he went right to work? Well OK, maybe. I was a doctor's wife, but I don't know everything.

In old records the names of the three men were entwined with that of Milton Hospital for a while. When Schermann returned from Philadelphia, Raymond, who wanted specialized training "for eye work," left Fronske to attend to his patients. After he came back, the two "doctored" together. Fronske worked with Schermann at the hospital for five years or so; when Schermann went to New York for Eye, Nose and Throat studies, he left Fronske in charge. Finally Fronske opened his own office.

In 1914, the year he came to Flagstaff, news about Mexico's civil war appeared briefly in the paper. And treaty trouble was building into a major storm in Europe. On June 28 Archduke Franz Ferdinand, heir to the Austria-Hungary Empire, and his wife Sophie were assassinated in Serbia. Austria-Hungary made demands and a month of bellicose debate followed. The *Sun* had nothing to say about it.

Within four months, starting at harvest time (What were they thinking?) nations declared war in all directions beginning with Austria-Hungary against Serbia and Russia. Medicine hasn't been the same since.

Austria, Germany, and Turkey were arrayed against England, France, Montenegro, Russia, and Japan. England's Royal Navy confined the German fleet in the Baltic, blockaded German ports, and placed mines in the Channel. Germany declared the waters surrounding Great Britain a war zone and warned America and other shippers. I'm sure it was all terribly rational.

There's no forgiveness, I say, for men in governments who start wars, no matter their reasons, which usually aren't very good anyway. Those men in 1914 had no idea how their actions would permanently change everything. Some historians claim they ended everything but war.

German armies occupied Luxembourg, ravaged neutral Belgium and invaded France. Italy mobilized troops on its northern border and prudently waited to see who was going to win. Add the far-flung British Empire, Asia, and Africa, most of which was claimed by a European country, parts of South America, and that was just about everybody who was anybody except the United States of North America. President

Wilson, sympathetic with England but convinced that virtue was not all on one side, urged Americans to be "neutral in fact as well as in name," free of the passions of war.

At the time another war in Europe seemed too far away to matter much. In Flagstaff the 4th of July celebration and its schedule of events were covered in the paper. An "immense" crowd, the largest ever, was in attendance. Dr. Slipher at Lowell Observatory announced that the nebula in Virgo was rotating, "throwing new light on the problem of stellar evolution."

Only during August did the *Sun* report on the world-wide war with BULLETINS on the front page but did not tell of half a million dead, men blown apart by 20th century weapons, men burrowed into trenches, a stench of corpses that spread for miles. It was committed to being a local paper. Range and Market News, Forest Service, a county election, weather, grazing law filled the pages. Voters in Flagstaff precinct totaled 1,272.

In Europe battles were fought at Ypres and the Marne, Liege, Arlon, Tannenberg, Mons. Hundreds of thousands of people died. Refugees moved along roads. The American hospital of Paris expanded to treat war wounded, and the French government made available to it large, nearly finished buildings that had been intended as a school. Within two weeks it was equipped to take patients by wealthy and prominent Americans, men and women who were part-time residents of France. The Ford manager in France donated ten Model T chassis which were finished as covered trucks to transport wounded men from the Paris train station to the hospital for treatment. The volunteer drivers were mainly Americans.

The U.S. government might have been neutral, but many American citizens were not so inclined. The American Red Cross sent a Mercy Ship carrying hospital supplies and trained personnel—129 nurses and thirty surgeons, all to be apportioned among six countries. The ARC put fifty women doctors in the field that first year. Hospital units were sent by Scots and by American universities.

They found chaos. Europeans had been fighting each other since who knows how long—you'd think by 1914 they'd have learned that war meant wounds and injuries, but they were completely unprepared. Patients were filthy and hungry. There were no supplies and no facilities.

In autumn the armies on the Western Front settled into a stalemate in a zigzagging line of trenches that stretched from the Swiss border to the English Channel. Outraged women from Britain and the United States, calling the war "obscene, bloody, pathetic and foul"—an accurate summary, it seemed to me—volunteered to serve in any capacity, including hospital orderlies. They formed their own units of women surgeons, nurses, drivers, radiologists and administrators and paid their own passage to France and Belgium.

Sitting in my little room in the library reading old newspapers on a machine, I was a spectator to the contrast between national news and news of the war in Europe. Over here, women were called into work in factories, where they wore (omigosh) trousers. At the same time eastern magazines reported that gigantic hats were out and a fashionable woman's silhouette was even narrower and sleeker, tubular, in a high-waisted Empire look. Hemlines were still just above the floor. Corsets still emphasized bosoms out of all proportion.

San Francisco was preparing an exposition to celebrate the completion of the Panama Canal. It was to be a fantasy world of towers, palaces, courts, gardens, sculpture and fountains along a two-mile stretch of the waterfront on the bay.

Equally bizarre: the difference between A) local news and B) war news. A) The new Flagstaff reservoir was nearly complete. Arizona voters chose prohibition of liquor by majority vote. B) The first of 90,000 American women in their groups and clubs organized more than fifty relief agencies to send aid to Europe, and a flood of American women, many with their own Model T ambulances, went to the war zones to help evacuate wounded men for the French Red Cross.

A) A lookout cabin was built on top of Mt. Elden, right above town, and another was planned for the summit of Kendrick. Both were to be connected with Flagstaff by telephone.B) English and German soldiers observed Christmas together between the trenches on the Western Front—when the generals heard about it, they gave orders that such friendly human contact would stop immediately. How like them.

Maybe it was because American women were so active in war relief—Margaret Wheeler Ross issued a request to the ladies of Flagstaff to join with her in forming a Women's Club (the local group having withdrawn from the state federation three years earlier), its object to be "mutual inspiration and concentrated action." When the first meeting was held on a Saturday at Emerson School, the ladies, 102 members strong, organized four departments—Household Economics, Music and Drama, Art and Literature, and Civic Education—and took as their first project the organization of a public library for their town. Hilda Fronske was an early member: she performed in a comedy skit for one of the meetings. There's a clue to who she was.

In December of 1914 the Flagstaff Women's Club opened a public library in newly cleaned rooms in the Pollock Block on Aspen with 700 contributed volumes and more coming in every day.

After my father's funeral, we walked back to the waiting cars and left his coffin sitting there above ground, waiting to be lowered when we were gone, and I was disturbed about that. I requested that Mother's coffin be lowered into the grave while we were there to see it, and that was just as hard to take.

Shame makes bad damage. You're supposed to talk to somebody about things that hurt you, get them outside, "process" them. But the worst of it is that you feel ashamed. The lockers at my high school had three chrome hooks in a cluster at the top for coats and such. One day I dialed the combination of my lock and pulled it open, and there was a dirty jock strap on those hooks, carefully arranged, hanging there like an insult.

I slammed the door shut and didn't go back until the end of the day when the hall was empty and there was no one to see me take that awful thing down and carry it pinched between two fingers to a trash can. Ashamed, as if I had deserved that kind of anonymous treatment, as if something about me made those boys think of me like that. The guilty victim. How could I talk about something that cut so deep?

If I'd known her then, I couldn't have told even Emily about it. She was a truly good person, a real friend, ready to see things in the best light. "Oh, Marlene, that woman lives to criticize, she thinks it validates her. She disapproves of everybody, not just you. You did a fine job for that committee. What she said reveals her, not you."

I trusted her, I really did. We laughed and sang and talked about all kinds of things. But I couldn't tell her that Don and I slept in separate rooms. I was ashamed to say, "He hasn't even kissed me for five years." Why not? Maybe I'm not kissable. Love is not an obligation. Sex is not a duty. Maybe I just don't appeal to him any more. How could I say that?

I can imagine what she might have said. Carefully. She'd have talked about men having hormonal phases in their lives too and they weren't all alike and Don was probably embarrassed. "In polite language it's called a 'dysfunction,'" she'd have said, "but golly, it's so common you can't use that word. The rare man is the one who doesn't experience it sooner or later. It happens to Travis more all the time."

Yeah, well, Travis was fifteen years older than Don.

But when I was growing up, we didn't talk about sex, not if we were "nice." There was a biology teacher at the high school, a woman, who was fired in the middle of a semester because some of the girls went group-hysterical when she tried to explain the nasty matters of human reproduction. I've wondered what that did to her.

Emily and I were in the middle of our lives. We'd borne children. Sex shouldn't have been a forbidden topic between us— we talked about politics and religion with no trouble, and those can be troublesome. We just knew the unspoken rule, and we never mentioned it.

For more years than I can count, I've been self-sufficient sexually. Given pleasure to myself, alone in the dark. And there's nothing wrong with that. I just don't want to talk about it, and I certainly never mentioned it to Emily.

I wish
...I had known my grandmothers
...my mother had lived longer
...kindness were easier
...truths came earlier

1915 Small didn't have to mean sleepy: Flagstaff was busy with debate on improvements. Should the small Protestant congregations in town unify into one Federated Church? Should a road be built down Pumphouse Wash into Oak Creek Canyon? Was the National Good Roads Association right about the need to work toward highway uniformity? Babbitt Brothers was building a "monster" three-story garage; street lights and paving were planned for downtown.

As part of a periodic effort to put the Rio de Flag where it would do the least damage, E. B. Raudebaugh had finished an eighty-foot reinforced concrete culvert to carry flood water under Railroad Avenue. The whole job cost three hundred dollars. With a map of the town in hand, I stepped from one railroad tie to another, figuring out what most people had known for a long time, but I wasn't sure I could identify Raudebaugh's culvert.

Local news included news of the whole state. Would it be a good idea for Arizona to register the births of all children? Had everyone heard that St. Joseph's Hospital in Phoenix, which had built a two-story nursing home the year before, now had a maternity unit? that Arizona had the first state old-age pension system in the whole country?

Items about doctors in 1915: Dr. Miller went to Phoenix for his health after suffering "a severe attack of illness." Dr. Fronske was called aboard the east-bound limited to dress the foot of the chef on the diner who had dropped a knife that "went though that extremity." George Babbitt had his face badly cut by the explosion of a tire, but the *Sun* didn't mention which doctor attended to him.

The Fronskes bought a frame house on the corner of West Aspen Street across from the Federated Church and Emerson School. Since 1902 Felix Manning sr. had been buying and selling the narrow lots on the south side of that block; in 1915 he owned six of them. Senator Ashurst's mother had two. One and a half lots between the Fronske House and the Manning house belonged to Sarah's daughter Henrietta and her husband, E.M. Brown.

Women, the usual small comforting details: Raymond's nurse Hazel Neer was living in a house on east Elm with Ida Leisling, who was employed as night nurse at Milton Hospital although she was not trained or registered.

Felix Manning and his wife Lois returned from Fort Grant; in December she and Josie went to San Francisco, where there was not yet a bridge across the Golden Gate. To see the Panama Exposition? It was built like a city with streets that passed through arches into courts with fountains and statuary. There were electric lights and fireworks, a Palace of Fine Arts, Navajo "cliff dwellings," Japanese wrestling matches, Samoan dancers who sang "It's a Long Way to Tipperary," a Dogs of All Nations display, milking machines, kangaroos, Hawaiian coffee served by Hawaiians. What a show!

Week after week ads in the newspaper for a new "clean and sanitary" Confection Den promised to ease the work of housewives by providing layer cakes and fresh-baked bread, as well as candies, ice cream, root beer and cream puffs with real whipped cream. Citizens were invited to stop in.

When the town council requested bids for nine miles of cement sidewalks downtown, some people said, "Give the job to the Women's Club. They'll get it done faster." They certainly were "go-getters." Under chairman Nellie Sult, membership had more than doubled, and the ladies had published a cook book and sponsored a dance at the Majestic Theater to raise money for the public library, which was thriving. By year's end 4,529 books had been loaned to readers. Every week's issue of the *Sun* carried news, prominently displayed, of the library and the club, perhaps because Editor Breens' wife Caroline was in charge of publicity.

In addition to Nellie Sult and Hilda Fronske, Josie Manning was also a Women's Club member. In the society columns written by Annie Noble, she appeared to be a worthy successor to Felicia Brannen: in almost every issue there were a few lines about her social doings. She gave "a delightful little luncheon" with a table color scheme of "delicate pink and white." She and Tom were members of the Southwest Club. His county duties kept him moving in his new Hupmobile; she visited Los Angeles. One evening the two of them entertained three tables of guests at cards.

Hilda Fronske visited for a month with her relatives in the east, came back and gave birth to a boy at Milton Hospital. On Christmas day she and Martin entertained two couples at a holiday dinner party—just a few days before a storm dropped five feet of snow.

Whether Editor Breen wanted to write about it or not, the horrible war in Europe, expected by combatants to end within weeks, dragged on and on—Zeppelin raids on London, men in trenches who suffered ghastly face and head wounds. In April, conditions were atrocious at Gallipoli because of bungling by British commanders, most of whom held commissions by virtue of social class.

Over here we were most concerned about naval matters—we established embargoes on food and supplies for Central Europe but not for England, and Germany of course considered the action anything but neutral. German submarines sank British ships with the loss of a few American lives. We protested; Germany announced a war zone around England that neutral ships could avoid by staying away.

In May the liner Lusitania, with 129 children on board, was sunk off the southern coast of Ireland by a German U-boat. 1,200 lives were lost including 291 women, 94 of the children, and 128 U.S citizens. Obviously the Germans were frightful people, and the Kaiser was a demon. Germany agreed to pay damages and allow neutral ships free sea voyages and went right on torpedoing. The American fleet moved out into the Atlantic for "war game maneuvers."

In June the Turks massacred Armenians in the eastern sections of the country. In November 30,000 Serbian boys between twelve and eighteen were ordered to retreat across mountains to save them from capture by the enemy. Only 7000 survived. People at war behave abominably, in case no one has noticed.

"Atrocity" was an appropriate word; it was wholesale atrocity. The first medical people who were there said:

> ...primitive and unhygienic resources...80% of the first wounded died of gangrene...no modern equipment of any kind...the generals are old, the surgeons are old, the hospitals are old, the nurses are old, the material is old...hideous mutilation is the rule, not the exception...

People shot shells filled with four kinds of gasses at other people on *purpose*:

- tear gas, which attacked eyes
- gas that caused incapacitating vomiting
- suffocants, lung irritants that resulted in pneumonia,pulmonary edema, failing circulation, fluids draining from nostrils, blood turning thick and dark
- skin irritants, mustard gas that caused burns and skin lesions, injury to blood vessels, separation of the epidermis from underlying connective tissue, gangrene in lungs, lesions in internal organs

From August 1914 through 1915, 2,622 injury cases had been admitted to the Ambulance Hospital in Paris. By the end of 1915 it had fifty wards with 575 beds and ten medical departments. From the front line men were carried by litter to a first aid station, then to advanced dressing stations where doctors cleaned and dressed wounds, immobilized fractures and amputated if necessary. After that the wounded were carried to triage hospitals where they were sorted into three groups: can't be saved, might be saved, can be saved. The third group was first to be evacuated to hospitals to wait their turn for loading onto railroad cars and taken to Paris, where they were placed on ambulances for Model T transportation to urban hospitals.

Estimated cost of the war for combatants at the end of 1915 was more than twelve million dollars.

In 1915 aspirin was available in tablets manufactured by the Bayer firm in Germany.

In 1915 almost a fifth of American doctors were women.

A cousin of a Flagstaff man drowned when his ship was sunk by a U-boat. A local man was thought to be on a British troop ship that was sunk. No one had heard from him.

A little geologic knowledge can confuse an amateur something wonderful. I thought I had figured out that the Kaiparowits Plateau, formed from muds and silts, was higher than the Grand Staircase and younger in time. That would mean that under the gray-black shale of the Plateau all the layers of the Staircase lay hidden, wouldn't it? If they were, none of my books came right out and said so.

Under the surface that I drove across were an estimated sixty-two billion tons of coal, so the books assured me, ten trillion cubic feet of gas, and an unknown amount of oil. That meant the land was once covered with forest, didn't it? It's not forested now.

The travel guidebooks I carried with me described the Kaiparowits as more than 800,000 acres of "fierce and dangerous …arid and desiccated …wild and remote" rock that contained "the best and most continuous record of Late Cretaceous terrestrial life in the world." About eighty miles to the south, where a maze of canyons dropped down to Lake Powell, there were a couple of creeks that carried water sometimes, but in the whole Kaiparowits not a single river and only one four wheel drive road, which "might become impassable in inclement weather."

Seventeen species of raptor—OK. Lizards. Mice maybe. But I'd have trouble believing the Anasazi ever tried to live there. Did Mormons actually trek across?

Highway 12 was almost deserted across The Blues, past Coal Bed Canyon, which was north of Death Ridge. Somewhere in there were the Burning Hills, red because underground coal fires had oxidized overlying strata. I thought fire needed oxygen, but maybe I was wrong.

The sun was only halfway to noon. Don was still sleeping behind me on the couch, and it was just as well. He'd have found plenty to complain about. Too much sky indeed. I drove toward Escalante, wondering about that Smokey Mountain Road down to Big Water. Who drove it and why? Who made it and why?

It's perfectly natural: I don't understand normal people who devote their lives to doing things that don't interest me—climbing Everest, diving into black ocean, shooting birds, driving race cars, drinking to insensibility. And those long-gone walkers into the unknown who wandered through the West. Maybe they were fleeing or seeking something personal. Who can tell?

When Don was in medical school, we didn't have much money, but every Spring I went without lunch to buy jonquils as soon as they appeared in the store—they meant that much to me. A bunch was twenty cents, which was what it cost to eat lunch. I've bought jonquils every Spring since then.

late April

Dear basic support group,

Official change of plans here. My assigned starting date for fire season 2001 was April 22. Now it's May 6. Nobody told me why, leaving me to make up reasons of my own. Snow is just as likely to be falling in May as April. And wind blowing. And me wrapped in a blanket.

This morning I left a town where fruit trees were blossoming in bright mounds of pink and white and drove up to Woody Mountain to see what has to be done before I can open the cabin and tower. A pair of ducks swam on the little pond below the gate, and there were small patches of snow here and there, and the ground was damp but not stuck-in-the-mud wet, and I had no trouble until I drove around a curve high on the east side to see a big dead tree that had fallen across the road. I did the practical thing: got out and looked at it. No question of lifting it or rolling it. I didn't have a chain saw and don't know how to use one anyway.

Under the seat in my 4Runner I have a heavy strap, and it didn't get there by accident: I put it there myself on the theory that any emergency you're prepared for isn't really an emergency. Moving delicately and fastidiously, getting just a touch of dirt on my knees, I looped the heavy strap—designed to tow air gliders—around the big base of the tree and fastened it to my SUV frame and backed up slowly. Well, I tell you, it was a thrill. While I cheered—yahoo!—that tree moved as if it were alive and kept moving and moving until I had pulled the whole thing to the side of the road. I don't know when I've felt more powerful, more capable, more macho.

I set the emergency brake, got out and freed the strap and coiled it and slid it back under the seat. If you aren't impressed with me now, there's no hope for you.

After that feat, I drove on to the top and climbed my tower. Oak and aspen trees were still bare. Snow shone on the Peaks. Despite those waves of storms that came through all winter, there was little water in Rogers Lake. The big horse barn built last year on the south shore by Georgia Frontierre (owner of the Rams football team) is still there. My wealthy neighbor— I'll probably never see her.

The shapes of the land around me were exactly the same. Voices on the radio were familiar. The firefinder was still accurate on its marks. When I unlocked the cabin and walked in, I heard the sound of my footsteps on the floor and realized it is distinct from the sound of the floor in town.

Last year's raging summer wildfires killed seventeen people in the West and destroyed 860 buildings. This year there have already been more than 2200 wildfires in Florida as a consequence of four years of drought. Fires are burning already in Georgia. In the West, fires could be even worse than last year: winter snowpack is at half its usual depth, and severe drought is expected for most of Idaho and much of Montana and Washington State. And Arizona? What will happen in Arizona?

News: an Intergovernmental Panel on Climate Change reports that warmer global temperatures could cause colder winters. What? What was that? The argument goes like this: warmer temperatures will result in efforts to reduce pollution in the air, which will result in clearer air with fewer greenhouse gases, which will result in lower temperatures. But fewer sulfate particles in the air to block the sun could result in warmer temperatures. Did I miss a step here?

News: After years of annual slashes, our fire prevention and recovery budgets will be doubled for next summer, thanks to Congress. The Coconino will have $10 million more than expected. Thus more firefighters, more thinning and burning to reduce fuels on more than 19,000 acres. Nothing has been said yet about money to paint and maintain lookout towers.

Muchas Smooches,
Mom

I had secret power fantasies. All I had to do was point my finger. I was standing on the sidewalk that day when the Germans marched into Paris. With my hand at my side, I pointed at the soldiers as they went past. Their testicles fell off and slid down their legs. At first they hesitated and stumbled; then they noticed the blood on their pants and began to howl. Lines of uniformed men came on, and I kept pointing. At the time I thought it was my revulsion against war; now I suspect there was more to it than that, and I'm surprised at how angry I was then.

Don's back was a slab without contours. Muscle lay on either side of Lyle's spine and made a valley from his shoulder blades to his waist. I discovered it the first time he kissed me, really kissed mouth to mouth with a full embrace, and my arms went around him and my fingers touched, and there was that wonderful groove beneath his shirt. At the time it seemed important.

He took Wednesdays away from dermatology, he said, and made up for it on "Pimple Saturday." Now and then he'd call. "I've just heard about some petroglyphs up a wash north of Carefree. Like to take a hike and see if we can find them?"

"A hike or a climb?"

"A stroll on sand. You're the only person I know who wouldn't freak out at being off pavement."

One of those people who fall for a compliment every time, I said, "Hey, I'm a girl of the golden west, I don't scare easy."

"I knew it. Can you be ready to go at ten this morning?"

It was a mile walk on a bright November day up a dry watch-your-feet watercourse from where he parked his Land Rover. The twenty-foot-high banks of earth closed in as we chose a route between mesquite trees and creosote bushes, talking about whether the desert was beautiful or forbidding.

"It's not tame, Marlene, not designed for human comfort."

"No, it's not, but it's fascinating. Everything belongs and nothing dominates. I'll grant you it isn't soothing."

He laughed. "Right."

"But it's honest."

"Honest?"

"Doesn't hide what it is."

"OK."

"The thing I like most about a desert is that you can see so far, see the shape of the land for miles. All the way to the bare mountains."

"You're a woman of broad vision. I tend to focus on the close at hand, and in the desert everything close bites, stings, scratches or punctures. Even the trees have thorns."

I did so enjoy being with him, trading opinions. "True. But they aren't hidden."

He was taller than Don, broader in the shoulders. It seemed to me that there was a glow about him. He smiled down at me, and I thought it was approval. "You're quite a debater, Marlene. I can relate to you on a mind level."

Where the main channel was only a few yards wide and big hills rose on either side, we found them, small shapes and symbols pecked onto rock, most of them in inconspicuous places, but high on one tall black stone face there were lines of goats, snakes, spirals, shapes we couldn't decipher. And not on paper in a book. Right there before us.

Awe tingled up and down my arms. "How old are they?"

"I don't know, but unless the artists were very tall, the ground has had time to erode by several feet."

"Who made them?"

"I don't know."

"Oh Lyle, they're wonderful, wonderful. They must mean something. See how carefully they were made."

He put an arm around my shoulders and pulled me close against his side. "You were arguing ten minutes ago that the desert has no hidden secrets."

I smiled up at him. "I take it back."

He bent his head, still holding me against his side, and kissed my cheek. An affectionate friendly little kiss. Like what a man might give his younger sister. Sun shone on his hair.

It was nothing to be offended about, nothing to step away from. I smiled an affectionate friendly little smile, but his eyes became solemn. Turning me to face him, he held me in both arms and ever so lightly kissed my lips. I stopped smiling, but I didn't move.

The next kiss lasted and grew, and it definitely wasn't brotherly. He held me tight against him wrapped in his arms. That's when my hands found the groove in his back.

I felt jolted alive for the first time in years. When we began to move again, walking back down the wash, rocks were alive. The leaves of every plant shone. Sun gave cholla cactus a soft halo. Birds—well, birds were painfully precious.

Twice on that enchanted walk Lyle stopped and pulled me close and kissed me again. And never said a word. When we got back to his Land Rover, he smiled at me and touched my cheek before he unlocked the passenger door, and that was perfect. Words would have been superficial compared to what I was feeling. As we drove away, he stroked his fingers once across the back of my hand. Oh, but he was a smoothie.

Back in town he pulled into the parking lot and stopped next to my car. Hands on the steering wheel, he spoke to the windshield. "We'll see each other again if you wish. It's up to you."

"Yes. I wish."

"I'll call one day next week?"

I'd have fallen on my knees and begged him not to extinguish the light, but "yes" was all I said.

Emily and I took the children to San Francisco for a week the summer when all of them were in grade school at once and did all the things we thought they'd like. Cable cars twice a day, Ocean Beach, Fleischaker Zoo, Golden Gate Park. Also watching fog come in through the Gate, a ferry ride to Sausalito, pastries in the coffee shop in the Fairmont lobby. They seemed to enjoy themselves, but I think I had the most fun. It was so different from home.

When I was sifting through things last winter, clearing away—entering a new millennium, new century, new phase—at the back of a drawer in my desk I found notes I had made in 1990.

I'd gone to the Medical Society Library and "combed," that's a good word, through bound journals that all looked the same, trying to free the text from polysyllabic terms, references, numbers, tables, passive verbs and such hedges as "may," "possible," "indication."

A meaningful proportion of depressed patients have a chronic or recurrent course with substantial impairment in functioning, morbidity and mortality.

Depression is associated with an increased risk of developing other psychiatric disorders: panic, bi-polar, anxiety, etc.

Depression is the most common contributing factor to suicide. It also contributes to the development of such physical disorders as cardiovascular disease.

It may come from within and appears to cycle autonomously, independent of stress.

Onset may be in childhood with a mean age of 8.

When I was thirteen or so, a nice-enough boy that I didn't know very well invited me to go to the state fair with him. I accepted, but when he developed a boil on his face, I made an excuse and got out of it. I wish I hadn't done that. I wish I had been a nicer person.

"Gwen, what a pleasure. How are all of you in my Denver contingent? Healthy, wealthy and wise?"

"Of course. We're fine. How are you? I haven't heard from you for weeks."

"I've written twice this month."

"I mean a phone call, I need to hear your voice. I worry about you, you know."

Control guilt and maybe you can control your mother. "Oh Sweetheart, I promise. If I were ill or injured, you'd be the first to know—I carry my cell phone with me everywhere."

"Mother, don't patronize."

"I wouldn't think of it. You'd be the first. I am no longer out of touch, thanks to Baxter. I've been busy, that's all."

"Busy? I thought you had time to do whatever you wanted."

"Usually I do, and I thoroughly enjoy it. Just now I drive up to the mountain for an hour or so every day to clean the cabin and the tower, getting them ready. And I'm packing into small boxes the things I'll need to live with this summer."

"You're moving? I thought you liked your place in town."

"I do. I'll be coming in every week to shower and wash clothes. But it's such a joy to live up there in the summer. Birds and trees and animals. Wind and clouds. It's anything but isolated. I'll be there most of the time for the next five months. Living on a mountain, I'm close to color and shape and scope. Every day I laugh."

"I wish you wouldn't go."

"Gwen. All those years I worried about you......"

"What did you mean by animals? *Wild* animals?"

"No wilder than I am, I have an easier life, that's all."

"*Dangerous* animals?"

"Ask mice and mosquitos if I'm dangerous."

"Mother, *answer* me."

"All right. I see Abert squirrels and golden mantle ground squirrels and chipmunks. Hummingbirds. That's because I feed them. Ravens, hawks, doves and an occasional eagle—I don't feed them. There may be bears and lions up there, but I haven't seen any. We have an understanding: I leave them alone, and they leave me alone."

"*Mo*ther!"

"It's worked so far. At dusk I hear coyotes singing down the slopes and a funny high sound that I think is elk. I've seen a few elk but no coyotes."

"What am I going to do with you?"

"Allow me freedom. This is the first time in my life I've been free, and I will not give that up willingly."

"But you could be hurt."

"Gwen, I don't think you hear a thing I say. Try listening to me—you might learn to like me."

"I do like you. I love you. You're wonderful. Just flighty. Wilful. Unconventional."

"A ditz? Not what a mother should be?"

"Well, maybe."

"Thank you."

"Mother!"

"I'm telling you something important, Gwen. Pay attention. In thirty-five years you'll be glad to remember. Now, tell me what you've been doing lately that's interesting."

Silence. A sudden sniff. My oldest child began to cry. "Nothing!" A quaver, a choked voice. "I don't have time for anything interesting. I cook and clean and shop and drive Beanie and Cazz places, and wash clothes and pay bills." It rose into a wail. "I don't do anything interesting or fun. How did you do it?"

She was in the hardest time of her life, being responsible to everybody for everything, trying to do it right, and having an awful time taking care of me. Poor darlin'.

"It's just another phase, Sweetheart. A phase that won't last, none of them do. I speak from experience."

Baxter was such a sweet little boy. He laughed in his sleep. Once I heard him singing. I'll have to ask his wife whether he still does that.

1916 The hospital in Milton was closed sometime in the early 1930s—when a "modern" facility was opened on north Beaver Street—and destroyed by fire in 1979. Few of its records seem to have survived. There was that scrap that Kathy found in the Riordan house dated 1907. A sketchy register for twenty-eight months, October 1916 to January 1919, is held in NAU's Special Collections Library. Far as anyone knows, everything else was lost.

By 1916 Milton Hospital had developed a long way from the original treatment facility for injured logging company employees. In the last three months of 1916 ten people died there. Fifteen babies were born, delivered by Doctors Fronske, Schermann and Raymond, and listed under the names of the fathers, not the mothers.

Sometimes there were as many as two dozen patients per day. In a beautiful script, which I thought might be Miss Neer's but maybe not, injuries, surgery, contagious diseases, obstetrics and births were listed with fees charged for each treatment. Sometimes Dr. E. Payne Palmer came up from Phoenix to perform operations.

All kinds of names filled the pages, people of different ages and genders and national origins. Names that appeared often in the *Sun*: Judge Doe, Percival Lowell, Professor Blome, Gustaf Pearson. Pollock, Sykes, Slipher, Babbitt, Moorman, Giclas, Verkamp, Prochnow, Costigan. By 1916 the big house in which the Sisson family had lived was a community hospital that served everyone in town except "the indigent."

In case anyone is interested in housing trivia, I can say that Dr. Tom Manning owned a house in what is now historic downtown. So did Dr. C. W. Sult. Between the Weatherford and the Bank Hotels on Leroux were the telephone exchange, a dance hall and a building for showing moving pictures, one of three in town. Silent movies, of course. I wonder who played the piano?

Right downtown on the northeast corner of Aspen and Beaver there was a corral for horses, a hay and feed yard. In voting precinct 4, north of Aspen and west of Leroux, voters were advised that their polling place would be in Lee Doyle's barn instead of the Campbell-Francis corral.

Another election campaign came around with the usual vituperation. Is politics of destruction inevitable in a democracy? I've been pondering for years, watching the show. Shameful invective, tearing down the other side, not much thought given to the general welfare. Will it ever be possible, in a democracy, to mature beyond demolition?

The top speed limit for automobiles in Flagstaff was only ten miles per hour, but the town council felt that frequent accidents at Beaver and the railroad tracks made it necessary to place a flag man there to control traffic. There were accidents involving autos in other places too and the usual ones caused by train and horses and logging and fights.

The injured may have been tended by three women who identified themselves as nurses in the Register of Voters: Alice King, born in Illinois; Cornelia Sleater, born in Mississippi; Sophronia Watson, born in Utah. County records are often a good source of information, but so far I know nothing else about those nurses.

The *Sun* still printed Annie Noble's social columns—local news was full of luncheons and dinners, dances and card parties. Maybe there had always been such activity in Flagstaff. Or was it cause and effect? Add a society column, and there will be society news?

In January when a heavy snowfall was on the ground and trains were slow and nights were freezing, Tom and Josie Manning held a "series" of dinners. That was apparently the thing to do, High Society, very showy—invite more guests than you could accommodate and entertain a few at time for two or three consecutive nights. Later in the year the Tom Mannings repeated: another series of six-course, 6 p.m. dinners on Wednesday and Thursday evenings. Table decorations were "dainty"—most dinners, every luncheon, "dainty." This high society was in a little Arizona town where the streets were still dirt.

In August Josie was hostess for "an elaborate dinner" at the Weatherford Hotel in honor of her mother and sister, who were visiting. In the fall she and Tom held a formal dinner at their home on Leroux Street. And there was a December dancing party at Herman Hall, "one of the smartest of the season," with 117 names on the guest list.

What a presence, that Josie. She was, of course a guest at fashionable parties about town. Her sister-in-law, Mrs. Dr. Felix (Lois) was quieter by comparison.

Hilda and Martin Fronske entertained at dinner parties too in their home on West Aspen. Hilda had twenty-eight ladies in for lunch and bridge; the next week she "gave" another luncheon. She and Effie Sipe were guests at afternoon bridge parties. With their men they were guests at bridge parties in the evenings. Sarah's daughter Althea Wilson and her husband had a series that included the Fronskes, the Tom Mannings, and the Sults on a Tuesday, the Felix Mannings on Wednesday. When daughter Julia Nance and her husband invited thirty people in for bridge, the guests included the Fronskes, the Sults, the Tom Mannings, the Felix Mannings, and Sarah Manning.

Sarah, fifty-eight years old, was finally a social item, her name on guest lists for afternoon bridge parties (She played bridge!) and luncheons every week, often in the company of her daughters-in-law. When Lois entertained at cards and luncheon, Sarah was there. She and her daughters-in-law invited eighteen other women to a sewing party and served a dainty luncheon. In early December, Sarah and Josie entertained forty women at an "elaborate afternoon auction bridge party"; that evening they welcomed twenty-six people for Five Hundred, a card game that was similar to bridge: bidding, trump suit, tricks.

Sarah's husband, Dr. George Felix Manning sr., who had arrived in Flagstaff twenty-eight years earlier, was not mentioned in any of that. He was eighty-four, in poor health. After Christmas, he and Sarah left on a train for Los Angeles ("the coast" as it was always called) for the winter. Their son Tom escorted them.

The wives of Flagstaff's doctors in those years were, like we were fifty years later, quite a visible group, members of clubs and circles. Josie Manning read her paper on "Vital Statistics of Infant Life in Flagstaff" for the Economics Department of the Women's Club. Effie Sipe was among ten delegates to the state convention of Federated Women's Clubs.

Hilda Fronske was a member of the Shakespeare Club, the Womens' Club, the Federated Church and—for whatever it meant in those years—the Republican party. She was a charter member when the local PEO was formed. PEO: an organization for women eighteen and over that dated from the mid-1800s, mutually supportive, offering educational opportunities for women, membership by invitation only.

"Leaders of the community" supported their positions by belonging. Mary Blome, whose husband was President of the Northern Arizona Normal School, was in the Women's Club; she and her husband attended the Federated Church, where Martin Fronske was elected president of the new men's club. Fred and Caroline Breen were also members of the church; Carolyn was in the Women's Club. Elizabeth (Mrs. William) Babbitt and Carolyn Breen—Women's Club. Annie Noble—Shakespeare Club. Marjorie Sisson—Federated Church and new president of the Flagstaff Women's Club. Vice Presidents were Elizabeth Babbitt and Carolyn Breen.

Late in 1916 there was word that a private Montessori kindergarten was planned for Flagstaff. Skating was fine at Lake Mary, which was "one glaring sheet of ice." Dr. Wilbur Sult and his "estimable" wife Nellie had moved to Clarkdale.

So Flagstaff's G.P. population was back to seven. Miller, Schermann and Raymond were not married; the others were one Fronske and three Mannings. Hilda, Sarah—the one continuing presence—and her son's wives, Lois and Josie, were the wives who were left.

The dresses they wore would have shocked Kathleen Brannen twenty-five years earlier. Underneath there were still corsets, but they were lightly boned and elastic and did not force women's bodies into a mold. Necklines did not rise to the chin. Skirts were narrow and less decorated. It was called "The New Simplicity."

In 1910 hemlines had risen high enough to reveal shoes. By 1914 they were just above the ankle. Critics blamed the war in Europe for what came next. Sometimes hems rose (gasp!) to midway between ankle and knee. At least they did in big cities, I doubt it happened often in Flagstaff. Women wore "sensible," tailored suits with loose waists and military pockets, easy to wear and care for. War time fashion?

The war. The ghastly war that was supposed to last four months and make the world safe for democracy slogged on its dreary way through the battles of Verdun and the Somme, the fall of Kut in Turkey, the sea battle of Jutland, the Brusilov Offensive. Britain instituted compulsory military service. English suppression of the Easter uprising in Ireland and Pancho Villa's attack on New Mexico were parallel struggles.

The U.S. threatened to sever diplomatic relations with Germany because of submarine warfare. Still "neutral," it shipped thousands of horses to the war in France. As the army began to expand, President Wilson appointed a Council of National Defense that included a medical division to organize the profession for war, which Wilson threatened if Germany refused to attend a peace conference.

The American Field Service provided France with ambulances, line divisions, field hospitals, military hospitals, and staffed them with volunteers, young people, many of college age, who paid their own passage and bought their own uniforms on pay that was no higher than French army wages. Many were women who insisted on being there despite what the generals thought of them.

In Flagstaff women appealed to the public for old linen and cotton to make surgical dressings for wounded men in European hospitals. What good were ambulance drivers without bandages? Donations were accepted in the children's room at the Women's Club library.

War proved the utility of x-ray machines for detecting fractured legs, knees, and skulls as well as shell fragments, shrapnel balls, and small pieces of metal in wounds. Some progress was made against typhus and typhoid fever. British doctors felt that the most important medical achievements of 1916 were:

1. discovery of an ideal antiseptic;

2. tracking down four germs which caused cerebro-spinal meningitis and preparation of a serum against them;

3. discovery of a drug for curing dysentery

Let's hear it for war's contributions to civilization.

9

When Abby was, oh, about seven, she sang, "My heels are alive with the sound of music." I wish I could remember how bizarre the world was for me when I was that age.

mid-May, 2001

My singular people,

Stop a minute and listen. Beanie and Cazz, you too. Hear the birds in the pines? Such a racket! Now try to separate the sounds—what do you think? I say there are three different species, probably LBBs (little brown birds) but I can't see them so I'm not sure. Hard to tell what they're saying to each other. It's a cheerful sound though, isn't it?

Beanie, in case you'd like to draw a picture of my mountain top with birds in it, you could look them up in a book to get them right. In the air above the trees there are a few turkey buzzards, two ravens, one eagle, and swallows that move too fast to count. Often the ravens sit on the very tops of the pines.

Every day the first week in May, I drove up the mountain and climbed the tower stairs in the wind, carrying up all the things I'd need for the next five months. Radio, clock, kleenex and paper towels and windex (gotta keep the windows clean), a magnifying glass for reading small print on the maps—all the things I carried down in the wind in October.

Don't ask me, it's probably illegal, but I've managed to provide myself with half a dozen plastic crates designed for carrying gallon containers of milk. I arranged them on their sides under the window bench to make shelves for holding all my necessities of living, and there I was, on the job for the summer— comfort, color, and organization. In a space so small, organization is absolutely necessary.

Once the tower was functioning, I began moving clothes, pots and pans, books onto the mountain. It's inconvenient to live in an 11' x 15' cabin: no bathroom, water from a pump outside, heat from an open oven. The apartment in town is only a mile from a grocery store. Mail comes right to the door. But up on this wind-swept mountain top the world is spacious and beautiful and free. It smells good. The first night I slept here there was a full moon illuminating white clouds floating above me, and I soared into the radiance. You're never too old for that kind of thing.

Oak trees on the mountain have only hard little buds so far—like clumps of buckshot on the branches—although trees lining the streets in town are in leaf. At night I stand on the doorstep listening to the moan of wind in the pines. The tower looms above me, black against millions of stars.

I can see the stars again! I've read that 2,500 can be seen by the "naked" eye on a clear, dark night far from city light. From here it looks like more than that to me.

Comfortable in the sky, cozy inside a little box where Spring wind can't reach me, I am watching cumulus clouds pile a thousand feet above the Peaks, brilliant white froth coalescing out of nothing, turning shades of grey in the middle. Bottoms are already flat and black, promising rain in an hour or two. They did that yesterday as well and produced flashes of lightning last night, booms of thunder, and .33 of an inch of rain. Baker Butte had 1.05.

May is traditionally the first month of a Spring drought, but nothing is traditional in weather any more. If the sky is a sign, we're well into the chaos of change. Mind, I'm not complaining. Drama in every direction is my favorite kind of weather.

Last night I was dry and warm in the cabin with rain pounding on the roof. Shelter from the storm, a safe place to sleep—haven't those been basic human needs, too often unmet, for many thousands of years?

This is my seventh day back at work…Oops, wait a minute, the lookout on Elden is reporting smoke at 340 degrees…I scan with the binoculars and can't see anything…sorry, no cross from me yet…Sunday morning, it's probably a campfire.

I didn't expect to be so glad to hear familiar voices on the radio, from the dispatch office and ground units and most of all—lookouts I recognize from last year. Shirley is Baker Butte again, sounding amused and friendly even when she's being proper. Sandy is Turkey Butte, and she talks with Ed.

"Patrol 2-4, Turkey Butte, you anywhere near Railroad Draw?"

"Could be in half an hour."

"I thought I saw a little smoke down there, but Hog Hill is in the way."

"I'll go on over and check it out."

"Copy. Thanks."

Friends can be fixed points, not as strong as family, not as permanent maybe, but good when you're in need of fixed points.

Seven large black military helicopters flew past a few minutes ago on a line west to east. Seven big helicopters make a huge throbbing noise. Then there were three more. I leaned out the window and shouted, "Where are you guys going?" Here come another six. Sixteen black helicopters, the origin of myth.

Elden's smoke is still invisible to me. Wind, which was two MPH at 0800 this morning has picked up to fifteen. Sun has moved off the east windows, and it's getting cold in here. Cumulus is massing in all directions except—wait a minute, I'll look—except right overhead. I think rain is falling north of Hochderffer Hill and out in Black Bill Park, maybe a light sprinkle south in Sedona.

Up here alone in the sky, I wonder about things. The electricity crisis seems to be spreading—Brazil is apparently the latest spot. There were more blackouts in

California and everyone was upset. I wonder whether the two ravens, glossy in sunlight, that circle my tower on the wind and dive through the pines are a mated pair with a nest nearby.

The daily Fire Weather report mentions twenty foot winds. For a while I played with the idea of a similarity to twenty foot waves and decided that it meant above the ground—a case of whimsy in a meteorology office somewhere. Oh, I think about a lot of things, busy all the time.

I watch cloud shadows sliding across the forest. The first time I saw that, I was seventeen. Your grandparents had taken the family to the Grand Canyon for three days and rented a room at the El Tovar. The first afternoon I noticed with a shock that little clouds moving overhead were making moving shadows down in the canyon. I've heard people say that seventeen is the age when you begin to see the world outside yourself, so I suppose I was right on schedule.

As the sun sank toward evening, shadows on the eastern sides of buttes and side canyons grew and deepened, outlining cliffs and ledges, hiding deeps in Bright Angel, the Inner Gorge, Trinity. The changes from hour to hour were a revelation.

The next morning I read the Park Service signs spread along the rim and turned to look at what I was seeing: a six-million-year reality of water wearing on stone and before that several hundred million years of making that stone. The numbers I could repeat, but numbers so far back in time just weren't real.

For the next two days I roamed up and down the rim trail, seeking a place where I could be alone with the canyon so I could come to terms with it, wrap my mind around what it was, what had happened there. Even though there were not so many tourists then as there are now, I wanted silence, and I couldn't find a place away from voices. The mystery of deep time open at their feet, falling away straight down, and people walked briskly along talking talking talking in every accent and language, talking trivia and gossip. A Hopi boy stood beside me at Yavapai Point and asked his father, "Who did that?" but the rest of them—why did they come? Why did they bother?

There are places you should see alone. I got up early the third morning and shivered on the rim in moonlight. I was so earnest at seventeen, such a pilgrim for Truth. The canyon is not on a human scale—but the tame Village, the sounds of present wind and birds and voices got in the way, I guess. I never could know.

Omigosh, here come six more big black helicopters. Two more way back behind them. Somebody call Rush Limbaugh. Look, there's a red tail hawk, silent and graceful riding the air. A swallow flashes across in front of the binoculars, and I laugh.

Smooches,
Mom, etc.

P.S. Cazz, I have another curiosity question that you might be able to answer. Some mornings when I climb the tower stairs, the sky is absolutely blank; other mornings it's a maze of long white lines left by planes flying very high. I assume traffic is fairly standard from one day to the next. So why are there contrails some mornings and not others? Any ideas?

P.S. Beanie, here's a Woody Mountain bird story. Just at sunset I heard splashing outside in the rain barrel. A hummingbird had hovered too low and was unable *to lift off because of the weight of water in its feathers. Poor little thing was close to drowning. I cupped my hand under it, lifted it out and circled my fingers around it so water could drain off, then took it into the cabin and dried it with a wash cloth.*

The sun was gone by then. In the doorway I opened my fingers to let the little bird fly home, but it hopped to my shoulder instead. I lifted my hand up to it, and it hopped onto a knuckle. And stayed there all night! I slept on my back, careful to keep my hand level when I wanted to move.

Next morning I eased out of bed and opened the door and held out my hand. The hummingbird flew away into the sunrise.

One more smooch

Windy afternoons early in May the city library kept its outside doors open; petals from the blossoming trees blew in and spilled across the floor. On my way to read more microfilm, I paused to smile at them—it was quite magical, especially in comparison with the news of an earlier time.

1917 Since 1914 the United States had been claiming to be neutral in the wholesale slaughter that Europeans were calling The Great War and making a lop-sided show of it. Aid and volunteers sailed from New York and flooded into England and France; official indignation was directed at the Central Powers—Germany and Austria. In January Woodrow Wilson delivered an address to the Senate speaking of rights for all peoples and asserting that the horror of the war gave neutrals justification to intervene. The Kaiser approved continued unrestricted submarine warfare around England anyway, and the Germans sank a few more American ships, thinking that it would take so long for the United States to mobilize that this country was not an imminent threat. Wilson called for more troops and broke diplomatic relations with Germany.

As the winter in the newspaper moved through February—the Manning name on guest lists for card parties, Hilda Fronske's too—there was talk of installing a wireless telephone system on top of the Peaks and of financing for a public library. Citizens were reminded that all parts of town south of the tracks, including the Normal School, were without sewers (outdoor privies on campus!) and bonds were urged to remedy the deplorable situation.

In March, during speculation about a diplomatic break with Austria, Congress made 100 billion dollars available to President Wilson "for measures necessary in case of war." Meanwhile, back at the ranch: in cooperation with Flagstaff merchants, a Library Day raised money for the purchase of new books; Dr. Fronske's paper on "Feeding of Infants" was read to the Woman's Club by Mary Herrington; the *Sun* announced that Josie Manning and her son Frankie were visiting in Los Angeles and that Dr. Raymond had gone to Rochester, Minnesota, although it didn't say why.

The Czar was overthrown, and the Bolshevik revolution took Russia out of the war. Famine in Berlin, mutiny and strikes in France, cynicism in the ranks of all the armies, carnage on the Eastern Front—given the circumstances, the United States seemed certain to become a combatant.

Congress was called into extraordinary session. It was estimated that the navy needed 18,500 men to bring it up to war strength. The Arizona National Guard regiment was retained in service after returning from the Mexican border. I think they'd been there because of Pancho Villa.

On April 2, 1917, Woodrow Wilson spoke in careful language to the House of Representatives. The United States was already in a state of war, he said, requesting that Congress "accept the status of belligerent" that had been forced upon it. It had been brewing. Congress declared that a state of war did indeed exist. Was that constitutional?

It was as much an economic contest as a diplomatic or military affair. Nevertheless, the heavy impact, as always, was on people. Flagstaff had collected immigrants like marbles for thirty-five years. The federal census of 1910, Flagstaff precinct, had identified thirty-four adults who had been born in Germany, another forty-two whose parents—one or both—had been born in Germany. That didn't include their children. Within the next seven years people like the Fronskes arrived. So at an estimate, somewhere around a hundred residents here in 1917 were "German," people with names like Schultz, Michelbach, Yeager, Prochnow, Molenpah, Dietzman. That total did not include such residents as the Raudebaughs, people of German ancestry whose family had been in the U.S. for several generations, people who were called "Pennsylvania Dutch."

The war situation was difficult for German-Americans with their conflicting loyalties—American by choice, they had relatives in the old country as well as customs and language that had meant family for generations.

Dr. Harold R.R. Blome, Ph.D. from Jena University, president of Northern Arizona Normal School since 1909, had been born in Germany, as had his wife Mary. Prussian militarism had bothered his parents, and they had left Europe in 1869 to become naturalized American citizens. During the eight years since his arrival in Flagstaff, Blome's name had appeared in the *Sun* often as he traveled on Normal School business.

Harold and Mary Blome had been active in the Red Cross since the war in Europe had started, but there were men in town who didn't like him and wanted him gone. War against Germany was an opportunity.

It was a shameful episode. A story was circulated that he had flown a German Flag from the campus staff, had even refused to fly the American flag. All but one member of the faculty signed a resolution in support of Blome and published it in the newspaper; the Pacific Division of School Superintendents elected him vice-president; the Arizona State Teachers Association elected him president; school superintendents of three counties supported him. The controversy went on for months.

Oh, what war does to us. Leopold Stokowski wrote to President Wilson to ask that Bach and Beethoven be dropped from concert programs. German-born Boston Symphony Orchestra conductor Karl Muck was arrested, imprisoned, and deported as an enemy alien.

Of course I married. Of course my husband would earn more than I ever could. Of course I served his career rather than my own. Culture imposes rules on us before we are old enough to think.

Highway 12 from Ruby's RV Park at Bryce to Capitol Reef is only 120 miles of paved road, but it's beyond "scenic", beyond merely "picturesque." More an experience of the soul. I drove my moving house into the treesy little town of Escalante at 10:30 in the morning, enjoying myself immoderately. Maneuvering a vehicle that size required special attention, but it wasn't more than I could do. Hey, power steering makes us all the same size.

Don was still sleeping silently on the couch. I had the road to myself, the scenery to myself, my thoughts to myself. Not quite free as a bird. Free enough though, free enough. I was back in red Jurassic stone that was somewhere around ten million years older than the Kaiparowits Plateau behind me.

The Escalante River drains occasional rainfall through a hundred miles or so of deeply eroded canyons with names like Horse and Little Death and Scorpion and East Moody and Coyote— all the surreal and colored country south to Lake Powell. Water, scarce as it is, makes the difference, sets the green of trees and grass in canyon bottoms against red stone walls and blue sky.

Getting down to the water must have been a problem for the Mormon wagon travelers along the benches high above it on the Hole-in-the-Rock Road. Driving, driving, I had to say I stood in awe of the women who made that journey with their families, and I wouldn't have traded places with them for anything. In a jeep maybe. Not otherwise.

Rounding a curve—look! white Navajo sandstone again in all directions, acres and acres of it, miles and miles of petrified, eroded dunes. How did they look, those dunes, glistening in the sun a hundred and thirty million years ago? Highway 12 ran right across the top of them, and before I could think about it I was clutching the steering wheel on a narrow ridge with a white cliff drop-off on either side. I was very glad that Don was not awake.

Down a gray shale monocline and into Boulder, where there are springs. Then slowly up to 9400 feet and around the flank of Boulder Mountain, black basalt and an ice cap long ago. Pull-outs and overlooks I could ease into and pause, engine throbbing, to scan broken country big enough to put the whole state of Connecticut in, so the sign said. Aspen brilliant. Sunshine. Air clear as a vacuum. And no vehicle on the highway but mine.

A long slow descent across a landslide apron, according to my books, probably Pleistocene. Was that the Vermillion Cliffs again? No. These were separated by 65 million years from those. Side roads and trails and campgrounds, most of them inaccessible to large motorcoaches like the one I was piloting. On into Torrey with only eleven miles to go to Capitol Reef. It was noon, and I was having a great day.

It's deliberate that I'm not calling this a story about murder. I'm not sure what the word means. Just exactly what is "malice aforethought?"

1917 There were plans to organize a home guard, just in case, and a State Defense Board too. Congress passed a selective draft law, minimum age 21, and Arizona boasted of being the first state with a draft statute of its own. Class 1 was single men without dependents, married men who failed to support their families, married men dependent on their wives, married men not usefully employed. The 1st Infantry of the Arizona National Guard, headquartered in Naco down on the southern border, appealed for 1300 volunteers, ages 18 to 45.

Military registration began immediately as training camps were established across America. Dr. Thomas Peyton Manning was among the first Flagstaff men who offered their names, but he wasn't in Class 1, so it was a year before he was called. Men who did not register or respond at all were called "slackers," part of a new vocabulary that appeared in the *Sun*. Isn't war glorious though?

Item: When the war began, there were only 400 nurses on active duty in the Army, 150 in the Navy. The Red Cross had 8000. In the next months it would recruit over 20,000 professional nurses, four-fifths of the total number of nurses who served in France.

Every week was a drum-beat of patriotic news. Something called the Women's Council of National Defense was organized—to work, of course, but not to fight. Money was needed to pay the cost of the war to end all wars, so citizens were urged to buy Liberty Loan bonds; Arizona was assigned a goal of three million dollars, Flagstaff $70,000, $30,000 of which was raised by June 1. No possible source was ignored: war revenue taxes were levied on liquor and tobacco.

I found the sudden excitement chilling, but then, I knew what was going on Over There; I'm not sure the citizenry did exactly. Newspaper censorship was proposed for Arizona. Three men were arrested for "treasonable talk." A series of parades and patriotic events thrilled the locals so much that flags were more expensive every week.

In June, when the first contingent of the American Expeditionary Force landed in France, war was finally prominent in the *Sun*. Flags decorated the first page, also drawings of Uncle Sam rolling up his sleeves. Annie Noble's column focused on "doing our bit...for the soldier boys."

Flagstaff answered the Country's Call with vigor. A chapter of the Red Cross was organized, with Mary Ann Pollock vice chairman. The executive committee included Harold Blome and Dr. Raymond; Dr. Miller chaired Civilian Relief. Annie Noble was in charge of Membership, a committee that included Carolyn Breen, Dr. Fronske, Josie Manning, Sarah and G.F. Manning sr.

Annie Noble reported that the Women's Club was for America First and concentrated on church news and the Red Cross (knitting two days a week at the work room in the Presbyterian church), but managed to squeeze in a little society comment. Lee and Pearl Doyle invited men leaving for service to a dancing party, where it was noticed that red, white and blue were the new fashion in clothes. Tom and Josie Manning entertained for cards; Felix and Lois were among the guests, and so was Sarah. And there were still dancing parties. I noticed no more reference to "series" dinners, just theater (movie) parties featuring such actresses as Theda Bara and Mary Pickford and Ethel Barrymore.

I found the newspaper depressing during those months. Horses were deemed indispensable in war. I knew what happened to them too. Part of every citizen's duty was a clean plate: no wasting of food. Patriots ate corn so that wheat could be sent to Europe—they called it "hooverizing" in recognition of the National Food Administrator. In Paris, training was being offered to amputees and other "war cripples" in a school that was a gift from a Philadelphia banker.

Flagstaff's Red Cross chapter planned to care for detachments that passed through town on the railroad: refreshments, a nurse on duty, rations in case of accident and delay. The first "selected" men from Arizona left September 6 for training camp in Kansas. There were three from Coconino County in that first group, twenty-two each in the second and third. By the end of the month, forty-five percent of the conscripted army was in camp. But the Arizona men were uncomfortable in Kansas—not enough blankets, they complained, and it was cold. Within the month Arizona soldiers were all transferred to Camp Kearney near San Diego. By December they were in Europe.

Before the troops were actively engaged, the AEF posted 1200 military doctors on the Western Front; scores of American doctors and nurses served as volunteers. (An aside: Dr. Alexander Tuthill, a Brigadier General, was the only doctor commissioned as a line officer and sent to France. The troops called him "Old Iron Pants.")

In Milton Hospital in 1917 twenty-one people died of the usual causes.

In high school we wore bright red lipstick that smeared teeth and drinking glasses and boys who kissed us. What an idiotic fashion. I suppose I have hippies to thank that I'm free from it.

"Abby, my sweet baboo."

She laughed. If she hadn't, I'd have felt like a clown, which is OK if people laugh. "Hey, Momsie. Howzit?"

"Fine and dandy, as Grandpa used to say. Yourself?"

"Also fine and dandy. What a nice old-fashioned phrase."

"Isn't it? I love having little memorials like that to say. A memorial to my grandfather."

"You know what I would say in memory of you? I love. You say it often."

"Oh, Abby, how nice. You have my permission."

"I need to say it after a week like this one. I passed my major field exams, six hours of writing over two days, I told you that. This week I spent three hours discussing my dissertation proposal with the five people on my committee. After satisfying themselves that the work would be worth doing, add to the body of knowledge and all that, they accepted the proposal, hurray hurray. Now I complete the dissertation, I hope in two years, and I'm ready to face the world."

"Get a job?"

"Right."

"Well, congratulations. I'm proud of you. But I'm not surprised—by now I expect you to do anything you decide to do."

"Vote of confidence never hurt anybody. I'm beginning to think books are part of the baggage I'll drag along as I go through life."

"Could be worse, Baboo. No books could be worse."

"True, true. How's your weather so far this spring?"

"Freaky. Arizona is in a drought, but now and then we get storms when we're not supposed to. Long-range doesn't look good. The prediction is that future weather is likely to be extreme, that's been happening more often than at any time in the Twentieth century because of a warming world. Insurance companies are calling it a "catastrophic trend."

"Which means?"

"Fewer frosts, more heat waves. More droughts, more intense rainfalls, tropical cyclones, and hurricanes in the Twenty-first century when and if C02 levels double."

"Not good, I hope they're wrong. Weather effects everything one way or another, everything—politics, art, health, wars, you name it."

"There's plenty of evidence. We've had more, longer, and stronger El Niños during the last twenty years than in the previous hundred and twenty. Weather, including unfriendly weather, might be locked in. See what you can learn by reading?"

"Nifty. Got any other cheerful news? How goes it with the past?"

"The Great War has started. I was hoping it wouldn't."

She laughed. "I know what you mean. Been saving women's history for me?"

"But natch. Let me find the page."

"Natch?"

"Naturally—slang from my youth."

"I like it."

"Here we go. The Army employed 30,000 women, thousands of them in France as part of the American Expeditionary Force, though they had no military rank or status. The Navy recruited 11,000, the Marines 269. Women."

"No kidding."

"I didn't know that either. The American Red Cross Nursing Service was the recruitment and training agency for overseas work. Approximately 23,000 nurses were assigned to the army and navy. They worked in field hospitals, evacuation hospitals and base hospitals but not at advanced dressing stations on the front lines."

"I'm surprised there were so many available."

"There was a big push. Vassar established a camp to train college graduates—a three-months intensive program—to enter schools of nursing. The result was college recognition of nursing and more picky standards of admission. And in May of 1918 the Army School of Nursing was organized; in 1920 rank was granted to women in the Army Nurse Corps."

"Amazing, the social changes that war can cause."

"You'd think they'd expect it before they start shooting, but they don't seem to. There was a sentimental popular song:

> Mid the war's great curse
> Stands the Red Cross nurse.
> She's the Rose of No Man's Land.

Everybody loved it."

"Still on a pedestal, by golly."

"On the home front, American women were urged to, I quote, 'put aside selfish female virtues and willingly give over their sons and husbands to patriotism and the nation's service'."

"What a load a'..."

"Oh, the ladies had important duties. The Flagstaff newspaper urged them to raise potatoes and plant truck gardens, conserve food and be aware of nutrition, limit expenses, practice economy in dress and entertaining and, of course, assist the Red Cross."

"Genius at work in offices somewhere."

"As we said in my youth—those guys were on the ball."

We also said "in the groove" and "zoot suiter", but I was a little young for "hep to the jive" and "hep cat".

At dusk I hear coyotes howling down the slopes, getting ready for a night of hunting. I won't tell Gwen that I've begun putting my meat scraps out on the opposite side of the cabin from where I feed the squirrels—it might be bad for her health to know that. I hear no sound of coyotes in the night, but next morning the bones are gone.

Some of the American draftees never went anywhere—more than one-third of the young men drafted were rejected on physical grounds. And then, training camps mixed together thirty to forty thousand recruits, including many rural men previously unexposed to the contagious diseases more commonly found in cities. Ultimately disease contracted in one of the military's thirty-two training camps threatened the health of drafted men more than battle wounds or injuries. Specifically, measles (100 to 500 cases a day) and resulting laryngitis, tracheitis, bronchopneumonia. Mumps and meningitis were prevalent.

By 1917 British doctors who treated sick or wounded men had identified four kinds of dysentery, sometimes with colonic gangrene that was transmitted by the swarms of battle-field flies. Dysentery, an indication of lack of sanitation and toilet facilities, was no joke. Amoebic hepatitis and hepatic abscess, secondary to amoebic dysentery, affected the liver.

Then there were:

- two types of Trench Fever, often misdiagnosed as influenza, and rheumatic fever, probably transmitted by lice;

- two kinds of paratyphoid fever, a bacillus infection similar in its expression to typhoid, also transmitted because of inadequate sanitation and mis-diagnosed in initial stages as influenza or trench fever but later developing into body spots;

- epidemic jaundice, another infection that was a result of poor sanitation;

- war nephritis, which affected kidneys;

- soldier's heart, secondary to any of the above, and to over-exertion and prolonged mental strain and insufficient sleep with damage to circulation through ductless glands, irritation of the central nervous system, dilation of both sides of the heart, and valvular disease.

All were more likely to occur in men weakened by cold and wet, which was everyone on the battlefield.

There were medical advances because of the Great War, oh my yes, such things as effective asepsis and antisepsis, portable x-ray units, improved methods of blood transfusion (useful in field hospitals), intravenous medication, tetanus antitoxin. A test to measure basal metabolism rate. Serum treatment for prevention or cure of typhoid fever, lockjaw, pneumonia, and meningitis—some of the compensations. Compensations?

The science of medicine advanced half a century in the four years of the war, so they said. The resulting medical revolution established new directions for surgical practice, especially in neurosurgery, and by the war's end other new contributions to surgery had been made in such fields as brain surgery to attempt repairs of head wounds and reconstructive surgery for facial injuries. Dentists learned to rebuild jaws and teeth. And let's not be naive: the war gave the American drug industry its start by ending German domination of the American market.

Curious, as is my wont, I looked up plastic surgery. It can be traced to nose reconstruction in India in 600 B.C. Duels and street fighting in 16th century Italy provoked Gasparo Tagliacozzi to develop new techniques for reconstructing noses. The specialty in its modern form dates from World War I. As a result of advanced techniques in plastic surgery used to repair faces damaged on battlefields, North American specialists who had worked in war hospitals organized in 1921.

Large-scale poison gas attacks with resulting gas gangrene (dead and dying tissue) brought development of gas masks.

I have not yet read of a new treatment for the widespread anger and hatred among the troops, but hey, Vitamin D was isolated from cod liver oil during the war years, resulting in advances in preventive medicine.

We took our ideas from a long past, from countries far away, and some of them have been disastrous failures. Here in Arizona in the year 2001 would it be possible to develop a few ideas of our own, something new and better?

Of all the demands on him in residency, Don was most anxious about diagnosis of the varied ailments that he saw every hour. Broken bones were easy enough to treat once routine x-rays revealed the problems. There were tests he could order and referrals he could recommend. Illness invisible on the inside though, symptoms that could be caused by a couple of dozen different conditions—headache for instance or fatigue or pains— he said his brain went into a whirl.

Now that I know more about it, how common his feelings were, maybe I could be of more help. Then I had only the vaguest clues to the stresses felt by residents and physicians in practice: constant patient responsibilities, ethical dilemmas, emotional burnout from work with sick and dying people. Courses in basic understanding ought to be provided for doctor's wives.

Afterward I learned important details by reading on my own through bound library issues of the *Journal of the American Medical Association*, JAMA as it's known in the profession. The death of a patient is usually seen as a failure of medical care by the physician, which sets them up, doesn't it? "Physicians and patients often conspire to deny the complexities, uncertainties, limitations, and tragedies intrinsic to medical practice." Conspire?

Sometimes there was open honesty. "Residents share five commonly held myths with older physicians: 1) Physicians should be all-knowing. 2) Uncertainty is a sign of weakness. 3) Patients should always come first. 4) Technical expertise provides personal satisfaction. 5) Only patients, not physicians, need support." They think that way about themselves. Yes, it's true.

Why weren't both of us told?"Those physicians who are vulnerable to stress may become unable to practice medicine without the intrusion of seriously neurotic or inappropriate behavior...Responses to stress include tendencies to compromise work goals, to blame the system for failure, to give up humanistic beliefs, and to increase emotional detachment."

We've heard about a blue wall of silence (police) and a grey wall of silence (West Point). Has there been a white wall all along that isolated doctors with their individual fears by pretending they don't exist? My poor Don, with a few changes his life might have been so different.

Astronomy info: If the whole universe as we know of it so far, could be compacted, it would fit into a ball smaller than the orbit of Mars. Sitting on my doorstep at night, looking up into the star-crowded sky, I find that almost beyond belief.

From the beginning when I first met Emily at a tea for wives, I liked her. Informal and unpretentious, pleasant, cheerful, she seemed the kind of woman who might wear well. I liked her shoes and her hair and her clean, un-made-up face. Her dress that day was blue.

She sat down next to me and introduced herself. "You're new?"

To a tea for wives, yes. "I grew up in Phoenix. So did Don. He came home from Colorado Medical School to do his internship and didn't want to leave again."

"Good idea. Travis and I were tired of winters in the mid-west—'where the wind comes sweeping down the plain'—so we decided to go into practice in the sun. We discovered there was more sun than we really wanted sometimes, in the summer, but we've been here six years now, and I think we'll stay. We like the small town feel."

She and I smiled and chatted and said "how nice"—just superficial get-acquainted small talk. Two months later she called and asked me to work on a benefit committee she was chairing, and by the time that was finished, she was the first real friend I'd ever had.

Once we tried to get together with husbands in the evening. It was her idea. "Why don't we go to dinner at the Biltmore, I love that place."

Don wasn't crazy about the plan. "Oh, Marlene. I wish you hadn't done that." We were in bed. I always made suggestions to him in bed where he was relaxed and comfortable.

"Why?"

"We can't afford dinner at a resort hotel, that's why. It will be expensive. Besides, he's an internist, and I'm only a G.P. We wouldn't match up."

"There's a doctor hierarchy?"

"It's understood."

But he put on his best suit that night, and we met them in the lobby. The Biltmore was north of town then.

Don and Travis shook hands; Emily and I smiled. I think it was maybe the seventies? before women in Phoenix began to hug each other in greeting. Or maybe not—maybe I just wasn't old enough then to notice. Travis didn't seem status-conscious to me; he followed all of us into the huge dining room and began talking to Don as soon as we were seated.

"I hear you grew up in Arizona."

Don picked up his menu. "That's right, a real desert rat."

"Born here?"

"Yes, I was. In St. Jo's."

"Not many of you natives around."

"Population's changed a lot since the war. It's like the rest of the world discovered we were here."

But I could tell Don wasn't happy, and it made me uncomfortable. Not that he was rude or stiff or anything, just not happy. Emily felt it too, I thought, and we chatted brightly to change things if we could.

"You know, Emily, this is the first time I've been in this room. Is it really big as an auditorium, or is it just me?"

She laughed. "It's really big. The first time we came here, I was intimidated, but then I thought, oh shoot, it's just a room, I'm big enough for it."

"Orchestra and dance floor and everything."

"They do it up, all right."

"There's a woman dancing with her grandson, how nice."

Emily's eyes followed the direction of mine. "Where? The one in silver? That's not her grandson, I know his family, he works here."

Don turned and looked, and I felt disapproval just radiating off him. "Works at what?" It was in his voice.

"Dancing. He's available to dance with guests who don't have partners, widows and such. He's very personable, handsome, a good dancer. I can see why they like him."

"Rich old women?"

"I suppose so. But he's not a gigolo or anything. Just a young man whose occupation is dancer. You know, women still like to dance no matter how old they are."

He turned away. "OK." Like a prude. I'd never thought that of him before.

It wasn't a successful evening, and we didn't try it again. There was plenty of time during the day for us to be friends without bringing husbands into it. I wonder whether the doctors were aware that they lived in compartments that kept them separate.

Emily and I became for each other the kind of company we weren't getting at home. Finally we could tell each other everything. "You know, Marlene, sometimes I wouldn't mind having my breasts removed."

"Oh, Emily!"

"I mean it. I don't need them for a single thing, and they get in the way. I just plain hate wearing a bra. That elastic around my ribs. Push-up bra to make me look sexy. Sports bra so I can run without jiggling." (Did she say that? Sports for girls and women weren't common then.)

"Nursing bra when you have a baby to feed."

"Right. Yuk."

"I guess I've just accepted mine as part of the way it is."

"I'd love to have a chest as smooth as a nine-year-old boy's."

This is what happened to Emily: her ovaries were irradiated to induce menopause and thus remove estrogen from her body because estrogen was known to fuel the growth of half of all breast cancers. Fat cells were thought to produce estrogen and thus stimulate breast tumors, so she was put on a weight reducing diet. Later they gave her a hormone-based drug to block the effects of estrogen on breast cancer cells even though it increased the risk of uterine cancer. With all of that, they did not cut off either of her breasts.

When the first Sputnik went up, reaction in this country was nearly hysterical: we're *behind* the Russians, how could that have *happened*? What I felt was personal worthlessness: this triumph of math and science, this technological world, and I was a housewife raising children and doing volunteer work.

1918 It was to be a year they would not forget, but they couldn't know that, of course, when it began. The war was still going on. Coconino County had organized a Council of Defense and something ominously called the Loyalty League. Armed with their new Winchester rifles, the Home Guard conducted target practice. A Congressional bill required an estimated 4,662,000 "alien enemies", German and Austrian and Turkish, to register with the authorities. Later women were added, all German-born women over the age of fourteen, registered alien enemies.

Patriotic propaganda shrieked from the pages of the newspaper:

The Hun Is At the Gate!

Buy Bonds to Beat the Beast!

You're a Part of the Army—Do Your Part—Do It Now!

Fearful Atrocities Committed by the Bestial Hun Hordes!
Thank God the Line Still Holds!

Help Crush the Kaiser…Bill the Baby Killer!

I cringed to read it.

Flagstaff men were finally in France: David Babbitt jr, "Peaches" Hock, Orrin Compton, Adolphus Treat, William Wilson, William Sisson, John Guthrie, Jack Williams, Charles McGookin, Henry Deutsch, Harry Embach—each name a conscious mind. More were called every month, as soon as they reached the age of twenty-one.

Those still in training camps had special railroad Pullman cars made available to them, cars outfitted and staffed for emergency medical use in case of epidemics.

True to its pre-war policy, the *Sun* was devoted to local activity, much of its space given to advertising, range and market news. Letters from local men In the Service of Their Country were printed in "The Soldiers' Corner"—Dear Mother, I am fine and in good health—but they were censored and said almost nothing about the war.

In the East there were shortages of food and coal, and plans were being drawn up for rationing. There was no sugar in Flagstaff, but that was all right because Food Control Means Victory. In an effort to conserve food, Congress had prohibited the "wasteful" misuse of it in brewing or distilling alcohol. That was not well received: right away there were bootleggers in Arizona. I mean, potato bread and corn meal cereal were one thing…

After passage of the Federal Food Control Act, T.A. Riordan was appointed the food administrator for Arizona, Alex Jurston the local administrator. They sent specific meal-by-meal guidelines to newspapers: meatless days, wheatless days, breads baked with half wheat flour and half other grain. Use war recipes. Raise more hens. Produce more eggs. Grow more vegetables. The Cattlemen's Association petitioned to have cowboys deferred from the draft with the argument that they were necessary in the push to produce more food for "our boys."

The women were responsible for changes in diet. Also for making bandages, knitting socks, sending books to soldiers and binoculars to the navy. Working for the Red Cross in its new quarters in the Masons' building. Buying Christmas seals for the prevention of tuberculosis. Writing cheerful letters. To me, eighty years later, there's a pathos in that mobilization of small-town housewives. And a transparency that's obvious from this distance. Illusion is better than being no use at all.

Pleasure didn't entirely end. A masquerade dance was "given" on New Year's Eve of 1917. Tom and Josie Manning entertained at card parties to which they invited Felix and Lois and Sarah. Parties could be construed as helping with home front morale, which the newspaper decided was important too.

Women's fashion during the war years—well months, for America the whole affair lasted from intervention to armistice only twenty months—featured a "slim line" with no discernible waist and then dresses with flared skirts and long jackets or blouses. Hems exposed a woman's ankles, no longer hidden inside high-topped, buttoned shoes. Patterns for middy dresses and modified naval uniforms appeared in sewing catalogs.

Was it war related, men gone fighting, that Mary Platten of Davenport Lake was hired as the first woman deputy game warden in Arizona, responsible for the western part of Coconino County? State officials announced that she would be paid the same wage as men doing the same job. Well, I'm so proud of them.

Another thing: though commercial radio was still in the future, a young Flagstaff woman, Mary Costigan, applied for and received a commercial radio broadcasting license, the first woman in the world to do that. She was also a licensed motion picture machine operator who kept the Orpheum operating for years.

Doctors Raymond and Miller traveled often, though not together. Hilda was expecting, and her doctor husband was elected a trustee of the Flagstaff schools. Dr. Manning sr. probably stayed close to home, but his sons, the Manning brothers, moved into new offices in the Masonic Building on Birch and San Francisco, four rooms on the lower floor in the north part of the building.

Dr. Felix was putting in "a major part of his time" working for the county Exemption Board. Still Superintendent of Public Health in Coconino County, Dr. Tom ordered quarantines for cases of smallpox, which continued to kill a few people now and then, as did typhoid, measles, tuberculosis, cholera, and chicken pox.Almost every week there was a still-born baby or death of a new-born or death of an infant. Nothing unusual for the time.

At forty-seven years old, Dr. Henry K. Wilson, who arrived in Flagstaff that year, was too old to be subject to a draft. Born in Illinois, a graduate of Northwestern University Medical School, he was registered by the state Board of Medical Examiners, and he and his wife Mary, also born in Illinois, thirty-seven years old, found? rented? bought? lodging on Birch Street. Henry's mother, seventy-one, was a member of their household.

Another doctor had come to town. Peter Paul Zinn, born in Utah, a graduate from the Los Angeles College of Osteopathy and the Pacific Medical College of Los Angeles, was also registered by the Board of Medical Examiners to practice medicine in Arizona. He set up an office on a corner of Railroad Avenue and Leroux (in the Bank Building?), phone number 93J, and advertised that he was available for medicine, surgery, and osteopathy, also for testing eyes and fitting glasses.

The Register of Voters of Coconino County described Zinn as 5'8" tall and 158 pounds. (For purposes of identification at voting polls?) He'd been married in Riverside, California, in 1915; his wife Annis, born in Kansas twenty-five years earlier to northern Italian parents, 5'6" tall, 150 pounds, listed her occupation as housewife. She had one child, Elizabeth, two and a half years old. Right away Annis joined the Women's Club and Rebekah, began playing bridge with the other ladies.

Those two men arrived just in time: something was coming that would be worse than anything they had faced before, worse than the war. It would be called Spanish, although Spain apparently had little to do with it. Pain began behind the eyes and spread to ears, neck, spine, legs. Explanations were offered, but no one had an answer. Nobody knew what caused the unfamiliar illness, what it was, how to treat it.

The United States did not yet have a uniform system of federal, state and local health authorities. Most cases of the strange spring complaint were not considered serious enough to report to health authorities; deaths were usually assumed to be caused by pneumonia. The first deaths documented under the name of Spanish Influenza were in Boston.

In March the first wave struck army bases, where men were crowded together for training and shipment. Then people in prisons and factories and big cities across the country became sick. The earliest reports of epidemic flu came in mid-April among American soldiers disembarking at Bordeaux.

The *Sun* reported in March five local people sick with pneumonia or grippe, in April only two. Now and then a case of erysipelas with chills and fever. No deaths. Flagstaff— on the trans-continental railroad line, an excellent route for contagion—apparently escaped the flu in the spring of 1918.

That early "flurry" killed tens of thousands of people around the globe, and then for a few months the epidemic seemed to be ending as the virus quietly shifted, mutating into something never before encountered by the human immune system. The big news here through March, April, May, and June was the "retirement" without a hearing of Dr. Harold Blome, president of the Normal School. Board of Trustees cited "the flag incident" and his German birth as reasons. Two of his assistants were discharged at the time.

That part of the controversy lasted in the newspaper four months. Editor Breen, who didn't like much about Governor G. W. P. Hunt, ran a column charging that the issue was statehouse politics not patriotism. Normal School students paraded through downtown Flagstaff in protest and threatened to strike against the school unless Dr. Blome received a fair hearing; Hunt suggested that the state militia would be an appropriate weapon for quelling a strike; the students responded that the militia was in France. Blome formally thanked them for their support and requested that there be no strike. He was already receiving offers of employment elsewhere, he said.

There were public petitions requesting a hearing and reconsideration of the Board's action and insisting that Blome's record was "without a blemish." The faculty protested that their patriotism had been assailed and submitted a petition in support of Blome. The local presbytery protested his removal from his position.

Governor Hunt conceded under pressure that a public hearing would be held in Flagstaff, then charged that since feeling was running very high and he feared mob violence, any hearing of the case would be held in his office in Phoenix. If there were citizens in that little town who hadn't been upset by then about the treatment of Blome, the governor's insult did the trick. "He's calling us a violent mob?"

Blome declined Hunt's offer of his office. In May the Normal School graduated its largest class ever—fifty-one students. Dr Blome was the commencement speaker at Bisbee High School. In late June, Governor Hunt traveled to Flagstaff, met in the Commercial Hotel with citizens concerned about "the Blome case," and left again "unmolested."

Nevertheless, Harold Blome accepted a position at Bisbee High. Carolyn Breen invited Mary Blome's friends to a dainty luncheon with Hilda Fronske as one of the guests. The Blomes left Flagstaff in August "with respect and esteem," after a reception for them sponsored by Normal School students and attended by 250 guests. Harold Blome died in Pasadena five years later.

Retreat from family life is probably the most common adaptation to the demands of medical practice. Retreat from the non-medical world usually begins in medical school and progresses to a nearly total avoidance of nonmedical socializing by private practitioners.

After that walk down the wash from the petroglyphs back to his Land Rover, Lyle didn't call for two weeks, and then he sounded casual, as if nothing had happened. "Hi there, sidekick. Got a couple of hours to keep me company for lunch? I've heard of a little place I'd like try."

I matched his tone. "I think so. Which two hours do you have in mind? I'll meet you there."

It was a cafe bright with color and mid-day sun through the windows. Wary about conclusions being made, I had already chosen a highly-visible table with separate chairs before Lyle came in.

Not knowing the situation—ignorant is another word for inexperienced—I didn't intend to say anything if he didn't. "How's your week gone?"

"Routine cases, nothing to challenge an idealistic dermatologist bent on preventing tragedy. You?"

Electricity crackled between us, at least it did for me. "I was curious about what those rock pictures might mean, the ones we saw a couple of weeks ago in the wash. Who did them? And why? How long ago? So I went to the city library."

He folded his arms on the table and leaned toward me, smiling. "And? Are those your notes?"

The papers were beside my right hand, sun-lit and obvious. A kind of shield. I had to have something. "You probably already know this: they were made by humans."

He threw his head back and laughed. I smiled.

"And they were pecked on the surface with a sharp rock. Most of the rock art in the Southwest is pecked. They had plenty of rock."

"That they did."

"Do you remember anything that might have been human shapes?"

He cocked his head. "Now that you mention it, no, I don't."

"No horses."

"No."

"There were all those goats or sheep with horns that curved backward. The legs were short, they didn't look like deer."

"True."

"Like this." I held up a sketch I'd copied from a book.

"Right."

"The squiggley lines were horizontal, so they wouldn't have been lightning."

"Looked more like snakes."

"There was a tight spiral thing, but I can't remember any marks that might have been used to indicate a position of the sun. Do you?"

"No."

"OK, here's what I guess based on what I've read. Because it was a long time ago, it's hard to say exactly when or why or by whom or what they meant, but I say it wasn't religious or by shamans, it was a hunting site on or near a stream and the pictures were pecked at least 600 years ago, maybe by women."

"Women? Pictures I've seen always show men, recent of course, but always men as the ancient artists."

"They do, yes. Shows you how we think, our thought habits. But that doesn't have to mean it's true. Why couldn't women have been ancient artists as much as men? Pecking at a rock wall, painting in a cave, that doesn't take muscle. Women now are as interested as men in making images."

"Maybe they were too busy cooking."

"In a subsistence economy men were busy too. Making tools and things like that."

"I have to admit you could be right."

"Look, suppose the older women were considered wise and some sort of magical, there's evidence of that in recent primitive societies, and they went along on the hunt to make images that would insure success. It's possible, isn't it?"

"I like it, I like it. Marlene, you're really something."

After that it was easy to talk, and he didn't even touch my hand, and we were friends. That's all. I was disappointed, but I was also relieved.

It's too late for me to take ballet or singing lessons, too late to become an athlete or a climber or anything that requires a strong young body. I can read philosophy though, and study art history. I can travel any place in the world I want to go and really see it. Strong young bodies haven't got it all, in case no one has noticed.

"It's me, Baxter, your one and only."

"Mom. So you are, the only one I've got. It's for me, honey."

"And you're the only son I've got."

"That's true too. How ya doin'?"

"Oh, not too bad. I just need someone to talk to."

"What's the matter? Where are you?"

"Oh Baxter, you're wonderful. You go right into help mode."

"Come on, where are you?"

"In my house in town doing laundry, safe and uninjured. It's my day off."

"Then what's wrong?"

"It's not an emergency. I've been agitated for a few days, that's all, and I can't get rid of it. I knew if I tried to talk to Gwen, she'd land on me with fifty pounds of advice and instructions. So I called because you're always so sensible."

"Well. Thanks. What are you agitated about?"

"It's the research I've been doing, the history. Gwen would order me to stop this minute, burn all my notes, and go out and have fun."

"She would, you're right. She would."

"She might not be wrong."

"True too. What's bothering you."

"I'm up to 1918, the U.S. entering World War One. So I've been hunting for news about medicine, how it might have changed things."

"Bound to have. War has always been an active force for change."

"What I'm upset about is shell shock. They called it that for a while because they thought it was caused by the sound of exploding shells, compression transmitted to the central nervous system or something equally ambiguous. Later they said "War Neurosis." But Baxter, I could cry…"

"It's okay, Mom. Tell me."

"It was awful, horrible. The armies in those trenches were under constant bombardment—endless noise—in hell for four years, trapped in sucking mud three feet deep. Pieces of human bodies poked out of shell holes and drew rats and flies. Lice were everywhere."

"My god. I didn't know that."

"The first sensation of a poison gas attack was coughing and choking. Then vomiting, gasping. Mustard gas blistered and burned their skin, poisoned their cells. Poison gas swirled in puddles of putrid water. There were no latrines—there was no such thing as sanitation. Soldiers were wet and cold and hungry, half sick from infections, short of food and water and sleep, afraid of mutilation and death. And there was no way out. A sane man would have run away, but they couldn't run. Where would they have gone?"

Bless him, he sounded angry. "Those poor bastards. The generals should have been arrested, all of them."

"They were safe and comfy behind the lines."

"The Big Bosses always are. Did the men rebel? They should have."

"Toward the end there was some rebellion, to their credit. And some of them managed to hold on to their sanity, at least for a while. But Baxter, some men began to twitch and tremble and cry. They developed nightmares, insomnia, depression, fever, hallucinations, convulsions."

"God."

"Blindness. Deafness. Paralysis. They couldn't talk, couldn't remember, couldn't concentrate. Some became catatonic."

"I'm not surprised. The doctors didn't know what was going on?"

"Symptoms varied from man to man. At first British officers treated them as cowards and ordered them shot. SHOT."

"That's criminal."

"I think so. I've read every book I could find, sent off inter-library loan all over the country for medical books published in those years. Most of them just described symptoms and told anecdotes. They were patronizing, you know, 'differences between officers and uneducated men.' There hadn't been much research. They classified: psych-asthenia, hysteria, emotional and psychic disorder characterized by impaired functioning. One English doctor said he would not attempt to 'describe the mechanisms by means of which emotional disturbances cause the disorganization of bodily functions' because it would make his book too long."

"Jesus, no wonder you're agitated."

"Another doctor wrote about 'organic changes in the central nervous system... minute capillary hemorrhages, chromatolysis of nerve cells' but said those conditions 'rapidly and completely disappear.' The soldiers had mostly psychological problems, far as he was concerned. They were cowards, traitors, malingerers."

"Pompous stupidity. Why do we let people get away with that kind of thing?"

"Baxter, something I learned not too long ago—during a depressive episode there are so many changes in the brain alone that it's overwhelming: neurotransmitters, synapses, neurons, genes, melatonin, metabolism in the frontal cortex, thyroid releasing hormones, cortisol secretion, disruption of the circuit that links the thalamus, basal ganglia, and frontal lobe..."

"Mom…"

"Sustained depression destroys neurons and neuronal networking tissue, results in lesions to the hippocampus and the amygdala. Ultimately it changes the structure as well as the biochemistry of the brain, for the worse and permanently. If that's depression, what must shell shock have done?"

"Mom?"

"Yes, I know. It hits close to home, doesn't it? Can you imagine the invisible damage of shell shock? It affected at least 100,000 American men. And do you know what the treatment was?"

"Not good enough, I'll bet."

"Right. Listen to this: encouragement, can you believe it? Complete rest, firmness, sympathy, relief of anxiety, isolation, suggestion, hypnotism. Kindness, work, hot baths. Psychological analysis and re-education. If that helped, they sent those men back to the trenches."

"Mom, I love you. You care about people. Grieve about the past."

"I love you too, Baxter."

"And I'm not hanging up until we've talked about something that makes us both feel better. "

"Like, let's see—one, two, three wars and eighty years later we've got a better idea what happens in there, in the dark?"

"Well, sure. It's encouraging. Think of all the people in lab coats slaving over their microscopes who got us this far. There are some bright spots in human history."

"In medicine too, a lot of them."

"There you go."

"Oh, Baxter, you know what I think? The whole history of humanity has been one long shriek, so I have an obligation to be happy if I can, you know, for the sake of all my grandmothers.

"It's a good philosophy."

"What else shall we talk about?"

"Can you plant flowers on the mountain?"

"Last June I did, marigolds, a long border of them. Something came the first night and ate every one down to the ground. Let's hear it for the natural world." I was crying.

Item: There are people with a genetic predisposition to develop depression.

Item: Depression can lead to premature death.

1918 More than 300,000 American soldiers were landing at French ports. A stream of young men had been called up, and the Coconino Sun began to mention casualties, prisoners, rehabilitation of the wounded. Doctors were desperately needed in the battle zones: both of the Manning brothers volunteered to the Army Medical Corps—as did twenty-two per cent of other Arizona doctors—and left for examination in Douglas. They passed and came back to await a call. In July Felix reported for service; Lois went to her former home in Graham county until his release.

The second American hospital in France, staffed by rotating units of doctors and nurses from medical schools in the U.S., was closer to the front than the big hospital in Paris. As the war intensified, the Surgeon General called for a thousand new nurses a week. A total of 25,000 were needed—a request went out for volunteers. Women who stayed at home were urged to work for the Red Cross, which Wilson called "an important auxiliary to the armed forces," and by the way, could the Red Cross provide thousands of stenographers to Washington?

In early August the first Flagstaff man was reported wounded in battle, Pantaleon Griego. The sugar shortage was growing worse. Food conservation meetings were held in the library, and citizens were told to eat less. Newspapers were informed they must conserve paper. There was a Fair Price Board.

It was probably inevitable: there were full-page ads for "Liberty Loans", and a "Badge of Shame" was proposed to mark those who hadn't contributed money to the war. Profiteering was defined as "inordinate greed and bare-faced fraud."

More than one-third of American doctors were in France when in late summer the flu virus, not dead at all, exploded to life again in Europe, in eastern cities, in army camps where hundreds of thousands of recruits were in training—and moved west in lethal waves that appeared to follow the lines of the railroad. Body temperatures soared to 104, 105. Blood was deficient in white cells. Wrenching coughs produced pints of greenish sputum. Body organs failed. Oxygen-starved skin turned blue, purple, mahogany brown, the color of wet ashes, as victims drowned in the fluids of their bloody lungs.

Against all reason, the war in Europe went on. In five and a half months of active combat, 60,000 American troops died in battle, 206,000 were wounded.

Most cases of previous influenzas had been "household" illness that lasted for three or four days and killed the oldest and most feeble. Most deaths from Spanish Flu were among people between fifteen and forty years old. The speed with which it acted was appalling: robust health turned to death in a matter of hours. Autopsies revealed lungs that were sodden, blue, swollen, bloody—they sank in water.

Bizarre mental effects were recorded: mild delirium, hallucinations, hypnotic trances, amnesia. When high fever broke suddenly, patients went into a state resembling shock with dehydration and hypothermia, sometimes encephalitis. Body and mind remained feeble for months, sometimes for life.

By 1918 there were vaccines for small pox, anthrax, rabies, diphtheria, and meningitis. There had been progress in limiting the spread of insect-borne diseases like yellow fever and malaria. But although research on viruses had begun by then, they were still largely unknown, and influenza was caused by a virus, a microbe that was borne on breath through the air. In one sneeze 86 million bacteria and 46 hundred viral particles hurtled into the air at a speed of 152 feet per second. There was, of course, no sulfa or penicillin.

The first death in Flagstaff was a teacher at the Normal School, but the situation was described as "not alarming." On October 4 the *Sun* mentioned Spanish Influenza clear back on page eight: sudden and extensive—"a bolt from a clear sky"—a new German war offensive? True, thousands of Americans had been prostrated over the past ten days, and there had been an unusual number of deaths, but that was no occasion for special alarm. No no, just a mild and humane disease that had resulted from a cold snap. It was "Flagstaff Flu", a few cases at the Normal School.

A week later it was a three-day fever on pages one and ten, a cold that turned into pneumonia, although its similarity to flu of other years was not known. Then word arrived that Sgt. John Yost had died of flu at Camp Funston. The Red Cross work room was closed. By October 12, eighteen people in Flagstaff had died. Lists of victims began to appear on page one, eleven in one week, twelve in another. In northern Arizona the epidemic was severe: Williams had 200 to 375 cases. Sickness all over: Holbrook, Snowflake, St. Johns, Prescott. In Winslow 500 cases (everybody in town) with 19 deaths. On the reservations the Navajos and Apaches were being hit hard.

Flagstaff had 400 sick, 228 of them at the Normal School. Dr. Schermann was sick. Dr. Miller had been called to Holbrook, where the resident physician was down with flu. The Manning brothers were gone to the war, Lt. Felix to Fort Douglas, Utah, Lt. Tom to Camp Funston, and their father was an elderly man with a crippled arm—nobody expected much of him. That left four doctors to cope: R.O Raymond and M.G. Fronske, both of whom had come to Arizona hoping it would cure their tuberculosis, and newcomers Wilson and Zinn.

With sickness in every family, Milton Hospital was full. The local Public Health Service took over Emerson School, removed the desks, turned the school into an infirmary, and used the domestic science room to prepare food for patients. Katherine Bader was in charge of nursing them after a nurse who had come from Phoenix died. When the school was full, rooms were used in the Ideal Hotel on Birch Street. At makeshift mortuaries, coffins were in short supply.

Public gathering places closed. Churches, schools, theaters, libraries, courts—closed. There were no newspapers, no police, no fire or garbage service. People began wearing gauze or paper masks when they had to go out; those who didn't were "mask slackers." It was unlawful to cough or sneeze or spit.

In Prescott it was a crime to shake hands. In Phoenix, population less than 10,000, the Women's Club building was converted into an emergency hospital, with two big tents erected on the grounds, and Jo Goldwater, trained as a nurse, was supervisor of Red Cross women.

In Flagstaff there were no "socials," no gatherings at the news stand on Front Street. Local women tried home remedies: mustard plasters, castor oil, Epsom salts. Jennie Switzer scrubbed her house daily with Lysol but nobody, including the doctors, knew what would work to bring people through. As it turned out, good nursing was more useful than anything else.

The *Sun* maintained a calm tone, reporting on October 25 that the epidemic was under control. If my count from the pages is correct, somewhere around sixty people had died of flu during slightly more than a month, forty or so at Milton Hospital.

Although deaths and sickness were reported through the winter, the epidemic appeared to be abating by the first of November. Voters were urged to wear masks in voting booths for the upcoming election. By the 8th, business had resumed, and the Red Cross work room was open again, although churches were not yet sure the situation was safe enough to hold services.

Can you believe it? The war was still going on. The military was engulfed as flu killed men on both sides. General Pershing was sick. Against all sense, the war went on in places with exotic names: Picardy, Belleau Wood, Marne, Argonne, Somme. Casualties were atrocious, starvation was widespread, hopeless German troops were revolting, sailors refused to put to sea—and the shooting went on.

Finally, on November 8th, terms with Germany were agreed upon at Versailles—unconditional surrender with abdication of the Kaiser. An armistice was signed on the 11th. There were joyful noises and a spontaneous parade in Flagstaff, all over America. Millions dead, millions wounded, and this is the way it ended: exhaustion, starvation, and influenza that killed more people than the war had. There were no real winners, not really.

Armistice. Worldwide morbidity rates were falling sharply, but that wasn't the end of suffering. Forty-six percent of fracture cases in the army resulted in permanent disability, chiefly by amputation. American army doctors had cut off 700 hands or feet, 600 arms, 1700 legs, and treated more than 2000 face wounds.

63,000 American soldiers and sailors had died from disease, nearly 10,000 more than those who died as a result of battle wounds—53,400 U.S. men died of war injuries, many of shock. Another 204,000 survived their man-caused injuries. Nine men from Flagstaff would not return.

Vick's Vaporub was advertised in the Coconino Sun as an effective treatment for flu, pneumonia and measles, which were made worse by a "run down condition." "Keep up your strength," was the sober medical advice. "Go to bed, stay quiet, and don't worry."

Flu and pneumonia lingered in army camps. The U.S. Health Service advised: "The worst is over but influenza is expected to lurk for months and increase susceptibility to all respiratory diseases. Take all measures. Stop all dances." Cases and resulting deaths were still reported in Arizona; the State Board of Health warned that influenza had not disappeared and urged universal vaccination. Stay clean, it advised. No coughing, sneezing, spitting, hand-shaking or kissing. Throughout the country flurries of flu continued through the spring of 1919, when the virus shifted, changed and changed again until it disappeared.

By the time it had run its course in America, 25 million people had been sick; 600,000 to 675,000 had died. (Compare that with a total of 423,000 dead in World Wars I and II, Korea and Vietnam combined.) Flu killed ten times as many Americans as were killed by bombs and bullets in the war. More than half the earth's population had been sick; between 21 and 40 million people had died.

There was an armistice that ended the shooting, but it should have been no surprise that the whole affair was not so easily disposed of. In America orders for the draft were suspended, and newspapers were shouting Bring the Boys Home, but it was anticipated that two years would be necessary for demobilization. Soldiers who did return that year were mustered out without pay, to the consternation of families at home.

The world food relief organization reported shortages, hunger and famine every-where in Europe, including the Armenians in Turkey, and the new cry was Hands Across the Sea. 10,000 more nurses were needed in Europe. The Salvation Army called for 800 women for war relief work.

Flagstaff received word that Corporal James Vail had been gassed in France and was in a hospital there. The Women's Club resumed its meetings, and the Red Cross ladies began sewing pajamas for men who were patients and clothing for Belgian orphans. A woman employed by the Anti-Tuberculosis Association of Arizona—a designated State Survey Nurse to work in connection with the influenza epidemic—traveled to each county looking over health and sanitary conditions.

When I was a child in Phoenix, my parents taught me to turn my shoes upside down and shake them before I put them on in case there was a scorpion inside. It still makes me uneasy to slide my foot into a shoe without shaking it first.

10

I watched a raven fly directly at the open tower window. Suddenly it flipped over and came on toward me upside down. I had barely had time to recognize what it was doing when it flipped over again, angled up, and flew over the roof. Now, I know I'm not supposed to be anthropomorphic, but it did look to me as if that raven was making a joke.

1919 Post-war inflation drove prices up all over the country. Cost of food rose 84 percent, clothing 114 percent, furniture 124 percent. Workers, four million of them, went on strike. Of course they did.

Thousands of people were starving in Turkey and desperate for American help—John Verkamp was chairman of the War Relief drive for Coconino County. President Wilson, in France for meetings on a peace treaty, was already under attack for his visionary support of a League of Nations.

In Washington Congress was debating giving equal pay to women for doing "the work of men" in government jobs. I wonder whether transcripts of those debates still exist—I'd be curious to read them. And probably annoyed.

Flagstaff's editor Breen, who opposed a League of Nations, favored women in the workplace. They were employed in every aspect of economic life, he said, in banks and offices and shops, on juries, and proving that they could "fill the bill." "A woman," he said, "should be able to do what she wants to do." Well, good for you, Fred.

He also printed a question being debated in Washington: are corsets underwear, thus a luxury, thus liable to federal tax? I ask you, who had decided that underwear was a luxury?

Despite Breen's attempt to keep his paper local, it could not escape the effect of decisions in Washington and the resulting waves moving outward. In 1919 two Congressional actions produced large waves that lasted a long time. One: idealism was defeated when the Senate refused to ratify the League of Nations. The treaty may have been seriously flawed, but I can't help speculating about what the Twentieth Century might have been if we had tried to make it work.

Two: people with, they claimed, the best of intentions, imposed on this huge and diverse population a constitutional amendment (!) which forbade the manufacture, transportation, possession, and sale of alcohol in most of its forms—that is, it abruptly outlawed a custom that had endured through several thousand years of European civilization. The result was wide-spread cynicism about law that still pervades American culture and, even worse, a virtual system of organized crime that metamorphosed as situations changed and remains with us still.

Nerves are part of a body-wide system of cells, fibers, axons, etc. that carry impulses to spine and brain and glands too, I think. It is complex, chemical and electrical. Then what does "nervous" mean? Does "nervous breakdown" mean a challenge or injury to or malfunction of some part of the nervous system?

I don't know how it is for other people. Criticism has a negative effect on me if someone is trying to modify my behavior, but I'll do almost anything to get another compliment. So I wrote a personal note to Beanie.

Hey, darlin',

Because I react right away to color, and because I like drawings done in bold happy strokes, I like your art and what it reveals about you. You do not cramp your pictures down into one bottom corner, nor do you work in all browns and greys and blacks. Unlike a lot of guys, I suspect, you do not draw shooting and killing scenes.

I think (my opinion) that people who are making art can't hide what they are. Your drawing is strong and cheerful and full of life. So are you. I've mounted all the papers you've sent to me on my refrigerator with magnets to hold the corners flat because I want to be reminded of how wonderful you are. And to remind me to try to be strong and cheerful and full of life myself. Thank you.

> *Love,*
> *Nana*

1919 The *Sun* trumpeted BUILDING BOOM HITS FLAGSTAFF! with a page of news about carpenters, painters, roofers, and cement men. George Babbitt was talking of taking responsibility for building a dam at the mouth of Switzer Canyon to create a reservoir. Though the town had not yet become "horseless," auto traffic was so heavy that the speed limit at street crossings had been lowered to six miles per hour.

Editor Breen was enthusiastic about a prediction that Flagstaff's population, currently above 3000—not including Milton south of the tracks—could reach 20,000 by 1930 if merchants were "wide awake" and people would show some ginger, hustle, snap, and go-to-it-iveness. He solicited suggestions from the locals and published them: let's have new houses, bigger hotels, improved and paved roads, a public health nurse. Beautification of City Park. Better phone service. A building and loan association. Boy Scouts. (There were already Camp Fire Girls.) One "wag" proposed that all the bachelors in town be made to get married. Get it?

Taxes were to be raised on vacant lots, that would be helpful, and George Babbitt offered for sale and subdivision his property at the north end of Beaver Street. The Forest

Service announced that it was having adjoining land on Knob Hill surveyed so that it could be leased and developed. Growth was already so fast that it was no longer possible to know where people were: all businesses and residences were being listed for publication in a City Directory.

As 1919 began, a few Flagstaff citizens were still down with flu and dying of it; the total deaths from the epidemic was finally more than 100 people. One late victim was Frank Hochderffer, son of pioneer George Hochderffer. There was an increase of tuberculosis—no one was sure just why—and Leo Verkamp died of double pneumonia (both lungs involved). Dr. E. Payne Palmer came up from Phoenix to consult with local physicians.

But the big scare had passed. The ban on public dances was lifted—the shimmy was a new craze—and the younger set went back to coasting on Observatory Hill. Club meetings resumed. Annie Noble continued to report Red Cross news but returned rather quickly, I thought, to writing about parties, dinners, luncheons, cards and "a delightful little series of dances" and "smart affairs" at which Fronskes and Mannings were frequent guests.

There were dark spots, of course. As it had from the beginning forty years earlier, Flagstaff was facing "water famine," so editor Breen reported. He urged that everyone use as little as possible.

A survey following the flu epidemic had determined Arizona towns, including Flagstaff, to be unsanitary because of inadequate sewers. A bond election was scheduled, asking all 297 qualified electors in town to approve the $65,000 needed to extend the sewers. Doctors who signed a statement that the system was needed were Schermann, Raymond, Miller, Manning (both Tom and his father) and Paul Zinn. By July streets on the south side were torn up as work began for installing a sewer pipe that was to be made of cement, quite a new method.

War-related news and letters from soldiers still appeared in the *Sun*. Local boys were on their way home from France, every one a hero. Wounded soldiers were registering at the Normal School.

This country is a collection of regional accents, that much is obvious. Not so obvious is the regional cultures. New York and Texas, for example: they don't assume what we do here in Arizona, you can recognize them in a moment. But what is the culture of the Southwest?

1919 Major Tom Manning who had been in Los Angeles "preparing to resume his practice" had come back with a new car. Dr. Felix and Lois and Dr. Tom entertained at a dinner; Dr. Tom was host at a birthday dinner for Sarah. The word was that Josie and her son were spending several months in Alabama.

In March Josie was back; she and Dr. Tom promptly entertained at a dinner party and played 500 cards with a group that included Paul and Annis Zinn, Felix and Lois Manning, and Sarah, who was sixty-one that year. Then for weeks, no mention of Josie and Tom. Why?

Curious, I went to the census of 1920 to see whether they had moved and found Thomas Peyton Manning, single, age thirty. Living as a roomer on North Leroux with Dr. Hays N. Nance, licensed to practice dentistry in Arizona in 1919, married—so the *Sun* said—to a daughter of the Mannings—Julia. Tom was single and rooming in his sister's house? What had happened?

In the Index to Civil Actions at the court house there was notice of a divorce action, Manning vs. Manning, with paperwork preserved in a separate book. The *Sun* gave the story one line; court records told the details.

In summer of 1919 Thomas P. Manning (plaintiff) sued Frances Josephine Manning for divorce, charging that she had accused him of relations with other women, specifically one with whom he had spent considerable time in the Adams Hotel in Phoenix, and then repeated such accusations so freely that it was "common talk and gossip" around town, harming his reputation. He denied "each and every, all and singular;" nevertheless she had taken their son Frank to Los Angeles saying that she would never return to Flagstaff.

In 1913 Dr. Tom had bought three narrow lots in Block 33 where he and Josie might have lived. After the divorce he sold them to her for one dollar. He gave her the house, the car, all household furniture, and custody of Frank. Gallantry or guilt? After all these years, it's impossible to say. He continued as county health officer. She sold the lots in 1920 and left this story, proof that those of us who came later did not invent "broken families."

What Annie Noble referred to as "the social whirl" went on with women who had already stepped into Josie's role. Paul and Annis Zinn entertained "in a most delightful manner" with dinner and dancing. Two nights later they played 500 at a card party.

Annis and Lois Manning were on the guest list at an afternoon gathering of ladies for bridge.

The Manning name remained prominent—a group of friends who met occasionally for pot luck suppers included Sarah, Dr. Felix and Lois, and Dr. Tom. In Annie's column Sarah and Lois were often identified as "Mrs. Manning sr. and jr." but there was no explanation for the social participation of Mrs. Manning sr. after thirty silent years. Was it Lois who was responsible for bringing her mother-in-law out of the house?

Now that I think of it, this is also a detective story. Trying to become acquainted with these women, these doctors' wives, was as much a matter of doggedly seeking clues as anything else. Hilda Fronske, for example, thirty years old. At five feet five inches tall, 126 pounds (Register of Voters in the County Recorders Office), described by those who knew her as "fun" (conversation with Terese, her daughter-in-law), she was something of a socialite herself—500, auction bridge, picnics (Coconino Sun). In one week in March she was a guest at two card parties, a luncheon, and an oyster supper and then went off to St. Louis with her two boys for "an extended visit" of two or three months. The Fronske house on West Aspen across from the Federated Church was being painted by G. N. Baty—which may have been why she decided to visit her parents. After she and the boys came back from St. Louis, the 500 Club held a party with cards, food, and dancing. She and Martin were there, also Sarah, Felix and Lois Manning.

Socially she behaved as we did in the second half of the century, entertaining, being entertained. But Hilda was not just fun and games. Active in Presbyterian affair, member of both the Shakespeare Club and the Women's Club, she didn't just step into a role, she created a new one and became a prototype: the doctor's wife as an active, functioning, useful part of the community. So was her husband: Martin was president of the Federated Church Men's League and a member of the Boosters Club. And by the way, for what it may mean: the Fronskes were assessed for taxes on a sewing machine but neither a piano nor a bicycle (County Treasurer's Office).

In the summer, picnic parties motored to Mormon Lake and Williams and Fort Valley. That was, parties of women, women driving. But not in August when Flagstaff was marooned by storms that caused washouts and bridge collapses along the railroad line.

In the Fall, what's this? Farewell parties were arranged for Edward and Henrietta Brown (Yetta, daughter of G. F. and Sarah Manning) who had rented a house in Los Angeles and were moving by automobile. Felix and Lois Manning were going too as guests of the Browns through the summer while they decided whether they wished to remain permanently and make their home in California. The big family was spreading, as families do in America.

If Felix and Lois did move, that would leave Dr. George Felix sr. and his son Tom, Martin Fronske, Paul Zinn, Ed Miller, R.O. Raymond, and A. H. Schermann in Milton. Is that all? Seven doctors in Flagstaff? And of the wives only Hilda, Annis and Sarah, always Sarah, since 1888 a Flagstaff presence, except for that brief sojourn to Texas. Ever more visible, she was elected treasurer of the local chapter of the Order of Eastern Star, a fraternal order affiliated with the Masons, a secret order for men, most of them white Protestant. Her daughter Althea (Mrs. Wilson? Yes, J. P.'s wife) served as associate music conductor. So the Mannings were probably not Catholic, but I still didn't know their church affiliation.

At Thanksgiving the big news was of a storm with high winds that dropped three feet of snow in eighteen hours and brought wires down. Nevertheless, people struggled through it to celebrate with family and friends. Dr. and Mrs. G. F. Manning sr. were guests at the home of Dr. Nance and his wife Julia.

Footnote: In 1900 there had been 11,804 graduate nurses in the United States; there were 103,878 in 1920. The names of four nurses were included in Flagstaff's register of voters that year: Alice King and Catherine O'Farrell, Mrs. Pearl Brown from New Mexico and Pearl Muncy, employed at Milton Hospital.

When General Tuthill returned to medicine in Arizona after the war, nurses at Good Samaritan Hospital in Phoenix referred to him as "King Tut." They weren't impressed by his military manner.

June 3, 2001

Report to my kith and kin,

    The days are hot now—they no doubt are hot where you are too—and the sky is empty. I move as the sun does, avoiding it, staying on the shady side of the tower and waiting for the summer rains to begin. Thank goodness nights are cool.

The regular storms that came through for four months last winter did wonders. Through May both the town and the forest were lush with grasses and leafy trees, all wonderfully spring green and tender. New oak leaves look as if they belong in a salad.

Wild flowers aren't blooming yet, but some of the grasses are already a foot tall and seeding. Soon they'll be dry. Cars are churning up clouds of dust along the roads. It's too early to predict what this year's fire season will be, but there's potential. On our mountaintops, we lookouts have been waiting to see what will happen if all the vegetation dries out.

Last year's wildfires were so horrendous that agencies around here—The Nature Conservancy, The Grand Canyon Trust, the Forest Service—have agreed that active prescribed (RX) burning has to be part of everybody's forest protection plan. The city has several subdivisions in forested land; it's taking responsibility too. $8.8 million has been appropriated by Washington to fund accelerated "prevention and restoration" in the "urban interface."

I can understand the prevention part: get rid of unnecessary fuels that spread fire. The restoration program puzzles me though. A professor at NAU has been saying for years that we need to return the forest to pre-settlement conditions, and I wonder how far back he wants to go. Probably about 150 years—he can't mean back to the Ice Age, can he?

It would be nice if a little of that federal money were to be spent on tower maintenance. Detection is a form of prevention, and we all work in structures that range from shabby to derelict. The East Pocket tower is so shaky the lookout limits his visitors to no more than four at a time. People hired for O'Leary have been refusing the job, the tower is in such bad condition. "Out of sight…" seems to be the attitude toward our old (1930s, mostly) shelters in the sky. We probably won't get much attention.

Work is proceeding on the ground. "Dog hair" thickets are being thinned, the scrawny little trees cut and stacked into neat tepees. Eight-hundred-and-some spindly pines per acre, "thick as the hair on a dog's back," in some places, ought to qualify as crowded even to the no-logging people. In May, on every day that offered good "ventilation" and moderate breeze, there were two or three huge columns of smoke roundabout with crews trying to "accomplish" hundreds of acres with agency permission.

It took at least as much of our attention as rising gas prices. And the effect of Senator Jefford's party change. Baxter, did you foresee that such an upheaval would happen? I didn't, although it should have been obvious that with the Senate 50-50, it could. What a show.

I was fascinated by the news that jet lag and other disruptions of sleep schedule, prolonged or frequently repeated, could result in shrinkage of the right frontal lobe in human brains. What does that mean for pilots, firefighters, business travelers, medical interns, new mothers? Heavy implications, everywhere I look.

Anyway—now that summer is here, people are out of school and vacationers abound among us. Prescribed burning is on hold because we know that we can count on the public to set things ablaze, and we want to be ready for them. On Memorial Day weekend we had three sizeable fires, burning up hill. Beanie and Cazz, do you understand why up-hill is the worst direction?

The first was in the bottom of Fossil Creek on the boundary between the Coconino and the Tonto, where a middle-of-the-day campfire got out of control, with campers right there, and started off in all directions. While crews from both forests fought with it, law enforcement arrested the campers, packed their gear up, and brought them into town.

One of our lookouts, who has been trying to ease up on his drinking after years of overdoing it, radioed that a man in camo clothing was up in a tree pointing a rifle at his tower, later that people were trying to break in.

Next morning the district FMO drove him into Cottonwood to the hospital. I feel bad about it. I ponder how far we can, any of us, trust what we can see. And I recognize a sad reality: shows you the kind of behavior we expect from the public. When I heard his reports and pleas for help, I believed him.

A wet spring doesn't last long around here. This last Saturday humidity was down to minus 15 per cent, winds of 30 to 40 MPH were expected and a strong low pressure system was moving through the Great Basin. We were working under a Fire Weather Watch and a Red Flag Warning. No lunch break for lookouts, extension of service hours until 1900. (Overtime! Overtime!) Clouds were drifting in from the north west. All we needed was dry lightning.

Everybody was in service until almost sunset, but the only fire of any size didn't start until nearly midnight. Voices came out of the radio for hours and into my sleep.

The next day the morning forecast warned that humidity was minus ten per cent, wind speed was up to fifty, and the low pressure system was still moving through. Another Red Flag Day was proclaimed; my tower was vibrating. Traffic on the radio was about roll-overs on the forest roads and mop-up of Saturday's fire.

Today is another Red Flag Day. Another day of noisy wind and noisy tower. People may think this is a quiet situation—not true. Forecast for tomorrow: a strong high pressure system developing with winds and warm temperatures. How low can RH go?

Oh for pity sake, here come six large black military helicopters, thumping along from the east this time, going west below the level of my tower. I wish I knew what they were doing.

> Kisses to all and sundry from
> a front-line fire detector

P.S. to Beanie

Darlin', I'm really impressed by the drawing you sent of birds above Woody Mountain. Not only is every one exactly right, there's open air and movement on the page. Some professional artists never do manage to get air into their paintings.

You made the front of the refrigerator again! You're a wonder, and I love you.

When I learned to drive, every car was a
stick shift, and the highest gear was third.
There was no such thing as power steering.
And no driver's ed in high school.

1920 The planet circled on its way around the sun, one revolution at a time, but
after the war the public was disillusioned, and idealism was a luxury. Portable
stills were offered for sale in hardware stores (!); speakeasies began to appear; Prohibition
was proving to be a failure.

American business activity increased—planes flying across the country began
transporting "air mail," and the Radio Corporation of America was founded. But
the economy was erratic—farm prices plummeted, and food prices fell seventy-two
percent. Prices on other goods rose, with a concurrent depression and more people in the
laboring class on strike: Amalgamated Clothing Workers against "sweat shops," railroad
employees against wage cuts of ten to twenty percent.

The census of 1920 told Americans about themselves.

Federal:

the population of the United States was 105,683,108;

the population earning a living through farming was less than thirty percent;

thirteen percent of Americans were first-generation immigrants;

median size of families was only 4.3 people; the birth rate was falling;

eighty percent of all women in their thirties were married; women working
outside their homes totaled 8.3 million;

State:

population in Arizona had almost doubled to 333,273 [that was the whole
state];

motor vehicle licenses were required;

County:

1440 children were in school in all of Coconino County;

Flagstaff:

the population was 3,515, a growth of ninety-five percent since 1910;

assessed valuation of real estate was $2,700,000;

citizens whose wealth required them to file income tax returns totalled 310.

Flagstaff was founded in what we've termed the Victorian Era—Romanticism
against Realism, revolution in the arts—and matured into a solid little town during the
Progressive Era between 1890 and 1920 when America—increasingly urban, industrial
and bureaucratic—came of age. Oh my, such progress. Movies, radio, phonographs,
automobiles, airplanes, telephones.

Women had influenced the shape of the new order with voluntary associations,
institutions and social movements that shook the traditional, the tried-and true. 1903:

the Women's Trade Union League; 1906: the International Ladies Garment Worker Union. Picking up the pace: the National Consumer's League, Young Women's Christian Association, National American Woman Suffrage Association, College Equal Suffrage League, Boston Equal Suffrage Association for Good Government, National Women's Party. TheNew Woman was followed hard upon by working girls, career women, bachelor women.

Worse yet, or better depending on how tried and true you were, the women had been busy through all that with "domestic" politics of reform, civic housekeeping (as in "sweeping the scoundrels out") and a new drive toward autonomy, toward economic independence and living outside their parents' homes, toward rejection of the old attitudes. Companionate marriage, who had ever heard of such an idea?

Even before the war, changes in the position of women were showing up around the edges: one-fifth of females in America over the age of ten worked for money. During the war they worked as nurses, doctors, drivers, motorcycle riders, on the home front in factories and offices. Arizona employed a woman livestock inspector, Coconino county a woman deputy county recorder.

The 19th century middle-class women's culture rooted in domesticity had been undermined. There were machines that could take over the most tedious of their accustomed chores. Plumbing, washing machines, commercially produced food—housekeeping no longer had to be a sixteen-hour-a-day job.

War always escalates change, always, which you'd think we'd have learned by now. The Parent-Teachers Association, League of Women Voters, Women's Bureau in the Department of Labor—all on board. Married women who did not work for pay engaged in ever more club work and volunteer services. The 19th Amendment giving women the vote was added to the American constitution after ratification by thirty-six states.

From the beginning Don expected me to navigate for him when he was driving, maps out, turns planned. At first driving was cooperation, and we'd laugh about it and feel intimate. Anyway, I did. Later, as he became more easily agitated, he was angry if I made a mistake and whipped me with angry words until I huddled in misery. I wonder whether young women these days would put up with that kind of treatment.

Beanie and Cazz,

Here's a special letter just for you. Your parents can read it too if they want to—you can decide after you've finished whether to allow them.

Sometimes before the sun goes down in the evening, I explore for a few minutes on my mountain. The top isn't very big. I've walked all over it. Out on the north side there's a ruin of a small shelter made of logs. I don't know when it was built or why, but I like to guess it was made by Boy Scouts who were camping up here one night long go.

Yesterday I walked past it and suddenly saw a big mother elk standing in the tree shadows not far ahead of me. She was not moving, just looking at me. I didn't want to bother her, so I turned around to leave. Right beside me there was a baby elk curled up in the grass. It was looking at me too. I guess it was hoping it was hiding.

I stopped and held still, but the little, long-legged elk jumped up and ran away down the mountain. I looked back at the mother in time to see her run away too in the same direction.

I wonder how many creatures live up here with me, creatures I never see. I have found narrow paths that wind among the pines, only a few inches wide. They look to me like trails made by deer going down to drink at the pond at the bottom of the mountain. Maybe coyotes use them too. Maybe bears walk along them. Who knows?

I probably live among many animals large and small who don't want me to see them. I try to be a good neighbor. When I go into town tomorrow, I will buy a salt block and put it down the slope and walk by it now and then to see whether my neighbors like to lick it.

Love, Nana

The color and light and beauty of sunset and evening are more precious because the day's work is done and there's quiet for seeing. I'm talking about life too.

1920 Despite enormous progress since the turn of the century, medicine was still helpless against the same old diseases. Pneumonia was one of the complications that followed measles, typhoid, etc. In the years following the war 588 per 100,000 people died of pneumonia and influenza, 125 of tuberculosis. There had been some advance in understanding measles, scarlet fever, typhoid, and diphtheria, and tentative use of vaccines, but the death rate for children was still high.

It was painful to read about. Treatment for encephalitis was to drain spinal fluid, give sedatives to "quiet the nervous system" and treat as any other disease, which was: administer cathartics, bromides, opiates and plenty of water. For typhoid, doctors "cleared" a patient's "system" with calomel or caster oil, administered aspirin and codeine to "quiet the nervous system"—whatever they meant by that—and prescribed a large fluid intake. The same went for colds and dysentery. For heart problems the favored treatments were strychnine, digitalis, and a large dose of caffeine. Tincture of opium was widely available.

When they looked around at the end of the war, the end of the flu epidemic, Americans saw a network of hospitals that had mushroomed in over 6000 communities all over the country, roughly a fourth of which housed nursing schools. By 1920 there were 180 such schools with academic standing.

Over the past decade the number of active nurses had doubled, and about half of them were in private duty work. Those who were employed in hospitals worked a routine twelve-hour day. The Arizona Deaconess Hospital in Phoenix had become Good Samaritan with its own nursing program.

A year of internship as part of medical training had finally become standard. Interns and nurses thus shared the dubious honor of being cheap hospital labor.

Reformers hailed the passage through Congress of the Shephard-Towner bill to

a. assist states in setting up programs in education to protect the health of women and children and teach preventive nutrition, sanitation, and child care;

b. address public health issues in maternal and child hygiene with a system of examinations, immunizations, and school health programs.

Traditional doctors opposed the bill, arguing that such matters were not properly the responsibility of government. I don't agree, and since democracy assumes varieties of opinion, I feel free to say so. I am working on a theory that the proper function of government, even in a competitive economy, is cooperative: any service necessary to public welfare that cannot be effectively performed by individuals acting separately is a group responsibility. I'm aware that the theory covers a lot of issues, and when I get the words just right, I'll discuss it with Baxter.

Partly as a result of the Shephard-Towner bill, the role of nurses was expanded, as was their prestige, and their education steadily improved. Before long, professionals would be required to study in universities. The same year a law was enacted in Arizona providing for a State Board of Nurse Examiners. According to the ledger in the County Recorder's Office, Josephine Phelan, whose family lived here, became the first registered nurse in Coconino County. Seven years later two other RNs—Ruth Lundell and Laura Bell Macdermid—filed with the county. Were there others? The State Board of Nursing in Phoenix holds a few records between 1935 and 1950 but nothing earlier. So that's another mystery.

As care for everyone was relocated from home to hospital, there was growing control by medical organizations. By 1920—who would have expected it—the number of women doctors had declined. An after-effect of the war?

I would wake to sit on the side of the bed and sing my version of a song that was popular then: "Morning, morning, one more day to get through." The job of stay-at-home mom can be pretty boring, in case nobody has noticed.

Still sleeping, Don missed the approach to Capitol Reef, but I saw every dramatic minute of it. What a spectacle! It's lucky the motor coach couldn't go fast, I could hardly keep my eyes off.

Grand Canyon and Zion and Escalante center on canyons cut down deep into millions of years of old sediment. Bryce and Grand Staircase are huge panoramas of erosion into ancient dunes and sea beds. Capitol Reef National Park protects fourteen layers of the same sediment pushed up in sharp north-to-south wrinkles in the earth's crust created by west to east accordion squeezing of the plateau at the time it was lifted a mile above sea level—the Pacific plate grinding against the North American plate on its way to Alaska. There were giants in the earth...

Deep-seated shifts in the basement rearranging the flat-lying sedimentary strata... active earth, landscape in motion... heaving, cracking, bending, upward arching—slowly I assume. What you end up with at Capitol Reef is a fold in the rocks three miles wide and a hundred miles long, most of it completely impassable, especially if you happen to be traveling by horse and wagon. The top seven strata, once almost a mile thick, are worn away now by sixty-five million years worth of erosion. Hot diggety, what a place.

It's not really a capitol, that's a case of whimsy on the part of somebody who thought a towering mound of Navajo sandstone looked like a capitol dome. It's a reef, not in the sense of coral barriers around ocean islands, but of no-way-through cliffs on dry land into which erosion has worn blind canyons and slot canyons and cathedral valleys. There are waterpockets, eroded little cavities in the stone that cup water after infrequent rain. If I were to try to do justice to it, I'd need words that are gritty to the touch, big words that scrape and bite and weigh too much to lift. (Hmmm. Is that a poem?)

On the west side of all that tectonic violence, all that stone desert that stretches away to the horizon, is Fruita, an old Mormon homestead on the banks of the Little Fremont River— log buildings and green grass and tall shade trees and fruit orchards surrounded by sheer red cliffs and, above, white clouds in a blue sky. Domestic, soothing, and completely incongruous in that landscape.

I had planned to stop in the little campground. At mid-afternoon on a week-day in October it was empty, every site available, and I didn't have to be in a rush to claim one. And Waterpocket Fold/Capitol Reef was a fascinating place.

Don was still sleeping, so I explored into the gritty sandstone maze, driving south through the park on the only road, which was ten miles of dirt. Staying close to the right on curves, glad I wasn't meeting other vehicles my size in the narrow places, I drove to the end at Pleasant Creek, grinning all the way with the most wonderful feeling in my chest. Turned around and started back, doing fine in a blind turn with an overhang, proud that I wasn't scraping a single surface, when Don sat up and shouted, "What are you doing? Are you crazy?"

It had been a glorious day so far. "I'm glad you woke up so you can see this—it's stupendous."

"We'll never get out of here."

"We're on the way back. Don, look. Look at the straight lines angling across those cliffs. They were laid down horizontal and then lifted. Lifted! Imagine the force underneath that could lift and bend a mile-thick slab of solid rock."

"Big deal."

"You must be feeling better. Elevation here is only 5400."

He climbed into the passenger seat. "Where are we?"

"Waterpocket Fold, fifteen minutes from the camp ground."

"This is what they call an entrance road?"

"No, I drove on, I wanted to see as much as I could."

"Why? This is only rock, what's it got to do with you?"

"With me? I'm part of the earth, so I'm this old."

"I'm not."

"You can be as old as you want to."

"Damn straight."

"So can I."

"You're a loony."

He was just realizing that?

Despite his anxiety, there was no problem with the road. Trying to hold onto the happy feeling of the day, I turned into the oasis campground at Fruita. We were the only vehicle there. "What are you doing?"

"It's a good place to stop for the night."

"No it's not. Not one of these slots is long enough for us."

"Our rear bumper is ten feet beyond the wheels. If I back into a site on the edge, we'll fit fine."

"There won't be good reception for television."

"That's what we have the satellite dish for." In reverse, using both mirrors, I maneuvered between two pine logs.

"This is ridiculous, you don't know what you're doing."

"Damn it, Don, *damn it.*" I hadn't ever shouted at him before. "Get out and tell me when the rear wheels are at the barrier."

He went out the door without another grumble. I parked neatly, wondering whether I should have shouted at him years earlier. Got his television going for him, poured Scotch into a glass. "Here you are, Don, everything you need. I'll get food ready, you must be hungry." I turned the oven on.

"What's for dinner?"

"Lasagna."

"You know I don't like that stuff."

"No, I didn't know. After all these years. I thought maybe we could sit outside to eat."

"It's cold out there."

"We can sit in the sun."

"I don't want to."

"All right. OK." What was I doing being nice to a selfish old bully? I was angry, my throat so tight it hurt. "You can have bread with your Scotch in here alone, and I'll eat lasagna outside in the sunset."

"I want you in here."

"Tough."

He looked straight into my eyes for the first time in I don't know how long, intense, threatening, and I was afraid he was going to hit me. "I'm not going to let you do that."

Not going to *let*? He wasn't even anybody I knew. "Not going to *LET*?"

The keys were in my pocket. I went though the door numb in my chest and sat outside alone, watching shadows grow until dusk. Thinking, "What am I doing with this person, this mean, grumpy old man?"

In the Southwest, sky blue is a noisy color,
young and in-your-face, boisterous as a shout.
The college boy who takes my money for
twelve-grain rolls looks out the window. "Isn't
it a beautiful day!" They like loud, these
kids, vibrating through their bones from one
horizon to another. I long for the soft grey
sound of clouds.

1920 By golly, Flagstaff was up to the minute. There were seventeen, count 'em, seventeen small grocery stores in town. Mail was delivered free twice a day to houses in town—no more going to the post office—and seven pick-up boxes sprouted on street corners. Free delivery three times a week was promised to Doney Park, where the ladies had organized a Domestic Club and spent the meetings quilting.

Through spring and summer another election loomed, with Editor Fred Breen, as usual, shamelessly partisan. Reporting the Republican convention, he published the entire platform and all of Warren G. Harding's acceptance speech (Calvin Coolidge was the vice-presidential candidate), but you'd have thought the Democrats had no candidate, so little was said about him.

For the first time the ladies would be voting for president. That might have been one explanation for the outcome; more likely, I think, was that it was the first election after that horrible war and resulting scandals. Breen published a three-inch headline: Harding was the new President, and the business of America was business (Coolidge). "Normalcy" (Harding) was re-established. Arizona had gone Republican, almost completely, for the first time ever.

In the initial issue of the *Sun* for 1920 Annie Noble announced that Mrs. Muncy had entertained with a "delightful little luncheon" (Hilda was one of the guests) to announce the engagement of her daughter to Dr. A. H. Schermann who had been in residence at Milton Hospital since 1912. Pearl Muncy, a nurse at the hospital, born in Washington, was 5'7" tall, and weighed 140 pounds.

A few weeks later a bridal shower was held at the Fronske house with "gifts of every description and the guests revelled with the happy recipient." Later in the day some of the guests stayed on to hold a quilting bee for the bride.

In mid-April of 1920 Albert H. Schermann, age 41, and Pearl Regina Muncy, age 29, were married, Rev. Cyprian Vabre officiating. Dr. Miller and the Fronskes were in attendance.

It was the second wedding to a doctor in Flagstaff's history. The newspaper reporting Clara Coffin's wedding to Dr. Cornish had been lost, and Annie Noble made use of her best florid style, so I copied the paragraph.

> *One of the loveliest of home weddings was solemnized last Wednesday night when Pearl Muncy became the bride of Dr. Schermann. The bride, who is unusually attractive, was lovely in an apricot gown of crepe de chine, the bride's bouquet a dream of white roses with a graceful shower of orange blossoms caught with myriad droops of soft white ribbon.*

The color scheme was pink and white; music and dancing and dinner followed the ceremony. Annie was pleased to report: "Dr. and Mrs. Schermann...happily will remain among us as a cozy little home will be erected for them quite soon."

When they returned from their wedding trip to Los Angeles, San Francisco and Lake Tahoe, they entertained a few guests (among whom were the Fronskes with their sons) at a dinner, "a felicitous affair," at which Pearl was "a lovely cook and a charming hostess."

Well, all right! Another doctor's wife added to the list:

Sarah Manning—1888
Kathleen Brannen—1889
Clara Cornish—1890
Felicia Brannen—1896
Mira Robinson—1899
Ethel "Effie" Sipe—1905
Margaret Adams—1905
Nellie Sult—1910
Josie Manning—1911
Lois Manning—1912
Hilda Fronske—1914
Annis Zinn—1918
Pearl Schermann—1920

The *Sun* didn't say whether Pearl left nursing to take up socializing and volunteering, but her daughters wrote to me to say she did. See there, doctors' wives didn't work for money.

Hilda "gave a most delightful" series of parties and luncheons, at which Lois, Annis, Sarah and Pearl were guests. For the rest of the year her name didn't appear in the *Sun*—Fronske and Manning and Zinn were.

Don and I had years of slim pickings ahead of us. We saw no sense in putting ourselves and our parents into major debt with a dramatic production. When the orange trees were blooming, we were married in the back yard that I'd grown up in, with our families as witnesses. We thought that put the emphasis on what was important.

I drove Emily to the oncologist's office and sat beside her. The hurrying doctor smiled. "It's good news, not alarming at all. What we're dealing with is a DCIS, a ductal carcinoma in situ, highly curable with non-invasive methods. But the cells are receptor positive, so I recommend a lumpectomy, removal of the tumor with some healthy tissue, maybe three-quarters of an inch all around, as a safety margin to be sure there's been no metastasis. It's a new approach, very effective. Take about an hour, another hour in recovery."

I glanced at Emily. "She won't lose her breast?"

"It looks right now as if she won't, not the whole breast, therefore no reconstructive surgery."

"No chemotherapy?" We'd read about chemotherapy: drugs injected into a vein followed by nausea, vomiting, hair loss.

"Possibly not. But the edges are not entirely clear. We'll use some anti-cancer drugs, hormone therapy and radiation therapy with high intensity to stop cell multiplication. A few minutes a day, five days a week, five to seven weeks. Normal cells will recover rapidly. Have the office make an appointment for a simulation unit."

I wrote the words into my notebook. Cancer, tumor, whatever they called it. Lumpectomy. Radiation. My hands were shaking.

But probably no full removal of a breast. No chemotherapy drugs that would destroy her immune system, her intestinal lining, her bone marrow. No plunging a needle through the flesh of her hip and drawing out marrow for a transplant. I'd been reading: one in five women died directly from the treatment; others could be left with permanent damage to heart, kidneys, lungs, liver, nerves. That's the way cancer was then.

In the car again, Emily spoke with a voice that was unsteady. "Well. It could have been worse. I've been worried for the children." She covered her face with her hands and cried silent shuddering sobs, and I couldn't think of anything to do except put my hand on her shoulder.

A doctor we barely knew had made the decision, and it was all matter-of-fact for him. "Radiation is a newer treatment widely used since about 1960, but there's a slightly higher risk of recurrence than with mastectomy. Thirty per cent of choice is for lumpectomy, but we prefer to combine the two."

He did it all the time. We didn't, though, and we thought the whole affair was barbaric, and we sat in her kitchen and raged about it.

"Darn it, Marlene. Darn it. Part of my body might kill me, so they're going to cut it out. It just seems such a crude approach."

"Like a mechanic. This from people who would have us think medicine is an art."

"Maybe a hundred years from now, there'll be a more civilized treatment, but for now they're going to subject me to a lumpectomy."

"Who thought up that ugly word?"

"I was fairly symmetrical up to now." I could tell by the way she laughed how upset she was. "I'll be lop-sided."

She pulled a tissue out of a box and wiped her eyes. "Darn it. I feel trapped."

"Emily, I'll be right with you every step. You'll still be my friend, lop-sided or not." I laughed too and reached for a tissue.

Sitting alone in the waiting room for an hour, I thought of Emily under anesthesia, part of her breast being cut away. Travis had left as soon as she'd disappeared through the doors. "Marlene. If I'm not back by the time she gets to recovery, tell her I'll be there as soon as I can."

I remember men just out of the army at my high school in 1948, older *boys* really, who were very interested in the girls around them, much to the alarm of our parents. I wonder what effect the veterans of 1919 had on Northern Arizona Normal School.

1920 The first two decades of the Twentieth Century had already gone by, and the third was beginning. In January mild cases of small pox spread through Coconino County.

Influenza was not serious in Flagstaff—only twenty or so cases for January and February, although one two-year-old child died—but it was enough to make people nervous. Doctors Schermann, Fronske and Felix Manning, interviewed for the *Sun*, agreed that whiskey used as medicine did no good and was probably harmful.

Scanning the Local Items column, trying to confine myself to Flagstaff's general practitioners, I was having trouble keeping track of everybody. Dentists were referred to as Doctor, and so were astronomers and veterinarians and clerics and academics and state livestock inspectors and doctors who had come in briefly from other places to visit and specialists making regular trips up from Phoenix. The print was salted with such information as the registration in the county of Dr. A. J. Mackey from Texas who went into practice with Dr. Nance, but both were dentists, and it was M.D.s that I was after.

Dr. Miller and Dr. Raymond traveled frequently; both were ill for a while and went to Phoenix for treatment. Dr. Raymond had frequent guests. Dr. Felix and Dr. Raymond found a nest of rattlesnakes "out east of town" and killed most of them. When Flagstaff organized an armory as home for Battery A of the National Guard, Dr. Raymond donated the land for it. Raymond's name was never in Annie Noble's society column, although Dr. Miller appeared occasionally as being in attendance at picnics and other such events. I wish I could find a personal description of him and his disposition.

When Dr. Raymond was sued by an AL&T employee for malpractice on the charge of inadequate treatment for a dislocated hip, I checked the Index to Civil Actions in the office of the Clerk of the Superior Court and read through old records of suits in which Manning, Raymond, Fronske, Schermann and Robinson were involved for one reason or another. I am thus confident about saying that the 1920 suit against Dr. Raymond was the first legal malpractice claim in the forty years of Flagstaff history.

Dr. P. G. Cornish came from Albuquerque to testify on Raymond's behalf. It was reported on the front page when the case was decided: the doctor was not guilty of the charge against him.

Dr. Miller, who had been active in the Elks' Lodge for many years, was presented with a diamond Elks button. In July he was called twice to the depot to tend to accidents Breen found unique enough for reporting. A passenger had been standing on the rear observation platform with a pistol in his pocket. A bump discharged the pistol and shot him in the hip and foot. A woman passenger "dislocated her jaw while yawning." Two dentists who were also passengers were unable to put it back in place. Miller boarded while the train was stopped at Flagstaff and tended to the unfortunate woman's yawn.

In the Voter Register I learned that the skinny doctors were George Felix Manning sr. at 5'7" 110 lbs, Martin Fronske at 5'8", 127 lbs, R.O. Raymond at 5'11" 138 lbs.

That might be of interest to nobody but me.

mid-June, 2001

Hi guys,

That term is not age or gender-specific, is it?

I hope you're all thinking about me being happy up here on my mountain. Just before nightfall the cabin is loud with the noise of hummingbirds through open windows, hummingbirds zooming in to the feeders under the eaves for one last sip of sugar water to last until morning.

When stars appear, I stand in the doorway and say "good evening" to them before I slide between my sheets with a book and a battery reading light. Later, after I've turned off the light for the night (I couldn't resist that rhyme), I look at the stars again to see how far they've moved in their nightly circling. Sometimes the Big Dipper has sunk almost out of sight.

Did you see this Mom-related news? It's full of numbers.

More than $1.6 billion was spent by taxpayers to combat 90,000 fires last year, double the cost of a typical year. For every dollar spent on prescribed burning, thinning and training firefighters, $7 worth of savings are realized in putting out big fires. At least 56 million acres in the West alone are currently at high risk for catastrophic fire.

On the Coconino we've had some activity that built as we went along. I remember that last year I sent you notes I made from the forest radio, so that you could imagine what my job is like. Actually, I make notes often. I thought this week's were worth sending, we had arson, and neighborhoods threatened, and a 12,000 acre fire up on the Peaks that had the people in town alarmed.

June 10

There hasn't been a stroke of lightning for weeks, but every day we have four to ten fires, man- or kid-caused. (Who ever heard of a woman-caused fire?) Often a campfire has been abandoned and come to life in the wind, human negligence compounded by human inexperience.

Or malice: half a dozen small fires, one after another in a straight line within an hour—obviously deliberate. Law Enforcement is called to those. Yesterday was high school graduation; this morning there are two fire series burning near forest subdivisions. Four days ago a fast-moving blaze threatened Mountainaire, Kachina Village, Forest Highlands, and the airport. So many engines and people were dispatched to "get a handle on it," that they parked middle-of-the-road.

White smoke began to drift above the trees a mile west of me from a place that's popular as a camp site. Despite my telling the dispatcher that it was small and white and not growing, she sent two big engines, a heavy water tender, and a twenty-person Hot Shot crew. Size-up was a quarter of an acre on the ground.

If the fire had grown out of control, my exit by car would have been cut off and I'd have seen my closest slurry drop ever. I wasn't worried though. Wind was blowing the smoke briskly in the other direction, and there was not going to be a threat to me unless something very surprising happened.

Humidity is still low; wind blows and blows. I was on extra hours (extended into overtime) every day last week. Since the only big weather news has been rain and floods in Texas and Louisiana, all our firefighters are still here, and they've "caught" the flames before they spread far.

One positive thing I can say about human-caused fires is that the distance from my tower is easy to figure—they're almost always right on a road.

June 11

Saturday the newspaper reported that Bellemont, ten miles northwest of me, had recorded 32 degrees, the lowest temperature in the nation. What? Montana, Wisconsin, Alaska—and Bellemont was the lowest? It has been cold up here in the wind; I keep my tower windows closed most of the day. But a nation-wide record? C'mon.

Today a low pressure system is approaching from the Pacific, and a FIRE WEATHER WATCH as well as a RED FLAG WARNING have been announced on the forest radio. All kinds of response procedures go into effect automatically under those conditions: dozens of people show up to fight a fire no bigger than a table top.

In the afternoon a fire started forty-eight miles to the southeast near Buck Mountain and grew to thirty acres. I could see the smoke rising high, hear the firefighters dispatched.

Then smoke was spotted ten miles from me at Little Leroux Spring just off the Snow Bowl road, south side of the Peaks, a few hundred feet down the Friedlein Prairie Road. So small I could see it at first only with the binoculars. North-end Coconino firefighters rushed up there. Firefighters and every official on the district. They named it Leroux.

Voices on the radio from both fires were fast, urgent, breathless.

"Order air assistance, tankers and helicopters."

"Send out the hose cache."

"Request permission to use dozers and chain saws in the wilderness."

"Go to tac."

"Order Type Two crews."

The Buck Fire was held at those thirty acres, but the Leroux Fire was spotting half a mile ahead, climbing the mountain with a strong wind behind it. Clearly visible to everyone in Flagstaff, it surged ahead to forty acres, no estimate of control.

"Close the Snow Bowl Road."

"Clear hikers off the trails."

"Order more tankers and a lead plane."

"Order six more crews."

"A TV crew is here."

"The head of the fire is crowning and torching."

"The governor is here. She'd like a view of the fire."
"Place the Northern Arizona Team on alert."
"Activate the Team."
"Set up fire camp at the Hot Shot Ranch."
Smoke made its own shadow across the face of the Peaks, placid green below—trees standing helpless—boiling black and grey and white above. Flames were backing downhill into the wind, moving slowly toward town.
"Lead plane 3-5 over the fire." (a woman's voice, casual).
"I can't see the head for smoke."
"Crews are going up each flank, but nobody's out ahead."
"Drop slurry on the south flank."
Circling low, she led tankers into the smoke and came out the other side. One of the big planes lost an engine and droned into the Winslow airport to set down.

By 1500 (three o'clock) the Leroux Fire was at 300 acres, and smoke was rolling over Doyle Peak, draping across a ridge, dropping down into Doney Park on the east side. Fire was in the wilderness, but had not yet crossed Kachina Trail. All lookouts and ground units not assigned to the fire were told to stay in service until dark. Three hundred people had been ordered for immediate deployment.

At 9:30 p.m. I climbed the tower in a cold wind to look at golden red flames glowing on the dark mountain, knowing that there would be tired sooty people digging line through the night.

June 12

This morning wind is blowing twenty to thirty MPH with gusts to savage speed, and the Leroux Fire is 600-plus acres. KNAU reports ten "highly-trained, elite" Hot Shot crews. Slurry drops were continuous until dark yesterday and resumed again at dawn today. Smoke on the section that was burned yesterday is thinner now—I can see through it to slopes that were hidden behind it.

Fire is burning high up, through the aspen zone, into fir and spruce, almost to tree line. It's definitely headed for Doyle Saddle. If it goes over the top in this wind, it will go down into the Inner Basin, which has provided Flagstaff's water supply for more than a hundred years.

The Buck Fire is still active. We have six smaller burns here and there. But the Peaks are personal scenery for Flagstaff residents. This one hurts. Black smoke means pines are dying.

There's a slurry line on south side, the downhill slope, along the Friedlein Prairie road, but burning is hot above it. Air tankers are circling in the turbulence above. Mt. Humphreys, Hart Prairie, and the Snow Bowl to the west are untouched, but there's intense fire in the pines below Agassiz and Fremont peaks.

June 13

A thousand acres have burned on the Leroux fire, which is only five percent contained, and the black stretches up to 10,000 feet, across Kachina hiking trail. Firefighters, equipment operators, water tender and engine crews are there—500 people committed. No injuries so far.

With winds above thirty MPH and erratic, four air tankers are dropping borate-based retardant. Flagstaff, Coconino County, Highland and Summit fire departments are cooperating. Thirty-three crews from New Mexico, California, Utah, and the northwest plus the Northern Arizona Type II Interagency Management Team—seven hundred people in shifts—are trying to keep the fire away from populated areas, corral it within a perimeter, then run it upslope and out of fuel, but the terrain is rugged, the path of fire is erratic and spotty, there's torching in some stands with flame length sometimes 100 feet. GAWD!

June 14

1240 acres, 760 people, 300 of them on the line at any one time, steep terrain: the Leroux fire is still burning.

June 15

831 people from six states, $1.5 million so far, plus $3 million more projected before mop-up is finished. Only three injuries: dehydration, injured knee, minor burn.

June 16

The Leroux fire is 85% contained; it might not be completely out until summer rains begin.

June 17

In spite of all the news from the mountain, Ed drove up on a camp of sleeping drunks whose escaped camp fire was burning toward their sleeping bags. Give those boys the Charles Darwin Award.

The calendar refers to next week as the beginning of summer, which may be true in some places, but not in Arizona—in the desert it's been hot for a couple of months. For reasons that are not immediately apparent, the sun stops moving to the north and begins to move toward the south. I track it daily by the place on the western horizon where it sets, with Bill Williams Mountain as my guide.

On my days off in town, I love my part of Flagstaff. June light is intense; shadows are dark; streets are framed and over-hung by vegetation; air is scented by new-mown grass. I see from the windows in my little town house how enchanting the big trees are when sunlight comes through their leaves and a wind is blowing. When I live with them next winter, there will be no moving leaves.

Love from your ear in the air,
M

 I remember the Little Orphan Annie comic strip in the newspaper. That's how old I am. Little Orphan Annie and her wealthy step-father, Daddy Warbucks—heavens, what a name.

"It's me, Baboo."

"Hi, Momsie. Laundry day?"

"Yep. Two days in town with all the civilized conveniences, and I miss my primitive cabin on the mountain. Go figure, as people were saying not long ago."

"My heart bleeds. Tough life you're living."

"Isn't it though? My neighborhood in Flagstaff is flowers and big shade trees; from my tower windows I look across miles of pines."

"You're some example for the rest of us: there's life after menopause."

"Thank you, thank you. I intend to keep it up too, in fact, I do not intend to go downhill at all."

"You…are…my kinda girl."

"That's a real compliment. I turn it back—you're my kind."

We both laughed; I love her laugh. "How's the dissertation going?"

"Slow. I keep realizing there's more that has to go in, and I'm off in hot pursuit. But even with this Teaching Assistant job taking up so much of my time, I think a few more months'll do it. Unless my advisor decides to give me a hard time."

"You looking forward to finishing?"

"I'm planning a celebration. Like sitting on the balcony and doing nothing at all for three whole days. Getting reacquainted with the real world."

"No loud noises and frenzied movement?"

"I think I've about worn out my interest in all that. At least for now. And sitting on the balcony won't cost anything."

"Mind if I come and celebrate with you?"

"You like sitting on balconies?"

"You bet."

"You're invited."

"I'll be there."

"And leave your research for a few days? I look forward to your tidbits. Tell them to Janey, and we shake our heads amazed. All that wasn't so long ago. Eighty or ninety years?"

"I'm reading the 1920s now. American women could vote, smoke and drink if they wanted to, show their legs, become educated, wear comfortable clothes. A former Arizona schoolteacher caused a commotion in New York City by wearing trousers in public, saying, 'I consider trousers more sensible and comfortable than corsets and skirts.'"

"Let's hear it for rebellion!"

"Cosmetics were respectable in some places, bobbed hair was beginning to appear, hems were ankle to calf length, hats were head-hugging."

"The cloche?"

"Right. And the brassiere was invented."

"Oh, yippee."

"Well, girls and women were taking up active sports. A Woman's Athletic Club was flourishing in Flagstaff."

"No kidding."

"So the newspaper said. There were policewomen in some of the big cities. When George Babbitt died, his wife Philomena was administrator of his estate, I don't recall a woman taking that responsibility earlier. The Society Editor for the *Sun*, Annie Noble took a three-month break to take courses in psychology and primary education at Colorado State University. Her grown daughter attended summer school there too."

"What year was this?"

"1920."

"Holy Moley!"

"I had no idea that sort of thing happened so early. And listen to this: in the southwest, women were being hired by the Forest Service as lookouts and dispatchers and on-the-front-line firefighters."

"So much for the weaker sex and brain fever if the poor girls thought anything strenuous. I'm proud of them."

"Here's something that pleases me: women who held public offices were referred to in the paper by their own names, not their husbands'. When Mrs. Lenore Frances Dumas resigned as Coconino County school superintendent, Mrs. Charlotte M. Acker assumed the office. That's the way it was reported, marital status still required but personal names for married women permissible. It ought to make figuring out who they were a little easier for me. The society editor still used the old-fashioned form though, most of the time. I think there were threemaybefour women in town named Mrs. Wilson."

"Still not a golden age."

"Not by a long way. More women died in childbirth in this country than by any cause except tuberculosis."

"That's almost unheard of now."

"Stinks, doesn't it? One in every five babies died before its first birthday."

"That was more important than cosmetics and bobbed hair and trousers, seems to me."

"I agree completely. But Flagstaff had no city health officer although the law authorized one, and the county health officer had no authority within the city limits."

"Rather uneven progress, wouldn't you say?"

"Oh yes. After the war there was a woman's Social Service Circle in Flagstaff organized to take care of local needs. It arranged to have a community nurse hired to address such problems. She arrived in March of 1920, Miss Frieda Johnson, office in the court house. One of the first projects she organized was an examination of all school children."

"Hurray for nurses."

"A letter to parents urging that they cooperate was placed in the newspaper, signed by Dr. Fronske, who was president of the Board of Trustees. You know what that nurse did? She joined the Woman's Club and Shakespeare Club right off the bat."

"Oh, clever."

"You know, I had to feel sympathy for the men: the newspaper printed the profound wisdom that a "real man" was not a "mollycoddle", he joined the National Guard."

"What was a mollycoddle?"

"I can only guess. I don't think it was a compliment. A woman, on the other hand, could be known as a "sweet patootie," which sounds like a compliment to me.

Insomnia. Self-doubt. Hope was the saddest word I knew. Suicide was a reasonable way out. For fifteen years I used pills so I could sleep.

1921 My, what a heady time it was to be a woman. The Supreme Court decided the suffrage amendment was indeed constitutional; the Women's Bureau in the Department of Labor reported that eight million females were in the work force, eighty percent of them in clerical work. Put them all together, it was a second American revolution. Really.

Bryn Mawr College established summer schools for Women Workers in Industry. Independent citizenship was granted by Congress to married women. The word obey? Episcopal bishops deleted it from their marriage ceremony.

Women's fashion continued its rapid revolt against the past. Silk stockings and strapped pumps with heels two to three inches high were exposed by slim line skirts that varied from ankle length to calf length. Fabrics, like crepe-de-chine, were soft and romantic. Underwear was lacy ("Fragile Frills"). Corsets and the new brassieres flattened breasts instead of emphasizing them, making it more difficult to recognize a feminine woman when you saw one.

Shocking, all of it. Jantzen presented clinging knit one-piece bathing suits in men's and women's styles. Advertised as "the suit that changed bathing to swimming," it featured a scooped-necked, sleeveless tunic attached to trunks. On Atlantic beaches, girls who wore them were arrested for "indecent exposure"—their arms and legs were bare and their natural shapes were revealed. Zounds!

And they could have anticipated it: the first Miss America pageant was presented in New Jersey with "bathing beauties" a new phrase in America. It was all about money, of course, keeping the tourists in town after Labor Day, keeping the hotels full, but it gave ordinary American girls a chance at the limelight.

In 1921 more than forty women's groups joined together to form the nation-wide Association of Junior Leagues, rooted in the belief that a group of females can be a powerful force. Business and executive women—a new species—organized the Soroptimists, dedicated to the economic advancement of all women. There was an earnest club to suit just about any woman's taste, and I say Hurray.

In Arizona women were on the move: the State Federation of Business and Professional Women's Clubs met in Phoenix. There were a Child Welfare Congress, an Arizona Congress of Mothers, the PTA.

And in Flagstaff? The Costigan family (mother, daughter and son) ran the Orpheum theater, which showed silent films—Charlie Chaplin, for example. Daughter Mary Costigan was managing the Orpheum by September, a first for northern Arizona women.

Established by the Women's Christian Temperance Union and taken over in 1915 by the Women's Club, the Flagstaff library on the southeast corner of Leroux and Aspen was given to the town, which planned to maintain it by a special tax levy. The affairs of the library were complex enough to justify a Board of Trustees, both men and women, to pay bills, buy books, hire librarians, establish policies, and maintain the existing collection.

In April of 1921 Milton, population 400, successfully petitioned to join its neighbor north of the tracks and brought with it the Arizona Lumber & Timber Company sawmill but not the lumber yard or stables. The *Sun* reported:

> *Milton, now part of the Flagstaff Corporation, is consistently merging its identity into the town, and the name "Milton" will soon be used merely as a neighborhood designation if at all. Probably it will, after a time, be forgotten and mentioned only occasionally, as is "Old Town," and other similar sections having nicknames.*
>
> *The Arizona Lumber and Timber Company informs the Sun that from now henceforth the hospital will be known as Mercy Hospital, and the store as the Arizona Lumber and Timber Company store department.*

Again I went through records in the county court house and found no record of incorporation or transfer of deed. The name of the hospital may have changed; apparently nothing else had.

"Don, please. Just sit up against the pillows. Please? I'll spoon a little into your mouth. Don, you have to. Come *on*. Why are you doing this?"

Lyle's voice. "It's a beautiful Spring day in Arizona, and I have to drive up to Prescott. Will you come with me?"

It had been three weeks since I'd sat in a sunny little cafe and told him that the petroglyphs had been pecked onto that stone by women. I'd wondered whether I had offended him, but I kept my voice calm.

"I should be able to rearrange my day. When do you propose to leave and return?"

"Right away. I have a package I promised to deliver to a friend, and then we'll turn around and come back. Return by two o'clock."

"Then, yes. I'd like to go out into a beautiful Spring day in Arizona."

"Meet you in the Bayless parking lot?"

"I'm on my way."

I combed my hair, decided the big shirt I was wearing over jeans was good enough, and was out of the house in five minutes. No need to put on the dog (wonder where that term came from) for a friend. By the time he pulled up beside me at the Bayless store, I was out of the car with the door locked.

Spring in the desert is a brief intoxicating time, no more that six weeks long, a thrill to savor in dread of the relentless heat that will follow. My mood was holiday. "Feel the air? It's like silk. March in Phoenix is the best season of the whole year."

North on I-17 to Cordes Junction we talked and laughed and traded stories. He asked how I felt about Bob Dylan, I asked how he felt about Viet Nam.

"You know, Lyle, I haven't been on this stretch of highway since I was in high school, I'd forgotten these bare hills. They're essential, basic, shape and line with not much color or vegetation to distract. Maybe I'm old enough finally to appreciate them."

"Marlene, I doubt anyone else I know would see that in them. You're a real find."

I laughed, delighted by the compliment. "You bring out the best in me. I'd forgotten that the road climbs like this. And the occasional cluster of buildings. Oh. We're turning?"

"My friend lives a few miles east of Prescott on ranch land that's just been opened to subdivision. Wait until you see it. Art lives in the top drawer."

A high valley among soft hills. Here and there half a mile off, houses that were new and attractive but not ostentatious. "Oh Lyle, it's lovely. Serene. The land parcels must be large."

"They are." He turned into a long unpaved driveway. "That's Art's place up ahead. He left a key out for me so I can put the package inside. If you'd like to tour the house, I won't tell."

"There's no one here?"

"He's in L.A. this week."

"I've been curious about how houses look on the inside since I was a child."

"Then let me be your guide."

We inspected rooms for cooking, eating, conversing, reading—all bright and spacious, all comfortable as if they'd been used for a long time—and poked our heads into bedrooms.

"Oh Lyle, everything's just to my taste. I feel a little squirmy about the owner being absent, as if I'm doing something I shouldn't. But you could be easy here." I'd been smiling since we'd come through the front door.

"This is the master bedroom."

"It's wonderful! Big bed, cozy feel, doors that open to an uncluttered view. I love it."

"Marlene, you're a joy." He put an arm across my back, squeezed my shoulder, looked down at me and smiled. A movement smooth as choreography—or practice—he turned to me. Put the other hand to my face. A long soft kiss, his mouth to mine.

My brain must not have been working well, I truly do not remember, truly, how we shed our clothes. The feeling of his lips, that I have to this day, his hands on my skin. I'm not sure what he was whispering.

One thing, though, I did not protest or struggle. I can't say I expected or even consciously wanted, but I did not refuse. Thick, gently moving cloud. Bare shoulders under my hands. A long humming moan. Moving colors behind my eyelids. I turned my head from side to side in a steady rhythm that brought my cheek next to his and moved it away. A growing urgency that animated every inch of me and focused low, deep within.

That's how old I was, old enough for sex to be an encounter with God. At least, it seemed so at the time. Now I suppose I'd call it endorphins.

Once I took my largest kitchen knife out into the back yard and knelt and stabbed it into the ground a few times. Displacement therapy, or something like that. But I felt a fool doing it, and I stopped.

1921 Sarah Manning was sixty-two years old, Lois Manning thirty-seven, Hilda Fronske thirty-four, Pearl Schermann thirty, and Annis Zinn twenty-five. Sarah's daughter Althea Wilson lived at 418 North Leroux, Annis Zinn at 610. Hilda was at 401, west Aspen, Sarah at 411, and Pearl at 416 west Birch.

Bridge remained an important part of "the Social Whirl" in Flagstaff. There were several afternoon bridge parties every week, some large, some no more than a table or two—even in stormy weather, ladies entertaining each other in their homes. Now and then a luncheon, occasionally dinner to which husbands were invited, but most of the society news was of bridge parties where the women played for prizes.

Sarah and Lois and Hilda and Annis and Pearl were members of the Women's Club (Hilda and Pearl in the Home Economics Department), devoting themselves to "bettering social conditions." Scarcely a week went by when they missed playing bridge, not always together but always somewhere. All five entertained—Pearl with a series in her "very attractive home," Lois and Sarah usually together.

As a doctor's wife, I played bridge too sometimes and thought I wasn't completely incompetent, so I feel assured in saying that Sarah Manning, a generation or more older than many of those women, would not have been invited to card parties out of duty or sympathy. Maybe she was funny or pleasant or full of stories, but most definitely she was intelligent when she played a hand. Real bridge players don't tolerate for very long partners who can't keep track. Ask anybody.

Lois Manning and Virginia Lockett, city superintendent of schools, were reported as the first white women to "brave the hardships of the Bright Angel Trail." The newest Mrs. Doctor, Pearl Schermann was mentioned in the society column more frequently that year. She "honored a house guest" from L.A. with "an old-fashioned afternoon candy-pull party," at which Hilda was one of the ten guests, and the next month delivered a baby girl (Marjorie) in Milton Hospital. Pearl, that is.

Other activities deemed worth notice: in the summer Dr. and Mrs. Schermann traveled out to Mormon Lake for a picnic at which Dr. Miller was also present; at Christmas the Schermanns entertained a group that included Dr. Miller, whose social life was picking up. He was good company, maybe?

11

They were fantasies that I told myself in bed at night, alone, waiting for sleep. Escape was a common theme, running and hiding. Heroic rescues—I enjoyed those. Often in later years I invented what my life could be if Don were to die. Divorce wasn't so common in those days nor so respectable, and the craze for Freudian analysis was past its peak.

1921 Trivia is the best part of history, it seems to me. This, for example: the American Medical Association endorsed prescription of alcohol for a range of complaints, a maximum of 2.5 gallons of Prohibition beer per person per year. And: thirteen percent of Americans owned telephones. The Census Bureau released the news that fifty-one percent of Americans lived in towns of more than 2500, and that included Flagstaff. Just barely.

Like the rest of the country, it had taken on a different character through the past forty years. In 1921 786 autos crowded the streets; in 1922 the number would be 866. Warren G. Harding arrived at his inauguration ceremony in an automobile (a Packard Twin-Six) the first President-elect to do so. Later he would be the first President whose voice was heard on the radio.

Financially the Twenties were not one homogeneous "Roaring" block in Arizona. When the 1919 post-war boom gave way to recession, farm prices fell. With a collapse in copper prices, mines in the state closed; so did sawmills in Flagstaff as lumber sales slowed.

But the mood was Improvement. At 8:00 in the evening a curfew whistle blew, warning children under sixteen that they must be off the streets, which would soon be completely paved if things went according to plan. Vacant lots were a disgrace, so said Editor Breen, a fright to behold, a menace to health. Much excitement: a bi-plane flew over the Peaks toward the Grand Canyon.

Life went on for the town's doctors with no substantial changes. Martin Fronske continued to be A Pillar of the Community. Elected to the School Board, appointed as county chairman for National Cancer Week, he was also a charter member of Flagstaff's new Rotary Club for business and professional men and one of its five directors, as well as company surgeon for Cady Company when it took over the Flagstaff Lumber

Company. He and Hilda were everyone's guests—when May and G. A. Pearson at the Forest Experiment Station in Fort Valley invited friends out to dinner, the Fronskes were in the party.

Dr. Miller, still a frequent traveler who occasionally was reported as present at social events, took a man who had been hiccuping for a week to Los Angeles on the train. Dr. Schermann took Pearl's brother there for the same reason. Dr. Zinn accompanied a boy to Los Angeles on the train for some kind of medical treatment.

Such notes, printed in the *Sun*, were hints of problems that the doctors hadn't the experience nor the equipment to treat. You begin to see the limits. The community hospital was in a house south of the tracks. The closest diagnostic laboratory was in Phoenix. Population in Flagstaff was under 4000. At seven doctors the per patient ratio was around one to six hundred, so it's questionable whether any of them could afford expensive equipment. The doctors, that is. They treated sickness and injuries, delivered babies and performed amputations, but didn't attempt difficult surgery unless they had to.

The story was in the details. Dr. Zinn attended a man injured in an overturned-auto accident. One of his patients that year was a two-year-old boy who had been leading work horses into a barnyard when one horse kicked him in the forehead. What a picture—a two-year-old leading work horses. The boy was not seriously hurt. (!) But when a case of appendicitis came into Mercy Hospital, Miller and Raymond and Felix Manning called Dr. Hannett of Gallup or E. Payne Palmer of Phoenix, whichever could get here first, to take charge. Palmer joined Raymond and Felix to operate on Jack Crabb who had been brought in from Rogers Lake with a ruptured appendix. Crabb died.

Since the Great War, medicine had developed quickly on several fronts, requiring doctors in Arizona to keep up if they could. Dr. Felix and Dr. Schermann went to Phoenix for a clinic; Felix and Dr. Raymond traveled to the Mayo brothers' hospital in Minnesota to train in "the latest methods."

There was still no specific remedy anywhere for infections or bacterial diseases. Neurological and brain surgery was well established in big Eastern hospitals, and electro-encephalographs could study those brains, but such "methods" would have been of little use to the men who worked in Mercy (Milton) hospital.

Well then, what might institutes and research hospitals have had to offer to Flagstaff doctors? I went hunting for an answer.

New words had moved into public use—vitamin, calorie, germ, antitoxin, vaccine, antibody—as emphasis shifted slightly toward prevention. Intensive work was being done through those years into diseases caused by nutritional deficiencies, and the value of calcium, vitamins A and D were being confirmed. Rickets was definitely a vitamin D deficiency which could be cured by sunlight. Anemia could be cured by eating liver, they knew that too, as well as the existence of Vitamin C.

Other changes: phenobarbital was introduced for the treatment of epilepsy; a tuberculosis vaccine was developed; between 1920 and 1922 rapid progress was made using insulin to treat diabetes. Diagnosis technology included electrocardiographs and Wassermann Tests.

News of an innovation was moving through the West along the railroad lines. Pre-natal care—a brand new idea. And previously unmentionable illnesses of women were being addressed. A Pap test could detect uterine cancer. Lydia Pinkham's medicine (fifteen per cent alcohol) for "women's complaints" was selling all over the country. Back East, Margaret Sanger was crusading against the multiple pregnancies that many women considered an affliction worse than illness. Somebody had to. Contraception and planned parenthood were still judged obscene in influential circles.

The war had brought new ideas about asepsis and antiseptic precautions as well as neurological damage due to shock and trauma. Information of that sort might have been valuable in Flagstaff. So might recent developments in diagnostic techniques, in cardiology, in glandular research, in immunology, urinalysis, use of sedatives and narcotics. OK, visits to clinics in the East were essential to northern Arizona's doctors in those years of expanding understanding.

Not that they didn't go on setting bones and sewing up cuts and treating accident injuries. In October of 1921, duck hunting at Rogers Lake with thirty or so other men on the water, dentist Mackey was in the stern of a boat being paddled by J. P. Wilson, Althea's husband. Mackey picked up his shot gun, which discharged, shooting Wilson in the hip at close range. Drs. Raymond and Manning, on the scene, dressed the wound. Mr. Wilson was away from his desk at Arizona Central Bank for a few weeks.

Reminders of the past: P. G. Cornish, still in Albuquerque, was elected a fellow in the American College of Surgery. Dr. and Nellie Sult, who had gone to Clarkdale in 1916 and then moved on to Phoenix, visited in town. Nellie had been active in the Flagstaff Woman's Club; I wonder what she'd been doing for the past six years.

As always, there were continuing developments in the Manning family saga. Dr. G. F. sr. and Sarah began spending winters in Los Angeles with Yetta and her husband. Sometimes Julia and Hays were also houseguests, sometimes Dr. Tom was too. One winter the senior Manning, eighty-five years old, was knocked down by an auto with injuries that were not serious. Dr. Tom brought his mother and father home.

Dr. Felix and Lois decided against L. A., returned to Flagstaff and lived for a while in his parents' house. Felix resumed practicing medicine with his father and was appointed captain in the medical corps of the National Guard to examine applicants. The county health officer, he drove to Sedona to see a sick man at the beginning of a snow storm and, unable to get back up the hill, came home by way of Jerome, Prescott and Ashfork. The next month he bought a big new Buick touring car.

Julia was a member of the Women's Club. Her husband Hays was in the Boosters Club, which was working toward an "aero" field for the town. In June, Hays went in California to take the dental examination for admission to practice in that state; Julia visited with her sister Yetta while he was doing so. Now they were considering leaving? Sounds like my family.

With a partner, Tom bought a drug store in Gallup and moved over there. In August, he married a girl from Bisbee, Lula Chancey, who had graduated from the Normal School that spring. Sarah and Julia and George Verkamp traveled to New Mexico to be among the witnesses. Later Tom and Lula visited his parents for a few days.

I still shake the milk bottle. When I was a child, there was no homogenization—milk always had cream on the top, and you shook the bottle to mix them together. That's how old I am.

"Hi, Abby."

"Mom! Hello hello."

"I have a question for you."

"Oh good, I love questions." Bless her, she never disapproves of me. That's important to a mother, in case nobody's thought about it.

"You're a student of history, aren't you, my Abby?"

"And proud of it."

I laughed before I could go on. "I've read that Willa Cather said, 'The world broke in two in 1922 or thereabouts.'"

"Willa Cather, the novelist?"

"Yes. I'm reading that year now, and I can't figure out what she meant. Why 1922?"

"Why?"

"I could understand 1914, when that obscene, criminal, pointless war started, cost millions of lives and billions of dollars and left the old cultures crippled. Or 1919 when this country refused to join the League of Nations and established that stupid Prohibition and made a mockery of law."

"You say stupid?"

"OK, ignorant. Ignorance of what people are and how difficult it is to force them to do what's good for them."

"As Barry Goldwater—I think it was Goldwater—said in another context, you can't legislate morality. Or health either."

"Right. Well said. My problem is this. If I were going to say the world broke in two, I'd put the divide in 1914 or 1919. But why 1922? Medicine and science and technology were different after the war ended. There was a shift in what women could do. But the country had been working up to those changes for a while, it wasn't sudden. Cather cared about the arts, repudiated modernism, but modernism was at least a decade old by then."

"Yeah, I see what you mean."

"I read a biography—she thought the Jazz Age was cheap, tawdry and ugly. Materialistic. It eliminated possibility for heroism."

"I'd have to agree with her."

"Me too." I laughed. "So that's a possibility. In 1922 she was awarded the Pulitzer Prize for her sixth novel. It got some savage reviews and focused a lot of attention on her, criticism and expectation. Gave her problems with anxiety. She might have thought she was happier before the Pulitzer."

"True. Maybe she meant her world broke in two. How old was she?"

"Nearly fifty. You can be pretty disgusted with life around that time."

"I can hardly wait."

"You'll love it."

"Now fifty is only half way through for a woman—you're a good example of that, Mom—but life expectancy was shorter then. She could have felt the best years were gone. Did she have any pair-bond losses around then?"

"Nothing recent."

"Did she go on writing?"

"Nine more novels. I haven't read them all. In the early books she seemed to have a strong feeling for what had gone before, Nebraska pioneers and so forth."

"I can think of a few depressing items in world events that she might have known about."

"I knew I could count on you, Baboo."

"The Progressive movement was pretty well finished by then, if she cared about that. Mussolini became Prime Minister of Italy in 1922. You know, fascism and all. Hitler had organized the Nazi party and was already making noise. Stalin was high enough in Russian Communism to have been part of the change to the U.S.S.R. That was before '22, I think. "

"I can't stand it. The first ghastly insanity was barely finished, I haven't gotten over it yet, and the next one was already building? It's too awful."

"Yeah, things are usually grim. In this country too, Mom. Graft and scandal in the Harding administration were in the news. I think you could make an argument that the big Bull Market in stocks was just getting started. Tabloid newspapers—you know, lurid, sensational ugliness, sex and violence, murder, such profound matters as flagpole sitters—they had a huge circulation."

"Mmmmmm. That on top of the war and all, maybe it became too much for her."

"I seem to remember that Gershwin's 'Rhapsody in Blue' dates from 1922. Would that have cheered her up, do you think?"

"I doubt it. I like it, but I'll bet she didn't. Odd, Cather was defiant when she was younger. It's hard to think of her as being more comfortable on the older side."

"Are you more comfortable in what you think of as the past?"

"Only when it comes to computers. I operate mine on the principle of illusion, which is better than no understanding at all."

I would like to see, in the maybe thirty-forty years left to me, whether it is possible to learn from happiness rather than always and only from sorrow and mistakes.

Tears were running slowly from under Emily's eyelids. I stroked the hair back from her forehead, from the sides of her face, as softly as I could, and her eyes opened slightly.

"They shouldn't do that to people."

"No, they shouldn't."

"It's not nice."

"You're right, it's not."

"They ought to think up a better way." Her eyes closed again, and the tears kept coming. "Is Travis here?"

"He said to tell you he'll be here soon."

"Am I all right?"

"The nurse says yes."

"How much did they take?"

"Hard to tell."

There was a long pause. "How did you get in here?"

"I told them I was your sister."

Then Travis was there on the other side of the gurney. He bent and kissed her, she raised her hand to his shoulder, and I stepped back. I was probably not at the top of the list right then.

After a lumpectomy the patient can expect numbness and tenderness andshooting discomfort in her breast. So the books had told me, the books that didn't mention tears. In addition, there will probably be an accumulation of lymph fluid in the soft tissues of the adjacent arm with accompanying swelling that can affect the whole arm or the hand and wrist, everything below the elbow.

Lymphatic fluid, which contains nutrients, is an easy target for bacteria. Therefore the patient—I almost said victim—should keep her arm clean, moisturize her skin, do anything to minimize infection, and seek immediate medical attention if infection does occur. Charming, yes?

I stopped by Emily's house every day to offer company and admire her children, who were old enough to organize themselves into a support group. The woman who came in three days a week kept the house clean, so the kids could concentrate on oiling their mother's arm, bringing in the mail, filling her water glass.

"What can I bring you, Mom?"

"What do you want for lunch?"

"Stay right there, Mom, I'll do it."

One of them was always with her, "dancing attendance," she said. "You know what they're doing? They read Dr. Seuss out loud to me and sing lullabies to encourage me to nap. They've used their allowance to buy me a teddy bear to hold and named him Jefferson because he's smart and practical. I discuss things with him. It's really quite soothing."

I laughed and squeezed her good hand. "Bully for them."

"Travis is treating me extra nice. He actually comes home at a reasonable hour and sits down to talk with me about his day, about anything I've been thinking. By the time I get used to being pampered, they'll probably be back to taking me for granted."

I laughed again. "Enjoy it while you can. In one more day you're supposed to be out taking short walks."

There was some lymphedema in what she called her "downstream" arm, so I drove her to the grocery store, but every day we walked, strolled really, around her neighborhood. Early December, so the desert days were perfect, the relentless heat of the summer sun relaxed for a few months. Without saying anything about it, I walked on her upstream side so I wouldn't bump her.

If she was suffering emotionally, she didn't say, she was like that. "It could be worse. Some of the photos I've seen—half a breast gone or huge jagged scars—are grotesque. I can't imagine what it would take to get used to that."

"Probably be easier to say 'My breasts are not me'."

"You're so right. Remember when I used to sing 'There'll be Spring every year without you' and 'I get along without you very well'? It doesn't seem so funny any more, now that I'm missing part of one."

"It's not as if you used it for anything."

"No, I didn't. I guess it was nice for hugging."

I touched her good arm. "You're a heroine, Emily."

"You think so? Is there such a thing as a tired heroine? I'm worn out. Physically. Emotionally."

"I've been reading. Fatigue often follows surgery, the books say, it's a natural response that may be related to red blood cell counts being low."

"Isn't it just great to have an explanation?"

"It makes you feel so much more cheerful."

Learning how valuable friendship can be, I treated her as if she were porcelain and made up a new aphorism: Decide who you can't afford to lose and behave accordingly.

There's overlap in the symptoms of anxiety and depression. Anxiety: insomnia, fatigue, headache, depression. Depression: insomnia, fatigue, headache, anxiety. Just how different are they?

"Hey, Mom."

"Baxter, how nice, I was hoping I'd talk with you today."

"How you doing?"

"Just fine. Days are long and slow and hot with no fires. I'm looking forward to summer rains. How are you?"

"Pretty good. The Enron debacle has been a negative event for business here in Texas, but we're holding on."

"Did it affect you personally?"

"Not much, except for being part of the general mood. I didn't own stock, despite all the excited advice. Glad I resisted."

"I'll bet. Reassure me that I didn't lose anything. I mean, I trust you without question, but the way things have been going lately…"

"No problem, Mom, I've got you invested in such conservative issues it would take another Ice Age…"

"Good, thank you. I'm relieved. Lately I've been reading about business in the 1920s, and what with the news from Texas, I've been thinking about you."

"How so?"

"I'm into 1922 now, the depression of 1920–1921 easing, America moving slowly into the beginning of what it would call 'Prosperity,' 'the Fat Years,' when projections came in every month of increased corporate profits, and all Americans with 'get up and go' assumed life would improve indefinitely."

"I see what you mean, it does sound like the recent irrational exuberance."

"At first the advance was not spread evenly—it was a crazy time. Listen to this: Standard Oil established an eight-hour day for its oil field workers in 1922; U.S. Steel did the same in '23. Then the Supreme Court invalidated minimum wage legislation, and the Railroad Labor Board announced a thirteen percent cut in employee wages. But business was expanding on most fronts. Zenith Radio was founded, for example. Audiences for the movies: fifty million a week. Want to buy something? Use installment plans. Go for a drive in your Model T."

"I would think it would be difficult for business men to make rational plans in all that confusion, signs pointing in all different directions."

"You know, Baxter, I doubt reason had anything to do with the economy for quite a while. They may have believed they were behaving rationally..."

"I'm beginning to suspect that economic trends are the result of some kind of contagion. Don't repeat that in the wrong company."

"I promise. Economics is described as 'the dismal science,' but it doesn't seem like science to me."

"Don't quote me—doesn't seem like science to me half the time."

"So Baxter, tell me. As I understand the 20s from reading about them, a major factor in the growth of trading in stocks was buying on margin: the buyer paid only a percent of the selling price, the rest was paid on loan—banks were involved—and the stock remained with the broker. Earnings on the stock were less than the interest paid on the loan; speculation was supposed to take care of the difference. Paper moved around. The volume of brokers' loans ("call" loans) was an index of the volume of speculation. Have I got that right?"

"I'm impressed, Mom. That's about the way it was."

"Seems like a shell game."

"Well, when there's money involved, people aren't exactly at their best."

"You've noticed that too? Those wheeler-dealers didn't know what was going to happen. I'm looking at it from the opposite direction, and I do."

"That gives you a definite advantage."

"It was unreal—millions of shares were traded, and the price of securities began to rise. I'm curious about how the economic boom affected a small town on the railroad line way out west. Did life go on in Flagstaff pretty much as usual? Or was there spending on new public buildings, a real hospital maybe? Public services? I've been reading the microfilms of old newspapers searching for clues."

"And...?"

"Local bank officials said business conditions were improving and growth was healthy. The town was shipping away more freight—things like oats, hay, straw, potatoes, lumber, livestock—than was being shipped in."

"That was a good sign."

"They thought so. The Future Holds Great Promise was a current motto. One month six pages, six, in the newspaper were required for printing Articles of Incorporation—sixteen different trading posts and livestock companies."

"I suppose that was healthy growth, I hope so."

"Well, there were problems. Population was increasing steadily, and a prolonged drought made the water system inadequate for all those people. The town feared it would have to shut its saw mills—the reservoir was down to only nine feet of water, and they were using more than they had coming in. The Santa Fe railroad had a contract for a specified amount for its steam engines. That was a definite complication.

"Big, powerful company..."

"It claimed it was prepared to cooperate in developing a new water source, but the town council objected to the plan it offered. Somebody had the bright idea of building a dam up in Schultz Pass to create a reservoir."

"How'd that go over?"

"Some engineers said it would hold water, some said it wouldn't, some said it would be expensive and unsafe. Finally it was, to use their word for it, 'nixed.' They went on debating and decided the only choice had to be another concrete reservoir below the canyon to store water from the mountain."

"Is that what they did?"

"First they had a bond election."

"I suppose so."

"And complained that taxes were too high."

"Even then?"

"Some issues last a long time."

"Yes. Yes they do."

"I loved an ad I noticed in the local newspaper—it seemed relevant to the water discussion: 'Protect Your Health—Drink Budweisser—A Liquid Food Drink'."

"You're kidding."

"Nope. For science news it was right up there with 'Wrigley's Chewing Gum Aids Digestion'."

I remember roller skate keys, tinkertoys, cootie catchers. I remember when you could put a coin into the list of records against the wall at your cafe table and play the jukebox. I remember when you were kept back a grade if you failed. I remember wringers on washing machines. That's how old I am.

The effect of shouting at Don didn't last long. Next morning he quite emphatically started the motorcoach. "I'm driving. You haven't got the sense God gave you." They were the first words he'd spoken to me. I wasn't expecting a thank you for breakfast, but "good morning" wouldn't have been too much to ask.

Refusing to talk, he drove the only road across Capitol Reef/Waterpocket Fold, east along the little Fremont River. Leaves on bushes at the side of the road were yellow. I looked out the window, thinking: "If the world is beautiful, so am I. And amazing, fantastic, full of surprises around every bend. Pew to you, Doctor Don."

He roared right past the junction that turned north to Green River, and I didn't say anything. He drove half an hour in the wrong direction, and I didn't say anything. It was a silly kind of revenge, I knew it at the time, but I felt so hurt and isolated I didn't want to say a single thing to him. Pew.

When we reached the fork with the sign that pointed to Lake Powell, and he realized what he'd done, he had something new to complain about. "God damn it, you're supposed to be reading the map. What's wrong with you? Can't you even get that right?" Nothing was his fault.

I turned and looked at him. "You want me to feel bad, don't you?"

He stared straight ahead, mouth tight.

"For almost forty years you've been the only person who's criticized me to my face. Like it gives you power if you can hurt your wife."

He drove back to the Green River turn-off, stony, silent, angry, as though he had a right to behave any way he wanted.

If I had known before hand, I'd never have married a doctor. All those decades the children and I had lived essentially without him, as if he'd barely existed—he was too busy and too important to be involved with us—yet he'd controlled our lives with orders and anger and disapproval.

We drove along the San Rafael Reef, turned east onto the interstate, and crossed the Green River where Powell's first expedition had floated by a hundred years earlier when no buildings had been there on the bluffs. I felt like a fifty pound bag of cement was lying on my chest.

When Don wasn't home, we'd been independent enough, but it takes everybody to make a family, and if you never see your husband, your father, all the money in the world won't stop you from becoming bitter. If I tried to tell him, you know what? It was my hang-up.

"Turn right at Crescent Junction, 191. South." I gathered my geology books into my lap and held the big one for company. Lineaments and wrench faults and ancient crustal unrest—company. The few white clouds above were pink on the bottoms with reflections from the Entrada sandstone.

Arches National Park is different from the other parks in southern Utah. There are 100 million years of erosion, colored stone, not much vegetation, like the other parks. Time is also visible, measured by words of many syllables. Arches is different because it lies above an underground salt bed thousands of feet thick in places—salt deposited by evaporating oceans 300 million or so years ago, then buried by other sediments that may have been more than a mile thick.

And there's contorted bedding, wrinkled as if a fifty-foot layer of mud had been wet last week and all the smooth layers above it had been too heavy. When I try to describe southern Utah, I want to write in capital letters and underline everything.

The road that climbs up from the Arches visitor center and out of Moab Canyon is a bit of a thrill, steep and crooked, but then it opens out on top into an amazing terrain, free-standing red formations with names like (yuk) Courthouse Towers, Tower of Babel, Park Avenue. To the east is a vista of petrified dunes and, twenty-five miles beyond, the La Sal mountains. The Colorado River is hidden in rough country to the south. It's all so gorgeous it's almost grandiose.

The Great Wall is a sheer cliff of sandstone two miles long. Balanced Rock, two hundred arches of all sizes, the Fiery Furnace (double yuk), Salt Valley—all of them carved into sedimentary deposits by wind and water. All of them temporary, still wearing away.

Don surprised me, "This is weird. You're the one with the books, what caused it?"

I tried to explain about salt deposits that drained away slowly on groundwater, causing a collapse that shattered overlying sedimentary layers into hundreds of parallel fracture lines, giving erosion places to work. "What we're seeing is all that's left. All that's left of an enormous block of solid rock that stretched to the tops of those mountains over there—covering the tops of those mountains."

I don't think he heard me, probably wasn't really interested. Exploring ideas is not part of your average doctor's approach to the world? Refusing to pause at viewpoints, he drove to the end of the road, where he ignored an ideal camp site with a stupendous view.

"Look, Don, here's one long enough for us. Imagine waking up in the morning to that panorama. Let's stop here for the night."

He didn't answer, and I felt like a fool for giving him the opportunity for another power display. Living alone couldn't be worse than that kind of treatment.

In 1932 Charlotte Perkins Gilman, suffering from breast cancer, chose suicide instead of mastectomy. Rachel Carson died of breast cancer in 1965, Ingrid Bergman in 1982. Mary Roberts Rhinehart had a mastectomy in 1947, Alice Roosevelt Longworth in 1956, Betty Ford in 1974, Nancy Reagan in 1987. Marvella Bayh had a modified mastectomy in 1971, Shirley Temple Black in 1972, Happy Rockefeller in 1974.

GETTING AROUND

1922 Does anybody remember "The Song of the Open Road?" How about "In My Merry Oldsmobile?" "He had to get under, get out and get under, to fix up his automobile."

The year before, the state highway department had printed the initial issue of a small, black and white, monthly newsletter named Arizona Highways to inform the motoring public about conditions. Maps included keys that identified established roads as paved (around Phoenix and Tucson), graveled, graded, dirt and "inquire locally for conditions."

Most of Coconino County's "highways" were dirt or inquire locally, despite such figures as:

- In 1922 85,000 tourists drove to the Grand Canyon Park although the road was sometimes impassable. The next year there were more than 100,000 visitors.

- In 1922 1037 cars were registered in Coconino County: by 1923 the number had increased to 2155.

- An estimated 20,000 tourist autos passed through Flagstaff in 1923; the town's auto camp ground was crowded with tourist cars in the summer.

- The county sold 62,500 gallons of gas in November of 1923 and issued 1429 auto licenses in 1924, 250 to 300 more than the previous year.

Despite a Good Roads Association that had been active for quite a while, no concrete or asphalt pavement surfaced the roads around Flagstaff—none completed, none under construction. Over the years between 1922 and 1924, roads to settlements round about (Mormon and Stoneman Lakes, Munds Park, Schnebly Hill, Cameron, Leupp, Fort Valley, Kendrick Park, Maine and the Grand Canyon) had been graded and graveled, "a vast improvement" in the opinion of motorists.

The best north-south highway in Arizona connected Flagstaff to Phoenix west through Williams to Ashfork, then south to Prescott, Congress Junction and Wickenburg, a long tedious 222 miles in a 1920s automobile, and it was "improved" but not paved. The *Sun* was full of ads for Dodge, Hupmobile, Maxwell, Willys-Knight, Durant, Star, Chevrolet and Ford autos as well as ads for tires (balloon and otherwise), oil and gasoline. As the pace increased, the phrase "speed demons" appeared in reports of accidents.

When Dr. Felix Manning went to Phoenix for an appendectomy, he motored back up in his Studebaker. Dr. Raymond always had a Packard. Hilda and Martin drove their own car to Phoenix to a conference of Boy Scout executives.

It was agreed that roads needed to be built in all directions out of Flagstaff, including a decent connection between Flagstaff and the small farming community in Sedona, something better than the steep track down Schnebly Hill. The Flagstaff Chamber of Commerce (Dr. Fronske a member) requested the Forest Service to construct a road through Oak Creek Canyon. Jerome wanted an Oak Creek road too. The list was impressive: the governor, both Coconino and Yavapai counties, Clarkdale American Legion post, Cottonwood, Arizona state engineers, the Flagstaff Rotary Club (Dr. Fronske a member).

All argued that roads on both ends of the canyon had been constructed, leaving only twenty-three miles along the creek to connect them. Modern times, you know: the engineers sent up a plane to make photos—a View Map of the proposed route. Late in the year work began and plans were made for two bridges over the creek—for $2000 each.

Coconino County negotiated through several months the sale of the Bright Angel Trail in the Grand Canyon to the United States. Sale price $200,000. Part of the deal—an understanding that $100,000 would be spent to build a road from the Old Trails Highway to the canyon and construct other trails in the park. Not everybody was happy about the sale, specifically Ralph Cameron, who had sold the Bright Angel Trail to Coconino County for not nearly that much.

A bold headline in the newspaper shouted "Wake Up Flagstaff; Open the Door; Opportunity Knocks; Others Awake." That was about a road from Flagstaff to Kayenta. Senator Hayden introduced a bill in Congress to fund a bridge across the Colorado below Lee's Ferry.

Meanwhile, chances were good that federal money would be made available to put a surface of oil and crushed rock on the road to Winslow. The town was waiting for a paved road from Flagstaff to Angell, a few miles beyond Winona on the railroad line. There was talk, too, about the place where a road crossed the Santa Fe tracks at Winona. It was, according to the *Sun*, the first "overhead grade crossing" in Arizona, and it can't have been surfaced with dirt, can it?

Because accidents in Flagstaff were increasing steadily, citizens wanted the Santa Fe Railroad to construct crossings that would go under the tracks at Sitgreaves and Agassiz. The Santa Fe said there wouldn't be any problems if motorists were to slow down at the tracks and look both ways before going onto the rails.

Another message went to the railroad company from Flagstaff's town council: train engineers were blowing their whistles unnecessarily all night and disturbing the sleep of citizens—be less noisy, please. The nighttime whistling stopped.

The men of the Rotary Club requested a new depot from the Santa Fe, saying "present accommodations are almost intolerable." The Santa Fe offered a blueprint for what, so Breen reported, would become "a national attraction."

The summer I was fourteen, my family did a summer vacation in the White Mountains, and I wandered alone for hours feeling terribly romantic in the Great Outdoors. Girls could do that then. There was a big meadow lush with grasses and flowers—ah! the perfect place for Communion with Nature! I lay down and composed myself in a spiritual attitude, ready for feeling to sweep over me, but a slight movement—omigosh, the flowers and grasses were full of bugs crawling on, up, along. Let's hear it for Romanticism.

Ladybug beetles can walk right across spider webs without getting stuck. I've seen it for myself. I don't know how they manage, on an old web, maybe? Everybody else gets stuck, including me. I don't walk actually, but my meaning is clear. I've seen fabulous insects here on the mountain, creatures with fragile blue wings. Creatures with transparent orange bodies or fuzzy red bodies. I suppose they all bite something.

A foot away from me in the tower a small brown moth and a yellow jacket wasp fell together with a thud to the deck of my firefinder map, the moth beating its wings, the wasp clutching it and bending its thorax to sting. I was horrified. Wasps are carnivorous (so are ladybugs) and they like to eat moths, but I've been very painfully stung by a yellow jacket. The struggle for life and all that notwithstanding—another bizarre word—I smashed them both. The moth wouldn't have lived, and I didn't want the wasp to.

You remember for a long time things you've learned for yourself by watching, by noticing, that is, you can if you look at what you're seeing. I think I miss a lot by not knowing enough.

A fact can lead to speculation. Example: if weather is movement of the atmosphere, as I've read, and there is no atmosphere on the moon, there is no weather on the moon, right? Example: if clouds are water suspended in the atmosphere, if two per cent of air is water, do some clouds weigh more than others? How could you weigh them?

Clouds were discussed by Greeks in the 7th century B.C., Chinese in the 4th century B.C., Romans in the 1st century A..D., Descartes in the 17th century, balloonists in 18th century but none of them developed a precise observational language.

In 1802, during the Enlightenment, the Age of Reason, a time when natural science was a matter of acute public interest, a thirty- year-old English chemist named Luke Howard announced his names for the clouds: cirrus, stratus, cumulus, nimbus. Clouds may have individual shapes, he said, but only a few basic forms, a few types. His bringing of order into constantly changing phenomena, naming of something that did not hold still, was very typical of the Enlightenment. We use his Latin terminology still. What did people see in the sky before Luke Howard named the clouds?

The atmosphere is always moving in thermals, currents, eddies, layers, all the winds, but as I've said before, it's invisible unless there's something in it like clouds or smoke. If someday humans develop a way to see atmosphere itself, what will it look like?

 Another thing I learned from Lyle: People who are willing to do harm have the advantage.

1922 Yes indeed, the prosperity boom of the 20s was beginning to affect Flagstaff. Officials boasted that the town had spent more than one million dollars on school buildings and were proud to announce plans to construct a new high school. The town was "alive" in every direction.

Members of the Federated Church intended to add a three-story community center, including a gym and a boys' club, to their existing structure. Cress, Nackard and Mayflower were planning new construction downtown. The Elks had decided to put up a new lodge building; the Gun Club planned one with space to share with the Boy Scouts. It must have been an exciting time to live in Flagstaff.

There was a new athletic field at the Normal School, but even better were the plans for a city recreation park to be built near the grounds for the new high school, a park that would include a dance hall, baseball and football grounds, tennis courts, a race track, a grandstand that would cost $13,975, and a dam on the Rio de Flag to create a lake. A bond issue that would provide funds was passed.

The Women's Club announced its intention to construct its own building soon on a West Aspen lot which it had purchased (across the street from what sixty years later would be the front door of the City Hall). Room would be provided to be used as a museum to preserve Indian "curios," which were being shipped out in carloads to museums in other states. Thus the small beginning that led to the Museum of Northern Arizona.

Applauding, the *Sun* described the Women's Club as "a tremendous factor in bettering social conditions in Flagstaff," and said, "Comparison with other towns throughout the west will not find a more enlightened and up-to-date community than right here in Flagstaff due to a great extent to the endeavor of the women." Breen urged local men to boost for the new Women's Club building.

Lots were cleared and ground was broken and plans were revealed to the *Sun*: red brick, one story with a high roof, cost $15,000. The ladies held fund-raising bake sales, dances in Ashurst Auditorium and on the tennis court at the Normal School, and were jubilant when a cornerstone was laid. Two months later the club building was formally opened. Fund-raising continued for purchase of furniture.

I stood in the parking lot across from the city hall, looking at a good-sized tree that is growing there and wondering whether the Women's Club planted it in 1924.

Come to think of it, anything that includes the Colorado Plateau is also a fantasy thriller kind of story. Rising intact for millions of years. All 130,000 square miles of its history visible. It's like an alien planet, like no place else, a setting for strange stories.

June 2001

Dear Progeny,

There was a song Gwen used to sing about the seasons going around like a carousel. "…and the painted ponies go up and down…"

When your father (and grandfather) and I traveled though the southern Utah part of the Colorado Plateau, time spread out of sight in all directions, plunging down under our tires, standing in cliffs above our heads, and I found it exhilarating—that I could learn to think in hundreds of millions of years, that I was part of a species that could make the planet's age part of its knowledge.

Now I'm living with a brief annual cycle, an annual trip around the sun. Such a snippet.

Winter slipped past, and spring with all its changes slid easily away. Now June's relentless sun and savage winds are half gone. Banks of cumulus build in the southeast every afternoon as moisture begins to seep up from Mexico as it did last year. Soon, I hope, there'll be afternoon lightning storms and rain and rainbows.

Painted ponies come around. Every stage is precious because it won't last. I'll see it all again a few more times, and then I'll spin off and away. And that's OK with me—another phase. The thing to do is to treasure this while I have it. (Is 'treasure' a verb? As in 'to cherish something precious'?)

While the heat of June beats upon the front wall of my little cabin, I take refuge in the sky where the cool breezes are. For the past two weeks I've been extended into overtime each afternoon, but even if I weren't, I'd stay up until sun settles behind the pines and shades the cabin.

It's especially private to be above everything late in the day. Dark shade thickens in the pines; needles at their tops shine in low sunlight. Shadows on hills and mountains grow long into folds and canyons that weren't visible at noon. I love it, glad for its goodness. If I were twenty again, I'd be moving too fast to see it happening.

I don't imagine there are many places anymore in this country where people could live in untouched wilderness. Most of the trees on this mountain are all second growth thanks to logging almost a hundred years ago. I look down on two ranches, and the Arboretum is only a mile and a half away in one of my blind spots. Without binoculars I can see three observatory domes, an airport, a golf course, half the city of Flagstaff, and the Purina dog food plant east of town. I could see houses in twelve subdivisions if their roofs weren't hidden by their pines. Probably a thousand campers and hikers and bikers are also down there, hidden by the trees. There are roads and beer cans everywhere. But illusion is better than no wilderness at all. Especially compared to Phoenix.

Cattle were brought in to Rogers Lake weeks ago. I can see them down there grazing in a group. Sometimes I can hear them calling. Rather an ungraceful sound. Yesterday I thought I heard sheep for the first time this year, at least the clack-clack of the wooden bells, but I haven't seen them yet moving beneath the pines, eating grass as they go, herded by dogs, followed by Basques.

The only voices I hear are on the radio. The only faces I see are on squirrels and ravens, and that's OK. Everybody needs a private place—in addition, of course, to the space inside.

I'm working on a new theory. Now, don't laugh, I'm serious about this. It's a common historical point of view that in the 1700s, removed from the traditions of centuries in Europe, America managed to devise a government and a society that lacked sophistication, perhaps, but achieved a vigor and equity new to humanity. It's possible, isn't it, that the same process might explain the differences between this continent's eastern coast and the newer culture that has grown here in the Southwest? that we need not apologize for ourselves? need to feel no inadequacy? I hope that makes sense to you.

Cazz, I'm working on a poem that I want to be, how shall I say it, true to the place where I've lived my life, something that connects me and the Arizona land. So far I have:

How to Write an Arizona Poem

Get out of town.
Hike the Grand Canyon
in flash flood season.

Choose words that are gritty
to the touch, big words
that scrape and bite
and weigh too much to lift.

Drive up Fish Creek Hill.
Up, not down. Up is on
the outside above the cliff.

Beware of similes that don't
stick like a cholla ball
on your ankle. Write lines that can
see through centuries.

Love to the whole kit and Kaboodle.
Kit I can guess at, but what does kaboodle mean?

The family's elder.

In 1900 the estimated number of deaths in America caused by breast cancer was 3,780. Eight of those deaths were white men.

1922–1924 Medicine made steady advances in the early 20s, despite the same old diseases. Cerebral meningitis was still around. Measles, scarlet fever, and polio were common problems. Nationally 90,452 people died of tuberculosis every year. Incidence of smallpox was climbing in Arizona—69 cases in 1919, 176 in 1920, 192 in 1921, 468 in 1922. But clever scientists in the East had discovered white corpuscles and their function in human blood as well as the strepto-coccus that caused scarlet fever, and they'd proceeded to develop an antibiotic. Wasn't it a marvel?

After the death of an eight-year-old girl in northern Arizona, it was announced that an antitoxin could reduce diphtheria fatalities. The State Board of Health circulated through newspapers its advice for avoiding the disease. For example: remove the tonsils and adenoids of carriers. (As a result, mine were cut out surgically when I was about six years old. Does that still happen to children?) Within a few weeks E. Payne Palmer was traveling north to Flagstaff to perform tonsillectomies.

Flagstaff's doctors continued to deal with routine frontier cases. Manning, Schermann and Fronske treated a boy who had been sick with grippe and had developed convulsions. They pulled him through. Felix Manning and Martin Fronske, working at Mercy hospital, patched up a man with self-inflicted knife wounds and served on the panel that judged him insane and ordered that he be taken to the state hospital in Phoenix. Dr. Zinn gave first aid, after a house fire, to a fourteen-year-old boy who had tried to save his mother. He died.

The *Sun* reported that flu was in style. Drs. Schermann and Felix were down with it, and physicians were busy—Dr. Miller was in Tuba City, where 125 people were sick—but the professional diagnosis was bad colds or old-fashioned grippe. Breen was equal to the situation.

> *Dr. Felix Manning became his own patient the latter part of last week, called himself up and asked himself to call at his house and prescribe for himself, which he did, ordering himself to stay in the house for a few days. Having considerable confidence in his doctor, he obeyed, with the result that he got down to his office again the first of the week and is again all right.*

Felix, who was both the city and the county health officer, reported that there were about ninety local deaths annually, part of that due to the number of tourists passing through in the summer. Probably he meant sick tourists died here, not that they ran people down.

In the winter, when snow was deep, coasting on Mars Hill produced the usual injuries, and Dr. Schermann made professional calls with a horse and buggy instead of his Studebaker. Footnote: Breen told readers that the doors on the doctor's car were hinged at the rear and confided that twice he had torn them off going into his garage with them open.

Dr. Miller, evidently a versatile man, was in charge of the Orpheum Theater while Mary Costigan was ill. In 1922 he became a member of the library board and remained a fixture on it through 1929.

Arizona had a State Nurses Association by then. Seeking locals, I ran my finger down the pages of the register of voters for Flagstaff, 1922. Nine women identified their occupation as "nurse": Edna Davis, Adaline Johnson, Sallie Watts, Frieda Johnson, M.J. Dwiggins, Catherine O'Farrell, Mollie Flynn, Mary Dougherty. The *Sun* mentioned Clara Brown as a nurse at the hospital. The Coconino County register of medical licenses has no reference to eight of those names. Were they "practical" nurses, not "registered"?

Frieda Johnson was legitimate. She had been Flagstaff's school nurse for more than two years, conscientious and efficient, an advocate of public health programs. "The health of the public school should be everyone's interest."

As part of her job, she had provided tooth brushes for the children, arranged vaccinations for them, treated them for injuries and for ring worm, scabies, pink eye, pediculosis. As part of "hundreds of home visits annually," nurse Johnson had found four families with cases of diphtheria. Flagstaff's Social Service Circle, impressed by her work, had bought a Ford for her use in home visiting, running expense for eight months $72.25.

But Frieda Johnson left the community because her mother was ill elsewhere. Virginia Phelan, the first registered nurse in Coconino County had moved as well, to a position in San Diego.

> I lived in a chronic state of simmer through those years of wifehood. I wonder what it did to my body.

No man could possibly be as handsome, as intelligent, as funny as I thought Lyle was. Or as inspired a lover. It was a magic few weeks. I sang from one room to another, sang to the children, sang in the back yard—"Good morning, starshine"—and danced on the grass. It wasn't a normal condition. Nobody can be that happy for long, worse luck.

He phoned now and then, as he had for months, with jokes or little stories that left me alive to my fingertips. Now and then, breathless, I'd meet him for lunch in an ordinary place, and we'd sit on opposite sides of the table trading opinions as if we were merely friends like always, and I'd go home and change my underwear. High school was never like that.

I don't know when sex drive peaks for a man. I've read it's about seventeen. For me it was closer to age forty. My body yearned for Lyle day and night; whatever I was thinking was pale by comparison. I wonder whether there's anything in medical literature about what effect, long or short term, it had on my biochemistry. I could check the indices for the journals in the NAU library, I suppose.

Once Lyle drove to a motor court in Camp Verde, and we spent the afternoon tangling sheets. I was in such a frenzy, I barely saw beyond the bed. It wasn't that he was so, well…he could last a long time and be ready again half an hour later. To every climax of his, though, I had four, gasping, shuddering.

Another time we met at night on a golf course in a soft rain and lay on the grass moving, slow and quiet, and mist touched my face like a blessing from heaven. A brief noon meeting in a room in Glendale. A walk with a blanket up a desert wash. Later I wondered whether he'd been to those places before, he found them so easily, but at the time I was too intoxicated by him to have any doubts or to wonder how long it would last.

And that's all I want to say about that.

—— —— —— —— —— —— —— —— —— —— —— —— —— —— —— —— —— ——

"Physicians rely on rationalization and denial constantly." *New England Journal of Medicine.*

1922–1924 America moved into the Jazz Age, into mah-jong and Louis Armstrong, young and handsome then. In Flagstaff Victrolas and records were for sale in stores; anyone who was young enough to do the Charleston was going to dancing parties. There were efforts to control those who were even younger—children who roller skated on the new street paving were held guilty of violation of a town ordinance.

A woman, Ana (Anastacia) Frohmiller, was appointed treasurer of the County Board of Supervisors. At the same time, girls who bobbed their hair and kept it sleek with brilliantine were warned that girls with long hair received better grades in high school.

Despite Prohibition, it was no secret that strong liquor could be bought in Flagstaff. From distilleries in Sycamore Canyon, kegs were sent up on the backs of sheep. Home hooch was coming in from ranches on the east side. Kendrick Park was full of stills and bootleggers, and rumor had it that one of the fire lookouts was making illegal gin in his tower. The south side of town had "Bootleg Row" where anybody with money could buy wild berry wine from the mountain.

The mood in town was still for Improvement. Editor Breen, who had been elected to the state senate, advised homeowners to "doll up the garden gate," that is, to paint their houses as part of the annual Spring Clean-Up Campaign. The Rotary Club—"growth and progress," "Big Things Are Ahead"—suggested that ancient ruins in the surrounding country should be made national monuments. When the Women's Club petitioned the town council to appoint an inspector for restaurants and food stores, the responsibility was referred to Dr. Felix.

The county physician was paid $600 a year. As county Superintendent of Health, Felix Manning received $2400. He reported 252 births in the county for 1921, 118 deaths. Thanks to the Shephard-Towner bill, I suppose, there was a County Child Welfare Board.

The sewer system that was intended to prevent certain kinds of diseases had been completed to the satisfaction of most forward-looking people. City Clerk Clarence Pulliam notified property owners that they must connect to the sewer or a penalty would be invoked, but the ordinance, "a modern health law," was not enforced at first. As Flagstaff's health officer, Dr. Felix recommended that town camp grounds be connected and warned while he was about it that some people with a cow or two were selling milk without sanitary precautions.

Hardly a week passed without a report that confirmed the town's image of as being "up and coming." An aeroplane, would you believe it, landed in the Babbitt pasture east of town and took off repeatedly, taking daring citizens up for a ride. Coconino County, agreeing that no development would be possible without a pact that would apportion Colorado River water among seven states, voted three to one for a dam on the river. The Riordans had plans to double the capacity of their sawmill, saying it would be "a great boost for prosperity".

Oh my. M. J. Riordan suggested that, a new name for Milton road being called for, "Logway" or "Go-Devil" might be appropriate to commemorate Flagstaff's beginning as a lumbering town. The parade, speeches and sporting events of the 4th of July celebration were still "right smart fun."

 I remember when the Pledge of Allegiance we recited in school said "one nation indivisible" and made no mention of God. That's how old I am.

"Woody Mountain."

"Mother, hello. You're in town, why are you answering your phone that way?"

"Oh, Gwen. I guess I did. That's the way I respond to the forest radio, I must have been confused, so much to do, you know. How are you?"

"School is out now, so I'm spending my days trying to keep Beanie and Cazz from breaking something. Yesterday I heard pounding on the flat roof of the rumpus room, and I rushed out to find those two little devils running across it and leaping into the deep end of the pool. They couldn't figure out how I knew."

I laughed. "Isn't it fun to have kids though?"

"Is that what you call it?"

"Might as well."

"Their father reads your letters to them, hamming it up, especially the parts about wildfires. He loves it. So do they."

"Oh, I am glad. Ask them if they can guess what it meant in the 1920s to say, 'He's all wet,' or 'She's the cat's meow,' or 'That's bunk' or 'That's horsefeathers'."

"I'll bet they won't. They'll like the horsefeathers though."

"Wonder how they'd react to the ads for automobiles, open to the air, flimsy-looking things, but they were 'spiffy' at the time."

"It might be fun to try that, I'll get a book with pictures of old cars."

"Too bad they aren't old enough to realize how familiar eighty-year-old news can be. Dr. Charles A. Cale, a local chiropractor, wrote a column for the *Sun* titled "Diet and Health"—evidence that the national movement for preventive medicine had reached the West. A book titled *Diet and Health* was on the best seller lists in 1922. It contained a key to calories."

"That sounds like today, one diet craze after another. I can't keep up with what's supposed to be bad for me at the moment."

"You too? Neither can I."

"Any more Arizona deja vu all over again?"

"Flagstaff was worried about drought and water shortage and pine bark beetles—ten percent of the pines of the Kaibab forest had died. A headline read FLAGSTAFF FACES WATER FAMINE."

"That's perpetual in Arizona."

"The town was using twenty million gallons a year, more than the average annual supply."

"Have you found any more gossip?"

"I have—another doctor divorce."

"No kidding."

"The divorce rate was rising. In 1900 it was three per 1000, in 1910 four and a half, in 1920 nine."

"So it wasn't just World War One."

"No."

"Let's have the gory details."

"Annis Zinn applied for divorce from Dr. Peter Paul Zinn, charging cruel treatment and outrages. That was one of only a few possible grounds in those days, and it might have been exaggerated out of necessity. Anyway, she claimed that P. P. told her he had had "improper and immoral" relations with other women; that he said he did not love her and one woman was the same as another and he would go with whoever he pleased. Further, she said, he had repeatedly suggested that she procure a divorce so he would not be answerable for his relations with other women. Also he said he would not live with her under any circumstances."

"Sounds outrageous to me, she should have just punched him. I would have."

"He denied all charges and asked that the divorce be denied. Who knows why. The court granted Annis her appeal, gave her custody of her four-year-old daughter AND their two Flagstaff lots, household goods, and the bank account, leaving him a Ford car and his office equipment."

"Was that excessive?"

"Well, a few months later he married in Prescott a woman who the previous year had been a member of the Normal School faculty."

"Oooooh, that looked bad."

"It did. You can't know from this distance what really happened, but it did look bad. Annis sold the lots, and left town, back to California, maybe. Peter Paul announced that he'd be gone a year for special post-graduate study in surgery, and Dr. Flett would take over his 'extensive' practice while he was gone. I haven't noticed that he came back to Flagstaff—next thing I knew he was in Phoenix on the staff of the mental hospital."

"Was Dr. Flett new?"

"Eric St. Clair Flett, graduate of Pacific Medical College in 1915. He'd been in Arizona previously, gone west, and come back to establish an office in the Bank building. Before long he was elected to the town council. I don't think he was married—a wife wasn't mentioned in the newspaper, even when he went to Los Angeles to spend Christmas with his mother."

"You're amazing, the facts you turn up." I heard her take a breath. "You know, I've been wondering. Maybe enough time has gone by so you won't mind my asking…"

Uh oh—she was after my secrets. Every woman, every mother, has a right to secrets. That may not be widely known.

"What happened to Dad, it wasn't deliberate, was it?"

"Deliberate? You mean the accident?"

"The accident and afterward. It was such a strange thing, I never could understand it. If you don't want to talk about it, just say so."

"I haven't…it's not pleasant. And his condition was complicated. Are you suggesting that he…that I…?"

"I don't mean you. I just wondered whether it was possible that he…"

"I didn't think so at the time. Whatever made you ask that?"

"It was a pop-psych article I saw in a magazine at the dentist's office, what happens to you is not really accidental, reasons are buried in your sub-conscious."

"That's absurd."

"Well, it was a dumb article, but it made me wonder."

"There was no way he could have planned that or foreseen it or avoided it. It's just, sometimes pop-psych writers, as you call them, are so glib with their theories, they don't begin to understand the complexity of the human mind. Who knows what harm they do."

"Have I upset you? I didn't mean to."

"Sweetheart, you have every right to ask. It was a dumb accident, caused by a stupid kid, and your father was a victim. You didn't know him when he was young, he would never…"

"Mother, you were there, you should know."

"I was shaking and shocky. He was almost catatonic…"

"Dad?"

"…unable to talk to the Highway Patrolman or the helicopter pilot or the men who came to evacuate the bodies."

 I wonder whether anyone plays Chinese Checkers anymore or knows who Lamont Cranston was. Can anyone sing all the words to "Give a Little Whistle"?

1922–1924 It was long ago in Arizona, before I was born, yesteryear when people were sparse in the landscape. Long ago on the Colorado Plateau. Different from my time in most ways, but I feel familiar with those women. They danced at the Women's Club and the Elks Club and the city park. Saw movies at the Orpheum, "Flaming Youth," for instance. Entertained with bridge parties and dainty luncheons in their homes. I feel as if I almost know them. At least, I think I do. Illusion may be better than no understanding at all.

I read the ads in the *Sun*—

> *Penny's Lady-Lyke, the perfect elastic corset! No lacing. Fitting the figure with the ease and gracefulness of contour so much desired by all women and so necessary for prevailing dress styles.*

I know those long elastic tubes that suppressed their curves and made red marks on their skin. My mother wore one. I heard about a woman who rode a mule down the Bright Angel Trail wearing one and couldn't get it off when she reached Phantom Ranch.

And the shoes: needle toes and cross straps and chunky heels. They went to the French beauty parlor in the Babbitt building to have their hair cut into a "shingle" with a single curl pulled forward from each ear onto each cheek, and then they went downstairs to buy face make-up and cloche hats that pulled down low on their foreheads, the perfect hat for the shingle cut. At home they plucked their eyebrows out and re-drew them to trendy shapes.

In the newspaper's Women's Page they read about food, furniture and churches. About washing machines and sewing machines, the mechanical servants that made life easier for housewives. And fashion: skirts above the ankles, the boyish look—youthful, pre-pubescent. About slide fasteners—patented zippers. About artificial silk (rayon) stockings, often seamless and flesh-colored. Some of them decided to buy a long string of artificial pearls to accent the flat-chested look their new elastic corsets achieved for them. I doubt that Sarah Manning wore such styles; probably Hilda Fronske didn't either, but I'll bet the young unmarried girls in town did if their parents allowed it.

Years ago those women faded into memory like the town they lived in, leaving photographs of their faces and their houses and their cars and their clothes, recordings of their music, some idea of what they might have thought, but they are gone from here. Impossible for them to imagine that would be true—as it is for me—and there's nothing I can do about it except find the evidence. That's not much, considering how heart-breaking their disappearance was. Oh, I get so involved.

A young Flagstaff woman died in childbirth early in the 20s; so did her baby. A national study reported that seventy-five per cent of America's married women approved of birth control. Banks were urging them to open their own accounts.

I'll bet Hazel Neer, Dr. Raymond's secretary/bookkeeper/ office assistant, had her own account. Somewhere around forty years old, she'd been in Flagstaff for ten years, but there were only hints in the old records about the kind of person she was. She wasn't married—that doesn't prove much. For a month she visited with relatives in Pennsylvania. She was with the doctor sometimes when he "went for a spin" in his Packard. "Known by all for his civic pride and thoughtfulness," Raymond had ordered small black walnut trees and was distributing them to his friends for planting about town—he and Miss Neer may have driven about to see them.

Some of the doctors' wives I knew better than others. Pearl Schermann gave birth to another girl, Mary Caroline, born on Easter Sunday. They were patients at St. Joseph's hospital in Phoenix for two weeks. Lois Manning went to Phoenix to consult specialists and "underwent" (what a strange word) an appendectomy at St. Jo's.

The Manning family was still an old fashioned bloc. The grown children came home for Christmas, celebrated New Year's Day together with their parents with "jolly parties." Felix and Lois lived next door. J. P. Wilson, Althea's husband, was promoted to Vice President of Flagstaff's Arizona Central Bank. How gratifying.

Past eighty-five, Dr. Manning sr., slight but erect, still saw a few patients and walked the two blocks into town from the house on West Aspen almost daily. But he was almost as invisible in the newspaper as Sarah had once been.

Hays Nance, Julia's husband, had been working as a dentist in Denver for the past year; they visited often. Dr. Tom was living first in Kingman and then Los Angeles as an eye and ear specialist for the Santa Fe line between San Francisco and Albuquerque; he and his wife were in town now and then. Henrietta was only an overnight train ride away in California. The older Mannings still went to Los Angeles to spend the winter with her.

The Fronske name continued to be prominent in the *Sun*. Hilda and Martin and their boys camped for two weeks in Oak Creek Canyon. Martin delivered a paper titled "Medical Ethics" to a Rotary Club meeting.

Driving one night with six other people in his car, Dr. Fronske saw one headlight approaching in the middle of the road. Not knowing where the other vehicle was, he swerved to avoid a possible collision and went off the road. His car overturned, but there was no serious injury to anyone despite the absence of seat belts in those days.

You see? It's easy to recognize those people, easy to imagine their lives.

Dysthymia, a chronic low-grade depression, a)may be a different phase not a separate illness, b)may have superimposed major depressive episodes, c)may be associated with several other disorders.

There were some words, some events, I knew only second-hand: Vietnam and anti-war protests, civil rights demonstrations and fire hoses, hippies, marijuana. They didn't really touch me, safe in my big house, cocooned in money. I hoped that my children were protected by their youth, although you never know about kids.

Gwen was outspoken enough to get involved, but she was still in high school, and most of the activists were college age. Baxter was too young to be drafted; besides, we could have kept him in college. Abby though, little Abby had some of her ideas changed, I suspect. She clamored for a tie-dyed shirt, bell bottom jeans.

Oh, the sympathy I felt for the young people I watched on television news facing police dogs or fleeing to Canada; I was old enough finally to see them as distant kin, whatever their color or the length of their hair. They were so brave in their rebellion, such idealists in their assurance that they could make a difference. They wanted to believe "The times, they are a'changing."

I took "You were only waiting for this moment to arise" as a personal paean. Our cherished old assumptions were not only wrong but destructive. Submissive was not a female virtue and neither was dependence. So I thought.

The youth who were loudly marching along streets to challenge the values of their parents wouldn't have welcomed me to join them, wouldn't have acknowledged that I too wanted to see things overturned. No one saw my fierce protests and rebellions—they were all internal, all invisible even to Emily. I always have hidden the things that go deepest. Don never imagined how much time I spent wishing he was dead.

It made no sense. I truly believed (I still do) that war is immoral, justified only as a last resort, yet I fantasized about killing my husband. Divorce was possible, but it was a degrading battle, probably still is. I was afraid of what he'd do if I tried it, afraid that he'd sue for custody or leave us destitute or see me pilloried in court.

He controlled the money, he always had, doling out an allowance for household expenses only when I asked for it. I couldn't write a check; I didn't have a credit card. If I asked for discretionary money of my own, he said, "No." A prisoner of old ideas, I was mad enough to think of killing.

It wasn't like that in the first sweet years. Before he entered medical school, Don brought little gifts, things he saw that made him think of me: a flower, a mesquite seed pod from which I raised and tended two little trees. A biography of Abigail Adams from the library. Pictures cut out of the newspaper that he'd written his own captions on.

He'd been a medic in the South Pacific during the second big war, in a hospital in the New Hebrides, moving and tending wounded men. "Marlene, it broke my heart. They were so young, their bodies shattered and broken apart, and there was nothing I could do to make them whole again. It still haunts me."

When we were first married, we were short of money, broke we said, but not broken, and I worked at jobs that made me tired. The G.I. Bill gave married couples all of $90 a month. We'd never heard of scholarships.

On our first wedding anniversary we drove up Oxbow Hill to Kohl's Ranch to spend the night. A bridge on road 260 crossed Tonto Creek there and small one-room cabins were for rent under pines across the road from the lodge. A generator ran lights until ten o'clock at night. I was happy lying in the dark close to my husband, listening to the sound of water flowing by.

Evenings my strong young father would settle down with the newspaper. I'd climb up into his lap and lean back against his chest while he read Will Rogers' column to me. I love my father. I still do. He's been gone for twenty-five years.

In the late 1940s, there were only two high schools in Phoenix. Carver, which had been for black teen-agers, was closed by then, its students integrated into Phoenix Union. Do I have that right? And North High had just recently been opened. Now there are ten comprehensive schools in the Phoenix Union High School District and three alternative schools, and Phoenix is no longer the town I grew up in.

1923 Dr. Fronske said that Flagstaff was a town of "come and go people." In the early 1920s three new doctors—Francis, Hendricks, and Ploussard—arrived to confirm his opinion.

Richard McCleneld Francis, born in Missouri, was fifty-eight years old. He had graduated from the Missouri Medical College in St. Louis in 1889 and registered with the St. Louis Board of Health in 1891:

> *The State Board of Health of the State of Missouri having received satisfactory evidence that Richard M. Francis…having received the degree of Doctor of Medicine…in 1889 hereby authorizes him to pursue the practice of medicine in this state.*

Francis apparently came to Flagstaff in 1891, at least there are hints that he did, but if he practiced here in those years, he left no trace of it, none that I've found slogging through old records. He was certified in Arizona in 1915 (license #605), then served in the army during World War I as a medical officer.

Thirty-two years after he had graduated from the Missouri Medical College, Dr. Francis and his wife Elizabeth returned to Flagstaff, where part of his family was living, according to the *Sun*. (Mrs. M.O. Dumas was Elizabeth's sister.) He renewed his credentials with the Arizona Board of Medical Examiners in 1923—"recorded at the request of Richard M. Francis"—and opened an office in the Weatherford Hotel.

His daughter made a visit from Denver. He went fishing in Oak Creek. There was no hint that trouble was ahead a lot worse than Dr. Raymond's malpractice suit.

...On July 14 of 1923 he was issued by the Collector for the District of Arizona a special tax stamp as a "practitioner dispensing opium, etc."

...The next day (the 15th) he was visited by a woman to whom he sold "a certain quantity of cocaine."

...He did so again on the 17th.

...On the 18th he was arrested on the complaint of a federal narcotic agent on two counts that he did "willfully, unlawfully and feloniously deal in...cocaine without first having registered with the Collector of Internal Revenue (Hadn't the Collector issued him a tax stamp?)...and without first having paid the special tax"..."thus constituting a fraud against the revenue of the U.S. government."

...He pled not guilty and was released on $5000 bail.

...A search of his office under a warrant issued on the 20th produced no narcotics.

Those details came from Criminal Case Files, Folder Title 453; National Archives and Records Administration, Pacific Region (Laguna Niguel), but something about them doesn't quite make sense to me.

The sympathetic story that Fred Breen told was of a Good Samaritan undone by his own kindness. The story that Breen printed was that a woman employed under-cover went to Francis with a plea that a man who was her friend was in pain because of an amputated leg and unable to walk. Could Dr. Francis give her something for him? Licensed to dispense drugs, the fifty-eight-year-old doctor sold cocaine to her rather than writing a prescription.

A sting? Coming at him from his past? I don't know.

On September 10 a Grand Jury reported an indictment and witnesses were subpoenaed to appear for a jury trial in the federal court in Prescott. (I don't think there was a federal court in Flagstaff yet.) On September 20th Dr. Francis was found not guilty on the first count—the sale on July 15—guilty on the second—July 17. Did the undercover agent neglect something when she bought cocaine the first time?

Francis was removed to the federal prison at Fort Leavenworth, Kansas, to serve a term of two years for failure to pay a tax. Seven months later he applied for Executive clemency. The District judge recommended against it.

How many variations on the doctor story will I discover before I'm through?

1924 Toward the close of 1924, two more physicians arrived in Flagstaff to join the—wait a minute, Zinn was gone and Manning sr. was not very active but let's count him, Francis was out of commission for a while, that makes—six

Fronske   Manning jr.

Miller   Manning sr.

Raymond   Schermann

Add Flett, making seven, and two more newcomers who were formally introduced by the newspaper, a total of nine.

Both the Apache Lumber Company and the Flagstaff Lumber Company had been recently purchased by the Cady Company from Louisiana. The *Sun* reported that Dr. William C. Hendricks, one of the Cady Lumber physicians …

> *…and his family, formerly of Alexandria La., who for the last six months have been at McNary, have moved to Flagstaff and are living on West Aspen avenue near Emerson school. Dr. Hendricks will be physician to the employees of the Flagstaff Lumber Co. He is much taken with Flagstaff and says he hopes to build a home here before long. Coming from southern Louisiana where game is plentiful and every boy and man a born huntsman, he expects to try for some of the high scores at the Flagstaff Gun Club's endeavors.*

A graduate of the Memphis Hospital Medical College in 1908, Hendricks was licensed to practice medicine in Arizona by the state Board of Medical Examiners in 1924.

And there was Dr. Charles Nicholas Ploussard…

> *… St. Louis physician and surgeon, a graduate of St. Louis University in 1922…coming here to associate with Dr. Schermann, both to have charge of Mercy Hospital. His wife's sister is Mrs. Herb Anselm.*

Charles Ploussard was born in Illinois. His wife Elizabeth, born in Missouri, 5'1" tall, 110 pounds, was an instant hit in this frontier society. Within a month she and Charles had been guests at four bridge parties.

That made four doctors in the little town with St. Louis training: Fronske and Raymond and two of the newcomers, Francis and Ploussard. Did Francis know Raymond (1904) and Fronske (1914) before he came to Flagstaff? Possibly.

I can say that 1924 was the first recorded inspection of nursing schools in Arizona— St. Joseph's and Arizona Deaconess in Phoenix, St Mary's in Tucson. The total number of their graduates that year was twenty six.

As a woman, I catch a glimpse of Blacks and Indians. It can do no end of damage to your self-esteem to be told constantly that you are second rate, that difference proves inferiority.

Five days a week for five weeks I delivered Emily to the radiation oncologist and waited while she changed to a paper gown, paper shoes, paper cap, and lay down on a form that had been molded to her body.

"So they can position me the same each time. And I have a tatoo."

"*Tatoo?*"

"It's a tiny mark so they can focus on the right place. It will always be there. Kind of a souvenir."

"Oh gosh, Emily."

"The people are good to me, very nice, but the machine is so big. I don't like it. I don't like anything about this whole process."

She learned all she wanted to know about the lingering side effects of radiation therapy. Bruising from intravenous lines. Burning caused by the rays, skin pink or red and raw. Swelling. Her breast tender, her nipple sore. The cancer was ghastly, and so was the treatment.

"I'm just so tired, Marlene. It takes all day to do one thing. And I'm stiff. Aches and pains."

"Oh, Emily." I tried not to cry. My sweet, funny friend, so good, that wonderful soft voice.

"I know it doesn't make sense, they're doing the best they know, but I'm so resentful. It's high-tech and all, but it seems barbaric. Travis says it's normal to be angry when what they're doing makes me feel worse. You know, that doesn't help at all."

"Of course not."

"I'm depressed too. Sad."

"I'm sad seeing you sad. Oh, I'm so helpless. If I just had magical power…I'd wave my hand, say a few words, banish the cancer…"

She tried to laugh, but it sounded weak.

I groped for ideas. "Tell you what, tomorrow's a day off for you. Let's go someplace. I'll surround you with pillows and we'll drive up I-17 to Oak Creek Canyon. Have you been on that highway yet?"

"No. It's finished, isn't it?"

"For a while now, all the way to Flagstaff. I went to the canyon once with my parents in the '40s, when construction was just getting started. The only road was through Wickenburg and up Yarnell Hill to Prescott and over Mingus Mountain. It took all day—Sedona was relatively isolated from the rest of the state then. Now I'll bet we could do the drive in a couple of hours."

She wasn't wildly enthusiastic. "What's the canyon like?"

"An oasis in this dry country, full of shade and leafy trees. A clear cool stream too wide to jump across. There was one place where it poured over a long slide of slick rock. Hardly anyone else was there, so I sat down with my clothes on in water to my waist and whooshed down laughing my head off."

"I don't think I'm up to that."

"No, of course you're not. But we could drive up the canyon and back down. Have lunch in Sedona. When I was there before, the population wasn't even 500, the town wasn't much more than a grocery store with a wooden porch, and the main street wasn't paved. Now with tourists and all, I'll bet we could find a cozy place to eat. Want to? All you'd have to do would be sit and look around."

"Sounds wonderful, Marlene, just wonderful. Isn't it nice of you to think of it. Maybe next month. I think today I'll just lie here on the couch and feel sorry for myself."

"Shame on me for suggesting, I should have known."

"No, please don't. I like it when you're enthusiastic."

So for most of the day she lay on the couch, and we talked. Discussed the current President—I don't remember who it was—and where we hoped our children would go to college and what we thought of *The Catcher in the Rye* and whether we would ever dye our hair or get face lifts. An assortment of topics. As was our wont.

According to the *Journal of the National Cancer Institute*, there is an association between exposure to light at night and breast cancer risk. That doesn't seem right to me, but what do I know?

1925 Felix Manning was invited to consult about whether library books should be loaned to houses in which there was a contagious disease. Felix advised against it, and the Board so voted.

Mrs. Lee Doyle, sick with diphtheria, was having trouble breathing. An antitoxin against the diphtheria bacillus had been in use since 1890, and the death rate (571 in 1910) had begun to decline from epidemic levels. However, it was not until well into the 20th century that efficient vaccines became available. Most of humanity still died of infections for which doctors had no antibiotics or sulfa drugs.

American researchers had learned by then that iron was a major factor in formation of red blood cells and that a diet rich in liver could control pernicious anemia. But when Jack Fronske had measles, his doctor father put him to bed in a darkened room to protect his eyes and watched for complications of secondary infections. Martin Fronske did not know what else to do to save his son. No one did. No drug was effective against measles nor mumps, whooping cough, scarlet fever or chicken pox. A few weeks later both Jack and his brother Bob were sick with bad colds, which still have no real cure.

TB: Through two centuries, the 19th and the 20th, tuberculosis killed a thousand million humans around the world. At the turn of the 19th century the death rate worldwide was an estimated seven million people a year, one in every seven. In the early 20th century it was pretty well established that the disease was caused by a microbe that lived in soil, but it would be another thirty years before a search for a cure was productive. By 1930, when 90,000 people a year died from tuberculosis in the United States, sanitariums had been established, and patients were treated with fresh air, good food, rest, and exercise. Ultra high-tech scientific.

Polio: The polio virus had been around since at least the time of the Pharaohs. Millions of people were attacked by it in the United States—Louisiana 1841, New England 1884, several places in the 1890s and 1908, but the first American outbreak of size was in the summer of 1916 in New York and the northeast. In the 1920s the numbers were rising steadily, and people were frightened. The worst was still ahead.

Don't talk to me about The Good Old Days.

Appendicitis: Inflammation of the appendix had been known of in Europe since the 16th century. The first case of appendectomy with recovery was in 1736 in Paris, but most patients died painfully of gangrene and peritonitis for another century and a half. In 1865, after the end of the American War Between the States, Joseph Lister in England pioneered antiseptic surgery, which was to dramatically change mortality rates for appendectomies. The operation was known to English surgeons by 1880, but medical opinion was divided about its advisability.

The American pathologist Heber Fitz published a detailed paper in 1886 implicating a diseased appendix in several deaths ascribed to a multitude of abdominal conditions. In 1887 a Philadelphia surgeon became the first to successfully remove an inflamed appendix after making the correct diagnosis.

Thirteen years later the technical approach was outlined, and medical schools began to teach students the procedure; probably Charles Ploussard learned it at St. Louis University.

Until he arrived in Flagstaff, all cases of inflamed appendix were sent to Los Angeles or Albuquerque on the train or treated by E. Payne Palmer up from Phoenix. In 1925 the *Sun* reported the first abdominal operation performed by a resident doctor in Mercy Hospital—Dr. Ploussard did an appendectomy on a mill employee. The death rate from the operation in those years was fourteen per cent.

The older Flagstaff doctors did what they could to catch up. Martin Fronske took Hilda and the boys and drove to St. Louis so he could do two months post-graduate hospital work at Washington University. For those months they lived in the home of her parents, retired doctor H.J. Harnish and his wife Lizzie, who came to Flagstaff to stay in the Fronske house. They decided to stay in the West. Their son E.J. was here.

Footnote news of the M. D.s:

Martin Fronske moved from the Babbitt building to offices in the new Hensing building. Dr. Hendricks planned to occupy Fronske's previous office, but he was soon transferred back to McNary, and Flagstaff was back to eight doctors.

Eric Flett, who was still on the town council, succeeded Dr. Hendrick as Flagstaff Lumber Company physician.

Fronske, as president of Flagstaff's Rotary Club, traveled to a national convention in Ohio.

E.S. Miller went on as usual, heading the American Legion poppy fund drive, attending a Shrine convention.

Felix Manning, president of the Hiram Club, was still county health officer, full-time instead of part time as in previous years. As health officer he inspected the little school in Sedona.

Felix and Lois and E.B. Raudebaugh went camping and hunting quail in the Verde Valley.

R.O. Raymond was granted a temporary injunction in Superior Court against David, Charles and William Babbitt and Jake Hennessy in a sheep trespass case.

For most of my life I was a standard size. Now all these long-bodied, long-legged kids: I'm short. What happened while I wasn't looking?

One night about thirty years ago I dreamed I was running. It wasn't quite a dream, not exactly, because it was in brilliant color and I remember it still so vividly, but I have no better word.

I was running through golden light. Not on anything solid, not on ground. Running through light. Just the light and me, running easily, gracefully even.

OK, melodramatic, but I've kept the memory because it seemed significant, although I couldn't think why. I still won't try to guess what it might have meant—as I said before, explanations are usually so small. I've thought of it lately, that's all. Sitting here in the tower, air washing across me, miles of the Earth spreading out around me, I feel that in this late part of my life I'm running through light. I can't see where I'm going, but that's all right.

Probably no one likes what happens to aging faces and bodies, can't see anything beautiful in the wearing out. I'm trying without much success to teach myself to find beauty in the thin, soft skin that drapes the bones of my arms now that the muscle beneath it has dwindled. It's easier to concentrate on what I've learned while the years were doing that to my skin.

Example: there's as much fun in being as in doing. That's an important thing to know.

I remember after all these years the names of the cosmetics my mother used and the way they smelled, remember how her dressing table looked. Now I'm older than she was when she died.

For the first time since, going north, we'd looked up at the Vermillion Cliffs, we drove across the Colorado River, heading south this time to Moab. Don turned into the first RV park beyond the bridge, announcing, "I'm tired, I need to rest," and I didn't mention that a month earlier I'd made a reservation for a parking place there.

All day I'd been thinking that his face looked rather grey, although we were down to 4000 feet. He'd been so unpleasant I hadn't mentioned it. Who wants another insult?

His hands stayed on the steering wheel. "Go in and see if they have room for us."

Thinking "Yes, Massa," I checked in with the woman in the office. "How many days will you be staying?"

"I'm not sure. My husband isn't well, he may need to rest. And he may refuse to. Write us down for two nights at least."

"I'll put you close to the river—maybe the sound of the water will be soothing for him."

"I hope so. Thank you."

We parked in a slot on the edge of the property. I leveled the coach while Don settled onto the couch with pillows and the TV remote. "Bring me a drink. Bushmills on the rocks."

Orders were coming too close together for my liking. "You intend to be here for the rest of the day?"

He didn't answer.

"I think I'll go for a walk into town." I slid my bank card and the motor coach keys into my pocket, just in case he might decide to do something unexpected. Probably he wouldn't miss me until he was hungry.

It was mid-afternoon. We'd been on the road five days by then, and I was overdosed on arid, overdosed on uninhabited, overdosed on space. Time in the millions. All that gorgeous red rock—Entrada, Wingate, Kayenta, whatever. Natural wonders. Geology puzzles. Stupendous scenic beauty. I'd seen the word "scenic" until I wasn't sure what it meant anymore. So I walked the two miles into Moab in autumn sunshine, what else?

Moab, the Mountain Bike Capitol of the World. On the main street—motels, restaurants, jeep rental businesses—were throngs of muscular young people in shorts. A banner announced the Fat Tire Festival to be held the next week. I browsed in two bookstores and an art shop and felt easy for the first time that day. Not entirely secure, of course: the seventeen-mile-long Moab Valley is a collapsed salt structure above two faults, and walled by sandstone cliffs a couple of hundred million years old, and dotted with uranium mines. Not real security.

The next morning Don, looking not much better, turned on the TV and ordered breakfast on the couch. "I'm going to stay right here all day."

"You don't want me to drive?"

"Don't be silly."

That was all right with me. I walked back into town and rented a car and drove to Island in the Sky in Canyonlands National Park. Which would hold Los Angeles and its suburbs, including the San Fernando Valley, the California cost from Santa Barbara to the Mexican border. The whole park would, not just the island. Is that in scale with the Colorado Plateau or what?

The Grand Canyon contains older rock, but Canyonlands has wider views. From the Island in the Sky rim, one hundred plus miles of various rock structures spill out south, east and west. Twelve hundred feet straight down is a deeply eroded sandstone mesa, one hundred feet even farther down the confluence of the Green and Colorado rivers, once hidden and secret. Up? Up to the tops of the La Sals, laccoliths—igneous (lava) domes that did not break the overlying surface when they cooled. Their elevation is 12,721 feet high now, after millennia of erosion, a difference from river to summit of approximately two miles. How many tons of stone once filled the space where I parked, how many tons had gone down the river?

Canyonlands is labyrinths of stone, light, space, four-wheel-drive dirt roads and mountain bike trails. All stunning, but it was the Shafer Trail I especially wanted to see. I had read about it, but I wanted to see for myself.

Two hundred years past there were trails in that broken, eroded country, old trails used by deer, maybe, and Indians. Some of them by Spaniards like Escalante. By a few wandering Anglo explorers. Definitely no roads wide enough for a wagon until late in the 19th century after Mormon colonies began to spread south.

St. George was founded in the 1860s, Kanab and Lee's Ferry in the 1870s. The first settlers had an awful time getting to where they were going. Sometimes they took wagons apart and lowered them down cliffs with ropes. There was no point in trying to go around and hunt for easier routes. There weren't any within hundreds of miles.

When houses had been built and fields cleared, when cattle and horses and sheep needed to move between summer and winter pastures, when supply wagons and pack trains were traveling back and forth, the pioneers began to look for ways to improve travel —and dugways became a fixture in southern Utah.

They're hard to define and even harder to imagine. Sometimes crews paid by traders, sometimes one man working alone, hacked out with pick and shovel short cuts and cut offs and rough routes, barely developed, narrow enough for one animal at a time or barely wide enough for a wagon if there were a shallow trench that would give one wheel some purchase and prevent the whole rig from going off the cliff. It was impossible, but give those Mormon settlers credit: one thing they were good at was hard work.

> *Dictionary of the American West:* A dugway is a road or trail going through a high land form which is dug out of the land form or excavated into the land form to provide a path for transport. Also a path scraped out of a steep hillside allowing cattle and wagons to travel the hillside.

I'd read in a book about a dugway known as the Shafer Trail which crawled down a red, thousand-foot cliff from Island in the Sky with staggering drops on the outside, no guard rails, and had trouble believing it. The story was that the Shafer brothers, second generation of a pioneering Moab family, had worked on an old Indian trail from 1914 to 1922, using an existing shelf for much of the way, to move cattle off the high plateau. When they were finished, they had only a bad stock trail. That was about forty years after the first dugway had been built at Lee's Ferry. Determined to see for myself, I walked to the edge and peered down. Now I'm able to say for myself that the Shafer Trail does indeed crawl down the face of a red sandstone cliff with sharp hairpin curves, and that it's been improved considerably since 1922. It's driveable now; maybe it would be possible for a car to pass another one. I guess it's been done. It made my stomach cramp just to look down at it, though, and that was before eight bicyclists and their support truck started down.

OK, it can be done. But I knew right away I would not, repeat NOT, try it in a 36-foot motor coach. I'm old enough to know about what can happen to people in automobiles.

I think I've said it before (I'm also old enough not to be sure what I've already said): the Colorado Plateau is a unity of stone. The red cliffs in Oak Creek Canyon show up again in the Grand Canyon, in Canyonlands. You round a curve and say, "Here's Navajo sandstone again, way over here." The same oceans and deserts made them all. The Plateau would be a state to itself if geology had had anything to do with it (Have I already said that?) and you need to see it all if you're to catch a glimpse.

It's not Disneyland, not loud music and moving fast. Hikers and bikers are everywhere, but the heart of the plateau across southern Utah has no human scale. It is what it was and what's left above ground. Ragged remnants: a few arches, impassable cliffs, canyons cut deep, a butte in the distance. All that's left of a massive block of stone what? two, three, four miles thick? that once covered significant parts of Arizona, New Mexico, Colorado and Utah. There's air now where a major part of the stone once was. But for me no spiritual insight. It's too big, too old—500 million years—for something so human as spiritual.

Doctors made house calls in the days after World War II. Don kept his medical bag in the trunk of his car. In one hot Phoenix summer the mercury in his thermometer blew up in the heat.

1925 "Business fever" was what some observers were calling it. The nation watched a building boom, an ever more active stock market, an economic index that continued to rise month by month. President Calvin Coolidge was saying, "The business of America is business," but too many investors were becoming involved with too little knowledge of how the game worked.

With enthusiasm Flagstaff had pitched right in with a building boom of its own. There was talk of a big new community-sponsored hotel—they needed one didn't they? The Santa Fe Railroad went ahead with construction of a new depot between Beaver and San Francisco streets. Arizona Lumber & Timber Company doubled the capacity of its sawmill, Flagstaff Electric Light Company the capacity of its generating plant. How about a forty by sixty foot addition to the county courthouse?

"Boosters" called for increased work on roads and continued to agitate for "development" of the Colorado River with a dam in Glen Canyon. Voters approved a bond issue of $475,000 for improvement of the town water system and applauded construction of a new pipe line from springs on the Peaks, and none too soon: by August there was no water reserve in the town reservoir. None.

The Library Board voted to inquire into a Carnegie grant to improve its service and was told the foundation had not given such grants since 1917. Never mind, they'd do it themselves. Population had increased by somewhere around twenty per cent. School enrollment was up by twenty per cent as well. Two thousand automobiles were registered in Coconino County. Everywhere the signs were positive.

Northern Arizona Normal School had become a state teachers college. Its mostly female students were wearing their skirts above their ankles, up to their calves, sometimes even up to their knees, and their waistlines dropped to their hips. The result was linear, a "boyish" look, so they thought.

Imitating Eastern fashion, the girls powdered and rouged their knees, used skin lotion and moisturizers on their newly fashionable tans. The national cosmetic industry was selling $141 million on its products by then.

Young wives, hair marceled at the Powder Puff Beauty Parlor, went to "radio" dances (music on the radio) and bridge parties in dresses that were made of silk, a "ravishing fabric for momen's apparel."

That is, some of them did. Business woman Mary Costigan became the first woman in the United States to be licensed for radio broadcasting and had her set installed backstage in the Orpheum Theater, of which she was still manager. When KFXY went on the air in mid-December, Wilson and Coffin set a loudspeaker on the roof of their Necessity shop and Flagstaff's station could be heard up and down the streets for blocks. The next day Wilson and Coffin sent up a floating aerial between bouquets of balloons. Oh, they must have been excited, the people in that little town.

Some of them, though, thought old-fashioned decorum had gone right out the window. Women were proud to be seen in men's roles: local agent for the New York Life Insurance Company was Lulu Robinson. Lulu Hall, who had built the Kinlani Apartments in 1924 on the corner of Leroux and Aspen Streets, across from the Weatherford, was adding space to that "desirable" location (the Ploussards lived there for a while) and planning another downtown building. Marie Hensing erected one on the east side of

Leroux, from Front Street to the alley. No wonder the Federation of Woman's Clubs was urging women to enter state politics.

The town's modern matrons, no longer stuck at home, motored about cheerfully, driving visiting relatives to the Grand Canyon, taking picnics out to Mormon Lake. Hilda Fronske and four other women went camping with their children in Oak Creek Canyon. Pearl Schermann took her little girls on the train to visit her mother in Los Angeles.

Lois Manning and Dr. Felix were gone for three weeks on a trip to San Francisco with Dr. Raymond, who was happy for any excuse to take friends out in his Packard. He and Felix went to San Diego for two weeks. In October he drove Lois Manning and Hazel Neer and William Coburn to Roosevelt Lake. He and Dr. Miller seemed always off somewhere. On the move.

I felt the same excitement when I was sixteen and got my first driver's license. Didn't we all?

Early in 1925 Sarah Manning was ill for several weeks, alarming her "many friends." Then Dr. George Felix Manning sr., age eighty-seven, came down with influenza and pneumonia, and his children gathered from other states to keep watch at his bedside. A Confederate veteran whose arm had been injured in a Texas gun fight, a doctor who had lived in Flagstaff for thirty-nine years, he died and was buried as a Mason after a brief Episcopal ceremony in his home on West Aspen. The notice on the front page of the *Sun* said, under the headline "A Notable and Useful Career Ended," that he "met death as became a gentleman, a soldier and a man whose life had been clean and honorable."

George Felix had been the third doctor to arrive in the little frontier town. Until his death, he and E. S. Miller and R. O. Raymond had been the only medical survivors of Flagstaff's first twenty-five years. Dennis Brannen had died in Washington D.C.; P. G. Cornish was practicing medicine with his son in Albuquerque. Robinson, Adams, Slernitzauer, and Sipe had all moved to other places. Younger doctors were taking their places: Felix Manning, Albert Schermann, Martin Fronske, Charles Ploussard, Eric Flett. Back to seven.

Sarah Manning had been the first doctor's wife and the first doctor's mother in Flagstaff, finally the only doctor's wife from the 1880s. In 1925 she became the first doctor's widow.

Sarah had the company of Hilda, Pearl, Lois, and Elizabeth Ploussard—and that of her children, of course. As she had for several years, she spent the spring months of 1925 with Tom and Lula in Los Angeles, then traveled to Texas to spend the winter with relatives. What did the big Manning family do for Christmas? The *Sun* didn't say.

In April of 1925 Elizabeth (Mrs. Doctor) Francis, who had been in Los Angeles for the winter, returned by train and was met in Williams by friends who brought her on into Flagstaff in a motor car. In May the *Sun* reported: "Dr. R.M. Francis will be back next week from the east," which was tactful, I think. He had been gone for twenty months. I've found no record of how long he was in Fort Leavenworth. Possibly good behavior, non-violent crime and all, he was released early.

Dr. and Mrs. Francis resumed their residence in the Weatherford Hotel, entertaining guests, inviting family and friends to Thanksgiving dinner. The next year, identifying himself as a doctor, he registered to vote and continued to do so for the years he remained in Flagstaff. I thought on conviction of a federal charge his voting rights would be revoked, but maybe it was different then.

In public records he didn't appear to lose any privileges as a result of his imprisonment. For the rest of his life he referred to himself as a doctor. That winter his nephew, out sledding, suffered a deep cut on his leg, and Francis repaired the damage. A few weeks later he was called to an AL&T logging camp to attend a child with bronchitis.

The Revised Statutes of Arizona, 1913, state "The Board of Medical Examiners must revoke a certificate to any applicant guilty of unprofessional conduct." Specifically:

- abetting in procuring a criminal abortion,
- betrayal of a professional secret,
- deceitful advertising,
- advertising medicine designed to regulate the monthly periods of women,
- conviction of an offense involving moral turpitude,
- habitual intemperance in the use of alcohol or narcotic drugs,
- impersonation of another doctor.

The list does not include conviction on a felony tax charge.

There was provision for revocation or cancellation of a medical license, the most serious option that could be taken, barring the doctor from practicing. But it was not self-executing: the Board needed to take action and apparently did not do so in his case. There is no record of discipline taken against Dr. Francis while he was licensed in Arizona.

And life went on. Remember, it was "The Jazz Age," and blues music was spreading across the country. So were songs by George Gershwin—"Swanee," "Fascinating Rhythm," "I'll Build a Stairway to Paradise." Anyone in Flagstaff could have heard them—and Rhapsody in Blue—on plate-size records played on phonographs.

The doctors might have danced to the Big Band Tunes, maybe to one jazzy little number, "We're in the Money," but most of them were old enough by then to be at least slightly dignified and protective of their reputations. Edwin Seymor Miller was sixty-seven, Raymond O. Raymond forty-nine, Albert H. Schermann forty-six, Martin Fronske forty-two, Felix Manning forty-one. Eric St. Clair Flett, (residence 1 N. Leroux) in his 30s?

The youngster was Charles Nicholas Ploussard, 28. He and Elizabeth hiked into the Grand Canyon and played bridge with the 500 Club; Elizabeth joined the Friday Club (bridge) with her sister. Driving one day "at a brisk pace" near the county hospital, the couple was shaken but not injured when the right front wheel came off their Dodge coupe. They took their new baby daughter back to St. Louis to show her to relatives. On their return to Arizona the Dodge had to be pulled out of mud by a team of Missouri mules.

My favorite medical anecdote for that year: Ploussard and Elizabeth went to Tuba City so that he could set a leg broken in a polo game. Polo? In Tuba City? The Lasky-Famous Players movie company was there filming Zane Grey's The Vanishing American.

More people die as a result of medical errors than from motor vehicle accidents, breast cancer, or AIDS. Some estimates of error-related deaths are as high as 180,000 a year. *Discover: Science, Technology and Medicine.*

late June

Letter to my core group,

Hey, y'all, as my great-grandmother might have said growing up in North Carolina. How you keeping? I want you to know that I appreciate the letters you write to bring me up to date. Some of you have said that you know me better through what I write than you ever did, and the reverse is also true.

Here in the desert a fire rages overhead half the year, scorching the land and blistering skin. Snakes hide in holes underground. Panting coyotes wait until dark to hunt. Shade is shelter, and so are clouds. So is night.

Even here at 8000 feet shade is shelter in the summer, when sun sears human skin. At least, it sears my skin after two unprotected minutes. I am eager for clouds and wind and rain.

I'm completely baffled by these helicopters, haven't the foggiest what's going on. There are the small medevac machine that flies from the roof of the hospital and the police copter that lifts off from the airport—I'm accustomed to those. During fire season, contract and Forest Service helicopters come from Green Base east of Williams for initial attack or air-to-ground cooperation.

The ones I don't know a function for are the big black military dragonflies that thunder past like something out of Revelations. When they go by at night, I can feel my mattress vibrating and hear the cabin windows rattle.

But there's been nothing like this month. I've lost count. Last year I saw a few flying on a straight east-west line. Now they're going in every direction, including turning-and-going-back. Are there army maneuvers nobody's told me about?

Sometimes when a big wildfire is burning, the huge Erickson with a tube hanging out the end is brought in from California to siphon water into itself from ponds and lakes, then dump it onto burning trees. An aircraft powerful enough to carry a useful amount of water—which is very heavy—impresses the bejeebers out of people who didn't see it coming.

Last week I was surprised by a mustard-yellow monster with a tidy compartment up front just big enough for a person or two, then a long, straight beam connecting it to a separate cargo hold (door but no windows), large blades churning above, another beam, and the tail rotor. I'm sure it made sense to somebody. It looked bizarre to me.

Probably while I'm at it, I should mention that few of these contraptions fly above me; when I say "past", I mean eye-level or lower. Helicopters, I'm told, fly most efficiently not too far above the ground, which around here is mostly 500 feet lower than my mountaintop. I look out at or down on the tops of helicopters. As I do on the backs of large birds.

Wind rushed wildly at me without a pause for the first six weeks of this season. Safe in my tower or my cabin, I liked it, although it wasn't much fun while I was on the tower stairs. But one morning as I was leaving for town with laundry and grocery list, I rounded a curve on the south slope of the mountain to see that two trees had blown down and blocked the road.

Both were smaller than twelve inches DBH (Diameter Breast Height) but twenty feet long and slanted down the road so that I'd have struggled to pull them aside with my tow strap. Calmly I pulled on the emergency brake and got out. Wearing sandals, a skirt, a filmy blouse, I managed to lift the top of the smaller tree, using the big end as a pivot, and walked it in a curve to the side of the road, very proud of myself. The other tree was too heavy to lift, so I got a hold on the top and dragged that tree far enough aside to allow me to drive around. Dusted off my hands and went on into town. Shamelessly smug. And why not?

Finally the forest was so dry that campfire, smoking and chainsaw restrictions were imposed. Three hundred acres were burning on the Grand Canyon's north rim, so the Northern Arizona Team was activated.

Sometimes at dawn and dusk there was a smell of moisture in the air; sometimes in the afternoon puffs of cumulus moved across the sky. Monsoon patterns were moving up from Mexico, so the radio said. But weather forecasting has about a fifty per cent chance of error despite four Weather Service satellites, Doppler radar, and $100 million a year spent by the National Oceanographic and Atmospheric Administration. Nobody was being so bold as to state that the summer storm system was imminent, certainly not a week ahead of time. Weather is even more chaotic than human behavior.

The day after the Summer Solstice, cirrus then cumulus advanced from the southwest, cumulus piled up above the Peaks. And turned black, covering half the sky. Ground strikes! Thunder! Falling temperature! Big fat drops of rain on my steel roof, the first of the season! In the sudden cold, a dozen moths crept out of hiding places in the tower, soft brown wings fluttering against the window glass. The tower was shaking in the wind, and the world was so noisy I could barely hear my radio. There were twenty-three fires on the forest that day and, bad turn of events, my rain gauge measured only three hundredths of an inch.

Saturday the word was that high pressure had trapped moisture over the region, and we could expect storms for at least a couple of days. No guesses about farther ahead than that. Sky was black and overcast when I climbed the stairs at 08:00, but the expected precip did not materialize. The forest put out twenty-one fires, including half an acre at the Boy Scout camp, where the kids were organized into a line-digging crew until Forest Service trucks could get there.

There was no rain the next week. An unstable flow of moist air was coming up from Mexico, another headed our way from the Gulf of California. That usually means summer storms. We did see some gorgeous cumulus build-up but no rain. Just a couple of dozen small fires every day, all human-caused.

I send love.
Mom or grandma, as the case may be

P.S. I have in great excitement developed an idea that explains for me why I have so much trouble with sophisticated physics like quantum mechanics and string theory. If it makes sense—that is, if it agrees with my sense perceptions and my experience and thus my rational mind—if it makes sense to me, it's probably wrong! Conversely, if it doesn't make sense, it's probably right. You have no idea how much this clears things up for me and releases tension. I'm not necessarily stupid, just that I should have been looking at the problem from a different angle. I wonder whether this has a wider application, like to economics. I'll have to work on that.

My earliest memory is of the twelve inch square piece of cardboard with a different number on each of the four sides. My mother put it in the front window with the number of pounds of ice she needed turned to the top. The horse that pulled the wagon stopped at our house and a man carried in a block of ice with a pair of big pointed tongs. This was in Phoenix when I was five.

1926 The decade moved past its mid-point toward the height of the stock market frenzy, though only a few observers recognized it at the time. Ninety percent of the country's washing and sewing machines had been bought on credit, installment plan. One of six Americans owned an automobile, seventy-six percent of them on credit. Secretary of Commerce Herbert Hoover said he was concerned over the "growing tide of speculation."

Buildings continued to sprout: hotels and homes, banks, office buildings, chain stores. In Flagstaff, progress was positively dizzying. The Santa Fe's new depot was dedicated, and Breen called it "the railroad's gift to the town." The Federated Church dedicated the expansion of its building. Mary Costigan installed an electric sign on the Orpheum and put in new seats.

A big new water reservoir was completed, giving the town a storage capacity of 105 million gallons. After three weeks of summer rain, it was full to overflowing, much to everyone's relief.

Arizona law prescribed that a community could be incorporated as a town when it had a population of 500 or more people and two-thirds of the taxable inhabitants voted to petition the state. By order of the town council, Dr. Flett a member, Flagstaff officially became a city in 1926: it held a population of 3000. The council remained with new powers and responsibilities and a new name, city council, but the mayor would henceforth be appointed rather than elected by popular vote.

In November at the Flagstaff Armory a business exposition of more than thirty stores and companies was "one of the most progressive moves that this section of the state has ever exhibited." Breen also boasted that Oak Creek Canyon was becoming famous.

But the big news, the front page headline news, for most of the year was of a modern hotel that would cater to tourists and commercial travelers. The Weatherford was twenty-six years old, the Bank Hotel thirty-two, the Commercial about the same. Surely the town should provide something up-to-the-minute.

In early Spring a bold headline spoke to Flagstaff: "Do We Want a Hotel? Yes, We Do!" The prospects looked good, then seemed assured. A site had been chosen on the corner of Aspen and San Francisco streets, and architects were offering plans for a building of seventy-five rooms, seventy percent of which were to have private baths!

The sensational innovation was that it was to be owned by the people of Flagstaff. A California hotel chain had been engaged to furnish and manage, but ownership would belong to a Community Hotel Corporation with local stockholders.

Campaign headquarters for the subscription drive were set up, and a committee of more than twenty local business men—all of them with pep—was organized to raise the $250,000 that would be needed. Dr. Fronske was on the executive committee, of course; the sales organization included Drs. Flett, Miller, and Ploussard. They all got right down to the task.

By noon of fourth day of the drive, $136,000 had been subscribed. Within a week 350 citizens had bought $200,000 worth of stock, the bulk of it raised by the Rotary Club, and in hardly any time the goal was met. If you can believe the *Sun*, locals were quite proud of themselves.

A weekly front page column in the newspaper reported progress. Ground was broken, a foundation poured, then concrete floors for each story. Within three months plumbers and brick masons had moved in; windows and doors had been installed; an elevator (!) was being put into position; furnishings were being selected for a kitchen and coffee shop. By the end of August there was a concrete roof. After a city-wide contest to choose a name, the Board of Directors settled on "Monte Vista."

By the way, a new building for the *Sun* was constructed that year across Aspen from the hotel. And in case anyone is interested, Rudolph Valentino died in 1926. The Dempsy-Tunney fight was a big attraction.

During the first eight months of the year, 13,250 people in America were killed by automobiles; 350,000 were injured. (How would that compare, I wonder, to the number killed forty years earlier by horses?) In Flagstaff injuries and deaths from "car smashes" and roll-overs were reported on the front page.

Hey, maybe this is a coming-of-age story, like coming into the next phase. For me, I mean, but maybe it's true of Flagstaff as well.

My big love affair, the whole romance, lasted about six weeks. From that day near Prescott to the last hello—six delirious weeks. I suppose I should be grateful it lasted that long.

Now I know how naive I was, how flat-out dumb. Dumb in love, what a cliche, what a redundant phrase. The strongest revulsion I feel now is that I was such an easy target. As Abby used to say, totally clueless. I must have been visible for miles away.

I had never phoned Lyle, just waited for him to call me. And he did, steadily, patiently, for a full year. It didn't occur to me that anybody could be so calculating, could have a reason to be so calculating. I've wondered since whether he hated women, to so deliberately cause that kind of destruction. Maybe. Maybe he was just thinking of himself.

Even during those six weeks I didn't once call him, though I longed to. Just to hear his voice. He called me now and then, joked for a minute, as he always had, back when we were friends. "Did you see this morning's paper? What do you think of Johnson now? Should he have said that?" "Can you tell me what a Tambourine Man is?" "If you were filthy rich, would you go to Arabia on vacation? Why not? It's hot and dry—that's your reason?"

My skin came alive at the very sound of him, my toes, the inside of my mouth, alive. Completely enveloped by a voice—I loved the feeling. Giddy with it. Maybe once a week we'd meet someplace with a bed, and each time the body loving was more transcendent, knowledge beyond the limits of the possible. I felt supremely wise. I felt beautiful.

Then he stopped calling. No warning, just stopped. The first week I thought he was probably busy. Dermatologists could be busy too. He hadn't always called every week. Then I began to wonder, to doubt, to fear. I was nearly crazy finally—crawling numb through my days—and trying hard not to show it.

Don said, "Why are you so tense? Your face looks drawn and ugly." I could always count on Don.

I wouldn't be tricked again as Lyle tricked me. I thought he loved me as I loved him, anything else wasn't possible. I've heard women say, "I know he loves me; he must," and I realize I wasn't unique. Just typical. How humiliating.

I'm proud, though, that I didn't call him, not even once. Sick, consumed with grief, drowning in a bubbling broth of emotion, I didn't cry or plead or beg for explanation, didn't even look up his number. A song popular then had a line—"I'll never have that recipe again"—that cut me in half. I stood staring out the kitchen window, my ears ringing with the hurt of it, wondering where he was. Week after week I lived in a body that was a swollen blob ten feet wide until I didn't want to live any more and locked myself in the bathroom and sliced at my wrist with a razor blade, trying to open a vein. I was that devastated. What a fiasco—I've drawn more blood shaving my legs.

And I didn't pick up the phone to hear his voice again. Not once. After a while, of course, I didn't want to hear it, declined invitations to social events to eliminate the chance of seeing him. Slowly I stopped caring. Didn't hate. Wasn't angry. Just didn't care.

In my memory the words "vacant lot" have an almost mythical ring. There probably aren't any in Phoenix now, but when I was growing up there was a vacant lot at the end of our block, a flat bare stretch of dirt that we could turn into anything our imaginations needed.

"Gwen, my sweet patootie,"

"Mother, you're so…"

"…full of applesauce?"

"More slang?"

"Hurray for the Jazz Age. I have some new ones for the boys."

"They thought 'horsefeathers' was a hoot."

"Good! They probably know 'upchuck' and 'scram', you think?"

"I can ask."

"Try this on them—that's banana oil."

"Banana oil?"

"Or 'that's hokum'. 'It's the berries'."

"Mother, where do you get these things?"

"Oh, here and there, I read. Research isn't all gloomy, you know."

"I've been thinking about you."

"Really."

"I was reading that lightning kills seventy to eighty people annually in the United States, with three hundred reported injuries. Naturally I thought about you up there on a mountain top in a steel tower. Aren't you a target?"

"You'd think so, but considering how many bolts strike all around me and how seldom the tower is hit, I don't feel particularly attractive."

"Mother! Do you go down the stairs when a storm comes?"

"Oh no. The tower is grounded. I lock all the windows and turn off the Forest Service radio and sit on a chair that has phone-line insulators on all four legs. My odds are probably better in the tower than if I were standing under a tree."

"Mother, do you know what you're dealing with?"

"Well, I think so."

"We're talking up to three hundred thousand amps."

"What's an amp?"

"I don't know, but an average household circuit carries only forty-five of them. Or less. And that can electrocute a person."

"Gwen, where do you get these things?"

"I read too, you know."

"My reading is more fun."

"Mother. It's dangerous to be up there. The core of a lightning channel one finger thick can be up to fifty thousand degrees Fahrenheit, five times hotter than the surface of the sun. It has a current of several hundred million volts, and don't ask me what a volt is."

"Hey, I can top that. I'm bombarded with showers of high-energy cosmic rays that have one billion volts moving at close to the speed of light."

"*Mother!*"

"So are you, so don't tell me I'd be better off in Denver."

"I'm just trying to take care of you."

"I know, darlin', you're wonderful that way. You take responsibility for everybody in the family, it can't be easy. But look on the bright side: if I'm struck by lightning, maybe I'll develop some kind of superpower or a higher IQ or something."

"You're kidding."

"No, I've read that in people who've been struck there can be a slight but measurable rise in IQ score. I think I'd rather have the superpower. It might be nice to be able to fly, although that does look like a lot of work."

"Mother, you're so strange."

"Thank you. I hope so. I'm working on a theory that strange is better than no change at all."

"What?"

"If you don't change as you go through life, what's the point?"

"Oh, I don't know why I bother."

"There used to be a comic book hero named India Rubber Man. When I was a little girl, I wished I could stretch out my body like he did twenty feet or so to look at something or throw my arm out and around a corner to pick something up. Haven't you ever had secret fantasies?"

"I guess I did. When I was ten or so, I made believe I was invisible. It was a kick. But I'm not a little girl anymore."

"Neither am I. I have a different kind of fantasy now. Like, at night before I go to sleep, I lie in bed imagining what the world might be if everyone received a compliment every day. It could make a huge change."

With surprise and, I'll admit, shock, I can see blue veins under the skin all down the insides of my arms below the elbows. It's as if the skin were becoming transparent, I'm sure I've never noticed that before. What will I learn about myself next?

1926 Industrial technology had changed the reality of American life. Because most homes were electrified, the revolution included housework: irons, central heating, water heaters, washing machines, a variety of labor saving appliances. Electric stoves in kitchens—no more starting coal or wood fires before meals could be cooked. Housewives had soap powders—no more shaving a block before laundry—and electric lights—no more cleaning lamp chimneys. Convenience foods like breakfast cereals and canned vegetables eased cooking tasks.

Nevertheless, women labored fifty to sixty hours a week in housework. The job was less burdensome physically but no less time-consuming because of new duties and higher standards of cleanliness. American bathrooms, evolving rapidly in those years, needed daily cleaning and so did carpets, thanks to vacuum sweepers.

Life for women had changed, it was true. Women were playing golf, baseball, basketball; they were diving, bowling, entering track and field competitions in (gasp!) short trousers and other revealing clothing. Gertrude Ederle had become a popular heroine by swimming the English Channel two hours faster than the men's record. Helen Wills dominated American women's tennis; Mae Washington might have beaten her if she hadn't been black and thus eliminated from competition. It was difficult to put Eleanor Sears into a category, she was so good an all-round athlete. ("Babe" Didricksen was still in school in Texas.) But most wives were not involved in sport of any kind.

Flappers were going to speakeasies, wearing breast binders and chemise dresses with no sleeves and long strings of beads and silk stockings and sometimes loose trousers—in public!—but flappers were young, literally footloose. Wives in small towns like Flagstaff had too many responsibilities to engage in such behavior. Doctors' wives not part of the youth culture of the 1920s, not in any big way.

They voted, though, for other women who were elected to county and state offices: in the primary election of 1926 five women were candidates for Recorder and Superintendent of Schools in Coconino County. (Democratic votes in the county: 2064, Republican 1470.) Ana Frohmiller, Coconino County Treasurer, was elected to the office of Arizona state auditor. Women were the majority of election officials. In 1926 there were ten women in Congress.

Nationwide the rate at which they had children had declined to 2.5; the divorce rate had risen to one in seven. But the League of Women Voters was a mere one-tenth the size of the Woman's Suffrage Association which it had replaced, and women had surprised everyone by not voting as a bloc. Most school boards still refused to hire married women teachers with the argument that it would "break up the family." Medical schools imposed a quota on female students; most hospitals refused to hire female interns.

The general opinion had been that voting rights would cause American women to run wild and destroy civilization entirely. General opinion was disappointed that they hadn't. In Flagstaff the Business and Professional Women opened a women's employment bureau, but for the most part the ladies settled into the security of their traditional positions.

The Women's Club retrenched into private and conservative activities. In Flagstaff it offered a three-day school in cooking with electricity and established "at home" open house on Thursday evenings in their new club house—offering quiet conversation, light refreshments, a reading table, cards for those who wished to play. They'd earned the rest, I suppose. Later there was summer "open house" on Thursday afternoons. Tea was served and out-of-town guests were welcomed.

In the pages of the *Sun*, the brief bits where the names of the doctors' wives appeared, they seem to have been playing bridge most of the time. If they joined the new national craze—crossword puzzles and mah-jongg—the newspaper did not report it. Flagstaff's ladies could order groceries on the phone and have them delivered to their kitchens the same day, freeing them to play bridge. Their husbands (Schermann) or their babies (Ploussard) were sometimes sick and needed tending, but in social column paragraphs their names peppered the reports of bridge parties.

There were still only six of them, three over forty:

> Sarah Manning, a sixty-seven-year-old widow, born in Tennessee, was a member of the Women's Club and Eastern Star. One or another of her five grown children visited often; she went off to Denver or California to visit them. In 1926 she had her house painted and entertained other women, including all of the doctors' wives, at a series of bridge parties.
>
> Lois Manning, forty-two years old, married to Sarah's son, was also born in Tennessee. She played bridge too, and was a member of the Women's Club,

but she had no children. She and Felix went down to fish in Oak Creek that year with a group of friends.

Elizabeth Francis, wife of a physician who had spent several months in a federal prison, mother of grown children, was quite ill that year with flu/pneumonia. She had not registered to vote. I haven't discovered yet where she was born or how old she was or whether she played bridge.

The younger three were:

Hilda Fronske, thirty-nine years old, born in Missouri, another bridge player. She had two young sons. An active member of PEO, the Shakespeare Society, the Womens' Club, and the Presbyterian Church, she found time to take her sons and seven other boys to Elden Springs for an outing and to arrange a picnic for eight women.

Pearl Schermann, twenty-nine years old, former nurse, had three small daughters (Regina "Jean" was born in 1925) and a son, Albert jr, born in 1926. A bridge player, she was a member of the Women's Club and the altar society of her church.

Elizabeth Ploussard, born in Missouri, played bridge despite her new baby. She and her husband had bought a house on north Beaver.

When I was growing up in Arizona, most people had never heard of Kokopeli.

early July 2001

Hi kids!

How's everybody? I'm fine, in case you're curious, and enjoying my life with gusto. I'm happy to say that there's so much to see and do and think and read that I have no time for feeling bored. When I was in the library the other day, I came across a reference to Sophie Tucker, and ever since I've been strutting around in my cabin singing, "You got to see Mama every night or you can't see Mama at all." I try to sound like Sophie did, but I'm afraid I just don't have what it takes.

Here on this modest peak there's no light among the trees on a moonless night. Down the slope in all directions, not even starlight. Dense and black beyond the trees at any edge of the clearing, but the one-room cabin is bright inside with color and propane lamps, warmth and safety. I hear sounds, but it's only the animals outside. I've never felt so comfy any place.

Nights are a little longer now and days shorter. When I open the door in the morning, there's no morning on treetops or the meadow below, but the walls of the tower far above my head are colored a deep red by the rising sun.

Yesterday I took notes again in my tower to show you what I mean: too interested to be sick, too thoughtful to be sad. I hope you like my notes; for me they're sort of an all-round diary.

11:00 a.m.

Everyone agrees that there was more rain and snow in Flagstaff a hundred years ago, and some of us look for a place to put the blame. Probably people of European ancestry arrived during a wet phase in a long climate cycle and ever since have considered it the norm, which ain't necessarily so. Though they describe the past eight years as Drought, these years may be part of a commonplace fluctuation. Whatever, we are having a turrible hard time.

Dry. Relative humidity is below ten per cent; moisture in the wood of trees is likewise low. All the ponds and stock tanks are lined with cracked mud for the first time in memory. The basin at my water pump is empty twice a day, so many birds come to drink from it. Oak trees have not fully leafed out, and it's mid-July! There are no green grasses, no flowering plants for deer and elk to graze on. Abert squirrels are eating the tips of ponderosa branches—starvation food.

Every afternoon dramatic cumulus clouds build masses into the sky, their bottoms turn flat and black, and I think hopeful things. There is wind to go with the clouds, so I am cool up here in the tower. But rain doesn't come. Dust stays powdery on the roads, on places where animals walk.

I am surrounded by silent anguish. I wish I could gather up the creatures and bring them here for food and water. Would that be considered environmental interference?

This morning gorgeous clouds are developing across the southeast but not over the Peaks. Up on Schultz Pass, Horse Patrol 2-1 is calling for assistance: two mountain bikers sped away from him when he stopped to cite them for closure violation. He hoof-beated after them and saw them throwing their bikes into a car with a Colorado license plate.

Some people don't like being excluded from recreation they feel is their "right." Environmental sentiments go only so far with some of us.

Would anybody be interested in debating with me the meaning of "right?" Natural rights, legal rights, civil rights, animal rights, and are they the same or different? I don't mean this as a frivolous question. The dictionary I keep here in the tower lists right mind, right honorable, put things right, knocked right down, mine by rights, right of search, but says nothing about political rights except to refer to the first ten amendments to the American constitution, and I doubt the word is even defined there. It's so bandied about these days that I really think we should come to some agreement about what it means. If possible.

1:00

There is a river of grey-white-black clouds pouring across the sky from the southeast, their shadows dragging behind them over the tops of pines. A twenty-mile-wide city of clouds rises through piled-up shapes and colors to the northwest. A storm is reported east of Kingman, and black rain is falling beyond Sitgreaves. Over Flagstaff, blue sky is flat and empty and glaring with sun.

Today is my first day back in the tower after one off. A day of laundry and grocery shopping and intense research, so I'm tired. Usually on the first day back I lie around and try to write history that wouldn't bore y'all, I hope.

Below me ladybugs are everywhere in swarms and baseball-size clusters. Branches and stems of grass bend with the weight of them. I looked it up—they're little carnivorous beetles. We find them appealing with their red and black carapaces, and we're fond of them, but I'm here to testify that when you have that many ladybugs around all at once, they aren't so cute any more.

2:30

Cumulus clouds are crowding closer together; there are more haphazard shadows across the forest. But above this mountain and the Peaks the sky is still blue and empty. It would take just the slightest change to pull the clouds over me, shut out the sun, wash dust off my pines. But I'm not expecting anything today, see if I care.

Well! A voice over the radio: "All lookouts on the Peaks district, we're out of money. Go back to your regular schedule, eight hours, five days." OK. Wonder if he means out of 'prevention' money and they're having to go to 'fire' money—charge overtime to nearby fires instead of a general fund.

For two months we've been on until six p.m. Now hours will be extended only if there's fire or lightning.

4:30

My cloud city has collapsed into a uniform grey across the west. The river-in-the-sky has thickened. Around most of the horizon there might be rain falling, but I don't see any lightning. Still clear above the Peaks and me.

Until midnight last night a contract helicopter flew above the forest looking for campfires which, as I may have mentioned, have been prohibited because of fire danger. Each time they spotted one, a crew on the ground was dispatched to put it out and cite the campers sitting around it.

They probably made noises about "a free country." My opinion is that in the interest of public safety, free people can't be allowed to run completely amok. I don't know where that puts me on the liberal/ conservative continuum.

Cazz, your poems are better every week. I'm very impressed by the sounds of your words. Trying to keep up with you, I've written something a little more ambitious than my usual effort.

Moon
   rises a hundred miles away here.
      Condors fly above the canyons. Arizona
                  is not England.

This land is silence on hot stone,
   vanished oceans, seeds that wait for rain.

                  Cactus spines.
We learn to live in caves that move
   with shifting earth and southwest wind,

                  Some of us,
see dinosaurs crossing the plateau
   and the length of our lives in rocks.

(Note: I chose "rocks" instead of "stones" to be the last word because it is hard and sharp-edged like this land. And I think there is air in this poem; it's my opinion that all Arizona poems should have air in them.)

Love from my sky university,
M

Something deadly was ahead of us, and we were getting closer with every mile we drove. So was everyone else, for that matter. That's a horror story, isn't it?

1926 It would be easy to assume from reading the pages of the *Sun* that some of Flagstaff's doctors spent more time traveling than doctoring. There were sick babies, as usual. A twenty-six-year-old man died of typhoid fever at Mercy Hospital. Dr. Ploussard performed three tonsillectomies. Not much in the way of medical news for such a bustling city.

For me the most memorable was of a lumberjack who tried suicide by hitting himself twice in the head with his axe. "He is a Swede," the *Sun* reported, "and is a steady, reliable man when normal."

Naturally the doctors attended to civic and professional duties. The Fronskes were involved all over the place. Albert Schermann was president of the Coconino County Medical Society, E. S. Miller secretary-treasurer. Miller and Charles Ploussard served on the Chamber of Commerce. A three-man team that delivered ballots on the border of the county included R. O. Raymond. Eric Flett, who moved his office from the Bank Hotel to the new Nackard building that year, was medical advisor of the Northern Arizona Teachers College football team. Felix Manning and Lois went to Phoenix for a medical conference and to Globe to attend the state medical convention. Felix and Lois, Martin and Hilda, Albert and Pearl all went to Tucson for sessions of the Southern Arizona Medical Association. Standard behavior—doctors in my generation did the same sort of thing.

Nevertheless, they traveled. Since the years of Dennis Brannen, Flagstaff's doctors had moved around the country a goodly amount. Charles Ploussard seemed to be preparing to do the same thing, replacing his coupe with a sedan, saying that some cars were too small to hold all of a baby's gear.

Dr. Fronske went to Prescott overnight; so did Dr. Miller.

No surprise that the two bachelors, Miller and Raymond, were the prime travelers. Together they spent Christmas on the coast (California) and went on to Mexico. Later Raymond toured California and New Mexico in his Packard, then drove Hazel Neer and his sister and a woman from Santa Monica to San Francisco and Los Angeles. Oh, and he went off to St. Louis for two weeks.

Dr. Miller traveled to San Francisco on the railroad to bring home a sixteen-year-old girl he had taken to the Shrine hospital for crippled children two years earlier. The *Sun* reported, "She is now walking with braces."

Eric Flett—what was going on there? First he drove to Los Angeles "in his new Dodge coupe" to visit his mother, according to the newspaper. He went back again "to visit" while Edwin Miller took care of Flett's practice. Later he went again "on business," then to Phoenix "on business." Was he planning, in another Flagstaff tradition, to move someplace else?

The dinosaurs lasted 150 to 225 million years. So far homo sapiens have been around, from the primitive beginnings, for 400,000— less than one-third as long.

After the war, when Don got to med school, the other students were mostly veterans, men who had come back from a war they didn't like to talk about. They worked hard, avoided younger guys with no memories who still wanted to play. I typed outlines of chapters, quizzed Don before exams while I ironed. It wasn't easy for men who had fought a war to spend their days memorizing books.

The student they envied, the one with photographic memory, was a suicide two years into practice. Why? Why was Don so changed by medical training and practice? For that matter, why were some medical students drop-outs? Why do some people in battle develop "shell shock" and others don't? Maybe there was no answer beyond "too sensitive," but I needed one, needed an answer.

With no great glee, I sat for hours in front of a computer in the NAU library, figuring out how to find medical journals and titles of their articles. Clutching my list, I climbed the stairs to the room that holds hundreds of bound periodicals.

My forte is not science, so I may have misunderstood the abstruse and deliberately tentative technical articles. But I think they said that extroverts and introverts are differentially sensitive to stimuli. Because of two neuronal systems, neurologically based—I was nearly lost already—people with one or the other of these systems react to reward or punishment stimuli in quite different ways.

There is a good deal of evidence, particularly from electrodermal and electrocortical recording procedures, that introverts exhibit greater reactivity to sensory stimulation than extroverts.

Fifteen to twenty percent of the population can be classified as "sensitive"— that is, it takes less to overwhelm them.

There is a positive relation between cortical arousal and sensitivity.

Cortical arousal means messages from the visceral brain, the hypothalamus, hippocampus, amygdala, cingulum and septum. I think what that means is that, for inherited biological reasons, about one-fifth of all people are more easily distressed by stimuli—overaroused, frazzled and jangled—than other people in the same situation, even when they seem to be coping just fine, until they reach a shut-down level termed "transmarginal inhibition."

Arousal produces cortisol, a hormone which can be measured in blood, saliva and urine at higher rates in people who react strongly to stress. That's also true for norepinephrine in their brains. They tend to have more stress-related and psychosomatic illness and greater risk for depression and anxiety.

So some of us might be perfectly nice people if we had less intense stimulus? And it has little to do with character? Whatever that means. Maybe so. Environment may have a strong influence on individual reaction—sensitive children who are criticized or beaten, for example, can experience intensified response. Does that mean we shouldn't be blamed for what we become? I don't know. Brains are obviously very complicated.

The bones that are ever more obvious under my skin, they will still be recognizable and distinct long after the rest of me has disappeared. Now there's a thought.

13

mid-July, 2001

To my family,

One morning I stood on my cabin doorstep with my face lifted, sniffing at the breeze—definitely moisture coming in on a forecast of monsoon movement. Happens every year. I'm still not sure I understand why, but it happens every year.

At first it honored us with lightning that started fires and a frenzy of human activity. Constant traffic on the radio. Continuous thunder. I was on my feet for hours hunting for smoke, figuring locations, half deafened by the noise.

Lightning in the Pine Mountain Wilderness started a fire that burned hundreds of acres for two weeks, putting a smoke lid on the Verde Valley and blocking the whole south end of the Coconino from my view. Incidents like that provoke flurries of phone calls from the General Public to the dispatcher: "I SMELL SMOKE!"

Finally, finally the rainy season settled in. At least, we thought so at the time. Every day by 10 a.m. black-bottomed cumulus filled the sky and began to shed rain—there, around Sitgreaves, and there, behind Mormon Mountain, and there, over Lake Mary. Below me, tree tops swayed. Water sluiced down my window glass.

But it was never the same one day to the next. Lashing rain that lasted twenty minutes, thus flash flood warnings. Three hours of what the Navajos call female rain that sank into the ground. Dark clouds that boiled toward me at tree top level, seethed up around me—and stayed unmoving for fifteen hours, shrouding dark wet trees, hiding land below. I was a remote island, a ship becalmed in fog. Safe. Hidden. No one could see me snug in my tower, wrapped in blankets, cheerfully reading.

Except for the weather, days in the tower go on the same. I climb the stairs with my Forest Service radio, deciding on wind speed and direction as I go up. A pause on the top flight to unlock the trap door, the last few steps, and I'm out of the wind recording weather data in my log, reporting to the dispatcher—"Flagstaff, Woody Mountain in service, southeast ten to twenty." The first of the daily exercises. There. Ready to begin.

I've been awake three hours by then, on my feet, sweeping etc. Even in a little cabin I have what Abby calls "a raging case of the neats." So I'm ready to rest. If the morning is cold and windy, I lie in the sun on the window seat reading for an hour. Ah, the luxury, to lie down in the morning and read.

311

I'm still living with clouds. They block the sun, carry rain and lightning, cold and wind. But so delicate, soft as soap suds. You could fall through one without a pause, stand in the middle of it and suffer no damage.

Watch, I'll show you today's spectacle. Are you watching? It's the same; it's always different.

Ten miles to the north, rain is a dark wall from Sitgreaves Mountain to the Peaks (twenty-five miles of dark wall) beneath serene masses of soft white and grey that are moving to the southwest. Thunder rumbles. But there is no wind here, no air movement at all.

Far to the southeast, at least forty miles away, is a low bank of whipped cream. Maybe rain has started to fall over Anderson Mesa—I can't tell yet.

Now look, tree tips ten feet away from my windows are moving gently. A few small friendly white clouds have appeared out of nothing above I-17 and Mexican Pocket. Rain to the north is two miles closer. Thunder is louder. The whipped cream has spread around a quarter of the horizon.

Does it feel a little cooler in here? The tops of the Peaks have disappeared into black clouds.

But what's going on up there? Those white puffs are larger and darker, moving from the west. Whipped cream is rising fast in the southeast. To the north, rain has almost reached the cars I can see driving on I-40, and A-1 Mountain is going under. Sun is shining overhead.

What time is it—12:05? Rain falling to the north is only three miles away; thunder begins with a sharp crack. In a sudden cold wind I grab at my papers, put weights on them, and rush to close down the windows.

Tops of the innocent little clouds have soared into the overcast, which is darker now with well-defined shapes. Do the people in town realize there's rain in Schultz Pass?

That black wall that was moving southwest? It's now headed right for me.

It's cold in here. Darker by the minute. Trees around me are whipping back and forth. The first drops of water hit my steel roof noisy as pebbles dropped. I have no visibility at all through 180 compass degrees, but I can see the Mazatzals eighty miles to the south. I think I'll put on my heavy slippers. And a sweatshirt.

You like this so far? I love it. Woo hoo!

To the south clouds are a jumbled mass that is also moving in this direction. What will happen if there's a collision? Yikes!

12:58. Rain has backed off—the whole show just skirted me, moving to the southwest, taking thunder with it. I can see for five miles now in my 180 degree arc. There is snow on the Peaks.

But wait. Rain is falling over Flagstaff and Oak Creek Canyon. Sky is black behind Mormon Mountain. Clouds are sagging dark and heavy all across the south and now they are headed this way.

I notice that a string of black clouds that just passed over me is coming back. I shout, "Hey! Change your mind?" With no apparent pattern, clouds move away. Afternoon turns sunny.

There's heavy rain in Colorado, fire in Oregon and eastern Washington, all dry due to lack of rain. Four firefighters died recently when the blaze they were working on blew up. I try not to imagine their last moments and concentrate on the girl who saved two hikers by putting them under her when she deployed her one-person fire shelter. She was burned on her side, but all three survived. In the middle of news of scandal in government and business, it's good to hear of heroism.

Cynics claim altruism does not exist, that we always act in our own interest. Maybe. I would need to know how much time that young woman spent on her decision, how aware she was that it could result in her death. It sounds like heroism to me.

Love,
Your personal first-line defense

P.S. Baxter, I'm still thinking about your question—"Is there such a thing as an Arizona love poem?"

1927 What a year! Lou Gehrig and Babe Ruth were hitting home runs. (The World Series was twenty-four years old by then.) Al Jolson was starring in *The Jazz Singer*, a "part-talkie." Charlie Chaplin was having divorce and income tax troubles. People loved "Fascinating Rhythm" and "Old Man River," and they were "sitting on top of the world."

Prohibition was still the law of the land, with 65,000 citizens arrested so far and $15,000,000 worth of booze coming in from Canada every year. Speakeasies, you bet. Somehow it didn't fit with Calvin Coolidge as President or Oliver Wendell Holmes as the oldest jurist on the Supreme Court, but never mind.

A new dance called the Lindy Hop was named for Charles Lindberg, who had claimed a $25,000 prize after the first solo crossing of the Atlantic by plane, non-stop, thirty-three and a half hours. When he arrived at Orly near Paris, he was carried around the field on French shoulders.

In the U.S. all leading economic indicators were rising. Day after day and month after month the price of stocks went up—brokers' loans alone totaled $3,480,780,000 by then. (Three billion) Wireless communication between London and New York City was established for public use.

Had poverty been eliminated yet? Ford Motor Company, which had recently completed its Rouge River plant, announced that some of its workers would be put on a 40-hour work week at the same pay they had been receiving for working longer hours. General Motors reported a $2.60 per share dividend totaling $65 million, the largest dividend in American history. J. C. Penny made a public offering of stock in his chain of stores.

Farmers did not share in the national prosperity. In Arizona general conditions were reported good—tourism, banking, range and livestock, mining, sheep and wool were all up—but income in agriculture—lettuce, cantaloupe, cotton—was not as good as it had been in 1925 or the first quarter of 1926.

A new state law cut labor hours for women (who had been working ten hours a day) to eight hours a day, six days a week. It excepted women in fields and packing sheds at harvest time. Also not included, for reasons apparent to somebody, were maids, nurses, and telephone switchboard operators.

Everywhere they looked, there was progress and rumors of progress. Flagstaff boosters were trumpeting More Prosperity For This County! Bidding opened for a "wagon" bridge at Lee's Ferry. Two months later a contract was awarded. There was talk of more new highways, of a Flagstaff-to-Denver phone line, of dams in Boulder Canyon, in Glenn Canyon, in Marble Canyon.

Flagstaff population, over 5500, supported nine churches, 201 businesses, 722 telephones, and 907 houses. Streets were being improved, and there were new buildings downtown, a new restaurant. Mary Costigan (did I mention that she was 5'8" tall?) had plans for a new movie theater. Brannen buildings were being remodeled; Wilson and Coffin were building a fireproof garage. Houses too were being remodeled—Sarah Manning was having a heating system installed in her home. The Fronskes had their big frame house painted again.

Hot diggety! The city council bought four ranches in Doney Park to use as an airplane landing field and named it for Mayor L. B. Koch. Flagstaff had a city garbage disposal system that amounted to more than just people taking trash to the dump south of town. The city health department was involved in that innovation.

There was a Country Club, with Dr. Felix Manning as its president. No houses surrounded green grass, it was just a nine-hole golf course with links of dirt and bunch grass where the Elden lookout road left the Schultz Pass road, but by golly, they could call it a Country Club if they wanted to. The hazard on the first hole was the water reservoir, which did not have a cover.

Bigger News—the Monte Vista Hotel opened with hundreds of visitors and stockholders present to look at the facilities. Congratulatory telegrams poured in from everywhere. Events scheduled for the new hotel included receptions, bridge parties, dinner dances, club meetings. The Business and Professional Women's Club held a dinner meeting in the hotel. For those addicted, there was a bridge party on New Year's Eve.

A committee (architects, artists, astronomers, academics) sponsored by the Chamber of Commerce and chaired by Dr. Grady Gammage of the Normal School urged the formation of a museum for science and art to study and preserve Northern Arizona historical artifacts, etc. T. A. Riordan and Mayor Koch were among those who spoke in support. Artist Mary-Russell Colton, wife of Dr. Harold Colton, wrote a letter published in the *Sun* to say that such an institution would be "the intellectual apex of the town" and "show the effete East that Flagstaff had taste and vision," and who wouldn't want to do that? Knob Hill, where the big hospital is now, was suggested as a possible site.

In response to complaints or lawsuit following death or serious damage the state Board of Medical Examiners can issue a letter of reprimand or revoke a doctor's license after official findings of wrongdoing (i.e. misdiagnosis operation on the wrong body parts, removing healthy organs, ignoring test results).

For the first few weeks after the radiation treatments, we walked slowly, strolled really, and never more than a quarter of a mile. Emily was so fatigued.

"It's not that I *get* tired, I *am* tired. Darn it, tired is my new state of being."

She looked tired and sick and older. Not old, just older, and it made me want to cry. I took her elbow so she wouldn't stumble over a rough place.

"And it gets worse, Marlene, it accumulates. Every day I'm more tired than I was the day before."

"Let's stop here in the shade for a minute. What does Jefferson have to say about it?" Treating Jefferson as a wise and thinking creature was a joke we shared to make things easier.

"Oh, he's so sane and practical, it's annoying. 'Fatigue often follows surgery,' he says. 'The prognosis for noninvasive ductal carcinoma is good. Each case is different, of course, but the survival rate is eighty-five to ninety-five per cent.' That bear reads too much."

"Well, he's right."

"I know he's right, I just don't want to hear rational reassurance from my teddy bear."

We both laughed. She didn't want to worry Travis and the children, but she needed to talk with somebody, even a stuffed bear. I examined all the books I could find, but that's not the same as facing cancer. The idea of support groups wasn't widely accepted then.

After the first month, when November mornings were cool under bright blue skies, we built up to ambling half a mile. Emily wore blouses that buttoned down the front so she wouldn't have to maneuver clothing over her head. She was still uncomfortable lying on *that* side.

But she tried to make me smile. "That breast is smaller than the other one now. Maybe I'll just have the other one reduced."

"That's a great idea. Big breasts are a nuisance, I think I'll have mine reduced too."

In January, walking along the canal bank, she confessed as if it were a weakness. "I'm a mess, Marlene. Lumpectomy isn't that big a deal, not like mastectomy. They didn't even take any lymph glands. Everyone thinks I'm back to normal, I should be back to normal. The family is expecting me to pick up where I left off. But I don't feel normal, I don't feel good, and I can't do anything, can't get anything done."

"Watch it—that rock—"

"I see it, thanks."

"People react differently to trauma, you realize that."

"I know they do, Jefferson tells me every day. 'Why do you think you should be like everyone else?' he asks me."

"That's a rare bear you've got."

"I know, I know. I'm glad for his company. But, Marlene," her voice wavered, "I cry and can't stop, hours at a time. I wasn't nearly so scared while the treatment was going on—there were plans that other people managed. Now I don't know what might happen. Every little ache, every twinge, scares me. I feel nowhere."

I stopped and took both her hands in mine. "My friend, that just proves how good you are. You're aware and thoughtful and sensitive, of course this whole thing has upset you. I agree with Jefferson—you're not like everybody else."

"I feel so fragile. Imagine me fragile? The doctor asks whether I have pain in my legs and back. Do I have a persistent dry cough? And I can't help worrying about whether the cancer will come back. Every day I check the scar for lumps."

"Oh, Emily."

She took her hands out of mine and fumbled for a tissue in her pocket. "I'm amazed at how I took my life for granted. I'm overwhelmed, that's all. You want to hear my symptoms? Fear, stress, bewilderment, loss, and I wouldn't be surprised if there were separation anxiety too."

We both laughed unsteadily.

"I'm angry, depressed, despondent, afraid, guilty. And I resent young women who can wear low-cut necklines."

I put my arm around her shoulders. "You know what I think? Bodies heal faster than minds do."

At the University of South Carolina neurologists have been applying weak electric magnetic fields above the left ears of patients to alleviate symptoms of depression, obsessive-compulsive disorder, mania, and schizophrenia. They say sometimes it helps. Don would have said it was just so much hokum.

1927 Flagstaff's doctors were seldom mentioned by name in the *Sun* when they were called to tend patients, not in the 1920s, but I could guess the kind of practice they had. The paper reported:

- broken bones, a broken elbow, a cracked rib
- infected wounds, a near amputation suffered by a local man while he was chopping wood
- measles, heart disease, scarlet fever, tonsillectomies
- logging accidents, fights, train wrecks
- a four-year-old who caught his arm in an electric wringer
- deaths in house fires
- two cases of frozen feet, a severed thumb tip
- babies born at Mercy Hospital
- an abandoned baby found dead of exposure
- auto accidents, an ear severed in an auto accident

(It was reported that nationally during the past eight years deaths from auto accidents had exceeded the number of Americans who had been killed in the Great War.)

Two operations, unidentified, were performed at Mercy Hospital, and Dr. Ploussard operated on a tourist for a ruptured stomach ulcer. (Note: People who could were still going to L.A. or to E. Payne Palmer in Phoenix for surgery.) Despite patent medicines advertised in the newspaper, there were a few cases of influenza.

After heavy storms in September, Dr. Schermann was called to Lake Mary, where a pine tree had fallen on a car ("It's coming down!"), injuring two people and killing one.

Poliomyelitis appeared in town, first in a baby. Vera Raudebaugh, age fourteen died of it. So did Mary Margaret Nichols, age thirteen. Front page headline news was that two adults born in Flagstaff, Arthur Riordan, age thirty, son of Michael and Elizabeth Riordan, and his cousin Anna, age twenty-six, daughter of T. A. and Caroline Riordan, had died of polio within hours of each other, Drs. Ploussard, Raymond, Schermann and E. Payne Palmer in attendance. Two other polio patients recovered.

The bereft Riordan mothers were sisters in the Metz family. I ached for them, for all the deaths and all the women, the mothers whose children died, usually ignored in formal histories. Statistics are offered of the thousands and thousands of men who were killed in our Civil War; I've never seen a tally of all the women, casualties too, who suffered because of those deaths. It's enough to bow you right down to the ground.

Felix Manning reported that general health in the county was good, but the milk supply was not. Before the year was out, city and state and U. S. Health Service regulations required that milk be graded on a scale from A to D.

But Editor Breen was not shy about reporting non-medical items about the doctors. Dr. R.M. Francis, apparently a respectable resident again, went to Phoenix to visit his son. Later he and Elizabeth went south for Christmas.

R.O. Raymond, fifty-two years old, moving slowly out of doctoring, bought a half interest in the Howard Sheep Company with Ramon Aso. He and Dr. E. S. Miller, fifty-nine (not to be confused with Dr. E. A. Miller, dentist, or E. G. Miller, Forest Supervisor) traveled to San Francisco and Vancouver by car, also to Washington, D.C. Dr. Raymond visited Los Angeles and Phoenix, all that within three months.

Dr. Miller went off to North Dakota and took a patient to the Mayo clinic. Breen reported that, back again, he was sick for a while. Miller, that is.

Dr. E.S. Miller receives plenty of attention from the ladies. But this week he decided he wasn't getting his share; so he entered Mercy Hospital with a mild attack of flu while girls of the nurse's registry competed in trying to please him.

Martin Fronske, rapidly becoming known as "the baby doctor" because he delivered so many, was a member of a Federated Church committee formed to supervise a community gymnasium program for boys and girls with classes in the church recreation center.

He spoke to the Rotary Club three times during the year, first seriously on Physician's Ethics. On the occasion of inauguration of officers, Fronske advised the new secretary on 1001 ways he could go wrong. Serious again, he appealed to the Rotarians to consider that Flagstaff needed an emergency hospital.

Mercy, he said, had been designed and equipped and maintained by Arizona Lumber and Timber Company for the care of its sick and injured employees. The Riordans had kept it "ever open to others," although it meant financial loss for the company. But demands on the facility had become greater than it could cope with. Witness a recent train wreck nearby which had swamped the doctors and crowded the rooms with strangers. Two injured tourists were brought in to Mercy nearly every week, Fronske argued, no appeal was refused.

The Riordans had not complained, he said, but their company should not be expected to maintain a community hospital without support in taxes. Could an emergency facility be established under a church management? It would be several years before action was taken on his suggestions.

Then there was Eric S. Flett, who had arrived six years earlier from Los Angeles. He'd had a term on the town council, served as county registrar of vital statistics for a year, been medical advisor of the Northern Arizona Teachers' College football team. Several times a year he went to L. A. to visit his mother, so the paper said. Back and forth, back and forth.

In May of 1927 Flett drove to the coast, "straight through without sleep," came back and "fitted up an apartment for his mother and sister" to use when they came to visit him. A month later he traveled again to Los Angeles and returned with a woman named Ruby Parks. A marriage license issued by Coconino County identified them as Eric St. Clair Flett, thirty-five years old, and Ruby Parks, thirty-one. The *Sun's* notice of the wedding described Ruby as "a family friend of long standing," and informed curious readers that the doctor was fitting up an apartment near his office where they would live. Same apartment?

Maybe people in town knew that Flett was traipsing off to L. A. to see someone besides his mother, but it was a surprise to me. Editor Breen had maintained a discreet silence about it. He also did not explain why they were married here rather than in California nor whether representatives of their families attended. What I wanted was the story.

Through the decade, Flagstaff's doctor population had remained quite stable: Raymond, Manning, Miller, Schermann, Fronske and Flett. Francis had been gone a while. Dr. Charles Ploussard had arrived three years earlier from St. Louis. Qualified to perform abdominal surgery, he associated with Dr. Schermann at Mercy Hospital. In the same week in the spring of 1927, he was appointed local railway surgeon for the Santa Fe and commissioned First Lieutenant of the Medical Reserve Corps, Department of Surgery of the United States Army.

Ploussard addressed the Rotary Club on the history of surgery and the value of hospitals to a community. Then he and Elizabeth and their two daughters traveled to St. Louis where the doctor enrolled for post-graduate training. They were back in time for Thanksgiving.

Within a month of his return, Ploussard announced that he had been invited to join E. Payne Palmer in his Southwest Clinic in Phoenix for work that would be primarily surgical. He was leaving immediately; his family would join him as soon as he could arrange housing for them. Pearl Schermann invited Elizabeth Ploussard as guest of honor to a farewell (what else?) bridge party.

Editor Breen wrote that a replacement surgeon was being sought but had no opinion about who it might be.

Things You Can Learn by Reading *Who's Who in Arizona*

Doctor Errol Payne Palmer was fifty-one years old in 1927, a prominent Phoenix physician and surgeon. Born in Mississippi, he had attended Barnes Medical College in St. Louis and taken up a practice in Phoenix in 1900, a new doctor twenty-four years old.

In the quarter century since, Palmer had done post-graduate work in all of the larger medical colleges of the United States and Europe. His record was impressive: member of the medical associations of America, the Southwest, Arizona and Maricopa County; founding member of the American College of Surgeons and chairman of its regional committee on fractures; busy staff member of Good Samaritan Hospital in Phoenix; chief of the surgical staff at Saint Joseph's; author of many articles read before medical meetings and published in medical journals. Does it need saying that he had an excellent reputation?

A mild-mannered man, he could have boasted, if he had been so inclined, of a home on North Central Avenue, two sons who were also doctors, and membership in the Phoenix Country Club. He seems to have intended to make his Southwest Clinic the largest and best equipped between Los Angeles and Albuquerque.

I don't know whether these ads in the *Sun* should be included with medical news, but here they are: "Coca Cola will give you pep." "Hires root beer is good for spring fever."

"Hey, Mom, how ya doin'?"

"Abby, I was just thinking about you."

"Absolute proof of telepathy. What were you thinking?"

"Something nice, of course."

"Well? Tell me. Something nice would be a compliment. It's a well-known truth that you should always tell a compliment."

"Oh, is it?" I smiled.

"Sure. Your individual contribution to the evolution of the human spirit. Even if told on a cell phone."

"Abby, what a wonderful philosophy."

"It's true. So tell me."

"Something happened to tickle me on my lunch hour, that's all, and I was thinking you were the only one I'd dare tell."

"Dare? What was this funny event?"

"You won't tell Gwen? She'd be on the first plane, prepared to abduct me and carry me off to Denver."

"I'll keep it deep and dark."

"Ed came up this morning…"

"Ed?"

"The patrolman on this district—I invited him and his wife to dinner at Christmas?"

"Yes, I remember."

"He was delivering fire shelters to all the lookouts."

"Fire shelters?"

"Aluminum, I think, I'm not sure—one-person bags—uh, sort of a thermal sheet that keeps heat out—emergency last minute protection in case a fire looks as if it's going to sweep over you. It folds into a package the size of a canteen."

"That's protection?"

"So they say—saves your life if you don't wait too long to get into it."

"They think fire will sweep over you?"

"I guess you never know. And then, my theory is that an emergency you're prepared for doesn't turn into a crisis."

"Well, that's profound."

"I wasn't aiming at profundity."

"Profound happens."

I laughed. "I guess you're right. Anyway, this little thing has two sides like a folded blanket, sealed top and bottom and split down the middle of one side so you can get in between. There are two straps inside at the bottom for your feet and two at the top for your hands so you can hold it down."

"Down?"

"Fire makes an awful wind. Could blow your shelter away if you don't have a tight grasp."

"This is tres bizarre. I can see why you don't want to tell Gwen. She'd call out all the troops."

"When I told Ed I'd never seen one, he was indignant. "'Those turkeys in the office didn't give you fire shelter training? You're up here in the forest on top of a mountain in a drought with no fire shelter training?'"

"'I didn't have any training at all. They were busy.'"

"'My goodness gracious, this'll never do. Your lunch hour's coming up. Come on down to the ground, I'll show you how this thing works.'"

"So there we were standing in sunlight in my little clearing while he pulled the fire shelter out of its carrying case—canvas, with straps so it can be slipped onto a belt. First he gave me a stern lecture—stern for Ed—about not waiting until the last minute to deploy (that's the accepted word, "deploy") because if the fire wind hits, the whole thing could be torn out of my hands and blown away. He had me repeat it, 'Better too early than too late.'"

"Good general advice, seems to me. Covers a lot of life situations."

"Then he had me shake this fire emergency gimmick out like a stiff plastic bag and lay it flat on the ground. It looked pretty small and flimsy."

"Oh, Mom."

"'Now,' he said, 'be easier for you if you sit down in the opening, right here, and get your feet set first.' 'OK,' I said, sitting down."

"Mom, the image of you…"

"Hey, a crown fire is roaring up the slope toward me, it's no time for worrying about dignity. I found the straps and got my feet into them. Found the straps for my hands. Pulled the end of the bag over my head, and there I was, inside peering out."

"Damn, you're a good sport. I'm proud of you.

"Thank you, Baboo. Wait till you hear what comes next. Ed said, 'You need a pair of heavy gloves, you'll never be able to hold on without gloves. I'll bring you some. Now keep the front side tucked around you, lie down and roll over so you're face down in the dirt.'"

"In the dirt?"

"Supposed to keep one from inhaling overheated air, thus searing one's lungs. So I lay down, pulled the split together and rolled over. Face down in the dirt."

I could tell Abby was grinning. "Wait till I tell Janey. She'll envy me. My mom."

"Ed, standing above me, said, 'You got a good hold on it?'"

"'Yes,' I answered from inside, feeling a little foolish."

"'Push your elbows out and flap 'em,' he said. 'If you pull the shelter too tight, you'll get a burn on your back.' I flapped, at my age, I flapped and began to giggle."

"'Now,' he ordered. 'You'll have to stay there for half an hour to be sure the fire's gone past. It's gonna sound like a jet landing on you, but don't panic. Don't come out. Half an hour. Start counting.'"

"'Oh, Ed!'"

"'I'm kidding for this time. Just remember that you can't come out too soon. Your life depends on it.'"

"You can see why I was tickled. I lay there on the ground like a baked potato and couldn't stop laughing."

In World War II they called it combat fatigue— afflicted soldiers had lived through prolonged and violent emotional experiences and been very fatigued. The U. S. Army estimated only ten percent of men in combat developed the neurosis. Of those only one third who had been in prolonged combat recovered and returned to duty. If treatment was delayed, only ten per cent recovered. This is according to *The Encyclopedia Americana*, which had nothing to say about unadmitted cases or those with only moderate symptoms.

1927 A doctor in Virginia, advising that feminine modesty was disappearing because of suffrage and "sex magazines," had absolutely no effect on fashion, to nobody's great surprise. Styles for the young were straight with no waistlines and slim with skirts to the knees. Ads read "smart and dashing" and "escape from the obvious and conventional." They all looked alike to me, which goes to show.

Attitudes about women had changed dramatically. Fewer than fifty years had passed since the railroad had been built across the plateau, and there they were—voters, public officials, drivers of automobiles. They could join the DAR, the Soroptimists. Infant mortality rates had decreased; the maternal death rate was also moving downward. The American Birth Control League had fifty-five clinics in twelve states and 37,000 dues-paying members.

Marion Wallace, twenty-one years old, was county recorder, the youngest elected government official in Arizona, maybe in the whole country. Born here to pioneer settlers, a member of the Business and Professional Women, she was recognized as a "live wire."

Early in 1927 the doctors' wives watched The Biggest Storm in Years, more than four feet of rain and snow in five days and, despite the weather, went out for their usual bridge luncheons. That wouldn't have been difficult for the women who lived close together, Hilda and Lois and Sarah side by side on Aspen, Pearl down the block.

Mary Costigan was featured in an article in The Independent Woman, a New York Magazine for business and professional women. Member of the local Chamber of Commerce and the Woman's Club, owner of the first radio station in Flagstaff, Costigan ran the first radio station in the world licensed to a woman. The antenna was in her yard, the machinery in her house. The studio was in the Monte Vista, in a little room off a hallway between the lobby and the dining room.

A member of the American Legion Auxiliary, Lois Manning lived rather quietly, with the exception of bridge parties, of course. Her mother-in-law, Sarah, continued to play bridge too and traveled to Los Angeles now and then to visit her daughter Henrietta. Pearl Schermann was chairman of the Altar Society Committee bridge party and contributor to the annual Catholic bazaar. She traveled to Phoenix and Los Angeles, organized a birthday party for her daughter Marjorie, six years old already. Nothing spectacular—the usual settled lives.

The Fronskes were the active ones; their names were in nearly every issue of the weekly Sun. Martin dressed up as a girl for their "jolly high-jinks" party to benefit the Women's Society of the Federated Church. Hilda and the boys drove down to Oak Creek Canyon for picnics. With her parents, Dr. and Mrs. Harnish, the Fronskes went to the Smoki dances in Prescott. Dr. Felix and Lois went too with Sarah and E. B. Raudebaugh.

I have no idea what Ruby Flett was doing. Her name did not appear in the newspaper any place for five months, not even as a guest at bridge parties which other doctors' wives attended. Not any place. I watched for it carefully. The announcement of her wedding in the Sun had carried the information that she had "a considerable number of friends here, made in former visits." If she did, I don't know who they were.

But it had been a double wedding. The other couple was Charles Kunsman— partner in and manager of the Flagstaff Pharmacy, a "wide awake" businessman—and Louise Switzer—one of the nine children of W. H. "Uncle Billy" and Nettie Lockwood Switzer, both from prominent pioneer families. Charles and Louise had to have been at least acquainted with Eric and Ruby, wouldn't you think? Witnesses were dentist Vaughn McGuire and his wife Elizabeth, whose names often appeared in the paper. With contacts like that, why wasn't Ruby mentioned in local doings, church parties, anything?

Ladies, even here, had formal calling cards, so concerned were they about social niceties. Ruby must have had invitations, it would have been expected.

In December the Fletts left for "an extended vacation" of several months in Los angeles supposedly to visit his mother and Ruby's relatives. I didn't believe it for a minute. Something was definitely going on.

With Elizabeth Ploussard gone, the wives were back to a tentative total of four: Lois and Sarah Manning, Pearl Schermann, and Hilda Fronske. Elizabeth Francis' husband was no longer in general practice; neither was Lizzie Harnish's husband. And Ruby Flett was iffy.

"From out of the past come the thundering hoofbeats of the great horse Silver. **The Lone Ranger rides again**. Bu-du-dum, bu-du-dum, bu-du dum-bum-bum…" I loved that radio program when I was in grade school.

"Hello."

"Hello, Beanie. Is that you?"

"Yes."

"Well, darlin,' I haven't heard you answer the phone before. To think you're old enough."

"Yes."

"This is your lookout grandmother."

"Hi, Nana."

"You're out of school now. You finished first grade?"

"Yeah. I did."

"Congratulations."

"Thanks."

"What are you doing with your extra time?"

"Drawing."

""Birds?"

"Yes."

"What kind?"

"Flying."

"You haven't talked on the phone much yet, have you?"

"A little. No, Mom, it's Nana, she's talking to *me*."

"The biggest birds I've seen so far this summer are vultures. Do you know them?"

"Yes."

"Vultures are beautiful in the air, circling and soaring above the mountain, coasting on their big wings, swinging out above Woody Ridge. This year one is missing a few primary feathers on the left wing."

"Oh."

"What's your favorite bird?"

"Ravens."

"Why?"

"Why what?"

"Why do you like them?"

"Because they're big and shiny and they aren't afraid of me."

"Those are good reasons. Ravens are astonishing as they flash past my tower, riding the wind. I think a breeding pair lives on the mountain—I see only two at a time, sailing together or grasping the prickly tops of pines with their feet, sitting there, calling back and forth. I've read that they are very intelligent, as birds go."

"Yeah. They are. I feed them."

"What do you feed them?"

"Anything."

"That sounds like ravens all right. I like violet-green swallows too, they're a circus act. Sometimes there are a dozen darting around the tower scooping flying bugs into their mouths, making instant turns so fast I can barely follow them. My books say they are so adapted to flying that their feet and legs are almost useless."

"Oh."

"They migrate here in summer from Mexico and Central America."

"Flying?"

"Yes, flying. In forests they nest in holes dug in dead trees by other birds. They would, wouldn't they, if their feet aren't useful for holding them onto bark?"

"I guess so."

"Hummingbirds were here the day I arrived, a dozen swarming around me demanding sugar water. Every day I wash and fill five feeders."

"We have hummingbird feeders too. I like those birds, they aren't afraid of me either. They fly all around my head if I stand still."

"How many do you have?"

"They move too fast for me to count."

"True, true. The males chase each other around, zipping high into the air and diving down. I like the sounds they make."

"So do I."

"Now and then one comes right into the tower to say hello."

"Neat."

"It may too late for egg laying, I don't know."

"Neither do I."

"I've learned a few things about the bugs up here."

"What kind?"

"Lady Bugs. I have them by the thousands, which is way more than I want. And wasps—they're related to bees. They don't make honey, but they need to drink. They cluster at my pump and fly around and make a loud noise when I go out for water."

"I don't like wasps."

"They're hard to like. Did one sting you?"

"No.

"Do you have Daddy Longlegs spiders?"

"Yes."

"With thin thready legs that move quickly and silently?"

"Yeah, and little red mites fasten onto the legs. The bodies are ugly and they stink when you squash 'em."

"I wonder why."

"So do I."

"So much to learn; so few hours in a day."

"Yeah. Well, bye."

One in every five people reports
the symptoms of depression.
What is this, an epidemic or
something?

Hit just about anything hard enough and fast enough in just the right place and it goes to pieces. A nut. An egg. An airplane dives into water at high velocity and, even though the water absorbs much of the force of the impact, the plane breaks apart. I'll bet I could drop a watermelon from the window of my tower and watch it evaporate when it hit the ground.

I've seen photos of a bullet fired into an apple—the interior of the apple exploded backward from the point of entry. Counter-intuitive, but there you are. I've read that a small car struck at high speed by an eighteen-wheeler virtually disintegrates.

But I didn't know the physics. 'Explode' means 'burst with a loud noise,' burst implies action from the inside, doesn't it? What I was wondering about was something hit from the outside.

Would mass and speed, squared or not, affect the outcome? Would the structure of the impacting and impacted objects matter? Would there be something like metal strain?

In town on a day off, waiting for the washing machine cycle, I went into my upstairs computer and found 2,150,100 hits on high velocity impact. An entry on high velocity impact blood spatter—a police page with photos. High velocity impact on airplane structures. High velocity impact on athletes in the long jump event. Planetary matter in high velocity impact. Ice. Temperatures and pressures reached. Swiss groups. UK groups. Space debris. All at the tips of my finger—this is not the world I grew up in.

Under high velocity auto collisions there were 174,000 entries, many journal articles. Objects of unequal mass. Newton's laws of motion.

Auto speed and erotic associations. I stopped a moment or two on that one, wondering if it explained why so many spectacular speeders were young males. Very public indecent exposure.

Then an article cited in the *American Journal of Forensic Medicine and Pathology*: "Complete Transection of the Trunk of Passengers in Car Accidents." The abstract referred to damage to vehicle and people when the point of impact in a broadside collision was at the column between front and back door just in front of the rear axle at a speed as low as seventy-four mph.

All passengers flung out of the car. Car torn into two parts. Passenger in back on the impact side cut in half. Traumatic amputation of his extremities.

Problems caused by being struck by lightning
may show up three to five years later:
serious neurological injuries, damage to the
autonomic nervous system, tiny holes in the
membranes of nerve cells, as well as impaired
memory, concentration and organization. Is
there no end to the neurological damage that
can come our way?

1928 The economy was skipping cheerfully right along. It was the year of Will Rogers and Mickey Mouse and color movies, of Gerber's baby food. Democrat Al Smith was the first Catholic candidate for President. Herbert Hoover, Republican, won the election a few months before the collapse of the stock market. Lucky Herbert.

In northern Arizona engineers were drilling in Meteor Crater, hoping to find and analyze the rock from space that had caused it. After all the plans and preparation, the first steel girders were put into place for the Lee's Ferry bridge across the Colorado River, and a heated debate erupted: should it be Lee's or Lees? A big new hotel was going up on the North Rim of the Grand Canyon.

Flagstaff was full of conventions that summer: Knights of Columbus, Chambers of Commerce, Wool Growers, Southwest Missionaries, Arizona's Business and Professional Women, directors of the Arizona Industrial Congress.

For three days a convention of the Southwest Division of the American Association for the Advancement of Science discussed the organization of a Northern Arizona Society of Science and Art, proposed the previous year, and decided to sponsor a study center and museum. Dr. Harold Colton was to be President and Director. The Women's Club offered a room in its building as temporary housing and, with local collectors donating the relics they'd accumulated over the years, an opening date was set for September. The first issue of Museum Notes came out in July.

The golf course at the Country Club had been moved to level ground seventy-five feet below the old one, and a carload of cotton seed hulls brought in for a surface on the "greens."

Rustic foot bridges crossed the "ravines." Dr. Felix, still president, appointed a committee that would have charge of women's golf tournaments—his wife and his sister Althea were enthusiastic players.

Babbitt's retail store had a lending library. Attention was being devoted to cleaning up the straggly cemetery. Midgley's grocery promised that within fifteen minutes of a phone call, your order would be delivered at your door by its Minute Man. Midgley's employed teen-ager Henry Giclas to make that promise good on a motorcycle.

Progress was moving so fast in every direction that when I read a proposal in the *Sun* to stock the Rio de Flag with herring, I believed it for a moment—until I realized it was a joke.

In the last edition of 1928 a bold headline read:

THE SUN OF PROSPERITY SHINES BRIGHTLY ON FLAGSTAFF

*With the New Year Will Come Even Greater Prosperity
to the Finest City in the Best State in the Union*

There'd be odd sensations in my arms: my hands would feel numb and above my elbows was a kind of tingling pressure that I wanted to flee from, anything to escape. One day I drove half way to the California border but turned back so I'd be there when the children came home from school.

"Hi, Mom. I thought I might catch you in town today."

"Baxter, how nice."

"How's your summer so far?"

"Going well. Full moon is due any night. It seems to be larger and brighter on the mountain than in town, I suspect because it has no competition from artificial lights. I love it—it fills my little cabin with radiance."

"I'm calling for a general welfare check: wanted to know whether you survived July 4th unscathed."

"Oh my. Yes, just barely. You?"

"The usual back-yard friends and in-laws barbecue. No crowd, no noise, no stress."

"Aren't you civilized though. Around here the first salvo from the General Public was fired four days ahead of time—an abandoned camp fire burning half an acre, close by two dead elk full of bullet holes. Not really my kind of guys, those campers."

"Mine either. Some people we shouldn't let out of town. We probably don't want them in town either with the idea of fun they have."

"I couldn't agree more. It turned into an exhausting holiday. Campgrounds full. People swarming. Little lightning fires all over the place. I was on my feet for hours trying to see through rain on the windows with my binoculars."

"Sounds like something of everything."

"Oh yes. When the rain stopped, a motorcycle race roared round the mountain with shifting of gears and whining of motors. It turned out to be one teenager."

"You saw him?"

"He roared up here as fast as he could."

"On muddy roads? Sounds like a boy headed for an early death."

"I'm afraid I'm far too old to understand it."

"I'm afraid I am too."

"Who can explain it, who can tell you why?"

He laughed. "Mom, you're developing a nice sense of absurdity—the human kind. Are you still studying weather?"

"I'm watching it and puzzling about unseen rules. One morning I climbed the tower and saw ribbon of smoke from a fire in Fry Canyon lying across the land for twenty miles. I assumed some kind of invisible ceiling. But I've put weather study on hold for a while. Too busy watching the 1920s build to the Crash. I'm up to 1928 when Hoover—Herbert not J. Edgar—was saying that the end of poverty was in sight."

"Rather premature."

"It's wonderful how hindsight makes one smarter."

"Do you find yourself wanting to shout, 'Sell now'?"

"Yes! It's just pathetic. People risking their savings. Or borrowing. Or buying on credit. They all thought it was perfectly safe: if automobile sales were up and construction was up and production was up, then the economy was sound. They were so smug, so confident."

"Do you remember any of that?"

"Good heavens, Baxter, I'm not that old. I can recite facts and figures, but I'm just now learning what they meant. For example: ten million households had radios. Two hundred thousand factories manufactured seventy billion dollars worth of products. But costs were ever up, so most companies were going public to raise capital. Speculation was rampant and so was manipulation of stock prices, surprise, surprise. Brokers' loans totaled five billion dollars, up one and a half billion. And there was no government regulation worth mentioning."

"Hey Mom, I'm impressed, you reeled that right off."

"Kids don't have all the learning advantages, in case you haven't noticed. Besides, I have my notes open in front of me."

He laughed again—three times in one conversation, I was doing very well.

"But, you know, the crash wasn't for lack of warnings. Prices on the Berlin stock market had collapsed, and economists were saying the prices of American stocks were beyond the point of safe return. A few bankers and financial editors were calling the whole hysteria 'unrealistic'."

"You know, I never wondered before—what was the situation in Arizona?"

"The same buying and building orgy, just on a smaller scale. Despite headlines that blared 'Arizona Makes Remarkable Gain in Wealth in 1927,' business had been slower in the second half. Cattle values had risen over the past three years, and that had attracted speculators who sometimes had little cash. There was danger of over-inflation. The Corporation Commission ruled that the Santa Fe's rates on lumber were excessive. But Arizonans were giddy with their own optimism—there were ten thousand more automobiles on state roads than there had been three years earlier."

"You said not long ago that you wanted to see how Flagstaff reacted to the Boom. Did you find out?"

"Little town, same wild dance. They were building or planning to in every direction. New houses, new business buildings, a new hotel. Out on the Lake Mary Road there was a new plant nursery complete with greenhouse. In the other direction a new water works with a reservoir of fifty million gallons capacity. They wanted a bigger hospital, paving for Route 66. Wool prices were up, so was tourism, so were property values, so was business, to more than eleven million dollars in the previous year. A monoplane had made the first landing at Koch Air Field. And you know what? They finally had a bathing beauty contest of their very own. People who warned of over-extension were 'crepe hangers'. It was beyond euphoria, it was crazy."

After the accident, after every-thing had stopped moving and there was only a sound of water dripping, I groped down from the motorcoach and sat in dirt beside the road, numb, shaking. It had happened so fast.

Don said he was beginning to resent the big hurry in the morning "Like we're in some kind of race. I want time to eat a leisurely breakfast if it's all right with *you*." I was the one who'd been pushing him since we'd left home?

After a late start, we drove south from Moab on 191 through more redrock and rugged country accented by deep green cedars, through small, comfortable towns with big shade trees. An unchallenging road, nice, a more human scale than some of our roads had been. I entertained myself reading signs to places with wonderful names:

Sixshooter Peaks, Wind Whistle Campground, Dark Canyon Wilderness, Newspaper Rock. Don was actually driving at a moderate speed.

I thought we were headed on down to Bluff on the north bank of the San Juan River, but he saw a sign that pointed to the west—Bicentennial Highway, Natural Bridges National Monument—and made a sudden right turn.

"Hey!" I grabbed for a handhold.

"I'm tired of you telling me where to go."

"Fine," I said. "Fine. Give me five second's warning next time."

"I want to see what a bicentennial highway looks like. And what makes a bridge different from an arch."

A couple days behind the wheel, and he was Mister In Charge again. I unfolded the map.

We weren't far from the right turn to Natural Bridges, another few miles of cedars and dirt, when we approached a large sign on a road that branched to the left.

NOT RECOMMENDED FOR RVS
OR TRUCKS OVER 1000 POUNDS
THREE MILES 10% GRADE
SWITCHBACKS
5MPH

He made another sudden turn, to the left, past the sign. "Don!"

"I'm sick of people telling me what to do."

"We weigh over a thousand pounds!"

"You're a Nervous Nellie, Marlene. Shut up and let me drive."

He went doggedly on for twenty uneventful miles of fairly level ground and sage and junipers, stopped briefly at the ranger station at the head of the Grand Gulch Primitive Area. According to my books, Grand Gulch is a deep canyon that hides the best collection of Anasazi ruins in Utah. I'll take their word—I couldn't have seen it from the road, even if I hadn't felt so tight about what was ahead.

The road was still nice enough, and Don was enjoying lording it. "You and your signs." But a quarter of a mile beyond, the ground dipped a little and then disappeared. All I could see ahead of me was sixty miles of empty space and more red cliffs way over there. Now I can guess what it would feel like to be approaching the head of Niagara Falls.

I gasped. "Don! It's a dugway! Oh god, Don, it's a dugway." A narrow dirt road wound down the face of a red sandstone cliff about 1000 feet high with steep switchbacks and no guard rails. Like the Shafer Trail—the "dugway drop." He turned onto it and plunged down, not even shifting gears, barely touching the brakes.

"Don! That's a hairpin turn down there! Stop, please stop and let me out."

"What for? I can do this."

"If I'm not in here, I can tell you where your wheels are. Let me out."

He wasn't gracious about it, but he did it—stopped in the middle of the turn—and it's a good thing he did. His right rear tire was poised to go over the cliff. I talked to him through the window. "Don't go even an inch forward. Not an inch. Back up slowly if you can and come forward toward the left."

"The left?"

"Yes, slowly. We'll have to do this a bit at a time."

After fifteen minutes of me signalling and him jockeying back and forth ponderously, we were positioned to go forward again to the next sharp turn. By then his mouth was cinched up tight.

I ran down that whole cliff in the sun and the wind, easing him around tight inside curves, scouting ahead on blind outside curves, guiding him as he eased around them taking the whole road. It was a stupendous view—the kind of place where gods might be born—but I couldn't give it more than a few glances. The motorcoach crashing down onto rocks hundreds of feet below would have been a stupendous view too.

When we reached the long slope at the bottom, I thought Don wasn't going to pause long enough to pick me up, but he did finally and I caught up with him. He did not say thank you when I climbed in. I did not say Tonto sit down now. But hey, it could have been worse—I could have been running uphill, not down.

Recently I've learned, thanks to a Colorado man named Steve Allen (of Ducks Unlimited) who was recommended to me as reliable source about southern Utah, that the road I hurried down follows a faulted scarp but it was never a proper dugway, never a stock trail hacked out by hard muscle work.

In 1956 Texas Zinc, a mining company, paid Isabel Construction Company a reported three million dollars to construct the thirty-three mile road from Natural Bridges to near Mexican Hat. This included the section down the south face of Cedar Mesa now known as the Moki Dugway. The construction of the road allowed uranium ore to be shipped to a processing plant.

Well. What's in a name? It must look like an improved dugway to people other than myself. But what I really want to know is how big were those ore trucks?

Neurasthenia, a syndrome: impaired functioning in interpersonal relationships, fatigue of body and mind, depression, feelings of inadequacy, headaches, hypersensitivity to sensory stimulation like bright light or loud music and by psychosomatic symptoms. Sound familiar?

Late July

Dear group,

I probably said this last summer. If so, I'm saying it again. I love living in the sky, intimate with Arizona clouds. If I were in some other place, like London or Seattle, where all day many days is a grey overcast, I wouldn't feel so enthralled, I'm sure. I live in Arizona though, and I'm intimate with summer cumulus, and I love it. Day after July day, it's always new to me.

When I climb my tower early in the morning, the sky is usually blue and empty except for a few low-level cirrus clouds here and there, nothing serious. (I make a pun. Sort of.) Maybe a small line of small cumulus off to the southeast, innocent and white, that's all. The day is young yet, and the air is still cool.

I fill out my daily paperwork and open the windows and look around for smoke, and a few small clouds hang above the big mountain where they weren't before. They haven't moved in; they've just appeared. Half an hour later they're piling up, spreading out, growing in all directions like living creatures. I can see them swelling out of themselves, changing every five minutes, and I have time to watch the show. Lucky me.

I never tire of the spectacle. Another half hour and the clouds to the southeast have doubled in size. Over to the southwest cumulus are definitely developing, and the huge piles to the north are beginning to merge. Greys and blacks are showing up, and I'm feeling a twinge of anticipation. Dare I hope for rain?

Hummingbirds zoom in, cheeping, and are promptly baffled about how to get out again. They bump their bills and beat their wings against the fixed glass panels. I say, "Wait, wait, sweetie, you'll hurt yourself," and make a cup of my hands over them and move the tiny creatures down to the sill, where they collapse with their wings drooping wide and give up. A hummingbird that has given up is a pitiful thing to see.

Slowly I enclose them in my hands, careful not to press against them and hurt them. When I put my hands out an open window and spread my fingers, the little birds zip away into the air above the pines as if their release had been their own clever doing.

The trees, which are these days regarded as almost sentient by sentimentalists—that includes me—stand stolid as statues below me, unlike those formations in the sky. I may not know enough, but part of the wonder of clouds is that they are unlike anything on the ground, anything else on the Earth. They seem alive, but you can move easily right through them. They move and change, soft, evanescent, yet they contain an energy so powerful it can blast a tree to splinters with a deafening explosion. Different from all the rest of us, unlike anything else. And from down here they're silent.

By noon a heavy black mass is skimming the top of the Peaks and growing in this direction. Towering white piles are building everywhere, all around me. Where is that shadow coming from? Overhead? I lean out the window—a soft dark cloud is right above me.

Rain in dark columns is falling on the Hochderffer Hills, on Mormon Mountain, on Anderson Mesa, hiding the land beyond. There's a distant mutter, but where in all this skyscape is it coming from? Lightning strikes the ground in miles-away places.

When I was in the fourth grade, I think that's when it was, I asked the teacher in class why it always rained at night. This was in Phoenix, you know, the desert. As I remember it, she gave me an excellent summary of temperature and condensation and such factors, an excellent explanation. But what I really meant, I suppose, was why rain didn't fall until it was dark and I was in bed and I never got to see it. Rain was too precious to miss, and I longed for it.

The distant mutter has become a rumble coming from at least two storm cells. The black columns are several miles wide; there are grey scarves of rain now and white veils. Oh, yipee!

When the rumble in the clouds has become tympani, has become cannons, and lightning stabs into earth in all directions, and rain is a 180 degree arc around me, I fear for the hummingbirds and the nuthatches, all the little birds. What do they do in a summer storm? Hide among branches in the trees, maybe, as they have for centuries.

Rain streaks my windows, washing off the dust, and rattles on my steel roof. In my dinky room it's still and dry, but wind blows cold through cracks, and thunder booms, and it's noisy in here. I am apart from the ground, a part of the storm, and I am very happy. I love living in the sky.

I love you too.
Marlene

Evidence is growing that depression is a risk factor for illness and death and that depressed people have weak immune systems. Caregivers also suffer from comprised immunity. This is one dangerously communicable disease.

1928 It was the year of Vitamin C, penicillin, the Iron Lung. Flagstaff's doctors were apparently as prosperous as everybody else: A. H. Schermann bought a new Buick, E. S. Miller a Chrysler. Martin Fonske provided Hilda with a new Fordsport coupe. Was she the first woman in town with a car of her own?

The Fronskes were all over the place. Head of the Coconino Chapter of the Red Cross, Dr. Fronske spoke on polio to doctors of the County Medical Society. After frequent visits and picnics, the Fronskes built a cabin in Oak Creek Canyon, where they spent several weeks that summer. In August they invited Lois and Feliix Manning to join them as guests. Both couples drove to Tucson that year for medical meetings.

In July the *Sun* printed this paragraph under "Local Brevities:"

Dr. C.W. Sechrist of St. Louis arrived Sunday to spend the summer in Flagstaff as a guest of Dr. and Mrs. A. H. Schermann. He was formerly associated with the St. Louis City Hospital and may locate here.

Charles Sechrist, born in Kansas thirty-two years earlier, was of average height, 5'8" tall. He had taught school, worked in a bank, attended the University of Kansas at Lawrence for four years, spent three years in medical school in Kansas City.

While he was at U.K., he met a woman named Ethel, born in Kansas in 1893, who was working toward a Master's Degree in Home Economics. World War I started; Charles Sechrist, twenty-two years old, enlisted in the Navy. Ethel worked in Washington, D.C. during the war with Herbert Hoover's Allied Relief Administration. They married in 1923, when she was thirty and Charles was twenty-seven.

Ethel was early in the tradition of women who worked their husbands through medical school. (Did she teach at Central Heart Pain College in Missouri? She was there for a while.) It also means she was the first doctor's wife in Flagstaff who had graduated from college. Well, let's hear it for Ethel!

Trained in surgery, Charles had finished his internship by 1928. In 1929, when Dr. Schermann inquired at St. Louis City Hospital for a surgeon to replace Ploussard, the new Dr. Sechrist was recommended. He arrived in Flagstaff in July, worked with Schermann for two months, decided to stay, and sent for Ethel and their son Milton. In September they moved into an apartment across from the new high school.

Charles made house calls, kept office hours on Sunday mornings to accommodate working people. They joined the Federated Church. Ethel became a member of the Shakespeare Club.

After they were settled, the Schermanns introduced them to society with an informal dinner and bridge party. On Thanksgiving Dr. Felix and Lois were hosts at dinner and bridge for sixteen, almost every medical person in town: the Schermanns, the Fronskes, Hilda's parents the Harnishes, the Sechrists, Sarah Manning, Dr. E. S. Miller, and three dentist couples—the Millers, the Mackeys and the Murpheys. Dr. Raymond was probably traveling somewhere as usual.

St. Louis. The Sechrists came to Flagstaff from St. Louis. I went back through my notes—I'd written that name often. It seemed to me that St. Louis had had quite an influence on the medical care provided in Flagstaff.

The Doctors' Schools

Brannen: E.M. Institute in Cincinnati
Cornish: Jefferson Medical College of Pennsylvania
Manning: Universities of Virginia and Alabama Medical Colleges
Miller: University of Buffalo Department of Medicine
Robinson: ??
Sipe: Hospital College of Medicine, Central University of Kentucky
Adams: College of Physicians of Cleveland, Ohio
Raymond: Washington University Medical School, St. Louis
Schermann: University of Pennsylvania School of Medicine
Sult: Georgetown University, Washington D.C.
Manning: University of Alabama Medical Department
Manning: University of Alabama Medical Department
Fronske: Washington University Medical School, St. Louis
Wilson: Northwestern University Medical School
Zinn: Los Angeles College of Osteopathy, Pacific Medical College of Los Angeles
Flett: Pacific Medical College
Francis: Missouri Medical College, St. Louis
Hendricks: Memphis Hospital Center
Ploussard: St. Louis University
Sechrist: University of Kansas Medical School, St. Louis

Missouri had a long history of disreputable medical schools and diploma mills—ranked at the bottom of the AMA's Council on Medical Education. But St. Louis? I wrote to the National Library of the History of Medicine in St. Louis, and the archivist answered with this information:

H. J. Harnish, St. Louis Medical College, 1881
Richard M. Francis, Missouri Medical College, 1889
R. O. Raymond, St. Louis Medical College, 1899
Martin Fronske, Washington University in St. Louis, 1907

All four had received their training before the Flexner Report of 1909 had evaluated the quality of American medical education. So had Albert Schermann, Western University of Pennsylvania, 1903.

Charles Ploussard, St. Louis University, 1922, and Charles Sechrist, University of Kansas in St. Louis, 1926, were both trained after the Flexner Report had changed medical schooling.

Harnish and Francis had learned what they knew about medicine in an era when many medical schools were more concerned with numbers of graduates than the quality of education they provided. That's not to say that Harnish and Francis were not good doctors, just that their schools had not been particularly good.

In 1891 the St. Louis Medical College was designated the Medical Department of Washington University; in 1899 when R. O. Raymond was there, it merged with Missouri Medical College. In 1904 the combined schools began planning for a new medical science building that would accommodate a major teaching hospital. Martin Fronske's education probably benefitted from the change.

Nevertheless, the 1909 Flexner Report was critical: "uneven" laboratory instruction, "wretched" clinical branches, "inadequate" hospital. Whew! Flagstaff's earliest doctors evidently had to rise above their education. That was probably true of doctors in most of the small cities and towns of the time.

In Flagstaff in 1928, they treated such cases as a woman who had been knocked down by a cow and suffered a wrist 'knocked out of place" and a woman "in critical condition" after a nervous breakdown.

Footnotes about women, 1928:

- Flagstaff ladies began to invite friends to "a series of bridge luncheons." And golf luncheons at the Country Club.

- Hilda was a guest at almost every party, even after her appendectomy performed by a doctor called from Albuquerque, Charles Ploussard having gone to Phoenix.

- Sarah was hostess to fourteen at a Tuesday Bridge Club meeting.

- Pearl's name was often in "Society Notes." So was Mary Costigan's.

- President Hoover's wife's hemlines skimmed her ankles. For younger women hems were just below the knees and had no waistlines. The brims on cloche hats were so low and close to the face, they restricted women's vision. In New York a doctor declared that fashion and life style were primary causes of tuberculosis.

- Nurses in Flagstaff—Virginia Phelan was the school nurse. Ruth Lundell and Laura Bell Macdermid were both registered as RNs with the state. In the Voters Register Mrs. B.A. Boenitsch, Mrs. F.A. Massey and Emarose Smith listed Nurse under the heading of occupation.

Humanity includes a long line of women. I learned to crochet from my mother, who learned from her mother, who went out into the woods to make "pretty lace" because her mother wanted her to do useful work instead.

Things You Can Learn While Reading Medical Journals

- Doctors placed under examination and probation because of professional misconduct have a rate of suicide as high as 20,000 per 100,000. The rate of suicide in the general population is 15 per 100,000.

- Such doctors tend to be socially and professionally isolated. A high degree of serious psychopathological conditions manifest early in their careers and are recurrent throughout their professional lives. They are long-term heavy drinkers.

- All have a history of serious, formally diagnosed psychiatric disturbance before probation status. Depression is present to some extent in all of them…Younger men have serious endogenous emotional problems associated with instability early in their lives. Most are described as introverted and sensitive, with anxiety and depression.

14

Well, maybe "breakdown" is not quite a precise term. Maybe "overload" would be better. I wonder whether what we call a "nervous breakdown" is like what we used to call shell shock or combat fatigue.

"Gwen, how's my eldest?"

"*I'm* fine."

"You're fine. Who's not?"

"Your grandsons, that's who. Why didn't you tell me it would be so hard to raise boys?"

"You probably wouldn't have believed me. What have they done now?"

"They've been boys, that's what. They haven't stopped moving at Mach speed since school let out. I've been driven right to the edge for weeks trying to keep them from some kind of major destruction. Are girls easier?"

"For a few years they are. Then they hit twelve, and after that it's a toss-up."

"I can't watch Beanie and Cazz every minute, I have other things I have to do. My neighbor Estelle called a few days ago and said, 'Gwen, do you know what your boys are doing?' I thought they were watching tv, but no…"

"Where were they?"

"On their bikes out on the street. You know how it slopes downhill north of us for a couple of blocks? They were trying to see how fast they could coast. Estelle said she'd been driving up and passed them, both of them holding the handle bars and lying stiff and flat out on the seat! She wondered if that was all right with me. Her opinion was that it was a traffic hazard."

"Oh Gwen…"

"I rushed outside still holding the phone, and there they were. They'd pedaled to the top and pushed off again, and Estelle was right, they were straight as boards head to toe on top of those bikes, headed for an intersection. Just as I saw them, Beanie wobbled and hit Cazz and they both went down on the pavement and bounced and skidded and I don't know what all. Mother, I was just plain horrified."

"I'll bet."

"I raced down there—they were screaming and covered with blood—I dialed 911—an ambulance came—we went to the emergency room, sirens screaming, boys screaming, me crying—"

"My poor Gwen…"

"They both have broken arms, and they're covered with abrasions, but the doctors say there's no permanent damage. Not for the boys. I'm not so sure about me. You know what their father said? He called it a science experiment!"

"Well, that's one way of…"

"He's so cheerful about it. They're covered with casts and bandages, there's no way they can have a shower or a bath, so he uses a wash cloth on them every evening and tells stories in funny voices and makes them laugh."

"Good for him, Gwen."

"Oh you're right, it would be awful if he were mad at them. Or at me. Actually he helps a lot, he comes through the door at the end of the day and takes my little barbarians off my hands."

"It must be several days since you've thought to worry about me."

"That's right! I forgot all about you."

"See there?"

"Shame on me. My mother, and I forgot."

"It's OK, really. Let me worry about you instead."

"Me? As much money as we have?"

"You're in a very stressful phase—mother of growing boys is one long learning experience."

"Mother, your phase is too, whatever it is, has to be."

"I've never done it before—that's how it is with phases—but this one is not very stressful."

"I worry that you'll think you can do what you used to do and hurt yourself."

"Hey, Sweetie, I'm enjoying this phase. It's the best one yet."

"Your fire season will be over soon—what are you going to do then?"

"I'll stay on in Flagstaff in my little town house. I'm quite happy here."

"What will you do this winter, go on with history?"

"I'm nowhere near the end of the story. If indeed stories ever have an end."

"Don't you ever do anything for fun?"

"I think I'll buy a purple sweatsuit."

"Mother."

"And a red hat."

"Mother, that's a cliche. The Red Hat Society is all over the country by now."

"Can you imagine? A poem by a woman starting a nationwide movement? 'When I am an old woman, I shall wear purple with a red hat which doesn't go.' It must mean a great deal to a nation of women…"

"But I hate to think of you as a cliche…"

"…of defiance, of rebellion against the stereotype of age as a time of giving up…"

"…you've always seemed so independent."

"That's it exactly. Old is the time to cut loose, and it doesn't hurt to wears a symbol to flaunt it."

"But you aren't that old, not yet."

"The poet, Jennie Joseph, is only a year younger than I am. I wonder whether she wears a red hat."

"It's too much, first the boys and now you."

"Hang on, Sweetie. You may want to get a red hat for yourself before you know it."

When I was in high school, there were dances with live bands. It was after the jitter-bug phase. We danced quite calmly. Sometimes the girls wore long, full-skirted formal dresses. At the end of the evening the band always played "Goodnight, Ladies" at the end of the evening.

1929 **January through May:** Calvin Coolidge, leaving office, said stocks were "cheap at current prices." However, the boom had changed into a speculating orgy with people swarming to buy stocks on marginal down payments. Share prices had risen 38% in the last year, and some observers were saying that the situation was not supported by the general condition of business. A few, a very few people were using words like "hysteria" and "inevitable collapse." They were considered virtual traitors. The consensus was that stocks were not over-valued and that a severe depression was outside the range of probability. Which goes to show.

Banks organized securities affiliates. Mergers grew into corporate chains. Holding companies controlled holding companies which controlled other holding companies. Investment trust companies—their only property the stocks, bonds, debentures, mortgages and cash that they owned (!)—sponsored investment trusts which sponsored investment trusts at the rate of about one each business day.

In March a trading pool caused a sudden rise and then an abrupt fall in RCA stock prices within four days. The market rebounded. The whole set-up must have looked insane to anyone who knew what was going on, but markets in New York, Boston, San Francisco and Cincinnati were booming. Corporations speculated instead of using money to build business.

Flagstaff may have been on the fringe, but it was not immune from the national fantasy. The *Sun's* front page headline for its first issue of the year was FUTURE LOOMS BRIGHT FOR THIS CITY. A financial speaker to the Hiram Club reassured its male members that prosperity would last another ten years.

The increase of advertising in the *Sun* was proof that business was active. The Country Club was flourishing; Babbitt Brothers were building a new warehouse; a city zoning commission was organized. John Weatherford remodeled his hotel.

The Orpheum Theater incorporated, its articles signed by Dr. E. S. Miller, Mary Costigan, and Philomena Babbitt. Interesting combination. Costigan was considering buying equipment that would make "talkies" a reality at the Orpheum.

And did they ever have plans—it must have been quite heady. Was there money enough to pave residential neighborhood streets on Aspen, Birch and Sitgreaves? They could at least install curbs and gutters. United Dry Goods chain was coming to town. Definitely in the works: an air taxi service to fly twelve passengers at a time between towns in northern Arizona. With an enrollment of 107, the three rooms at Brannen

School were no longer adequate—new classrooms would be built right away, as well as a new building for the Normal School/Teachers College.

The electroencephalogram (EEG) was developed in 1929, which probably would not mean much to Flagstaff for years. The Nobel Prize for medicine was awarded to the discoverers of Vitamins A and B—that could have been within the reach of every household. Could have, but was it?

Dr. Sechrist went east to Kansas to attend a surgical clinic, Dr. Fronske farther east to New York for "intensive study" at the Lying In Hospital, which had provided short courses to physicians since 1902. Dr. Mackey and Dr. Felix both went to Los Angeles for sinus operations. Dr. Raymond, fifteen years into his sheep business, spent "numerous days" in southern Arizona.

In January Mary and Tom Rees (Clerk of the Superior Court) entertained eighteen guests at a dinner party followed by bridge. The Fronskes and the Sechrists were—as Fred Breen put it—"among those bidden."

All the clues indicate that life didn't change much for the doctors in the months leading up to the Crash. Dr. Felix was elected head of the new Arizona Public Health Association—that was no surprise given his years of service to the cause. Dr. Miller stopped to take something into the Orpheum Theater, left the keys in his car, and came back after a few minutes to find it gone, stolen. It was soon found abandoned out of gas seventeen miles west of Winslow.

When they were little, I sat on their beds and rubbed their backs and sang to them. "Living for you is easy living." Light from the hall came into the darkened room. "It's easy to live when you're in love." It was the best of all times for me. I sang my children to sleep.

"Hi there." Breezy way to answer the phone.

"Hi yourself, my Abby."

"Mom! I've been thinking about you. How are you?"

"Fine, thank you. We're well into what's supposed to be the rainy season, but so far I haven't seen much rain here, just now and then. How are you?"

"My advisor is driving me nuts. She says my final chapter needs expanding. Probably take another four months and turn the whole thing into something I don't want."

"Oh, how irritating. Is there anything you can do?"

"I've talked to some people. We'll see. One man on my committee told me he thought they ought to let students write their own dissertations, not the dissertations the professors want. I was so grateful to him."

"What an enlightened person."

"Isn't he though. You know, Mom, I'll really be glad when this academic hoop-jumping is finished."

"Learning should be fun, I say."

"Right on. I hope I'm not your age before I can say that from experience. So how's your research?"

"I'm into 1929 now. A Big Crash coming up."

"You learning anything fascinating?"

"Yes, I am. Did you know that there were seven elected women in Congress in 1929?"

"No. I didn't."

"Twenty-two New York brokerage firms had women partners."

"In 1929? Now that's a surprise."

"Well, women were investing in increasing numbers. They owned fifty-five percent of Tel and Tel stock, for example."

"No kidding. That doesn't fit the stereotype, does it?"

"They were as happy to be making money as men were. But not all of them—only one and a half million people, out of a population of 120 million had an active association with the market. At the peak in 1929 the number of active speculators was less than a million. The key word there is active, another half million had invested."

"Must have been a popular topic for conversation."

"Oh yes. Even people who hadn't bought stock thought prosperity would go on and on: there was a mass market for cars, radios, refrigerators, vacuum cleaners."

"Spending money they didn't really have?"

"Yep. Everybody was buying on credit."

"Like today."

"Disturbingly like. Half of what I'm reading reminds me of now. For example, a man named Birdseye introduced frozen foods."

"Really!"

"Editorial cartoons in the Flagstaff newspaper made political points that weren't far short of propaganda. The past never stops."

"Never. Even ancient Egypt. Even ancient Greece. Never stops."

"The other day it hit me that I was born when Herbert Hoover was President. I hadn't realized that before. Do you know who was President when you were born?"

"Come to think of it, no, I don't."

"It changed my perspective on American history."

"I'll bet."

"I remember when FDR was running for a fourth term as President. I knew names like Dewey and Wilkie and Frances Perkins. And Eleanor. That's how old I am."

"Whooee."

"Then in the middle of the accumulation of several millennia, not to mention several decades, I'm brought up short by the new and different. When I was growing up the words LONG DISTANCE were tinged with almost sacramental importance. You didn't make Long Distance phone calls lightly then, they were expensive. And here I am talking to you a few hundred miles away like we were in the same room and thinking nothing of it."

"Magic is afoot."

"Everywhere."

When I was raising children, there were no safety car seats. I still throw my right arm out across the passenger side when I have to brake hard. That's how old I am.

1929 **Summer:** Between 1925 and 1929 the number of American factories increased from 183,900 to 206,700. In 1926 4,301,000 automobiles were produced, in 1929 5,358,000. By the summer of 1929 the stock market dominated the national news—the whole society, it seemed, was preoccupied with money.

Through the decade farmers—people who produced the food—had not enjoyed the prosperity that was making the rest of the economy giddy. Cattle prices were down in Kansas City. When Congress passed a farm bill and trumpeted Brighter Farm Prospects, well, that took care of the problem, didn't it?

There were warnings. Demand for manufactured goods was falling, and American loans overseas were being reduced.

Professional brokers were noticing what they called "ripples of uncertainty" in the stock market—I love that description. Cautious dealers were warning that good times were coming to a close. The Federal Reserve Board suggested that it was unwise for banks to lend money for speculation.

The economy was moving from sluggish toward depression. Purchases of personal items were up, but wages were not—five hundred women were on strike in Tennessee textile mills. Industrial and factory production turned down; steel production declined; freight car loadings fell; home building slumped. Henry Ford warned about the dangers of speculating.

Reading the *Sun* gave me the impression that those omens had no effect on Flagstaff. There was the usual buying and selling. New buildings and businesses, plans for more. In a paid statement in June, the Arizona Investment Service, office in the Monte Vista Hotel, offered reassurance:

> *The stock market is more or less influenced by mob psychology—governed by fear of what may happen—and that fear on the part of the trading public caused the break that was witnessed in the past week... Intrinsically, good stocks are worth just as much as they were when they were selling at much higher levels. Market fluctuations cannot take away values.*

I look at those people from seventy-two years later, and they seem so innocent. There had been warnings. And they went right on. George Babbitt and his partner announced that they were placing on the market their new Elden Heights subdivision, with restrictions on buildings that would be erected there. A. E. Dubeau of Los Angeles began construction of a tourist bungalow hotel on southSan Francisco Street. John Weatherford hired repairs for his "boulevard" on which sightseers could drive right to the top of the Peaks.

Koch Air Field was leased to Western Air Express, which planned improvements that would make it a "big junction," and two other airlines promptly applied to use its "privileges." More good news: the new museum reported "many accessions." Plans: a new rail link with central Utah; National Monument status for Sunset Mountain; a big dam on the Colorado River in Boulder Canyon.

The doctors' work went on as usual. Sechrist took to the Prescott Veterans Hospital a man whose arm had been amputated at Mercy Hospital following an accident. Albert Schermann was called to the scene when lightning struck seventeen-year-old Tom Piper—Dr. Miller, deputy county health officer, examined him and certified his cause of death. A "well-known physician" (Did I mention that he had a luxurious mustache?), Miller was the new president of the Hiram Club.

They still felt prosperous, apparently, they traveled as if they did. Dr. Felix and Lois went off to the White Mountains on vacation. The Fronskes were in their Oak Creek Canyon cabin for the summer. Hilda's parents, the H. J. Harnishes, went to Florida. Charles and Ethel Sechrist traveled to the Grand Canyon and back by plane. Albert and Pearl Schermann had a new baby boy (Thomas William) which cost money too, and then she and the children—five by then—-spent two weeks in Los Angeles.

The Ladies Golf Club played once a week. Mrs. J. B. Francis (not the doctor's wife) "gave" two bridge parties for a total of eighty-five guests. Ethel Sechrist did not attend—she was hostess at a birthday party for her five-year-old son Milton, maybe that was why. A member of the Women's Society of the Federated Church, she was admitted to the new Eastern Star, which met for a regular social gathering at her home, thirty-five women present.

Traffic problems were increasing in town, so were auto wrecks with injuries and deaths. In that long-ago summer Hazel Neer, who had worked as Dr. Raymond's secretary since 1914, was injured in a head-on collision while riding in a car which the doctor was driving. Hazel was an invalid in a wheelchair afterwards, tended by Ida Leissling in a house behind Raymond's office on north Leroux.

mid-August

Dear fellow voyagers:

There are mysteries wherever I turn. Weather forecasters around here won't commit themselves more than five days ahead, and then they say things like: "An upper-level disturbance may lead to a chance of rain this afternoon, heavy in places. This trend may continue into next week." Not very confident, if you ask me. But this morning on the radio I heard that the National Hurricane Center in Florida is predicting twelve big tropical storms for the next two months. What can they be seeing to forecast that far ahead?

I know this much, at least I think I do: like all weather it's complicated. A hurricane forms out of a disturbance over western equatorial Africa and gets involved in contending air masses between the Sahara and moist air over the coast. Hot dry air, warm ocean temperature, resulting low atmospheric pressure, and it all moves to the west, picking up tons of ocean water as it comes, developing extreme wind, thunderstorms and a counter-clockwise rotation.

I've acquired wonderfully exotic terms like "tropical depression" and "Southern Oscillation" and "African Easterly Jet." And here's something that intrigues me: "It is suggested that nearly all of the tropical cyclones that occur in the Eastern Pacific Ocean can also be traced back to Africa." What a planet.

Over here in the southwest sector of the Colorado Plateau, San Francisco Mountain volcanic field, we are officially into summer storms, but local precipitation is wayward. I can see weather forming and moving a hundred miles out, but I never know who's going to get it. I shiver through three-quarters of an inch of rain in the afternoon and go for several days afterward in sunshine while everybody else gets soaked. On the 4th I recorded all the lookout reports as an indication. My rain for the day was .82, and I was quite proud of that until Mt. Elden twelve miles away reported 2.85. Turkey Butte twelve miles in the other direction was completely dry. Kendrick Peak measured 2.35, East Pocket ten miles south of me had only .11.

Storms during July amounted to more than a drop in the bucket but not by much, at least in this neck of the woods. (Isn't English wonderful?) In August I've witnessed daily melodrama. A sky full of white cream puffs and black giants, piled up, heaping. Moving. Thunder a constant cannonade. Lightning striding across the forest pushing cold wind ahead of it. Rain is dense curtains here and there. Shifting patches of intense color and sunlight. Clouds at different altitudes moving in different directions. I'm up here in a thin-skinned little box at the mercy. I love it.

For the past three weeks I've watched clouds and urged them to move this way, watched half a dozen rain cells blotting out portions of the forest. The ground isn't particularly muddy up here, despite 2.68 inches of rain through those weeks, but there's been enough to make life chancy for lightning starts. Anything we spot is small and stays that way. At the moment a wispy little smoke is drifting up out of the trees on the southeast slope of LeBarron hill a mile away, and we are letting it do that as long as it doesn't get too big.

It's just as well. There's been a long-term drought in the Northwest. All our Hot Shot and Indian crews, some of our engines, miscellaneous overhead and people I probably don't know about have gone off in the direction of the forty-two fires that are now burning in ten dry western states, 600,000 acres black so far, but not all in one place. Twenty-seven thousand people are working fire lines, five thousand of them Army and Marines, promoting the general welfare.

I have no trouble imagining the big heavy trucks roaring off to Nevada, but one of them left last week for Oregon. The three-person crew must have had a noisy, tedious, uncomfortable ride.

Grass and wildflowers are blooming and seeding now. Leaves on the oaks below me aren't turning color yet, but nights are longer and quite cold. Sun comes in the south windows of the tower. "The days grow short when you reach September."

I'm sure it wasn't this spectacular last year. Do you suppose, weather being seasonal and not uniform, it always seems unusual, always something new?

RX burning, restoration ecology, forest health, preventive thinning in the urban interface—there's a new philosophy visible from a tower these days.

In the 1800s trees were saw-timber, a crop to be harvested. Early in the 20th century fire was bad and should be controlled by 10 o'clock the next morning. Then forests were public land to be used as many ways as possible, including recreation. Conservation vs. preservation was a controversy for a while. There was a movement to exclude commercial mining, grazing, and so forth. Though it was obvious that second-growth trees were so stunted and close together they could barely stand *upright, logging companies were driven out. Logging was bad.*

Now here we go into another turn. Fires rampaging through the West in these drought years have burned whole neighborhoods that lay between towns and forests so tight with spindly trees that the spread of blazes couldn't be stopped. It's quite apparent from here that Flagstaff is an island among pines, and unless something is done, it's only a matter of chance before catastrophe.

Huge tracts of the Coconino are being evaluated and thinned. One block sweeps across Woody Mountain in the fifteen or so miles from I-40 to the Volunteer Canyon rim. Good idea, I say. The mountain, clear cut in 1904, has had no attention since, so there are standing dead trees, snags that have fallen into other trees, dead trunks lying on the ground. The slopes are covered with eighty-year-old trees that are less than twelve inches in diameter, The place is a firetrap.

So far I've seen little activity, only timber markers in a couple of trucks who came up to figure out where things are. But now that we've had a little rain, crews are busy in other areas burning ground fuels and slash piles, sending white clouds of smoke high above the treetops: preventive treatment meant to forestall wildfire. When it's finished, the forest will look something like it did before whites arrived with their logging machines. At least, that's the plan.

Thus RX. There's medicine everywhere I look.

It's 9:30 a.m. Sky is turning black and promising. Safe up here, I will not say "ominous."

Lovelovelove

1929 September: The great stock market collapse was a total surprise to most Americans, who'd been unwilling to see the signs. Early in September an economist warned, "Sooner or later a crash is coming," but investors went right on buying shares. On September 3rd an erratic downward drift began and was not recognized for what it was. The bull market of the 1920s had come to an end.

In the Flagstaff paper news of the Graf Zeppelin was not as important as ground breaking for a $50,000 Catholic church on the northeast corner of Beaver and Cherry. The architect's drawing published in the *Sun* was of the church that is there now. The Teachers College announced it was building a new library. Again the drawing was of a structure that still stands on the northwest corner of the campus. Both remain as visible proof of Flagstaff's cheerful confidence that the economy would continue to provide plenty of money.

John Weatherford, who owned the building where Mary Costigan had been operating the Orpheum Theater for years, decided not to renew her lease when it expired at end of October and signed a contract for a ten year lease with Fox West Coast Theaters instead. Costigan owned the seats, the equipment and the name Orpheum, so she decided to build a new $100,000 theater with sound nearby on West Aspen, a site she'd owned for years, and leased a building around the corner on Leroux to run as an Orpheum until her new theater was ready. The architectural drawing was of a huge, elaborate structure. There's no sign of it now—I wonder, did she build it? Not if she delayed past autumn of 1929.

Dr. Felix was still county health officer. Dr. Miller received praise from a Red Cross magazine for his years of service. Dr. Fronske brought the eight-year-old daughter of Carl Mayhew up from Oak Creek Canyon to Mercy Hospital with appendicitis. Dr. Sechrist operated.

His wife Ethel was one of the 111 guests (111!) invited to a bridge luncheon series at the home of Lois Manning. Everybody who was anybody was present including the other doctors' wives and Sarah, seventy years old, who traveled afterward to Los Angeles for the wedding of a granddaughter. She told the *Sun* she didn't know just when she'd be back.

There were only four women in town that year whose husbands were active physicians: Lois Manning age forty-five, Hilda Fronske forty-two, Ethel Sechrist 36, Pearl Schermann thirty-one.

When I was growing up years ago in Phoenix, I didn't wear a helmet when I rode a bicycle. Nobody did.

Emily's recovery was slow. Long after the doctors had finished everything they could think of to do to her, she was still tired. Not complaining, but I could tell, tired and depressed. We never did get to Sedona.

She looked good. Her girls took advantage of her when she was resting to kneel beside the couch or on the bed and try various make-up on her face. Then hold up a mirror for her.

"What do you think, Mom? I like it, it makes your face look longer, don't you think?"

They rejected the lipstick she'd worn since high school—too red, old-fashioned—and concentrated on her eyes. "They need to look bigger, Mom. I'm going to try blue eye shadow." I thought her patience was saintly.

Both of them went with her when she consented to buy a wig—"We have to be there, Mom"—and were ecstatic when they saw the result. "Come right over, Marlene, and see. She's a strawberry blonde!"

They hovered while Emily and I played roles for them.

"It's really flattering. Turn around. Oh, they're right, Emily. You are just beautiful."

"It's the new me. There's nothing like surgery for making you feel old and bored, but my daughters have rescued me, bless their little hearts."

We took the girls out for ice cream so they could show off their new mother to the public, and we laughed and joked and generally behaved as if we'd come out of a dark canyon. I nearly cried it was so good to hear Emily laugh again.

Days later, when the children were all in school, we sprawled on opposite ends of her couch in morning sunshine, and she said she thought she was going into a new phase. "No, really, Marlene, this has been a good point if ever there was one. I got just about all I could out of the old phase, not that it was bad, just that I learned all I needed to know about babies and primary school. It's time to move on. Heaven forbid I should go back."

"Do you have something in mind?"

She laughed. "That's the problem." Yes, that's always the problem. "I haven't heard of any daily exercises for moving into the future."

"Well, Emily, what did you want to do when you were a child that you haven't done yet?"

"Except for being Ozma of Oz?" She grinned and waggled her tongue.

"You did? That's wonderful. I wanted to be Polychrome the Rainbow's daughter and dance down every road."

"Marlene, really!"

"Her hair floated around her in a cloud. But seriously, what did you want to do when you were a child that you haven't done?"

"Sail to Tahiti."

"That was definite. On your own boat?"

"Yes!"

"It would take a bit of learning."

"I don't think Travis would go for it."

"Maybe the kids would though."

"If they could take their friends."

"So what else could your new phase be?"

"I guess it's too late to become Ginger Rogers."

"Or Shirley Maclaine."

"One thing…it's probably ridiculous…"

"What?"

She pulled a pillow out from behind her head and settled lower in the cushions. "I never told anybody…when I was in high school…I used to imagine that some day I would be very wise."

How like Emily, she didn't say rich or smart or famous, she said wise. "That's not a bad idea, is it?"

"Hey, it's good. I'm proud of you."

"But it's another case of not having daily exercises you can do."

"Could you keep a sort of journal of what you're thinking?"

She laughed. "Probably read like a shopping list."

"Then what? First you'd have to live to be very old. I've never heard of a young sage."

"Socrates said we are wise by what we know—I learned that in a Western Civ course."

I was impressed. "I like it. By what we know. It would be hard to be wise if you knew nothing. Book learning, do you suppose, or experience?"

One hand went up in the air…"I'd think it would take both…" and came down. "All kinds of book learning, all kinds of experience, but maybe some kinds of experience should be vicarious."

"Like from a book."

"Right. I could get by without hands-on learning about being a diamond miner in Africa."

"Or being at sea in a typhoon."

"Exactly. I'd rather read about it, given the choice. How's this for a suggestion—my former phase was domestic and bringing up babies, my new one could be self-taught student and seeker of knowledge. I wouldn't have to leave home or abandon the kids or be an athlete. You can read lying down."

"Especially right now. Later you can climb Denali. Learn to sail."

"Right. Start slow and see where curiosity leads me."

"Good thing Phoenix has a library. What would you start with, big issues like astronomy, little ones like flowers, medium-sized ones like humans?"

"Golly. Where to start is a good question. For years I've been curious about earth history, you know, geology. That's pretty basic, understanding what's under my feet, right in front of my eyes."

"Hey, hiking trips in the Grand Canyon. Later, not right away."

"Human history is basic too. You know, like where your ideas came from. Your own culture. Any of it could be a search for perspective, a journey."

"Adventure. Make you late for breakfast."

"All the time I'd be learning about myself. How could you get tired of that?" She grinned at me.

"Well. It sounds like an ambitious plan. Would you mind if I were to join your class? We could read the same books and talk about them."

"You want to, Marlene?"

"I wouldn't mind seeking knowledge."

She laughed. "Book buddies!"...more alive than I'd seen her in weeks.

I sang. "On the road again."

"I love it. This is the best I've felt since I was diagnosed. We'll have fun. Not that we've ever needed an excuse for a conversation, and we certainly won't now. Thank you, my friend."

Emily was killed the next morning on her way to the library. A seventeen-year-old boy who'd left school mad at a teacher slammed into her car in the middle of an intersection. The coroner said multiple fractures including C-spine, trauma to brain and internal organs.

I didn't learn about it until Travis called that afternoon, crying.

"No, Travis. No."

"She skidded twenty feet on the pavement."

"No..."

"...skin bloody and torn..."

"No. She's all right now, the cancer is gone."

He could barely talk. "...knocked out of her shoes, they were still in the car."

"No, she's all right now..."

"...moderate bleeding...near instantaneous shut down..."

He couldn't say death, I couldn't say death. Dead. Killed.

For weeks all I could say was no no no. It was a fact, I knew it was true finally. I knew it. But I didn't believe it. How could I believe it? At the funeral I was thinking Emily, don't do this, come back. I rejected the date on the marker, the date of ending. I couldn't say grave. Buried. Head stone.

I'd pick up the phone and think "I can't call, I don't know the number." My soul would howl.

Every day I walked miles, until I could barely push myself to get back home. I talked to her, sure that she knew what I was saying, sure that she answered. "Don't feel bad," she'd say. "We can go on learning to be wise."

I don't know why—who can figure brains?—I was often afraid. I'd see something unusual like a man up a power pole, and it would fill me with fear. Once Baxter ran into the kitchen and I dropped a plate and huddled against the counter shaking.

The children became quiet around me. And kind. They had known Emily all their lives. "I love you, Mom." We'd hug each other and cry.

I don't think Don noticed any difference.

> Doctors not only deny their own problems but minimize any weakness of their colleagues as well. They cover up for each other. My husband's friends at the hospital refused to admit he had a drinking problem.

More Information You Can Find in a Library

When the Arizona State Board of Medical Examiners receives a complaint, it has options ranging from dismissal to revocation of license. It can dismiss the complaint even though civil juries have found the doctor to be negligent or incompetent.

Or it can decide to use:

…an advisory letter, a non-disciplinary action if the board decides the violations are minor;

…a letter of reprimand in cases where negligence has contributed to death, sometimes coupled with probation;

…continued practice with monitoring and possible restriction of practice;

…a decree of censure, considered a serious discipline but carries no punishment;

…suspension of license to practice for a specified period.

> I was fourteen, I think, among the dozen or so light-skinned girls who stood at the door and tried to shout the dark-skinned girls away, and I was as rude and raucous as the rest of them. Two weeks later I was ashamed and raw in my soul for what I'd done, for the harm to other girls. In all the years since, trying to apologize, I've been courteous to people with dark skin, and I never could tell anyone how cruel I was once.

The dugway that wasn't a dugway was behind us, lost in the expanse of Utah cliffs. I couldn't find it in the side mirror. Don wasn't talking, and there was nothing I dared say to him. We were on pavement again. I was numb with fatigue, driving down the road with a stranger. A long-time stranger.

Mexican Hat and the bridge across the San Juan gorge. Arizona again and Monument Valley, further proof that there's more of the ancient sea beds gone than there is left. Kayenta, an old trading post. I wondered whether Navajos are uncomfortable living close together. Have they got used to it?

Another stretch of road and soothing beauty, people thin on the land. I was curious about the culture that had grown out of those cliffs and dry washes, but I hadn't brought with me any books that tackled that. Then Tuba City, which would not look like a city in the East, no doubt, but traffic! traffic lights! set in that country.

On through rocks under a clear blue sky and a junction finally: U.S. 89, an arrow pointing left to Flagstaff. Don turned right.

"Don. This will take us back to Utah."

"I don't want to go home yet."

I was stunned but not surprised, if that makes any sense. "Where are you going?"

"Lee's Ferry. Don't you want to see it?"

"Of course. Uuhh, we have a reservation for tonight at Cameron."

"So we won't be there. Isn't there a campground or something at Lee's Ferry?"

"I think there is, Park Service."

"So we'll stay there."

I had enough food in the freezer for a few more days. OK, change in plan, adaptable is my middle name.

Now I think it was as pathetic as anything he'd ever said. Poor guy. "I don't want to go home."

So there we were again, driving between striped mounds that looked like mud and felt like sand, along the same line of red cliffs that stretched far ahead. You can see such a long way on the Colorado Plateau, in distance and in time. I'd learned to love it. Made me feel light as foam.

The second time around I knew enough to see more. The layers in the Echo Cliffs were not cleanly horizontal as sedimentary layers should be. The whole mass was tipped away toward the east so steeply that it looked as if it had no back. Across the highway on the west side, rock was tipped at the same angle toward the east, but it was much lower. A block fault? A slump?

Delighted that I had words, possible explanations, I scooped books and maps into my lap and began searching. Don didn't ask what I was looking for.

Faults, some in the "basement," are all over the Plateau, as if the strata had cracked with the bulging and bending of movement. I put my finger on the Echo Cliffs. There were short faults cutting across them, but what I was seeing from the highway was an eroded monocline, a one-way change in elevation, that swelled up toward the west, part of the big East Kaibab Uplift, part of the dome into which the Grand Canyon was carved. We were driving along a trough worn into it. Let's hear it for the Big Picture.

On a ledge on those barren cliffs there was a spot of green in trees way up there, then another spot and afternoon sunlight flashing from a window. Houses and hanging gardens? High up looking out across the miles? What a place, I would live there and feel myself rich. Would but couldn't—I'm not Navajo.

We passed a lone cyclist in stretchy shorts and a helmet pedaling along on the edge of pavement. Going where? Coming from where? Strong, obviously, but he seemed vulnerable with cars zooming past him. Training his ephemeral body among the ancient rocks.

Mile after mile, we drove north along the trough, the Little Colorado invisible somewhere to the west, the Big Colorado ahead, the Vermillion Cliffs on the other side of the river. Higher than the Echo Cliffs and different, smoother, firm and strong and level. Level. So close together I could see both without turning my head. They had to be the same formation, didn't they? The Plateau had formed as a huge sedimentary unit.

Back to the books. Yes, the two cliff systems were similar formations, Jurassic sandstone topping both, but the steep monocline had separated them and lifted the Vermillion Cliffs higher. Not only that—the Colorado River had cut across the Echo Cliffs, which continued on the other side and wrapped around the end of the Vermillion Cliffs. Fellas and girls, there was a lot going on in that country a long time ago, and it did not quite compute, not in my mind.

The river, when we came to it suddenly, was deep in a narrow canyon of sheer walls, so far down, 500 feet down, that in the ten seconds crossing it in the motorcoach on a steel bridge fear squeezed my chest. A few people were standing on a second bridge. the old one, looking down. The Colorado River. Then it was gone, hidden again, and I held a map in my hands, a perfectly safe map.

"Turn right. At the sign."

"I can read signs, remember?"

Two lanes, paved, wound down and down among boulders fallen from the cliffs above. No trees. The scantiest of vegetation. As a human I was completely alien in that hard towering place, sure that I was there only because some giant reptile hadn't noticed me yet. My nerves were wearing just a bit thin, right?

Then we were at the bottom, and the river was right there, moving powerful and fast, sunlight sparkling on its surface. Water, all that water. A minute before there hadn't been any. Days before there hadn't been any.

"Camp ground." I pointed to the sign.

"I see it." Don pulled up onto a bluff.

"Nobody's here."

He drove past empty sites to the one on the edge of the bluff and stopped above the Colorado. Upstream it came out of a narrow gorge. Downstream it disappeared again. At the wide bend in front of us, below us at the base of a cliff, there it was.

I didn't say a word, afraid Don would leave if he thought I liked it, just opened the door to a wet smell, a sound of water foaming over stones.

"This will do, I guess."

We stayed two nights, one long day. In the morning I strolled along the river to the Lonely Dell and wandered about wondering whether I could have lived there as Emma Lee had if I thought my religion called for it. Lived between the overwhelming reality of those stone cliffs, worked the way a frontier woman did. Greeted river-crossing groups but not companions.

I couldn't say what I'd have done as a woman one hundred years earlier, but I did have an opinion: "lonely" is too mild a word for a place in which humans have no place.

A river-running company was working at the boat launch preparing for a two-week raft trip down to Diamond Creek, so I sat on a rock for a hour and watched. Fascinating. Young men, of course, organized (as my mother used to say) "to an nth degree." Colored rubber bags layered and strapped into fat rubber rafts with no room to spare. Far as I could tell, each man who'd be rowing was responsible for his own organization. They were all tethered—the rafts, not the men—to the shore on bow lines, swinging in the eddy current.

It was a fierce sensation. I wanted to climb aboard and push off into the river and float out of sight into unseen canyons. Across the river, was that part of the Chocolate Cliffs, looking like Hershey's Kisses? Behind me on my side was the same candy layer but higher, noticeably higher. Hmmmmm. Back with my books that afternoon, I located one line: "The river bend is controlled by a monocline, lower on the southeast." I'd had a very satisfying day.

Don had not. Television reception was practically nil so far below the surface of the Plateau, and he'd spent the day sitting outside in the October breeze with nothing to do but look at the river and think.

"This wasn't a good idea. We're leaving in the morning."

I borrowed slang from a different generation. "Whatever."

Next morning we were laboring up hill away from the river, air transparent and sun at our backs, and Don was making irritated noises, when five seconds changed everything. We were nearly to the top, past the balanced boulders on a blind left curve with a low mound at the shoulder on the right, when a little sedan appeared in front of us going way too fast, maybe eighty, across the center line. Three young men were inside.

The driver tried to correct, it looked like, brakes, steering wheel, but there wasn't time. The car went into a skid broadside of the road and slammed into the front of our motorcoach, just like that.

I wasn't aware of anything. I'd been thrown hard against my seat belt and hit my forehead against the console in front of me. When I finally sat up, I realized that we'd been shoved backward, against the mound on the shoulder, but we were still upright, tipped slightly to one side. Red paint and gobs of something covered our windshield. I couldn't see the little car.

Don was slumped over the steering wheel, not moving. I touched his arm, then clutched it. "Don?" His arm twitched. Slowly he moved, raised his head, but he made no sound and he didn't turn toward me in his seat. His face was grey.

"Don?" He didn't answer me.

Shaking, I opened the door and climbed up onto the mound and walked forward, and my god! a headless torso with no arms lay in the middle of the pavement. A leg was ten feet away. I didn't see a whole body anywhere.

The little sedan had been cut into pieces as if it had exploded. The hood and engine were off to the left, what looked like the trunk and a wheel to the right, but the rest of the car had plowed under our heavy RV. A smell of gasoline was strong, and something else, maybe blood. Slowly, slowly—I looked for something clean to lean against, but there wasn't a square foot that wasn't red, and I knew it wasn't paint. The gobs on the windshield were pieces of flesh. My hands and knees were on the pavement, I don't know how, and I was looking at part of a hand.

A truck, an official Game and Fish truck, drove up and stopped and a man in a uniform shirt called DPS Highway Patrol on his radio, ordered a helicopter. He looked shaken himself, I remember that, but he helped me up carefully and led me to the mound on the shoulder, turned me away and had me sit down.

"Let me just check you for injuries." He looked into my eyes, felt my pulse. "Do you think there might be broken bones anywhere?"

I had to look at him for a while before I realized what he was saying. "No. I don't think so. I saw their faces looking up at us. I saw their faces."

"There was someone with you?"

"My husband is inside."

I didn't see him leave. He disappeared, and I sat staring without seeing anything. I don't know how long. Then the man in the uniform shirt came back.

"His eyes are open, he's breathing, and his heart is beating, no injuries that I can see, but he doesn't respond. Shock, probably. What's his name?"

Slowly I turned my head toward him. "Don."

"I'll move my truck so it'll block the road and turn on the flashers. Will you sit right here and rest?"

Everything was so slow. "Yes."

"Good. I'll be back. You just stay right here."

It didn't occur to me to do anything else. I'm not usually so obedient.

Then, "How you doing?" He was crouching next to me. "You OK?"

"They were young. Three of them, I saw their faces."

"Yeah. I'll try talking to your husband again. Don?"

"Yes."

A woman was there. "I just drove up. I'm a doctor, can I help?" She looked into my eyes and felt my pulse.

The helicopter arrived before Highway Patrol did, very loud. Very loud. A strong wind blew sand and dirt. Voices.

"She says there were three of them."

"Jesus! You couldn't tell if you tried, look at this mess. They don't need us. Let's see those injuries."

"She's had a concussion, I think, but she's responsive. He's the one in trouble."

"OK, we'll take both. She gonna need a stretcher?"

"I don't think so."

A hand appeared in front of me. "Can you stand up?"

I looked at the hand, then reached up, and he pulled me to my feet, the nice man in the uniform shirt.

"Where did the doctor go?"

"She's inside. I'll hold your arm and we'll walk down the road a little way. Can you do that?"

"I can walk."

We stopped beside the helicopter.

"What's your name?"

"Marlene."

"Nice name. Been on the road long?"

"I think so, yes, a week."

"Arizona plates. Where's home?"

"Phoenix."

"I live in Phoenix too."

I looked at him.

"I came up to meet with some people who've been doing a fish survey in the river."

"Oh."

He kept me talking until two men came from the motorcoach holding Don between them. His legs moved, but his eyes looked unfocused, and his face was grey. They had to pull and boost to get him up and in.

"Now, Marlene, just put your foot here, and we'll help you."

"But the motor coach. Our things."

"We'll take care of it. If it's driveable, we'll take it into Flagstaff. If not, we'll have it towed. Don't worry about it."

"Thank you."

"You bet. Best of luck."

From above I looked down at the river and the cliffs and the motorcoach sitting crooked at the side of the road. It looked small to me.

Nervous breakdown is a term that has no precise medical meaning. Psychiatrists and others who study and treat mentally ill patients do not use it, just those who believe it is an accepted medical term or who want to avoid using "mental illness."

end of August

To my people, my own people,

There are voices in the wind. I can't make out what they're saying—but I hear voices. Sometimes they sing. It's a pleasant, happy sound.

No, I'm not losing it, thank you, all alone up here. I know the source. Summer storms, weak as they've been, have backed off for a while leaving no clouds to block the sun. I have windows open on all four sides of the tower, and the trap door in the floor too, to any breeze that might wander by. I hear moving air murmuring around edges and corners.

Took me a while to figure that out. At first I thought people were walking up the road, talking to each other as they came, but no one ever arrived. Now I know what's causing it, and I treasure the idea of voices in the wind. They aren't threatening.

Crickets begin to shrill at dusk—I didn't notice them earlier in the summer, before the rains began. Most of the hummingbirds have gone somewhere else, Tucson maybe, so I don't need to wash and fill the feeders so often. Sun is noticeably farther to the south, especially when it sets, which is almost an hour earlier than sunset was in June. The planet has its own rhythms, and nothing is permanent.

About the Colorado Plateau: 1) Two people have been killed by a summer flash flood in one of the deep, narrow slot canyons that have been eroded into sandstone over millennia. 2) The Bright Angel Trail, closed three weeks ago by torrents of rainwater that left mud and boulders across it, has been reopened in time for Labor Day.

Here on the Coconino we're down from three dozen little fires a day to only one or two. Most of our firefighters are gone to other states. More than two dozen large fires are still burning in the West. Tests have revealed high levels of mercury in the smoke—maybe emissions from coal-fired power plants that has settled in vegetation?

News this morning was of two planes, air tankers carrying hundreds of gallons of water or slurry, that collided over a wildfire in California, killing both pilots. I stand up here and watch tankers working on fires. Usually they are escorted on a "drop line," one at a time, by a small "lead" plane flown by a man or woman who tells their pilots precisely where to put the wet cargo. My guess is that the two who collided were circling, waiting to go into the smoke, or pulling out and turning for home base, or one of each. I doubt the radio will report exactly what happened.

I didn't know the pilots. I don't have to, do I?

The orbit of the moon shifts through the season, north to south and back again. Living in a city, I didn't notice that. All summer I've seen a golden planet in the same place every evening—Mars, I'm told, although it hasn't looked red to me. Searching in the library, I discovered that planet-size dust storms up there lately have given Mars a more golden tint than usual. Well!

Late afternoon is richly beautiful in the mellow light, peaceful and reassuring. The night sky is as spectacular as it's been all summer. Stars jostle each other in every inch, sharp and clear, leaving me full of questions about possibilities. When the moon is waxing toward full, it illuminates cumulus clouds sailing past, luminous white against the stars in a black sky. Glory. Also hallelujah.

Analogies to life occur to me, the last quarter of life. It should be rich and mellow and peaceful, serene and beautiful, illuminating. That assumes the last quarter should be passive, doesn't it? I want more activity than sideline appreciation. Maybe I'll feel differently twenty years from now, more content to watch and enjoy.

Adios

Cazz—Do you think poems about Arizona should have echoes of Indian drums in them?

A number of studies indicate that prolonged, major depression is associated with a selective loss of hippocampal volume long after the depression has resolved. Overt neuron loss may be a factor to the decrease in hippocampal volume.

1929 **October:** By October the value of stocks held on margin had declined until they were no longer sufficient collateral for the loans that had paid for them. Speculators were asked for more cash.

On Monday October 21 trading was jittery. Tuesday share prices dipped. Wednesday they fell again. Thursday, October 24th, panic began and stock prices plummeted as major investors began to sell. Politicians and commentators said it was only a "technical correction."

It was a warm autumn in Flagstaff. In the first week of October the Fronskes called Felix Manning to come next door and surprised him with a birthday party. The third week Wong June and his wife Dew Yu entertained thirty guests at the Bright Angel Cafe, including Felix and Dr. Mackey, in honor of the birth of their eighth child. There was the usual going and coming.

As I've said, it was Fred Breen's policy to publish the *Sun* as a local newspaper that dealt with local affairs—he hadn't written much about the lead-up to the Great War either—so there was nothing in its pages that month about the financial crisis. Several logging trucks were foreclosed because the operators were unable to pay off their loans. Prices were declining in Kansas City stock yards. But an air mail route was planned between Albuquerque, Flagstaff and Los Angeles. Banks, hotels and car dealerships reported that business was good. The headline on the front page of the paper published on October 25 was "Flagstaff State Teachers College Plans 6th Annual Homecoming for Gathering Hordes."

Hilda Fronske's name was in every issue, playing bridge, going to parties. She and Mary Rees were among the twelve ladies who were charter members when a chapter of PEO was organized. Martin said he wanted to take her away "for a rest," and I could believe she needed one. Despite all her activity, Martin insisted that she had not been well for several months and took her to Los Angeles to be examined by specialists.

Black Tuesday, the 29th, was the most devastating day in the history of the New York stock market. And then things got worse.

In three weeks stocks lost 30 million dollars in paper values. No hope of recovery was held out for U.S. Steel, General Electric, Westinghouse, American Can, and General Motors. The Vanderbilts lost an estimated 40 million dollars of their railroad holdings.

Investment trusts went down to nothing.

The student body president was the kind of golden boy who was charm incarnate. He knew everything and everybody. I saw him thirty years later. He hadn't changed, but as a fifty-year-old man he was embarrassing.

More bulletins from medical journals:

- Investigators have shown that depression is associated with an increased risk of coronary heart disease in general and myocardial infarction in particular.

- Depressed persons have more than a two-fold higher risk of developing heart failure compared with non-depressed persons.

- Depression is independently associated with a substantial increase in the risk of heart failure among older persons with isolated systolic hypertension.

- Investigators have shown that depression is associated with an increased risk of developing coronary heart disease in general.

- In addition, depression has been associated with excessive activation of the sympathetic nervous system. Heightened activation of this system is thought to be one of the processes involved in the pathogenesis of heart failure.

- Depression-induced sympathetic nervous system activation represents a separate pathway by which depression could increase the risk of incident heart failure.

I remember when there were no cell phones. The first television I saw was in a store window; people were standing on the sidewalk watching it. We had radios that were three feet tall and sat on the floor, pieces of furniture.

Labor Day Weekend has come and gone again. I just love major holidays and the American idea of fun.

Saturday was clear beyond mere clarity. There was no atmospheric perspective—the effect that distance has on colors, making them fade to gray. The Mazatzals eighty miles away were almost as dark blue as Mormon Mountain eighteen miles away as Volunteer eight miles away. Nothing was in the air to interfere.

Small, fair weather cumulus laid shadows across tree tops. Sun was warm and breezes were cool, a delicious combination. I had no visitors, not one single person, much to my delight; the only voice I heard was the raven which sits on pines and talks to me. I couldn't hear noises from the county fair at Fort Tuthill four miles away. A lightning-caused fire that was contained two weeks ago two miles away from me began to smoke again, quietly.

Even the radio was silent most of the time. The only outrages of the day concerned a sheriff's deputy and an animal control officer called because of defiance from campers and their dog, which attacked a Forest Service patrolman. And carousers on quads—fat motorcycles with four big tires—off the road in a closed area. They're usually off road in the wrong places.

Last week at six o'clock one morning I heard roaring and whining and grinding of an engine as a man gunned a quad up the west slope of Woody Mountain and burst into the clearing at the top. Two bow hunters, camoed up, hoping to sneak up on a deer or two, I guess. "We didn't know this place was up here." Sincere voices and honest expressions.

1) Middle-aged high school liars, I see them often, 2) men who couldn't read a map, 3) city boys up from Phoenix, 4) lousy hunters, 5) probably all four.

Sunday morning Ed Piper, patrolling, came on the radio to say that the dirt road through this area was the 231 Freeway, packed with cars going Mach One. In the cold air, smoke was rising out of Pumphouse Wash, probably coming up from campgrounds in Oak Creek Canyon: the manager at Garland's called the dispatcher to say that Banjo Bill campground was full, that cars trying to get in were backed up in a tangle, that his driveway was blocked, that congestion was a danger on the highway, and could the Forest Service do something about it?

It's the pressure of recreation, not grazing or lumbering or mining or even fire, that is the real threat to forests now. Those campers, balked from setting up in a developed area, go on to "throw-down" sites and leave wildfires in their wake. What's the solution—more campgrounds?

At noon on Sunday the first call came in on the radio for an ambulance, and I thought, "Here we go." Shirley phoned from Baker Butte and said helicopters came and went all day carrying people to hospitals—she'd had one hundred visitors in eight hours.

James Brooks on Apache Maid tower reported shooters killing turkeys out of season. I heard repeated gunshots.

By noon on Monday seven hundred and something people had been arrested in Arizona for driving with elevated blood alcohol. Requests were coming in from Forest Service patrolmen—Law Enforcement Officers needed. Operators of heavy equipment were digging lines around their tractors and reporting wildfire in their area. I tell ya—you want to develop a bad attitude, live and work in national forests on a three-day holiday weekend.

In the Pacific Northwest sun shines through most of every day. Alaskan glaciers are melting. Wind in Arizona blows through my cabin, clean and cold across my face all night as I snuggle deep into blankets.

 As the song says, believing in living is a hard way to go.

1929 **November–December:** The scope of the Crash became evident slowly. In mid November the market stopped falling for a while, but prices of commodities continued to decline, as did consumer spending, factory payrolls, freight car loadings, department store sales.

Politicians were saying that it was not the job of government to run money markets day to day and insisting, "Hands off the Economy." J.P. Morgan and a few other bankers began buying stocks, but that helped for only a few days. Henry Ford raised employee wages and cut the prices of his cars as a "contribution." The gesture cost him twenty million dollars but did little good.

The *Sun* continued to ignore the situation except for syndicated cartoons on the editorial page that

1. labeled a burning building "Wall Street Stock Disaster" while "Farm Loan" saved the wheat market (November 8),

2. labeled clouds "Threatened Post-Stock Crash Depression" while Hoover responded with a trade parley (November 29)

3. showed Hoover's income tax giving "Economic Pessimism" a boot out the door (December 13)

All three encouraged the reading public to have courage and be of good cheer. With the country's economy falling off a cliff, Flagstaff was told about a Big Road Program for the Grand Canyon, $625,000, another for the Oak Creek highway, $150,000, work on both to begin in 1930. The town had been selected as the site for a permanent National Guard camp. A silver fox farm had gone into operation at the foot of Elden Mountain with twenty pairs of adult animals. Sixty local families were needy, but an Air Circus at Koch Field raised sixty dollars so that Flagstaff Associated Charities could provide Christmas baskets. See? Nothing to fear. Read our Christmas ads.

Life went comfortably on through Armistice Day and Thanksgiving and Christmas. Dr. Felix went to Phoenix for a Southwestern Medical Society meeting. Ethel Sechrist joined the Woman's Club. She and Lois were among the eighty-five guests at one of Nettie Switzer's bridge luncheons.

Hilda Fronske was not there—she was in Los Angeles through November having a "major operation." (I wondered whether it was a hysterectomy but didn't find an answer.) Laura Macdermid, for the past year one of Flagstaff's registered nurses, was there to tend her recuperation and accompany her home on the train late in the month.

The front page headline on the *Sun's* last issue of 1929 was "Flagstaff Most Prosperous City in Arizona—1930 Will Be Banner Year." On New Year's Eve, President Hoover reassured America: "The economy is sound." We didn't have Alan Greenspan then.

As an aside, I should mention that the names of the doctors' wives did not appear in any list of membership for the Business and Professional Women. Sarah, Lois, Hilda, Pearl and Ethel—they didn't work for their money any more than we did half a century later.

Depression is not contagious like flu, but it can't help but have an effect on people who live with the patient, and one result of Don's long illness had been a virtual maze of dark symptoms in me—thirty years worth of symptoms that became habitual.

Dear Baxter,

I hope you understand what a pleasure it is for me to be able to discuss politics with you. There's simply no one else I can express my thoughts to. I don't know whether I need to express them, but I want to. I'm glad I have a son of sober mind and considered opinion.

Today I'm bothered about the popular judgement of Herbert Hoover. I have no personal memory of him nor of the Depression, and we didn't always get that far in history classes, but my impression is that he has been widely reviled ever since as an aloof and passive president who spoke encouraging platitudes but did nothing about the national catastrophe. I've just worked through 1929, read three books on the subject, and I want to say that the do-nothing perception isn't completely fair.

Hoover was an engineer, an organizer, a scientist, a businessman, an intellectual—but not a reactionary. He was an able, activist, modern man willing to expand the powers of the presidency and the government and to use both to combat the Depression. Many men in his own Republican party thought he was too strong a president, socialistic even. (Horrors!) At that time there was a widespread fear of communists, socialists, and labor unions, and I don't think they thought there was a whole lot of difference.

His philosophy of government was what they called "associational": anticommunist, scientific, patriotic, pragmatic, and (this was important) belief in government/business cooperation and voluntary associations of citizens. Yes, he believed that government should not interfere in the private sector, but he also thought that government could act where private enterprise was not able to.

Look what he was up against—conventional wisdom was that it was the job of the people to support the government not the obligation of the government to support the people (I'm not making that up; it was part of the dogma) and that to interfere with competition would cause damage to the nation's social and moral fabric, whatever that is. And he truly believed in individuals with initiative and vitality as the basis of a democratic society, which could be eroded by government action.

Furthermore, ten years earlier in 1919, '20 and '21 there had been a post-war panic with 30,000 bankruptcies, 500,000 farm foreclosures, and five million unemployed, and the country had soared out of that one into the Big Boom. Very few people in 1929 and 1930 believed that the current crisis would be long-lasting. The Wall Street Journal considered the crash a "shake-out" after which prices would rise again. The Guaranty Trust Company said it was a favorable development, you know, purge the weak and the unfit from the market place. Ergo, politicians should keep their hands off the economy.

Hoover did not go beyond his powers as president to interfere with the banks and brokers and importers and trust companies or with the stock exchange on Wall Street, and he did not ask Congress for new powers. He did:

- *announce a cut in income taxes*

- *expand public construction*

- *authorize work on Boulder Dam*

- *speed up highway programs*

- *support a tariff to protect business*

- *hold conferences to elicit the cooperation of business*

- *obtain a 50% reduction in railroad rates for food shipments*

- *persuade Congress to create a Federal Farm Board*

Now, tell me, given all that, has it been simplistic to demonize the man? Could he have accomplished more if he had tried? And—this is probably a legal

*question—if we can allow the president extra-ordinary powers in times of war, can
we give him the same freedom to act in times of economic emergency?*

Love,
Mom

I still don't know what it is, that sudden and permanent disappearance that's called death. Can't get my mind around it any more than I can the age of the universe. Those of us who are left behind for a while, as we become older and older, live on with ghosts in our minds, traces of people who aren't here any more. I have a difficult time trying to find words for the feeling.

My ghosts aren't the throng that some people have, just a few. My grandmother who died of influenza in 1919—I've lived twice as long as she did, and sometimes, like when I'm in the NAU library, I wonder what she would think if she could see what I'm seeing.

My parents, sometimes I talk to them in my mind. Emily, I talk to her every day almost. "I can't tell whether I'm wise yet, but look what I'm reading, a book about the Little Ice Age." Don. The man he was before he went to medical school, loving and happy.

Some people I didn't know were nevertheless personal for me. Eleanor Roosevelt. Ella Fitzgerald and Louis Armstrong. And whatever happened to Danny Kaye?

Footnotes:

- In 1929 state law limited a nurse's shift to eight hours.
- Wilbur Sipe died—AMA *Directory of Deceased Physicians*
- Flagstaff's first case of spinal meningitis was diagnosed.
- The Chamber of Commerce was thinking of taking in women members.

15

For weeks I've been setting out across the clearing any scraps of food that I think would be acceptable to coyotes, separating it from the seeds and things I offer to the squirrels near my water pump. During the day I see squirrels and chipmunks rush in for apple cores. Although bones and strips of fat are always gone next morning, I've never glimpsed the coyotes nor heard a sound from them at night. Wasn't really sure they were there.

Yesterday early, sitting on the doorstep brushing my hair, I realized that off to my left a fine-boned animal the size of a young dog was standing, facing me straight and looking directly at me, feet planted square on the earth, head held below the level of its shoulders. How long it had been there I don't know, I didn't see it arrive. For several moments I stared back, and it didn't move or look anywhere else, just right into my eyes.

Once I had a dog that watched me with that posture when I was driving away from the house in the car and it didn't want to be left behind. Yesterday morning I recognized in a completely undomesticated animal an attempt to communicate without words that I hadn't recognized in my dog.

A stranger was at my gate. "All right," I said. "OK, just a minute." I stood, and the little coyote didn't move. I thought it was a female it was so delicate, but I couldn't be sure.

When I carried a handful of hamburger and a couple of slices of cheese outside, she moved away to the trees at the edge of the clearing. I laid my offering down the slope a step or two, far enough so it couldn't be seen from the cabin door and walked back inside, hoping that would be understood as courtesy. Later when I looked out, she was gone; when I walked out, the food was gone.

I don't expect to see her again. Probably I shouldn't want to. But the encounter has left me feeling that all these years I've lived in a world full of possibilities I didn't begin to comprehend. I love it.

Freckles are developing on the backs of my hands. I'm not pretending anymore or denying or trying to will them away. Therefore—I have to accept that I will die some day. When I was younger I refused to consider that.

I still think it's preposterous.

1930 Seventy years ago the population of Flagstaff was up to 4000 people living along the railroad line on the vast Colorado Plateau, old beyond the reach of anybody's poetry. They and the ranchers roundabout were tended to by six active general practitioners lined up in order of their arrival:

Edwin S. Miller, who had come to Flagstaff in 1894, was seventy-two years old. Active in civic and social affairs, he was a Mason and a member of the BPOE.

R.O. Raymond had arrived in 1907, hoping to be cured of tuberculosis. Fifty-five years old, Raymond spent more of his time on his sheep business than on doctoring and a good deal of his money on philanthropy.

Albert H. Schermann had moved to Flagstaff in 1910. Doctor in charge at Mercy Hospital, he was married to a former nurse. Fifty-one years old, he had five children.

George Felix Manning jr., born in Flagstaff, had returned as a graduate doctor in 1910. He was forty-six in 1930, well-established in a career of public health. Married, he lived next door to his widowed mother.

Martin Fronske had stepped down from a train in 1914 with diagnosed tuberculosis. Forty-seven in 1930, married with two sons, he specialized in obstetrics and participated in civic affairs.

Charles Sechrist, who had moved to Flagstaff in 1928, was thirty-four years old, a surgeon at Mercy Hospital. He was married with two sons.

They stand there in the northern Arizona sunshine, looking old-fashioned in their stiff collars and high-buttoned coats. Who knows what they were thinking? In 1930 they were presented with the usual colds and such diseases as measles plus a variety of less common cases...

> ...an infant, kicked by a burro, who had a cut just above the bridge of his nose;

> ...a baby with a cold that had "settled" in his ear, which was lanced;

> ...a nine-year-old boy who had lost two fingers and a thumb when a dynamite cap he had been beating on with a rock exploded;

> ...a six-year-old boy killed by an automobile;

> ...an eleven-year-old boy whose arms were broken when, playing in the street, he had run in front of an automobile;

> ...a two-year-old boy killed by a fractured skull when the automobile in which he was riding turned over;

> ...the twenty-year-old nephew of George Hochderffer who was killed in an automobile accident;

> ...a thirteen-year-old boy who broke his arm pole vaulting;

> ...a sixteen-year-old boy whose nose was bitten off in a fight (!);

> ...a woman who died after she was burned in a gasoline explosion;

> ...a four-year-old who had been stabbed in the abdomen by a five-year-old;

> ...a man under the influence of alcohol who died after he had set his clothes on fire;

...a man whose knee was broken when "a giant buzzard swooped down on" the burro he was riding;

...a girl who had lost three fingers and suffered head wounds when she fell from a train;

...a girl whose hand was smashed in a laundry iron;

...a seven-year-old boy who died of "heart failure;"

...a three-year-old girl who died of "heart failure."

Add to the list a modern innovation in treatment: little Rosemary Babbitt, referred to a Los Angeles hospital by doctors here, was taken to the coast by an airplane that had a propeller for its single engine.

A spectacular explosion that year strained the resources of Mercy Hospital. The Pathe Company of Hollywood, filming for the movie "The Painted Desert" fifteen miles northeast of Cameron in Dinosaur Canyon, set up a scene which called for an explosion in a mine and a resulting landslide and destruction of the set's mine buildings. Several people from Flagstaff drove out to watch.

Two tons of gunpowder and dynamite had been buried in a 400- foot cliff by men experienced with blasts in metamorphic rock. They had overestimated the amount needed to blow up sedimentary shale and sandstone. Three shots were planned. The first two blew not out and down but up into the air, hurling fragments of rock everywhere. With debris falling on crew and visitors, the technicians canceled the third shot.

Forty to fifty people were injured, some seriously. The father of county recorder Marion Wallace suffered a fractured skull. Half a dozen victims were brought in to Mercy Hospital. Others were taken to Tuba City. Come on, let's all sing together now—"There's no business like show business."

mid-September, 2001

To my loved ones,

Before sunrise on the 6th of September, wind began to blow. All day it raged across the Coconino, bringing a cold front in from the west. Suddenly daytime temperatures were down sharply and nights were in the 30s, almost to freezing. Wind never stopped. Temperatures stayed low, and I kept the windows in the tower closed all day. I love the comfort of sunshine through the glass when trees around me are thrashing.

Days are two hours shorter now. In Phoenix summer lingers till December, but here at 8000 feet autumn surprises me it's so sudden. I've begun to carry a few of my least necessary things into town on my days off, things I like to live with but don't actually use.

An area of low pressure off the California coast and a high off New Mexico indicated clouds and rain again, and we had an extension of our days of spectacular beauty. Leaning away from the wind, grey and white clouds drifted across the sky.

The morning of September 11, I woke before sunrise and stood in my doorway looking at drifting pink clouds. Birds were barely awake. The world was quiet and beautiful and peaceful. And good. Then I switched on the radio and heard the news from New York and Washington: hi-jacked planes full of people deliberately flown into buildings full of people, explosions, fire, towers collapsing into streets.

People have always done vicious things to other people, and I don't understand it. My chest ached and I felt loathing, outrage, sadness. And pride. Those passengers who went down in Pennsylvania fought back and foiled an attack—on the Capitol building? Some New Yorkers went toward the trouble to help others. People all over the country sought a way they could help from where they were. A team from the Coconino Forest was deployed to a building three miles from the Trade Center site to facilitate emergency efforts there.

I was also disgusted. But I'm not impressed. It's easy to kill people. Negative is easy. The hard thing is not to kill and destroy. Anybody can do that. Making the world better, that's the hard thing. Love, create, praise and support, so behave that for the first time in its history humanity has a chance to develop to the fullness of potential. Do something hard, and then I'll be impressed.

Fewer than six thousand people died, including passengers and crews, including fire and police personnel, including the attack on the Pentagon. A single earthquake can kill more than that. Aids has killed more; the Spanish Flu epidemic killed more. Automobiles kill more every year.

I'm supposed to be impressed by this? I'm supposed to refer to the man who ordered it as a Master Mind?

In this neighborhood, traffic over Hoover/Boulder Dam was blocked, and lines of cars stretched back to Las Vegas. Camp Navajo, the old army depot four miles from my mountaintop, was on heightened security.

Now we're being told to return to "normalcy." All three of our Hot Shot crews are out to fires in New Mexico. There's a motorcycle accident on Highway 180 with an ambulance called. The city is doing prescribed burns five miles east of here. Normal.

Autumn is in the sunlight. On the ends of their branches, oak trees hold bouquets of gold leaves. Nights are cold and twelve hours long. The forest stretches away serene. Ancient sand dunes half a mile high, covered by water and turned to stone over hundreds of millions of years, still stand as testimony to Bigger Issues. I suppose Northern Arizona is back to normal.

But I know something about trauma. Some of us will never get back.

Lovelovelove

1930 Popular songs from that year were revealing. Sure, people were singing "I Got Rhythm," but remember these? "Brother, Can You Spare a Dime?" "I'm Goin' Down the Road Feelin' Bad." "It's a Mighty Hard Row."

The economy of the whole planet was sliding down into the Great Depression, which was more world-wide than even the Great War had been. At the conclusion of an era of explosive stock speculation, President Hoover called for industrial cooperation to convince the nation that business was on a sound footing. Despite his efforts, unemployment, declining trade and productivity, bank failures, monetary instability, et cetera spread across the land.

In India, Gandhi marched 165 miles south to the sea. Hitler's Nazi party captured, by election, 107 seats in the German Reichstag. Japan invaded Manchuria. The American Communist Party increased its membership nearly fifty per cent. That kind of thing can't be what people mean when they say they'd like to have lived in an earlier, simpler time.

In March hundreds of thousands of American men were out of work, by the end of the year perhaps three million, perhaps six? Finally eight million. Breadlines in New York stretched for blocks; there were protest marches in New York and Chicago. Americans were going hungry—"political discontent" was the polite term for their reaction.

In May and June stock prices again declined sharply, the Federal Reserve Board lowered its discount rate to two and a half, and before long corporate earnings were down by twenty per cent from their 1929 high. Output of American factories declined by fifty per cent, automobile production by eighty per cent. Banks foreclosed on businesses, homes and farms—and then collapsed, declaring bankruptcy. Cities could not collect taxes: local governments were bankrupt.

President Hoover said, "We have now passed the worst." Congress established Federal Farm Loans, but in the mid-West drought was building toward the Dust Bowl. Homeless families were camped in parks and in shanty towns they called Hoovervilles. There were hobo jungles, soup kitchens. Americans were hungry. My father held onto his job through the Depression, but he never forgot the sick fear of those years.

I was reading the other day that a black hole can never really form because its gravity would slow the flow of time to almost nothing. Thus: never. That makes no sense to me at all, but I learned long ago not to assume that my mind is an accurate instrument with which to measure reality.

After the accident, Don didn't communicate with me or anybody else, not at all. He lay all day curled up tight in his bed. At night sometimes he sat in his study drinking whiskey or roamed the two acres he'd bought years before to make an impression on other doctors. Once I watched from my bedroom window as he raced around and around the pool in the dark and suddenly collapsed into a chair. Weird. Or pitiful. Either way, it scared me. I never saw him eat more than a bite or two at a time.

The hospital ER had found no overt injury. Shock though, arrythmia, low blood pressure, and they'd held him a few days for observation. His partners ordered what they called a "battery" of tests. Does that sound martial to anybody but me?

They decided I'd had a simple concussion and released me the second day to Abby, who'd come over from California for the weekend to help. Together we dealt with the company that had driven the motorcoach down from Lee's Ferry. We unpacked it, moved it to storage. All the time I teetered right on the edge of frantic crying.

When Don left the hospital, the other two doctors in his practice asked me to come in late on a Tuesday afternoon for a "consultation." They perched side by side on the edge of the desk wearing formal faces.

"You see, Marlene, Don was making mistakes."

"What mistakes?" There in the chair, I sat with my hands squeezed together.

"Potentially fatal mistakes. A few months ago he prescribed for a child a dosage that would have been suitable for an adult but would have caused a dangerously elevated pulse in the little boy. The pharmacist called to confirm and warned him in time. The parents were not informed what had almost happened, but it was a red flag for us."

"Nobody told me."

"After a teen-ager hemorrhaged when Don had prescribed an unnecessary anti-coagulant, and his parents asked angry questions, we talked the situation over between us and agreed we had to interfere for our own protection."

"Interfere? What does that mean?"

"We decided to reorganize the practice and shift all routine exams to Don. Insurance and that sort of thing. Procedures where he couldn't do any harm."

"But that would…"

"Frankly, we didn't want…we couldn't afford a complaint review."

"Complaint…"

"A person or a health care institution files a complaint against a doctor with the state board. The board investigators review the accusation, call the complaining party to discuss the case and ask for additional details. Then the investigation starts."

"Oh god. Don would have…"

"The investigators call for a written response from the doctor. Medical records are requested. Witnesses are interviewed."

"How humiliating…"

"Well, yes, it would be. Frankly we didn't want the experience. You can see that."

"But did you…"

"After a review by a medical consultant, a determination is made whether the doctor involved performed up to the expected standard of care. The case goes to board members for review. If discipline is being considered, the doctor is invited to a formal interview, a hearing before the board, with an attorney if he wants one." It wouldn't have occurred to them to say "or she."

"Did Don know about this?"

"We debated telling him we were worried about it and decided it would be worse for him to face a vote to discipline or a hearing before an administrative law judge than for us to try to head off the process by reassigning responsibility in the office."

"That's when he decided to retire."

"Well, yes. Frankly, we thought it was a good decision. We were relieved."

"No wonder. No wonder he wanted to keep moving, to watch television all the time. He was trying to escape. It must have been awful for him."

"Yes, I suppose it was. And that's something else we wanted to talk with you about." I was already stunned. "There's more?"

"We're afraid so. We suspect that Don has been depressive for years and managed to function pretty well in spite of it. His avoidance of treatment, maybe his refusal to recognize the condition, simply made matters worse."

"Depressive? Oh, come on. Grumpy, yes, but he never said anything—I was the one who was depressed."

"That's quite possible. Depression spreads through the family. Happens all the time."

"He was mean and angry and distant…"

"Now, hold on, Marlene, let us explain. Until recently medical opinion was that depression was more of a psychiatric disorder than an organic brain disease. The patient needed to talk it out."

"He wouldn't talk—he shouted and lectured and insulted…"

They were a doctor duet, first one, then the other. "We've been doing some research. Recent brain scans show that both the frontal cerebral cortex and the hippocampus are abnormally small in people who have suffered major depressive episodes."

"One possibility is that people prone to depression are born with a less-than-normal amount of brain tissue in those areas."

"Less than normal brain tissue…!"

"Another theory is that depressive individuals react to stress by secreting excessive levels of stress hormones that are toxic to neurons in high dosages; thus depression may occur when acute or prolonged exposure to stress damages mood centers in the brain."

I thought I was understanding. "…medical school…"

"Exactly. Or, frankly, the responsibility of practice."

"It's serious. Depression can kill. It's associated with heart disease."

"Alpha and beta blockers can cause a drop in blood pressure, with associated fatigue, weakness, heaviness of the legs…"

"His blood pressure's low…"

"The heart is regulated by a nerve network with connections to the brain."

"A change in the brain is likely to have an effect on the heart. People who have episodes of depression are more likely to have a heart attack than people who have never had a depression."

"Nerves that regulate the heart may malfunction in depression."

"Blood elements that help in clotting may become overactive."

"Higher activation of the adrenal gland creates more stress hormone."

"Stop!" Tears were running down my cheeks. "Stop. Please stop."

"We thought you ought to know, Marlene. Research is just starting, but there are indications that if you have too many episodes, it changes your biochemistry for the bad, possibly permanently."

"If I hadn't been busy all those years with the scholarship committee and the Kidney Foundation, I might have recognized…"

"Now, you shouldn't blame…"

"I tried to save myself. I closed him and his nasty disposition out as much as I could…"

"Would knowing have done any good? Would he have taken medication? This recent accident has made the whole process that much worse but didn't cause it."

"Frankly, we thought if we explained, it might be easier for you to deal with it. But maybe not…"

"Frankly, we don't know what to do for him. We mentioned drug therapy, but he didn't react positively."

I sat in that office curled around the pain in my chest, rocking and sobbing, choking on tears, but they didn't seem to know what to do for me either except prescribe warm milk. Frankly, I thought they were both a couple of creeps.

Gwen came home furious one day from high school. "This boy said we had met before but I had been in no shape to remember. Was that supposed to mean I was drunk in public?" Adolescent boys don't change much from one generation to another, do they?

"Mom!"

"Abby?"

"Guess what! My advisor told me I'm the best student in the department! Guess what else. I've got a job! Not another T.A., I mean, yes, I have a T.A. for fall quarter, but for winter. I'll be an adjunct professor with my own class! Or at least, I will if I have my dissertation accepted by then. I'm so excited!"

"Oh, Abby, how wonderful. At Riverside?"

"I won't have to move or change anything. I'll be a U. of C. professor."

"Professor—the little girl I used to sing to sleep. My goodness. I'm proud of you, Baboo."

"It's only one class, American History from 1900, I won't be making much money, just enough to pay my share of the bills, but it's a start. Janey and I are dancing around and laughing like maniacs. I just found out, I had to call and tell you."

We both laughed into the phone lines.

"...the little girl I used to take water skiing...like the Cole Porter song, "Who'd a thunk it?"

Sometimes I'm just a little off balance, just a little, and I reach out to touch something to steady myself. So I'm fascinated by all that's been automatic for so many years, like what happens in my brain, my muscles, when I walk around a corner. It's actually marvelous. I've never paid attention before.

1930 Of course the Great Depression affected doctors as surely as it did everyone else. The good news: the number of hospitals in America had risen to 4309; the number of doctors per 10,000 people was a respectable 42.74.

American medicine had improved rapidly over the past decade.

The key word had become science, the science of medicine, at least in big-city hospitals and medical schools with laboratories. Life expectancy was up to 59.7 years. The rate of infectious diseases was dropping due to national standards for water and milk. A National Institute of Health was in the works. That was good—let's hear it for the good news.

Johns Hopkins scientists were perfecting a new method for diagnosing brain tumors: injecting air into the brain under local anaesthesia, then using X-rays. (That high-tech technique was probably not really useful to doctors in Flagstaff's Mercy

Hospital.) Harvard Medical School scientists announced that lack of vitamin B caused the symptoms of pernicious anemia. The year's Nobel award for medicine was awarded for the discovery of blood groups. The American Board of Obstetrics and Gynecology was established.

The bad news: the biggest health concern was how to pay for the medical care that was offered. Average national income fell to less than half of what it had been a year earlier; therefore doctor and hospital earnings began to fall as well. Average hospital receipts per person fell from $236.12 in 1929 to $59.26 in 1930.

Making the situation even worse, due to a drop in tax revenues, there was a sudden halt in new Public Health Departments. Private charities could not meet the nation's needs. There were no Blue Cross or Blue Shield insurance programs. Lot of stories behind that.

Acute problems were being replaced with an increase in chronic conditions such as heart disease. The National Commission on Federal Legislation for Birth Control (twenty million members) endorsed lifting restrictions on dissemination of birth control information as part of medical practice, but Pius XI condemned contraception. The death rate from childbirth in America was higher than in other industrial countries.

Tuberculosis still topped the list of deaths for infectious diseases. Riboflavin, Thiamine, and vitamin K had not yet been identified. There was no cure for polio and no prevention; no sulfa drugs; no sodium pentothal to anaesthetize patients for surgery; no dried human blood serum; no blood banks; no National Cancer Institute; no electron microscope. There would not be an American Board of Pediatrics until 1933.

And by the way, after ten years of Prohibition, deaths from alcoholism were soaring.

I can see now how much of my life was influenced by what boys and then men thought of me. I'm glad I've finally grown out of that phase.

"Residence."

"Baxter luv, how are you over there, deep in the heart of Texas?"

"Just fine, Mom. Honey, could you take him, please? I can't talk to my mother and wrestle with a puppy at the same time. Thanks. How are you, Mom?"

"I've called to confess to a deep embarrassment."

"What for?"

"You remember last year I was trying to find out what's causing the drought northern Arizona is suffering through?"

"I do. I admired you."

"I was so naive. 'What's causing this drought?' What a simpleton."

"It wasn't a good question?"

"No, it was ignorant. Short question, book-length answer. I didn't know enough to ask a good question."

"And now you do?"

"Now I know enough not to ask. You know why? There's no final answer."

"I'm lost already."

"We know what happens in the ocean and the atmosphere, but we don't know why. Why does the jet stream shift? Why do ocean currents change? Why do ocean temperatures change?"

"Why..."

"Look. Principle number one: Politics may be local; weather is global."

"Global..."

"Air circulates around the planet, doesn't it? A volcano's eruption affects crop conditions continents away."

"I've read that."

"Water in the oceans is always going somewhere, moving, moving on different levels, out of this ocean, into that one."

"It does?"

"I think so. It's all of a piece, all part of a large, mysterious (so far) global— climate—phenomena of large scale. Air and sea interactions. One book I read calls them 'global teleconnections'."

"And you understand these books?"

"Oh heavens no, but I've finally realized that you don't have weather in your county that has no connection to weather somewhere else. Can you talk about whether there's enough water in Lake Powell to make electricity for Arizona without talking about rain in the Colorado mountains?"

"OK. I can see that."

"And that's not big enough. Atmosphere-ocean interactions in one part of the world have drastic effects thousands of miles away. It's fascinating. Wet here, thus dry there, all connected."

"Are you talking about El Niño?"

"Yes! It's very important. It affects Peru and Brazil too, Australia, southeast Asia, southwest America, Japan. Climate is vast, gigantic, driven by ocean circulation and constantly changing air. And not just recently. Over hundreds of thousands of years the earth has been in climate transition more than three-quarters of the time."

He laughed, but it sounded pleased. "Mom, you don't mind thinking big, I can see that."

"The Anasazi here in Arizona? Between two major sources of moisture, the Gulf of Mexico and the Pacific Ocean?"

"Ahhhh, yes, I guess so."

"Both influenced by episodes of the El Niño Southern Oscillation?"

"I'll take your word for it."

"The Anasazi left their stone buildings empty and went away because fifty years of drought settled over the Colorado Plateau in 1130 or so causing crop failure and famine. And that was a short-term episode on a much larger scene. So when I asked what's causing our drought, our five years of drought, I was thinking small and restricted about what was happening way beyond my sight. And I had no idea of the mystery of why."

"And now you have a new view of your world?"

"You do understand. I knew I could count on you. Oh Baxter, the world is full of excitement. I've never looked so old and felt so alive."

I would not go back to any of it, any of my life. Once I was pretty. Once I could ride my bicycle all day. But now I'm free to make of myself what I want to. It's obvious, to me at least, that geology, weather, history—I'm doing what Emily and I planned to do together.

1930 Hemlines were down again, past the calf; hair was longer, and there were ruffles on ladies' clothes. Mary Costigan had spent $10,000 to improve her new Orpheum Theater with sound photophone and a bigger screen. Flagstaff was planning its first All-Indian Pow Wow for July 4—three days of Hopi, Zuni, Navajo, Apache, Hualapai, Supai, Mojave and Ute in races, parades, dances, tug-of-war. (I don't know here to put the 's' there. Tugs? Wars?)

The town's population had grown by twenty-two per cent in the past decade. Not seriously hurt right away by the national down-turn, they applauded Senator Ashurst when he told the Rotarians that The Depression was a trivial thing for America.

Citizens were "making do," but in March twenty-two hobos came through town on one freight train. The livestock market was in a slump, and when sheepmen shipped two million pounds of Arizona wool, they were hard hit by market conditions. The city Water Department managed personnel changes and retirements so that it could save $4000 yearly in the city payroll. Road construction was planned to employ men who needed jobs. The signs were there for anyone to read if they wanted to: things could get a whole lot worse.

In June the Flagstaff Electric Light Company announced a reduction in rates that might be as much as twenty-five per cent. Then in October it began construction of an addition to its plant to house a new 500 KW generator that would increase capacity seventy-five percent. Then in November it decided it would burn wood not oil though the winter to help cutters and teamsters hurt by the "local unemployment situation." As confused as anyone, I guess.

As usual the *Sun* was positive: "Local Business Outlook For 1930 Good." The economic situation was not being helped by Reds and Socialists, it said. All we needed was to work together for production increase, employment, and lower prices to achieve a revival of prosperity.

Just look at business in town if you wanted proof, look around. The Sprouse-Reitz chain was going to open a 49 cent store. The Chamber of Commerce had decided to erect a building for itself on the railroad station lot. Post Office directors were looking for a new site. Local businessman Wong June had announced plans to open a restaurant, the American Kitchen, modern and up-to-date. Mountain States Telephone and Telegraph had bought three vacant lots at the northeast corner of Aspen and Beaver for an exchange building with new equipment. Surveys were being made for a new road up Oak Creek hill that would be eighteen feet wide. Movie companies were filming all over northern Arizona. Who could see all that and doubt that Flagstaff's economy was sound?

The year had started with drought and thirty to forty tank cars a day, 10,000 gallons a car, of Flagstaff water shipped on trains to Winslow, Williams, the Grand Canyon, Ash Fork, and Seligman for railroad and Harvey House use. A week-long snow storm that closed roads followed by a wet summer with heavy rains in August and a good snow storm in November had relieved the situation, so that much was all right for a while.

There were seven churches in town and seven lodges. Stop signs. A flower show, a rodeo, a "grueling" auto race up the Peaks with thirteen autos entered. The year's Pulitzer Prize novel, Oliver LaFarge's *Laughing Boy* set in Navajo country, was being printed as a serial in the *Sun*. The museum had conducted its first annual Indian Art Show, its first Arizona Artists exhibition.

If the 1st National Bank of Flagstaff was in default with a shortage of accounts, well, that was because a cashier had embezzled and misappropriated money.

On long-ago summer evenings in Phoenix all the children on the block played Kick the Can together, running, hiding, running in low evening sunlight until our mothers called us in.

"Mom, it's me."

"Gwen, how nice to hear from you. I hesitate to ask how everyone is."

She sighed. "We're all pretty good at the moment. The boys' casts will come off any day, and so will their scabs. Their parents are relaxing a little. It's been a chore to keep them occupied the past month—I'm really tired of playing canasta. I never thought I'd long to see them active again."

"I can sympathize."

"But school has started, and they seem to think their casts give them a kind of glamour. They're collecting autographs on what is by now a very dirty surface."

"And you have a few hours to yourself."

"Never thought I'd be so glad to be alone. I notice you're not saying that if you were here, you could play cards with them. You used to play cards with us."

"So math would be fun for you."

"Was that it? I didn't realize."

"I thought your education wasn't a responsibility I could turn over completely to the school."

"Really! I'll get it for you in a minute, Beanie, I'm talking to Nana. Was that why you had us read to you while you cooked?"

"Yep."

"Mother. You were quite enlightened."

"Thank you. I took the mother job seriously."

"How about taking the grandmother job seriously?"

"I do—all those letters…"

"You're kidding. But come to think of it…Beanie, I said wait a minute."

"Grandmothers can be a civilizing influence, you know."

To my surprise and great delight, Gwen laughed. It wasn't a sound I had heard often lately. "I've almost exhausted my reasons why you should move up here. Aren't you tired of climbing the tower every day?"

"Not yet. I'm slow and steady. People a third of my age, sturdy types with muscles and fire boots, come through the trap door breathing harder than I do."

"You don't have trouble doing the job? Beanie, get off that! A drawer is not a ladder."

"I can see and hear and talk and read a map, which is what's required. That and sense enough to stay off the radio unless I have something useful to say."

"You aren't bored? I'd be bored out of my mind."

"Good heavens no, the day's not long enough."

"So you're going to stay in Flagstaff through the winter?"

"I love my little townhouse, love the neighborhood. And I haven't finished the story of doctors and medicine, I have only the first fifty years done—1881 to 1930. I find it fascinating."

"You'll do what you did last year?"

"Well, I have some ideas. I'm booked for a Grand Canyon river trip next month."

"What!

"Two weeks on a raft..."

"Mother..."

"I hurried on. "And I'd like to do that drive through southern Utah again now that I know what to look for."

"But you don't have the motorcoach any more. Beanie, don't pout."

"I thought I'd stay in hotels at night, safe and comfy."

"Are you going alone?"

"Not exactly. I'm taking a ghost with me."

"Mother!"

"I was hoping you'd understand, Gwen: the memory of what your father was as a young man before he went to medical school. Loving, interested in things. We were so close at first. I need to resurrect the young man I married and show him the Colorado Plateau and live with him young in my mind instead of the man he became. So I'm taking him with me."

"Mother, you are so weird."

"I'm glad you think so. And maybe I'll fly up to Denver for a visit this winter."

"That would be something anyway."

"For a couple of weeks."

"Good. You and I can go places and have fun. Now, let's just go back a minute to what you said about a raft trip on a river. Through the canyon? You mean camping?"

"Right on sand. Floating through the days."

"Will there be seat belts in the raft?"

"The thing is, Gwen, I've been young and middlle-aged, but I've never been old, and I've had no training for it, just some wisdom gained through the years. I'll have only one chance, you know, at being old. I'd like to do it well. I'm thinking of taking drawing lessons."

"Drawing...*BEANIE*!"

"Go take care of him, luv, I'll talk with you later."

I suppose I expected my life to be fine and clean and strong with clear colors and noble purpose, instead of the muddy mess it was through the whole middle. I've lived long enough to redeem it, I hope, long enough to care about strangers I pass, long enough to treasure connections.

1930 Ever upbeat despite the economic news, Flagstaff's newspaper printed encouraging items about doctors, reporting that Charles Sechrist, addressing the Rotary Club on progress in medicine, had said that the past fifty years had added more to scientific understanding than had the preceding five centuries. In his opinion, the work was only well-started.

Take public health, for instance. Diphtheria anti-toxin was administered to 880 children by Drs. Felix Manning and Edwin Miller with help from state nurses. Felix as county physician, Miller as his deputy, also Sechrist and Fronske had combined for an examination of school children at the college training school and found nothing unusual. To guard against epidemics Felix and state chemist Jane Rider had inspected water at nearby tourist camps and lakes.

Sometimes the news about doctors was chatty. Percy and Clara Cornish visited now and then from Albuquerque. Felix hunted quail in Chino Valley. Sechrist went hunting on the Kaibab; he went fishing. Dr. Raymond was often traveling, which comes as no surprise.

The doctor news could be professional. The Sechrists and Dr. Miller drove to Winslow to attend meetings of the Navajo and Apache counties medical association. Dr. Miller went to El Paso to attend the annual meeting and clinical conference of the Medical and Surgical Association of the Southwest. Dr. Felix, busy as always, was Arizona's delegate to a Texas conference of American public health associates. With Lois and Sarah he drove to Phoenix to attend state medical and health meetings. And he was elected councilor for the northern third of Arizona by the state's Medical Association.

Fred Breen was unable to resist teasing them. He had a wonderful time with the report that Dr. Miller's car had lost two door handles, twisted off by the attack of "a huge steer with widespread horns." And he was gleeful when the Rotary Club engaged in high-jinks at a regular meeting: Martin Fronske solemnly addressed his brethren about court procedure, then called in a sociologist who spoke to them about taxation. In November when the newspaper printed that Dr. Felix was sick with a cold, then that he said twenty-five school children had measles, I wasn't sure whether it was a spoof or not.

But Editor Breen was properly sad and respectful when he reported that Dr. Raymond had accompanied M. J. Riordan of Arizona Lumber and Timber Company to the Mayo Hospital in Minnesota, where he had surgery for cancer. Mike Riordan died after the operation.

The *Sun's* "Local Brevities" and "News of Interest to Women" columns were the only real clues to what the doctors' wives were doing. Going by that, I'd have to say that economic collapse hadn't affected them much yet.

The ladies went on with bridge luncheons and golf club luncheons as they had in previous years. The annual Fall Festival at the Federated Church claimed the attention of a few of them. Hilda and her boys opened the Fronske cottage in Oak Creek Canyon. Lois Manning had always been fairly decorous. She and Hilda and Pearl, as members of the Friday Club, met regularly over luncheon and bridge. In June Lois won first prize in a golf handicap tournament conducted by the Women's Tuesday Morning Golf Club. In September Lois and Pearl were hostesses for a bridge luncheon at the Monte Vista Hotel. But was it all less frequent, less spendy? I couldn't tell.

Pearl entertained the Friday Luncheon Bridge Club at her home. Late in the year she traveled to Phoenix as a representative to the state convention of the Arizona Council of Catholic Women.

They were always open to new social wrinkles. The Fronskes were hosts at dinner for eight guests, including Felix and Lois, at La Posada in Winslow. Felix and Lois entertained the Fronskes and seven other guests with pinochle and a Chinese dinner.

In December Ed Miller, Felix and Lois, and Sarah—just before she went off to L.A. to spend the winter visiting Tom and Julia—were among eighty-six guests of Mr. and Mrs. Wong June for a Chinese dinner at the Mandarin Cafe.

Nurses, important as they were, seldom appeared in social news. Laura MacDermid was back at work in Mercy Hospital; Mrs. James Doyle was office nurse there for doctors Schermann and Sechrist; two nurses resigned from the hospital staff and left Flagstaff. That's all I found. There was not much about Ethel Sechrist either, but then she had a new-born son—an excellent excuse.

The part of life that requires the most courage may be not the last but the next to last or maybe the phase just before that.

Ah, the memories we accumulate, the weight of them. I haven't ever recovered from childhood hurt, adolescent hurt, not really. It's always there. Or from foolish things I did when I was young and the shame of knowing I did them. I wish I could erase all that.

My head is so full of memories it's a wonder there's room for anything new. The faces of my parents. The house we lived in. Dresses that I liked. The thrill of Christmas morning. Books I read. Trees I climbed and the dreams I had when I was up in them. Songs, all the songs. My sweet babies—how I miss them. Your babies are always left behind in the past.

I'll never get over losing Emily. I remember her voice, the shoes she wore, the way we laughed together—little pictures like Emily on water skis with sun glittering on the lake behind her, Emily sitting on grass in the shade of a tree—and I can hardly bear the pain in my chest. My friend. My dear dear friend, gone all these years. Sometimes I talk to her in my mind, sometimes I can't find her and don't know where to look.

I remember Don when we were young, before life damaged him the way it did. How sweet his smile was then. How strong his hand felt when it held mine. He cared so much about science and medicine in his college years. My young husband.

He was so somebody else, so…so peculiar after the accident…I don't know how to say it—fogged out. There was no connecting with him on any level. I mentioned it to Gwen, who went right into efficient mode. Of course she did.

"Mother, who's paying the bills?"

"I am. I have for a long time."

"Good. Be sure you keep everything up to date. How many bank accounts do you and Dad have?"

"Just two, checking and savings."

"Are they joint?"

"Both names are on them? Yes, joint."

"Do you know whether Dad has any separate accounts? You should find out. You don't want any nasty surprises."

She didn't come right out and say "…in case he dies." Neither did Baxter, he was ever so calm and mature. "You know, Mom, it would be a good idea to talk with your lawyer, just in case Dad is incapacitated for a while."

"I don't have a lawyer. At least, I haven't talked with one since we made our wills—that's been years."

"Does Dad have a lawyer? Maybe through his practice? They might have made investments together. You should find out."

Abby mentioned doctors. "Mom, I think you should call the men Dad's been in practice with. Somebody. This sounds serious."

"I don't particularly like those men."

"But they might know something, didn't they see him in the hospital?"

"I didn't know who else to call."

"But they know something about him, don't they?"

"Yes, all right. I'll call."

I don't remember whether anyone asked if Don had a Living Will. He was way past signing one by then.

My wonderful grown-up children, they called every day, talked me through those weeks. I did what I was supposed to. Everyone knows what women are supposed to do. But I had been stretched too tight for too long. That happens to people.

Finally Don wouldn't look at me, wouldn't open his eyes, wouldn't taste the soup I tried to spoon into his mouth. He was as bad a patient as a doctor can be—how can you save a man like that? I'd sit and stare at the wall an hour at a time.

Since 1980 researchers had been studying causes of death in patients with serious depression and suspected it doubled the odds of mortality in cases of cardiac disease and cancer. In the 1990s biological psychiatrists looked at suppressed immunity and neuron loss with decrease of hippocampal volume. The statistics were there: forty percent mortality rate before the age of sixty-five. They knew that suicide was not the only way depression could kill. But that didn't save him.

Nothing saved him. He'd been gone for a long while before that morning when I walked into his bedroom and found him dead. I don't know how long I stood there, looking at his body…I don't know…before I realized I should do something, and I didn't know what. My father and my mother had both died in hospitals, and it seems to me that people there had made initial decisions. Finally I called Gwen, my Gwen.

"Have you told Baxter and Abby yet?"

"Just you."

"I'll take care of it."

"There's supposed to be something I should do."

"Mother, maybe you should call the police."

"Police? Why police?"

"Dad died at home. Do you know cause of death?"

"No. I'm not sure. Heart, maybe."

"So, police. You need a doctor to write a death certificate. If the cause can't be determined, there might need to be an autopsy. For the insurance company. Never mind, I'll take care of it. It'll take me a few hours to make arrangements here and get a flight, I can probably be there tomorrow. But I can make phone calls from here. Do you know anyone who can come and stay with you for twenty-four hours?"

"Emily."

"I'll take care of it. Is there a doctor you want for the death certificate?"

I was barely able to think, crying by then. "No." Completely useless.

"One of his partners?"

"I suppose so."

"Never mind, I'll take care of it. Go get something chocolate to eat."

"Chocolate?"

"It couldn't hurt. Do you have a funeral director?"

"I don't want a funeral. Who would come? Who would care? Do we have to have a funeral?"

"Mother. Of course we do."

"I don't see why."

"I'll find out, but right now someone has to, you know, be responsible for the body. I'll take care of it. Go sit in the kitchen and eat something chocolate."

I've been told that one of Don's partners came immediately and reported that I seemed to be functioning, just a little spacey, but I have no memory of it, no memory at all until Abby arrived that evening. Ten hours were completely gone. I've never recovered them.

Someone had come and taken Don's body, but I don't remember. If there were police, I don't remember. Nothing is left of that day until I was sitting in my room and lights were on and it was dark outside and Abby was kneeling beside the chair, holding my hand.

"Hey, Mamacita, I came as fast as I could."

I was slow to recognize her. "Thank you." The room seemed very large.

"How you doing?"

"I don't know."

There were tears on her face. It seemed natural.

"Did Janey come with you?"

"I drove over by myself."

"Oh. Why?"

"You don't remember?"

"Your father died."

She bowed her head to our hands and cried, and I was aware of how the light from the lamp looked on her hair. Quite beautiful. My Abby. I loved her so.

The world seeped back in a little at a time over the next days, every detail marvelous. I was fascinated by light on things. Colors were awesome. In the office of the Cremation Service I watched Baxter arranging details, and I knew what he was doing, but mostly— as a spectator of miraculous reality—I was interested in how mature he looked. "Copies of the Death Certificate for notifying Social Security and the IRS, yes, we'll need that. For insurance companies, the bank, the County Recorder, yes, yes, I suppose so." I loved him too. I loved everything, but I don't think I mentioned it to anyone.

Gwen searched Don's desk, looking for income tax returns, bank records, titles to the cars, insurance policies.

"Mother, I don't find any safe deposit box keys. Do you know whether Dad had a safe deposit box?"

"I don't think so."

"Did you keep separate check registers?"

"Just one."

"Where is it? Where would receipts be?"

I admired her tremendously. Who would have thought my little golden-haired Gwen would grow up to be so efficient? "Mother, I found the deed to the house, thank goodness you're tenants in common. But didn't Dad own his share of the office building? I haven't located proof of that."

I look back now and I can't believe I drifted and let her do all that as if it did not concern me. There was something wrong, but they assumed it was grief and they were too busy to notice. It wasn't grief, I didn't feel anything. I walked, I talked, nothing was bleeding or broken, nothing visible. But something was wrong.

"Did you transfer title to the motor coach? Sell it?"

"Ask Abby."

"Abby? Why Abby?"

She found our wills—"Thank goodness he left everything to you"—Abby took Don's to the Registrar of Probate of the Superior Court and made appointments with his lawyer and his partners. "Didn't those three own the building where they had their offices? Mom, did you hear me?"

"Years ago they bought the land, yes, and built those connected offices on it. We had a party when they moved in."

"But did they have a mortgage? Was it paid off? We can't find a deed."

"It was nothing but problems. Maintenance and upkeep. There were vacancies and no rent coming in."

"Mom, I'm going to see them this afternoon, and I need to know so I can ask the right questions."

Months later I realized that no one could have done all that alone. I am deeply grateful to my grown children, tackling the job for me. And impressed. When did they become so capable?

Don's funeral was what I wanted. One chilly afternoon the four of us climbed Tempe Butte with a small box full of ashes. A pinch at a time we emptied the box and put traces of Don among the rocks. I don't know whether it was legal.

Those years when he and I were in college I'd had the real Don, and I'd loved what he was then, and I wanted him to be there again, overlooking ASU and the places where we'd been happy. So I could remember him that way.

Nobody was there who thought it was a duty. The four of us stood close together under the sky, touching, crying a little, saying nothing. There is nothing that can be said that is adequate to death.

For another two days Gwen and Baxter and Abby worked at "wrapping up affairs," "giving notice," talking with a lawyer. Will there be an estate tax? Will Mom need a new will or can she just change her beneficiary? Do we need to go into probate? They changed my insurance policies, my bank accounts.

Finally they looked at me straight and asked impertinent questions.

"Have you been sleeping?"

"Do you even hear what we say?"

"How many fingers am I holding up?"

"Mother, are you all right?"

How do you answer the all-right question? "Fine. I'm fine."

And I did manage for a while. Said goodby to them. Set up a routine for such daily tasks as eating a little. Showered regularly. Changed clothes morning and night. Walked for hours along the Arizona Canal every day and got back home before dark. Gwen called every day and insisted that I move to Denver to live with her, but I always said, "I'm fine, Sweetheart. Fine."

…until the day I realized I was standing on an unfamiliar canal bridge with sun in my eyes while cars whizzed past, and I didn't know where I was or how I'd got there. I suppose I looked lost. A very nice young policewoman saw me and stopped.

She stood close and shouted over the traffic noise. "Can I help you, ma'am?"

"Where am I?"

"Sun City. Do you live here?"

"Scottsdale, I live in Scottsdale. What time is it?"

"It's going-home time. All these cars are going home. Tell you what, for you that's about twenty-five miles away, why don't I take you? What's the address in Scottsdale? Is there someone I could call to say we're coming?"

She was pretty in her dark blue uniform, and I loved her too. I gave her Gwen's phone number in Denver.

It must have been a burden for my three, but they didn't say so, just took turns staying with me for a few days at a time, complaining about how much weight I'd lost, taking me to doctors for exams and blood tests. I had an MRI, which I hated, and a small camera was forced down my throat to examine my heart, which I also hated. Finally medical minds came up with a name for what had happened, which is better than no explanation at all.

"It's called a transient ischemic event, apparently a brief interference with arterial blood. We don't have a clear idea of what goes on, but it probably won't happen again."

"I'm going to prescribe an anti-depressant and some mild sleeping pills."

"I'll give you a list of counselors and therapists, it would be a good idea to choose someone to work with."

For a year I "worked with" the counselor, a pleasant woman—I liked her. We talked about Don and the individual ways human brains react to stress and ideas for dealing with that. I still take an anti-depressant and a sleeping pill every evening.

I'm not the person I once was, but maybe that's good. If we ended as we began, there wouldn't be much point to living, it seems to me.

If anyone were to ask me what I've learned from so many years, one thing I would say would be this: it's hard to defend yourself against people you love.

More medical news to upset popular assumptions:

About a quarter of all schizophrenics may owe their symptoms to spontaneous mutations in paternal sperm. And the older the father, the more likely his sperm is to carry such mutations. Among the diseases more likely to occur in children with older fathers are dwarfism, premature aging, predisposition toward a certain kind of skin cancer, and some congenital heart defects.

By the time a man is forty, each of his sperm cell precursors has divided 660 times. Egg precursor cells in a female divide only 24 times. The more replication, the greater the chance that a mutation will occur. Also, DNA repair enzymes become less efficient as a man ages and more frequently fail to fix a mutant sperm.

I did not make this up. I read it in a medical journal.

His father was fifty-five when Don was born. I don't know whether that had anything to do with what happened.

Brief summer rains in Phoenix were celebrations when I was a child. I'd hurry to pull on my swimming suit and run outside to frolic in water falling right out of the sky. After all these years, I see it from the inside the way I saw it then and from the outside, a little girl in a red swimming suit running around the yard in the rain.

DETAILS I LEARNED WHILE READING ABOUT OTHER THINGS

Dr. Cornish and Clara both died in 1932 a few months apart. They were survived by a son in Albuquerque, Dr. Percy Gilette Cornish jr.

In 1932 and 1933 Dr. Martin Fronske took post-graduate courses in pediatrics in St. Louis and obstetrics at New York Lying-In Hospital.

Dr. E.S. Miller died in 1936.

Sarah Manning, widow of a doctor and mother of two more, died one month short of 85 in Phoenix at the home of her daughter in late January of 1941. The dean of Trinity Episcopal Cathedral in Phoenix officiated at her funeral, which was held at A.L. Moore and Sons.

The headstone in Flagstaff's Citizen's Cemetery is double—for both G.F. and Sarah. Obituary records state that Sarah was buried in the Phoenix Greenlawn Cemetery.

Felix Manning, after serving as Coconino County health officer and head of the State Health Department, died of a heart attack in 1954 at the age of 70.

Hilda Fronske died in 1955, Dr. Raymond in 1959, Charles Sechrist in 1965, Martin Fronske in 1984 at age 101, Ethel Sechrist in 1987.

Mercy Hospital burned in 1979.

End of September, 2001

To my grandchildren and their elders,

Since Labor Day, the forest radio has been quiet, so my only company in the tower is the sound of wind, but that's enough. Clouds in the sky are sufficient for interest but not adequate for drama. (I do love drama in the sky.) An annual necklace of gold circles the Peaks in the aspen zone; below me spots of gold appear as oak leaves begin to change.

September looks like autumn in Flagstaff after a month of late summer lush. Sun still shines on flowers that are everywhere in every color, but one by one, yellow leaves are falling. Have you ever noticed the smell of fallen leaves?

I've been in this little tower for five months this summer, and I ought to be antsy to get out of here, but oh, it's so beautiful. Moisture left in the air heightens colors on the land. Sun, a punishment in June, now feels soothing on my shoulders. It's farther south, softer, shadowing hills I haven't noticed before. There's something nostalgic about these long quiet afternoons.

When I'm back in town, I miss the night sky, the swarms of neighbor stars. This month the Big Dipper has nearly set before I turn out my reading light, and the Milky Way stretches all across the sky. I open the cabin door into a cold black wind, lean out and look up at deep masses of stars. Before sunrise Orion rises and Venus is brilliant in the sky.

Humans who strive for control, mastery, dominance, power must not be in the habit of looking up at night.

Beanie and Cazz, I would like to show you my stars. Maybe next summer. Did you see the Harvest Moon? For three nights I watched it from my bed through the cabin window as it shone through the pines, enchanting the mountain. All night it moved across the sky, shining on my roof while I slept. In the morning it was low in the western sky.

I'm in love with this mountain. I'll be packing up and moving out in one week, free again from duty to the forest radio, from a schedule set in the office. Time will be mine to arrange as I choose. But I'll also be excluded from the landscape stretching away into the distance, from the huge picture I've seen for the past five months. I'll be able to see no farther than down the block, unable to watch weather changing half a day ahead of time.

Down in town people of all ages are back in school. Golden leaves drift in the wind, falling from the big old trees around the library. I look forward to packing away my flimsy summer clothes and getting out the soft, sturdy jackets of winter. Look forward to snow and Christmas and seeing Shirley and Sandy again. And to another summer on the mountain.

What's more, I look forward to adding colors that might turn the piece-by-piece thing I call my life into something that makes sense. If I can't do it in the un-beholden years from here on out, I'm a pretty sorry specimen. Late is better than no sense at all, in case you didn't know.

I send love.
M

Sources

Published, Books:

Abram, Ruth J. *Women Doctors in America.* W.W. Norton and Co., New York. 1985.
American Medical Directory, 8th edition, American Medical Association, Chicago. 1923.
Anderson, Paul G. "One Hundred Years of Innovation," *Washington University.* Winter 1991.
Aron, Elaine N. *The Highly Sensitive Person.* Broadway Books, New York. 1996.
Ashurst, Henry Fountain, ed. George F. Sparks. *A Many Colored Toga.* University of Arizona Press, Tucson. 1962.
Baron-Faust, Rita. *Breast Cancer.* Hearst Books, New York. 1995.
Bates, Barbara. *Bargaining for Life.* University of Pennsylvania Press, Philadelphia. 1992.
Beard, Bernice. *At Your Own Pace: Traveling Your Own Way in Your Motorhome.* Arbor House Publishing, Westminster, Maryland. 1997.
Beckman, Edward and William R. Leber, editors. *Handbook of Depression,* second edition. The Guilford Press, New York. 1995.
Block, Adrienne. *Amy Beach: Passionate Victorian.* Oxford University Press, Oxford and New York. 1998.
Bond, Courtney C.J. *City on the Ottawa.* Queen's Printer and Controller of Stationery, Ottawa. 1961
Bonner, Thomas Neville. *To the Ends of the Earth: Women's Search for Education in Medicine.* Harvard University Press. Cambridge, Massachusetts. 1992.
Brittain, Vera. *Testament of Youth.* Penguin Books. New York. 1933.
Bruno, Richard L. *The Polio Paradox.* Warner Books, AOL Time-Warner Books. 2002.
Bullough, Vern L. and Bonnie. *The Emergence of Modern Nursing.* The Macmillan Company, London. 1969.
Bullough, Vern L. and Bonnie. *History, Trends and Politics of Nursing.* Appleton-Century-Crofts, Norwalk, Connecticut. 1984.
Christensen, Larry. *Diet-Behavior Relationships: Focus on Depression.* American Psychological Association, Washington, D.C. 1996.
Chronic, Kalka. *Roadside Geology of Arizona.* Mountain Press Publishing Company, Missoula, Montana. 1983.
Chronic, Halka. *Roadside Geology of Utah.* Mountain Press Publishing Company, Missoula, Montana. 1990.
Clements, Kendrick A. *The Presidency of Woodrow Wilson.* University Press of Kansas, Lawrence, Kansas. 1992.
Cline, Platt. *They Came to the Mountain.* Northland Press, Flagstaff, Arizona. 1976.
Cline, Platt. *Mountain Town.* Northland Press, Flagstaff. 1994.
DePaulo, J. Raymond jr. *Understanding Depression.* John Wiley and Sons, New York. 2002.
Diamant, Anita. *Good Harbor.* Scribner, New York. 2001.
Directory of Deceased Physicians. American Medical Association.
Donahue, M. Patricia, Ph.D. R.N. *Nursing, the Finest Art.* C.V. Mosby Company. St. Louis. 1985.
Downum, Garland. *A Flagstaff Heritage: The Federated Community Church.* The Federated Community Church, Flagstaff. 1983.

Duffy, John. *From Humors to Medical Science*. University of Illinois Press, Urbana and
    Chicago, Illinois. 1993.
Duke, Martin. *The Development of Medical Techniques and Treatment*. International
    University Press, Madison, Connecticut. 1991.
Eggleston, Wilfrid. *The Queen's Choice*. The Queen's Printer and Controller of
    Stationery, Ottawa, Canada. 1961.
Elkins, Rita. *Depression and Natural Medicine*. Woodland Publishing Company Inc.,
    Pleasant Grove, Utah. 1995
Ellis, John. *Eye Deep in Hell*. Johns Hopkins University Press, Baltimore, Maryland. 1976.
Evans, Sara M. *Born for Liberty: a History of Women in America*. The Free Press: a
    Division of Macmillan, Inc., New York. 1989.
Fagan, Brian. *Floods, Famines and Emperors, El Nino and the Fate of Civilizations*. Basic
    Books, New York. 1999.
Fenn, Elizabeth. *Pox Americana*. Hill and Wang, New York. 2001.
Feinberg, Barbara. *Black Tuesday*. The Millbrook Press, Brookfield, Connecticut. 1995.
Fine, Carla. *Married to Medicine, an Intimate Portrait of Doctors' Wives*. Atheneum, New
    York. 1981
Fity, Reginald Heber. *American Heritage* Vol. 37. American Heritage, New York. 1986.
Foster, Vanda. *The Nineteenth Century: A Visual History of Costume*. Drama Book
    Publishers, New York. 1984.
Fowlkes, Martha R. *Behind Every Successful Man: Wives of Medicine and Academe*.
    Columbia University Press, New York. 1980.
Galbraith, John Kenneth. *The Great Crash: 1929*. Time Incorporated, New York, 1954.
Geller, L.D. *The American Field Service Archives of World War I*. Greenwood Press, N.Y. 1989.
Goff, John. *Arizona Constitution and Government*. Arizona Historical Society, Tucson. 1987.
Goren, Charles. *The Sports Illustrated Book of Bridge*. Time Incorporated. New York. 1961.
Graham, Katharine. *Personal History*. Alfred Knopf, New York. 1997.
Greeley, Andrew. *The Irish Americans*. Harper and Row, New York. 1981.
Griffin, Gerald and Joanne. *History and Trends of Professional Nursing*. C.V. Mosby
    Company, St. Louis. 1973.
Haiken, Elizabeth. *Venus Envy*. Johns Hopkins University Press, Baltimore. 1997.
Halaes, Dianne. *Depression*. Chelsea House Publishers, New York. 1989.
Hamblyn, Richard. *The Invention of Clouds*. Farrar, Straus and Giroux, New York. 2001.
Hansen, Arden J. *Gentlemen Volunteers*. Arcade Publishing, New York. 1996.
Higonnet, Margaret, ed. *Nurses at the Front*. Northeastern University Press, Boston. 2001.
Hirschfeld, Robert. *When the Blues Don't Go Away*. Macmillan Publishing, New York. 1991.
Hoff, Brent and Carter Smith III. *Mapping Epidemics*. Franklin Watts, New York. 1962
Hurst, Arthur F. *Medical diseases of the War*. Edward Arnold, London. 1917.
Iezzoni, Lynette. *Influenza 1918*. TV Books L.L.C., New York. 1999.
Jackson, Marie. *Stone Landmarks*. Piedra Azul Press, Flagstaff, Arizona. 1999.
Karolevity, Robert F. *Doctors of the Old West*. Superior Publishing Company, Seattle. 1967.
Kennedy, John W. M.D. *Arizona Medical Association :the First Hundred Years*. Heritage
    Publishers, Flagstaff, Arizona. 1993.
Kennedy, John W., M.D. *Arizona Medicine: Historical Essays*. Heritage Publishers,
    Phoenix, Arizona. 1990.

Kerber, Linda K. and Jane DeHart-Matthews, editors. *Women's America: Refocusing the Past.* Oxford University Press, New York. 1987.

Kocsis, James H. and Daniel N. Klein, editors. *Diagnosis and Treatment of Chronic Depression.* Guilford Press, New York. 1995.

Kravetz, Robert E. and Alex Jay Kimmelman. *Healthseekers in Arizona.* Academy of Sciences of the Maricopa County Medical Society, Phoenix, Arizona. 1998.

Lange, Vladimir. *Be a Survivor: Your Guide to Breast Cancer Treatment.* Lange Productions, Los Angeles, California. 1998.

Lee, Hermione. *Willa Cather: Double Lives.* Pantheon Books, New York, 1989.

Luckingham, Bradford. *Epidemic in the Southwest, 1918–1919.* Western Press, El Paso, Texas. 1984.

Mangum, Richard K. and Sherry G. *Flagstaff Historic Walk.* Hexagon Press, Flagstaff Arizona. 1993.

Marion, Robert, M.D. *The Intern Blues.* William Morrow and Company, New York. 1989.

Marks-Maran, Diane J. and Barbara M. Pope. *Breast Cancer Nursing and Counseling.* Blackwell Scientific Publications, Oxford. 1985.

McKawn, Robin. *Heroic Nurses.* G.P. Putnam's Sons, New York. 1966.

Mendes, Valerie and Amy de la Haye. *Twentieth Century Fashion.* Thames & Hudson, London. 1999.

Migneco, Ronald, and Timothy Levi Biel. *The Crash of 1929.* Lucent Books, San Diego, California. 1989.

Miller, Brandon Marie. *Just What the Doctor Ordered: the History of American Medicine.* Lerner Publications Company, Minneapolis. 1997.

Mondimore, Francis Mark, M.D. *Depression: the Mood Disease.* Johns Hopkins University Press, Baltimore and London. 1993.

MotorHome. Volume 37, Number 8. TL Enterprises. Ventura, California. August 2000.

Mulasky, Robert. *Medical Technology: Inventing the Instruments.* The Oliver Press, Minneapolis. 1997.

Narland, Sherwin B. *Doctors: the Biography of Medicine.* Knopf, New York. 1988.

Pfeuffer, Charyn. *Breast Cancer Q&A.* Avery, New York, 2003.

Plant, Jane A. *Your Life in Your Hands.* St. Martin's Press, New York. 2000.

Pohl, Amelia, Paul B. Bartlett and Barbara J. Simmons. *When Someone Dies in Arizona.* Eagle Publishing Company of Boca, Boca Raton, Florida. 2000.

Quebbeman, Francis E. *Medicine in Territorial Arizona.* Arizona Historical Foundation, Phoenix. 1966.

Parlett, David. *The Oxford Guide to Card Games.* Oxford University Press, New York. 1990.

Peacock, John. *20th Century Fashion.* Thames and Hudson, London. 1993.

Podell, Ronald. *Contagious Emotions.* Pocket Books, New York. 1992.

The Revised Statutes of Arizona, 1913, Civil Code. Compiled and annotated by Samuel L. Pattee, Code Commissioner. The McNeil Company, Phoenix, Arizona. 1913.

Reyes, Gary. *The Automobile.* Mallard Press, New York. 1990.

Rice, Trudy Thompson. *St. Joseph's: the First 100 Years.* Heritage Publishers, Flagstaff. 1991.

Ritchie, Andrew. *King of the Road: An Illustrated History of Cycling.* Wildwood House, London. 1975.

Rosenberg, Charles E. *The Care of Strangers: the Rise of America's Hospital System.* Basic Books, Inc., New York. 1987.

Ross, Margaret Wheeler. *History of the Arizona Federation of Women's Clubs and Its Forerunners.* 1944.

Ross, Stewart. *Causes and Consequences of the Great Depression.* Raintree Steck-Vaughn Publishers, Austin, Texas. 1998.

Rothstein, William G. *American Medical Schools and the Practice of Medicine: a History.* Oxford University Press, New York. 1987.

Ryan, Frank. *The Forgotten Plague.* Little, Brown and Company, Boston. 1992.

Ryan, Mary P. *Womanhood in America.* Franklin Watts, New York. 1983.

Rydell, Robert, John Findling, Kimberly Pelle. *Fair America.* Smithsonian Institution Press, Washington. 2000.

Rydell, Robert William. *All the World's a Fair.* University of California dissertation. Los Angeles, 1980.

Schaefer, Vincent and John A. Day. *Atmosphere,* Peterson Field Guide. Houghton Mifflin Company. Boston. 1981.

Schafer, William J. and Johannes Riedel. *The Art of Ragtime.* Louisiana State University Press, Baton Rouge, Louisiana. 1973.

Schlesinger, Arthur M. jr. *The Food and Drug Administration.* Chelsea House Publishers, 1988.

Schneider, Dorothy and Carl. *Into the Breach.* Viking Penguin, New York 1991.

Scholl, Albert B. *Rock Art and Ruins for Beginners and Old Guys.* Rainbow Publishing, Tucson. 2001.

Shannon, Joyce Brennflect, ed. *Stress-Related Disorders Sourcebook.* Omnigraphics. 2002.

Smith, Cynthia S. *Doctors' Wives: The Truth About Medical Marriages.* Seaview Books, New York. 1980.

Smith, Dean. *Brothers Five: The Babbitts of Arizona.* Arizona Historical Foundation, Tempe, Arizona. 1989.

Smith, Dean. *The Goldwaters of Arizona.* Northland Press, Flagstaff in cooperation with the Arizona Historical Foundation. 1986.

Smith, G. Elliet. *Shell Shock and its Lessons.* Manchester University Press, London. 1917.

Sobel, Robert. *Herbert Hoover at the Onset of the Great Depression, 1929–1930.* J.B. Lippincott Company, Philadelphia. 1975.

Solomon, Andrew. *The Noonday Demon: An Atlas of Depression.* Scribner, New York. 2001.

Paul Star. *The Social Transformation of American Medicine.* Basic Books, Inc., New York. 1982.

Tanner, Faun McConkie. *The Far Country: A Regional History of Moab and La Sal, Utah.* Olympus Publishing Company, Salt Lake City, Utah. 1976.

The Times History of the War. 22 volumes. The Times, London. 1921.

Teague, David W. *The Southwest in American Literature and Art.* The University of Arizona Press, Tucson. 1997.

Tompkins, Vincent, editor. "Medicine and Health." *American Decades 1910–1919.* International Thomson Publishing Company. 1986.

Tucker, Jonathan B. *Scourge: the Once and Future Threat of Smallpox.* Atlantic Monthly Press, New York. 2001.

Ulseth, Hazel and Helen Shannon. *Victorian Fashions: 1880–1890.* Hobby House Press, Inc., Cumberland, Maryland. 1988.

Voyage Through the Universe: Stars. Editors of Time-Life Books. Alexandria, Virginia. 1988.

Webb, George. *Tree Rings and Telescopes.* University of Arizona Press, Tucson. 1983.

Wells, Kenneth, et. al. *Caring for Depression.* Harvard University Press, Cambridge, Massachusetts. 1996.

Wilder, Laura Ingalls. *West From Home.* Harper and Row, New York. 1974.

Zeiger, Robert H. *America's Great War.* Rowman and Littlefield, Lanham, Maryland. 2000.

Published, Journals:

Abramson, Jerome, et al. "Depression and Risk of Heart Failure Among Older Persons with Isolated Systolic Hypertension," *Archives of Internal Medicine*, Vol. 161. July 23, 2001.

Colford, J.M. and S.J. McPhee. "The Raveled Sleeve of Care: Managing the Stress of Residency Training," *Journal of the American Medical Association*, Vol. 261 N. 15. 1989.

Council of Scientific Affairs, "Results and Implications of the AMA-APA Physician Mortality Project," *Journal of the American Medical Association*, Vol. 257, No. 21. June 5, 1987.

Cranshaw, Ralph. "An Epidemic of Suicide Among Physicians on Probation," *Journal of the American Medical Association*, Vol. 243, No. 119. May 16, 1980.

Deaconson, T.F, et al. "Sleep Deprivation and Resident Performance," *Journal of the American Medical Association*, Vol. 260. 1988.

Edmund, G., D. Schalling, and A. Rissler, "Interaction Effects of Extroversion and Neuroticism on Direct Thresholds," *Biological Psychology*. 1979.

McCall, Timothy. "The Impact of Long Working Hours on Resident Physicians." *New England Journal of Medicine*. Vol. 318, No. 12. March 24, 1988.

McCue, Jack D. "Effects of Stress on Physicians and Their "Medical Practice," *New England Journal of Medicine*. February 25, 1982.

Nadjem, Hadi M.D.and Ropohl, Dirk M.D. "Complete Transection of the Trunk of Passengers in Car Accidents," *American Journal of Forensic Medicine and Pathology*. Lippincott-Raven. June, 1996.

Peitzman, Steven. "Thoroughly Practical: America's Polyclinic Medical Schools," *Bulletin of the History of Medicine*, Vol. 54. Johns Hopkins University Press, Baltimore. 1980.

Stelmark, Robert M., "Biological Bases of Extroversion: Psychophysical Evidence," *Journal of Personality* Vol. 58. March 1990.

Swetnam, Thomas H., Craig D. Allen, and Julio L. Betancourt. "Applied Historical Ecology: Using the Past to Manage for the Future," *Ecological Applications*. The Ecological Society of America. 1999.

Published, Newspapers and Magazines:

Garner, Joe. "Dangerous Equation Leads More Counties to Order Restrictions," *Denver Rocky Mountain News*. June 10, 2000.
Haseltine, Eric. "The Quiet Killer," *Discover*. Buena Vista Magazines. January, 2002.
High Country News. Vol.32. Paonia, Colorado. May 8 and June 5, 2000.
Klawonn, Adam. "A Dry Rain: Arizona Still in Drought's Grip," *The Arizona Republic*. Phoenix. November 8, 2000.
Kocin, Paul J. "The 1998–1999 Snow Season," *Weatherwise*. Vol. 53. March/April, 2000.
The Moki Dugway. San Juan County Visitor Services, Monticello, Utah.
Scott, Stephanie. "Healers, Hucksters and Heroes," *Vim and Vigor*, Fall 1994.
Stevens, William K. "Ocean Change Making Winter More Volatile," *New York Times*. January 20, 2000.
"Vital Signs," *Discover*. Buena Vista Magazines, Walt Disney Company, New York. 2000 and 2001.

Primary:

Richard M. Francis, M.D., Criminal Case File, July 14 to September 20, 1923; Record Group 21, Records of District Courts of the United States, District of Arizona, Prescott Division; Criminal Case Files, Folder Title 453; National Archives and Records Administration, Pacific Region (Laguna Niguel).
U.S. District Court, Prescott, Case #165, 1930.

Flagstaff City Library:

microfilm of *Arizona Champion* 1883–1885
microfilm of *The Coconino Sun* 1883–1931
Riordan, M.J. "The History of the Catholic Church in Flagstaff." Published by M.J. Riordan. 1930.

Coconino County records:

Coconino County Recorder's Office
    Index to Deeds
    Index to Corporations
    Index to Physicians' Diplomas
    Register of Physicians, 1918
    Register of Physicians' Certificates
Coconino County Treasurer's Office
    Duplicate Tax records
Clerk of the Superior Court
    Case #884, Book 2 Page 263, Coconino County Civil Actions
    Case #1804, Book 3, Page 610, Coconino County Civil Actions

Historical Society Pioneers Museum:

Miscellaneous archives
Welch, Art. *Chronological History of the Coconino County Indigent Hospitals, January 1892 to July 1938.*

Northern Arizona University Special Collections Library:

"Alexander Mackenzie Tuthill." Vertical File
"Mercy Hospital." Vertical File
Oral History 28, boxes 18 and 37
Milton Hospital Register October 1916–January 1919

Correspondence:

Steve Allen, Ducks Unlimited
Ruth Gentle, Librarian, Arizona State Board of Medical Examiners.
Mary Caroline Mackey and Regina (Jean) Mason, daughters of A. H. Schermann, 2004.
Richard Mangum, Northern Arizona historian.
Crystal Smith, Reference Librarian. National Library of Medicine, History of Medicine Division. Bethesda, Maryland.
Pat Sullivan, Librarian, Maricopa County Medical Society Library.

Email:

Arizona Board of Medical Examiners (http://cgi.docboard.org//cgi-shl/nhayer.exe)
Steve Grimm, *Old West Gravesites*, <sgrimm@dimensional.com>

Index

Vermillion Cliffs 71, 351
Zion 109, 134, 241
Cornish, Clara 33–34, 39–40, 58, 80, 127, 136, 159, 245, 382
Cornish, Dr. Percy Gillette 22, 40, 50, 58, 64, 80, 84, 127, 132, 157, 159, 247, 261, 295, 376, 382
Costigan, Mary 219, 254, 275, 294, 299, 314, 322, 334, 339, 345, 373
Depression, Anxiety, etc. 23, 42, 60, 71, 101, 103, 123–124, 143, 153, 163, 185, 198, 224, 225, 232, 265, 282, 309–310, 316, 325, 330, 332, 335, 355, 356–357, 359, 368–369, 378
Doctors, Flagstaff
   See Adams, John E.
        Brannen, Dennis J.
        Cornish, Percy Gillette
        Flett, Eric
        Francis, Richard McCleneld
        Fronske, Martin G.
        Halstead, J.L.
        Hendricks, William C.
        Manning, George Felix
        Manning, George Felix, Jr.
        Manning, Thomas Payton
        Miller, Edwin Seymour
        Ploussard, Charles N.
        Raymond, R.O.
        Robinson, Wilbur S.
        Schermann, Albert H.
        Sechrist, Charles
        Sipe, Wilbur P.
        Slernitzauer, W.M.
        Sult, C.W.
        Wilson, Henry
        Zinn, Peter Paul
Doctors' Wives
   See Adams, Margaret
        Brannen, Felicia
        Brannen, Kathleen
        Cornish, Clara
        Flett, Ruby
        Francis, Elizabeth
        Fronske, Hilda
        Manning, Lois
        Manning, Sarah
        Ploussard, Elizabeth
        Robinson, Mira
        Schermann, Pearl

Lockett, Virginia 257
Lundell, Ruth 241, 335
Mackey, Dr. A.J.(dentist) 247, 261, 333, 340, 356
Macdermid, Laura Bell 241, 335, 359, 377
Malpractice 247, 349, 368
Manning, Althea (Wilson) 23, 136, 235, 257, 261, 281, 326
Manning, Dr. George Felix 22, 39, 58, 65, 83, 98, 117, 118, 136,
    157, 159, 185, 187, 192, 202, 211, 233, 235, 248, 261, 281, 286,295
Manning, George Felix Jr. 23, 127, 144, 159, 167, 174, 185, 192, 211, 219, 220, 225,
    226, 227, 234, 235, 247, 260, 261, 270, 275, 277, 281, 286, 289, 290, 295,
    296, 314, 317, 322, 326, 332, 340, 343, 346, 356, 359, 364, 376, 383
Manning, Henrietta (Brown) 23, 136, 192, 235, 261, 281, 322
Manning, Josie 167, 178, 187, 192, 201, 202, 208, 211, 219, 233, 234, 245
Manning, Julia (Nance) 24, 159, 178, 185, 202, 235, 261, 281, 377
Manning, Lois 174, 178, 192, 201, 202, 232, 233, 219, 226, 234, 235, 245, 257, 261,
    281, 290, 295, 304, 308, 322, 326, 333, 346, 359, 376,377
Manning, Sarah 23–24, 65, 84, 102, 118, 127, 137, 159, 167, 178, 185, 202, 211, 219,
    233, 234, 235, 245, 257, 261, 281, 295, 304, 314, 322, 333, 334, 346, 359, 376,
    377, 382–383
Manning, Dr. Thomas Payton 65, 144, 167, 185, 187, 192, 201, 202, 211, 219, 220, 225,
    227, 233, 234, 235, 261, 281, 295
Marshall, Eva 33, 125
Medical history, general 52, 82, 103, 112, 124–125, 144–145, 147, 174–175, 185,
    240–241, 260,261, 275, 289, 290, 340, 370–371, 382
    See World War I
Medical schools 52, 102, 333–334
Medical training 20, 102, 168, 175, 215, 216
    See Flexner Report
Medicine, Arizona 16–17, 21–23, 39, 48–49, 63, 92, 178–179, 192
Medicine, Flagstaff 17, 39, 45, 57, 58, 60, 61, 84, 97, 98, 126, 132, 145, 260, 316, 361,
    364–365
Mercy Hospital 255, 260, 275, 287, 308, 316–317, 365, 383
Midwives 23, 43
Miller, Dr. Edwin Seymour 48, 69, 83, 84, 98, 101, 102, 117, 118, 119, 127, 132, 144,
    157, 159, 174, 185, 187, 192, 202, 211, 219,227, 233, 244, 247, 248, 257, 259,
    260, 275, 286, 290, 295, 296, 300, 308, 317, 332, 333, 339, 340, 343, 346,
    364, 376, 377, 382
Milton Hospital 146–147, 159, 167, 187, 188, 192, 193, 200, 212, 227, 235, 255
Museum of Northern Arizona 272, 326, 314, 374
Murphy (dentist) 333
Navajo Army Depot 130–131
Nance, Hays 247, 261, 281
Neer, Hazel 187, 192, 281, 295, 308, 343
Noble, Annie 192, 201, 202, 211, 233, 234, 244, 245, 252